Saving The Dark Side

Book 3: The Unbound

Joseph Paradis

Saving the Dark Side Book 3: The Unbound is a work of fiction. Names, Characters, places, and events are the product of the author's imagination. Any resemblance to actual persons, places, or events is entirely coincidental.

From the World of Aeneria

For all Hate mail and love letters:
AeneriaIsComing.com/contact/

This book is dedicated to those to braved it first.

Mike Waitz
Timothy Charest
Trevor Hornbeck
Melanie Kasparian

And to Brandon Courcy,
who lit the path for me and many others.

CHAPTER 1

DELIVERANCE

Cole took a long, steadying breath. Brisk air rushed into the stone room that was the center of his mind. Water flowed from the domed ceiling, running down his cone of memories like a blanket of liquid diamonds. The water collected in a neat line, shooting down to the pedestal where Cole's pain lay condensed in a single ingot of grief. The water collided with the miserable lump, dousing it with pacifying clarity before evaporating in a cloud of steam. Cole exhaled, sending the steam away.

He knew he'd been in his center for a long time, perhaps too long, but that was where he needed to be. Over and over he called the crystal waters down to his pedestal with slow breaths, melting off layers from his ingot; Hate, Fear, disgust, shame, insecurity. He was quite good at the process now, but try as he might he was unable to relieve himself of the grief that clenched his heart with the hand of loss. Chiron was dead. Roth was now Harbinger for Grotton. And Alvani was not long for this world. She was perhaps already gone.

Opening his eyes, Cole was first aware of a breeze flicking Lileth's raven hair against his neck. She was asleep now, leaning into Cole with her back against his front. The rest of the unit was still lined up safely on the golden plumage of Gale's back. Valen clung to Alvani at the front, his head bobbing with an exhaustion that he denied with a shake of his head. Cole couldn't tell if Alvani was still alive, and he was afraid to use his Passion to find out. Sitra and Eliza sat bolt upright, though fast asleep. Cole saw emerald rings securing the two women safely together, which he realized must have been conjured by Valen. Lileth stirred suddenly, waking halfway as Cole put his arm around her and gave her a squeeze. She wrapped her fingers around his forearm and fell back asleep at once, nuzzling deeper into Cole.

Cole peered over Gale's flank. They had gone far. They were now flying over a lake carved into a forest of lush pines. The mountains were far smaller than the razor towers near Fangshard Valley. Gazing past the misty summits, Cole saw swaths of farmland peppered with cozy hamlets, their citizens still blissfully ignorant of horrors yet to come. His eyes fell to the lake below. Its mirror smooth surface showed Gale's belly, white as the snowy peaks they had departed from. Oberon glimmered up from the lake like a fat coin. Its churning surface of cobalts and fuchsias seemed to match the melancholy that hung in the air. Cole gave Gale a gentle pat on the rump, imbuing the touch with a pulse of lavender Passion. Gale raised his cat-like snout to the stars and released a mournful keen that echoed across the lake. Cole knew the source of the creature's suffering, for he felt the twist of grief upon his heart as well.

Searching within himself, Cole found the candle that represented Valen. It was tired and tepid, but it was there. Cole immersed himself in Passion and spoke to the candle with his mind. *"Is Master Alvani still alive?"*

Startled, Valen jolted upright and looked back to Cole. He sighed with relief and replied through their Passion link. *"I am sorry, Brother, I have yet to accustom myself to our link. Yes, Master Alvani is still alive, but barely so. We should land soon."*

"How long have we been flying?" Cole asked.

"I'm not sure. Half a day, perhaps longer. We're still within the Fangshards, but I think we're closer to The Sill now." Fear and vulnerability trilled through from Valen's mind. *"Cole, what are we to do?"*

"I don't know," Cole replied. Their link fell quiet for a time. Cole felt Valen slipping almost imperceptibly into Despair, so he willed Passion into his friend, bolstering Valen with magic and words. *"Don't let Sorronis into your heart. We still have much to fight for. This is far from over."*

Valen sat up a little straighter, throwing his shoulders back as the breeze carried a sparkling tear from his cheek. *"Thank you, Cole. It is…*

difficult at times. Too much. But you are right. This is far from over. We will land and rest, then we will discern the brightest path out of this darkness."

"That sounds like the Valen I know." Cole sent another burst of Passion through their link, lifting the remaining shadow from Valen's face. *"Everyone's got their limits, but that's what friends are for. You've helped me out plenty of times so it's only right that I pay you back now and again. Even if you did kick me out of a tree the first day we met."*

"If only I knew what you would become," Valen said with tones of regret and awe. *"I would have shown a bit more reverence for the man who carries Varka's burdens. I am lucky you did not master Rage in that moment or else my crippled arm would have been the least of my injuries. Master Roth likely would have seen my death as a Trial of Honor and granted you custody of the unit, though I suppose you would have made a better leader than I. You certainly are a better leader now."*

"Don't you go pawning your job off on me," Cole jested. *"I think the rest of the unit ought to have a say before you start promoting people to unit leader. Especially not the least experienced of the group."*

"You sell yourself short," Valen replied. *"And at this point I do not think you have much of a choice. Experienced or not, you are the most capable of us all, and more importantly you inspire the others in ways that I could never. Your Rage has no equal, and certain aspects of your Wisdom match mine. Furthermore, I am confident that you mastered Passion while fighting Sorronis. The lovers magic feels different for you now, does it not?"*

Cole was about to refute the claim, but knew he couldn't prove Valen entirely wrong. His Passion certainly felt different. Even now he was acutely aware of the little candles that represented the rest of his unit. He felt Gale too, and with a swoop of his heart he felt what was left of Alvani. Goran's torch burned hot somewhere near Fangshard Valley. Cole smiled inwardly, thankful for proof that his first friend was still alive.

"It's different alright," Cole said. *"I can't tell if I've mastered it though. Mastery of Rage is pretty easy to spot; either you're fully shrouded or you're not. Passion isn't so clear. It's just there when I need it, though there does seem to be a lot more now. What makes you think I've mastered it?"*

Valen twisted around and gave Cole a look of incredulity. *"Look around you. We are all alive because you saved us. It was your Passion that cleansed us of Sorronis's black rain, which was a potent manifestation of Sorronis's Despair, a god's magic. None of us could withstand it, yet you cleansed it from us with Passion. Despair is the counter-magic to Passion, and so your spell ought to have been ineffective. Furthermore, you just initiated a direct Passion link with me without my knowledge. That is expert-level at the very least, though some would call it rude."*

Cole chuckled quietly. *"I didn't want to wake the others. I'm not doubting your claim, but I'd like to get Eliza's input when she wakes up."*

"She would tell you that only a mastery of Passion could have made a mirak grow taller than one of The Sill's bull-pines." Valen's gaze drifted to the mountains behind them. *"How is Goran by the way?"*

At the mention of his friend, Cole's link to Goran broadened to a wide river. The mirak was certainly alive and well, but Cole had a hard time finding his exact location. It was as if Goran's presence had spread itself across the whole of the Fangshards. *"Goran is okay I think. He feels so strange though. The connection isn't as sharp anymore, he's too vast, like he's everywhere. There's so much of him now."*

"I wonder if he would be willing to help us again. I imagine there is not much in this world that could oppose him, including The Three. Could you call him to us?" Valen asked.

"I... think I could," Cole replied, withdrawing from Goran's link before he lost himself in it. Navigating the mirak's mind felt like wandering alone through an unknown forest. *"If our need was great enough I think I could grab his attention. It's so weird. It's as if all he cares about is the entire Fangshard mountain range. The animals, the peaks, the snow, all of it. It's hard to compete with all that. I wish master Alvani could help me understand it."*

As Cole said her name, a sobering spark reverberated across his and Valen's link. Valen pressed a hand to Alvani's neck.

"Her flesh is as ice," Valen said. *"We need to land now."*

Cole gave Valen a brotherly nudge through their link and withdrew. He opened himself to the golden song of Gale's mind and asked the beast to bring them down. Gale released a pained cry and tilted to the right, descending towards a cove big enough for him to land. A minute later Gale pounded the air with his massive amber wings as he slowed himself. Bearded willows hissed at their blustery approach, their curtains of ropey leaves swaying away as though in an underwater current. Cole gripped Lileth a little tighter, ready to work his Wisdom should they fall. With three mighty flaps Gale's momentum came to a halt and his claws sank gently into a plush blanket of grass. Rainbow streams of Oberon's light shot through the beards of the willows, illuminating the cove and a shoal of butterflies caught in eddies of twirling air. The water of the cove looked like rippled obsidian festooned in flowering lily pads.

Lileth stirred, sitting upright. Valen dismissed his conjured rings that secured Eliza and Sitra as the two women woke as well. Gale laid himself flat, allowing the unit to slide down his flank to the ground. As soon as Cole landed, he felt Varka's cape shift to a carpet of damp grass, mimicking the cool blades between his toes. Seeing the exhaustion in the others, Cole took the initiative and walked a ways into the tree line, probing the area with magic. He sharpened his ears with Wisdom. Sounds of scurrying rodents and clicking beetles came to him as he sensed their tiny life candles with Passion. His probing yielded nothing of concern. However, he laid a few spells over the immediate area just to be sure. So long as the unit stayed within the bounds of his magic, nothing would hear them, smell them, or see them. He expected a heavy toll from each spell, but Varka's cape bent the Wisdom for him, tuning the magic to a melody that better suited the nuances of his mind. For a moment a glittery dome shimmered around the area as the concepts solidified into facts.

Cole returned to the unit. Their eyes were heavy with lingering Despair. Eliza swayed on the spot, her short pixie cut flattened on one side from where she had leaned on Sitra. Sitra plopped herself down cross-legged and hugged herself. Lileth curled up like a cat against the soft white feathers of Gale's underbelly. The winged beast laid himself comfortably in the grass; however, his feline head was upright and alert, his tufted ears twitching about for signs of danger. His molten eyes were locked onto Alvani, whom Valen had just set down in a patch of moonlight surrounded by curtains of willow branches.

"How is she?" Cole whispered to Valen, crouching next to him in the grass.

Valen rubbed his eyes and stifled a yawn. "I know not how she still clings to life. Her heart beats too thin and too slowly. I cannot feel her with my Passion. Can you try yours?"

"I can't feel anything either," Cole replied, feeling Alvani's forehead. She felt like a cold rock. "I'm afraid to try and heal her. That thing in her chest, the needle that Habbad used on her, it's interfering with the magic. Do you have any idea what it is?" Cole gently pushed aside the white robes on alvani's sternum, revealing a wound as wide as a finger with a lump of knotted metal in its center. The needle was very long. There was no doubt that it was in her heart.

"I've not the slightest idea," Valen said, setting his fists upon his hips. His face was slack with drowsiness, though his eyes were wide and alert, as if yanked open by magic. "We must do something, however, as soon as we are rested. Go Sleep with the others. I will take first watch."

"I don't sleep anymore," Cole replied. "You go ahead and rest." He saw the question blooming in Valen's zombified gaze. "Chiron's training was extensive. Trust me, I couldn't sleep if I wanted to. Go sleep, Valen."

Valen shook his head, then sighed, "I trust you, Cole."

Cole watched as Valen trudged over to the others and lay on the ground next to Gale. The beast unfolded a wing and extended it over the four warriors like a golden shield. Gale curled his head around and set it on the grass, closing them in. One amber eye remained open, locked unblinkingly upon Alvani.

Cole heard a weak, yet incessant thumping coming from one of the saddle bags at Gale's rear, the faint sound only apparent now in the quiet of everyone's breathing. Lexy was still inside the heavy canvas bag, or whatever was left of her. Cole had almost forgotten he'd rescued her from the depths of the Colossus in Fangshard Valley. She may have been free of Sorronis's clutches, but she was still Chosen. Still charred beyond recognition, burning with potent Hatred while writhing in endless Despair. As Chosen she could never die, or else Cole would have ended her suffering as soon as he freed her. To be Chosen was a fate no one deserved, let alone an innocent child who had already experienced suffering far beyond her tender age. Cole knew the spells to release her soul from her body, and he considered casting them now, but the recent growth of his Passion gave him an idea. Once the others woke and Alvani's fate was clear, he would ask his unit to help him with the idea. He would need Eliza's help for sure.

Cole flicked a beetle off Alvani's shoulder, then chuckled quietly. Alvani loved all creatures. She would have welcomed the little visitor with a gift of Passion, not batted it away like some pest. Keeping the elder in mind, Cole left the protective dome of his spells and set out to find some food and firewood. He paused, checking over his shoulder. There was no trace of the unit whatsoever. Just a patch of moonlit grass nestled in between the beards of the willow trees.

Varka's cape grew little roots as Cole stepped near the base of the tree. He was grateful Chiron had gifted him the garment as it made using Wisdom much easier; however, Cole had learned enough about magic to realize the risk. If he relied upon the cape too much, his inherent Wisdom wouldn't develop properly. If he took it off now he was quite sure the focus required by his protective spells would put him straight into a coma. He resolved to train without the cape as soon as he could.

Cole wandered in ever expanding loops away from the unit. Whenever he found a dry stick or fallen branch, he trickled some Wisdom into the dead wood and sent it cartwheeling gently back to the unit. He knew they would love to wake up to a sizzling meal and a cozy campfire. Cole found a few species of edible mushrooms and recognized the spiked leaves of a plant with tasty roots. He thought back on Chiron's private lessons and how he loathed going over the basics of Aeneria's flora instead of learning how to fight. He silently thanked the old Wisdom walker for his patience. The thought of his master brought up a question Cole had not yet had the time to think on: What happened to Chiron? While Roth and Alvani struggled with the needles buried in their chests, Chiron simply vanished. Just a puff of green smoke and nothing more. Cole used Passion to search both within and beyond himself, but just as Alvani and Roth were masked to him, so was Chiron. Hopefully with the aid of the others he could glean some answers from Master Alvani before the needle took her.

Cole made a few additional loops, this time searching for game. His studies with Passion gave him a newfound respect for all life. He had spent countless hours linked to creatures small and large, sharing in their struggles and triumphs. It took a tremendous amount of luck and ferocity for something as seemingly inconsequential as a hawk to make it to maturity. Respectful or not, Cole and his unit had to eat. He did his best to mitigate his effect in the environment. He took only a few eggs from a nest while fueling the rest of the clutch with Passion. Farther out Cole noticed a swath of vegetation torn and plowed by something with strong claws or horns. He followed the destruction to a pack of sleeping feral swine. With a whisper of Wisdom Cole broke the spines of several of the beasts, levitating them away without a sound.

Back at the cove, Cole lit a fire and dressed the kills with his munisica, burying the viscera at the base of a bearded willow. The work was grisly, but it reminded him of the time he and Roth feasted by a campfire after their flight from Costas. Though Cole had been exhausted beyond his limits, the Bonebreaker had given him the laborious task of cleaning a pair of animals larger than Cole himself. He'd never appreciated Roth's lessons in the moment, but Cole had always come out stronger after completing them. Cole missed Roth already, though it had barely been a day since Grotton had taken him for Harbinger. While Kreed and Talin were the deadly hosts of Decreath and Sorronis, Cole dreaded facing Grotton the most. Grotton's Hunger was the exact counter to his Rage, and Roth was already beyond Cole's equal in overall power. The unit would have to become stronger if they ever hoped to face such a nightmare.

Hours passed, and the only sound to be heard was the gentle breathing and snoring of the unit. Even Gale found sleep after a time. While sleep was no longer available to Cole, his body did require certain functions to be carried out to remain healthy. Recalling yet another of Chiron's lessons, Cole invoked the necessary Passion to mimic the benefits of restorative slumber. He panned through his memories of recent events and siphoned the impressions into his subself, where they could be stored and process on a deeper level. He ran his mind over his body, healing tendons, patching up strained muscles, and stimulating the production of certain hormones. He wasn't acutely aware of the finer details of the spells, but he had run through them enough with Chiron that it was as easy as humming a song that he'd forgotten the words to.

A soft rustling of bare feet over grass drew Cole from his meditations. He didn't turn to meet her eyes as his Passion had revealed which of his candles drew near.

"No sleep for the vigilant?" whispered Lileth as she sat next to him by the fire.

"Hello Lileth," Cole said in a low voice. He turned his head, drinking her in. She was as beautiful as the first time he saw her. Her raven hair was held in a high knot while rebellious strands swept down across her cheeks. Her eyes held equal parts of intelligence and ferocity, and filled Cole with a longing for her touch. Throwing caution to the fire, he placed a hand on her knee, and to his delight she shuffled closer and set her hand over his.

"You've been through so much, Cole. How do you feel?" she asked, voice softening with concern. It pleased Cole that he had grown so tall that she now had to look up to meet his eyes. She seemed even more beautiful from this new angle.

Cole took an unabashed moment to paint his gaze over every curve of her face before responding. "I'm…very tired. Not of body or mind, but my heart feels like it's worn out. I'm tired of losing people I love."

"Not everyone you love," she said, squeezing his hand. "There are still a few of us left who can breathe some vigor back into your soul. We are with you, now and forever. You are important."

Cole's gaze escaped to the fire. The pulsing embers and dancing flames baked his cheeks. "I'm no more important than any other member of this unit. I love you all, but I've learned enough about Passion to know that love is not a universal thing." Cole shrank away from her, bracing himself for the impact. "How important am I to you, Lileth?"

For a moment the only sound was the popping and hissing of the fire. Lileth was silent for so long that Cole forced his eyes to be brave enough to meet hers. Her breath was heavy and her lips trembled. Her face was awash with such alarm that Cole thought a Corpulant might have just sneaked up over his shoulder. She blinked hard and confusedly, pushing a single tear out. She took a deep breath and said in a tiny voice, "I think I am in love with you."

All of Aeneria seemed to freeze before the significance of the moment. Though there were only a few reasonable responses to his question, this wasn't one that he thought possible. Never in his life had he been so stricken by a few simple words.

Cole swallowed hard and time seemed to resume in a whirlwind of sensation and emotion. "I...I think I feel the same about you. I mean...I love you too, Lileth."

The worry lifted from Lileth's face, and Cole was filled with such giddy relief that he felt a queer laughter flutter up in his throat. He had to hold her, to give her the kiss he had yearned for since they first met. But as Cole reached for her, Sitra rolled behind them and emitted the most sonorous example of flatulence he'd ever heard in his life.

Sitra giggled, farting even louder this time.

"Have you no decency!" cried Eliza. "My head was right behind your knees!"

The thumping Fear in Cole's heart vanished. Holding his breath, he looked back to Lileth, but she was doubled over and chuckling into her fist.

"SITRA!" Eliza bellowed, springing to her feet and casting an emerald shield over her mouth and nose. "That smells worse than a bog angel's breath! What in Oberon's light did you eat?"

Sitra fell onto her back, choked silent by her mirth while kicking her legs into the air.

Valen spun to his feet, hands and feet flashing to ebony munisica as he scanned for danger. "What happened? Is anybody hurt?" His face suddenly twisted as the stench struck him. "Oh Sitra, that is atrocious."

He tucked his nose into his elbow as he dismissed his bladed claws and cast a strong wind across the cove. The fire roared jubilantly.

When the air had been cleansed and Sitra thoroughly threatened, the unit approached the fire with starved expressions.

"Look at this feast! Someone's been busy," Sitra said, poking one of the skinned boars spinning on Cole's invisible rotisserie.

"Did you not sleep at all?" Eliza asked, placing a hand on Cole's shoulder after he stood to his feet. "You were fully shrouded for quite some time while you fought Sorronis. You need rest to ease the toll taken by the Rage. Do you need my Passion?"

Cole felt Lileth's eyes raking over him, and he chose his next words very carefully. "No, thank you Eliza. I worked my own Passion while you all slept. And I consumed one of Chiron's cyphers back at The Sill—he called it the dreamsource. It changed my need for sleep, or completely erased it I should say. I couldn't sleep again if I tried."

"But that's a top-shelf Wisdom cypher!" Sitra exclaimed through a mouthful of roasted boar. "Storn used to save every drop of Rage he could spare for one of those, that and a set of focusing shards. *Stars* he was so bad with Wisdom." Sitra shook a sad smile from her face before narrowing her eyes to Cole. "How'd you afford something like that?"

Cole laughed. Not because he thought her question funny, but because he was deeply grateful that they were all here with him now. He cared for each of them more than he cared for himself. He sighed, then gave Sitra a warm smile. "Why don't we eat before I catch you all up? Then we'll see what we can do for Master Alvani. She's still alive, but I need everyone's help before we decide what to do with her."

All eyes went to the patch of moonlight just beyond the luminance of the fire. Alvani lay like a lone flower petal, her alabaster robes tainted with a bloody wound set in her chest. Without another word the unit set themselves upon Cole's meal, not to enjoy themselves, but to fuel their bodies and minds for the task ahead. It may take every ounce of Passion and energy they possessed to help Alvani, or none at all if it was too late.

After a few minutes of eating without tasting, Cole rose to his feet. Smoke from the fire wafted over his eyes, stinging them, but he was too nervous to move. He was afraid to find out how bad it was.

He wasn't ready to lose another person he cared about. A hand found his, drawing him from his thoughts with a gentle squeeze.

"We must do what we can for her," Lileth said. The rest of the unit was on their feet as well, waiting for him to make the first move. "Come," she whispered, guiding him with a gentle tug.

The unit converged around Alvani. Gale stalked silently behind them, his wispy ears low and sad. Insects chirped and buzzed between the beards of the old willows as Oberon's glow waved over Alvani's form. Cole knew they were all waiting for him, but he had no idea where to start. He took a deep breath and looked to Eliza.

"Eliza, do you have any ideas?" Cole asked.

Eliza bit her lip and shook her head. "I'm afraid not. I've never seen a wound like this before. That needle, it doesn't belong here, on Aeneria I mean. It's wrong. It feels like some sort of malignant void, as if it's intentionally siphoning her life force to another place. I'm afraid it will steal what little is left of her if I so much as scan her body with magic."

"I sensed something similar," Cole sighed, seeing the defeated looks on everyone's faces. "If we *were* to try and help her, how do you think we should go about doing it?"

"Why are you asking her?" Sitra interrupted. "You're the one who trained with Chiron, and we all know you mastered Passion. If you can't do it then Liza sure as hell can't. Just get on with it already." Sitra's eyes became glassy and her jaw started to tremble. The others shot her horrified looks, but she stood a little taller and continued in a croaky voice. "She's not going to survive this. The sooner we confirm it, the sooner we can start grieving and move on."

Once more all eyes fell to Cole. He rubbed his forehead, trying to massage a headache that had started to sink its claws in. He approached Sitra and set a hand on her bulky shoulder, then spoke in a slow and steady tone. "I'm not ready to lose her either. Even if we all mastered Passion I think she'd still be beyond our help. We don't know how that thing in her chest works, but it's taken too much from her. I have my ideas on how we should handle this. However, I know her the least, and while my Passion might be the most powerful, Eliza is the one who's best with fixing people. We need to do what's best for Alvani, even if that means saying goodbye to her."

Sitra's face had hardened to stone, and Cole worried she might strike him, but she threw her arms around him and sobbed into his chest. He slid his hand under the thick rope of her braided hair and rubbed her back. He would have cried with her, but that part of him felt too numb, as if covered by a layer of dead scars.

"What are your ideas then?" Valen asked when Sitra's weeping relented. "Inexperienced or not, you have accomplished more than any of us. Your opinion carries weight."

Cole gave Sitra a hug before releasing her and crouching low next to Alvani. A ghostly pallor filled her flesh, making her skin even more pale than her snowy robes. He placed a hand on her chest, feeling the quivering breath beneath. "We enter her mind and her body, all of us. We'll have to link with Passion first—I'll be the hub. Then we'll try to remove the needle while simultaneously healing her and searching her mind. She'll probably die as soon as we try, but we might be able to keep her alive long enough to ask her a few questions. Or, like I said, we might just be saying goodbye to her."

"That seems as good a plan as any," Lileth said, crouching next to Cole. "I'm with you, Cole."

"Me too," Sitra said, squatting at Cole's other side.

Valen and Eliza joined him on Alvani's other side. Eliza's hands lit with a dim rosy light as she waved them slowly above Alvani's body. She scanned for a few minutes, avoiding the area above the needle. After completing her search, she rubbed her hands together as the dim light faded from her palms. She spoke in a steady, confident voice: "Sitra, you will use Wisdom to keep her lungs working. Make sure the air going in is clean and oxygen-rich. Lileth, I need you to cover her vasculature. Contract every vessel that doesn't involve her vital organs, but gently expand those in her heart, lungs, and brain. Valen, you're going to keep her heart pumping and heal the wound as Cole and I work."

"And what exactly will you and Cole be doing?" Lileth asked, leaning closer.

"We will try to remove the object and touch Alvani's mind," Eliza replied. "He is the most powerful with Passion, but I am the most experienced with the art of it. Together we stand the best chance of mending her. We should start now, unless anyone else has a better plan." Lileth looked as if she wanted to say something, but seemed to think better of it. No one else said a word. "Then let's get started. Cole, if you would."

Cole felt Eliza's mind pressing into his, beckoning him to connect with her. He opened himself to her and the familiar song of her soul entwined with his. This was not like the communication link he used with Valen. This link was special, deeper. Every errant thought, guilty urge, and physical sensation thrummed through the bond, naked and raw. Lying was impossible, and at times it was difficult to see the world through one's own eyes. There was something different about their link, however. Cole raised an eye to Eliza as his curiosity bled through to her.

Eliza's words bloomed in his mind as if he'd thought them himself. *"You weren't supposed to see that. Please, disregard it. I won't let it affect anything."*

Cole felt a riotous blend of incredulity and amusement pour from him. The bond felt different because it was no longer fraternal, at least not from Eliza's end. Her feelings for him had apparently grown beyond mere battle-brother. Compassion flowed from him next as he gave her a look of understanding. *"Don't worry, I won't tell the others. I'm going to bring them in now."*

Cole shut his eyes and gathered his candles close, hugging them into his consciousness. He felt each one ring with recognition as they linked themselves to him, creating a mental network among the five warriors. Their links weren't as broad or deep as his and Eliza's, but they were enough to communicate mentally.

"I SAID CAN ANYONE HEAR ME?" Sitra's voice blared through their link. Everyone winced as the words shocked their minds.

"Clear as cannonfire," Eliza chimed. *"Is everyone ready?"*

"Yes," everyone replied in unison.

"Then let us begin," Eliza said, closing her eyes.

Alvani's breathing was the first thing to change. Her shallow rattle was immediately replaced by a steady pattern of full, healthy breaths. Her hands blanched bone white as some color returned to her face.

Apprehension trickled out from Eliza's mind as she reached out and grasped Cole's hand. *"Can you sense Alvani's mind at all?"*

"No," Cole replied. *"I'm afraid to get too close with that thing still in her chest."*

"Then lend me your Passion. I think I know how to find her, but I need your strength to do so." A bubble of Fear rose up from Eliza's mind, but she seared it away with a quick surge of Rage. *"If I can find Alvani I'm going to join minds with her, but in doing so the needle might take me as well. It might kill me."*

Valen interjected, *"Then we find another way, or none at all. Eliza don't be foolish! Cole, stop her!"*

Before Cole could utter a response, Eliza's presence vanished from their link. Her and Cole's bond was as strong as ever, but he could no longer sense her nearby. Maintaining the magic, he opened his eyes to see Eliza kneeling upright, her fingers interwoven with his and her face hard with concentration. Fearing for her life, Cole summoned every ounce of Passion he could spare and pushed it across his bond to Eliza. The magic surged through their bond, bending it to its limits before vanishing into the unknown. Eliza's face relaxed, and so did her grip on Cole's hand. Then she fell sideways into the grass.

"Eliza!" Cole's cry blared to Eliza, only to end in a void on the other side. He could hear questions coming from his links with the others, but they were too quiet before the calamity of his distress. Through his worry he found deeper reserves of Passion and pushed them to Eliza. She remained motionless. Panicking, he reached for the base of the needle in Alvani's chest.

"Do not touch it," whispered a weak voice. "Not yet."

Lileth's, Valen's, and Sitra's eyes popped open and went to Alvani, whose rosy cheeks twitched with a weak smile. Cole moved his hand away from the needle.

"Ask your questions quickly, Cole," Lileth said. "We are forcing her body to stay alive, but we cannot maintain it much longer."

"Eliza...is fine," Alvani said, pausing in between aided breaths. Her voice was faint and she had yet to open her eyes. "She found me...but the pithing shard found her. I've shielded her from it.... for now. It warms my heart to hear your voices."

"Master, tell us what to do!" Valen pleaded. "Tell us how we can save you. Cole mastered Passion, he can help you."

Alvani's chest rose and fell several times before she spoke again. "I...am beyond help... It is up to you now...You must be the next Unbound."

Sitra leaned in, her long braid falling across Alvani's legs. "What about Roth? Are you still bonded to him? Can we save him?"

Alvani's smile vanished. "Rothael was lost to me as soon as his pithing shard struck him.... He is Grotton now... Chiron vanished, but where I do not know..."

Sitra winced, slumping back into the grass as fresh tears streaked down her face. Lileth and Valen wilted, their expressions somber and defeated. The elders had been three pillars holding up not only the unit, but the whole populace of The Sill, and anyone else who defied The Three. Without them what hope did the five of them have? Eliza began to stir in the grass. Her body trembled, then thrashed in a violent seizure.

"We need to end this," Lileth said, looking up at Cole with a grim expression.

"Lileth is correct," Alvani sighed. "I can only shield Eliza a little longer. You will have to kill me to save her."

Cole nodded. While he had no issue sustaining the heavy flow of Passion, he knew he could do no more for Alvani. He placed a hand on the elder's forehead and her small smile returned. "Just...just one more thing before we say goodbye. Can you tell us anything, anything at all that might help us against The Three?"

"The Three are united... Their Harbingers have all been crowned...They are stronger now...Too strong." Alvani paused for a few breaths before continuing. "The Cold Crows... They made the pithing shards... But they were not alone...The shards... The shards are..."

Alvani's face drooped, lifeless. Eliza's thrashing intensified, now accompanied by agonized moans.

"Do it, Cole," Lileth demanded, tears staining the Fear on her face. "Do it now before we lose Eliza."

Cole's eyes darted back and forth from Eliza to Alvani. The pithing shard began to glow a ruddy shade of copper. The air seemed to drip with an evil presence, as if the eyes of The Three had found them at last. Cole's bones chilled, and he had the sensation that something was creeping up just behind him.

"The shards are *what?*" Cole blurted as the others covered their ears. A noise chuckled up from nowhere, a sound that had no business in the world of the living. "What about the shards?" There was no answer. The presence was overwhelming now. All of his Passion flowed into Eliza, leaving him utterly vulnerable to the evil presence that rose from nowhere. "Release your spells!" he cried. "Do it now!"

"We did!" Valen exclaimed, cupping his ears and rising to a defensive position. "Something has her now!"

Alvani's chest rose once more as she hissed in a wet voice that was not her own.

"BETRAYAL."

Lileth roared and her hands exploded into munisica. Her bladed fingers whipped through the air as she grasped the pithing shard and yanked it from Alvani's chest.

Chapter 2

Commemoration

Lileth hurled the pithing shard. It whirred through the air and, with a loud crack, it buried itself halfway into the trunk of the willow. The evil presence vanished at once, and so did the otherworldly noise. Gale rose to his hind legs and flapped his wings, then released a mournful keen to Oberon.

"Is it over?" Sitra asked. Her face was pale and her hands shook. "Is Alvani okay?"

"She's dead," Cole said, hovering a hand over Alvani's body. "But her soul... I have no idea... that thing."

The air around Alvani's body seemed to drop several degrees. Her rosy cheeks faded to a lifeless grey as she embraced the quiet of death. The cove took on a somber silence, as if every insect and bird had fled to faraway lands, never to return to a place of such horror and sorrow.

Eliza was as quiet and still as Alvani. Just as Cole began to Fear the worst, her hand reached up for the stars.

"Eliza!" Valen darted to her, kneeling down and cradling her head. "Sister say something!"

Eliza's eyes opened halfway and gazed off at something none of them could see. Cole felt her presence return to the other side of their bond, her mind apparently whole and unharmed, though she was unaware of him or anything else. He ceased the flow of Passion to her. A chill of lethargy crept into his limbs, leaving him diminished, but he could feel the magic begin to slowly replenish itself almost at once. The song that flowed from Eliza was profoundly sad, as if she were dreaming of the end of the world.

Lileth and Sitra approached Eliza with a timid crawl, hands aglow with Passion and Wisdom as they inspected her mind and body.

"What's wrong with her?" Lileth directed the question at Cole, though her eyes flicked between Eliza and the pithing shard buried in the willow. "What does your bond tell you?"

Cole reached down and caressed the side of Eliza's face. "I'm not sure. It feels as if she's sleeping, like she's just having a bad dream. I could try to-"

Cole froze. Whatever had plagued Eliza's thoughts was now rushing to the surface. He withdrew from their bond, but Eliza held him fast with an urgent bolt of Passion.

"Get away from her. Now!" Cole cried, jumping to his feet.

Valen swiftly set Eliza's head back in the grass and everyone leaped back a few paces.

"Farther," Cole said, though he took a step closer. Whatever was welling up in Eliza was immense, but he had a feeling she would need his help. As if to confirm his suspicion, Eliza sent him another jolt of Passion and a message.

Come to me, Eliza said, though her tone felt more exhilarated than desperate.

A deafening crack split the air as rich amethyst flames engulfed Eliza's form. She rose several feet into the air, arms outstretched to either side. Her eyes had turned a brilliant white as sparks zapped from her fingertips.

Come to me, Eliza repeated.

Cole knew the magic coming from Eliza was Passion, so he grasped his reserves and willed what was left of his own Passion into the moment. Cole withdrew from the minds of the others and leaped up to her, hoping he had guessed right. He was just a few feet away when a powerful force resisted him like an opposing magnet, but then the force flipped on itself, slamming him into her body. His flesh and soul collided with hers in an explosion of lavender and amethyst.

An ocean of Passion flowed into him. It was the most euphoric thing he'd ever experienced, though it was too much. A whole world of compassion erupted within him, striking the multitudes of details of every memory in which he had felt love for another. His mother laying him to bed, kissing him goodnight. Joshy crying because he couldn't figure out how to work his toy. Nana Beth wrapping him in warm blankets fresh from the dryer. Lileth in the meadow, despondent and lost as the demons of her mind tore at her, and the joy Cole felt at lifting her from her darkness.

Cole opened himself to the Passion, no longer caring if it killed him or drove him mad. Eliza needed him, and he needed this moment.

The tide of magic memories eventually ebbed to gentle solace. The storm cleared and he found Eliza on the other side of their bond, right where she should be. She was similarly embroiled in her own torrent of love. Together, their bare feet alighted upon the slick grass as the light of the magic dwindled and dimmed around their bodies. Cole opened his eyes. She nuzzled herself into his embrace, crying and smiling.

"You did it," Cole whispered to his friend, squeezing her tight.

"*We* did it," Eliza said. She pursed her lips together, then broke down in happy sobs and buried her face in his chest.

"You did *what?*" Sitra hollered, taking a timid step closer. "What the hell just happened?"

Cole released Eliza and turned to the others. "Eliza just mastered Passion." Valen's and Sitra's expressions lifted from worry to shock, though he noticed Lileth's gaze fall to the ground.

"It's true!" Eliza exclaimed, bounding over to Valen and throwing her arms around him in a tight hug. "It's so wonderfully, beautifully true!"

"But how?" Valen asked as Eliza's infectious mirth spread across his face. "We thought the pithing shard was killing you."

"It nearly did," Eliza replied. "After I found Alvani I felt myself slipping into another world, a terrible place made of every nightmare I've ever had. It was as if a plane of existence had been crafted from the worst parts of myself. It would have taken me if not for Alvani's protection. Before she faded she gifted me a piece of herself, a key that unlocked the Passion within me, showed me its true meaning." She withdrew from Valen and gazed at Alvani's body. "She's gone now, isn't she?"

"Yes," Cole said, feeling the grief crash over him at last. He wasn't sure if the pithing shard had killed her or done something much worse, but the ache of loss pained him all the same. "What should we do with her?"

"We could bring her to The Sill," Sitra offered in a croaky voice. "We could set her up with a tree right next to Deekus. I'll carry her."

"It could take weeks for Gale to fly us home, and that is even if he consents to bear us without Alvani," Valen said, eyeing the winged beast. Gale's wings trembled as he kneaded the ground with his claws in an anxious manner. "Unless you intend on preserving her body the whole way, I do not think that will be a viable option. Time and travel will ravage her remains with each passing second."

"Well we're sure as hell not abandoning her!" Sitra cried. Her jaw trembled as she spoke in a shaky voice. "Lil, you'll use your Wisdom on her while I carry her, right?"

Lileth kept her eyes downcast as she shook her head slowly. She hugged herself, and spoke to the ground. "I... I don't know. That would require a prodigious amount of focus, and if I wavered for but a second..."

Cole approached Lileth and put an arm around her while Sitra and Valen continued their argument. She stiffened like wood at his touch, then wept openly and leaned into him. "It's going to be all right. She's not suffering anymore." Cole only said the words to console her, but the sickening truth was that her soul may have been trapped in eternal agony at that very moment.

"It's all my fault," Lileth said as she sobbed into his chest. "It's all my fault. I'm the one..."

"Stop that." Cole gave her a firm squeeze. "You did the right thing. Eliza would be dead or worse if you hadn't acted."

Lileth looked up at him, not with the sorrow he had expected, but with a wild Fear of one on the brink of coming unhinged. She breathed in a whisper so low that the others couldn't hear, "I'm a horrible person, Cole. What I've done... no decent person... I need you."

"I'm not going anywhere," Cole reassured her, turning her away from Alvani's body. Inside he blamed himself for risking Eliza's life and not pulling the pithing shard out sooner. "Whatever you need, I'm yours."

Lileth's eyes peered right through his own, then beyond to somewhere only she could see. "You don't understand. I am not whole."

Cole was about to question her, but Sitra's and Valen's contention had risen to a level they could no longer ignore. Sitra's munisica were out, her shroud nearly up to her shoulders and hips. Valen leaned back cross-armed with an icy expression, though his fists glowed a dull jade.

"This isn't a time for practicality, you ass!" Sitra snarled, taking a step closer to Valen. "Would you leave her corpse here as a hotel for rats and ants? Or would you like to see if something larger will eat her first? Can't have the enemy finding traces of our presence, right?"

Valen's chin rose in defiance. "I am suggesting none of those things. I am only pointing out that bringing her back to The Sill would cost us resources we cannot afford. I do appreciate the gravity of the moment, truly. However, I *do not* appreciate you assuming that I am so cold-hearted that the loss of our elders does not affect me. I feel pain too, Sitra, I just choose a different way to deal with it. Now stop putting words in my mouth and let's—"

"I'll put something in your mouth!" Sitra stormed at Valen, her munisica swelling ever larger as she balled them into bladed fists.

A ball of fuchsia light hummed across the grass, sinking into Sitra's chest. The anger melted from her face, then her munisica shrank away. Eliza strode over to Valen and Sitra, placing a loving hand on each of their backs.

"Still your Rage, Sitra, and your Wisdom, Valen," Eliza said. "Now isn't the time for either. You're both right, but a graveside brawl isn't helping anyone. What Alvani valued above all else was the life around her, so we will make her a part of the life in this cove."

"That sounds beautiful, Eliza," Valen said in a soft voice. "I think Alvani would love that."

Sitra gave Valen an apologetic look before turning to Eliza. "Are you sure you can do it? Just like Deekus?"

Eliza's eyes fell at the mention of her old lover's name, but she steadied herself with a sad smile. "With Cole's help I think I can. We don't have a gratia stone, so we must get it right on the first try." She turned and looked to Cole. "Do you feel up to the task?"

Cole felt Lileth's shoulders harden under his arms as her face resumed its usual stoicism. He released her, then clipped his budding concern. "Of course. I'll help however I can. Just one thing before we start."

Cole trotted over to Gale, who had been stomping and snorting like an angry horse while biting at his saddle bags. He connected to the beast with Passion, opening himself up to the pain and grief. The sorrow was as deep as it was potent, but Cole's Passion allowed the emotions a safe place next to his memories of Joshy. Gale relaxed and folded his golden wings as Cole snipped the saddle bags free with a single bladed finger. From within the rearmost bag Lexy thrashed with renewed Hatred at the world. Cole shouldered the bags and stowed them beyond the firelight. Her torment twisted his heart with guilt.

"Are you familiar with botanomancy?" Eliza asked him as he returned to the warmth of the fire.

Cole looked to the draping willow leaves around them. He knew what she was getting at. "The most I could do was grow saplings from seeds while training with Chiron, but that was before my fight with Sorronis. I think my Passion could do a lot more now."

"Wonderful." Eliza beamed at him, then continued through their Passion link, *"Then let us give Alvani a proper send-off."*

Cole welcomed her into his mind, broadening and strengthening their link as never before. The air between them thrummed with power as the others took a step back. Cole dismissed his protective spells over the cove, focusing entirely on the task at hand. The Passion coming from Eliza felt almost too much to handle, affecting Cole with involuntary sobs and a maddening ardor for all things.

"It's good you returned some of my Passion to me. I'm still a bit diminished," Cole said, joining hands with Eliza as together they approached Alvani.

"I had to," Eliza replied, holding a hand out as a snowy butterfly landed on her finger. *"Your Passion kept me anchored to this world, but you gave me too much. It nearly killed me."* At the swell of remorse coming from Cole, she added, *"Don't worry over it now. Alvani needs us."* She reassured him through the bond, bringing the butterfly to her lips and kissing it softly upon the tip of a wing.

The butterfly pulsed with fuchsia and flapped away at once, dancing between the ropy strands of the willow leaves. Still hand in hand, Cole and Eliza stood beside Alvani and began pouring their collective Passion into her with beams of fuchsia and lavender from their free hands. Cole had no idea why they poured so much love and life into Alvani, though after a moment he saw the same butterfly return, a fat seed of butterscotch yellow clutched in its spindly legs. The butterfly hovered above Alvani's wound and deposited the seed before fluttering back beyond the firelight.

Alvani's wound shone with blinding white light as her body took on an iridescent sheen. A warm wind spiraled around the cove, sending glowing embers up into the sky as the bearded willows danced around them. Gale cried a baleful tone and took flight with a single stroke of his wings. The beast landed above Alvani, encircling her protectively between his front paws. The others rushed in to help, but Cole and Eliza had sensed Gale's intentions, and gave them a mental urge to hold back.

"Should we stop him?" Cole asked as Gale scooped Alvani's body into his front paws. *"He'll die too."*

"He will, but it's his choice," Eliza replied. *"And it's already too late, look at the roots. Just keep the Passion flowing."*

Cole strummed his acknowledgment through their bond as he beheld the effects of their magic. The iridescent sheen spread from Alvani's body to Gale's, giving his feathers the appearance of having just emerged from a pool of liquid opals. White roots crawled from the glowing diode in Alvani's chest, wrapping and weaving their way down her front and into the grass at her feet. The roots grew thick and dark as they propagated, lifting Alvani into a graceful pose, making her look as though she had been frozen while dancing. Vines spread from her outstretched fingers as they wove up into Gale's feathers. Gale sat back and bent his feline head low, sniffing her one last time before bringing his head up high and spreading his wings. The opalescent sheen flashed over their bodies, filling the cove with a blinding light and a symphonious peal of crystal windchimes.

"Is this supposed to happen?" Cole asked Eliza, holding up his hand to shield his eyes.

"I don't know. It feels as if Gale is crafting the spell now. We are merely fueling it. Don't relent until he's finished," Eliza replied, turning her head away from the brilliant light.

Cole began to wonder how an animal could use magic, but then Goran came to the fore of his mind. The mirak's explosive growth and command over the Fangshards involved a primal magic that Cole couldn't begin to grasp. But Cole trusted Goran with his life, and so he would trust Gale with Alvani's body. He surged on, funneling his Passion into the unknown spell before him.

The ground beneath their feet began to rise, pushing them backwards as if some large animal had burrowed below the damp grass. Blinded by the luminance of the magic, Cole and Eliza took a few timid steps backwards, careful to maintain the stream of magic. Wet wood creaked as the hissing of wind through the willows rose over the sound of windchimes. The light dimmed at last, and Cole opened his eyes.

Alvani and Gale stood before them reposed in the heart of a great willow. Their flesh, feathers, and robes had been transformed into pearly crystal, casting them in perfect statues of grace and pride. The trunk of the willow continued to grow around them though it left the majority of their bodies uncovered, as if the tree knew their beauty was a thing to be seen and loved by all. The willow's branches flexed ever larger over their heads as thousands of leafy ropes descended to the ground, budding as they unraveled. With their reserves of Passion ebbing away, Cole and Eliza ceased the flow of magic, leaving the two statues partially embedded in the base of what was now the largest tree in the cove.

Cole released Eliza's hand, feeling a dull ache where his Passion had been, knowing it would be days before his Passion would replenish itself. He looked to Eliza, seeing his weariness mirrored in her heavy breathing and sunken eyes.

"Need a little pick-me-up?" Cole said with a smirk, sending an invigorating jolt of Rage across their link. His fingers and toes lengthened with gratifying pain into ebony blades.

"Oh!" Eliza gasped as her munisica sprang forth. "That feels much better."

"What on Oberon's backside did you guys do?" Sitra said, striding past them on her way to the tree.

"We don't really know," Cole explained, following her. "Gale knew though. We only intended to grow a tree around Alvani, but he jumped in and commandeered the magic. We had no idea what he was doing with it, but we trusted him, so we just kept the Passion flowing."

The unit approached Alvani and Gale. Solemn silence reigned for a few minutes as they all gazed upon their lost friends. It was as if they had been sculpted from pure opal by a team of master artisans. Alvani's eyes were closed, her face hinting at one of her warm smiles. Her hair and lashes were frozen in individual strands of crystal, delicate yet sharp. Gale stood sentinel over her, fierce and protective. His feline features looked almost playful with his eyes wide and teeth slightly bared, making him look as though he were about to pounce and chirp. The snowy butterflies wasted no time chasing each other between his tufted ears.

Lileth brushed Cole's arm as she stepped around him for a closer look. "It's beautiful." She reached a hand out, caressing the side of Alvani's face. "Is it too late to make a contribution?"

"I'm afraid so," Eliza said. "When Gale took the spell from us he left no room for us to let anyone else in."

Valen ran his hand over the feathers on Gale's forearm. A curious smile spread across his face as a green spark jumped from his fingertips and into the crystal, sending an emerald ripple throughout the statue. "It appears Gale *did* leave us some room. This material seems similar to the bio-crystal of a gratia stone." He pressed his palm flat against Gale's arm and deposited a great current of emerald Wisdom.

Sitra cupped her hand over Alvani's shoulder and closed her eyes. A torrent of crimson light pulsed throughout Alvani as though a fire burned within the crystal. Cole made a deposit of Rage as well, offering half of his reserves. Eliza and Lileth chose Wisdom, each making several moderate contributions.

Cole watched the statues closely as the crystal absorbed each donation. He recalled how he once broke a gratia stone by overloading it. However, his worry now was for nothing. The sheer mass of the crystal was equivalent to dozens of gratia stones, if not hundreds.

Furthermore, as soon as an offering was made, the magic seemed to dissipate in earnest, as though someone was using it. Cole looked to the leaves and branches of the new willow, but it showed no signs of new growth.

"What's happening to all that energy?" Sitra asked. She screwed her brow up in frustration as she made an even greater offering of Rage. Both statues shone a brilliant crimson before rapidly fading back to an empty opal. "I hope we're doing this right."

The others inspected the crystal, peering into the depths of Alvani and Gale as if attempting to divine the future. Confused, Cole took a step back and broadened his inspection. The tree looked to be in the prime of its life, but it hadn't grown an inch beyond the original spell. Perhaps they had made a mistake. Cole shut his eyes, broadening his awareness further still, but there was nothing. Disappointed, he turned away from the tree, but something brushed his hand as he stepped. A plant that had not been there a moment ago was sprouting before him. A large bell flower erupted from a knotted bud, its throat an electric magenta with frilly azure petals. There were dozens of new flowers of various species, each shooting up from the grass and displaying their beauty for the night.

"I think I found where all that energy went," Cole called to the others while gazing up at a nearby willow. The tree rocked gently while growing steadily taller.

"The life around her indeed," Valen said as he admired the sprouting garden. "Most of these are very rare, and some are only found on the Light Side. I applaud you, Gale, this is marvelous work." He offered Gale's statue a quick bow.

"Look at the water," Sitra said, pointing to the shore. "Was it that clear before?"

Cole sharpened his eyes with Wisdom as they all jogged to the shoreline. The murky blackness in the cove receded out towards the main lake, chased away by a shimmering water so clear that it appeared like liquid glass. A few fish jumped excitedly out of the water, making little splashes as though in celebration. A breath of balmy wind passed over the cove, carrying with it a spark of something vibrant and wild. Cole's hairs stood on end, and he suddenly felt an urge to strip bare and run through the willow grove. A measure of his Passion returned to him, allowing him to sense the rising waves of life candles about him.

"This is Alvani's and Gale's final gift to us, to Aeneria," Cole said to the others, who all bore flush cheeks and yearning expressions. "If we ever find Chiron or free Roth from Grotton, we should bring them here."

"They would love it," Eliza said. "It feels like home."

They all nodded in agreement. Lileth then broke free from the group, stalking half crouched towards a willow that had not grown like the others, and looked feeble in comparison. Cole followed, and on closer inspection noticed it was sick. Its leaves frayed and broke off to a crunchy carpet of death around its base. Its branches drooped and wilted far too low. Buried in the center of its trunk at eye level was the pithing shard.

"We need to get that thing out of here," Cole said, startling Lileth, who had been so captivated by the shard that she hadn't noticed him behind her. "Sorry."

"It's fine," Lileth replied, looking sullen and wounded. It pained Cole to think she blamed herself for what had to be done. "You're right, the pithing shard cannot remain here. I would remove it myself, but my hand hurts terribly from touching it. I've never felt pain through my munisica before. Do you have any ideas?"

Cole took Lileth's hand, holding it tenderly in both of his. If only his Passion had replenished enough to heal her. Her hand was swollen and scorching. She smiled at his touch, however, giving him a look that made Cole's heart swoop with delight.

"We can't use magic to interact with the shard, that much I know," Cole said, indulging in the way Lileth gazed at him with genuine longing. "There might be another trick to it though."

Releasing her hand, Cole summoned an emerald cylinder and with a twist of Wisdom, pushed it into the trunk around the pithing shard. The magic cut through the wood with a high-pitched whine. Smoke billowed from the circular incision. Cole dismissed the cylindrical saw and with a solid crack, withdrew a long column of wood with the pithing shard at its center. Bringing forth his munisica,

Cole grasped the length of wood with a bladed hand and hammered the base of the pithing shard with the other, burying it completely within the confines of the wood. Lileth hadn't exaggerated about the pain. Even through his munisica the heel of his right hand throbbed with debilitating pain, as if seared by Hatefire cast from Sorronis himself.

With the pithing shard secured, the unit broke down the campsite and disassembled Gale's saddle bags, modifying the canvas into workable rucksacks. Alvani had packed enough provisions in the bags to last them a few days, as well as several cases of various potions and a collection of fully-charged Passion stones. Lileth volunteered to carry the pithing shard, setting its wooden case into her bag with the tender care of laying a loved one into a coffin. The unit attempted to ease Lileth of her guilt, assuring her that removing the shard had been the right thing to do, and any one of them would have done the same. Lileth became increasingly distant, however, giving curt responses and withdrawing to the outskirts of the group.

Cole shouldered his rucksack containing Lexy's ruined form. He did his best to keep from disturbing her, but her scabbed voice and charred fists pounded against the canvas as soon as he picked the bag up.

Valen experimented with the crystal while they packed. He managed a clever facsimile of Cole's protective spells, setting them over Alvani and Gale to keep potential looters from discovering such an abundant source of gratia stone. He tied the spells to their statues, offering a heavy dose of Wisdom for fuel while the remnants of Gale's consciousness maintained the framework for the magic.

With a heavy heart, the unit said their final goodbyes, making their solemn vows to return to the cove someday. Cole was last to leave, taking a moment alone to say his farewell so he could weep with some privacy. He didn't want the others to see him in a moment of weakness. Even though Cole had grown from a pudgy teenage boy to a spell-casting giant, he had never felt so powerless and vulnerable. Roth, Chiron, and Alvani were no more. The enormity of their absence seemed to hit him all at once, taking his breath and legs out from under him. He fell to his knees, wrapping his arms around the warm cyrstal that had become Alvani's legs. He felt like a little boy, cast out into a storm far from the safety of his mother and Nana Beth, drowning in an ocean of his own inadequacy. He couldn't do it. He would fail in this war, just as he had failed to save Lexy and Joshy. There was no hope for them now.

Cole slumped lower, crying into Alvani's feet, but something tickled his nose. Where his tears fell into the grass, a green stalk sprouted up, its tip balling up into a chubby bud before blooming in earnest. The flower was plain, but it released a wonderful scent that reminded Cole of happier times, of days spent wandering The Sill and exploring the Arts District with Lileth. A snowy butterfly landed on the flower. It flexed its wings and probed through the petals, entirely unaware of the evils and tragedies outside its little world. Cole felt a swell of Passion return to him, soothing a Despair he was only now aware of. Emboldened, he took hold of a sliver of his Rage and felt the Despair flee back to the dank pits of his mind. Cole rose to his feet and gave Alvani a swift kiss on the forehead before charging after his unit. Alvani was right; they were now the Unbound. With his help the unit would master themselves and their magic. Together they would be the bane of The Three. The war was far from over.

CHAPTER 3

BLOOD IN THE WATER

The unit kept to the ground instead of flying. Everyone was exhausted from their contributions to Alvani and Gale, and no one had fully recovered from the battle in Fangshard Valley. They kept at a steady jog as their magic replenished, sustaining themselves through Alvani's supplies and the purified water they found along the way. They agreed they needed to get back to The Sill. They would muster up any remaining troops and train them while coming up with a way forward.

After replenishing himself with Alvani's gratia stones, Cole found that his recent accomplishments in Passion revealed the life candles of everyone he'd ever been close to, including the baby girl he'd saved in Brimhallow village. Her candle was dim and distant, but it was acute enough for him to sense her general direction. Cole felt a flutter of anxiety upon facing her again. He had left the baby with the old man Naythan, who was as ornery as he was ancient, but also a master healer. Naythan had informed Cole of a grave mistake made while rescuing the baby. While attempting to remove the girl's wicked memories from the sacking of Brimhallow Village, he had inadvertently damaged the girl's mind beyond repair. Cole was honor-bound to the girl's wellbeing now, but part of him Feared meeting her again and seeing her affliction blossom in person.

After several days of meager respites and trudging through game trails, the unit's Rage had entirely recovered, hastening their progress commensurately. They chose to remain on the ground, however, as their conjured wings would be too easily seen by enemy forces, and no one was eager for another fight just yet. Conversation was as scarce as their dwindling supplies. Though they ran in tight formation, everyone seemed content with being alone with their thoughts for a while. They continued on for two days after they exhausted their supplies, fueling their bodies instead with Rage, as well as an eagerness to gain as much distance from Oberon City as possible. After a week's hard travel the unit made proper camp, complete with protective spells and a roaring bonfire full of sizzling meat and roasted vegetation collected along the way. After eating their fill, they stripped to their undergarments and took a much-needed bath in a nearby river.

While the others busied themselves with washing up, Cole caught Lileth's eye and beckoned her to a deep eddy. She followed, wading out until the water rose up to her chin. Cole waited until she was out of earshot of the others before asking, "Do you want to talk about it?"

Dark thoughts swam behind her eyes as she pondered his question. At last she shook her head, her chin sending little waves across the surface of the water. "No. What's done is done and I won't perseverate further. I will miss Alvani dearly, but her death is the fault of Habbad and The Three, not mine."

Cole didn't like how her expression hardened back to her usual mask of stoicism. He could tell she was suppressing her feelings, but he knew her well enough to know she wouldn't come out of her shell until she was ready. "Well, just remember I'm here for you. I'll always be here for you."

Lileth swam closer, and as she did Cole felt the water temperature rise to that of a hot tub. Steam hissed and curled up around them. Her hands found his under the water, pulling him so close their noses were less than an inch apart. Her lips parted and she spoke through an alluring smile. "I think that's all I really need, for you to be here I mean. I don't know if I'll ever figure it out, but there's something about you that makes me feel... together. It's as if part of me that I never knew was returned when we met, or perhaps that part simply grew in the hollows of my soul. Regardless, I feel whole when you're around."

Cole had forgotten he was supposed to be paddling and most of his head dunked under the surface. He popped back up to find Lileth chuckling at him. He cast a quick spell over both their bodies. She let out a gasp as his magic tugged her nearly naked form against his own.

"Well then it's a good thing I'm not going anywhere, because I feel the same way about you." Cole followed his heart before his brain could stop him, and kissed Lileth deeply. He expected her to withdraw, but her hands wandered over his back as she pulled him closer.

"You're freezing," Lileth said, rubbing her hands over his shoulders and arms. "Do you not know how to warm the water around you?" There was a quick flash of green in the water around them as Lileth made the water even hotter.

"I do," Cole replied, indulging in the soothing warmth and Lileth's massaging hands. "But without Chiron's cape, Varka's cape I should say, I still struggle with Wisdom. I have much to learn, especially if we're supposed to be the next Unbound."

"We all must grow," Lileth said. "But you least of all. Mastery of both Rage and Passion, and you haven't even been on Aeneria for a full cycle. Your Wisdom will develop quickly enough, I'm sure of it." Her eyes suddenly fell to the water between them and her brow furrowed with concern. "I worry though, about your Passion. It scares me."

Cole laughed softly, shaking his head. "I thought my Rage would scare you the most as I almost killed you with it a couple of times." Seeing the concern tighten on her face, Cole stopped laughing and cupped her cheek with his hand. "I'm sorry, I thought you were joking. What about my Passion scares you?"

Lileth eyes fell to the side. "It's foolish. I shouldn't have said anything."

"You've seen me make a fool of myself countless times," Cole said. "Please, tell me."

"It's Eliza," Lileth said. "I worry that your Passion extends certain feelings to her, especially while you're so closely bonded with the magic. Even the superficial link that you've connected to me with is somewhat intimate in nature. I can only imagine what you and Eliza must share now that you are both masters of the magic. Your Passion scares me because I'm afraid you'll love her over me in the end."

As Lileth spoke, Cole withdrew from his link with Eliza, thinning their connection to an almost imperceptible strand. Eliza was a dear friend and they had shared almost everything since they joined minds, but he didn't want her hearing this. Especially not after she'd revealed her feelings towards him. After ensuring he wouldn't be overheard through magical or mundane means, he spoke in a low voice. "That won't happen. Ever. Eliza and I are friends, nothing more. My heart burns for you and no one else. It's always been you, Lileth, ever since I dreamed of you in that meadow."

Hope lifted Lileth's features as her smile returned. "That was so long ago. You made a beautiful soul fly by the way. I wished I could have gone with you when you left."

"I promise if I ever figure out how to Travel on purpose I'll take you with me, to all the local planets." Cole gave her a gentle squeeze.

"Not if I figure it out first," Lileth said with a mischievous grin. Cole felt her survey him with a pulse of Passion. "Your Wisdom really is terrible."

Cole gazed deep into her eyes, wishing he could live in this moment forever. "I'll follow you anywhere."

Lileth's eyebrow curved up. "Then how about you follow me underwater." She pressed her palm flat against his bare chest and sent a blast of Wisdom into him. Before Cole knew what hit him, she disappeared beneath the surface.

Cole's lungs began to burn in earnest. If Lileth hadn't cast the same spell on him once before, he would have panicked. Dunking his head under, Cole forced the air out of his lungs and sucked in all the water he could, dousing the choking conflagration in his chest. It was painful and went against every instinct he had, but after a few heaves Cole was breathing water as though it was no more than heavy air. With a quick spell of his own design, Cole flattened the lenses of his eyes, granting himself crystal-clear vision.

He found Lileth swimming near the bottom, her raven hair billowing behind her bare shoulders as she laid herself on a patch of light sand. The moonlight cast flattering shades over her body, showing the soft curves of her hips and hard muscles across her back. Cole met her with a few powerful strokes. A tiny school of mirror fish darted out of his way as he swam. Lileth twisted onto her back to face him, pointing somewhere to the surface. Cole spun and put his bare back to the sand, enjoying the pleasant scratch of the sharp granules against his skin. He followed Lileth's outstretched finger and saw

Oberon looming above like a rainbow ghost. The current distorted the moon's shape, making it appear even more indecisive about what color it wanted to be. Her hands found his, her fingers weaving in between his as she pulled herself onto him, kissing him through the water, which now seemed ready to boil around them.

When Cole and Lileth finally emerged from the water, the rest of the unit had long finished bathing and eating and preparing for sleep. Sitra greeted Cole with a volley of jokes, all centered around his and Lileth's lengthy absence. Lileth refrained from rising to the bait, donning her usual expressionless mask as she set up a makeshift bed beside the campfire. Cole's face on the other hand seemed stuck in a permanent grin as the residual Passion filled his chest and pulsed in his loins.

He ignored Sitra until sleep finally took her, instead watching Lileth as she lay with her eyes closed, a satisfied smile on her face. She was the most beautiful thing Cole had ever seen, with her black petal lashes, full lips, and hair still slick from the water. Just the sight of her made Cole's heart feel too wild for the cage of his chest, as though it belonged up in the sky chasing the stars. Even if he were capable of sleep, there was no way his dreams would find him tonight, for the dream before his eyes was far too sweet.

Cole patrolled the campsite while the others slept. He inventoried Valen's protective spells, checking for weak links and gaps, but there was none. Even while fast asleep Valen's Wisdom was far beyond Cole's level. With a pang of guilt he found Eliza curled up several yards away from the others, isolated. He felt for her link but it was completely gone. Cole spent the rest of the night in the stone room of his center, panning through thoughts and memories of recent events while temporarily emptying himself of all emotion. When the unit woke he had already disassembled the campsite and removed all traces of their presence. They set off after a quick bite of leftovers from the night before.

After an hour of steady sprinting, Sitra slowed the unit to an easy jog as she fell in to the center of their formation. "So are we ever going to discuss Alvani's cryptic message or are we just going to pretend like it never happened?"

"Master Alvani imparted quite a bit of grave news upon us before she faded," Valen replied. "Which part were you referring to exactly?"

"Oh I don't know, Val," Sitra said with a mirthless laugh. "How about that part when that demon thing spoke from her mouth and froze the marrow in our bones? Did anyone actually hear what she said?"

"Betrayal," Eliza replied. "It said betrayal. I felt the word from inside Alvani's mind, spoken by a presence other than her own."

"She was talking about the pithing shards, and something called the *Cold Crows*," Cole said as a sickly chill ran up his spine. He could almost feel the weight of that evil presence wrapping around him again. "Does anyone have a clue what the Cold Crows are?" No one replied, though all their eyes flashed to Lileth's canvas rucksack and the pithing shard buried within.

"I'm more curious as to what Alvani meant by *betrayal*," Valen said at last. "I Fear we may not have felt the final sting of that portent."

"That answer's obvious," Sitra said with a wave of her munisica. "That little bastard Habbad betrayed us. Big bastard I should say. How the hell did he grow so tall?"

"He could have altered his body with Wisdom," Lileth said. "He *was* unusually adept in the art."

"No, I don't think so," Eliza interjected. "He would need to possess near mastery of Wisdom for such a feat, and the process would take months of constant and very precise focus to do it right. None of us could do it. A few inches maybe, but to triple one's height would be a terrible waste of resources for little payoff. No, I think he used Grotton's magic to alter his body."

"How so?" Lileth asked in a polite tone, keeping her eyes straight ahead as she jogged. "Grotton's Hunger deals in lies and coercion, and if he took a large Domina into himself, he would look more animal than Underkin."

"I believe Habbad took an Aenerian thrall for his Domina," Eliza replied. Her words seemed to slow the unit's pace with the weight of the implications. "Or *many* Aenerian thralls."

"That is impossible," Valen said defiantly. "An intelligent mind would never submit to a Domina contract, it is too simple a trick to fall for. He would have to enthrall a king of fools, which would diminish his own intelligence."

"I don't think it's all that impossible," Cole said, attempting to catch Eliza's eye. "Habbad was as ferocious as he was cunning. He always found a way to weasel his way through a task, magical or not, and he never ended up worse off in our lessons. Habbad despised Aenerians, and where he came from all Underkin lived and died as slaves. I wouldn't put it past him to take an Aenerian soul for his own personal slave. He definitely had something to do with those pithing shards too, and seeing as none of us understands how the hell those things work, we really can't label anything impossible when it comes to Habbad."

Eliza nodded in agreement, but otherwise didn't reply. Cole felt Lileth's eyes burning on him, so he fell back to run next to her.

"You bring up some good points, Cole," Valen said. "Habbad is a prime suspect in terms of betrayal, but do we want to limit our suspicions to him?"

"Probably not," Cole replied. "We shouldn't rule anything out at this point. Or any*one*."

"What about that wart, Arcturus?" Sitra said through bared teeth. "The Speaker for the Celestial Council. He Hated us before we even met him. Probably wanted payback for Cole and Chiron leaving against Council edict. Stars, I wish Roth had broken his jaw so we didn't have to hear his sniveling voice."

"Arcturus is a Speaker," Valen said in a slightly patronizing tone. "His every thought and memory is wide open for the entire Council's perusal. From what I understand the connection works like a Passion bond, accept Arcturus is a conduit for the minds of all twenty-one Council members. Lileth, your home village uses a similar form of higher government, does it not?"

"Yes," Lileth replied. "The Speaker is a mental hub for the others."

"You mean he's a puppet," Sitra said through a snarl. "I'm still not counting him out though. Maybe we should sneak back in the temple and have a little chat with old Arcturus just to be sure."

"Clean your ears out, Sitra," Eliza snapped. Sitra's face went slack, as though she had just been slapped. "If you doubt Arcturus then you bring the entire Council under scrutiny, which is a reach beyond foolishness. It is possible, however, that an individual Council member could deceive the others. Especially if they partition any secretive memories before joining with the Speaker."

"Do we really want to accuse the Celestial Council?" Valen asked the group. "They are the leaders of the entire Dark Side. Such treachery would cast a bleak future for us all."

"We can't rule them out," Cole said as a horrible memory of his last night in Oberon Temple crept up. His munisica flared painfully as his bladed feet elevated him a few inches taller. "The Corpulant that attacked me in my sleep... Chiron said it could only have infiltrated the Everglen with help from someone inside the temple. Someone involved in this betrayal was inside Oberon Temple at the time I was attacked."

Grim silence fell over the unit as the dirt path under their feet gave way to a soft cushion of fallen pine needles. Cole let his words hang, knowing full well the weight of the insinuations tied to them. Not only had he shed doubts over the Council and the many thousands living within Oberon Temple, he extended the possibility of blame to their elders and each member of the unit. The only innocent party he was certain of was Eliza, as their Passion bond would have made any treachery plain to see.

Valen was first to speak, addressing Cole but speaking loudly enough for everyone to hear. "The only way to know for sure is to inspect the minds of everyone who was in Oberon Temple at the time, including each of us. You and Eliza are the only ones with the Passion to do so. I for one refuse to have my every secret laid bare for all to see, and should anyone here have their mind invaded against their will I shall intervene."

"Agreed," Lileth said.

"I'm not suggesting we start breaking into anyone's head," Cole said, though in the calm of his center he felt it was the only logical course of action. He was confident he could do it too, so long as Eliza didn't try to stop him. If betrayal was a real possibility then they needed to start with a clean base of fact, not blind trust. Followers of Grotton used the trust of good people as tempting rope to climb, which made it all the easier to hang them later. Now was not the time for contention, however, so Cole tried another approach. "If we start forcing our way into each other's minds, then we might as well head back to Oberon City and go join The Three. A mental inspection would have to be voluntary, and I'll be the first to volunteer."

"Cole is trustworthy," Eliza said. Her eyes flicked over Cole as a doleful shadow fell across her face. "I have been inside his mind for months at a time. There is no treachery within him, though I'd be happy to search him more thoroughly once we reach The Sill."

Sitra trotted up behind Eliza and clapped her on the backside with a bladed hand. "You can take a look up my ass too, Liza. I've got nothing to hide. It's no secret I think you're all as stupid as a pile of bog angels, though you're only half as ugly. Just make sure Valen removes that stick from *his* ass before you take a peek up there."

"*Ha Ha*," Valen said with a mirthless laugh. "Leave it to Sitra to make light of betrayal and murder. Perhaps I shall join Eliza's inspection of your mind to see what exactly makes you so charming."

Conversation took on a refreshingly playful tone for the rest of the push. The rise and fall of the terrain became less pronounced as the surrounding pines became thicker and fuller. Another few days passed and they neared the limits of the Fangshards, a fact made all the more apparent to Cole as he felt Goran's waning presence in the rocks and soil under his feet. He still had his Passion bond with his friend, but as before the mirak's focus was spread across the whole of the Fangshards, with a slightly heavier concentration at the valley near Oberon City.

Every now and then Goran sent brief glimpses of shifting rock or torrents of snow pouring over the recently closed Fangshard Valley. The power required to close an entire mountain pass was near a thing of gods, and the fact that Goran now possessed such strength meant that Cole must have been affected somehow. As Eliza once told him, the Passion bond with an animal was reciprocal, so as much as Goran had advanced, Cole must have grown as well. The thought of so much power both intrigued and scared him. Every night while the others slept he probed his mind from the safety of his center, searching for sources of his own Goran-like power, but he only found his reserves of Rage and Passion with his Wisdom trailing far behind. Cole was certainly powerful in his own right, but his magic was nothing compared to the might that Goran now wielded.

After days of cutting through game trails and sneaking through shadows, the salty air of the lagoon outside The Sill greeted them like an old friend. They could see Oberon's light rippling off the water through the trees, and hear the waves whispering up the wending shore. As they neared the edge of the tree line, Eliza halted the group with a flick of thought. The unit crouched low, sharpening their ears and eyes with Wisdom as they took up a defensive formation. Cole scanned the surrounding area with his Passion and discovered the source of Eliza's alarm at once. Just off the shoreline were several dense clusters of life candles gliding over the water. Cole brushed against the minds of one of the strangers, which turned out to be three separate entities held together by a ravenous Hunger. Peeking through the leaves, Cole saw a hulking ship topped with a blood-red flag on its main mast. The flag had a black fist set inside a pair of jaws with jagged teeth; the banner of the Domina.

Cole shifted his Passion to the life candles around him, inviting the unit to join in a mental network as they did while examining Alvani. Each mind connected to his own with an air of caution, though Sitra latched right on, gripping them all with excited Rage.

"Oh come on, let's go for it," Sitra urged. She reminded Cole of a cat ready to pounce. She peered through the leaves, flexing her munisica and bouncing on her toes. *"Look at that one! He looks dumb as a stump. They'd never see it coming."*

"Domina are unpredictable," Valen reasoned. *"A head-on assault would be foolish. We should glean what we can from a distance before acting. We don't even know what they have for thralls. They could be venomous, or armored, or flyers."*

"And my munisica won't care what they're made out of, I'll tear their hearts out just the same," Sitra said with a bloodthirsty growl. She gripped a nearby trunk so forcibly that her claws creaked into the wood. *"We're the Unbound now, Alvani even said so! We've been sneaking and hiding from these things for weeks, and now we have a chance to catch them with their pants down. I'm not wasting time with planning when I should be killing."*

"We are pretty close to home," Cole said, showing them the proximity of the life candles at The Sill. *"Those boats are headed right for The Sill, and by the looks of it they'll be there within a few hours. This might be our only chance at surprise."*

Valen shook his head. *"There are too many variables, not least of which is how many and what variety of priests are aboard those boats, but you do have a point. This may be our best opportunity."*

"Allow me to make this choice a little easier for us then," Sitra said with a tone of savage glee. She dropped her rucksack and leapt for the tree tops. Jade wings snapped out from her back. *"Study me for a minute if you want, Val."*

"Sitra!" Eliza's voice blared across their minds, then she leapt up into the air without another word, dropping her bag as well. Her emerald wings sliced through the canopy of sun lily leaves as she twisted out of sight.

"Maybe we can plan it as we go?" Cole chuckled aloud as he watched the frustration grow on Valen's face.

Valen gave a resigned sigh and conjured his own wings. Setting his rucksack down, he tore up into the sky in a burst of wind.

Cole set his own bag down as gently as he could so as not to disturb Lexy. Lileth watched him closely, as if waiting for something. Cole looked up to see her grinning wide with an eyebrow raised. "Something funny?"

"The last time we were on this beach I had to carry you," she replied with a smirk. "Just checking to see if you need a lift."

"Not a chance," Cole said defiantly. With a twist of thought, Varka's cape tuned Cole's Wisdom to the perfect pitch. He shot straight up into the sky without the aid of wings as the cape shifted from black soil to rippling glass. He felt Lileth's life candle trailing close behind him.

Once above the canopy, Cole surveyed the three vessels plowing their way up the shoreline. Each ship had three masts, though the sails were furled and black smoke poured out of iron pipes in their afts. The vessels appeared large enough for fifty Aenerians apiece, but the figures stalking about the decks were so large that the ship appeared to be a toy model. From what Cole could tell, the Domina were comprised of the same variety the unit first encountered. They were each nearly twice the height of a tall man, with a mismatched blend of claws, hooves, horns, or giant hands clutching crude weapons. Their snouts and finger-length teeth were easily large enough to swallow a child whole. The ships rode low in the water, hinting that the decks below were full of supplies or perhaps more Domina.

"Don't forget to maintain your mental links," Cole urged the others, keeping a firm grip on each of their life candles. *"There's got to be over a hundred Domina down there, which means there's likely a few of Grotton's priests to control them all. Keep your Rage in check so they don't turn it against you."*

"But that takes all the fun out of it," Sitra whined before tilting into a steep dive aimed at the rearmost ship. Valen and Eliza followed close behind her.

Cole climbed a little higher, hovering above the center of the fleet and hopefully out of sight of the Domina below.

"Don't you want to follow them?" Lileth said as she floated up beside him.

"I want to see how the Domina react," Cole said, watching carefully as Sitra's hands ignited with magical flame. "The Domina won't expect you and me to join in, not while they're focused on the others."

"How very tactical of you," Lileth said.

"I'm just trying to do what Roth would do," Cole replied. He took a deep breath and made a quick visit to his center, granting himself clarity before the impending violence. "Actually I'm more worried that one of Grotton's priests will capitalize on Sitra's Rage. We'll be able to see it and stop it from up here."

Lileth nodded, impressed. "You're getting good at this."

Sitra passed over the rearmost ship in a streak of emerald wings and roaring flames, spraying liquid fire along the top deck as she went. The Domina reacted quickly, manning harpoon guns and blaring their war horns. They hurled spears and fired at Sitra with deck guns, but Valen was there in a flash, hovering just above the main mast, where he wove his hands through the air as though conducting an orchestra. The missiles followed unnatural paths, sailing away from Sitra and looping up to the sky, where they made a sharp u-bend and flew back to their owners. The Domina screamed and threw up a few shields. The spears clanged off harmlessly, but the heavy harpoons pierced the metal like rock through wet paper, skewering the Domina beneath. Eliza made a low pass around the hull, spraying the wood below the surface with rays of fuchsia Passion.

The Domina howled and retreated back into the growing fires as more of their comrades came bustling out of the lower deck. They seemed torn between a desire to kill their attackers and a need to put out the fire before it spread across the entire ship. After a moment of snarling and shouting, they did both poorly. Claws and axes cleaved at the burning wood, then the Domina chucked the timber at Valen. Valen deflected the barrage as he did with the first; however, the Domina and their ammunition had grown too numerous. Valen swooped away from a spear and sent a flaming cross-beam back at its owner, only to sail right into a weighted net that was cast from a small Domina in the crow's nest. The net tangled itself in Valen's wings as he dropped to the water.

"Do not worry about me," Valen assured them all. *"I'll be free in a moment. Let them think they killed me."*

The Domina roared in victory. They focused their efforts on Eliza, who was still looping around, soaking the sides of the ship with Passion.

Sitra swooped to the aft of the ship and clung to the hull with her munisica. *"What the hell are you doing, Liza? Healing their ship?"* She plunged a flaming hand into a window, sending a river of fire into what Cole guessed was an engine room.

"You'll see in about a minute," Eliza said. She made one final pass around the hull before landing gently in the middle of the deck. The looks of shock on the Domina's misshapen faces quickly hardened to murderous Hunger.

"Eliza..." Cole said, preparing himself to dive down to her aid.

"Relax, Cole," Eliza said.

A surge of Passion rushed forth from Eliza, flooding their network with a dizzying pulse of euphoria. Cole blinked, steadying himself as he dropped a few feet in the air. Down on the deck, Eliza stood with her arms spread wide, a fuchsia aura radiating from her into the crowd of circling enemies. The Domina halted and dropped their weapons as their ugly faces drooped with stupefied expressions.

There was a loud bang from below deck as a cloud of grey smoke replaced the black billowing from the exhaust pipes. Sitra landed next to Eliza, fury and bloodlust in her eyes. She dismissed her emerald wings and her shroud crawled up her limbs and her long braid hardened to an obsidian whip. The door to the lower decks crashed open. A portly man in copper robes rushed out, hacking violently and hopping on one foot as he pulled his pants up from around his knees. He looked from the dumbstruck Domina to the two women in front of him.

The man's chins jiggled as he screamed, "What have you done to my Domina? And my ship!" He fastened a belt at his waist and stamped out a small fire by his foot. Flames lapped at the Domina's legs, but they stood moon-faced and swaying as though in a trance.

Sitra took a step towards the man, her bladed hands flexing menacingly. Eliza threw out an arm, stopping her.

The man's eyes sharpened as he took in Sitra's munisica. "Ah, very nice. A whore for the red Rage and a slut for the lover's Passion. Bring that fury over here, sweetie, let's see if you're as good a dancer as you look."

Sitra growled and crouched low. Cole recognized the ruddy orange glow in his eyes as Grotton's magic; Hunger. Grasping his Passion, Cole willed the magic into Sitra's mind. Her Rage fought back like a child squirming away from a parent's kiss, but within a few heartbeats Cole's Passion soothed her red magic. Her shroud and munisica reverted to bare skin.

"*Thanks, Cole,*" Sitra beamed through their network, then brought her attention back to the priest. "I'd love to dance, but you're not really my type. Little on the chubby side for me. I'm worried you'll be too rough for my tender frame."

The Hunger in the priest's face soured into a childish Rage. Tiny munisica enveloped his fingertips as he charged, screaming at the top of his lungs.

With a flick of Wisdom, Sitra yanked up a length of decking, halting the priest as his stomach collided with the plank. He fell to all fours, gasping as he tried to bring air back into his lungs.

"Into the air now, Sitra," Eliza said, flashing a sense of alarm across their network.

"But I'm about to rip his arms off!" Sitra whined, stamping her foot.

"That might still happen," Eliza said. She glanced about the deck, apprehension sharpening. *"The air, now!"*

Cole watched as the two women took flight in a gust of wind and flames. Cole was about to ask Eliza what was wrong, but something on the ship caught his eye. A shapeless mass of what looked like grey stone began to crawl up the exterior of the hull. The thing swelled up into bulbous rocks the size of wagon wheels, sinking the ship even deeper into the water as they sprouted across the deck.

"What are they?" Sitra asked.

"Barnacles," Eliza said plainly. *"This variety normally feeds off plankton and small fish, but at their current size I wager they'd prefer larger game."*

"That's disgusting. I love it," Sitra said as she watched the rocky crustaceans spread over the entire deck like dirty grey tumors.

Two barnacles sprouted long, feathery appendages and sent them squirming around a Domina, who was still stunned by Eliza's Passion. With a violent twist, the feathery tentacles sawed through the Domina's leg and torso, knocking back a nearby fire with a splash of blood. The priest had barely recovered from the blow to his stomach when he finally realized what the barnacles were. Fear blossomed in his eyes as he sprinted for the side rails, but a feathery rope slapped around his ankle, removing his foot as though plucking an apple from a tree branch. His scream died almost instantly as he fell right into a clump of barnacles, which promptly chopped him into dozens of pieces small enough to carry back to the mouths of their shells. In no time at all the barnacles consumed every Domina on the upper deck, gaining in both numbers and mass with every limb they carried back to their insatiable maws. Eventually their combined bulk dragged the entire ship below the surface, where it vanished in a cloud of steam and bubbling smoke.

"Valen, how are you doing down there?" Cole asked, eyeing the two other ships, which were now within harpooning range of Sitra and Eliza.

"I am free," Valen said, sending a spike of revulsion through the network. *"I was about to disable the rudder on this ship, but Eliza's little friends wouldn't let me near it. Are they going to be a problem? We ought not to leave such monsters running free in our waters."*

"They'll expire within an hour," Eliza replied with a prick of remorse. *"Once they grow beyond the fuel of my Passion and the meat from the Domina, they will starve."*

"That's so twisted!" Sitra exclaimed. *"I want to kill something with Passion!"*

Scanning the entire shoreline, Cole sent an image of the two remaining ships into their mental network. *"Valen, stay under and disable whatever rudders and propellers the other two ships have. Sitra and Eliza, you two take the ship farthest from the shoreline. Watch out for the priests this time. He almost had you, Sitra."*

"As you wish, oh mighty Varka," Sitra said, saturating her mental voice with heavy sarcasm. *"Are you gonna do any work or just bark orders from the clouds?"*

"Lileth and I are going to take the ship nearer to the shore," Cole replied. *"And when we're done we'll help you finish up. It took you almost five minutes to take down that first one. Roth would be ashamed of you."*

Sitra's Rage flashed hot across their link. *"Oh you're so dead. I'm gonna tickle you with my munisica when we're done here."*

"The Domina will die of boredom if you two keep bickering," Valen said, sending them all a fuzzy image of a pair of broken propellers sinking to the lagoon floor.

Laughing, Cole turned to Lileth. "Ready?"

"For what exactly?" she replied, giving him a quizzical look. "Cole, I don't like the way you're smiling. You better not do anything foolish."

"Here, put this on," Cole said as he unfastened Varka's cape. Ignoring Lileth's protests, he flung the crystalline fabric at her and felt the expected dip in his Wisdom, then dropped like a stone.

Cole's stomach flipped over on itself as the wind rushed through his hair. The thrill of freefall was almost overwhelming, and he was still hundreds of feet above the water. As he picked up speed he nudged Wisdom throughout his body, guiding his fall and accelerating him faster still. The wind stung at his eyes, forcing them shut. He attempted to shield his face with a spell, but his Wisdom was too slippery without Varka's cape. Instead, he opened himself to Passion, aiming himself for the cluster of life candles farthest from the shore. He pressed his arms to his sides, cutting through the air as fast as he could. Right before he collided, he ignited his Rage.

The shroud snapped over his body, armoring him inside and out as his munisica flared to ebony dragon claws. Hot and wild, the Rage demanded Cole's every thought and desire; however, Cole was well-acquainted with the savage urges of the red magic. He yanked the leash, matching his Rage to the necessity of the moment while promising it a bounty of blood and havoc.

Cole opened his eyes. He was only thirty feet above the deck. Twenty feet. The Domina weren't even aware of his presence. Likely they never would be. Time took on its usual slowness when Cole was engulfed in Rage. He savored the Domina for what felt like hours, indulging in their vulnerability, their weakness. When Cole was ten feet above the deck, he snapped his limbs as wide as he could.

There was an explosion of wood and tar as Cole smashed through the decking. He barely slowed, descending through two more decks, battering through heavy timber, flesh, and metal, though through the shroud it all felt like punching through stale bread. It wasn't until a sloshing noise filled Cole's ears that he knew he'd passed through the entire ship. The water brought him spinning to a halt. He looked up, his blurred vision revealing the vague outline of the jagged hole he had just passed through.

It was surprisingly difficult to swim while fully shrouded. His munisica were designed for rending and smashing, not paddling, and his body had become so dense that he was no longer buoyant. Cole dismissed the red magic, feeling the coolness of the water replace the dullness of his shroud. The ship was sinking rapidly now, so Cole took hold of his Wisdom and shot himself to the surface like a torpedo.

His head and torso broke through to the air, but he sank back down at once as his levitation spell wasn't strong enough for proper flight. Treading water, he looked to the ship, finding only the main mast above the surface with several Domina clinging to the crow's nest. Soon dozens of ugly snouts bobbed up around him, choking and struggling to stay afloat with their axes and armor weighing them down.

"Need a hand?" called a clear voice above him.

Cole wiped his eyes, looking up to discover Lileth floating just above him with Varka's cape whipping behind her shoulders like liquid glass. He beamed up at her, spitting out a mouthful of salt water.

"No way. I'm not having you carry me again," Cole said, screwing up his face in concentration. A second later his Wisdom took hold of his body, and he rose steadily out of the water. He leveled with Lileth, but she shot off away from him, hovering above the churning masses below.

Lileth's eyes were ablaze with calculated fury. Varka's cape shimmered as her hands erupted with emerald light. She swung her arms in a wide arch before bringing her palms together, aiming them at the Domina like a gun. A few priests popped up at the surface now, clamoring orders to their minions while fighting to stay afloat in the chaos. The Domina wailed as emerald light shone off the wet fur of their scalps. The surface of the water looked like a boiling stew as the Domina splashed and thrashed away from Lileth, but they were far too slow.

Emerald orbs exploded from Lileth's palms, raining down upon the Domina like starfire. Their eyes rolled as they watched the magic pass by them and dissipate in the water. At first nothing happened, but then a deadly quiet replaced the splashing and the snorting. The Domina ceased all movement, though they did not sink. The water was hardening. Within a few seconds an entire acre of surface solidified into ice. Some Domina had only their heads or noses above the water, emitting piteous shrieks while others were drowned in frozen silence below.

Lileth sent a beam of Wisdom into the ice. There was an explosion like cannonfire as the swath of ice shattered along with the victims trapped within. Cole watched, half disgusted, half awestruck, as the surface of the water became a cocktail of broken bodies trapped in bloody ice cubes. Lileth took a quick lap above the wreckage, checking for survivors. There were none.

Cole trailed Lileth with his feeble Wisdom, following her to aid the others in taking down the final ship, but when they arrived it was clear they required no help at all. The prow of the ship had already sunk deep underwater, its aft hanging up in the air with broken propellers exposed. Eliza stood on the rear hull, locked in battle with a tall priestess weilding a conjured purple spear. Sitra danced around a few Domina beside Eliza, laughing her head off while spraying the beasts with electric pink Passion from her hands. The Domina appeared to be growing larger by the second, but as Cole neared he saw it was only their fur, which quickly swelled into unmanageable tangles, turning them into blundering tumbleweeds of wiry brown hair. The Domina tripped over themselves, rolling down the deck and into the water. Valen was waiting for them. He swooped over the bobbing Domina like a hawk on the hunt, sending bolts of blue lightning down into the water and electrocuting those who dared come up for air.

Cole and Lileth alighted on the aft of the ship, surprising the remaining priestess with their sudden appearance. Eliza seized the moment and drove a bladed hand through the woman's chest. Life drained from the eyes of the priestess, and she toppled down the hull and vanished with a splash. One of Valen's blue bolts followed her body down into the water.

"Well that was fun," Sitra said, leaning back against the broken propeller. "Are there any more? I've just thought of another way to kill someone with Passion."

"Just the priestess in the crow's nest," Valen hollered as he landed on the slanted deck. "I believe she is calling for help, but I cannot imagine why. Perhaps she thinks another fleet will fare better?"

Cole looked up to the crow's nest. A woman was swinging an odd hammer against the top of the main mast, striking a long, narrow bell covered with intricate engravings. The bell made no sound; however, Cole noticed a deep vibration under his feet with each blow. Sitra took a step towards the mast with Passion glowing in one hand, but stopped as a jade disc went buzzing over her shoulder, cleaving the mast from the deck. The priestess jumped out of the crow's nest right before the mast thunked to the water. Valen stepped in front of Sitra, jade Wisdom ready in his hands. With an almost lazy flick of his wrist, he smote the priestess with a final blast of lightning, killing her instantly.

Sitra punched Valen in the arm. "Dammit Val! You already cooked half an army with your stupid lightning. I wanted to try blowing up her heart with Passion."

Valen rubbed his arm while scanning for additional threats. "Sitra relax, Now is not the time for silly experiments. We need to get the job done and get home."

While Sitra and Valen argued, something drew Cole's attention away from the shore out to the open ocean. Something massive was coming, and fast. A shadow tore across the water from the horizon, though there was no cloud in the sky. The shadow grew larger, closer, darting from side to side as if searching for something, then appeared to make up its mind and shot straight towards them.

"Is something the matter?" Lileth asked, sensing Cole's unease.

A drop of Fear settled between the beats of his heart. "We should get off this boat."

"What's wrong?" Sitra asked.

There was a wave forming behind the shadow now. They didn't have much time. He instinctively reached for his Wisdom, intending to levitate himself as high as he could. However, the Fear had spread through his chest like cold fire, crippling the green magic.

"The sky, now!" Eliza cried, taking flight in a whirlwind of ocean mist and emerald wings.

The others followed her while Cole fumbled with his Wisdom. Fortunately Lileth grabbed him under the arms and rushed him up to the stars. When they were safely above the water, Cole glanced down. His Passion told him a massive beast was right below them.

An explosive force suddenly yanked the entire ship to the deep as a geyser of foaming water shot up in its place, carrying with it a menacing bellow of some hidden monster. A gust of hot, fetid breath rushed up around them. Cole probed the mind of the monster with Passion, sensing a familiar sadness blended with prodigious Hunger. The mind felt ancient, and held echoes of purity and innocence, but the Hunger lashing within its soul dominated all, demanding flesh and power with every thought.

CHAPTER 4

COMFORT OR COMMITMENT

"What is that thing?" Sitra asked once Cole and Lileth had joined their circle.

"An abomination," Eliza replied, looking at the murky water with a look of utmost disgust. "Grotton's minions have no limits on what animals they take for Domina, though I never thought I would live to see the day a baileen became a thrall. Several baileen actually, judging by the creature's mass. We have to kill it. For its own sanity and the safety of Aeneria."

"Or we could just get the hell out of here," Sitra said. "That thing feels enormous. I say we notch our belts and call it a day."

"I am inclined to side with Sitra on this," Valen said, peering down at the bubbling remains of the ship. "But what would the baileen's—" Valen clapped his hands over his ears as a horrible keen pierced the sky.

The surface of the water erupted, revealing a gaping maw large enough to swallow the entire ship. A massive creature rose into the air, rising straight for them as though launched from a cannon. It looked as if it may have been a whale at one point, with its long nose and curving jaw, but its teeth were human-like, each larger than a man and jutting out from puffy gums. Its skin was a supple shade of pink with patches of black hair clinging to its hide. Instead of flippers, the creature had nubbed appendages that looked like half-formed hands and feet, pruny and useless. In place of eyes were two solid black orbs sunken in the sides of its head. The creature reminded Cole horribly of a large naked baby, a single-minded toddler rushing for a snack.

"Move!" Cole jolted the message through their Passion network, forcing the concept into their minds. The unit disappeared in a blur of

emerald wings, leaving Cole struggling to corral his Wisdom into something productive.

The monster continued its ascent at an alarming rate, higher than any creature born of fins and water ought to be able to jump. A fact slid alongside Cole's growing dread, confirming his suspicions; the thing was capable of flight. Cole wasn't going to make it. He abandoned his Wisdom and drew upon a measure of his Rage instead. The red magic was all too eager to come to his aid. The world slowed as the shroud snapped over him, then a solution presented itself to him at once. He allowed himself to fall, colliding with the monster's flank and sinking his munisica deep into its skin. The collision was jarring, but holding on was easy enough. The beast released a sickening wail that rattled Cole's armored teeth, sounding like a thousand demon infants crying in pain.

"It can fly," Cole said through the Passion network.

"We can see that," Lileth replied. *"Are you harmed?"*

Cole held on tightly as the creature banked hard, nearly throwing him off. His grip was unyielding, but he felt his munisica slicing through the beast's skin like knives through soft fruit. He sank another claw in before replying. *"I'm on its back. I'm going to try to work my way to where its brain might be and do what damage I can. In the meantime I need everyone to try and draw it farther inland. I have an idea."*

The unit relayed their acknowledgment in unison. Crawling along, Cole drove a bladed hand or foot deep into the monster's skin, but every time he did, one of his other munisca would cut free from the layers of slick fat. He timed his movements with the sharp turns and flips the creature made as it chased his friends through the sky. After a few minutes it became clear he wouldn't make it near the skull, but the unit had succeeded in luring the monster over a mile inland. Abandoning the kill, Cole released himself partway and carved his way down the creature's back like a cat on a curtain, then kicked off, spinning out into open air. The monster wailed again, though it sounded more out of frustration than pain. Cole glimpsed one of its black-diamond eyes as it banked sharply back towards him with a clumsy flap of its webbed tail.

"Do you want me to catch you?" The message came from Eliza.

"No, I need it to follow me to the ground," Cole replied. *"I need your Passion, however. All you can spare."*

There was a fleeting hesitation from Eliza, then her mind joined his, reestablishing their private bond. Cole felt an ocean of Passion join his, along with every thought, memory, and desire Eliza possessed. Maintaining hold of his Rage, Cole spun uncontrollably through a canopy of sun lily leaves before colliding with the forest floor. The shroud protected him from the force of the impact, though he knew the danger was far from over. Jumping to his feet, he looked to the sky to see the whale's mouth wide open, each crooked tooth draped with thick ropes of mucus. He seized his Rage and launched himself off a nearby tree stump, landing safely thirty paces away. The Domina crashed through the trees, smashing to the ground with the force of a toppling skyscraper.

The baileen shrieked once more, then crawled out from its crater of upturned earth and broken trees with indecent, jerky motions. Green wings streaked down from the sky, followed by a hail of magic consisting of fire, lightning, and jade buzz saws. Each attack found pink flesh, but the damage was slight for a creature so large. The baileen hobbled out of its crater and crawled after Cole with renewed vigor, using its short webbed appendages to scuttle its mass over the forest floor.

With a few seconds to spare, Cole dismissed his Rage and shifted all his faculties to his bond with Eliza. His vision blurred as tears welled in his eyes. He plunged his hands into the black soil and willed the magic into the earth, sending it deep into the roots of the Fangshards.

"Goran! I need you!"

The baileen continued dragging its girth with alarming speed, its beady eyes and gaping maw bearing straight down on Cole. There was no response from the mirak. Cole swore, then sprinted perpendicular to the approaching abomination. He was too slow without his Rage, however. There was a thunderous clap of teeth behind him as something struck him in the back, sending him flying straight through a tree as thick as his chest. He tumbled several times over the ground before skidding to a halt on his back. He coughed up blood and forced his eyes open, wishing he hadn't. The tree he had just passed through was now falling inexorably towards him. Cole rolled to the side as the tree smashed to the ground. A thick branch collided with his back, pinning him down.

"Cole!" Eliza cried into his mind. Her vision bled into his mind, showing her in a steep dive. The Domina was in her periphery, charging directly for him.

Voices from the others rang through their Passion network with Lileth's standing out like a clear bell. Cole spat out a mouthful of blood and ground his teeth together. He managed a single word in his mind, sending it to everyone. *"Don't..."*

The ringing in his ears wasn't loud enough to drown out the din of the charging baileen. He could hear the wetness of its breath, the snapping of its teeth. Lileth called his name again, and at the thought of her in danger, Cole's Rage finally exploded through the confusion.

The shroud flowed like quicksilver over his skin, armoring him inside and out while healing his injuries through hot power and strength. It was time at last to give himself to the full measure of his Rage. His munisica snapped open along with his eyes as he forced the branch off his back and spun to his feet, ready to kill. Time slowed. The abomination was on top of him now, its head twisted sideways as its jaws dropped over either side of him. Cole roared, charging and leaping into the creature's bottom jaw, tearing his munisica in wide arches over and over as darkness closed in around him. He struck at everything he could reach, using what he guessed was the beast's jaw bone for leverage as he cleaved through the flesh. All too soon Cole beheld starlight and felt himself falling through open air. He landed twenty feet below to the beautiful sound of the Domina's agony. A tongue the size of a school bus landed next to him.

There was a buzz of emerald wings, and a flutter of foreign thoughts attempted to enter his mind. He knew they were no threat, so long as they didn't get in between him and his quarry. The Domina wailed again, throwing its massive head from side to side, wetting the forest floor with a waterfall of blood from its puffy gums and human-like teeth. Cole reveled in its weakness for an entire heartbeat before preparing for another attack, intent on removing the entire bottom jaw this time.

Something happened then, so fast that not even his Rage could react quickly enough. Through the fallen trees Cole beheld a gargantuan stone hand erupting from the ground. There was a sound of rolling thunder as the hand crunched around the Domina's tail. The monster's cry cut to silence as the hand yanked it backwards towards what appeared to be a mountain rising from nowhere. Cole's Rage settled to a gratified simmer as he beheld his battle brother, Goran.

The mirak was almost more mountain than animal. His arms, each as broad as a city block, were made of a flexible stone, covered with striped lichen and small trees. His chest was broad and black as charcoal, while his belly was a field of jade moss. The mirak blocked out half the sky as he rose to his full height, which Cole guessed to be just shy of a mile. Even his Rage-sharpened eyes could barely make out the crest of snow and ice than had replaced his fluffy mohawk, but the mirak's eyes were as clear as blazing fire. Ruby-red and filled with ancient savagery, Goran's eyes locked into Cole's, rooting him to the spot with the weight of their intensity.

The Domina kicked and flailed helplessly as Goran brought it to the sky. With one chomp of his cavernous jaws and diving canines, Goran bit through more than half of the Domina's body, swallowing it after a lazy chew. A cascade of blood and viscera ran down his chin, filling the valley of his chest muscles with crimson gore. He swallowed the remainder as easily as throwing back a deka seed.

Unable to contain his excitement any longer, Cole leaped as high as he could. Wind took the laughter from his mouth as his bladed hair clinked over his ears. He landed upon Goran's knee, sinking his munisica into what felt like tree bark before scooting up the mirak's leg like a tiny lizard. Goran brought his cleanest hand to Cole, holding out a finger large enough for his unit to stand on several times over. Cole kicked off Goran's thigh, landed on the rocky surface, then rose swiftly up into the air. The trees below shrank until they appeared no larger than the grass and lichens growing in the crevices of Goran's hands. His Rage cooled, and Cole became aware of the life candles of his unit flying up after him in wide formation. Their network had all but vanished in the heat of the red magic. He poured Passion back into the mental web, reassuring them with soothing thoughts of safety and victory. Cole was sure he could see The Sill from here, but at the moment he had eyes only for his friend.

Goran lifted him to nose level, taking such a blustery inhale that Cole had to hold on with his feet to keep from being sucked into a nostril. With the mirak's exhale he released a searing wind that might have come from the heart of a volcano. Goran gave a slow blink as a single word bellowed into Cole's mind.

"Cole." Goran's mental voice was slow, yet methodical, taking nearly ten seconds to say Cole's name. Memories of chasing prey near Costas, eating deka seeds, and exploring the forest swam forth. The word was simple, yet the impact was profound, leaving Cole gushing with affection for his friend.

Laughing and wiping happy tears from his eyes, Cole felt his shroud recede. His Rage yielded to the relief of his Passion. *"I missed you too, Bud. I'm glad you made it out of that valley alive."*

A grating rumble stormed out from Goran's chest as his massive ruby eyes closed halfway. *"Cole"*

"You were incredible," Cole said, taking a seat on Goran's finger. *"How did you get so powerful? So big? I used to be able to hold you in one arm. Do you remember that?"*

Goran blinked again, replying in his wild and ancient mental voice, *"Cole."*

Cole wanted to ask what Goran meant, but for the moment he was simply happy to have his friend back. Goran was his first friend on Aeneria, his first sense of safety and stability in an unknown world full of magic, liquid stone doors, and carnivorous grubs the size of motorcycles. He wished he could hold Goran again, or at least give him a good headbutt, but Cole settled for staring into the blazing ruby novas that were his eyes.

The unit landed around Cole in a gust of wind, mouths agape at the sight before them. Valen stepped forward, placing a hand on his chest and bowing low. "Greetings, Mountain King. It warms my heart to see you again."

"You have rid this world of a perverse nightmare," Eliza said, holding her hands in front of her heart while beaming up into Goran's eyes. "I would expect nothing less from one so deeply bonded with Cole. The two of you now rival the greatest powers that have ever walked Aeneria."

"Hello Goran," Lileth said. She gave him a polite nod, which Goran returned with a thunderous grunt.

Sitra cupped her hands and hollered in a tone of mock reprisal, "Took you long enough! We've been hoofing it halfway around Aeneria while you've been fussing over a little Colossus. Sure could have used a lift."

Sitra kicked out at a lump of rock, breaking a boulder free from Goran's finger. The others winced, looking warily up to Goran, but Cole knew it was nothing to worry about. Goran pressed his lips together, then his cheeks bulged as he sent a gust of wind at Sitra. As soon as the breath hit her, she flew backwards, swearing and spinning as she fell out into open air. When the laughter of the unit finally faded, Valen sidled up to Cole, a question burning in his eyes.

"May I ask him something? I mean, will he understand?" Valen asked.

"Oh he'll understand you alright," Cole replied. "Just make sure to hold on tight and fold your wings if you think you'll annoy him."

Valen did not laugh. He looked up to Goran, his expression softening with hope and wonder. "Goran, will you join us? Will you help us fight The Three? Your help would alter the balance of power, saving this world and every other."

Goran remained silent for a long while. However, he spoke with Cole through a series of desires and images, revealing intimate details of the entire Fangshard range. There were birds that remained in flight for months on end, only landing to birth their young in a certain coastal bluff where the chicks could hunt their own fish. Without Goran's pruning of the cliffs, their nesting grounds would erode and fall into the ocean, dooming an entire species. There were the mountain folk, simple Aenerians who lived off the ever-rising population of snow rams, farming and taming the animals for pelts, meat, and manual labor. Without Goran maintaining the wind and guiding blizzards, merchant trails would melt and shift, blocking trade and allowing ice wolves free reign over their farmlands. At the roots of the mountains, tectonic plates needed a steady hand, while others needed encouragement. Even now, miles and miles away there was an avalanche mixing with a landslide, all because Goran wasn't there to keep an underground river in check. Countless thousands of creatures ranging from insects to giant elk would breathe their last because Goran came here to rescue Cole and his friends.

The sheer volume of information strained Cole's mind to its limit. His head throbbed as guilt pushed fresh tears out of his eyes. Steeling himself, Cole looked into Goran's ruby eye, conveying all his remorse through their bond while offering appreciation for the cost of his actions. Goran replied with a slow blink of understanding.

"Cole," Goran said again.

Cole nodded. Shaking himself, he addressed the unit, ready to give them Goran's reply, though the somber dejection on their faces told him they already knew what it would be. Sitra returned with a joke ready on her lips, but then seemed to think better of it.

"Goran can't come with us," Cole started, struggling to find words meaningful enough to translate Goran's message. "He's...part of the Fangshards now. He pretty much *is* the Fangshards. It cost him dearly to come help us, and even now things are dying every second he remains with us in this form. The mountains need him more than we do."

"I don't understand," Valen began, "but I do not think I am meant to. Goran was always beyond my understanding, now even more so. But I trust him as I trust you." He lifted his gaze to Goran, projecting his voice across the gap. "We are honored to count you as a friend, Goran. May the mountains thrive under your care, and Oberon shine its warmth on them till the end days."

Goran hummed like a summer storm.

"We should go," Cole murmured, stifling thoughts on what other havoc currently ensued while they chatted.

The others said their goodbyes. Valen gave a quick bow while Eliza crouched down and hugged Goran's boulder of a knuckle. Sitra produced a lump of rock she retrieved after Goran blew her away. She set it into the hollow where she had kicked a piece of rock from

Goran's finger, then sealed it with Wisdom. They each took flight, leaving Cole and Lileth alone. Tender hands caressed Cole's neck as Lileth replaced Varka's cape around his shoulders, finishing with a swift kiss on the cheek. Cole felt the familiar trill of Varka's magic guiding his Wisdom, allowing him the clarity to cast the spells for proper flight. He floated away, hand in hand with Lileth as together they stared into the fading bonfires of Goran's eyes. He wished he had just a little more time with his friend.

"*Cole,*" Goran repeated, saturating the name with affection and admiration.

Goran's eyes dimmed to empty slate as his features shifted from brindle fur and leathery snout, to plain rock and damp soil. The mirak sat back as slowly as a passing cloud. His chin dipped to his chest as though he were falling asleep, while vines and trees sprouted over him like a creeping blanket, crumbling and eroding his form back into the foothills of the mountains. His presence faded from Cole's mind, but not entirely. Goran had the whole of the Fangshards to look after, but he left a large measure of himself nearby. Cole knew he was just another bird for Goran to look after, one that flew the winds of fate and had his own nest to tend, but he would always be his first and favorite friend.

"Do you want to talk about it?" Lileth asked in a careful tone.

"No. Not yet," Cole replied. He tugged her along, picking up a burst of speed and aiming them towards the life candles of the others.

The unit retrieved their bags from the shoreline, then flew as high as their wings would carry them, aiming for the home they longed to return to. Cole trailed close behind, held aloft by the ironclad aid of Varka's cape. Lexy thrashed with renewed fury as he threw her canvas prison over his shoulders.

The Sill was far away but well within view, nestled within the warm arms of the lagoon, which shimmered like a million mirrors under Oberon's gaze. They talked the whole while through Cole's Passion network, regaling each other with happy memories of days spent training and adventuring within The Sill, though in between the lull of every tale there was an unmistakable pall of grief. Cole joined in reluctantly after several failed attempts to elicit a response from Goran, but before long the ache in his heart melted before a blossoming appreciation for all he still had.

The journey took longer than it should have as they had to skirt enemy camps in wide arches, backtracking and adding hours to their travel. Still, it was faster than running. Once over The Sill they descended in a wide spiral, checking the surrounding waters and shore lines for danger. Cole could see the vibrant colors of the Arts District. He could almost hear the orators performing in the theater, and he could nearly smell the savory aroma of baked sweets from the traveling vendors. He saw the markets and their webwork of ramps and walkways, which incited a strong desire for a perusal through the cypher shop, The Cordial Compendium. His mastery of Passion would unlock whole shelves of cyphers that were once beyond his reach. The dancing gardens came into view, as well as the blue glow of the necropolis where the fallen warriors of The Sill were laid to rest. A pang of sorrow reverberated between his and Eliza's bond at the sight. Try as he might, Cole couldn't find Chiron's house. He searched for the floating platform among the canopy, finding nothing, but they were still very high in the sky. The house had to be down there somewhere.

"Perhaps we ought to use the Lurkwood Gate," Valen suggested. *"Given recent events I wouldn't be surprised if Whind set defenses in case of an air assault."*

"Roth used to jump over the walls all the time," Sitra scoffed. *"Even after the barrier went down and the war reignited. Whind is probably too busy polishing all the gratia stones in the outer trees to notice us dropping in. Never liked that guy. He seemed more plant than Aenerian."*

Cole knew what she meant. Whind had a certain stiffness to him, as though his bone and brain were made of unyielding hardwood, incapable of the sway of casual conversation. Even his clothes had been crafted of leaves and bark, and he had an unusual affinity for things like moonlight, weather, and the quality of the soil beneath his feet.

"We should use the gate anyway," said Cole, angling himself towards the Lurkwood Gate, pleasantly surprised that the others followed his lead. *"We should speak to Whind first. He can give us an*

update on events both inside and outside The Sill's walls. Besides, he deserves the courtesy of knocking first."

"I agree with Cole," Eliza said at once. *"He is a queer man, but I miss him. It seems like a lifetime since we've been home."*

Lileth flew nearer to Cole, settling herself between him and Eliza. *"It has only been a couple of months, but we have been through much in our absence. Too much."*

They continued their spiral, looping in ever tighter circles, then finally landing on the same harsh, rocky shore where Cole first met Roth. He recalled the memory with nostalgic relish. He was so small, not by human standards, but to the Aenerians he was barely a halfling, and Roth was tallest of all. The elder had given him a warrior's greeting, challenging Cole to a duel within seconds of meeting him. He walked away from the encounter with a bruised ego, collapsed lungs, and a lead coat of dread at his enlistment at The Sill. As Cole retraced his steps from another life, he laughed inwardly, thinking on how scared and inadequate he was at the time. He was still no match for the Bonebreaker, even before Grotton took him for Harbinger, but as Roth had promised he was certainly more deadly than the day he arrived.

The briny aroma of the lagoon and the familiar sights set an air of comfort about the unit, relaxing their gait from poised vigilance to loping grace. They were home at last. Whispers of melancholy wove throughout their Passion network, carrying thoughts of those missing among their number. Storn, Deekus, Goran, the elders, even Habbad. Each held a moment of their silence as they trudged their way up the slippery rocks and pink sands leading into Lurkwood Forest. The monolithic trees of The Sill's outer wall winked at them as their embedded gratia stones flickered through the surrounding foliage. They picked up their pace. Everyone was eager for the comforts of their own bed and the safety that lay beyond the gate. Cole had other intentions for the unit, however. He kept the ideas locked within his center, where no one, not even Eliza would be able to find them. He would wait and only reveal his plan after they spoke with Whind.

Cole halted the unit fifty paces outside the gate. The air felt too heavy, charged almost. He scanned their area with Passion, finding no trace of Whind, though the nearby flora rustled with an angry hiss, as though the plants were coiled to strike. Eliza sensed it as well. She crouched and turned her ears this way and that, probing the area with her own Passion. Cole was about to announce their arrival when the subtle flutter that preceded violence whispered from the nearby leaves.

Seizing his Wisdom, Cole spun his glowing emerald hands about him, crafting two spells at the speed of thought. There was a collective gasp as the unit was lifted off their feet with the first spell, carrying them several feet into the air. He poured the majority of his focus into the second spell, imbuing it with one simple rule: Nothing shall enter. A translucent orb of seafoam green crackled into existence around them. Cole used his Passion network as well, galvanizing the others into action, and they bolstered his second spell with the might of their combined Wisdom. The spells materialized in a blink.

Something collided with their magical shield from every direction, assaulting it with bone-crushing strength while spreading like forked lightning. Roots thicker than Cole's arm came into view, flexing and writhing over the surface of their shield with unrelenting ferocity, each spreading hundreds of hooked thorns oozing with violet oils. Within a heartbeat the roots had completely covered their barrier. Cole looked to the others. Their faces were all locked in stony determination, though through their network he felt a unified confidence. Thoughts darted among their minds like a hive of angry bees. Someone cast another spell, igniting the air around their shield with snaking ropes of scarlet flames. Someone else sensed a waning of their enemy's strength, suggesting they expand their shield. The unit poured their combined Wisdom into the magic, snapping and burning the poisonous roots, their power snowballing ever greater.

The severed roots fell to the ground while their stumps retreated to the surrounding trees. The hands of the unit filled with liquid fire and blue sparks, or else morphed into ebony dragon's claws, daring anyone to come within range of their wrath.

"Most Impressive," said an airy voice barely audible over the din of the spells. "Welcome back, Warriors of The Sill."

Whind stood on the path between the unit and the Gate. He was as still as winter tree, wearing battle robes of woven vines embellished with leaf-shaped plates of amber. His arms were crossed behind his back, and while he appeared not three feet from their shield, his gaze was far beyond the unit, as though they were nothing more than a passing day dream. Most unusual of all was the look on his face. For the first since Cole had known him, the gatekeeper was smiling.

Whind continued, spreading his arms wide with his palms forward in a gesture of supplication, "Please children, pardon my attack. Minions of The Three have called upon us on thirty-four separate occasions while you were gone. Their gambits have expanded in both cunning and desperation with every failed attempt to enter The Sill. I had to verify your identity."

"How do you know we aren't minions of The Three?" Cole asked, urging the others to maintain their hold on their spells. "And how do we know you're really Whind and not some illusion meant to trick us?"

Whind turned his head, looking directly into Cole. "You are the first to defend yourselves with proper magic. The others were simple Domina, or low-level priests wielding magic of torment and plague. They were ill-prepared to deal with a few angry roots. As for my identity, you are welcome to enter my mind and see for yourself. I will not resist."

No one moved. Cole spoke to the minds of the others, asking if they had any ideas, but none were forthcoming. Seeing no other alternative, Cole handed off the reins to his spells, severing himself from the flow of Wisdom. He dropped to the path below their shield while summoning just enough Rage to shroud his entire body in protective armor.

Whind's expression didn't change as Cole approached, towering over him like an ebony demon, nor did he flinch when Cole touched the flat of a bladed finger to his forehead. Eliza's mind rubbed against Cole's, persistent and protective, finally forcing her Passion into him in case of treachery. Few could resist the combined power of two masters of Passion.

Upon first contact there was no doubt it was the real Whind. Like needles on a pine, his mind teemed with verdant thoughts and urges, all of which concerned the walls and wellbeing of The Sill. There was simply too much to sift through, even with Eliza helping him. With Whind's focus dispersed throughout every leaf, root, and budding fungus, the fact that he had faculty enough for simple conversation was astounding. Satisfied, and silently thankful that they hadn't felt the full might of the Gatekeeper, Cole dismissed his Rage and withdrew from Whind's mind.

"It's him," Cole said to the others.

The seafoam barrier dimmed and the snaking fire puffed to harmless smoke as the unit floated to the ground. As they drew near, Whind turned on his heel and strode for the gate, beckoning them all along.

"Quickly now, into The Sill," Whind said in his ethereal voice. "As powerful as you all have become, you would be better off within my walls. Evil tides are rising."

"We know," said Cole. "We just came from Oberon City. The Three have each taken a Harbinger. We saw it ourselves."

"That confirms my suspicions," Whind said. At the gate he stretched out his hand, which sprouted wire-thin vines that spiraled out towards the titanic outer trees, burrowing into the bark. "My heart weeps for whoever bears Sorronis. To carry the burden of Aeneria's Hatred and Despair is a fate I wish upon no soul. Do you know the name of the victim?"

"One of our own. Talin," Cole said, recalling his fight with the Harbinger.

If Whind was upset by the news, it didn't show in his face. There was a sound of creaking wood so loud Cole felt it in his chest, then two of the outer trees stood up on their roots, revealing the tunnel of the Lurkwood Gate.

Whind ushered them inside. "Talin was one of the brightest students and fiercest warriors among us. It is most unfair that Sorronis chose him, for he has brought much good into this world. His wife and daughter went missing after the failed mission in Costas, perhaps to look for him. I pray they never found him. Penelope and Pineah were their names."

Cole didn't have the heart to tell Whind that Talin's daughter was the other half of Sorronis's Harbinger. Her body had been fused to

Talin's chest like some half-melted tumor, a tortured creature of pure suffering. While Talin was Sorronis's hand of Hatred, the girl wielded the god's Despair. Cole had managed to overpower Talin with raw Rage, but he had been utterly crippled by a single touch from the girl.

Whind stopped at the end of the tunnel. With another nudge from his vines the hulking gate trees closed, planting themselves on the ground with a massive groan. Whind turned and addressed them all, though his eyes fell to distant things only he could see. "While I am relieved to see you safe once again, I am concerned as to why Masters Alvani, Roth, and Chiron are not with you. What has befallen them?"

No one replied. Cole couldn't bring himself to recall their final moments in Fangshard Valley. The sting of loss was still too fresh.

Cole moved aside as Valen shouldered his way to the front of their group, taking a calming breath before speaking with a tone of cold pragmatism. "The elders were struck down by Sorronis and Habbad. The Underkin used something called *pithing shards*, wicked needles to which there seems to be no defense. The shards struck the elders in their hearts, disabling them instantly. Chiron vanished with an unknown spell of Wisdom, but from what we saw of Alvani he couldn't have lasted long. We managed to escape on Gale and bring Alvani to safety before she expired."

"And what of Roth?" Whind asked.

"Master Roth was taken by Grotton... as Harbinger," Valen replied, his voice cracking slightly.

Whind shut his eyes and said in a low whisper, "Aethers save us." A shadow fell over his face as he seemed to lose the ability to speak.

A blanket of Despair draped itself over them. Cole broke the silence after a sullen minute. "Whind, we have some clues, questions really, about what happened when the remaining Unbound died. Will you answer them?"

Whind resumed his usual countenance of tranquility. "For you, child of Varka, I will try."

Cole was taken aback by the title, but drove on. "Do you know what the Cold Crows are?"

Whind's eyes hardened slightly. "They are an ancient cabal of assassins who work directly for The Three. Stories of their treachery stain our history books. As far as we know they are as old as Aeneria itself. Other than the scant anecdotes recorded in our library, I know little about them."

It wasn't much, but it was a start. Cole continued to his second question. "What about the pithing shards? Do you have any idea how they work, or what they do?"

Whind's eyes darted from side to side, as if perusing invisible books in front of him. "Every story of the Cold Crows contains the horrors of the pithing shards. They are a tool crafted exclusively by the Crows, and each shard seems destined to a single individual, rendering it harmless to anyone other than the intended victim. They are designed to kill, and they do it well. As to how they work, I cannot say, other than they are crafted with evil magic of the highest order."

"Then you probably don't know where Chiron vanished to," Cole said with a frown. "If you don't know how the shards work, I mean."

"Chiron's understanding of Wisdom was far beyond my own," Whind replied, crossing his arms behind his back. "Though I attained mastery of the school myself, no two individuals perceive reality in precisely the same manner, especially when manipulating the limits of the mundane. I cannot say with certainty where or what Chiron did in his final hour. I could guess, but my guesses would be as useful as gleaning fact from dreams."

A dead end, but not unexpected. There was only one question left for Cole to ask. He steeled himself, staring into Whind's eyes until the Gatekeeper looked directly at him. "Is The Sill ready for war?"

"I'm afraid I do not understand your question," Whind replied. "We have been at war ever since the day you first arrived."

Cole shook his head. "That's not what I meant. What is our overall readiness? Is there anyone left to fight with us, or did everyone leave? The Three won't wait long to come finish us off. Sooner or later they'll come knocking and we have to be ready to fight."

Whind took a moment to think it over before responding. "There are just over three hundred remaining in The Sill. Of that number there are forty-four warriors; however, they are merely students and have yet to see battle. The other citizens consist of craftsmen, artists, scientists, and healers, though as news of our failures reaches their ears, many decide to seek their fortunes elsewhere on Aeneria. The people of The Sill have abandoned this war; however, The Sill itself is not without defenses. Not while I have yet to breathe my last."

"Then what the hell are we supposed to do?" Sitra demanded. "Everyone else is giving up. What's the point of risking our necks?"

No one said a word as no one could find a good response to Sitra's question. The situation was bad, even before the fall of the elders, and now there was only a handful of student-warriors and a few civilians, none of whom were ready for the evil outside their walls. The foundations of Cole's mind softened as Despair undermined his resolve. The doubts whispering through their Passion network certainly didn't help matters.

Whind raised his chin, his distant gaze sharpened as he brought his focus to the unit, surveying them now with an air of pride. "That is up to you. You are the only true warriors who still call The Sill their home. I can offer advice, and keep you safe within my walls, but I cannot decide for you. My mind and body are bound to The Sill, and so I cannot leave it, even if my heart longs to join you in battle." He paused and spread his arms, his hands aglow with a mixture of coral and juniper light. A refreshing breeze washed over them all, invigorating and cleansing, and replaced their murky Despair with budding hope. "Listen to me well. You are all we have left. You have been trained by those who fought in the first war alongside Varka. You must now become the Unbound. Remove your shackles of doubt and Despair and embrace the power which you have yet to unveil. The evil arts may be potent and our enemies great in number, yet against an Unbound mind they are but a passing squall before a mountain. Do not abandon hope. I believe in you."

And without waiting for a response, Whind strode forward, flowing between them like water through rocks. He pressed himself to the outer wall. Within a few seconds his skin and clothes grew a crunchy layer of mahogany bark, then his entire form sank into the tree.

"I am not giving up," Lileth said, breaking the pensive silence. She looked energized and defiant. "If nothing else we can still learn and train. We may not be able to defeat The Three directly, but our recent success was no small victory. The five of us alone managed to defeat a fleet of Domina and their priests. If we are careful, and with enough time, we could give The Three no end to their troubles."

Eliza approached Lileth, placing a hand on her shoulder. "There is still much worth fighting for. I'm with you, Lil."

"As am I," Valen said, throwing his shoulders back.

Sitra let out a sigh of annoyance, though she bared her teeth in a wolfish grin. "I suppose I'll stick around then. I like killing Domina too much to let Cole get all the glory. After we rest I say we head back out for a little hunt, and see if we can't kill one of those baileen-Domina without Goran's help."

Valen's mouth stretched wide in a heavy yawn. "We could all use some rest. Let us find our beds and enjoy a peaceful respite for once."

The weeks of hard travel seemed to crash over the unit all at once. Mumbling their agreement to Valen's suggestion, they set off down the path towards the barracks, dragging their bare feet as they walked. Cole, however, did not follow them. Now was the time for them to make a choice.

Cole uncorked a sliver of his Rage, leaped high into the air and landed on the path in front of his friends. They stopped, though out of respect or annoyance he couldn't tell. He chose his words carefully, and spoke with an authority he certainly didn't have when he first met them. "Before you go to the comfort of your beds you need to make a choice. First option is you run off to bed, sleep for as long as you like, then wake up well-rested and ready to tackle another day."

"Yep," Sitra blurted. "Say no more, that's exactly what I want. That and a decent meal or two."

Ignoring Sitra, Valen gave Cole a wary look, stifling another yawn as he spoke: "Hush, Sitra, I'm sure this isn't unimportant. What is the second option?"

Cole did his best to recall Chiron's words, which now felt like a lifetime ago, like a half-forgotten dream. Still, he needed to convince them if they were to have even the slightest chance. "Every second that you spend asleep is another second used against you by our enemies. While you crawl into bed and wrap yourself in your cozy blankets, they come. While you wander through the fantasies of your dreams, they come. With every sleeping breath you take, they come, killing and torturing everyone and everything along the way. Your second option is this: Go to the Cordial Compendium. On the top shelf in the Wisdom section you will find a cypher called *dreamsource*. It's expensive, and so it will drain you, but when you recover you will never need to sleep again."

Their lips curled into looks of disgust, as though Cole had just dropped a heaping pile of manure before them, but he raised his hand before anyone could utter a retort. "I realize it's a very personal and life-changing thing, but I wouldn't ask you without having already done it myself. I won't argue the point any further, and if you choose not to go through with it I won't hold it against you. After you've made your choice, come find me. I'll be in the Arts District."

Cole turned away without a backwards glance. He severed the Passion network, shifting his focus to Wisdom instead. He took flight with such force that he cracked the woven root path beneath his feet. This was one thing they needed to figure out without him.

CHAPTER 5

SWEETNESS RETURNED

Cole landed outside the home of The Sill's greatest healer, Naythan. It was a plain two-story house with chipped corners, constructed of red clay and void of windows, as if to shut the old hermit off from the outside world. The exterior wore a thick coat of vines, which did a good job of camouflaging it from distant eyes. The house was on the outer limits of the Arts District, with no neighbors in sight other than a few towering pines and passing birds. Cole rapped the back of his knuckles on the door three times, though after the first knock he heard a sound of breaking glass, then a hurried scuffle of slippers.

The door rippled like water, forming a hole in the center which expanded outwards into the frame. Naythan stood in the doorway, poised for battle with his voluminous fur coat of armor and a staff gripped within his tattoo-covered fingers. Shrewd eyes peered through a set of wire-framed glasses, perched slightly askew upon a crooked nose. His scrunched grimace popped into a look of open surprise as his eyes met Cole's.

"Hello Naythan," Cole said, flicking his gaze to the metal tip of the staff. "Expecting trouble?"

"Of a sort," Naythan wheezed in his dry, papery voice. He stamped the butt of his staff on the wicker doormat, leaning on it with both hands as he scrutinized Cole through his spectacles. "Not that you're much better. Trouble stalks you like a shadow, human. I don't suppose you're here to relieve me of the charge that you so unceremoniously dumped on my doorstep."

"I'm afraid not," Cole replied with a half grin. "Actually I've come to check up on her."

Naythan raised an eyebrow. "And?"

"And I will refill your gratia stones as promised," Cole said with an exasperated sigh.

Naythan cocked his head, then repeated himself slowly, "And?"

Cole's rucksack gave a little shake. He ignored it, but he was certain Naythan could sense something through the spells he put over the bag to muffle Lexy's screams. "I've come to beg your advice."

Naythan squinted, turning his head from side to side as he tried to peer behind Cole's broad shoulders. "I doubt that stink is just your soiled clothes and rotten hide. What's in the bag?"

"An Underkin," Cole said, holding the old man's inquisitive glare.

"The truth, boy!" Naythan snapped, rapping Cole on the forehead with the tip of his staff.

Cole hissed, kneading his fingertips into his brow. An egg had already started to form. How was the old man so fast? He healed the contusion with a flash of lavender Passion. "Her name is Lexy. She's been Chosen."

"Absolutely not!" Naythan shouted, barring the door frame with his staff. "You may come visit the child and pay your debts, but you will leave that thing outside. There's no way under Oberon's bloody light I'm letting that nightmare near the girl."

"You mean not unless I pay you for it, right?" Cole didn't bother hiding the venom from his voice. "You'll only help people so long as you have something to gain from it, is that it? Or are you one of those bigots who thinks all Underkin are trash?"

Naythan looked as if Cole had just spat in his face. "Fool boy! Pick up your tongue before you trip over it. You have no idea what you speak of. It's not a matter of payment or racism, you dolt, I'd cleanse the Underkin in an instant if I weren't so busy guarding your child from her own suffering."

A heavy ball of guilt fell into Cole's stomach. "What do you mean? Is something wrong with her?"

"I'm afraid so. Come in and see for yourself," Naythan said, deflating with a sigh. "Just leave the poor wretch by the door. I'll help you free her soul when we're through with our business here."

Cole obeyed, gently placing his rucksack down against the house, then nudging the blanket of vines with Passion so that they covered the bag completely. The door shrank shut behind him as a wave a stifling heat assaulted him, thick with the aroma of burning incense. In stark contrast to his last visit, the furniture and shelves were clear of clutter, arranged in a comfortable, inviting fashion. The walls were lined with candles caged in bronze animal statues set between neatly stacked books. There was a tapestry that Cole didn't remember seeing on his last visit. It was beautiful and marvelously detailed, depicting each local planet on a canvas stretching over an entire wall.

"Why didn't you sense me coming with your Passion?" Cole asked as he ran his hand through a basket of acid green flames set on the dinner table. "You must be an expert with Passion at the very least. I could sense you and the girl from miles away."

"And anyone capable of Passion or Despair can sense your probing, including those pestilent children that keep pounding at my door, demanding I join their little band of warriors. They're students, lost and crippled without a Master, and just because I know a trick or two with Passion they think me the Grandmaster of The Sill. But it's all parroted tripe anyway. Expert, master, novice, it's relative." Naythan huffed, then snatched a teapot and two cups from the fire and set them on the table. "To a fish, both a dung fly and a thresher hawk would be *masters* of the sky, but what would the hawk call the fly?"

"Nothing, it's just a hawk," Cole replied.

"Wrong," Naythan said, filling the cups with a black liquid from the teapot. "The hawk would call the fly lunch, but both would perish should they attempt flight in the meanest spring storm. The clouds would be their master, and then the stars and the Aethers beyond. There is no such thing as mastery of a school, just those more adept than others. Drink that," he said, sliding a cup to Cole. "You'll be glad you did."

"What is it?" Cole asked, sniffing the liquid. It smelled rich and roasted, and pleasantly bitter.

"Coffee," Naythan said, taking a long, slurping draught from his cup.

Cole felt a happy pang of homesickness as he took a sip. It tasted remarkably similar to the coffee his mom used to brew in the morning before school. The zing of stimulants hit him at once, exuberant and buzzing, filling his head with a gratifying sense of acuity.

"So what can you tell me about her?" Cole asked, unsure how to frame his question. "Did I... did I affect her development?"

Naythan lowered his head, boring his eyes into Cole's. Green light danced across the side of his face, making the tattoos on his neck look alive. He leaned close, speaking in a gravelly whisper, "Tremendously so."

The hammer of guilt broke across Cole's chest, heavy and crippling. "How bad?" Cole dared ask.

A derisive grin twisting his lips, Naythan leaned back with a satisfied huff, apparently pleased at Cole's dismay. "The physical changes were as immediate as they were apparent. The girl's body took on such rapid growth that I had to call off the wet nurses after the first three days. She went to solids right after. Ate like a starved pup, taking fancy in any fare so long as it kept coming. As the days turned into weeks her body seemed unable to keep up with her appetite. I'd bring her plate after plate, and she'd just knock them down one after another, then come snatching my own food if I wasn't quick enough. After one week she was no longer a toddler, and after two she looked a fat healthy child, and now I'd guess her body to be nearing adolescence. Her growth isn't what puts my guts in a knot, however, not by a long shot."

Fascination and dread mingled within Cole as he absentmindedly watched Naythan slurp at the steaming coffee. However, after a minute's silence Cole's anxiety won over his patience. "What's wrong with her mind?"

Nathan's blinked rapidly, as if Cole had just materialized from thin air. He seemed to choose his words with utmost care. "The girl *has* no mind."

Befuddled, Cole ran his fingers through his hair, struggling to grasp the meaning of Naythan's statement. "But of course she would have a mind," Cole started, unsure if he believed himself. "I felt it when I first met her, and how could she eat and breathe without thoughts? I only stole her first month of memories, just up until we fled Brimhallow together. Her thoughts, her mind, everything should have started over at that point. Shouldn't it?"

Naythan downed the rest of his coffee in a single gulp. "The girl can walk and eat on her own, heck, she even recognizes me when I come back into the room. But other than that there's not much else growing in that little flower pot head of hers. I've brought her to see other kids, given her toys, shown her magic and illusions from the Arts District, but there's simply no reaction from her. She just stands there, existing. No stimuli can rouse her, unless you have a piece of food. I've scanned every inch of the girl's mind, even tried planting memories of my own, but nothing seems to stick. It all passes through her like a rock thrown through flame."

At the mention of the word *flame*, Cole brought his eyes to the ceiling, staring at the spot where his Passion sensed the girl's life candle. "I want to look at her. I have to see it for myself."

"Of course you do," Naythan said. "But before you go up there I must warn you of the child's third oddity. Ever since her arrival, something strange has been happening around her. It became more potent as she grew, its range broadening with each passing day. It's the reason I had you keep your Underkin outside."

"Tell me," Cole said.

Naythan paused, his gaze drifting away, as though debating whether he should continue. "Within each of us live all seven schools of magic. Passion, Rage, and Wisdom are merely the dogs we at The Sill *choose* to feed. However, even the great Chiron had a capacity for Hunger and Fear, as well as Despair and Hatred. While this girl's mind is as useless as a cracked bell, the air around her bleeds with magic. The bad kind."

"But how?" Cole demanded. "How can a child produce Hatred or Fear without thoughts or memories?"

Naythan shivered, hugging himself in his massive fur coat. "The girl doesn't produce it. She absorbs it. I had to line my house with countless layers of spells to keep her influence limited to this space. I even took up the monotonous chore of meditating, just to keep her from pulling anything from me. She's pulling from you as we speak."

"But I don't feel anything…" Cole's voice trailed off as he began his own ritualistic meditation, cleansing himself in the waters of his center. He inventoried his faculties, easily finding his Passion, Rage, and Wisdom, but there was nothing else other than wandering thoughts and memories.

"Of course you don't," Naythan said. "She's pulling them from you. Bring your focus outside yourself, to the air and the walls. It all flows to her."

Feeling stupid, Cole sniffed the air, looking around him. Something was wrong. There was a scent so faint he thought he imagined it. It was nauseatingly sweet, as if someone tried covering a corpse with perfume, filling him with a sudden desire to run from the house as fast as he could. It was Fear. Cole shut his eyes and opened himself to the atmosphere around him, sensing facets of the other evil magics swirling about like smoke from an invisible fire. It moved with phantom grace, unchecked by the materials of the mundane as it flowed to the little life candle in the room above.

Cole looked back to Naythan. "What does she do with it all?"

"That has yet to be seen," Naythan replied, sending his and Cole's cups floating to the sink with a spark of Wisdom. "Are you ready to meet her?"

"Yes," Cole said without hesitation.

They rose from the table. Naythan led Cole to the landing of a staircase set at the back of his house, then beckoned him to go first. Cole did his best to remain neutral, anchoring as much of himself as he could into his center, but even that couldn't stop sweat from coating his palms. He pushed the door open at the top of the stairs and entered Naythan's chambers. It was a large room, consisting of the entire second floor, bathed in warm light from Passion stones embedded in the walls and ceiling. A horseshoe-shaped desk was tucked in one corner, stacked with towers of notes and neatly arrayed medical instruments. A basin full of soil lined the longest wall, soaked in warm gratia light that fed budding mushrooms and herbs.

A bed large enough for five people took up a quarter of the room. It had four carved granite posts and its satin curtains were drawn tight. Beside the bed was a nightstand bearing a haphazard stack of dinnerware. There were no traces of food, not one crumb or fleck of dried sauce, as though the plates and spoons had all been licked clean. There was a thick bedroll set up on the floor next to the bed, on which was a small mountain of fluffy blankets and pillows.

Cole followed his Passion to the bed and peeled back a curtain. She was far bigger than the last time he saw her, though still tiny. The girl lay face up atop the flower-patterned blankets, a curly shrub of fire-orange hair covering her face and flowing down to her lower back. She was clothed in a plain olive tunic with black leggings, though her hands and feet were bare. Her flaming riot of hair rose and fell with the motion of her breathing, making it look as though a large furry creature rested on her head.

"Is she sleeping?" Cole asked in a low whisper.

"Must be," Naythan replied, not bothering to lower his voice. "*Is she dreaming* would be the better question. Go ahead and scan her and see what you can find. I haven't let anyone else have a look at her, not even the other healers. I'm eager to see what you make of her."

Cole brushed aside her hair, revealing alabaster skin dotted with freckles. Her cheeks were plump and healthy, her ginger brows thick and upswept at the edges, giving her the appearance of a wizened cherub. Cole reached the tip of his first finger to her forehead, but stopped. Her eyes opened, azure blue and halting. She pushed herself up to a sitting position, tucking and crossing her legs under herself, all the while keeping her eyes locked into Cole's.

"Hello," Cole said, dropping to his knees and resting his elbows on the bed. "I'm Cole."

There was no change in the girl's expression. Her hard blue eyes bored through the tangle of ginger hair.

"You don't have to speak if you don't want to. Do you want to talk to me with your mind instead?" Cole asked, offering his hand.

Her empty gaze fell to his hand.

"I don't believe it," Naythan said in a low rasp.

The girl reached out and grasped Cole's first two fingers. Cole smiled. The contact wasn't necessary to reach her mind, it was the trust that mattered. Calling his Passion to the moment, he rubbed his consciousness against her life candle, taking immense care to be as gentle as possible. He sifted through her essence, starting from the blank space of her stolen memories, then working his way out and around. There was nothing. Not a single thought or urge, not even a fleeting observation or acknowledgment of his presence. Naythan was right. The girl was empty.

Cole withdrew from her mind, leaving a drop of Passion inside her with the hope that it might bloom into something. He took his hand from hers, but as he did her eyes opened just a little wider.

She reached out and touched Cole on the tip of his nose and spoke in a mousy squeak. "Hate."

Cole's mouth fell open. Before he could say a word she lifted her finger, tapping him twice more.

"Fear. Hate," she said, offering each word with a touch.

Cole felt a sudden swelling of the two magics she named, each writhing and spiraling out of him, siphoned away by her touch.

"Stars," Naythan gasped, taking a step back. "No child's first words should be something so foul. Boy, are you all right?"

Cole gave an empty sob as the girl took her hand away. "Y-yes. She knew. She saw it coming up inside me. I Hated myself for what I did to her, and I Feared for her future. I thought I emptied myself of those emotions before coming up here, but she must have found a bit more."

"Well I think that's enough for today." Naythan drew his fur coat about him, shivering as though a chill had somehow crept into the stifling room. "She's taken more from you in the last ten minutes than she's—woah now flower, not so fast."

Ignoring Naythan's protest, the girl leaped from the bed, her voluminous curls bouncing around her as she landed. Naythan placed a tender hand on her shoulder, then withdrew it immediately with a pained cry. She continued towards the door.

"Damn!" Naythan hissed, flapping his hand in the air. "The little shrike burned me!" He sniffed his palm and rubbed his fingers together, then scowled. "Hatred."

"Should we stop her?" Cole asked.

Naythan shrugged. "She's probably just looking for food. I don't know what you did, but at least she's acting on her own now."

The girl reached up and grasped the door handle, throwing it open as fluently as if she had been doing it for years, then she closed it behind her.

"Let's make sure she doesn't burn your house down," Cole said.

Naythan cradled his hand, giving Cole a nod of encouragement. "Lead the way."

Cole caught up to the girl halfway down the stairs. She moved quickly, though she was barely as tall as his waist. When she made it to the landing she turned not for the kitchen, but for the door, quickening her pace as she went.

"Don't worry, boy, the door only works when I..." Naythan's voice trailed off as the girl pressed her palm to the front door. The liquid stone melted like wax, spreading over the floor and emitting a bitter, sulfurous odor. As soon as the threshold was clear, the girl hopped outside.

"Hey not so fast!" Cole vaulted the kitchen table and ran after her, but she stopped right outside the door, looking directly at the spot where Lexy was hidden beneath the vines. Cole loomed over her, ready to intervene, but trying his best not to scare her. "Why don't we go back inside, just for a moment. We can play and eat all the food you want."

Ignoring him, the girl crouched by the bulge in the vines, probing the leaves with the same finger she'd touched Cole's nose with. The skin on Cole's neck tingled as something unsavory stirred in the air. The leaves smoldered and died at her touch, the taint spreading and killing a wide swath of invisible fire. The rucksack was now in plain view.

Naythan gripped Cole's arm. "Stop her."

"I don't want to do this," Cole said to the girl's back. He delved into his pool of Wisdom, bringing the power of his thoughts to the need of the moment. Before he could levitate the girl back into the house, something stabbed into Cole's mind, evil and incredibly powerful.

Cole's vision shrank to a small circle as darkness enveloped all five of his senses. Fear splashed over his Wisdom, dousing it to nothing. Before his Rage could react, alien Hunger stole the red magic from him, leaving him weak and shaking. Despair crawled up through his cracks of doubt, leaving him vulnerable to the ominous cloud of Hatred settling over his will. The evil magic crashed over him with alarming precision, crippling his defenses before they could form, though oddly enough the attacks seemed restrained, as if he were merely being held prisoner. Cole fumbled in the grass, not realizing he had fallen. His thin vision revealed Naythan lying beside him, the old hermit similarly affected, writhing and reaching from the confines of his fur coat. Cole watched helplessly as the girl unbuckled the canvas rucksack and removed Lexy's charred body.

She held Lexy at arm's length, measuring her as though picking out a doll for play time. Lexy wailed through the scabs and scars in her throat. She looked nothing like the adorable dancing girl Cole once knew. Her ringlets of brown hair were gone, as most of her features and all her fingers, all burned away by the odium of the Devotion. Shredded vocal chords groaned their Hatred at the world while Lexy beat her charcoal fists against the arms of the ginger-haired girl. Cole lay on the ground, an impotent prisoner to the evil magic.

Lexy's screams came to an abrupt halt as the girl pulled her into a tight embrace. Blood-red gas billowed from Lexy's mouth as purple light shone from the sunken divots that were her eyes. The crippling magic lifted from Cole then, returning to him clarity of mind and use of his limbs. His own magic was beyond reach, but it was still there, unharmed and whole. He could sense the Despair and Hatred leaking from Lexy, siphoning from her tortured form to the soul of the ginger-haired girl. Cole felt Lexy's life candle dim as the evil bled from her. While her Hatred and Despair made her every moment a living hell, they were the only things keeping her from succumbing to her wounds. Now she would die the death she earned so long ago.

Lexy's arms went limp as the last of the evil magic left her body. Cole rose to his feet. Naythan was still on his back, alive but now unconscious. The girl approached Cole, cradling Lexy to her chest like an infant, then offered the blackened corpse to him with a look of dire urgency on her face.

Unsure of himself, Cole took Lexy in his hands. She was as light and stiff as a paper doll. He glared at the girl. Inside himself he felt a stirring Rage and Passion, righteous and potent. "You shouldn't have done that. I was going to ask Naythan if he knew a way to free her without killing her. Now there's no chance at all. You better not have hurt him by the way. I won't be caught off guard by you again."

The girl ignored him. Her brow furrowed as she jabbed a finger at Lexy's corpse. Seeing that Cole wasn't getting it, she strode forward and kicked him in the shin. She pointed again, this time at Cole first, then Lexy. Her lips parted as her eyes began to plead, but for what Cole couldn't guess. He felt for the girl's mind, intending to invite her into a mental conversation, but her thoughts were as blank as ever. An idea came to him.

Cole shifted his magic away from the girl's mind and towards Lexy's body. His Wisdom revealed a still heart while his Passion showed no flame of life, but he would try anyway. Cole shut his eyes and took a long breath. He trickled Passion into Lexy's body, just a little to see if it would even work. To his surprise he felt a shift within the little ribcage; a single thump of her heart. Careful not to overdo it, he uncorked a bit more of the lover's magic, focusing on the vital organs of her core. The heart thumped again. And again.

As he worked, flakes of char began to fall from Lexy's body like black snow, and in their place healthy pink skin grew from knotted scars. While his anatomy lessons with Chiron had been cut short, Cole's Passion made up for the lack of understanding with the raw power of love. Eyes watering, he watched as a perfect little girl took shape from the tortured creature in his hands. A network of veins grew over the exposed skull, followed by woven layers of flesh, then a canvas of unmarred skin. Hair sprouted like a thicket of brown moss, flowing and swirling down over her shoulders. Fingers reformed, plush and pink and flexing into tiny fists. As the rest of her body took shape, Cole found a scrap of her old wrapping that had somehow survived the flames. He drew upon his Wisdom and Varka's cape, multiplying the threads and wrapping her body snugly in the springy cloth. After a quarter of an hour her blood and breath began to pulse on their own power, and her mind began to spark with activity. Cole could do no more.

"Lexy," Cole whispered.

Her eyes rolled behind her lids. The ginger-haired girl looked up at her, concerned.

"Lexy," Cole repeated, speaking her name with his mind as well as his voice.

Lexy's eyes opened. They stared through Cole for a moment, then snapped wide.

"No!" Lexy screamed. "No-no-no, stop it! Help me!" She slapped her hands over herself and gasped for air. Her legs kicked madly into open air. Cole held her gently, his hands tucked under her arms while her little heart thrummed like a frightened bird.

"Lexy you're safe! The fire's gone!" He sensed Fear pouring out from her. It saturated the air around them, but the ginger-haired girl drew it all into herself. Grudgingly, Cole forced himself into Lexy's mind, transferring a drop of Rage to quiet the Fear. He gave her a little shake and repeated her name, more loudly this time.

Lexy tensed as her eyes and nostrils flared wide. Her hands balled into little shaking fists. She drew a quick breath as though to scream, then growled through pursed lips, finally settling into a steady calm. Confused, she blinked as she took in her surroundings. Her gaze settled upon Cole.

"What's your name?" she asked. There wasn't a trace of malice or sadness in her voice. Just pure, childish innocence.

A fluttering laugh flew from Cole. Shock and relief rushed through him, stealing his breath away. He wanted to hug her, to kiss her wrinkled forehead, but he didn't want to scare her.

The wrinkles on Lexy's face deepened with concern. "You have sad eyes. I could sing you a song if you'd like? You should sing with me, then your sad eyes will turn into happy eyes." She grinned hopefully up at him.

Cole dried his tears on his shoulders. "Lexy, it's me, Cole. Do you remember me?"

Her eyes fell to the ground between her dangling feet, darting about in search for an answer. Recognition flashed as her face lit up. "Naked one!"

Cole smiled. He had forgotten she used to call him that. "Yes, it's me."

Her legs kicked in a running motion while her arms reached for him, giggling. Cole pulled her tiny doll frame into a gentle hug.

"Cole I missed you!" she squeaked. "I missed you so much!"

Cole patted her back with the tips of his fingers. "I missed you too Lexy. More than you'll ever know."

Lexy grunted, pushing herself away from him with a soured grin. "You smell, Cole."

It felt like a lifetime ago since he'd seen her last, and he had spent the entire time believing she was lost forever to the madness of her torture. Yet here she was, whole and healthy and poking fun at him. "I bet I do," he sighed. "It's been about forever since I washed these clothes. Will you help me pick out some new ones?"

Lexy pinched her nose. "I'll help you. I can pick the best clothes." She then took on a befuddled expression as she surveyed Cole's body. He was twice as tall as the last time she had seen him. "You got big, Cole. Very, *very* big."

Cole watched her, enamored by the simple fact that she was alive, even more so that she was exactly the same Lexy he remembered. There would come a time when he would have to explain everything to her, from his growth, to the rise of The Three and the fall of the Dark Side, as well as the fate of her brother, Habbad. But now was not the time. He wasn't ready, and as far as he knew there was no precedent for the magic he and the ginger-haired girl had just performed. No one had ever been released from Sorronis's Chosen.

Cole set Lexy down on the grass. She was barely taller than his knee. "You and I have a lot of catching up to do, but first I need to check on my friend here." Cole jerked his thumb towards the ginger-haired girl. He sharpened his mental defenses before scooping the girl up in one hand. She didn't resist.

Cole plopped her down by Naythan's head and gave her a stern look. "Wake him up."

She looked up at him with a blank expression.

"Now," Cole growled.

She crouched down and promptly flicked Naythan in the eye. Naythan's skinny limbs shot up from his fur coat, giving him the appearance of an overturned sheep. He scrambled to his feet, disoriented and disheveled, as though waking from a thousand-cycle coma.

"Draw your blades, bastards!" he roared, reaching a glowing emerald hand into the air. His staff zoomed from the entranceway of his house, spun once in the air, then slapped into his outstretched hand.

Cole approached the old hermit with outward-facing palms. "Calm down, Naythan. Everything's fine. How do you feel?"

Naythan scanned the area, then set the butt of his staff into the grass. "Never better, though I'm right miffed the brat caught me off guard. That won't happen again." His eyes sharpened as he took in Lexy, who had just popped her head out from behind Cole's leg. "Aethers save me, is that the Underkin? But how? You said she was Chosen."

"She was," Cole said, scooping Lexy up and setting her on his hip, "but no longer. She is free. You can inspect her yourself, if she's okay with it that is."

"But that's impossible," Naythan said. He adjusted his glasses and stepped close, his lips working soundless questions as he looked over Lexy's body like an open book. "Chosen die when separated from the Hatred that sustains them. How can this be?"

Cole tried his best to explain everything that had occured after Naythan had been knocked unconscious, though he hadn't the slightest idea how Lexy had been saved, other than his part of healing Lexy.

"This is unprecedented," Naythan said, rubbing his chin as he began pacing around the girls. "But if this could be duplicated, or even distilled into a simple spell... This could turn the tide of the entire war, or at least give Decreath a good kick in the seeds. The spell would of course need to perpetuate itself to undo something as complex as a Colossus, then of course there would be no way to heal the quartered victims, no, none at all, but at least they would be at proper peace."

"Naythan!" Cole blurted, interrupting the hermit's train of thought.

"Spit it out quick!" Naythan said. "But it better be important, my mind's running full gallop right now."

Cole waited until he had Naythan's wandering gaze before proceeding. "I need you to look after Lexy as well as the girl. I'm going to be busy training with the rest of my unit, but I promise I'll come by every day to pay you and help out any way I can. Is this acceptable?"

Naythan glanced from the girls to his house, no doubt thinking of his many gratia stones Cole could fill for him. "You ask to double my charges, then I would ask double the price. Is that acceptable to you?"

If Cole hadn't recently mastered Passion, he would have doubted himself. However, even after his exertions from his travels, and having just healed Lexy, he knew he could fill every gratia stone in the hermit's house several times over. "I accept. However, if you plan to scan Lexy's mind I'd prefer you do it now while I'm here. Is that okay with you, Lexy? Can Naythan take a peek in your ears for a second?"

Lexy squirmed in his arm, nuzzling herself into his chest. "My head feels sick. I don't want anyone poking and sneaking right now."

"There's no need for anyone to go snooping around your pretty head, my little comet," Naythan said, placing a hand on Cole's shoulder. "If Cole says you're a good girl, then that's just fine for me. Beauty and innocence twinkle like starlight in your eyes. Such things leave no room for bad thoughts. I do need your help with something, however. Something big. Will you help old Naythan?"

Lexy nodded against Cole's chest. "I'll help."

Naythan beamed at her. "I've got a whole batch of apricream cookies that will be ready any minute now. There's no way I can eat them all, not even if I asked all the birds in the sky to take a bite. Will you help me?"

Lexy's wrinkled cheeks bulged with an eager grin. "Only if Cole helps too."

"An excellent idea!" Naythan exclaimed, tucking his staff under his arm and clapping his hands together. "We need a poison-checker. The whole batch could be tainted with windviper venom, and we might very well taste the sweetness of death while munching on our delicious dessert! Come Cole, save us from our savory demise!" Naythan threw his arms into the air and let out a dramatic cry for help as he ran to his house.

Lexy giggled and writhed in Cole's arm in an attempt to chase after Naythan. Cole set her on the ground and she shot off with a flurry of belly laughs and kicking feet. The ginger-haired girl remained by Cole's side, staring up at him, silent but expectant.

"I'm sure there's going to be plenty of cookies for you too," Cole said. "Are you going to behave yourself?"

The girl shot her hand up, holding it out for Cole. Cole placed two fingers into her palm and she gripped him tightly, then she stepped off towards Naythan's house, pulling him along.

As it turned out, the cookies were in fact not poisonous, though Lexy and the ginger-haired girl wasted no time tearing into the batch before Cole had swallowed the first bite. The two girls soon became inseparable, perching themselves on the same chair, and chatting away as if they'd known each other their entire lives. The conversation was one-sided of course, as the ginger-haired girl was content to watch and listen while Lexy waxed on about the finer points of dismantling the apricream cookies.

Cole appreciated his time in Naythan's house. It felt peaceful, almost normal, as if he was simply visiting with family. For the moment there was nothing to worry about, nothing to fight for. He was happy to just watch the two girls enjoy their treats and catch up with Naythan on the recent goings-on of The Sill. He couldn't completely ignore all worry, however. The other members of his unit, or the Unbound as they would now be called, were either in the middle of making a life-changing decision, or sleeping their troubles away in wasteful, wonderful sleep. Nor could he ignore the storm clouds of war that drew ever closer. With every bite he took, another Corpulant swallowed a fresh victim. With every story he shared with Naythan, schemes blossomed into strategies to be used against them. With every passing second, an inch of ground was taken from them. The shadow of the enemy was coming.

CHAPTER 6

REBIRTH

The darkness weighed heavily on Habbad, as crushing and unforgiving as the miles of rock and dirt that surrounded him. He couldn't remember the last time he'd seen the stars, or tasted the sweet freedom of open air. He felt as if his entire life had been spent beneath the bones of the Fangshard Mountains, crawling and carving his way through the unknown, every foot a fight for his life. He chipped his way through solid stone and scuttled eagerly whenever fate had been generous enough to bestow an opening to him. Habbad had no idea how many weeks had passed, or if he even labored on the quickest path out of his stone prison, but his Hunger to survive kept him going in spite of his failing spirit.

Habbad's definition of Hunger had changed quite a bit since waking beneath the ground. Once, it was merely a means for power, built on a bedrock of dominated souls and held up by the framework of his information empire. Now, however, Habbad Hungered for revenge. Grotton, the insatiable maw of The Three, had betrayed Habbad and chosen to bless that savage oaf with his grace instead. The god of Hunger and his new Harbinger would die by Habbad's hands, but first he needed to escape.

At the moment he found himself pinned between the floor of his tunnel and a boulder he knocked loose while digging. His fractured ribs and crushed organs would have pained him beyond his limits, but he needn't feel such things, nor accept the injuries. He had Domina for that. Dozens of Aenerians and a few powerful animals were bonded to his body and mind, slaves for his bidding. Their physical strength, intelligence, memories, all were tools for his use, given freely or taken forcibly. The sheer mass of Habbad's internal army had never been seen on Aeneria, and he would know, for he had enthralled a historian from the archives in Costas. This accomplishment was one of the many reasons he, not Roth, should have been crowned Harbinger.

Delving into his pool of Hunger, Habbad assigned his injuries and pain to the least useful of his Domina. He felt her body die within him, screaming and weak, then silence as his body consumed hers entirely. His wounds stitched themselves back together, granting him the clarity of mind to call upon his Wisdom. The boulder on his back crumbled and cracked to tiny pebbles, lifting the immense weight from his chest while filling the space in his tunnel. Habbad stood and raised a glowing emerald hand to the falling pebbles, halting their flow with another spell. He waited a moment for his wounds to finish healing, then braced himself as his sacrificed Domina entered the void. Unfortunately, her soul would go to Grotton's realm, where it would serve the traitorous god until the end of time. It wasn't ideal, but it was necessary.

Habbad continued digging with his hands and magic. He used his Wisdom every step of the way, granting himself light and fresh air, taking great care to probe the surrounding rock before removing material. He still carried a moderate supply of Domina, but he had already lost nine from the cave-ins, and there was no telling how much farther he still had to go. Every once in a while, after hours or sometimes days of digging, he would find clusters of bodies from the battle in the Fangshard Valley. His labors drained him beyond the sustenance of his Domina, and so Habbad had no choice but to feed upon the bodies of the fallen. He recognized some of the Wisdom Warriors from Oberon city. Habbad drew upon the minds of his animal Domina to complete the grisly task of consuming their flesh and drinking their blood. He found remains of his Domina army as well, Aenerian men and women who had each taken two or three thralls, making them more animal than Aenerian. They were all Chosen by Sorronis himself before the battle in the valley, and so they were still alive when Habbad ate them.

Time passed with agonizing monotony. Habbad grew more reckless as the wells of flesh became less frequent, or so badly decomposed that they were beyond palatable. He cannibalized more of his internal Domina when his body began to quiver from lack of nourishment. There were several more cave-ins, all of which occured when he least expected them and happened too quickly for him to muster any sort of defense. Habbad depleted over half his Domina before long, but he persevered without relent, ignoring his body's demands for sleep and food, fueling himself with his Hunger for revenge.

Eventually the digging became easier, almost effortless compared to the tedium of the past miles. The dirt loosened, yielding freely to his touch even without the aid of magic. A sickly dread filled him when he scooped a clump of earth away, finding the soil beneath damp and soggy. He labored on, hoping he could circumvent the source of the moisture, but as he bored on his clothes became soaked and his tunnel walls shifted to loose mud. There was no turning back now. Even if he didn't backtrack through all the cave-ins, he knew he wouldn't have the Domina to start another tunnel.

With his Wisdom nearly exhausted, Habbad resorted to manual labor, sticking his arm into the wall of mud. The chill of the soggy dirt sapped the heat from his flesh at an alarming pace, sending shards of ice throughout the rest of his body. His fingers were so numb he couldn't feel them moving, but he could feel something else creeping up towards his shoulder.

Water flowed around his arm like a fresh wound in the earth. He withdrew his arm, pushing mud back into the hole in an attempt to stop the water, but the wall disintegrated at his touch as buckets of icy water splashed down his front. Before Habbad could cast a spell to save himself, the entire wall fell apart and the river charged into him. The force of the impact knocked the air from his lungs and filled his mouth with the coldness of uncertainty.

He was submerged, tumbling and blind as the water swirled around him. His spells slipped from his mind as primal Fear wracked him from the inside out. Lungs burning, limbs freezing, Habbad knew this was it. This was the moment of his death. He wished he could give up now, submit to the unknowing, unfeeling void, but his instincts wouldn't allow it. He would suffer and fight to the bitter end. Habbad's foot found a rock, solid and still. He kicked, freeing himself from a thick jacket of mud, pushing and stroking his way into open water. Invisible fingers worked their way into his mouth, pulling and prying at his throat as they urged him to take a breath. Dirt clawed at his eyes as they opened on their own. There was light.

Battling his body's instincts, Habbad swam towards the ghostly luminance, but it was too late. His vision dimmed and his heart slowed. He couldn't move. Paralyzed, he was forced to wait for yet another Domina to die for him. In his panic he threw a few more Domina at his failing body, but each death brought clarity to his mind and power back to his limbs, and mercifully, a modicum of his Wisdom. Habbad forced his will to the moment, propelling himself through the water with a spell. The light rushed closer, brighter.

Habbad erupted into open air, dousing the fires in his lungs with full, gratifying breaths as he levitated away from his prison of mud and rock. He was alive. He was free. Oberon loomed overhead, its radiance warming him like a midday sun on Aeneria's Light Side. Once recovered, Habbad brought his focus back to the task at hand; his revenge. There would be time for savoring victories when his enemies were dead.

The starscape revealed that Aeneria had passed from the house of Jindaere to the house of Balmoray, which meant it had been at least two weeks since the battle in Fangshard Valley. He flew higher, pleased to discover that he had ended up on the Oberon side of the Fangshards, only half a day's travel from Oberon Temple, where Kreed ought to be waiting for him. He looked back to the Fangshard Valley, but it wasn't there. Surely he hadn't tunneled so far that he was beyond sight of the valley? Upon closer inspection he found a dark seam in the mountain ridge, a mile wide and completely devoid of snow or vegetation, as if the valley had simply closed in upon itself. He hoped Kreed would have an answer to the phenomenon.

Habbad alighted on the pebbly shore of the mountainside river and assessed himself. His Domina had done their jobs well in healing him, though his crimson suit was nothing more than a husk of soiled brown rags and his shoes were somewhere under the mountains. He cleaned himself with magically heated water and fixed his suit the best he could before setting off to Oberon City. Habbad traveled on foot, as his animal thralls made him more swift on the ground than in flight with his Wisdom, and he didn't know if Kreed's forces had taken the city yet. He made kills along the way, feeding on slow birds and foxes, eating the meat raw so as not to waste time. The flesh put fire back into his limbs, but the greatest meal of all was an unsuspecting soul fly he caught while crossing a starlit meadow. He saturated the creature with every one of the four dark magics before drawing its vitality into himself, leaving the soul fly grey and frail. He came upon the city gates far sooner and feeling much better than he expected to.

Habbad had never been to Oberon city, though a couple of his thralls had visited briefly. He drew upon their memories as he approached from the shadows skirting the main road, using Wisdom to hide his form while he peered around a statue. There wasn't a person in sight in either direction. A barrier of Wisdom should exist between the arches of the brass gate, and automatons should have been standing sentry, counting and verifying the citizens and travelers moving in and out of the city. Habbad inched closer. There were fragments of metal and broken gratia stones scattered about the entryway. A good sign. Habbad sharpened his senses with the aid of his Domina and emerged from the shadows.

The metallic pavement was pleasantly warm on Habbad's raw feet as he strolled down the middle of the thoroughfare. Several of Oberon City's flying cars were parked along the sidewalks, sleek and luxurious, but the doors had been left open on many, as though the vehicles had been abandoned in a hurry. Another good sign. The buildings grew taller the farther he walked, each lined with sharp corners and surfaces so shiny he could see himself as clearly as if looking at a mirror. No light shone from the windows, and like the cars, many of the doors were left open. Habbad eyed one of the vehicles as he passed it, admiring how its design managed to portray both opulence and athleticism. He would have to take one of the locals for Domina so he could gain the knowledge to operate the car.

Just when he began to think the entire city might be devoid of life, Habbad's ears twitched at a sudden noise; the distant tapping of approaching footsteps. The sounds echoed more loudly off the smooth walls and windows as the strangers neared, eventually settling into militant cadence. It sounded like a squad-sized element at the very least. Habbad could have concealed himself, but the rebellious Hunger within him planted his feet in the middle of the street, welcoming the potential challenge. He may have lost over half his Domina, but the twenty or so he still held put him leagues beyond the most prestigious of Grotton's priests. Or if he were very lucky, the strangers were a host of Oberon's forces. A ravenous shiver ran through Habbad's body at the thought of so many souls ripe for the plucking.

A formation rounded the corner, wearing battle robes and wielding conjured weapons made of emerald Wisdom; tall halberds with leaf-shaped blades, stout rifles, and broad shields. Their faces looked as though they were once as proud and dignified as the elegant silver and cerulean patterns on their robes, but now the group looked utterly defeated and bedraggled, as though they hadn't slept in weeks. Habbad recognized the shadow of Fear in their eyes.

A woman in the front rank noticed Habbad as soon as she turned the corner. She cried out a command to the others, who relayed it back to her, then the formation dispersed and closed in around Habbad. He grinned and waited for them to encircle him. His contact within the Oberon Temple had informed him about the soldiers of the capital city. Oberon's finest were all experts in Wisdom, shirking all other types of magic, which made them pitifully vulnerable to even the slightest prick of Fear.

"Who are you?" barked one of the soldiers in a voice much braver than his face displayed. He stepped forward with a white-knuckle grip on his halberd, which Habbad noticed had started to dim with every step.

"Why don't you come a little closer and find out?" Habbad said with a sneer. He had already saturated the air around himself with a broad bubble of Fear. Invisible, it throbbed steadily wider, chilling the hearts and minds of the soldiers around him.

The soldier stopped as his halberd shattered in his hands, showering the metal street with a tinkling chorus of emerald shards. He staggered backwards, wide-eyed and pale-faced, but it was too late. "Shoot him!" he cried in a feathery voice.

Conjured bolts whistled through the air. Most missed by a wide margin, shot by shaking hands whose owners were already under the effects of Habbad's Fear. The few bolts that managed to aim true exploded in puffs of green dust several inches from Habbad, where the Fear was too great for rational thought to exist.

Habbad readied his Hunger and took a step towards the soldiers nearest him. They all took a small step back.

"Don't tell me you've lost your nerve. There are so many of you, and then there's me, unarmed and alone. Do your jobs," Habbad said, amplifying their terror as he took another step. The air was so thick with Fear, Habbad could see a mottled purple haze starting to form.

The soldiers abandoned their conjured weapons and drew with trembling hands steel daggers and short rifles. One soldier mustered up the final dregs of his courage and charged with a wild cry, while several others turned and fled. Habbad's fingers twitched, dripping with dull magenta. Just another drop of Fear would paralyze most of them, and then if he was quick enough he could catch the deserters. His Hunger would be there for them at the end, freeing them of their terror through a simple, yet binding contract. He never expected to replenish his Domina so soon.

"Stop," said an oily voice.

The soldier charging at Habbad came to a crashing halt, as though colliding with a brick wall, then something yanked the fleeing soldiers back with invisible ropes. A man whom Habbad hadn't noticed stepped out from behind a cluster of soldiers, who all stiffened like corpses at his presence. Their Fear for Habbad was but a snowflake in a blizzard compared to the crippling dread they regarded this man with.

Habbad recognized him at once. He was an elite priest of Decreath, a bishop, which meant he had long mastered his respective school of magic. The man was hairless, his face gaunt, and unusually short, giving him the appearance of a child's skeleton bewitched to imitate life. He was thin as a ladder, with pale skin hanging loosely from his jaw and under his eyes. His midnight-grey robes slithered over the metal street as he approached Habbad with unnerving confidence.

"This part of the city has been decreed off limits to all," said the bishop. He surveyed Habbad with a look of disgust. "Congratulations to you. You just earned death by a hand of Decreath."

"You know who I am, Festin," Habbad growled.

A mirthless grin stretched across Festin's face, stopping well below his eyes. "I'm not sure I do. Everyone of importance is fully aware that this district is off limits to all besides me and my guard. For all I know you could be a citizen fleeing the city, or a scavenger perhaps, prowling and looting the very streets we fought so hard to capture. There's only one prudent option in my eyes." He presented his first two fingers in a gesture of benediction. Dark purple began to spiral from his hand.

Habbad chose his next words carefully. While he had pushed the boundaries of Hunger to unprecedented levels, his arts were best served in scheming and secrets, not for open combat with a master of Fear. "A priest does not attain the title of bishop without ambition, does he?"

Festin paused. His eyes narrowed. "And what would you know about it? Speak quickly, and do not think to delay your death with clever words. Every second you continue to live will be an eternity of suffering before I kill you."

Festin's curiosity, however brief, was all Habbad's Hunger needed to take root in the bishop. "It would be a waste to kill me before treating yourself. Your mastery of Fear is second only to Decreath himself, so what risk would there be in feeding upon me before killing me? Your district is quiet, which means you must have done your job very well. You've earned a little treat, don't you think?"

"What trickery is this?" Festin said with a snarl. "Wait, I've heard lies like this before. You're Father Kreed's apprentice, aren't you?"

"There's only one way to find out," Habbad replied in a silky voice. "Come bishop, taste my Fear. I promise it's the sweetest you've never had."

"Enough!" Festin snapped. He stormed over to Habbad, his hand locked into a gnarled claw. "I'll have your hubris as well as your Fear. Show me your shame!" With Habbad's Hunger blossoming in his eyes, Festin clapped his hand over Habbad's forehead, digging sharp fingernails into his scalp.

Habbad threw one of his more powerful Domina before the mental assault. He felt his thrall wither and wail before the torrent of Fear, a perfect diversion. The bishop was so enraptured by his Hunger, he didn't sense the mental trap closing in around him. Festin tortured the Domina with indecent terror, thinking he was attacking Habbad. As soon as the first drop of Fear bled from the Domina's mind and into Festin's, Habbad felt the Hunger slip into place. The contract manifested into binding law. Festin had unwittingly relinquished control over his body, mind, and soul. He belonged to Habbad now.

Habbad twisted the Fear upon itself. The hand upon his forehead loosened its bite. Festin fell to his knees, hugging and whimpering to himself like a child.

Habbad bent down next to the broken man. "Do you remember me now, Festin?" He indulged in the man's suffering for a moment. It took all he had not to take the Bishop for Domina. A master of Fear would be the crown jewel of his thralls, but he had already declared one of The Three as an enemy. Father Kreed and Decreath would not look kindly upon the loss of one of their elite bishops. Though they might not begrudge him one of Oberon City's soldiers. Or several. "Stand, Festin. Behold the fate that I spare you from, and don't you ever forget me again." Festin clambered to his feet, eager to obey.

Habbad approached one of the soldiers. The woman stood paralyzed, bathed in the Fear still clouding the air. She stared at a horror no one else could see while fine beads of sweat collected over her colorless face. Habbad entered her mind and whispered promises of release, freedom from the terror, if only she submit to him. She nodded. Habbad rubbed his fingers over her head as though sprinkling salt over a steak. Orange dots the size of marbles snapped into existence, rolling down from Habbad's hand to the woman's trembling lips. The orbs flowed over her face, each splitting neatly in half as the seams sprouted wicked teeth, then proceeded to bite clean chunks from the woman's flesh.

She screamed. Habbad held up his end of the bargain by freeing her from his Fear, but now it was her own Fear driving her mad. She clawed at her face, but the tiny orange mouths bit at her fingertips, cleaving chunk after chunk with sharp little clicks. With each bite the mouths propagated, producing two more. The woman's face and hands were first to vanish as the clicking marbles reproduced at an exponential rate, and screaming gave way to a wet rattle as the orange mouths consumed her head and throat. She was gone within a few seconds, though not a drop of blood had made it to the ground. There was now a swarm of the little orange marbles, clicking and snapping as they began to consume each other. Habbad opened his arms, and with no other prompting the swarm gathered and twisted high in the air, then funneled their way down Habbad's open mouth.

Habbad felt the expected surge that succeeded the act; the savage pleasure, the power, and to his pleasant surprise, the knowledge of operating the flying vehicles. The euphoric rush of a new Domina left his Hunger aching for more. Obliging himself, Habbad consumed three more of Oberon City's finest. The soldiers were easily worth ten of the pedestrian commoners from the Light Side.

Using every ounce of willpower he possessed, Habbad wiped his mouth and ceased his feeding, then approached Festin. The crotch of the bishop's robes bore a dark stain that trailed down to a shining puddle on the metal street. Habbad sneered. "Master of Fear indeed. Remember this, Festin. If you ever cross me again you can consider our contract in default, and I will collect. You may continue working for Father Kreed and Decreath, but you belong to me now."

Habbad left the formation in his lingering cloud of Fear, returning to the sleek sky car he'd passed earlier. Using the strength of his Domina, he gripped the seam of the driver's door and yanked it clean from the frame, where it fell to the metal sidewalk with a clanging gong. Habbad overrode the controls with a blast of Fear and the car roared to life, then shot high above the tops of the buildings, where it angled towards the dark mass of Oberon Temple.

CHAPTER 7

PROMOTION

Eliza was the first to join Cole at Naythan's house. It had been over half a day since he left the rest of the Unbound, plenty of time to get a good bout of sleep, but judging by the heavy bags under her glassy eyes, Eliza had indeed consumed the dreamsource cypher. She plodded like a zombie behind Cole, Naythan, and the girls as they made the long climb up a spiral ramp that twisted up one of the nearby trees. Eliza seemed too exhausted to speak.

It was the dawn of the changing of houses for Aeneria. Naythan sang for them as they climbed. The melody mourned the passing of Shaskien, then heralded the arrival of the house of Cigni, a local planet inhabited by a sentient race of aquatic folk with slippery skin and webbed feet.

Aenerian sunrises had never failed to leave Cole speechless with their awesome beauty; however, this time he kept a close eye on the two girls. Wonder swam in their eyes as they took in the distant clouds of soul flies undulating back to Shaskien, then they spun around to the sky opposite to catch a glimpse of the rising sun. They seemed innocent and pure enough, but Cole didn't fully trust the girls, not blindly at any rate. Lexy had just spent several long Aenerian months enslaved by some of the darkest magic Cole had ever seen, and the ginger-haired girl seemed as adept in evil magic as a high-ranking priest. Cole had experienced enough of Aeneria's nightmares to maintain healthy suspicion, even for sweet Lexy.

The golden beam of light from Shaskien's sun finally tipped over the horizon, bathing The Sill in the newborn day. But as soon as it appeared, the sun vanished, taking Shaskien and the entire starscape with it. The girls made a game of counting Cigni's stars as they popped into the empty sky.

They descended the ramp in awed silence. Cole trailed closely behind Eliza to keep her fatigue from wandering too close to the edge. To his surprise, Valen and Sitra were waiting for them at the bottom of the ramp, each looking as worn and lethargic as Eliza. Naythan offered to make more coffee for the new arrivals, but Cole declined, as it would only make matters worse for them when the caffeine wore off. Cole chatted around the subject for a time, but after a while Sitra bluntly informed him that Lileth had not chosen to take the dreamsource cypher, and was still asleep in her apartment. His heart sank low, but he kept his emotions off his face. Cole milled about with Naythan for an hour longer in case Lileth decided to change her mind, but the old hermit shooed him away, demanding that he take the other warriors with him. Cole paid the gratia stones and said a quick goodbye to the girls, leaving them with a promise to visit soon.

Cole led the others out of the Arts district, bringing them to the trio of sentinel pines where Cole first met them during Roth's lesson. He could tell by their wilted expressions and grumbles of dissent that he wouldn't get much out of them. The dreamsource would require weeks to fully alleviate the dregs of their fatigue. Even Eliza seemed close to her breaking point. Cole checked his sympathy before it flourished into compassion, as he knew soft hearts would offer no solace in this. He had survived the dreamsource, and so would they.

Cole cleared his throat and waited for each of their heavy lids to crack open. "I hoped everyone would be here, but that doesn't look like it's going to happen. I think we should get started."

"Get started with what?" Sitra croaked. Her long braid was frayed and partially unraveled. She glared at him with bloodshot eyes. "We already took your stupid cypher. If this is anything hard then I'm going to kick your face in."

"Actually, that's exactly what I want you to do," Cole said. He didn't want to go over anything important until Lileth joined them anyway. He unclipped Varka's cape from his shoulders and set the silky cloth near the edge of the training ground. "Rage will wake you up. Go on, draw your munisica."

"Cole, I'm not sure I can use Rage at the moment," Eliza said, wincing as though simply standing was causing her physical pain. "What exactly are we supposed to do?"

"Think of this as one of Roth's lessons," Cole replied. "I want you to try and kill me. You'll find your Rage soon enough, and it should sharpen up the rest of your mind to use the other magics."

Sitra stomped the ground. "But you're a master of Rage! I told you, nothing hard!"

Cole bared his teeth and stoked his warrior's magic. The black shroud snapped over his body, transforming his hands and feet into sweeping ebony claws with a satisfying ache. He gave Sitra a savage grin. "Where's that kick you promised me?"

Sitra stamped her foot down twice more, shaking with fury as her shroud began to crawl up from her hands and feet. She shot him a look of deepest loathing, then charged, munisica drawn with an unrestrained intent to kill.

Sitra was a near expert with Rage, but even her blazing speed was no more than that of a waddling child to Cole. He sidestepped faster than she could register. Reaching down, he hooked his bladed hand around her ankle, then used her own momentum to hurl her straight at Valen and Eliza. Sitra flew through the air, spinning and roaring as she collided with the others, who hadn't so much as raised a hand in defense.

The impact sent all three warriors tumbling to the edge of the training ground. It was a powerful blow, but Cole knew it was merely a warm-up compared to what Roth had put them through. They rose in unison, Eliza and Valen healing everyone with pulses of Passion while Sitra's shroud crawled higher up her limbs. Cole charged this time.

The intensity of the skirmish rose exponentially with each passing minute. Cole was simply too fast for them to aim a spell at, appearing as a flurry of slashing blades then vanishing in a blink, leaving their Wisdom to lash at open air. Their Passion had even less effect. Valen and Sitra were adept in the lover's magic, and Eliza was of course a master, but Cole's whirlwind of attacks kept their focus on defense. After several minutes Valen had deciphered some pattern to Cole's movements, and by unspoken command the others began to spread out.

Cole sensed them forming their own Passion network, no doubt with Eliza at its hub, but he couldn't catch any of their thoughts or make out any words. Good. They were waking up at last.

Seconds later the three warriors had Cole suspended ten feet in the air, where his munisica could find no purchase and his Rage would have no outlet. Using his Passion instead, Cole circled about their minds like a wolf prowling around a campfire, watching and waiting for a moment of weakness. Eliza's Passion was more than sufficient to protect all three of them, however, and without Varka's cape aiding his Wisdom, Cole was quite helpless.

"Do you concede?" Valen asked, flipping Cole upside-down with a twist of his hand.

"No!" Sitra barked. "I didn't get to kick him yet. Spin him right ways up so I can land one in between his legs. Let's see if that shroud really does protect everything."

Cole laughed and dismissed his Rage. Valen spun him upright and planted his feet back on the ground. "Thanks for the offer, but I'll pass if you don't mind. The only thing that ever hurt me through the shroud was Sorronis's Hatred, but I think I'd rather have another bout with Talin than take a kick between the legs from you, shrouded or not."

Sitra's munisica shrank away as Valen and Eliza released their spells. Her tone softened with tender curiosity. "You never did tell us about your fight with Talin. I still can't believe Talin betrayed us. He wasn't the friendliest guy, but he was one of us, you know? Was Sorronis really inside him?"

"Inside him and his daughter." Cole suppressed a shudder as he recalled the misshapen girl melted to Talin's chest. "Talin wielded the Hatred, while his daughter wielded Despair. Together they made Sorronis's Harbinger."

"Stars, no!" Eliza gasped. "The depravity of The Three truly knows no bounds. She wasn't even a cycle old. How could a mere child endure something so vile?"

"I have no idea," Cole said with a weak shrug. "I wanted to wait until Lileth got here before I talked about my fight with Sorronis, but I guess I could just fill her in later. It's important, though. You all need to know what it's like. Our little training fights here in The Sill make us deadlier than most anything else on Aeneria, but it can only help so much. We train using our three magics, which gives us the tools we need to win, but we have little experience actually fighting enemies adept in the darker magics."

"You mean *we* have little experience," Sitra said, crossing her muscled arms with a wry grin. "*You* have plenty experience. You fought and killed three priests on your solo mission for the Celestial Council. Don't think you're getting away with not telling us about that either."

Cole's gaze drifted towards the barracks, where Lileth slept in her bed, and where he wished he was. "Fine. But I'm not explaining it all verbally. It would take too long and I'm not a very good storyteller."

"Passion it is then!" Sitra said. She turned on her heel, her long braid whipping each of them, then found a soft patch of clovers and plopped herself down. The rest of the group took seats around her, forming a tight circle.

Cole opened himself to his Passion. Its soothing warmth flowed through him like a river of wholesome energy. He reached out with his mind's eye, then connected himself to each of the three life candles around him, basking in the familiar companionship of their collective souls. Holding tight to each of them, Cole emptied his mind and brought them all to the stone room of his center, a place he had never shown anyone else, save for Alvani. He focused their minds to the pedestal set beneath the cone of marble memories hanging from the ceiling. Cole took a deep breath and exhaled, releasing a cascade of cool water down the cone, where it caressed over each of their minds and melted layers of stress away. Steam billowed from them and the room filled with a heavy white fog, but Cole breathed again and the steam vanished in a crisp breeze. He repeated the process several times, until each of their minds was at a place of calm neutrality suitable to examine the horrors of his memories.

A marble clicked loose from the cone, landing without bouncing upon the obsidian surface of the pedestal. Black as oil, it rolled around as though restless, then cracked open and filled the room with shadow.

Cole's center surrendered to the growing darkness, then the memories of his mission to Brimhallow Village began to fill the void.

He stood with Chiron, standing in the elder's wandering treetop house and discussing the details of the mission. Fear, Ambition. Inadequacy. Duty. He crawled through the bushes around Brimhallow, filthy and tired, probing for signs of life while trying to hide his own. He entered the demon's nest, a temple once devoted to love and life, now a celebration of desecration, an insult to innocence. Fear. Pain. Rage. He passed through the wall of arms, killed the Domina beyond, then descended to the bowels of the temple. Three priests, one for each of the evil gods. They had him. Helplessness. Fear. Violation. Pain. Insanity. Despair. A foolish spell, whimsical and desperate, but enough to save him. The first two died slowly, the third with a mere stab through the heart. A child cried out, a flower blooming in a grave. Hope. Escape. Failure. He created another Joshy.

Valen and Sitra recoiled and attempted to wrench their minds from the horrible memories, but Cole held them fast. Eliza endured, for she had already experienced all of this through her private link with Cole.

Cole wasted no time diving into his battle with Sorronis. Those memories pained him just as much, and while he wanted to be as thorough as possible, he was eager to push through and be done with tracing his old scars. He placed heavy focus on Sorronis's use of magic; the Hatefire, the blood-red shroud covering Talin's body, the crippling black-tar rain, and the crushing touch of Despair from Talin's child. He showed them how the child's touch had brought about the manifestation of Joshy. Seeing his brother again felt like tearing open a half-healed wound, even though it was a mere ghost of his sorrows, but the details were necessary. Letting go of his guilt allowed Cole to master Passion, thus releasing him from Sorronis's Despair.

To emphasize the importance of the events, Cole concluded his recollections with a surge of Passion so powerful that it lifted his friends from the ground, their bodies aglow with lavender light. The weariness drained from their faces by the time their feet touched the ground. Happy tears welled in their eyes.

"You truly deserve to lead this unit," Valen said with a heavy sigh. "We have much to learn. I always knew of its significance, but I never would have guessed that Passion would play such a significant role in the war."

Cole's eyes fell to the side as he kicked at a clump of grass. "I don't consider myself your superior in any way, but I'll show you everything I know and offer what help I can. My first suggestion is that we stop referring to ourselves as a unit. We are the Unbound."

"Indeed," Eliza said with a proud nod.

A grin began to tug at Valen's cheeks as he mulled over the suggestion. "The concept is a bit daunting, but I believe you are right. There is no one left alive who has followed paths of our magic as diversely and as deeply as us five. We are the Unbound."

"Really?" Sitra said in a tone of utter disbelief. "Really? You think we're up there with the likes of Varka and Chiron? There were twenty or thirty people in the Unbound, and every one of them mastered at least one school of magic. Come on, Cole, besides you and Eliza, the rest of us are just kids. And you were cheating the whole time."

"How so?" Cole asked with a smug grin.

Sitra leaned over and punched Cole hard in the chest. "You've got one of the damned Unbound living inside you! I'd master a school of magic every other week if I had Varka whispering the answers in my ear."

"I wish Varka *was* that clear," Cole said as he massaged his chest. "Listen, I'm not saying this is going to happen overnight or anything. Varka and his crew spent cycles together, traveling the local planets, learning about magic, and picking up recruits along the way. We've got a good start though."

Sitra huffed. "I'm not trying to drop the axe on your plan, but our time isn't measured in cycles. Weeks more like. And in case you haven't noticed, Aeneria is a little light on recruits at the moment. Everyone willing to take up arms against The Three already lives here, and they're fleeing like Underkin with a hawk in the sky. We're in a bad way."

"Don't be so fatalistic, Sitra," Eliza said, rolling her eyes. "You speak as if there's no hope. We're not dead yet."

Valen nodded in agreement. "We have yet to hear Cole's plan. There is much to consider, and many resources yet to tap." Concern furrowed his brow as he cast Cole a sideways glance. "You do have a plan, correct?"

Sitra donned a haughty smirk. "Yeah *boss*, what's your plan to sail us through this shit storm?"

"I don't know if it's much of a plan, it's more like some ideas I've been rolling around," Cole started, aware of the uncertainty in his tone. He shook his head, releasing a pin prick of his Rage. He stood to his full height, forcing confidence into his words. "We don't sleep. We're going to spend the nights training, and when we can swing it we're going out on some missions. Real ones like Brimhallow. It's the only way we're going to find experience dealing with the dark magics, and it's the only chance you have to master our own. If there's one thing I learned from mastering Rage and Passion, it's that the situation needs to be dire. We're not going to do much more growing in The Sill. It's too safe, too controlled."

Sitra's look of derision hardened to a savage yearning as she stood next to Cole. "You sure know how to warm a girl's heart. Find me a few strong Domina to tangle with now and again and I'll dance along to whatever song you please."

"That seems well and good, but what are we to do with the rest of our time?" Eliza asked, rising to her feet as well. "Even without the need for sleep I don't think we could sustain a lifestyle of constant training and fighting."

Cole offered Valen a hand, hoisting his friend to his feet. He hesitated a moment while he pondered how best to respond. This was the part of his plan that he was least certain about. "As powerful as we might become, there are only five of us. Even if we were as strong as the original Unbound at the height of their powers, our numbers would still limit us. Most of our enemies won't be nearly as powerful as we are, but we can't take down armies spread across the whole planet, not unless we ask them to line up outside The Sill and fight us one at a time. We need to recruit."

Valen clapped a hand on Cole's shoulder. "I agree with you. Recruiting is far from impossible, but how do we inspire the masses to join the losing side? We cannot hide how woefully outnumbered we are."

Cole grasped his Passion once more and pressed upon them images of Brimhallow, of Storn's death, of the Devotion in Costas. They winced as each memory flashed in their minds.

Cole's next words were galvanized with a level of confidence and authority he never had before. "After everything we've seen, would you run and hide, or would you stand up and do something about it?"

The group fell silent. Cole could tell by their looks of fiery defiance that they would follow him through any hell.

"We start right here in The Sill," Cole continued. "Naythan said there's some students practically begging for new mentors. I'll go find them in the morning. The rest of The Sill might take some convincing, especially the folks in the Arts District, but I bet we can at least get a few healers out of them. Everyone here's been affected by the war. If they haven't then show them the memories I just gave you. If that doesn't make them want to join the fight, then we probably don't want them in the first place."

"There is an abundance of non-combat positions required as well," Valen added. "We need intelligence teams, equipment, sustenance, transportation. Most of our assets are likely still operational. We will need to assert ourselves at the Heart Tree, where The Sill's bureaucrats hold office. Cole's authority as Varka's echo ought to suffice for the staff."

"And what if they don't recognize Cole as the sole leader of The Sill?" Eliza asked.

"That's the *assert ourselves* part," Sitra said. "If anyone stands in our way, I'll invoke Roth's Trial of Honor."

"Wait a second," Cole said with an empty chuckle. "You can't just put me in charge of The Sill, no one would believe it. I'm not even qualified to lead the unit—the Unbound I mean. Who's going to listen to some kid from Terra, especially one who only just set foot on Aeneria a few months ago. I wouldn't know where to start."

Eliza gave his arm a gentle squeeze. "You are more than that, and we all know it. What you Fear is the unknown, not what you must do.

And don't believe for one second that you'll be alone for any part of this. Aeneria needs you. We need you."

Sitra gave his other arm a not-so-gentle squeeze, bruising him to the bone. "Face it, boss. You're in charge of the Unbound, and seeing as we're about to be in charge of The Sill, well that makes you top dog in the yard. Don't make us vote on it."

"No," Cole sighed, shrugging himself away from his friends. Anxiety whipped about his chest like a rabbit caught in a snare. "This is stupid. You're *all* being stupid, and I'm not doing it."

"Elder Cole, don't leave us!" Sitra wailed. She bounded after him and wrapped him in a tight embrace, crushing him with a shoulder-popping hug. "Guide us, Elder Cole. We are but wandering sheep without a shepherd. Please, give us an order!"

"Get off me!" Cole's Rage flared, shrouding him for a moment as he broke Sitra's grip and flung her several yards away. She landed gracefully, holding her belly and laughing her head off. "You want an order, go shower and put some clean armor on. You all look like you came out the wrong end of a Corpulant."

"If we're keeping track..." Eliza prodded. "You're the only one who has seen the inside of a Corpulant, Elder Cole. You could use a wash yourself."

Cole shut his eyes and retreated to the center of his mind to keep from saying something he would regret. He heard Eliza's and Sitra's playful banter fade as he stormed off towards the barracks, though he sensed Valen was still near. Cole turned his head, ready for another witty remark, but Valen sidled up beside him with a solemn expression.

"Eliza was right about one thing," he said, crossing his arms behind his back. "You are not alone. Not in the slightest. Your connection to Varka makes you a figurehead for the people. However, it is your talent, wit, experiences, and the merits of your character that make you worthy of leadership. No one will force you to take the position, and you are not the only candidate, but in my opinion you are far and away the best person for the job."

Valen then reached for Cole with Passion, embracing him like a brother through the link. *Call us when you are ready.*

A numbness fell over Cole as he watched Valen stride back towards Sitra and Eliza. The prospect of so much responsibility and so many unknowns troubled him to his core, but something else bothered him even more: Why hadn't Lileth taken the dreamsource cypher?

Cole brooded over the question as he took flight and soared aimlessly over the towering pines of The Sill. His guesses branched off into implications that troubled him deeper still, each worse than the last. A wild urge leaped up in his heart, demanding that he fly straight to the markets and purchase the dreamsource, then fly to Lileth's tree and convince her to take it. He took a few stabs at understanding why he took such offense at Lileth's choice, but his delving only showed him how deep his hurt ran. Only when he noticed his meandering had brought him over the Cordial Compendium did he change course, blasting off as fast as he could towards the uninhabited reaches of The Sill. He beheld the gentle glow of the Necropolis, with its turquoise waters and branches laden with moss, a graveyard for The Sill's fallen. Cole veered away so he wouldn't taint the place with his foul mood.

An odd forest peered up at him now. Its trees were somewhat narrow compared to behemoths dominating the rest of The Sill, and they displayed themselves in a grid-like array. Cole smiled. It was the same forest where he first found Chiron's house, a task which took him a frustratingly long time as he didn't know the house floated above the trees, not under them. Cole looked back on the memory with a tinge of chagrin, remembering how naive he had been to lean on Rage to solve the problem. Chiron's lessons were the most irksome of all the Elders, not because they were more difficult, but because the answer was usually in plain sight the entire time. If only he could talk to Chiron now, even for a moment. He would know what to do for The Sill.

As if fate itself could hear his thoughts, Cole spotted a small cabin set on a wooden platform resting on the tree tops. Chiron's house was dark and vacant, and sat crooked on the canopy instead of wandering around as it usually did. Cole alighted on the decking, leaning heavily to one side to keep from sliding off the platform. He had never been inside Chiron's house, and when he pushed himself through the liquid stone door he felt a sense of unease, as though he was trespassing through on an active ghost. He popped through to the other side and ignited an orb of light with Wisdom. Cole's trepidation soon gave way to a sense of familiarity. He felt as if he'd been here before.

The walls were lined with grey mushrooms as large as his fist, their roots cascading down and across the floor. Decorations were spartan, with a thin bedroll, a single round table with chair, and a bookshelf expanding over the entire back wall. Cole's circumspection revealed an omnistone embedded above the door frame. He clapped a hand over the glassy surface and deposited his Rage, filling the cloudy orb with pulsing red light. The slanted platform lurched, righting itself as the cabin resumed its slow crawl above the canopy. Cole peeked out a window, but couldn't tell where the house was headed, then decided it didn't matter. He busied himself with replacing some of the volumes that had fallen from the shelves, discovering several of Chiron's blackstout fruits scattered about the floor as well. He picked one up and gave it a squeeze. It was still firm. Cole skinned its black hide with a twist of Wisdom and devoured the meat in one huge bite, feeling as though a cinder block had dropped into his stomach. Almost at once, a steadying vigor began to spread throughout his body, nourishing and replenishing.

Cole downed a few more blackstouts and put the rest in a carved bowl set on the table. He paused mid-chew and brought his conjured light closer, blinking in disbelief at something odd. A piece of paper lay next to the bowl, folded in the shape of a six-sided star and sealed with a dollop of glittery silver wax. The words *Cole Carter* were etched in sloppy handwriting beside the seal. Cole hastily swallowed and wiped his hands on his pants, then picked up the paper as tenderly as he could.

As soon as he touched the wax, wisps of emerald light emerged from the creases of the paper, cracking the seal as a letter unfolded in his hands. The script was untidy and wandering, as though written by an unfocused child, but Chiron's name winked up at him from the bottom of the page.

My Dearest Friend,

If you are reading this, then one of two things has occurred: Either you have taken advantage of one of my many absences from The Sill, or our latest foray to Oberon City did not go as well as we had hoped. If it is the former, then I suggest you take a moment to peruse the bookshelf beside you. There you will find my personal notes on horticulture, including instructions on how to cultivate your own blackstouts so you won't go hungry after eating all of mine. However, if circumstances bring us to the latter outcome, then I have some parting words for you, as well as the humble blessing of a very old, and very foolish man.

You have grown faster than any student before you, not just in your magical talents, but in your command over yourself. If your arrival on Aeneria was but thirty cycles earlier you would stand equal to any of the Unbound, or even the Elites of old. I say this not only to recognize your accomplishments, but to beg caution from you. Take time to discover yourself as you grow, for the paths of the hero and the tyrant often stem from the same trail. Your friends will help you in this endeavor. Keep your heart open to them, and keep your mind open to life.

What I am about to say next is one of the most dangerous secrets in all of Aeneria, and as such I have placed a spell on this letter which will destroy it once your skin leaves the paper. The only ones privy to this knowledge are Ka Reine, myself, and The Three, so I ask that you not divulge this to anyone outside of your unit. The means to win this war lie not in strength or clever spells. Even if you were to kill each of the Harbingers tomorrow, The Three will linger on, and whether it be one or one thousand cycles, they will find new hosts to torment the Aethers with. According to official records, in the core of Oberon Temple lies a collection of Vaults, one each for Passion, Rage, and Wisdom. Unofficially, there are three additional Vaults, which represent Fear, Hunger, Hatred and Despair. They are named the Vaults of the Soul, and they were crafted eons ago by those long dead and with magic long forgotten. Each Vault is a gateway to the very source of its namesake, and no one in recorded history has ever emerged once they entered one. The first three to enter were named

Decreath, Grotton, and Sorronis, who each chose the Vault they are so famous for today. Before they entered The Three were as mortal and mundane as you or I, though rather more talented I must admit. While their bodies never emerged from their respective Vaults, their souls joined with the source of the evil magics they had devoted their lives to, and they have plagued the Aethers ever since. The last person to enter a Vault was Varka, who of course sought the answer to the last war in the Vault of Wisdom.

Your only hope of truly defeating The Three lies within the Vaults of the Soul. I would have brought you to them myself, but in my cowardice I was not ready to see you throw your life away so soon, not when you still had so much of it yet to live. Furthermore, I believe that as wonderful and talented as you are, you were not quite ready for the perils of the Vaults. Now, however, the only one who can assess your preparedness is you. When you are ready, you must go to the Vaults. You must go willingly, and with the understanding that once you enter, there will be no coming out. I'm afraid I cannot tell you which to enter or what you will find inside. That is for you and Varka to discover.

Now I must say goodbye. I pray that fate will look kindly upon us and you will never read this letter, that you and I will have a hundred cycles of uninterrupted learning and growing, but fate has ever been a capricious thing. Go now with my blessing. May you be a candle to light the flame in those you love, and may the fire of your life stay the darkness evermore.

-Chiron

And one more thing: Release the letter out of doors. I may have overdone the enchantment a bit.

Cole gripped the letter firmly with both hands and read it over twice more. Repeating waves of emotion crashed over him with each pass. Grief struck him first, leaving him with an aching, hollow sensation, as though someone had removed several organs from his chest. It was grief not only for Chiron, but for everyone he had lost, even Habbad. But as he read on, the void within him seemed to fill with something nauseating and ice cold. How could Chiron ask him to enter one of those Vaults? Hadn't Cole lost enough just by coming to Aeneria? His family may have been broken, and his friends back on Earth weren't the greatest, but it was his life. No one had a right to take it from him. Now Cole had a new life, with friends as close as family, Chiron had the audacity to demand he throw that away too. When would it be enough? How much of himself would he have to lose? He crumpled the letter in his fist, blasted the nearest window open with magic, then chucked the ball of paper as hard as he could, feeling it erupt with flames as soon as it left his touch.

A sudden urge to burn Chiron's house to the ground rose up in Cole. He was alarmed then when he detected an acrid smoky odor, worrying that he had unwittingly set something ablaze. Cole raised his hand and readied a spell to douse fire, then noticed threads of smoke curling from charred stubble on the back of his hand and knuckles. He rubbed his hands together, smothering the smoke, but the smell remained. Chiron certainly did overdo his enchantment.

CHAPTER 8

IN THE HEART TREE

As Cole's singed hand cooled, so did his temper. Chiron's demand meant the end of life as Cole knew it, but there was one very important part to the letter that brought Cole back to reason.

When you are ready, you must go to the Vaults. You must go willingly, and with the understanding that once you enter, there will be no coming out.

When he was ready, not *right this second.* And Chiron said he must go willingly, which meant that it would be his choice, no one else's. If Cole wanted to, he could keep this secret to himself and never tell a soul. The Unbound could kill the Harbingers, then the next ones, over and over for as long as they were able. Perhaps after a thousand cycles Cole would eventually grow bored, and only then decide to see what other adventures awaited in the Vaults. That's if he lived through the end of this cycle, however. His education taught him Aenerians could live indefinitely with the help of Wisdom and Passion, but he was human after all, at least partially. The same rules might not apply to him.

Before his mind could spiral down a winding contemplation of his own mortality, Cole decided upon one of Chiron's suggestions that he would follow. He flicked on a few of the mushrooms absentmindedly, bathing the interior of the little house in turquoise light. He suddenly realized why the house was so familiar. Apart from the windows, it was identical to the cabin where he first met Goran, only now he was large enough to fit the furniture. Cole smiled as he combed through the bookshelf. He found the horticulture section last, tucked down at the very bottom, but on his way Cole found hundreds of useful titles printed on the spines. The first one he opened was labeled *Sundries and Such.* Inscribed were various spells designed for household use, such as creating one's own laser-showers, growing furniture from living trees, and crafting one's own clothes. With the aid of Varka's cape, Cole showered himself raw, then cleaned and repaired his armored clothes, restoring them to pristine condition.

Cole wanted to spend the rest of the day going through Chiron's library, but his Passion revealed a restless unease growing among the other Unbound. He pocketed Chiron's notes on horticulture as well as the rest of the blackstouts, then popped out the front door and took flight.

Cole arrived at the barracks after a short flight from the Necropolis. For the first time The Sill felt small to Cole, as if he were a fish that had outgrown a pond. What would have taken him a couple hours to walk now only took him a minute of flying. To his surprise, he found Sitra, Valen, and Eliza sitting in a circle with their eyes closed, meditating like they would before one of Chiron's lessons. Cole hid his smile as he landed gently beside them. He felt Varka's cape transform into a blanket of soft grass across his back, matching the plush carpet between his toes.

"Anyone hungry?" Cole asked. He tossed a blackstout to each of them before they could respond.

"Always," Sitra replied as she lashed out with a bladed hand and caught all three blackstouts, spearing each on a separate finger in an impressive display of dexterity. "What is this, bait? We don't need to trick our prey with fruit when we can track them with Passion. Way too slow."

"Those are blackstouts," Eliza remarked as she plucked one of the dark fruits from Sitra's claw, hefting it with a look of curiosity. "Or are they? These are massive, and dense as rock."

"They're Chiron's special blackstouts, and they're not for bait, they're for us," Cole replied. He peeled his own as he continued. "They've been altered with Passion and Wisdom. They digest very slowly, and there's enough energy in one to keep a grown Aenerian full for a week, though I had eight in a day once. Go on, eat one." Seeing their hesitation, Cole forced the entire fruit into his mouth, spilling its juices down his chin and neck.

The others followed his example, though they took much smaller, more dignified bites.

"It certainly tastes like a blackstout," Valen remarked with a grimace.

Sitra made a gagging sound. She tried to speak, but could only manage a few words between heaves. "This is ... awful. Tastes like a... tastes like a ball of snot." She spat the rest out onto the grass beside her. "I'm not eating another bite."

Eliza held her peeled blackstout between her thumb and first finger, though she had yet to take a bite. "I'm sure Cole wouldn't have offered these to us without good reason." She then spoke directly into his mind. *"And it better be a very good reason if you expect me to eat this."*

Cole finished his blackstout with a grin. "Thank you, Eliza. There *is* a very good reason for eating these things. I know they're gross, but they're necessary. They save time for one. Once we really get into training, your bodies are going to burn through food faster than you can eat through conventional means. Think about it. If I needed nine in a day, and each blackstout is a week's worth of food, I'd have to live at the markets day and night to sustain myself. We'd eat all the food in The Sill in about half a day. Think of it as another sacrifice. You've already given up your sleep."

"You're not doing a great job of selling your stupid fruits," Sitra said in a dark tone. "Honestly, I'd rather starve than eat these things all day just to save a bit of time."

"Then let me sweeten the pot for you," Cole said. "These disgusting things are just one reason why I'm physically stronger than all of you. Yes, even you, Sitra. They're also one reason why Chiron was stronger than me. And they're why none of us will ever be as strong as Roth was."

"He's talking about condensing," Eliza said with a smile. "Cole went through the process while training with Chiron. He told us before we entered Fangshard Valley."

"Exactly." Cole brushed up against Eliza's mind with his own, embracing her for a moment. She alone had been with him while he trained with Chiron. "Chiron's done it a bunch, and Roth does one every cycle. You're going to eat these stupid fruits because that's what they did. You're going to train your asses off, grow big and strong, then when your bodies grow too bulky with muscle you'll do a condensing, because *that's what they did.* We're not just the new Unbound, we're better. We have to be if we're going to do what they couldn't. That's why you're going to make one more little sacrifice." Cole expected exasperated sighs from the group, but they were hanging on his every word, sitting tall in the grass and staring without blinking. It felt odd, speaking to them as a leader, but he hid the awkward feelings from his face and began circling around them. The weight of their gazes fell heavy over him. "From here on out you're each going to maintain a spell over your bodies. You're going to make yourself heavier, as heavy as you can stand. You'll keep it up when you're training, eating, teaching, even when you're resting. The only time you'll dismiss it will be in battle, which will make for a nasty surprise for your enemies. I'm not going to lie, it's going to suck at first, then it's going to get worse. But your bodies will adapt, you'll get bigger and stronger, then on those rare occasions when you take the spell off you'll feel lighter than air."

"That's ingenious," Sitra gasped. "I can't believe the Elders never brought this up. I wish Chiron was my private tutor and taught me all these neat tricks."

"Actually this was Cole's invention," Eliza said. "Chiron wouldn't let him use Rage or do anything physical because he relied upon it too much. Cole grew restless and discovered a new way to train his body, right under Chiron's nose," Eliza finished, blushing lightly at Cole's gaze.

"I'm surprised you caught that," Cole said directly into Eliza's mind. *"I thought you might have tuned that part out. If I knew I had an audience, I might have tried a bit harder with Chiron's lessons on Aenerian Economy."*

Eliza's rosy cheeks gave way to a knowing smile. *"Oh I checked out for most of the boring parts, but I did pop in from time to time. I almost flew back to The Sill when you knocked yourself out with one of your alchemy experiments."*

"You definitely weren't supposed to see that part," Cole replied, raising an eyebrow, to which Eliza gave the smallest of shrugs.

"You know," Valen said after clearing his throat. "We may not be able to hear what you're saying, but we don't need a master's grasp of Passion to know when you're whispering right in front of us. Please Cole, continue. This is most intriguing."

Cole instructed them with the spell then amused himself by watching them droop and lift as they calibrated their gravity spells. When it came time to stand, they all did so slowly, using their hands to push off their knees and grunting like arthritic old men.

Sitra made a few hops in the grass, landing with a heavy thud each time. "You keep this up all the time?"

"Of course," Cole replied. "I mean I took it off when I sparred with Chiron, and once more while fighting Sorronis, but I didn't have much choice in either case. I wouldn't ask you to do anything without doing it myself."

"Wait, are you saying you handicapped yourself while fighting all of us earlier?" Sitra asked.

Cole shrugged. "Well yeah, but that was only to wake you guys up. It wasn't really life or death."

"I want a rematch," Sitra said, taking a weighty step towards Cole. "No one asked you to take it easy on us. You probably didn't put much extra weight on anyway. I bet my spell's at least twice as heavy."

"Maybe, but not likely," Cole replied coolly. "I've been at this a while."

Sitra took another step towards Cole, slow and wobbling, then drew her munisica and shifted into an easy stride. A toothy smile stretched across her face. "Let's see who's heavier now."

Valen drew his own munisica and jumped between them. "Wait, I have an idea." He extended a clawed hand, which gleamed four times with jade Wisdom. Four pebbles took flight from around the training grounds, each landing neatly in Valen's armored palm with a little click. He tapped each pebble with a claw, and as he did a jade spark snapped into the stone. "Each of you take one. I've enchanted the pebbles so they'll mirror whatever Wisdom spell you have active when you first touch them. They're nearly identical in size, so there'll be no cheating. Just make sure you only have your gravity spell up when you take your pebble."

Sitra scowled as she always did when denied a chance to fight. Nevertheless, they each took a pebble from Valen. Cole pinched his with a vice-like grip, receiving a little green spark to his fingertips when the spell took effect. The pebble almost slipped through his fingers with the added weight. Valen dismissed his munisica and closed his hand around the final pebble. Eliza then crafted a set of simple scales, which they used to hold a tournament to see whose pebble was the heaviest. Eliza's lost to Valen's, though she didn't seem much bothered by it. Valen then lost to Sitra, but only just so. When Valen removed his pebble and Cole set his against Sitra's, the scales jumped like a catapult, launching her pebble two feet into the air. Sitra was much more subdued after the loss. Cole promised her they would reset their pebbles and hold a tournament every week until she beat him.

They still had a few hours before the rest of The Sill woke up, so Cole led the Unbound to the dancing gardens, where he planned to both learn for himself and teach the others how to grow Chiron's blackstouts. Sensing an air of uncertainty, Cole reiterated the importance of the fruits, assuring them that they would see results within a few days.

Upon arriving at the gardens they were met by a violent pack of flowering plants, each galloping about on roots taller than they were. They had neon pink petals with black thorns at the tips. The petals met in an orifice leading to a bulging, translucent sack full of liquid and the bodies of small animals. Sitra conjured a fistful of flames in each hand, but Eliza managed to send the carnivorous plants away by summoning an aura of Passion.

Following Chiron's notes, they probed the soil in search of a spot that met the blackstout's requirements for acidity, mineral content, and microbiomes of bacteria and fungi. After half an hour of searching and fighting off various flora, Valen discovered a swath of soil with the lichen-covered bones of a large animal sticking up like saplings. They scattered the seeds from the skins of their blackstouts, then poured water and Passion over them. Sitra chopped down the surrounding ferns to let Oberon bathe their garden in magically augmented light.

The plants exploded with the aid of Cole's and Eliza's Passion, and before long their patch of soil grew into a cluster of bushes the size of a small house, complete with dozens of fat black fruits.

Though it wasn't a particularly rigorous task, gravity had ceaselessly pulled at their bones with every step, dragging them to the ground as they worked. With the exception of Cole, they were all famished and sweaty by the time they trimmed up the finishing touches. They each picked and ate another blackstout without complaint. Eliza showed them how to place an enchantment over their garden, which would keep out parasites and scavenging animals, though only Cole had the strength of Passion to duplicate her spell.

It was early morning by the time they left the dancing gardens. They could hear distant shouts of convoy chiefs barking orders to their apprentices over the main gate, no doubt preparing for another day's worth of supply runs. A few sun lily leaves zipped overhead, carrying crates of food or passengers on their way to work. Moon birds trumpeted their songs for the new day. The Sill was awake.

Cole feigned interest in Oberon and slowed his pace so Sitra could catch up. She refused to use her Rage again to assist in her battle against gravity, and so she fought for every step, grimacing and panting the whole way.

"I've been thinking about how we should start recruiting," Cole said to the group. "I know we shouldn't play favorites with magic, but I think it's important to play to our strengths, at least at first. The Sill embraces all three of our magics, though you have to admit it's still somewhat segregated. Eliza, I think you ought to canvass the Arts District. Find us some Passion followers willing to fight. Valen, you should head over to the markets. There's bound to be some Wisdom users who are tired of tinkering with experiments in their shops. Sitra, head over to the barracks and see what we've got for students. They know nothing of combat outside these walls. Show them."

"With pleasure," Sitra said with a grin.

"I assume that means you'll be visiting the Heart Tree?" Valen asked.

"Yes," Cole said in a sour tone. "That doesn't mean I'm taking charge of the whole Sill, but we need to know what we've got left for resources." He stopped walking, and the others stopped as well. He addressed Valen and Eliza. "Show them our memories. Convince them. If you find anyone willing to take a more active role, tell them to meet us at the training grounds first thing tomorrow morning. I'll see you all tonight."

The Unbound parted ways, though at Eliza's urging they set up a Passion network so they could follow along with each other's progress. Lileth's absence left a hollow pain in Cole's gut. He considered flying to the barracks first to wake her, but decided against it, still brooding instead over the multitude of reasons she might have chosen not to take the dreamsource. The Heart Tree wasn't far, so he took his time walking there in order to clear his head before presenting himself to the staff.

The Heart Tree came into view. Solitary and proud, it stood in the middle of a field blanketed with flowing fog, giving it the appearance of an island plopped in the middle of a river. It was the thickest structure in The Sill, thicker even than the outer walls which took nearly half a minute to walk through. The entire tree had been altered with Wisdom and fed with Passion, shaping its many offices and the winding staircase that spiraled up its core, making its branches look comparatively thin. Cole neared the main entrance, surprised to find it unguarded, but even more surprised by the person standing at the base of the stairs.

"You clean up well," Lileth said with a wry grin. Her arms were crossed as she leaned against the bannister at the foot of the stairs. She wore a clean set of russet battle robes with silver accents and a hooded half-cape draped over one shoulder. Her raven hair was back in its neat and practical high bun. She greeted Cole with a look of private guile that filled his chest with warm desire.

"So do you," Cole replied. All of his concerns vanished in an instant. "I thought you were still sleeping! How did you know where to find me?"

"Passion," she replied, brushing up against his mind. "For someone so adept in the art you shouldn't be so shocked to find me anywhere."

"My mind was elsewhere. I have a lot on my plate," Cole said defensively.

"Like wondering why I didn't take the dreamsource as the others did?" Lileth asked. Her eyes fell, heavy with guilt.

"That might have crossed my mind at some point." Cole reached over and cupped her cheek in his hand. "Don't worry, I'm sure you had a good reason. You don't have to explain yourself to me."

A tender smile returned to her lips as she reached over and entwined her fingers in his. "No, I don't, but I will later. You must be in the middle of something important if you came to the Heart Tree."

"I was about to go take command of the staff," Cole said, gesturing up at the thick tree. "If there's anyone left, that is. Care to join?"

"I'd love to," she replied.

Cole pushed his way through the liquid stone door, popping through to a pleasantly warm atrium. Sconces were embedded high up on the walls, their enchanted flames snaking their way up to the ceiling without damaging the wood. Lileth popped through after him and they started up a staircase that wound up the exterior wall of the tree. They passed several doors along the way. The first one was labeled *Training Center*, the second *Intelligence Axis*, the third, *Strategy and Operations*, the fourth *Logistics Arch,* and the fifth, *Communications Web*. Cole's Passion revealed each room to be empty; however, the final room at the very top contained several life candles, all burning bright and strong like beacons in the night. He sensed an air of contention tightening among their minds, as though they were in the middle of a fiery debate. Cole paused at the top of the stairs and faced the door, more uncertain than ever.

Lileth leaned close and whispered into his ear, echoing Roth's famous words, "I hope you're not hesitating."

Cole let out a queasy chuckle, then pricked his Rage. His anxiety fled from him like moths before a hurricane. He pushed his nose into the stone door, which resisted him at first, as though it were partially frozen. Cole pushed harder and the consistency of the door thinned to that of suspended liquid, and he fell through with an ungainly wobble, landing flat on his face. He heard Lileth pop through behind him, her footsteps as graceful as ever. Cole rose to his feet, stemming the blood from his nose with a quick flash of his lavender Passion.

Five Aenerians rose from a round table in the center of the room, each wearing formal robes and expressions of fading alarm. The room looked the same as Cole's last visit, when he and Habbad had been summoned before their mission to Costas. The ceiling was open to the elements and the walls were made of the topmost branches, all woven together in a seamless braided fence. One man had spells ready in his hands, pointing them at Cole like weapons. A woman whispered something to him, and he dismissed the magic.

Cole showed them his empty hands before crossing them behind his back. "I'm sorry to interrupt, but would you happen to be the ones in charge of the Heart Tree?"

"Students are not permitted in the Heart Tree!" said the man who had almost attacked them with magic. "How in Oberon's bloody light did they get in here anyway? I thought Falinor was supposed to lock the door."

"Of course I did!" snapped Falinor, a stout man with a squashed nose and square jaw. He sat back in his seat and the others followed. "Only those with an Elder's authority could have made it through. No student could have entered, but these are no students..." he trailed off as he surveyed Cole and Lileth.

"How can you tell?" asked the first man.

Falinor gave an impatient sigh. "Open your eyes, Rayn. How many of our students wear proper armor and look like anything but lost pups? No, these two are warriors. These are Chiron's kids." He grinned and gave Cole and Lileth a respectful nod.

Rayn's jaw dropped. "Chiron's unit! Whind told us you were back, but he didn't elaborate on the outcome of your mission. Please, come in, come in." He stood briefly and with a twirl of his wrist, two more chairs rose seamlessly out of the floor, filling gaps around the table. "Yes, I recognize you, Lileth, and you must be the human. Cole, right?"

"Yes," Cole replied, taking a seat next to Lileth at the table.

"The Sill is in a state of calamity," Rayn said in a hard voice. "We are disorganized, dwindling, and there is no plan for the coming tide. Furthermore, the Elders haven't responded to us in weeks." He reached towards Cole and jabbed the table with his first two fingers. "You need to tell us everything that happened since you and Chiron left The Sill."

"You mean Chiron didn't tell you anything?" Cole demanded. "He was a master of Passion, he should have at least given you the details before we left."

A dark-skinned woman spoke next. She had a regal beauty, with strong features and curly black hair. "We had constant contact with Alavani, Roth, and Chiron up until the Alpha Colossus appeared in the Fangshard Valley. However, Chiron's reports left much to be desired, lacking specifically in details regarding you, Cole. And like Rayn said, Whind didn't tell us anything other than five of your unit returned." She gave Cole and Lileth a polite nod as she introduced herself. "Wareen, Sill Communications."

Cole braced himself for another rush of grief. "Alvani, Roth, and Chiron are gone. I don't know how to put words to it, mostly because I don't understand it all. I'll have to show you. Keep in mind that I won't show you everything. There is a traitor among us, and whoever it is may very well be in this room."

A grim silence fell over the room, broken eventually by Rayn, who spoke with venom on his tongue. "You dare accuse us? A mere human who's been here all of five minutes accuses us of treachery? You have it wrong, boy. *You* will tell *us* everything, even if we must straighten your tongue for you."

The air thickened with intent, ambiguous yet ominous. The slight scent of ozone that preceded magic wafted into Cole's nose.

"It is your mind that needs straightening," Lileth said in an icy tone. "You sit in the presence of Varka's descendant, a master of both Passion and Rage, the hero of Fangshard Valley, and the only man alive who stands a chance of defeating The Three."

Before the members of the Heart Tree could muster a response, Cole summoned his Passion from the depths of his heart, enveloping their minds with his own. He felt their life candles thrash and surge against him, but even their collective strength could only delay his embrace. He was gentle, yet firm, holding them still with the power of his will. If Cole were so inclined he could have plunged into their minds and pulled their memories out as easily as picking out clothes for the day, and he let them know it. But he didn't violate their privacy. Instead, he set up barriers of his own, granting them each a small, yet safe cage to simply be. He then plied his memories into them, showing them nearly everything that had occured since he and Chiron left to defend Oberon City. He left out a few things, including Goran's involvement, the location of Alvani's and Gale's tomb, the secret of the Vaults, and the fact that Lileth had retained the pithing shard. He trusted his fellow Unbound, but he didn't trust anyone in The Sill any more than he trusted the Celestial Council.

When Cole finished his recollection, the faces around the table relaxed, and he offered them each a dose of soothing Passion. Lileth stood next to him, confident and ready.

"It is worse than we thought," Rayn admitted, shaking his head slowly. "We knew The Three had crowned two of their Harbingers, but with all three assembled they will be nearly impossible to kill. And Rothael... I can think of nothing more terrible than Grotton and Roth united as Harbinger. I apologize for my impulsive response. You truly are Varka's heir."

"We were ever in a dire state," Falinor croaked. A fat tear rolled down to his chin and crashed to the table, followed closely by another. "But the loss of the Elders might very well have been the final nail in our coffin. They were the only surviving Unbound. *Stars*, they were our only hope. I can't believe they're gone."

The others wilted, too burdened with grief to contribute spoken word. Cole felt a swell of loss as well, twisting and groping its way up his throat and stinging his eyes. Lileth's hands slid over his shoulder, and a measure of her Passion flowed into him, sharing in his sorrow. With his conviction renewed, he addressed the staff.

Cole stood, summoning the shroud of his master's Rage. His hair lengthened into a mane of ebony blades while his hands and feet transformed into massive claws, elevating him several inches taller. He spoke with controlled ferocity. "There is still hope. Our Elders may no longer be here to help us, but that doesn't mean the Unbound died with them. The Unbound isn't just made of Roth and Chiron and some long-dead heroes. The Unbound is a path. Anyone willing to explore beyond the comforts of old traditions and the magic they were raised with has already taken the first step towards unbinding their minds. My Unit and I have traveled this path further than anyone alive, and so we have earned the title of Unbound. Anyone willing to join us will eventually earn themselves that title, and together we will find a way to stop The Three."

Every face around the table looked up at him with open awe. It was only then that Cole realized how young the staff was. These were not ancient warriors and scholars, rather they were men and women in the dawn of their maturity, intelligent and capable, but uncertain and untested. After a moment's silence, the staff seemed to collect themselves, and Cole detected the mutterings of telepathy among them.

Rayn's eyes flicked around the table, then he nodded and folded his hands close to his chest. "Before you entered this chamber, we were deliberating over how to best dismantle The Sill and mitigate our losses. Evacuations are already underway, but there are still many resources and powerful assets within these ancient walls that would further doom Aeneria should The Three find them. We thought it more prudent to scatter ourselves across the world, and so deny The Three the courtesy of placing all their enemies in one convenient basket. However, this was before you came to us." Rayn then took a deep breath and braced himself. "Though it may mean the doom of us all, we will support you. We five are no warriors, but we will stay and offer our services and advice. We will not, however, condemn the rest of The Sill to our fate. It is their right to flee, just as much as it is their right to stay and fight. Does this satisfy you, human?"

"It does," Cole replied. He looked to each staff member, but they dropped their eyes to the table, unable to bear the weight of his Rage. His Passion longed to soothe them, to dismiss his shroud and show them that he wasn't a threat, but his Wisdom told him this was not the time to be soft. "I'm assuming each of you is in charge of one of the offices I passed on the way up here." The five heads around the table gave him a collective nod. "I have absolutely no intention of undermining your authority, nor do I wish to assert myself as leader of The Sill. I think we should work together to figure out what's best for The Sill."

"We disagree, respectfully of course," Falinor said, bowing slightly in his seat. "The Sill needs a figurehead, the students especially.

If everyone knew Varka's heir was back, stronger than ever and leading the fight, why I think that would nip our little evacuation problem right in the bud. We'd certainly get more volunteers willing to take up ranks. The Sill needs you. We don't want to work with you, Cole, we want to work *for* you."

The others gave their vehement support of Falinor's opinion, bombarding Cole with a deluge of reasons why he should lead The Sill. Irritated, Cole's Rage began to fight against its leash as his munisica lifted him a few inches taller.

"Fine!" Cole barked. The staff shuddered from the force of the word. "I'll do it! But I'm warning you, things are going to get busy, and I won't have time to monitor everything that goes on around here. I can't babysit you, nor can I spend time worrying about every little thing that goes on around here."

"Oh, that won't be necessary," Rayn said in a rushed voice. "That's our jobs. We handle the day-to-day operations of our various departments while you tend to the big picture situations—it's exactly the arrangement we had with Chiron. We ought to meet at least once a day, however, as there will be certain issues that will require the full attention of all departments. And it wouldn't hurt if Wareen gave you a communications cypher, that way we can reach each other if an emergency arises."

"No thanks," Cole said. "I've already touched each of your minds. I can speak to you again whenever and wherever I am, so long as I'm not on the other side of the planet, and you should all be able to reach me."

"That should work," Rayn said.

"Good." Cole nodded. He strode around the table, feeling their furtive glances follow him, as though they worried he might lash out at any second. Their wariness stoked his Rage, pleasing it to no end. "One of the offices I passed on the way up was the Intelligence Axis, so I think it's safe to assume you know a great deal about me, but I know little about you. Please, tell me about yourselves and your departments. We don't need to go deep in the weeds, just a general overview so we can all get on the same page."

Falinor cleared his throat. "Well, you already know my name. I'm in charge of the students. I handle everything from sourcing new recruits, training, job assignments, and organizing new units."

"The Unbound and I were students here not long ago," Cole said. "Why haven't I met you before?"

"The elite units were managed directly by your Unbound predecessors," Falinor replied. "Your unit was among the best The Sill had to offer."

Disappointment churned within Cole. His unit had failed horribly in Costas. If they were supposed to be the elite, then what sort of helpless fools were left to defend The Sill?

"Thank you, Falinor," Cole said, hiding all concern behind his shroud. "You should know then, that two of my Unbound are currently scouring The Sill for recruits, and one is training your students as we speak. I planned on taking a direct role in training the students, but now I worry we're overstepping our bounds."

"Not at all!" Falinor exclaimed. A crooked grin tugged at his lips. "In fact, you just saved me the trouble of asking for your help. It's funny, you come begging our services, yet it is your team who is of service to us."

"Like I said, I'm here to work with you." Cole then addressed the person next to Falinor. The man looked so tired he appeared cycles older than he was. He had purple bags under his eyes, and his face looked as if he were under the weight of a gravity spell. Cole softened his voice before speaking, afraid the man might break if addressed too harshly. "Who are you?"

As bedraggled as the man appeared, he raised his head with all the dignity he could muster and spoke in an alert, clear voice. "Debjornik, Intelligence Axis. My department garners information from all reaches of Aeneria. We have, or I ought to say *had* operatives in every major city on the planet. My teams work outside The Sill, right in the thick of it, and so our losses have been substantial."

Cole frowned. "If they're the first to see how bad it is, then it makes sense they would be the first to flee."

Debjornik opened one eye wide and stern, though the other barely moved. "You have us wrong. We may not be your traditional warriors, but we are not cowards. My operatives bind themselves to an oath sealed in magic before departing, which prevents them from revealing The Sill's secrets upon pain of death. The Three have become adept at weeding our agents from their ranks. The losses we suffer are from suicide."

Even though Cole was shrouded with impenetrable armor, the words still cut to his core. "How bad?"

Debjornik gave a curt grunt. "We are still somewhat functional. For the safety of my remaining agents I cannot reveal anything precise, but know that we are spread thin, and we grow weaker every day."

"You look as if you're speaking for yourself," Cole said. "When was the last time you slept?"

"I am understaffed," Debjornik scoffed. "I've no time for luxuries such as sleep."

"Then let me help you," Cole said. "In the Cordial Compendium lies a cypher that will relieve you of your need for sleep. If you are willing to never sleep again, I'll get it for you."

"Your offer is as generous as it is permanent," Debjornik said. "I will have to think on it."

"Please do," Cole said. "And in the meantime I plan on making periodic scouting trips outside The Sill. I'll be sure to share anything I learn along the way. Just let me know if anything urgent comes up. Day or night." Debjornik gave him another grunt, and Cole looked to the rest of the staff. "Who can tell me about the Strategy and Operations office?"

"That would be my department," Rayn said. "We are a small group comprised mostly of analysts and strategists, but we have a few retired veterans who have seen enough battle to provide useful insight. The other offices report information to us, we analyze it, then advise the Unbound as to what actions The Sill should take, as well as the repercussions of those actions."

"Simple enough," Cole said. "I'm sure we'll be working closely. Just so you know, the rest of the Unbound will be involved with any major decision-making. You'll find most of them to be reasonable, though we do have one that's a bit of a hot-head."

"Different perspectives are always welcome," Rayn said with a polite nod.

Suppressing a chuckle, Cole looked to the next chair where the regal Wareen looked up at him expectantly. "What can you tell me about the Communications Web?"

Wareen straightened her posture. "Pretty self-explanatory. We maintain long-range communications to other cities and provide secondary means for individuals lacking the Passion to talk to one another. Since you and Chiron left we have been in a blackout state, and our only traffic coming in and out has been through Debjornik and his agents."

"Tell me about these long-range and secondary communications," Cole asked.

"For long-range we have the Seer Jar," she said, indicating a large, teardrop-shaped piece of crystal supported by a woven brass frame. Cole recalled seeing Arcturus, Speaker for the Celestial Council, in the jar on his last visit to this room. "That one is still receiving, but the others across Aeneria are no longer transmitting. Squashed by Domina no doubt. As for secondary communications we have cyphers that imbue the user with the knowledge of telepathy, though the magic is limited by the strength of the user's Passion. Unfortunately, most of our students have the mental capacity of a tea cup, which isn't enough to absorb the meanest of cyphers." She shot a sideways glance at Falinor as if expecting a rebuttal.

"We have two Passion masters in the Unbound right now," Cole said. "We'll show the students how to connect with one another, and while I'm out on missions I'll find out what's wrong with the other Seer Jars."

Wareen looked both satisfied and impressed with his response. Cole then turned to the staff member who had yet to speak. She was a large woman, with broad shoulders and bony hands covered in calluses. Sitting, she was head and shoulders above the rest of the staff. Cole saw traces of impatience in her eyes, as though his every word had been a waste of her time. She looked familiar to him somehow, but he couldn't quite figure out why.

"We've covered every office besides the Logistics Arch," Cole said. "I assume that's your department?"

"Very astute," she replied with heavy sarcasm. "I see why Chiron chose you as his favorite."

"Thessi!" Rayn said. "He is Varka's heir! Show some respect."

Thessi huffed and crossed her arms. "I'm well aware of who his is, Rayn, but this has all been a tremendous misuse of my time. My team is overworked and understaffed. I didn't have time for this meeting, and I certainly don't have time to cater to a single man, no matter who he descended from."

The other staff members drew away from Thessi, as if they might suffer Cole's wrath if they were too close. Cole's Rage demanded he silence the woman, perhaps take a leaf out of Roth's book and break a bone or two, but he had long ago mastered such urges.

"It's fine," Cole said. "I'm here to help, not take up your time, and I've already taken quite a bit. Before I go, there must be something I can do to help your department. Just give me a brief overview."

Thessi's eyes rolled so far back into her head that Cole thought she might tip back onto the floor. "You don't even know how to pose the question correctly, not that the responsibilities of my office can be diluted to a single question."

Cole walked over to Thessi and crouched so he was at eye-level with her. She held his gaze. "I'm ignorant. Educate me."

A slight smirk tugged at her cheek, accepting his challenge. "Everything in The Sill is my responsibility. Literally, every *thing*. The clothes you wear, the gratia stones that power this building, the building itself, armor, food, livestock, weapons, you name it and I am the sole person responsible for it. Every object in The Sill needs to be sourced, shipped, maintained, and replaced when no longer functional. Do you have any idea how many gratia stones we have, or what their average lifespan is?"

"I've no idea," Cole replied, sightly disarmed.

"Less than a cycle," she answered, all too gratified by his lack of knowledge. "And do you know where they grow, or how we ship them here, or what their value is when trading a Rage stone to a city of Wisdom users like Borla Dign?"

Cole had some understanding of gratia stones, but at the moment he thought it best not to offer a response. It disturbed him, however, that Deekus's death was all for some stupid rock that wouldn't even last a cycle.

"That's enough," Cole said, finally allowing his Rage to sear the edge of his words. Thessi's eyes fell to her hands. "I plan on coming back here first thing tomorrow morning, and every morning after. If you have time, write up a report of all your concerns for The Sill, and I'll see what the Unbound can do for you."

"Time is the resource I have the least of," Thessi muttered.

"Then I cannot help you," Cole said. He rose to his feet and addressed the entire table. "I'm heading to the training grounds to see what Falinor's students are capable of. I'll be back tomorrow morning, but if you need me or another member of the Unbound, then contact me through a Passion link. I plan to be inside The Sill's walls during the day, so you should all be able to reach me during normal hours. Debjornik, don't forget what I said about the dreamsource cypher. Actually, I'll extend the offer to the rest of you as well. You're all too important to waste half the day sleeping. Go take the cypher yourself, or ask me for help and I'll get it for you. Good day."

He turned and left them in silence. Lileth was already by the door, leaning on the wall and clicking the bladed fingers of her munisica together absentmindedly. Cole pressed his face to the stone and popped through the door, feeling her follow close behind.

CHAPTER 9

HOPE REKINDLED

"You were quite the sensation," Lileth said, striding alongside him.
"I was, wasn't I?" Cole said. His mind had already run through
the meeting several times since leaving the Heart Tree, and he built
himself a mental task list of every issue and promise made. Now that it
was only him and Lileth, another concern rose to the fore of his mind.
He could have flown to the training grounds, and he knew Lileth
would have no trouble keeping up, but he chose to walk instead so he
could spend more time with her.

The Sill was properly awake now. Sun lily leaves soared overhead,
laden with packages or letters that hopefully bore good news.
Whooping birds keened from the canopy, their songs perforated with
barking of rusty squirrels battling for dominance over their branches. A
distant heartbeat of drums from the Arts District rumbled underneath
it all, waking any who might have slept too late. While the fog had
long passed, something still hung in the air between Cole and Lileth,
preventing him from breaching the subject that troubled him the most.
They continued walking in silence, each apparently enjoying the sights
and music of The Sill.

At last Lileth spoke, but she kept her eyes on the grass between her
feet. "You must Hate me."

The statement took Cole by surprise, shaking his shroud loose and
melting his Rage. With the warrior's magic gone, compassion rushed
up to refute her statement. "Of course I don't Hate you. Hate is
disgusting. What I feel for you is quite the opposite, actually." To
exemplify his point, Cole initiated a Passion link with Lileth, which
she reciprocated in earnest. Thus joined, they enveloped each other's
minds like two rivers joining into one.

130

They walked in quiet contentment, captivated by the simple fact that they had each other. Lileth foisted upon him her genuine appreciation for all he had become, showing him how impressed she was by how he dealt with the staff of the Heart Tree. Cole showed her how comforted he was by her presence, that he never would have been able to acquit himself so capably without her by his side. Their thoughts became so interwoven that Cole's concerns began to slip through the link, just as Lileth's shame started to bleed into him.

Cole stopped walking and squared his shoulders to her. "Listen, you don't need to explain yourself to me. I know you must have had a good reason. I was only barely able to afford the dreamsource."

Lileth stopped as well, her eyes combing over the braided root walkway at their feet. "I told you I would explain myself, and so I shall. What I'm about to reveal to you I've never told anyone. Do you remember what I told you about my upbringing?"

"That you were born in a village of Wisdom followers," Cole said in a quiet voice. "And that you were born for the sole purpose of being sent away to train under Chiron."

Lileth nodded, but her gaze shot out far beyond the walls of The Sill. "Those facts alone would be enough to affect any child for the rest of her life, but there is more. In my home village, status is everything. The most prodigious Wisdom users earned themselves top ranks within our government, and were usually hand-picked for prestigious positions within Oberon Temple. More than one member of the Celestial Council was born in my village. While my mother wasn't particularly adept with Wisdom, she longed for a seat among the Council, and she was willing to do whatever it took to put herself as close to them as possible. Now that I think on it, some of her actions crossed the line of genuine Hunger."

"Are you serious?" Cole said with much more disgust than he wished. Lileth seemed unperturbed, however.

"Oh most definitely," Lileth said cooly. "She used to tell me, 'Every mind is a puzzle of needs. If you but solve the puzzle, you own the mind.'"

"The first part makes sense," Cole said. "But why would she want to own anyone's mind?"

"To earn her place among the stars," Lileth said. "She was incredibly manipulative. One of the first people she caught in her web was my father. His name was Jarnell. In his youth he invented a new spell for observing out-of-turn local planets, and was quite popular for it. She sought him out and solved his mental puzzle, then locked him into a lifelong betrothal, intent on riding the tail of his accomplishments to the stars. To her great disappointment, however, my father had no such ambitions. He, like a few others in my village, was interested in other magics, especially Passion. To stray from the path of Wisdom was a shame in my village, as it retards progress towards ultimate knowledge of the Aethers. My father turned out to be a total and utter failure among his peers, and a burden for my mother ever more. But she had yet to pull every string in her web. When The Sill's recruiters came calling, she coerced one to take her first born to train under Chiron, the greatest Wisdom Walker alive."

"How did your father feel about this?" Cole asked.

"He never knew," Lileth replied. "He was only happy to have my mother's affections again. She applied for a license to breed, and I was conceived soon after."

Cole's face twisted with sour confusion. "You need a license to have a child?"

"Of course," Lileth said. "Otherwise any irresponsible fertile pair could reproduce on a whim, which would hinder their ability to contribute to society whilst possibly creating a burden for the village. The parents must pass a competency test, genetic screenings, magical disposition exams. Having a child is regarded as the most important thing two people can do."

Cole was speechless. On one hand, the laws were extreme and socially unjust. But on the other hand he could think of plenty of people back in his neighborhood who ought to have passed a few tests before having more kids than they could afford. He looked back to Lileth. She watched him with a look of mild amusement.

"I was raised under my mother's ever watchful eye," Lileth continued. "My father was allowed to see me on visits, but only while teaching me my Wisdom." Lileth's expression softened into a look of reminiscent bliss, genuine and wholesome. "I loved my father very much. He used to call me his little comet. He would sneak me out of the house and perform dream shows for me, just like they do in the Arts District. He always let me play the hero, and I would rescue him from evil monsters or bands of marauders. My father saw the Passion in me, and when my mother wasn't around he showed me how to use it. I made friends with an animal, a glade horse named Smoke. I would wake up early every morning and sneak out to see him and feed him berries, then he'd let me ride him down by the river. I had an Aenerian friend as well, Marri. It was with her that I first performed a Passion link. My mother's lessons were only bearable because I had Marri there with me in my mind, reminding me I wasn't stupid or useless."

"You were far from useless if you were performing such advanced Passion at that age." Cole put a hand on her shoulder. She felt rigid as wood.

A grim shadow fell over Lileth's face. "My mother found out about my Passion, and Marri, and Smoke. She pulled the secrets from my father while he slept, then reported us to the village Council. Marri was dragged to the square, stripped of clothes and dignity. The elders sterilized her mind, burning all traces of emotion from her so that she would never again have a place for Passion to grow. It may as well have been an execution. My mother convinced the elders to spare me, but my punishment came the day after. My mother forced me down to the river with my empty Marri. Smoke was so happy to see me, he didn't even notice the berries we brought, or Marri's magic. She cut his throat with a spell, then my mother used her own Wisdom to carry Smoke back to the village, where we watched the butcher skin and quarter him out for the town pantry. I was sent to The Sill later that day."

"No child deserves that. There's no sense in it. Why didn't your father do anything?" Cole demanded.

Lileth's eyes filled with tears, but she held them back. "He tried. He appealed to the elders for Marri's sake, but my mother's webs had already been cast. He motioned for sole custody of me as well; however, the process takes several months to complete, and he didn't have a very strong case."

"Was he punished?" Cole asked.

"His rapport was such that he escaped sterility, though his name was sullied ever since." A tear finally wiggled its way out from Lileth's black petal lashes, diving like a falling star to the root path at their feet. "He fell ill shortly after I left, and then before his motion for custody ever reached the Council, he died."

"What sort of illness could take a man adept with Passion and Wisdom?" Cole asked.

"Poison," Lileth said, her face becoming her usual stoic mask. "My mother did it."

"That's horrible!" Cole gasped. "But how do you know, she might have..." The words died in his throat. He realized he ought to be supportive, not drilling her with questions.

"I took the knowledge from her," Lileth said with a tone of indifference. "Do you remember the first time I healed you?"

Cole rubbed his chin. "When Valen kicked me out of the tree?"

"No. When you washed up in the lagoon just outside The Sill," Lileth said.

"Chiron told me you healed me," Cole said. "And I remember seeing your eyes, but it was more like a fuzzy dream."

"Your lungs were full of water and your body was broken," Lileth explained. "You had no heartbeat. Everyone, even Alvani thought you were dead. But I felt something in you. I used Passion for the first time since childhood, and brought you back from the edge of the void."

"That explains why you were so weird after healing me," Cole said. "The last time you used Passion, your life changed forever. It couldn't have felt great using it again, especially with such a powerful spell."

"It did actually," Lileth said. "For so long I thought my Passion was broken, that I was incapable of using it again. Healing you showed me that all I needed was purpose, and in that moment a new purpose was revealed to me. I left The Sill one night and returned to my home for the first time since I left. I found my mother, and I punished her."

"What did you do?" Cole whispered.

"I took command of her mind and sifted through every memory she had. She was predominantly a Wisdom user, so she was powerless to stop me," Lileth said. "I learned the truth of her killing my father, but that wasn't nearly the worst of what she'd done. She had many husbands before Jarnell, and even had plans to kill her newly assigned husband."

"Did you kill her?" Cole asked, unsure if he wanted to know.

"In a way," she said. "In my time at The Sill I learned much in the ways of the mind, and how to use Passion and Wisdom to alter it. I sterilized her, but not in the way that Marri had been. I burned her ability to use magic of any kind, including Hunger, which she had been using to great effect among the entire village. I nullified all of her Hunger contracts in the process, then left her alive, a non-magical, non-contributing leech on society. It is the ultimate shame and her worst Fear."

"You killed the person she was," Cole said. "Did you ever find out what happened to her?"

"No," Lileth said. "I returned to The Sill soon after and relieved myself of almost all memory of her. I only left myself with enough to vaguely recall what I just told you. Her name, her voice, her face, all of it went into a gratia stone. I couldn't even tell you what my village was called or where to find it. I divested myself of nearly everything of my past life, though I held on to memories of my father and Marri. And Smoke."

"Is that why you didn't take the dreamsource cypher?" Cole asked. "So you could still see them when you sleep?"

Lileth's cheeks flushed. "It's selfish, but my dreams are the only way to feel them again. They still define me. It's no greater a sacrifice than you and the others made, but I'm not strong enough. I'm just not ready to let them go yet."

Cole was long to respond. It was true, that the dreamsource was no greater a sacrifice for her than anyone else, but still he could not blame her. He was mostly shocked that Lileth was capable of such creative vengeance in punishing her mother. While he couldn't say if she was justified in the act, it certainly redefined who she was to him. It was as if a layer of mystique had been peeled back, revealing something deeper, more intriguing. Lileth was dangerous, but she was all the more enticing for it.

Cole flashed her a wry grin, throwing an arm around her shoulder. "I knew there was more to you than the unapproachable ice-queen we all know and love."

Lileth wrestled against him in a half-hearted attempt to escape his grasp, settling with her head against his shoulder. "You still don't Hate me, even after all that?"

"Not even close," Cole said, pulling her closer. "When we have time I'll show you a few of the skeletons in my closet."

"What in the world does that mean?" she asked. "Is that some idiom from Terra?"

Cole gave her a squeeze. "It means I'm not perfect either. Now let's go check on Sitra. I'm worried she might have killed half the students while we were in the Heart Tree. You up for a little race?"

Lileth spun from his arms as emerald wings exploded from her back, sweeping twice as wide as she was tall. She gave him a smirk. "Think you can keep up without using Varka's cape?"

Cole knew he wouldn't stand a chance, but he tried anyway. She vanished in a whirlwind of leaves and grass clippings before he could so much as grasp his Wisdom. To his surprise he was able to conjure emerald wings of his own, but they were frail and stunted, and the effort left him with little focus to fill them with enough air to move. Abandoning the winged method, Cole simply levitated his body through the air, slow and steady. It wasn't quite so flashy, but it got the job done. He felt the influence of Varka's cape creeping its way into his spell, so he unclasped the garment mid-flight. He'd come to rely upon the artifact far too much lately.

Lileth arrived at the training grounds several minutes ahead of Cole, who landed like a drunkard from his prolonged exertion of Wisdom. Thirty or so students lay scattered about, each nursing a minor crippling injury. The clanging of munisica drew Cole's attention to a flurry of activity at the top of a nearby pine. Branches cracked and fell to the ground as clouds of needles rained from the chaos. Cole and Lileth approached the trunk of the tree, shielding their faces with their arms as they looked up.

Sitra's voice rang from far above, shouting to someone they couldn't see. "What, did you think I couldn't climb trees or something? Now stop running and fight me!"

There was another clang. Wood chips tumbled down through the branches, then there was an unmistakable tattoo of thumps and grunts. A spinning body appeared above. Cole lunged, catching a young girl in his arms before she hit the ground. Another body dropped several paces beyond the fingertips of the lower branches. Lileth's hand shone a brilliant jade as the body of a boy slowed to a gentle halt in the dirt. Sitra landed next to him in a violent crash, her munisica bared, her long braid glistening with the ebony shroud. She looked around, confused, but then her face broke into a wide smile at the sight of Lileth and Cole.

"Everyone, this is Master Lileth, and Master Cole." She bent down and picked the boy up by his collar, setting him on his unsteady feet. "Say hello."

There was a collective grumble of pained greetings. The students who could stand did so, giving Lileth and Cole a respectful bow. Their white and blue training armor had been stained brown with sweat, blood, and caked mud. In contrast, Sitra was clean and relaxed, without so much as a single blade of hair out of place.

Cole set the girl down, and she gawked openly at him before limping away. Though he trusted Sitra, Cole still reached out to every student with the Passion, ensuring that none of their injuries required immediate attention. There were many broken bones and bruised egos, but nothing serious. "How goes the lesson?" he asked Sitra.

Disappointment fell over Sitra's face. She approached Cole, speaking in a low whisper so only he and Lileth could hear. "It's worse than we thought. Less than half can draw munisica, and those who can only have their fingers shrouded. It turns out they've only been going over drills and magical theory. This was their first practical combat lesson."

Cole sighed. "It's a start. I did hope they'd be a little older. Most of them look as if they haven't even seen their second cycle. Are there any hopefuls?"

"None," she replied. "Though they all seem to have a mastery of talking back, the little jerks. Roth would have torn my arms off if I was half as mouthy as these kids. They all want to sound tough and strut about like warriors," she turned her head and hollered over her shoulder, "but the truth is, they're all soft as baby shit!"

"If they're soft then they should be malleable," Lileth said, surveying the crowd with a raised eyebrow. "I'm interested to see what we can make of them."

Sitra grunted. "Come on. Let's find out if we have any healers in the bunch."

The three Unbound split up among the wounded and divided them into pairs so they could practice healing each other. Most were unable to heal anything deeper than a scratch, but a few had the skill to mend broken bones and stitch tissue back together. In these instances, Cole used his own Passion to bring all the students into a mental network so they could feel exactly how the magic was performed. Their minds flinched and fled at his touch, making the task as difficult as corralling a herd of cats, but once Cole had them all wrangled into submission, they learned quickly enough. After an hour, nearly every student had managed to heal surface cuts, even those who'd never wielded Passion before.

As he made his rounds, Cole noticed a definite air of defiance among the students. Whispers met his Wisdom-sharpened ears, and with Passion he picked up every thought they shared. He observed quietly, unnoticed by anyone. Most complained about Sitra's methods because they didn't feel ready for such extreme training. There were others who believed the new Unbound were unworthy to teach anyone, as they had all been students here just a few months ago. The gripes initially struck a chord among Cole's Rage, and he seriously considered letting Sitra have another round to teach them a lesson in humility. What right did they have to complain? When Cole first arrived he was half their size, lacking any sort of conscious control of any magic. Not to mention he had to train under Roth, who thought the lesson wasted if he didn't beat the unit within an inch of their lives. Grudgingly, Cole chose to disregard their whining, though he did hear one individual he couldn't ignore.

"This has got to be the dumbest thing we've done so far," said a boy surrounded by six other students. "I swear that Sitra's half Domina, coming up with a lesson plan like this. Oh I've got an ingenious idea, let's beat some kids senseless and make them fix the wounds I give them. It's just lazy is what it is. Poor leadership."

There was a smattering of agreement from the surrounding students. Cole could tell by the admiration in their eyes that they regarded this boy as something of a leader. The boy then waxed on with several jokes made at Sitra's expense, to which the other students made no effort to hide their laughter. Cole wove his way closer to the group and the boy took notice, casting him a sideways glance before crossing his arms and turning away.

Cole walked into the middle of the circle and the boy's friends busied themselves with healing each other. The boy, however, did nothing except look up at Cole with a bored, haughty expression.

"What's your name?" Cole asked.

"Wilkin," he replied. His eyes flicked to one of his friends as an amused smile pulled at his lips.

"Nice to meet you, Wilkin," Cole said, giving him a small bow. "Why are you not practicing your healing with the rest of the students?"

Wilkin chuckled as he threw his shoulders back in a manner oddly familiar to Cole. "I'm more of a fighter, everyone knows that. There's no point dawdling with the softer magics when my talent's in killing."

Cole nodded in apparent agreement. "A fair point. Rage gets results after all. So what sort of injury did Master Sitra give you?"

"Just a couple of broken ribs," Wilkin said casually, patting his side. "One of the Passion users danced over here and patched me up though.

"I see," Cole said, though he sensed no trace of recent healing magic in Wilkin's body. "It seems like whoever did the patching missed a spot. Let me get that for you."

"No, I'd rather you didn't touch—" Wilkin protested, holding his hands out defensively.

Before Wilkin could say another word, Cole extended two fingers and shot a ball of lavender Passion into his ribs. It was not magic for healing, but for energizing. Wilkin's alarm shifted to relaxed wonder as the magic coursed through his body, fueling him far beyond his normal limits.

"That was… incredible," Wilkin gasped. "It was… it was…"

"Just a bit of softer magic," Cole said. "You know, Wilkin, we're looking for outstanding students to lead units of their own. You seem to already know what you're doing around here, so I think we'll make you a leader once we assign units." Cole turned to leave.

Wilkin bounded in front of Cole, panting from the rush of Passion. Worry tugged at his handsome features. "Human, about this leadership thing, I don't think—"

"It's *Master* to you, actually," Cole said. "And right now the only thing you need to be thinking about is what to do with all that Passion I just gifted you. I suggest you find an outlet soon so it doesn't burn you up. And while you're at it, think about what kind of leader you want to be." Cole strode away, leaving Wilkin stammering incoherently.

"Found yourself a favorite already?" Lileth said into his mind. *"Roth would be disappointed to see you let that one off so lightly."*

"Just wait until he has a unit," Cole replied. *"Then he's really going to be my favorite."*

Another hour passed with surprising productivity, revealing about a quarter of the students as promising healers. Sitra had already marked each person adept with Rage with a crimson mark on their forearms, so Cole and Lileth fell in with her distinguishing method by adding a pink mark for each student competent with Passion. They finished the day with a test of Wisdom, putting the students through a gauntlet of basic spells such as levitation, temperature alterations, and physical barriers. No more than a third of the students showed a natural inclination for the green magic. Throughout the assessments Cole paid special attention to those who had a knack for bringing out the best in others. For some it was through lighthearted teasing, while others chose blunt insults. There were various methods of motivation, but so long as the student lit a fire in others, Cole marked their arms with white for leadership. Wilkin was the last to receive such a mark.

The tree frogs began to sing their evening songs, signaling the end of the first day of training under the new Unbound. Sitra called the students into formation. She, Cole, and Lileth inspected each of their charges, offering words of encouragement and healing injuries that hadn't been patched up during the Passion exercise. Most students bore a colored mark on their arm, and a few had more than one, though some had no mark whatsoever. Sitra suggested they continue training until every student showed an aptitude for at least one school of magic, but Cole insisted that they wait until the next day, when Eliza's and Valen's recruits could join. The students were dismissed and Cole contacted Falinor, providing him with a detailed report so that he could start building units.

"Valen, Eliza, how did you two make out?" Cole said, projecting his thoughts so all the Unbound could hear.

Eliza was first to reply. *"I had to hijack a live show in the amphitheater, but our message reached just about everyone in the Arts District. I showed them the memories you showed us as well as a few of my own. We should have at least ten new recruits joining our ranks tomorrow."*

Ten recruits was far less than Cole had hoped, especially from the Arts District, but it was ten more than they had earlier in the day. *"That increases our numbers by at least a third. Well done, Eliza. Valen?"*

Valen's disappointment seeped through their network, then his thoughts solidified into words. *"Not so fruitful I'm afraid. The markets are full of scientists and entrepreneurs, not warriors. Many would be better suited for support roles than open warfare. I can only guarantee another three join our formation tomorrow morning."*

"It's better than nothing," Cole said.

The Unbound met in the upper levels of the markets, where one shopkeeper had convinced the topmost branches to grow into separate booths. Thousands of tiny gratia stones hung from wire-thin vines, reminding Cole of Christmas lights. Giant bell flowers swung from the ceiling using their roots like monkey arms. Unlike their violent cousins in the Dancing Gardens, these plants offered drinks in exchange for charging a gratia stone embedded in their hearts. Eliza had picked up a bushel of blackstouts on her way. The group tore into the fruits without complaint, famished from gravity's increased toll on their bodies.

They discussed the day's events in detail. They all agreed The Sill was in no shape for war, but their predicament was far from hopeless. While the others went over a lesson plan for the coming week, Cole talked with Lileth, catching her up on everything she had missed while sleeping. After the plan for the students had been set, discussion shifted to their own training, which would commence as soon as they left the table. Sitra wanted to fly out and capture a couple of Domina, explaining how they could cage the beasts in The Sill so the students could get some real training. Eliza wouldn't allow it, however, stating it would be inhumane for the enthralled creatures bound to the Domina. Cole settled the matter by informing them that they would be starting their evening training up in Chiron's house, where they would dive into the Elder's trove of knowledge recorded in his library.

After eating and drinking their fill, the Unbound departed straight from the canopy, hopping right over the edge of the booth into open space. Emerald wings snapped wide as they flew in a tight formation. Pedestrians gazed up at them from the catwalks below; the Unbound hoped the onlookers would be impressed enough by the display to join their ranks tomorrow morning.

Cole told the others how to find Chiron's house, then he split off towards the Arts District so he could spend a moment with Naythan and the girls. The day had all but burned away and he wanted to catch them before they all went to bed, but he was too late. By the time he arrived, Naythan had just tucked the girls into bed, and was too busy tinkering in his basement lab to play host to Cole.

Cole found Chiron's house floating above the trees near Lurkwood Gate. The others had conjured up chairs and were already nose-deep in books when he walked in.

"I'm glad you're joining us,' Cole said to Lileth. "Wouldn't want you falling too far behind."

Lileth snapped her book shut. "Nor would I, which is why I have decided upon a compromise to the dreamsource cypher."

"And what's that?" Cole asked, intrigued.

"She thinks she's going to get by on sleeping every other night," Sitra said. "I give it a week before she cracks. Maybe two."

Cole ignored Sitra. "Are you sure?"

Lileth nodded. "Eliza has graciously offered to instruct me on Passion-induced meditation, which will help delay my need for sleep. As long as I maintain this gravity spell over my body, I shouldn't miss much."

"I'll link up with her now and again to fill her in on anything she does miss," Eliza added. "I can copy my memories directly into her mind."

"There's that problem solved," Cole said. He looked about at the books they were all reading. "So I thought we could each read through a different book and teach each other what we find. There's too many books for me to do it all myself."

"Day one and you're already pawning off your responsibilities on us," Sitra sighed. "That's not very leaderly of you, boss."

Cole rubbed the back of his neck. "Believe it or not, most of my private lessons with Chiron were just getting me up to the same level as you all on basic Aenerian knowledge. It wasn't until the last few weeks that we started getting to the good stuff."

"There goes our hopes for an all-knowing leader," said Sitra. "So what does that mean for us?"

"It means you are going to open a book and start reading," Valen said, tossing her a heavy volume on how to enchant items. "Think of it as working on your weakest muscle."

For a few hours, the only sound to be heard was the turning of pages or the scratching of pens. Much of Chiron's library was too advanced for them to glean anything useful from. They shelved these master volumes for later perusal, focusing instead on subjects that bordered the limits of their understanding. When everyone had their fill of reading and writing, they marked their pages and made for the training grounds, eager to break their studying with some practical exercises.

To everyone's great surprise, Sitra was the only one prepared to teach. Seeing as she was the least scholarly of the group, Cole first thought she must have chosen an easy subject, but it quickly became clear that she was simply motivated to the extreme. She took Valen's jibe to heart, as though determined to prove she wasn't just some dumb grunt.

"Cole, do you know how Chiron's cape works?" asked Sitra.

"It was Varka's cape actually, but no, I only know how to use it," Cole admitted.

"That might actually give you an advantage," Sitra said, skimming through a small packet of notes. She read aloud. "The enchantment works best for the person who originally imbued the item, because like a Wisdom stone, the enchantment requires one to permanently forfeit part of themselves in order to sustain the magic." She flipped a page, then nodded to herself and looked to Cole. "So there's a good chance that since part of Varka is alive inside you, that cape will work better for you than anyone else. Why are you all looking at me like that?"

"Did you swap minds with one of the students today?" Eliza asked. "I've known you for almost an entire cycle and never once seen you open a book, let alone teach us about advanced magic. It's as if I'm meeting you for the first time."

Sitra's mouth twisted into a frown, but Cole swore he saw her cheeks flush. She buried her eyes in her notes. "Well then feel free to treat me as a student would her teacher, and shut the hell up so I can teach the class."

They all stood a little straighter. Just when Sitra got back into her rhythm, Cole felt a vaguely familiar presence buzzing around the edges of his thoughts. He took a surreptitious step away from the others and opened himself to the flow of Passion.

"Hello? Cole?" said a faint voice. *"Dammit my Passion's not strong enough. I'll have to send a runner."*

"Hello Wareen," Cole said. *"This is a late call for you."*

Wareen's words came into clearer focus as her relief rang through the link. *"Oh thank Oberon. Cole, we need you at the Heart Tree immediately. It's the Seer Jar. Someone is trying to contact us."*

"We'll be right there," he said.

"It would be best if you came alone," Wareen said with caution. *"We believe the transmission is coming from Oberon Temple. That makes it a secret of the highest order. Debjornik advises that we keep this to just the staff and you."*

"Fine," Cole replied, knowing full well he would keep the rest of the Unbound informed through their Passion network. He severed his

connection to Wareen and told the others what had just transpired, then took flight, keeping a firm hold on their minds so he wouldn't miss the lesson.

Since it was urgent, Cole dropped in through the open roof of the Heart Tree, cracking the polished wood floor upon landing. Falinor, Debjornik, Rayn, Wareen, and Thessi were already seated at the table, all wearing the disheveled looks of those who had just been dragged out of bed. About a dozen assistants stood around the edge of the round room, tired, but ready. Cole hastily mended the cracked floor and approached the table.

"Everyone else out!" Rayn shouted once Cole took a seat. "You two leave that Seer Jar on the table before you go."

Two assistants approached the table, holding between them not a Seer Jar, but a vague dark mass the size of a large fruit basket. The object was solid, and so profoundly black that it appeared to have been cut out from an empty void. The assistants set the thing roughly upon the table, sliding it to the middle, making no noise whatsoever. As if glad to be rid of it, the two Aenerians left the room at a dead sprint.

"Is the Seer Jar inside that thing?" Cole asked.

Rayn rolled up the sleeves of his robes, staring intently at the black thing. "Precisely. I've placed a spell over it that blocks all light and sound. I'm about to alter my spell so transmissions will come out, but not in." He extended a long finger, its tip glowing jade. He touched the black surface of his spell. A deep bell rang at the contact. Its surface shifted from black to that of a highly polished mirror, finally settling on a translucent shade of green that matched his finger.

The Seer Jar was as large as a child, with ornate brass wrapped around the girth of its teardrop crystal, keeping it upright. From the cloudy depths of the glass, a blue light flashed like a beacon, intermittently burning the image of a man's face in the jar. Fractured words crackled from the Seer Jar like an out-of-tune radio. Every head at the table leaned in, but the man's words were too broken to understand. The face flashed for a full second, revealing a terrified man.

"That's Terra's Wisdom Walker," Cole said, making the rest of the table jump. "Larkin, I think."

"Are you certain?" Debjornik said. He turned to Cole, but kept his eyes firmly affixed to the jar.

"Definitely," Cole stated.

"Well then lift your damn barrier already!" Thessi grumbled. "The sooner we find out what he wants, the sooner we can get back to bed."

Debjornik withdrew his glowing finger. "Therein lies an issue. I just received word that Oberon City has fallen to The Three. It's reasonable to assume Oberon Temple is under their control as well."

Horrified gasps hissed around the table.

Cole pinched the bridge of his nose. "This is the *let me know if anything urgent comes up* part that I was talking about."

Debjornik's tone hardened defensively: "Like I said, I only just found out. Can you contact Council member Larkin through Passion? Or any other member of the Celestial Council? That would be the safest option."

Cole shook his head. "I've never touched their minds, and the temple is so far away, I'm not sure I could initiate contact."

"Then what should we do?" Rayn asked. "We need to act now."

Debjornik's eyes scanned the table for an answer. His face lit with an idea. "Call up one of the assistants. It doesn't matter which."

"But this is secret!" Rayn exclaimed. "No one outside this room can know."

"Then kill whoever it is after we're done," Debjornik scoffed. "This is more important than any one person."

Rayn scowled. "Fine. We'll call up one of yours."

Cole sensed a spark of thought in the air, then a moment later a figure popped through the liquid stone door. She was young, but looked intelligent and carried herself with ironclad confidence.

"Over here, over here," Debjornik shouted, conjuring up a chair next to himself. "Take a seat."

Eliza's thoughts suddenly thrummed like a golden strand into his mind. *"You're not really going to let them kill the girl, are you?"*

Cole blinked in surprise. He forgot he was still connected to all of the Unbound. *"Of course not. I'll remove her memories if I have to, but no one's about to kill anyone while I'm here."* Judging by the incessant focus pressing in from the rest of the Unbound, they had long abandoned Sitra's lesson. They were currently hanging on his every thought.

The young assistant sat next to Debjornik, who pushed her seat closer to the table. "Right, now you are going to speak for us to whoever is in the Seer Jar. I'm going to encase you in a sensory web, which means you won't be able to hear or see us, but I will remain in contact with you through Passion. Do you understand?"

"Yes," she said without hesitation.

"Very good," Debjornik replied, reaching out to his web with fingers aglow. "You may want a light," he added.

The assistant conjured a candle of flame on the table as Debjornik stretched the web over her and the chair she sat in. Her eyes went wide, searching around her in the phantom darkness. She prodded her candle so it burned a little more brightly. The jar blinked once more.

"Go ahead and speak to the Seer Jar," Debjornik instructed. "Give your name and location, but nothing else."

The assistant nodded, then leaned closer to the jar. "This is Jahanna Dell of The Sill. Is anyone listening?"

A voice crackled once more, and Larkin's face flickered from within the glass.

"Grasp the frame," Wareen ordered.

Jahanna wrapped her fingers around the brass wire and repeated her greeting once more. Larkin's face solidified within the glass and he jumped back in fright.

"Not so loud!" Larkin hissed, shooting furtive glances around him. "You'll get me killed. Where are your superiors? Where is Chiron? Bring him to me at once! Hurry girl, the fate of Aeneria is at stake!"

Jahanna looked to her left, to where she guessed Debjornik to be.

"Tell him that we are indisposed, then ask him his message," Debjornik instructed.

She repeated his words to the Seer Jar.

Larkin swore, then terror snapped at his features before he vanished from the glass. It took him a full minute to return, and when he did his whisper was barely audible. "Tell him not to come. The capital has fallen. The Three have the temple and all of our resources. You must flee The Sill and hide, scatter yourselves across the farthest reaches of Aeneria and pray they don't find you. Do not come to Oberon City."

Horror thickened in the air. Debjornik shook off a chill and spoke through Passion. Jahanna blinked and gave a small nod before returning her gaze to Larkin. "You claim assumes The Three have taken the entire Celestial Council. For all we know your mind has been broken, and you now speak for our enemies. How do we know we can trust you?"

"Idiots," Larkin scoffed. "Debjornik is whispering right in your ear, isn't he, girl? Tell him he doesn't have to trust me, just listen. I'm not asking for information, I'm giving it. Just know the Council is still alive, but for how long I cannot say. Once The Three no longer need us they will kill us or worse. I'm offering you what intel I can, when I can, and at great risk mind you. If they found me now I'd be the next on Rothael's menu. He's already eaten Arcturus."

"What did you say?" Jahanna asked, unprompted.

"Well not Rothael, but Grotton," Larkin explained. "He took Rothael for Harbinger and they've developed a rather disgusting appetite for Aenerian flesh. All three Harbingers have been crowned. That is why you must flee, they cannot be stopped. Abandon your hope and hide."

Silence fell over the room. Jahanna's jaw worked and her lips trembled, but no words came out. Cole stood so fast that his chair went tumbling across the room. He rounded the table and yanked Jahanna out of the way, kneeling in her place to face Larkin. Cole's hair lengthened into black knives, but the shroud halted before covering his face.

"We are not done fighting, Wisdom Walker," Cole growled, pulling the Seer Jar closer with his munisica. "And neither are you. I know how to stop The Three, and seeing as I'm not dead, neither is our hope."

"Stars," Larkin breathed. "You're the human. Cole?"

"I'm much more than that now," Cole said. "Larkin, listen to me. There is a way to stop The Three, but doing it without help is going to be nearly impossible. We need you to stay alive as long as possible and keep us informed of anything you might hear on your end. For obvious reasons we can't tell you anything on our front, but know that everything you share will aid us in stopping The Three. Can you do this?"

"You expect…" Larkin shouted, then clamped his lips shut and continued in a whisper, "You expect me to risk my life and poke my nose around the affairs of gods? Did you not hear me when I said they were eating us?"

"They're not gods, and yes, I expect you to help us any way you can," Cole replied.

"And how did you come to that conclusion?" Larkin asked, cocking his head.

"Because we're *your* only hope of getting out of there alive," Cole snapped. "Provide us intel and we'll get you out if we can. Provide us nothing and we've got no reason to devote resources to helping you. The Unbound saved the Council once before, so think of this as your chance to repay that debt. And if this is to be your end, would you rather spend your final moments fighting death or waiting for it?"

Larkin's eyes widened in desperate wonder. "Are you saying the Unbound are still alive? The rumors… some say they fell to pithing shards."

Cole thought for a few seconds before responding. He had already said too much, and if The Three ripped Larkin's mind apart, they would know Cole was at The Sill. Cole, the key to the Aethers, the one who could unlock the means for The Three to Travel once more. Lileth pressed the comfort of her mind into his, presenting him with a memory. Cole smiled and brought his gaze back to Larkin.

"The Unbound isn't defined by any person or group," Cole said. "The Unbound is a path, and as long as there are those still treading it there will always be hope."

CHAPTER 10

WAKING THE GIANT

The staff of the Heart Tree were none too pleased after Larkin disconnected. Debjornik had taken particular offense, stating that by revealing himself, Cole had provided the enemy with valuable intel. The verbal assault rose to a crescendo when Cole flat out refused to explain what he meant when he claimed to know how to stop The Three. While Chiron's letter didn't exactly state how to use the Vaults of the Soul, he made it quite clear that no one else ought to know, which definitely included the staff of the Heart Tree. The thing that troubled Cole the most was the news of Arcturus's death. Not because he would grieve the Speaker, but because this meant that Arcturus was likely not the one who betrayed them.

Their discussions pushed on until morning, and before long the rest of The Sill was awake and ready for the new day. While Cole was as alert as ever, the staff of the Heart Tree were dead on their feet as the sleepless night dragged at their puffy eyes. They looked ready to cry when the obligations of their various departments came rushing up in the form of urgent messages from their assistants. Cole made the offer once more, and every single one of them grudgingly followed him to the Cordial Compendium.

Paying for five copies of the dreamsource cypher left Cole utterly drained of his Rage and Passion, though he didn't let them see it. To his surprise, the exertions left him too light-headed to command his Wisdom either, so when they parted ways, Cole hailed a sun lily leaf to carry him to the training grounds. He smiled to himself as the flying leaf came rippling up to greet him, and he remembered the time when he first left the cypher shop with Storn.

During his flight, Cole leaned over and watched people bustling about on the ground below, traveling in neat lines like ants. At first Cole thought them to be more deserters, but there were far too many, and they weren't heading towards The Sill's gates. When the sun lily brought Cole within sight of the training grounds, he was certain something was very wrong. There were well over one hundred people gathered. He tried calling out to the other Unbound, but his Passion had yet to recover.

The leaf slid to a halt on grass that had been stamped flat by the passing throngs. There were faces all around, hundreds now, all staring at him with wide-eyed expectancy. Some looked awed at his appearance, though most surveyed him with skepticism. Ignoring them, Cole donned a visage of confidence and began his search for the rest of the Unbound. The lack of Passion left him unnerved, as though he was suddenly blind.

"We're by the tree Valen kicked you out of," Eliza chimed in. *"Did you spend all of your Passion on the Heart Tree staff?"*

Cole waited until he was within range of them before responding. *"They needed it more than me. Who are all these people?"*

"Students," she replied.

"How many?" Cole asked.

Eliza found his eyes between the gaps of the students, and she greeted him with a warm smile. "That has yet to be seen," she said aloud. "They are still coming in."

Lileth, Valen, and Sitra were there as well. They all looked just as shocked as he felt.

"This is insane!" Sitra declared. "I didn't know we had this many people."

Valen brought his hand to his chin. "Perhaps their numbers appear so large because we have never seen such a gathering in one area. Still, considering how many have fled, their numbers are staggering."

"Indeed," Lileth agreed.

An hour passed, and still they kept coming.

Sitra tapped a bladed toe against a tree root. "How are we supposed to sort this mess into functioning units? Wait, I've got it."

Emerald wings snapped from Sitra's back and she took flight, hovering over the gathering mass. Rage fueled her lungs and orders erupted from her like cannon fire.

"IF YOU WERE HERE YESTERDAY, GET BEHIND THOSE THREE TREES." Sitra made the trees perfectly clear by lobbing a ball of liquid fire at them, which splashed against the trunk closest to the Unbound. Lileth extinguished the fire with a spell before it could do any damage. "IF YOU WEREN'T HERE YESTERDAY, FORM UP INTO RANKS STARTING HERE." She cast another ball of fire, which collided with the grass like a barrel of flaming lamp oil. "MOVE YOUR ASSES BEFORE I TORCH THIS WHOLE FIELD! DON'T YOU DARE LET ME CATCH YOU HESITATING!"

There was a stampede of activity as the crowd rushed to their places. After ten minutes the students displayed themselves in a massive rectangular formation, with the students from the day prior hiding from Sitra's wrath behind the trees. Once satisfied, Sitra returned to the ground, spraying the Unbound with clumps of grass as she landed.

"Three hundred and twenty-one, counting the ones from yesterday," Sitra said, smiling as though pleased with herself. She clapped Cole on the arm. "Well boss, it's time you go greet the kiddos. Fly up there and say hello."

Cole choked on his own saliva. The others waited politely for his coughing to subside, then he cleared his throat. "I think they all know why they're here. They don't need me to give them a *welcome to the losing side* speech."

"Of course they do not need your speech," Valen said. "But they deserve it. We are asking them to give up life as they know it for an existence defined by sacrifice and suffering, all in hopes that we shall prevail over evil gods. Many of them have already lost family to this war, yet here they stand, ready to give up what little they have left to us and our cause. They deserve to hear your words."

"But why me?" Cole said in a small voice. He glanced out at the formation. Its columns reached to the edge of the training grounds, and still more trickled in. He suddenly felt like a kid back in high school, walking to the front of the class to hand in a test he hadn't studied for. "I'm just a human."

"We've been over this," Sitra sighed. "You're a whole hell of a lot more than that. You're our leader, and our friend. Get out there and do your job."

Cole swallowed. His cheeks tingled with heat, and his heart felt as though it was trying to smash its way out of his ribs. He couldn't do it. He reminded himself that he'd faced monsters far greater than a field full of students, but in this moment none of it mattered. In this moment he was just a stupid kid, too weak, too dumb. In his rising panic he found Lileth's eyes, fierce and bright; they anchored him to the present. The world ceased its spinning as his breath came back to him.

Without preamble, the Unbound circled tight around him, each setting a hand on his chest. He felt the soothing calm of their Passion, the molten power of their Rage. Both magics swirled into him, replenishing what he had spent. Galvanized, Cole took command of his Wisdom. His feet left the ground as Varka's cape rippled from shaggy grass to flowing glass. The prospect of addressing a small army still terrified him, but it was no longer crippling.

He was only a few stories off the ground, but the training grounds seemed fuzzy and distant, and so did his worry. Their eyes were crystal clear, however. Cole felt Oberon's touch on the back of his neck, warm and nourishing. The rainbow moonlight painted each of their faces and glinted in their eyes, illuminating the entire formation in a nebula of hopes and Fears. They wanted to hear him, to feel him. For the first time Cole appreciated what he represented to the people of The Sill: the future.

Bolstered by a newfound sense of duty, Cole took command of his Rage and brought forth the master's shroud, simultaneously conjuring wings of corporeal Wisdom. A clamor of awe swept over the crowd. Cole brought himself lower so that they might see him better. The weight of the moment suddenly revealed to him not what he was supposed to say, but what he needed to say.

"The war is back, and it promises to bring out the very worst in all of us. But it also brings us together, as warriors, lovers, and friends. The bond that brought you all here is something beyond the powers of The Three. It's stronger than their armies, and burns too hot for the blackest of evil. Your training here will decide the fate of not only Aeneria, but every world she passes by, including my own. Every race, every child, every civilization, they're trusting you to win them a future. A future without The Three. Your training will not be easy. We're going to break you, and it's going to hurt. But look around you. You are not alone. We suffer together, and through our pain we will grow beyond ourselves. Welcome warriors, to your first step on the path of the Unbound."

Cole finished, leaving the air dead with quiet. A woman directly below him jerked as though waking from a daydream, then threw a bladed fist into the air, offering her battle cry to the stars. The crowd snapped from their stupor, reciprocating with such a thunderous roar that Cole's armored teeth shook in his skull. Flocks of birds fled the training grounds and sun lily leaves dropped from the sky. Even through the shroud Cole felt the tears slide down his cheeks. He looked to the ground behind him to find his friends, but they were hovering in the air beside him, gazing at him with pride in their eyes. Never in all his life had Cole felt such companionship, and so full of hope.

It took several minutes and a few fireballs from Sitra for the crowd to cease their applause. The Unbound resumed their place at the foot of the three sentinel pines. Cole's Passion revealed a familiar life candle nearby, and Falinor emerged from behind one of the trunks. The bags under his eyes were now a deep shade of plum, and his entire face looked as if it had been paralyzed by some venomous insect. His expression lifted somewhat when he beheld Cole, and his voice showed no trace of exhaustion.

Falinor gave Cole a jovial slap on the arm. "If your career as a warrior doesn't pan out, you might consider a job as an orator down in the Arts District."

Cole flushed. "I've never spoken to so many before. It seems like it went over well though."

"*Went over well?*" Falinor scoffed. "If The Three landed in the middle of that field there's not one person out there that wouldn't fight to the death. Stars, I feel the heat of battle lust boiling in my own blood. Mark my words, there will be half as many new recruits by daybreak tomorrow. This was exactly what we were talking about!" He grasped Cole's arms and shook him as they both laughed.

"What do you mean?" Cole asked.

Falinor stepped back and gestured at Cole's form. "The shroud, the wings, the commanding voice, this is exactly the symbol we need. You're our standard. It's more important than you know. This war might drag on for cycles, and kids everywhere are going to grow up hearing about the hero of The Sill. We'll have fresh recruits waiting for us at each village we liberate. I'll have to put that speech into a cypher for Wareen. This will do wonders for her propaganda machine."

Cole didn't like the idea of a war lasting for so long but at the moment that was the least of his concerns. "Falinor, you said you were in charge of training, right?"

"Yes, yes, that is my department," Falinor said. "Why, do you wish to replace me? I don't deny that you and your Unbound would be far better received than me and my staff."

"No, not at all," Cole said, glancing back at the sea of students behind him. "I'm going to be honest with you. I thought we'd be training forty or fifty students, and even that was pushing it. We have no idea how to deal with so many. I need your help."

Falinor scratched his head. "At our strongest we had about one fifty, but the theories should still apply. To give you the short of it, we're going to have to treat this crowd as a battalion, then divide down into companies and platoons and squads. It's not going to be quick, but it's the only way to control such a large force without direct Passion. With you and your Unbound overseeing the training, this batch ought to handle a force ten times their size, hell even a hundred times, but that's assuming The Three don't come knocking tomorrow of course."

Cole recalled their last skirmish with the Domina on the ships. They were outnumbered at least ten to one, and other than the grotesque baileen, the battle was ridiculously easy. Hope swelled once more in his chest.

"So where do we go from here?" Cole asked. "How do we split them up?"

"You let me worry about that," Falinor said. "I've enough instructors to get this lot divvied up. I'll adopt the system you used to mark the students yesterday and go further to identify levels of proficiency. Shouldn't take longer than the day, and if it does I'll just keep hammering them throughout the night. Don't think they'll mind, not after your little speech. I'll contact you with Passion when we're through."

"Actually, we're all going to stick around," Cole said. At his urging, the rest of the Unbound drew around him. "You can identify those who are predisposed to Rage, Passion, and Wisdom, but I want my team identifying the leaders."

"What's the matter, don't trust my judgment?" Falinor asked with a slight smirk.

Cole opened his mouth to answer, but Sitra cut in, shouldering her way to the front of the group. The shroud still covered the majority of her body and hair.

"It's not a matter of *trust*, little guy," she said, jabbing a bladed finger at Falinor like a spear. "It's a matter of preference. We would *prefer* the judgment of those who have seen battle. And since we've all killed more Domina and Corpulants and priests than any of you have ever seen, I think we'll be choosing the leaders. How does that sit with you?" Sitra's Rage flared hotter still as the shroud crept over portions of her neck and her munisica pushed her a few inches taller. Even her eyebrows hardened into strips of obsidian needles. Cole knew she was in complete control, however. Her calm ferocity made her look strikingly similar to Roth.

Falinor paled slightly, but his laugh was hearty. "Ha! Now there's the fire we need! That sits very well with me, warrior, very well indeed. I can think of no one better to groom our leaders than the Unbound. The Sill will have a force more powerful than anything Aeneria has ever seen!"

The field was full of students by the time Falinor's staff arrived. His training team set up a hasty gauntlet designed to test for basic proficiencies in each of their magics. One by one the students passed through, drawing munisica, bending the rules of the physical world, or healing the bodies and hearts of their comrades. Cole and the

Unbound hovered overhead, watching for those who showed the qualities a leader should have. Some leaders were easy to identify, as they had earned themselves a mark on their arms for all three schools of magic. Some were not so easy to find, because while they themselves were not particularly adept in any school, they had a knack for inciting proficiency in others. The gauntlet carried on into the late evening, and then dragged on into early morning before they finally finished. Cole wished it were feasible to offer the dreamsource to all the students, but he needed his strength for his own endeavors. When the last student passed through, Falinor had their battalion divided up into three assault companies of roughly one hundred warriors each, and a support company of one hundred fifty. The assault companies would receive training directly under Falinor's instructors and the Unbound, and the support company would fall under the guidance of the rest of the staff at The Heart Tree.

It was mid-morning by the time the last student stumbled off to bed, leaving the Unbound in an empty field of flattened grass bathed in Oberon's fickle hues. Falinor and his assistants left for the Heart Tree carrying a small mountain of paperwork in a cart between them.

"I think it's time for me to retire," Lileth announced. Her words were slurred, and her gait had lost its lithe confidence. "My mind yearns to stay and train, but my body demands respite. I shall see you all in the morning."

They said their farewells as Lileth took flight towards the barracks. Cole watched her emerald wings disappear through the pines, and he wished he could join her. With a jolt of guilt he realized he'd missed yet another day to check in on Naythan and the girls. He made a promise to himself to go see them first thing tomorrow morning, only to remember that was the time he needed to meet with the staff of the Heart Tree. The concept of leading the entire Sill became less appealing the more he thought about it. It was as if every minute of his time were not his own, leaving no room whatsoever to his own interests and desires. Even now he felt the eyes of his friends upon him, expectant and yearning, as if he even knew what they should do next.

Feeling a small storm swirling up inside him, Cole began their evening training with a bout of meditation, just simple nothingness to clear their heads. Finding his center was more difficult than usual, as the day's events had settled into layers of stress that coated his mind like hot steel. Once he, Sitra, Eliza, and Valen had found peace within themselves, they resumed Sitra's lesson on enchanted items.

After an hour, each of them had managed to imbue a stick with a quality of their choosing. The enchantments were weak, but the lesson was only meant to show them the basic concept. Valen's stick could double its length when dipped in water, but it could only do so once a day. Eliza's stick could glow forever, but it wouldn't shed enough light to be useful to the naked eye. Sitra's stick could produce a little finger of fire when tapped three times, but it ended up burning itself to cinders after the first use. Cole managed to slow the flow of time within the fibers of his stick. It wasn't the most practical spell, but it planted the seed of an idea for future training.

After the lesson, they fought each other with munisica and magic, starting as individuals, then pairs, then taking turns fighting three on one. Cole's Rage and Passion had not quite recovered from purchasing five copies of the dreamsource, and so his performance suffered commensurately. He was especially hindered when he removed Varka's cape to keep it from getting damaged. He knew he ought to do all his training without it, but he secretly enjoyed the feeling of power that came with it.

Exhausted and filthy, the Unbound retired to the barracks so they could clean themselves and mend their armored robes. Cole took a bit longer than the others due to a long tear Sitra made in his armor. Though he refused several times, the others insisted in joining him in his room while he made his repairs. Cole appreciated their enthusiasm, but he wished he could have had a little longer to enjoy some privacy.

Cole sensed the others walking up the ramp to his room, and hastily threw on some undergarments so he wouldn't greet them in the nude. As he expected, Sitra barged in first, not bothering to knock.

"Hatefire!" Sitra swore, her face twisting in revulsion. "It smells like a Corpulant took a shit in your bed. You live in this?"

Cole pulled on a shirt as Eliza and Valen popped in behind Sitra. "I haven't really lived anywhere since I took the dreamsource. I only come here to shower." He was about to offer them a seat, but he only just now realized every horizontal surface in his room was covered with his failed alchemy experiments. His bed, table, chairs, and every shelf was littered with jars of pungent ingredients and heaps of crumpled notes. He tiptoed his way through a small city of books stacked up on the floor like towers. "I did tell you all to wait for me outside."

"Oh dear," Eliza said through the crook of her elbow. Her palm flashed green and she slapped her hand on the door, forcing the liquid stone to retreat into the frame. "You know your apartment has windows, right?"

"Oh come on, it's not -wait, there's windows?" Cole asked.

"If you will them of course," Eliza replied. Extending a finger, she shot green beads of magic into the walls, creating holes in the wood that stretched and creaked into a round window. A breeze charged through the room and knocked a stack of paper off the table.

"What exactly have you been doing in here?" Valen asked, plucking a bottle of purple liquid from a shelf. "Did Chiron train you in alchemy?"

"No, this was just a stupid hobby of mine," Cole said. "Chiron would go out on his own missions for hours or days, and I had a lot of free time since I wasn't sleeping. I hoped some of these potions would make up for my lack of skill with magic, but the alchemist in the markets left a while ago so I had to teach myself. I'm not very good at it."

"What do the potions do?" Sitra asked, holding a vial of black liquid up to the light.

"From what I've read they can do just about anything if you know how to mix them up," Cole said, snatching the vial from Sitra's hand with Wisdom. "I cleaned out the apothecary before the shop closed, so I still have a ton of ingredients. It's the mixing and preparing that's the tricky part. This one will make the drinker invisible, or at least that's what it's supposed to do."

He uncorked the vial and threw it back, swallowing its contents in one gulp. His skin immediately began to itch, then the others let out cries of alarm.

"Cole, you- your skin!" Eliza stammered.

Sitra dry heaved then said in a shaky voice, "That's disgusting."

"What, you can still see me?" Cole asked. He looked down at his body, finding it still quite visible, though instead of arms and legs sticking out of his undergarments, there were what looked like raw meat from a butcher shop. He held out his arm and inspected it. The skin was entirely gone, revealing ruby muscle and thin swaths of bulbous yellow fat. Spiderwebs of pink and blue veins covered the flesh like tree roots. He worked his fingers, watching the muscles clump up as they tugged at his tendons. "Well that's better than the last batch," Cole said, tapping his invisible skin.

Valen's expression quickly turned to eager interest as he approached Cole's table, surveying the collection of alembics, crucibles, and other glassware. "Alchemy is a dying art, especially here at The Sill. I had an uncle who would travel to other villages peddling elixirs to those who lacked a certain disposition of magic. He did the bulk of his business in a village of Rage users. They were always fighting of course, and so they amassed a collection of injuries which they were unable to heal. He claimed some of his products could mend a gash in minutes."

"I've got one of those!" Cole said, reaching past Sitra with his skinless arm. Sitra's face went a sickly shade of green as she knocked over a stack of books to get away from him.

"Let's hold off on the trial sampling," Eliza said in a warning tone. "Alchemy can go horribly wrong if you don't know what you're doing. And I'm sorry to say it, but you have no idea what you're doing." She angled the mirror on the door of Cole's armoire, showing him his face.

"Fair enough," Cole said with a grimace as he beheld his gruesome visage.

Valen inspected a tall beaker, producing a clear ring with a flick. "Your equipment is superior. If you allow it, I would like to come here whenever events permit. I have not worked the craft since I was a child in my home village, but I believe with these resources I can make us some useful potions."

"Of course," Cole said, rubbing his face in the mirror. "The door's unlocked. Come to think of it we could all use some alone time. Not much, just an hour or so a day. That way we can work on separate things, like Valen with his alchemy, or Sitra with her enchantments."

"Or my cultivation in the dancing gardens," Eliza said. "I'm going to head over there now. With a little tweaking I'm certain I can raise enough blackstouts for the entire battalion by the start of our next bout of training. And while I'm there I'll keep an eye out for ingredients for Valen."

Eliza and Sitra left the apartment, leaving Cole to mend his armor while Valen took inventory of the equipment and ingredients. They each worked in silence. Valen became utterly engrossed in the alchemy books, clearly understanding more of the craft than Cole had. After devouring one slim volume on cataloging, he emptied every shelf of ingredients, replacing them in an order that Cole couldn't begin to understand. He then busied himself with cleaning the glassware, which was caked with burnt sediment and oily stains. Valen barely noticed when Cole left.

There was only a half hour until the students would be lining up in the training grounds for the new day's lessons. It seemed a shame to waste a whole half hour, but it wasn't enough time for Cole to start on a project, and he didn't feel much like studying from Chiron's library. What he wanted was to go to Lileth. However, she was likely busy getting herself ready for the day. Unsatisfied, he perched himself against the base of his apartment tree and retreated to the stone room of his center. Before long the morning birds raced overhead, heralding the new day with their song.

CHAPTER 11

DIVINE RETRIBUTION

As Habbad soared over the city, he noticed signs of their victory over the Dark Side, fruits of plans he himself created during his courtship with the traitorous god. Clusters of citizens had survived Kreed's initial assault, and had been corralled into segregated blocks and cordoned off by Decreath's priests, their numbers in the tens of thousands at the very least. To retain survivors was the intent of course, but their sheer numbers shocked Habbad at first glance. He expected a great many more to die in the invasion, but after thinking on how easy it was to disable a whole squad of their soldiers with the simplest of Fear, the numbers made sense. What fools the Council must be to think they could defend an entire city with Wisdom alone.

To his frustration, the information Habbad had garnered from his most recent Domina told him nothing as to the state of Oberon Temple. It concerned him deeply that Kreed had yet to make the slightest attempt to reach him after Sorronis struck him down in Fangshard Valley. Perhaps the Temple had yet to be won? Habbad discounted the idea almost as soon as it sprouted. He'd felt Decreath speak from within Kreed on several occasions, and the mere sound of the god's voice was enough to almost bring his heart to a stop. His blood froze in his veins just thinking about it. No, the god of Fear could not fail here, not with such a perfect plan in a city brimming with Wisdom followers. Kreed said he would be at the very top, so that was where Habbad would go.

Oberon temple was much larger than Habbad expected, even larger than what he assumed were exaggerated reports. Ten concentric cylinders rose up in gradually smaller rings to a lofty peak, too high to see clearly from the confines of the car. Habbad left the city limits, soaring over a body of water that appeared to surround the entire temple. After a while, the bulk of the lower tiers engulfed the entirety of Habbad's windshield, and he wasn't even halfway across the choppy sea. After an hour Habbad could finally see lit windows in the first tier winking at him. He aimed the car higher, but the engines gave a hollow cough, followed shortly by an altitude warning light which glared angrily at him from the dashboard. Habbad dipped the car to the bottom of the lowest tier, where he spotted a few other cars zipping in and out of an open bay like wasps in a hive.

Another sign of victory appeared to him as he approached the bay. A dozen of Sorronis's priests stood sentinel by the opening, garbed in the charred bodies of their Chosen in a perversely gruesome battle suit. They were not true Colossi, as they had yet to earn the right, but they were twice the height of a normal man with the strength of twenty or so. The heads of their victims were perched atop a barrel chest made from their torsos, positioned in every direction to grant visibility in all angles. As was common with Sorronis's craft, the legs were made of legs, the arms of arms, though the hands had been crafted into ramshackle weaponry of bone wrapped in white tendon. The priests themselves were only visible through a small opening in the chest of each suit, where their pale faces stood out against the blackened flesh of the Chosen.

Three of the priests attacked as Habbad entered the bay. Ropes of sinew shot from grotesque jaws that were their hands, their spiked tips stabbing into the hull of Habbad's car and stopping him dead. The car lurched to the side, nearly tossing Habbad out the hole where the door used to be. They were pulling him in. Habbad put the car into hover mode, silencing the groaning engines while keeping a keen eye out for another attack. The vehicle clunked to a stop along a walkway that looped around the entire bay, framing a small port of several large ships bobbing in the black water. Doors bordered the walkway, each topped with a gratia stone that flooded the area with soft white light, revealing dozens more of Sorronis's corpse-armored priests.

A priest tapped a bonemold sword on the hood of the car. A muffled voice hissed from a pale face. "Remove yourself now, or that car will be your coffin."

Habbad got out of the car and walked straight up to the man. Unlike the bishop back in the city, these were merely adept users of Despair and Hatred. Habbad could have dismantled the man in a second with Wisdom, especially with the soldiers he'd just taken for Domina.

"It is I, Habbad," he said, displaying open contempt on his face. The bodies of the Chosen smelled horrible, and reminded him of someone he'd rather not think on. "Do you recognize me, or do I need to show you who I am?"

"Forgive me, Underking!" The priest's blue lips parted in surprise. Remembering himself, he bent his fleshy armor into a stiff imitation of a bow. The other priests lowered their weapons and offered their own bows of respect, filling the bay with a cacophony of cracking joints. "We heard you died. Your arrival is unexpected, but—"

"Where are Kreed and Decreath?" Habbad demanded.

The priest pointed his sword arm three doors away. "The Three are congregated in the chambers of the Celestial Council. It's at the very top of the temple. That door leads to a lift that will take you there directly."

"The Three?" Habbad asked. "All of them? Are you sure?"

"Only as sure as my bishop is. She informed us not two days ago. I can summon her here, she can tell you much more than I." The priest inched back a step.

Habbad's eyes fell to the black water beside the walkway. The Three were united at last. He had known that much, though he only now realized he had been harboring hope that they were not, that Roth had not survived the coronation to Harbinger, that Talin and Sorronis had somehow been defeated in battle. Individually, The Three were near gods, far beyond the powers of mortal men. Kreed himself was certain he and Decreath alone could take the entirety of Oberon City. With all three Harbingers crowned and united, The Three amplified each other's powers magnitudes above their solitary states. Not only would Roth be harder to kill, Decreath and Sorronis relied on Grotton and his Hunger for their own powers. The other gods wouldn't stand idle if Habbad attempted to harm Grotton or his Harbinger.

Habbad glanced at the door, which seemed to beckon him as much as warn him. It could be a trap. Or perhaps he was so insignificant that The Three neither knew nor cared about his existence. But he needed to know. He needed to know why Grotton didn't choose him as Harbinger. All the work, the planning, assembling armies, his revolutionary industry of secrets, no one had done so much for Grotton. It was he who found where the Cold Crows had been hiding, he who brokered the trade for the pithing shards, and it was he who groomed the perfect traitor from the very heart of their enemies. None of this would have been possible without his efforts. The Three owed him an explanation at the very least. He had not escaped from the bowels of a mountain and died countless times for nothing. He had to know.

Habbad approached the door and pressed himself into the cool stone, entering a small stone chamber lit with sourceless light. He pressed the only button on the wall. There was a sound of grinding stone and the floor lurched upwards, buckling his knees slightly. The lift shot up into the heart of the temple, banking left, right, back, then left again, rising faster all the while. After ten minutes he had lost track of the turns, and the lift began to spin, making him dizzy as his guts twisted against his sense of direction. He assigned the discomforts of his flesh to one of his Domina and endured. Eventually the lift found a steady path and rose straight up, quiet and smooth, accelerating ever faster as the air about him became cold enough for him to see his breath.

There seemed to be no end to the temple, that the lift would bring him all the way to Oberon, never to return. Habbad began to consider using magic to stop himself, but then the lift slowed with a muffled scraping of stone on stone. When it stopped, Habbad felt a sudden chill grip his heart that had nothing to do with the freezing air. He pressed himself once more through the liquid stone door.

At first Habbad thought he had entered a void. There was no light, no sound, though there was a sweet, coppery taste in the air. He assigned his Fear to one of his Domina and stepped forward. His bare foot crunched on the floor, as though he had stepped out onto the dried bark of a fallen tree. He took another step, and then another.

An echo of a scream washed over him as the darkness suddenly vanished, revealing the chamber of the Celestial Council. The room was round and large enough for a hundred people to stand comfortably in. The floor and walls looked as if they had once been white, though now they were covered in what looked like a blanket of scabs. The ceiling held a massive gem twenty paces across, opalescent with ever-changing colors, as if the rock had fallen from Oberon itself. Lining the chamber walls were sconces of black flames, from which poured shadows that wandered about the chamber with minds of their own. The Celestial Council was nowhere to be found. The only things in the room were three thrones, each set equally apart along the scabbed wall on a separate dais.

"Now there's a face I never thought I'd see again," said a honeyed voice from the throne on the left. Unlike the rest of the chamber, Kreed's dais was meticulously clean, his high-backed throne of polished ivory. He wore his usual suit, its fabric the color of virgin snow embellished with flower patterns on the lapels and cuffs. Kreed uncrossed his legs and leaned close for a better look. "How are you, Habbad?"

"Did you know?" Habbad's voice shook with restrained fury. If he had been capable of Rage, he was certain munisica would have sprouted from his hands and feet.

Kreed smiled, then leaned back in his chair, slouching to one side as he tapped a finger along his jaw. "Did I know." He smiled and pondered the words, as if saying them carried some hidden joke he was on the verge of understanding. "I know a lot of things, Mr. Habbad. The Fears of every man, woman and child on Aeneria reveal much to Decreath. They whisper to me, in the spaces between their thoughts, when their hearts remind them of what they cherish the most. Right now your heart tells me of your Fear. Your shame. You Fear a life of normalcy, of irrelevance in this coming of the Shadow Tide. You were denied the title of Harbinger, and you want to know if I betrayed you. I'll humor your question with a question: What the fuck does it matter if I did?"

Hot air rushed out of Habbad's nose in puffs of steam. His Hunger for revenge flared, drawing his attention to the center dais. Roth sat on a throne carved from a single piece of oak. Grotton had swelled his proportions to at least twice the Bonebreaker's normal size, though his belly had bulged even larger, giving him the appearance of an obese gladiator. He was naked, save for the black armor of Rage that covered him from head to toe. His cavalier expression hadn't changed in the slightest at Habbad's appearance. He occupied himself with a haunch of raw meat, raining blood over his rotund belly as he tore chunks off with shrouded teeth.

Habbad noticed Talin sulking in a little black throne set farther back than the others. He held a soul fly in his right hand, a sad blue specimen dripping with Despair, he held it to the mouth of a disfigured child attached to his chest like a grotesque tumor. The child uttered pitiable moans as it suckled at the evil magic.

A recklessness took hold of Habbad as he returned his glare to Kreed. "Yes, it does matter. If you knew Grotton would betray me, even after all the work I did for him, then after I kill Roth and Grotton, I will kill you, Father Kreed."

Kreed's voice trilled with amusement, and he clapped his hands rapidly. "Oho! With ambition like that I wouldn't be surprised if Grotton leapt out of Roth right this very moment. I tell you what, Habbad, you and I have been faithful colleagues for some time now, so I shall refrain from tearing your spine out through your mouth, though that was rather rude you know."

"Answer the question," Habbad growled. He was in no mood for idle threats.

Kreed rolled his eyes. "Oh of course I didn't know! Don't be stupid, boy. I barely comprehend the whims of Decreath, and he lives in the quick of my bones! We may seem like old chums in here but I assure you, The Three don't share their secrets like little girls at a sleepover. The fact is simple. Roth made a better Harbinger than you. Deal with it."

A vein throbbed in Habbad's ear. "But how? How is that possible? I have done things with Hunger that no one in recorded history ever dared to achieve. I was the first to take an Aenerian Domina, and I was certainly first to take seventy-four."

"You told me it was only forty!" Kreed barked, slapping the arm of his throne.

"What did it matter?" Habbad said through a snarl. "Grotton was going to crown me as Harbinger. That was the whole point! All my training, all the torture and lies. It was supposed to be me the whole time! Grotton himself promised me, but instead he chose *him*!" He jabbed a finger at Roth, then jabbed a finger at Talin. "And *that* traitor nearly killed me with Hatefire! I've done more work to bring about the Shadow Tide than any before me, including all of you! My armies of Domina continue to devour Aeneria as we speak, and my agents still garner secrets from our enemies. And let's not forget, if it wasn't for my initiative with the Cold Crows, Alvani, Chiron, and *that* oaf would still be at large. *I* should have been crowned Harbinger. I was stronger, faster, smarter..." Habbad's voice trailed off as tears filled his eyes. Behind him, the child in Talin's arms let out a screeching keen.

"You are a child," thundered the voice from the oaken throne. Roth rose to his full height, the ebony blades of his hair tinkling against the surface of the gem in the ceiling. He took another wet bite of the haunch, licked the blood off with an indulgent slurp, then tossed the remains at Habbad's feet. It was a half-eaten leg of a man, its owner lying in a heap of robes and blood next to Roth's throne. "Your armies were never yours, whelp, and your secrets are no longer necessary. Aeneria belongs to The Three now, just as I belong to the lord of Hunger. You on the other hand, you belong to me." Roth stepped down the dais, towering in front of Habbad, naked and black as a starless night. Roth was somehow more than twice Habbad's height, making him feel small and helpless, like an Underkin. Grotton's gifts indeed.

"I belong to no one. You shall get nothing from me," Habbad said, voice trembling with fury. "And neither will Grotton."

Roth tilted his head to the side and surveyed Habbad with a toothy smirk, as though considering how best to eat him. "You denounce Grotton then? Even after all the gifts he bestowed upon you?"

"Careful, Habbad," Kreed interjected. "Consider your options before you do something rash. We're in a bit of a hiring spree at the moment. Grotton is in need of generals, assassins, information brokers, and agents of all specialties. I am too as a matter of fact. You are one of the most powerful and influential entities on Aeneria. Go wash the filth from your body and clear your mind, then reestablish connections to your resources. I'm sure you could walk into any position you please. I'd wager Sorronis would even take you, though you might have to butter him up with a few soul flies first." Kreed's voice then dropped to a dangerous, gravelly tone as a shadow fell over the chamber. "Don't go biting the hands that placed you on that pedestal you hold yourself on."

Talin's airy voice echoed from the other side of the chamber. "He has Hatred for you, Rothael. It consumes him. He will never forgive you. He cannot be trusted."

Roth showed no indication he heard what anyone had said. He continued to glare haughtily at Habbad, his smile broadening as he flexed claws nearly as long as Habbad was tall. A sea of Hunger boiled behind his shrouded eyes. "We don't have to trust him. He's weak. Insignificant. But he may still be of use. The Domina that reside in his body belong to Grotton, so I'll take them all in exchange for his life. He can consider it his first meaningful contribution to the Shadow tide."

It was Habbad's turn to smile. No one, not even Roth would take his Domina without a fight. He had long ago mastered the Hunger within himself, and so his Domina would only answer to him, the Underking. He would sooner kill every one of his thralls than give them over to some Rage-fueled simpleton who didn't know the first thing about Hunger. While the Harbingers droned on, Habbad had been busy casting layer upon layer of protective spells over himself, simultaneously corralling the collective physical strength and Wisdom of all his Domina. He'd spun webs of Hunger through the chamber as well, baiting each of the Harbingers with seemingly innocuous temptations, each framed with the magical contract of Hunger. He had never been more ready to kill, to dominate.

"Feed yourself, Harbinger," Habbad said through a savage smile. "You should know, I too can sense Hunger. I felt it the first time I met you, the thirst for challenge, the yearning for dominance, the unrequited victories of a forgotten age. You played your part of mentor well, better than any other, but you and I both knew your true potential lay far beyond teaching children how to climb trees and lift rocks. Come, Harbinger, feed upon my Domina. You deserve them. I promise they're even more savory than you imagine."

Silence ruled the chamber as Habbad's words echoed throughout the minds of the Harbingers. A minute passed. Then another. Habbad felt vibrations throughout his webs of Hunger, nothing more than little nibbles at his bait, but it was something.

A rumbling began to fill the chamber, deep and powerful like a stirring avalanche. Roth's armored belly shook as his laughter crashed through the air, shaking the shadows from the walls as another sound struck Habbad in the chest. Habbad shoved his fingers into his ears to blunt the noise, but as he did the laughter shifted to something foul, something unnatural, like a perverse secret whispered through the gates of another world. It was the voice of Hunger incarnate, of Grotton himself.

Habbad felt as if his skin were wilting to thin paper, his bones thinning to that of a bird's. There was a heavy churning sensation in his bowels, as though something were trying to wrestle its way out of him. He was falling apart. The chamber blurred and dimmed before him as the screams of his Domina raked across his mind. His guts twisted upon themselves in a stabbing lurch, then the screaming stopped, leaving him in an ominous quiet.

His vision cleared just enough to reveal black eyes shining down upon him, but they were not Roth's. The lord of Hunger set his gaze into him. Habbad did his best to scream, but something choked the sound off his throat. With horrible recognition, Habbad beheld a cloud of orange marbles pouring from his mouth and into the Harbinger's, just as he himself had done so many times before. Habbad resisted, but Grotton forced him to suffer the panic of death as one of his Domina tore from his soul. The pain of it consumed his senses, smothered his every memory and threatened to define him. Minutes passed like hours, each more agonizing than the last as his need to draw breath was denied over and over by the swarm of Hunger pouring from his mouth. When he could take it no more, Habbad felt the cold numbness of the void creep its way up from his limbs as his heart sputtered to a halt, granting him solace at last.

Just before he passed through the veil of death, Habbad jolted, coughing and hacking as his body drew a ragged breath of life. Iron claws wrapped around his middle, lifting him up into the air as his guts twisted once more. He kicked his feet and tried to beg for mercy, but another of his Domina was already rushing its way out of his throat.

CHAPTER 12

HIDDEN WEAKNESS

Two weeks passed and the students made remarkable progress. As with the preceding Unbound, Cole and the others rotated training the elite teams, running them through every grueling physical and mental ordeal they could think of. No unit was ready for battle, but at the rate they progressed, Cole felt they would soon be ready for supervised patrols outside The Sill.

As Chiron had suggested, Cole told his friends about the Vaults of the Soul, though for some reason he left out the part of it being a one-way trip. They spent an entire evening discussing plans to get Cole to Oberon Temple, offering their advice and encouragement as well as jubilation at the possibility of victory. Cole hid the sadness from his face and his mind as they celebrated, and with a sting of remorse he realized why he didn't tell them the whole truth; he was manipulating them. If they knew that he would never return, that his life would end as soon as he entered, then they wouldn't give everything they had to getting him to the temple. A seedling of self-Hatred took root beside his guilt.

The Unbound continued their training during the evening hours, which seemed to involve more studying and less practical exercise with each passing night. One evening while reading under the turquoise light of the mushrooms in Chiron's house, Cole discovered a small book labeled *Forbidden, Perilous, and Volatile*. The preface of the book was the longest part, composed of warnings and reasons to never use the spells listed. However, the more Cole read, the more intrigued he became. Most of the text was far beyond his understanding, but the final warning was very clear: *Use of any spells listed herein may yield terrible and permanent results, not limited to the alteration and utter destruction of time, space, or reality among the multiverse.* The preface carried on until the last few pages, where only three spells were listed. Cole memorized them, though he had no idea how to invoke them, or what made them so dangerous.

He continued to meet with staff of the Heart Tree every morning, now accompanied by the rest of the Unbound. Their meetings were brief, as the staff were so overwhelmed with their new recruits that they had to devote most of their time to training them. Falinor made a habit of tardiness, often complaining about how he was now even more short staffed. Debjornik offered the latest intelligence gathered by his teams, though none of it suggested anything urgent. Rayn and his team of analysts worked tirelessly devising plans for assaulting the various cities and settlements of Aeneria, as well as a defensive plan should The Sill face a siege. Thessi, who seemed to despise Cole at first, now seemed the least stressed and most amenable, agreeing with him on most topics and offering help when she could. The Unbound had solved her food sourcing issue by cultivating an entire grove of blackstouts, and the Logistics Arch had received the bulk of the new recruits. Other supplies were still hard to come by because there was still no communication with the other cities. Wareen and her assistants made attempts at hailing the other Seer Jars across Aeneria, but none ever replied. Larkin hadn't been heard from since his last contact, and was assumed dead.

Cole knew The Sill could sustain itself indefinitely, that sooner rather than later he was going to have to take the Unbound out to the nearby towns. Trade lines needed to be reestablished, allies reconnected, recruits collected. He shuddered to think what darkness grew outside the safety of their walls.

Lileth did her best while training with the rest of the Unbound, but since she was only with them half the time she soon fell behind. While she never had been the best fighter, she now lost nearly every match, even against Eliza. Cole could have sworn her munisica weren't as big as they used to be, and her Passion seemed to be getting worse as well. Valen and Eliza surpassed her Wisdom, and Sitra came close to matching it. After suffering a particularly demoralizing defeat where Cole bested her in combat without drawing his munisica, Lileth's stoicism finally gave way to a heavy melancholy. She missed the next two nights of training. Cole tried his best to console her, but it was as if she'd shut herself in a shell, locking him and the rest of the world out. There seemed to be less of her when she emerged from her room, but when she did, all she wanted to do was be with Cole, and all he wanted to do was be with her. This behavior was not lost on the others, but they were polite enough to not remark on it, even when it distracted them from their duties.

Though it took much longer than he wanted, Cole finally found the time to see Naythan and the girls. He knocked on the old hermit's door, but there was no answer. Then he pounded on the door, still with no answer. Cole's Passion told him all their life candles were nearby; however, a closer inspection revealed them to be not in the house, but outside in the back yard. He strolled around the verdant walls, noticing the leafy vines that blanketed the exterior now bore flowers and colorful paper crafts made by small hands. Shrill voices carried from the back yard, joyful and unbridled. Naythan's deep rasp punctuated the mirth with dramatic cries of warning or encouragement, eliciting thrilled screams or fits of giggles. Cole rounded the house and beheld the back yard. Naythan crouched low, pointing to a trio of golden soul flies dancing with each other not ten paces away. Lexy and the ginger-haired girl clung to his robes as if he were a sturdy tree in a storm. They all wore matching necklaces, which Cole recognized from the theater Arts District.

Naythan and the girls were utterly captivated by the soul flies. From his experience in the theater, Cole knew they were seeing not the grassy yard before them, but some sort of illusion brought on by the soul flies' dreams. Cole gave Naythan a polite tap with Passion. Naythan blinked and adjusted his spectacles. When he laid eyes upon Cole, he gave the girls a pat on the back and they darted towards the soul flies, where they skipped barefoot through the grass around the golden orbs.

Naythan strode towards Cole, removing the necklace and stuffing it into a pocket of his fur robes. A sad blue soul fly wandered into the yard, moping its way towards the girls. The old hermit aimed a kick at it, missed, then shot a bolt of fuchsia Passion at the fly, sending it scampering back into the surrounding brush.

"Miserable wretch!" Naythan snarled at the fly. He turned to Cole. "They're relentless! Soaked with Despair and keep trying to get the girls to play with them."

"Hello Naythan," Cole said. "It's none of my business of course, but shouldn't you be helping the soul flies if they're tainted with Despair? You're very talented with Passion."

Naythan grunted, then drew his robes about him as if there were a chill in the balmy air. "You're right, it's none of your business." Cole replied with a patient nod, which only seemed to infuriate the old hermit. "You're not even a tenth my age! Who are you to come to my home and question how I deal with pests. That's what they are, you know. Pests! I coddle one and ten more show up, begging and bothering. They're relentless! Bah, I don't have to explain myself to you."

"Of course you don't," Cole stated. He gestured towards the girls, who were now cradling the golden soul flies as though holding puppies. "How are they?"

Naythan scrunched half his face. "Took you long enough to get here. Lexy asks for you just about every hour. *When is Cole coming to visit? Can cole be my new daddy? Is Cole bigger than you? Is he stronger than you?* A father. Right. Are you even a man by Human standards?"

Cole considered the question for a moment. He hadn't done the math yet, but he knew he'd been on Aeneria long enough to make him an adult back home. Still, being an adult certainly didn't make a boy into a man. "No," he replied. Sensing Naythan's need for superiority, Cole donned a humble tone and dropped his eyes. "I was a kid when I left, and in a lot of ways I still am. I still have much to learn."

Naythan raked his eyes over Cole, then gave a satisfied nod. "You keep that attitude and this war will make a fine man of you yet. You might be well-listened-to around here, but don't you dare forget your responsibilities, no matter how small. I've seen many great men and women fall in love with the throne and forget the trappings of their past lives. Not that these two angels are mere accoutrements of your position." He gazed back at the girls and his stony visage softened.

"How are they?" Cole repeated.

175

"Tireless." Naythan sighed. "I've never seen a pair so full of life. Lexy still bears some residual trauma from her ordeal, which isn't unexpected given the extent of her horror. What *is* unusual, however, is that she's completely asymptomatic so long as Amorinanis is nearby."

"Who?" Cole asked.

"The other girl," Nathan said. "The redhead. Lexy named her. Took the girls to the library because Lexy wanted to learn more about you. I told the little fool you were too young and unimportant to be in any of those books, but we did find a small Terra book. I could barely read the damned script and the notes were made for Wisdom Walkers, not story time for children. Lexy took the name *Amorinanis* from a scrap I could read, and now it's the only thing the redhead will respond to. She still doesn't talk, by the way."

"Amorinanis," Cole said to himself. "That's quite the mouthful."

Naythan gave an agreeable humph. "Took some convincing, but she goes by Amori as well.

"Amori sounds much better," Cole said. "How is she? Have you learned any more about her... condition?"

"A bit," Naythan sighed, rubbing his tattooed neck. "And what I do know is only a fraction of what she's really up to. The girl surprises me every day. I gleaned two things from my observations, however. First, she is some kind of lodestone for the darker magics, which is to say that she draws them into herself. Fear, Hatred, Hunger and Despair, she absorbs all of it. What she then does with it I can't guess. I don't think even she knows. It manifests in the most peculiar ways, however, like making herself grow to the size of a middling child when she's the age of an infant. She made it rain diamonds in my bedroom one night when I was sleeping."

"That's not terrible," Cole said with a chuckle. "Aren't diamonds valuable on Aeneria?"

"Stars no!" Naythan growled. "They're one of the most common rocks out there, even among the local planets. Made a damned mess too. But it was harmless, which brings me to my second observation. Though she is utterly saturated with dark magics, she isn't tainted by them. She is not evil."

Cole's gaze drifted back to the girls. "Maybe not, but she's certainly capable of using evil magic. She paralyzed both of us with Fear when I tried to save Lexy."

"True," Naythan said with a contemplative frown, "but it is the intent behind the act that matters most. Do you think she meant us harm?"

"No," Cole replied. "I think she only meant to stop me before I separated Lexy's soul from her body. She caught me off guard, but the fact that she was able to affect me at all scares me even more. She's so young. There's no telling how the evil within will shape her throughout her cycles. What kind of woman will she grow up to be? We can't keep all sources of evil away from her. Not forever."

Naythan held out a hand. Confused, Cole reached for the old man, but a second later a wooden staff slapped into Naythan's palm. Naythan leaned heavily against the staff as he gazed at the two girls with a grandfather's stare.

It was a full minute before the old hermit spoke. "No one makes it through life unscathed, and those little angels are no exception. Amori and Lexy have already been exposed to the worst our world has to offer, yet here they are, gifting their innocence and wonder to a few passing soul flies. They both have evil in them, just as you and I do, but like I said it is the intent behind the act that determines the morality of a person. For instance, you carry the unmistakable stench of murder. To kill is an act of supreme evil. Do you even know the names of those you've killed, or how many?"

The question was as disarming as it was stinging. "Well, no but… that's different. It's not murder to protect yourself or those you care about. It was necessary."

"Was it necessary to enjoy it, oh mighty master of Rage?" Naythan asked.

"What? Of course I didn't…" Cole stammered himself silent before he said something that wasn't true. "My Rage enjoys it. Too much so. But I don't."

"That is because you are not evil," Naythan replied in a patronizing tone. "The morality lies in the intent."

"I see," Cole admitted. "But that doesn't mean I should enjoy it."

"No," Naythan said. "But that is why we must be aware of ourselves. Any magic used to the extreme takes the morality of the user with it. It is not wrong to feel Hunger, Fear, Despair, or Hatred, just as it is not wrong to feel Passion, Rage, or Wisdom. The Three have taken each of their magics to a level beyond fanaticism, which makes them evil beyond our understanding. If you were to devote yourself to your Rage as much as Decreath has with his Fear, then you yourself would be seen as evil, or mad at the very least. Even your Passion could turn against you."

Naythan's words made Cole think of the Vaults of the Soul in Oberon Temple. If what Naythan said was true, Cole could end up becoming what he'd been fighting all along. The Three could soon become The Four. He shook the thought from him and returned to Naythan. "In order to defeat The Three I need to become powerful in all our magics. How will I know if I'm straying too far down one path or another?"

Though Naythan was a foot shorter, he tilted his head back so he peered down at Cole. "That is for you to work out. Amori and Lexy will have to do the same. We can shield them from evil the best we can, but sure as starlight it will touch their hearts again. When it does it will be up to them to decide what to do with it."

Silence fell between them as they watched the girls. Cole saw a flicker of movement from across the yard. The blue soul fly was back, bobbing its way into the yard near the girls. Cole took a step forward to intervene, but felt a hard calloused hand on his arm.

"The girl must learn," Naythan said in a raspy whisper.

Cole relaxed, though he kept his magic at the ready. Amori's tangle of ginger hair perked up as the blue orb floated closer. She cast a furtive glance towards Cole and Naythan, who pretended not to notice her. Quick as a fox, Amori pounced on the soul fly, trapping it between her hands. She hugged the orb to her chest, grimacing as the blue Despair seeped into her body. Her jaw trembled as tears fell in neat lines down her cheeks, though her eyes were locked in composed determination. She gingerly replaced the soul fly to the ground. It was so dim and colorless that it appeared no more than a tiny ball of wispy clouds. Amori gave the soul fly a nudge with her bare foot, encouraging it towards Lexy and the other soul flies. Lexy, who had been watching Amori intently, carried her three golden soul flies and set them on the ground next to the empty grey one. The golden orbs danced and chased each other like a trio of puppies, bumping playfully into the grey. A moment later the empty soul fly swelled to a proud amber and joined the others in their mirth.

"Do you think she'll be okay?" Cole asked in a quiet voice.

"She'll be a little under the weather until she finds an outlet for the Despair," Naythan replied, frowning. Amori bent over, hands on her knees, and vomited in the grass. "But yes, she will be fine."

Amori wiped her mouth and rejoined Lexy and the soul flies. Her eyes were wet, but she was no longer crying. A small smile twitched in her cheeks as she watched Lexy and the four golden orbs. Cole couldn't help but admire the girl's resolve, and her selflessness. He also wondered about her powers, and what their limits might be. As young as she was, she was capable of taking pure Despair and converting it into something harmless, helpful even.

"Naythan?" Cole spoke to the old man without looking at him.

"Yes, boy?" Naythan replied.

"Do you think Amori has potential?" Cole asked.

"Everyone has potential," Naythan stated plainly.

Cole looked the hermit square in the eye. "You know what I mean."

Naythan sighed as an ancient sadness dragged at his brow. "If you value the girl's soul, never let her within one hundred leagues of The Three or their minions. A single soul fly's worth of Despair is nothing compared to proper evil. I shudder to think what might happen to the poor girl if she ever found herself face to face with even one of The Three. Probably lose her mind if she was lucky, or she might very well become the most dangerous nightmare in all of Aeneria."

Cole felt hot shame sting his cheeks. "It was a stupid question, I shouldn't have asked."

Naythan huffed. "You'd be stupid not to consider every option. Amori may very well decide to take an active stance in this war, though I hope that day doesn't come for a very, very long time. Now, let's go see what the little devils are up to before you take off for another week."

Lexy greeted Cole by diving into his arms and squeezing him tight around his neck. Cole's Passion revealed the extent of the damage her soul had sustained while Chosen; however, there were also signs of remarkable healing. He set Lexy down and offered his solemn gratitude to Amorinanis, who surprised him by offering one of the enchanted necklaces in return. Cole donned the necklace and watched the dreams of the soul flies with the girls for a while. The enchantment was weak, but safer than those found in the theater in the Arts District. Naythan's yard remained in clear view, but the soul flies emitted a small aura that revealed a hazy facsimile of their dreams. Each golden being contributed its creativity and emotions to an epic tale of wonder and discovery. To Cole, the dream was somewhat ambiguous and lacked context; however, the effect it had on him was profound. When the soul flies finally left, they left him with a strong desire to Travel. He could feel them calling to him, beckoning him upwards and onwards to the river of dreamers.

All too soon, Falinor pressed him with an urgent message, and Cole had to part company with Naythan and the girls. Tears filled every crease of Lexy's wrinkled face as she clung to him, begging him not to leave again. Guilt twisted Cole's throat as he deposited her into Naythan's arms. The old hermit pulled her into his plush coat and patted her back, cooing gently. Cole bade them all goodbye, and as he turned to leave he heard little footsteps pattering behind him. He twisted just in time to catch Amori as she leaped into his arms. She hugged him tightly, then gazed at him with pouting lips and accusing eyes.

"I won't be gone so long this time," Cole assured her. "Promise."

Amori raised a single eyebrow. Cole sensed Despair surge within her, heavy and sick, but he trusted her and so left his defenses down. She brought her tiny finger to his chest, tapping it against a torn seam in Cole's armored robes that he'd forgotten to mend. A dark substance bled from her fingertip, seeping into the fabric. The ripped cloth armor repaired itself as the shiny darkness spread throughout the rest of the material like creeping oil, passing over Cole's skin in a chilly wave. When her spell resolved, Cole's sturdy cloth armor had been stained with tones of dark bronze. The fabric glistened with a fine glitter of rainbow light reflected from Oberon. Curious, Cole set Amori down and inspected his armor with Wisdom.

"I don't believe it," Cole chuckled. He trickled Rage into his hand and tapped the armor with a bladed finger, producing a clinking sound. "That's Morthainian glass. How do you even know what that is?"

Amori inclined her head and gave him an arrogant smile, as though the answer was too complex for him to understand.

Cole departed Naythan's house and left for the training grounds. Using Varka's cape, he took to the sky and cut his way across the canopy to save time and avoid running into any citizens. While he had no problem helping the people of The Sill, he simply didn't have the time to assist them with their various issues such as charging their gratia stones or fixing their broken equipment.

"Hail, Master Cole!" Falinor barked from across the training grounds as Cole landed. He waved his arms and shouted again, though the effort was entirely unnecessary as Cole's Passion could pinpoint the man from across The Sill.

"I was in the middle of something important. What's the emergency?" Cole spoke directly into Falinor's mind and walked slowly so they would have time to speak privately. He noticed a group of students near Falinor.

"We need your expertise," Falinor replied. His mental voice was fuzzy and dim, but grew clearer as Cole neared. His telepathy was dreadful. *"I know you're busy, but we've got a group of elite students with no instructor. The elite units are taught by the Unbound as you know, but they're all occupied with their own groups. You're the only one left."*

"We have five elite units now?" Cole's astonishment beamed through their mental link. *"That makes one per Unbound. Pretty soon we'll be understaffed, though I suppose that's a good problem to have if it means our students are progressing. Who is the leader of this unit?"*

Falinor waited until Cole was close enough for him to speak his reply: "Master Cole, this is Wilkin. He's the leader of this unit."

Cole stopped a few paces away and inspected the unit. There were seven in all. The grass around them had been flattened by the hundreds of students mustering daily in their formations. Wilkin didn't look so sure of himself as the first time Cole met him. His eyes were sunken and dark, his face drooping in an expression of perpetual defeat. Cole knew the position of unit leader was difficult, and Wilkin likely hadn't slept in a few days, but showing such blatant weakness in front of his subordinates was unacceptable.

"I hear you've been promoted," Cole said. "Congratulations, Wilkin, and to the rest of you. To be distinguished as an elite unit is something to be proud of."

"Thank you…Master Cole." Wilkin offered the appellation with the slightest twinge, as if the word had burned his tongue on the way out.

"I'll take them from here, Falinor," Cole said to the department head. Falinor gave a grateful bow and a salute, then took off at a run towards the Heart Tree. Cole turned to Wilkin and the other students. "Sit yourselves in the grass and get comfortable." The students snapped at his orders, sitting themselves in a wide circle on the flattened grass. Apparently someone had already taught them Roth's rule of hesitation. "From now on you will arrive here a half hour before the start of training. You will do your best to clear your minds of all thought and emotion during this time. You can start now."

The unit let out a collective sigh of relief as they settled in to their meditation. They each shut their eyes and took on a methodical pattern of breathing. Cole strolled around them as they worked. He opened his Passion to the seven life candles before him, staying just beyond their awareness, but just close enough to sense what they were thinking. They each made a deliberate effort to quell errant thoughts that fluttered into their minds, which was of course impossible, but Cole appreciated the effort. He'd learned long ago that to try and force a thought from your head was about as effective as punching a mosquito in flight. As he passed by each student, he felt their minds and bodies tense, as though they expected him to attack at the slightest lapse in vigilance. Cole brought his Passion to each of their minds, disguising himself as one of their own thoughts, a favorite trick of Chiron's. He soothed their worries, offered them peace of mind, and gave subtle hints for the proper method of passive meditation. Once the unit had achieved an acceptable state of calm neutrality, Cole suggested they commit the process to memory, which they did.

Barely fifteen minutes had passed before the first student showed signs of restlessness. Cole felt the boy's mind wander, sending fleeting messages to the others and infecting the quiet of their minds with playful banter. Cole continued his silent patrol, listening to the flurry of mental words that zipped throughout the circle like excited bees. They shared private jokes, which then evolved into new jokes aimed at Cole himself. Still as statues, they hid the laughter from their faces, but the Passion network among them was a riot of humor. It wasn't until Cole laughed out loud that the joking died, leaving their minds dead quiet and alert.

"Meditation is as boring as it is important," Cole said with a chuckle. Their eyes popped open. "I never liked it. Still don't as a matter of fact. But the more you put into it, the more you'll get out of it. Master Chiron used to make us meditate before his lessons so that we'd start with a clear and open mind, which of course is the best way to tackle any problem. He said those who master meditation master themselves, and can achieve total peace of mind no matter how stressful a situation they find themselves in."

Wilkin sat a little straighter as a question bloomed in his eyes.

Cole inclined his head. "What's up?"

"Forgive me if I'm being too presumptuous," Wilkin started with a slight tone of derision, "but wouldn't our time be better spent learning how to fight The Three and their minions? The Sill needs warriors, not monks. Teach us how to kill, Master Cole."

The other students blanched and leaned away from Wilkin, as though afraid they might suffer retribution through association. Cole crouched low and placed a hand on Wilkin's shoulder.

"Do you know what Decreath uses against his victims?" Cole asked.

"Fear," Wilkin stated quickly, clearly eager to move on to something practical.

Cole held Wilkin's impatient gaze. "That's the answer given by those who have never felt him. It's not wrong, but it's vague. To be more precise, Decreath revels in the Fear of the individual. *Your Fear.*" Cole tapped Wilkin in the center of his chest. "He will steal your forgotten nightmares, bathe in your shame, and dance with your panic. Decreath will turn the worst parts of you against you. When he does, what will you do to stop him?"

Wilkin worked his lips like a fish out of water. Blinking hard, he finally found words. "I'll use Rage. Rage is an effective counter to Fear."

"Very good." Cole clapped Wilkin on the back and rose to his feet. He sensed messages of appraisal fly from the other students and into Wilkin. Cole smiled. Wilkin himself might be a bit arrogant, and his unit experienced, but their comradery was strong, which is what mattered the most. Cole continued, addressing the entire unit, "Wilkin is correct of course, but our enemies are cunning, and their magic dynamic. Rage is the most effective of our magics when it comes to stifling Fear, but what if Rage weren't an option in that moment?"

Wilkin snickered. "If I can't solve a problem with Rage, then the problem likely isn't worthy of my attention as a warrior." The other students' eyes lit up, impressed by their leader.

"Well put," Cole said. "Then you should find this lesson easy. Your task is to lay a hand on me. Even a fingertip will do. You may use your Rage, Passion, Wisdom, or any other trick you can think of."

"But you are a master of Rage..." Wilkin complained, sighing as though he'd just been asked to cut down every tree in The Sill by hand. "We'll never catch you. You are simply too fast. We tire of these impossible tasks. Why don't you give us something within our ability to accomplish."

It took Cole a surprising amount of willpower to quell his Rage before it spilled out of his mouth. His fingertips hardened into blades, cutting into his palms. He wanted to beat Wilkin within a breath of dying, then heal him and do it all over again, just to show the idiot what kind of pain their enemies were capable of inflicting. Enemies that crept closer every day, yearning for a chance to desolate everything they loved. Wilkin had no idea what lay outside their borders, the horrors of Brimhallow, of Costas, of Morthain. None of them knew.

Cole doused his Rage in the stone room of his center before replying in a calm, even tone. "This task is far from impossible. I won't use any magic to augment myself in any way. On the contrary, I'll maintain my usual handicapping spells, which slows me down considerably. There *is* one trick to this task, however. I've placed a spell on each of you, and it will take effect as soon as the lesson starts. You'll have to overcome the magic in order to catch me. I hope your heads are clear."

Wilkin shot to his feet and drew a sharp breath. "Wait just one minute! We don't need your tricks or ambiguities, what we need is clear and concise—" Wilkin uttered a soft squeak as he suddenly flew up into the air.

The unit cried out and scrambled to their feet, only to shoot up into the sky after him, limbs flailing. Cole smiled as their breathless wailing faded up into the starry sky. He wished Roth were here to see this. There were few things the Bonebreaker loved more than the sound of his students screaming for their lives.

It was a simple spell, and if any of the students had meditated properly, they would have felt Cole set the framework for it while they were seated. The spell simply inverted gravity's effects on each of their bodies. Instead of Aeneria holding them safely to its soft hide, the planet pushed them away as fast as if they were in freefall. Cole's smile faded as the moment passed. He could no longer hear the students, or see them.

"Oh shit," Cole swore as a cold needle of Fear poked his heart.

Going against his word to not use magic, Cole stilled his mind and hammered his Wisdom into action. Varka's cape snapped at his whim, tuning his magic to better suit the music of his soul. Clumps of sod tore from the ground as Cole shot upwards in a burst of pure force. He called Wisdom to his eyes, sharpening his vision, then focusing towards the seven life candles revealed by his Passion.

Relief washed over him. The unit was perfectly fine. Scared to the point of passing out but perfectly fine. He slowed his ascent, staying just out of sight. They continued their fall upwards for almost a minute before the first student made an attempt to right their situation. Her limbs were splayed out, her belly face down, perfectly stable. Cole sensed her cast a spell, which would send her body towards the ground, but she only shot up faster, passing by Wilkin in a blur of rippling cloth. She had yet to figure out the rule of Cole's spell.

Wilkin stabilized himself in time to notice her folly. Cole felt the spark of communicated Passion between him and the rest of the unit. Then, almost as if it were choreographed beforehand, the whole group spun to face the ground, spreading their limbs wide. Though they were now miles above the ground and terrified beyond reason, they found a sliver of comfort in the familiar minds around them. After a lengthy discussion which carried them to the ever-thinning air of Aeneria's lower stratosphere, they had finally deduced the rule of Cole's spell.

Wilkin's thoughts beamed into the minds of his unit. *"Up is down, down is up. Use Wisdom to send your body away from the ground, not towards it."*

One by one the students slowed to a halt, though their efforts sent them sailing away from each other. They readjusted, finally joining together in a stationary group, but they were now hundreds of feet away from their starting position. Cole sensed the Fear clouding their minds and numbing their Wisdom. He wanted them to figure this out on their own, but they would need help if they were to make it back to the training grounds. They were so high that The Sill had melded with the green and blue blobs of the landscape below. If Cole hadn't had several very important life candles burning at The Sill, he would never have found the place by sight alone. Looking around the starscape, he saw the planet Cigni beaming her seafoam green face at them while Oberon loomed nearby. The local sun stained the horizon blood red from the other side of the world.

Slow and uncertain, the unit began their descent. Cole fell far below them, careful to stay within range to save them, though not so close as to be spotted. They had already drifted several miles laterally from the borders of The Sill, and since the unit was nowhere near battle-ready, landing among a pack of Domina was out of the question. Cole entered Wilkin's mind and spoke privately to the unit leader.

"I knew you'd figure it out eventually," Cole said, offering Wilkin a soothing dose of Passion. *"Now would be the perfect time to use your Rage. Just a drop. It will clear the Fear from your mind."*

Wilkin's mental voice shook with terror. *"M-Master Cole you must help us, we've gone too high, I can't breathe. Where's The Sill! Oh stars, we're going to die!"*

"Your Rage, Wilkin." Cole repeated, thundering the words into Wilkin's mind. *"And don't you dare let the unit see your Fear."*

It took a minute for Wilkin to find his Rage while terror gripped him so. Cole knew how difficult it was. To ignite your Rage while so embroiled in Fear was like trying to start a fire at the bottom of the ocean. When Wilkin finally got hold of himself, he replied in a quiet, but even tone.

"Thank you, Master," Wilkin said. All trace of contempt had vanished. *"We are safe for now, but we are still miles high. I'm not sure I can find The Sill."*

"Clear your mind and use what tools you have," Cole said. *"You are in no immediate danger, a gift rarely handed to the Warriors of The Sill. Take as much time as you need."* Cole then retreated beyond the horizon of Wilkin's mind where he could observe unnoticed.

Wilkin deliberated for a moment, inventorying his memory of the landscape and limited catalogue of spells, but to no avail. His pride wouldn't allow him to ask for Cole's help again, though his frustration eventually led him to seek answers among the rest of his unit. One student had the idea to sharpen their eyes with Wisdom so they could zoom in on the ground, but no one in the group had focus to spare, as battling the inverted gravity took the majority of their efforts. The unit then worked out an idea so creative that Cole couldn't help but admire them. They each fixed a hand to the lightest member of the unit, a slender boy named Bennit, who then stopped fighting Cole's spell so he could sharpen his eyes. The unit floated back to the thin air and icy winds, eventually abandoning their attempt so they could descend to more manageable atmosphere. Bennit spotted The Sill on their second attempt.

Smiling and proud, Cole raced ahead of the students and returned to the training grounds. After half an hour seven figures descended from the sky, holding hands in a circle. They landed on the flattened grass, gripping each other for support as they bounced off the ground, still battling the inverted gravity. Ice clung to their hair and robes, their faces glazed with frozen tears and snot. Wilkin locked eyes with Cole, then set his face in a determined scowl as he detached from his unit and took an ungainly step. He floated several feet in the air before descending in an arch. His face drooped with the drunken look of one taxing his Wisdom to its limit, but he took one bounding step after another, and crossed the gap. Finger trembling, he reached out and tapped Cole on the chest.

The entire unit collapsed to the ground as gravity returned to its rightful place. Cries of relief rang from them, and they embraced the ground as if they had just been reunited with a lost lover. Wilkin rose to his feet, then bowed low.

"I'm sorry, Master," he whispered in a voice low enough that the others couldn't hear.

Cole still wanted to beat him all the way to death's door and back, but decided it was best to save that for another lesson. He reached out and shook Wilkin's hand. Cole pulled him close and whispered in his ear. "It's okay to be weak, but don't ever let them see it. You are their leader. You are never tired, you are never hungry, you are never scared or angry. This world is ugly, and our enemies are ruthless. One moment of weakness could get you, or worse, one of them, killed." Cole pulled away and looked Wilkin in the eye. Hot tears melted their way through the ice, clinging to his cheeks. "Do you understand?"

"Yes, Master Cole," Wilkin said, looking up at Cole with a resolute expression.

"Good," Cole said. "Now go to them. Discuss what you did right and what you did wrong. In ten minutes we're going to do this again, only this time there's going to be two spells you'll have to figure out."

Cole spent the rest of the day putting Wilkin's unit in predicaments of ever-increasing uncertainty, such as taking away one or more of their senses, removing the oxygen from the training grounds, or turning himself invisible. The unit fumbled at every step, but Cole was determined to break them of their habit of freezing up when faced with the unknown. The problem was, they didn't know what to do when they *didn't know what to do*. There was no assessment of their situation, no inventory of their available assets. It was as if their entire lives someone else had rushed in to wipe away every problem before they had a chance to challenge themselves. It wasn't until Cole locked them in seemingly life-threatening situations that they began to show any sort of critical thinking. By the end of the day they were still nowhere near battle-ready; however, they were certainly better off than when they started. When Cole dismissed them and departed the training grounds, the unit remained behind at Wilkin's instruction so they could meditate. Pride tugged Cole's lips into a smile as he flew back to the barracks.

The rest of the Unbound were already showered and waiting in their rooms for his return. Cole knew Lileth would be taking the evening to catch up on sleep, so he stopped by her apartment, hoping to catch her before she tucked herself in.

"Come in," Lileth said.

Cole hadn't even knocked on the door yet, but he pushed his way through. Unlike his own quarters, Lileth's apartment was scrupulously organized, lacking so much as a rogue sock on the floor. Lileth sat in front of an easel on the far side of the room, swishing a fine brush over a canvas of a half-painted wolf. Her raven hair fell down to the small of her back, held gently by several sprigs of flowering vine. A balmy wind slipped through the open windows, carrying the slightest hint of the sea.

"The illustrious leader of The Sill graces me with his presence," Lileth said in a sardonic tone. "You do me a great honor, Master Cole."

"Easy with the praise. I won't be able to fit my head out the door," Cole said. He stood behind her and set his hands on her shoulders. Hard muscles rolled under his hands as she worked delicate strokes on the canvas. "I didn't know you were an artist."

"It helps me to fall asleep," she replied. "After staying up for two days my mind is unwilling to slow itself to the speed of my dreams. How went your training today? You worked with Wilkin's group, no?"

"They're pretty bad, though not completely hopeless. I almost killed them." Cole massaged her shoulders, eliciting a soft moan from her. His calluses caught on her nightgown, snapping and tearing the lace, so he withdrew. Lileth's hands gripped his in a flash. She pulled his arms around her neck and nuzzled into him.

"Please, don't stop," she whispered.

Cole kissed her neck, astonished that anything could be so soft, so supple. Her fingers grasped his sweaty hair, jerking his lips to hers. Her breath was sweet and hot, like rum set by a fire. Her flames spread through Cole's chest and down to his loins. It had been too long since he'd had her. Blind with lust, he felt Lileth's hands wrestle with the buckles and straps of his armor.

"Lileth, I'm filthy," Cole said. "Let me shower first."

She gripped his hair once more and tugged him close. Her teeth raked over his ear. "No. I like you dirty."

A reckless thrill stole through Cole. There was a litany of responsibilities gnawing at him like a pack of dogs fighting over a kill, but when he looked into Lileth's eyes, none of it mattered. He was with her.

CHAPTER 13

RETURNING HOME

"*Cole.*"

Cole twitched. He glanced down at Lileth, who had fallen asleep with her head on his bare chest, her legs woven over his own. He had been in such a deep state of relaxation and meditation that he became detached from the world around him.

"*Cole,*" the voice repeated. It was Eliza.

Securing his thoughts so Eliza couldn't see through his eyes, he opened himself to the flow of Passion. "*Eliza, I'm here. What is it?*"

"*You are needed at the Heart Tree. It's urgent,*" she replied.

Lileth stirred and woke. Cole sat up straight in the bed. "*I'll be right there. How long have you been trying to reach me?*"

"*Only just now.*" Her tone had an uncharacteristic hardness to it. "*However, the staff of the Heart Tree has been trying to reach you for at least an hour.*"

Panic blossomed in Cole's chest. "*Why, what's wrong?*"

"*Go see for yourself.*" Eliza severed their private link, leaving a chilly void in her wake.

Lileth perched herself up on an elbow. "Who was that?"

Cole threw the sheets from himself and scanned the floor. "Eliza. There's an urgent message from the Heart Tree. Have you seen my underwear?"

Lileth was silent for a moment as Cole scoured the room for his clothes and armor. "You still maintain your Passion link to her?"

"What? No. I mean yeah, when we have to talk and we're too far away," Cole said, hopping across the room as he tried to force his sock over his foot.

Lileth's tone sharpened. "I told you how I felt about your relationship with Eliza. I don't know if humans are monogamous, but on Aeneria, once you partake in intimacy with another there are certain implications that follow, for decent people at least."

Cole paused and stared at Lileth in disbelief, but his momentum carried him forward and he crashed through her chair, splintering it to bits. Face reddening, he rose to his feet. "Eliza and I are friends. That means she and I are going to talk sometimes."

The concern on Lileth's face flattened to an expressionless mask. "Of course."

Unsure how to respond, Cole assembled the rest of his outfit and, after donning Varka's Cape, used Wisdom to repair the broken chair. Before he popped through the door he looked back. "Are you going to train with us tonight?"

Lileth's only response was the silence of her back and the steady breathing of her sleep.

Cole took flight as soon as he popped through the stone door. The air exploded around him as Varka's cape augmented his Wisdom far beyond his normal boundaries. He slowed to an abrupt halt above the Heart Tree, descending through the open ceiling and landing so hard that he cracked the wooden floor. The staff dove under their round table.

"Hatefire!" Rayn cursed. "Give us a warning next time!"

The staff rose from under the table, dismissing their various spells when they saw Cole. The only person unaffected was Jahanna, Rayn's assistant. She sat in a chair, staring blank-faced at the Seer Jar, where Larkin's face swam in the clear liquid. The web of magic surrounded her and Larkin, preventing any sight or sound in the room from reaching them.

Cole approached the table. "What's going on?"

Rayn closed his eyes and clutched the Fear in his chest. "*What's been going on* is that we've been trying to contact you for over an hour. Larkin appeared in the Seer Jar and he won't talk to anyone but you. What were you doing?"

"I was indisposed," Cole replied.

THE UNBOUND

Rayn scowled, dissatisfied with Cole's answer. "Never mind then. Get in there and replace Jahanna before we lose Larkin."

Cole walked around the table and reached through the magical barrier, tapping Jahanna lightly on the shoulder. She left the chair, and Cole sat in her place. The web of magic surrounded him with infinite darkness and silence.

"Wisdom Walker Larkin," Cole greeted him with a seated bow. "I'm sorry you had to wait so long."

"So am I," Larkin said. His face was sallow and thin. "They might catch me any moment so I must be brief. And keep in mind I will have to erase this entire conversation from my memory so The Three won't learn anything more about you. I wiped the details of our last conversation, so I will only update you on what I've learned since then."

"I'm listening," Cole said, leaning close. Delving into his Passion, he opened a broad network to the rest of the Unbound so they could hear as well.

Larkin jumped and looked behind him, then returned to Cole. "The Three have control of every city and village on the Light Side, and they've taken almost all of the Dark Side. They're boxing you in, choking your supplies at their sources so you will be all the weaker before they finally move on you. Even if you manage to escape, there will be nowhere for you to go. You must take footholds elsewhere on Aeneria before they besiege you, for once they do they will bring the full might of our world against The Sill."

"The full might of the world?" Cole asked. "You mean there are forces in addition to what minions they already have?"

"Yes," Larkin replied with a grim nod. "The Three aren't killing everyone, only the adults and elders. They leave the children alive, as well as anyone else they can win over with Hunger. Their intent is to indoctrinate the world and wash away the past. Magic is illegal, only to be used by the Divine Guard—that's what they're calling their priests now. The Three were already worshipped and loved by the Light Side. Within a single generation the entirety of the Dark Side will have forgotten all about The Sill, and they will worship The Three as their saviors."

193

"That's ridiculous," Cole said. "No one could forget crimes like Domina and Colossi. And Corpulants! No, not even a child would forget monsters like that."

Larkin let out a mirthless laugh. "Ah but the mind of a child is the most malleable thing in the world. Without their parents to guide them, the children have only Divine Guard to shape their minds. The monsters that come in the night are minions of The Sill, not of The Three. Only those who pray to our holy fathers shall be delivered from the wrath of the monsters from The Sill."

"There's no way!" Cole shouted, slamming his fist on the table. He soothed his Rage before speaking again. "There's no way. It can't be."

"It's been done to the Light Side," Larkin said. "And it has already begun on the Dark Side. Their lies are potent, and their methods work without fail."

Defeat washed over Cole. "Is there anything we can do?"

Larkin raised his head a little higher, regaining some of his lost pride and composure. "If you remain in The Sill you will die. It might take cycles, but so long as Travel to the local planets is still impossible, The Three will eventually come for you, for you are still the key to the Aethers. The longer you wait, the greater their war machine will be when they come knocking. You must stab out into the world. Seek out those who are not yet lost. Recruit them, show them the ways of the Unbound. Time is against you."

"That's... not ideal." Cole fell silent for a moment, thinking on how best to reply without revealing too much. There was still a possibility that Larkin already belonged to The Three. "I appreciate the risk you're taking to keep us informed. I really do. I wish I could offer you some news in return, but—"

"You'd be a fool's fool if you did," Larkin replied. "No, you're going about it the right way. Don't ever tell me anything you don't want The Three knowing. Even though I'll erase the details of this conversation, there is still a chance they could break my mind and somehow recover it. They are gods after all."

"Is there anything else?" Cole asked. "I'll talk as long as you want, but I don't want you taking unnecessary risk."

Larkin's eyes fell. "That is very gallant of you, Human, but I'm not long for this world anyway. The Council has been useful, and so The Three have not killed all of us. However, our utility is coming to an end. This will likely be the last time we speak. My final word of advice is this: Go to the city of Borla Dign. The Divine Guard plan to hold a Devotion tomorrow. Interrupt the Devotion and you will deny The Three an enormous resource, not to mention save an entire city of Wisdom Walkers from a fate worse than death. Go now. Time is against you."

Larkin's face shimmered, then vanished, leaving the teardrop glass an empty, pale blue.

Cole slid the chair back and stepped out of the masking web. The staff of the Heart Tree showed no reaction to his presence. They merely gazed at the Seer Jar with unblinking eyes and blank faces.

At last Rayn blinked and cleared his throat. "Well, I think I speak for everyone when I say this: You cannot go to Borla Dign."

Debjornik leaned forward on his elbows. "The Intelligence Axis has no knowledge of any portion of Larkin's testimony. There is still a strong possibility he is acting for The Three, so I advise we not act on his word, no matter how compelling it may be."

"Your agents wouldn't report anything from Borla Dign if they were Chosen for the Devotion," Thessi said, crossing her arms. "Borla Dign is a hub of commerce and transportation. The Borla river runs around the city, and used to be a main artery for barges carrying supplies directly to our lagoon. Securing Borla Dign would be a boon for the Logistics Arch. Everyone would benefit, including our new recruits."

"No." Falinor shook his head with deliberate slowness. "The recruits aren't ready for such a mission. They can barely crawl, and disrupting a Devotion would be asking them to sprint around the world. They would only serve to add fresh meat to the towers."

All eyes went to Wareen, as she had yet to speak her mind. She regarded them all with an air of ambivalence. "I think any mission outside our walls would be a fool's errand, especially if it involves throwing children into a fire." She raised an eyebrow and leaned slightly to one side. "However, disrupting a Devotion would be a mighty victory for the Communications Web. My propaganda team would make great use of such a victory, which would help us secure more recruits in the long run."

Rayn waved his hand dismissively. "Yes, yes, a victory would do us all some good, but the fact still remains: We cannot act on Larkin's word. Even if we *had* the warriors, there is still a strong likelihood that every word spoken through that Seer Jar has been naught but lies. Lies meant to lure us to our deaths. No, we wait for word from the Intelligence Axis before expending resources. Debjornik, do you have agents to spare? Could you send a few to verify Larkin's claims?"

Debjornik contemplated for a moment before responding. "Perhaps in a month I could trust one of the recruits for such a task, but I'd need a few volunteers to go with her. A lone traveler raises too many questions."

The Staff deliberated for several minutes, haggling over each other's resources like cutthroat merchants, each unwilling to give an inch of ground. Cole sat in silence the entire time, but he had not been idle. After reaching a consensus with the rest of the Unbound, he rose to his feet, speaking loudly enough to interrupt the staff in their squabbling.

"The Unbound will go to Borla Dign." His words sliced through the air like the crack of a whip. "If everything is fine, we will reactivate their Seer Jars and offer our friendship, which will hopefully reopen the trade route. If there really is a Devotion, we will stop it."

Rayn gave a look of such profound disgust that Cole checked behind him to make sure a bog angel hadn't just appeared in the chamber.

"Do you have any idea what you're saying?" Rayn asked. "Do you even know what that means? We have no analysis of the mission, no knowledge of the enemy, no way of knowing how long you'll be gone. You do know what a Devotion is, don't you? The Three will be there, and if they show up early they will have you and your Unbound flayed upon the towers like the rest of them. You may have power worthy of the Unbound, but what you flaunt in brawn you lack in experience. I beg you, shelve your arrogance just this once and let us do our jobs."

Falinor and Debjornik each gave an agreeable grunt; however, Thessi and Wareen looked as if they had more to say. Cole considered how to respond. He Ignored Sitra's urges to throw the staff out the open roof, following instead Eliza's advice to cleanse himself in his center. When he spoke, it was with the authority of the Unbound.

"I appreciate your concerns, I really do," Cole said. "But for reasons I don't have time to explain, we are going. Right now. No matter the outcome, we should be back in less than two days." Cole spread his hands as Varka's cape shifted from polished wood to the liquid crystal of flight.

"Too bull-headed to listen to reason!" Rayn spat. "Someone's going to die for this, mark my words." Cole's bare feet then left the floor as he rose into the air. Rayn then let out a derisive chuckle. "If arrogance were a school of magic then you'd be master of that as well! You're just like Chiron."

Cole paused in mid-air, glancing back at Rayn with a grin. "Thank you."

Cole found the rest of the Unbound dressed and ready in the center yard of the barracks, including Lileth. He stuffed some supplies in a bag, which included a week's worth of blackstouts and a few potions of Valen's creation. Once everyone was ready, they checked out with Whind at the Lurkwood Gate and took to the skies.

They enjoyed quiet for a time. They had spent every waking minute barking orders, training, or laboring over one project or another. The simple silence was a rare gift, and so they enjoyed it for as long as they could. They passed over the lagoon, right over the beach where they first drew munisica in real combat. A longing Rage boiled in Cole's belly as he recalled the event. The unit had been attacked by three double-thralled Domina, a battle which nearly killed them all. Then, Cole was nothing more than a frail liability, but now it would be no trouble at all for him to obliterate an army of Domina one hundred strong. Even a thousand Domina wouldn't cost him anything more than time.

The air grew warmer as they left the Lagoon behind them. Oberon's rainbow light baked the backs of their necks like a midday sun. They flew as high as they could, so that from the ground they would appear no more than a flock of birds. None of them had been to Borla Dign before, but the path was clear thanks to a geography cypher from Wareen's Communications Web.

Sitra shouted something to the group, but the roaring wind ripped the words from her mouth before they could reach anyone's ears. Valen tilted his emerald wings and cut his way close to her, then pointed a finger at his head.

"How much longer do you think?" Sitra asked in a broad mental shout. *"I'm getting hungry."*

"Hungry?" Eliza rang with astonishment. *"You had an entire blackstout before we left."*

"And a sereph egg, but Cole's gravity spell makes me burn through my food too fast. If we don't land and hunt I'm going to drop like a rock." To emphasize her point, Sitra projected herself through their network, infecting them with her ravenous cravings.

Cole reached into his bag and pulled out a blackstout. He flew close to Sitra and placed it firmly in her hand. *"Eat on the wing."*

Sitra gave him a sour look. *"Oh, perfect. Another snot rock."*

"I'll cook you a steak myself when we get back," Cole said. He then directed his thoughts to the entire group. *"Since we're not training at the moment, why don't we ditch the handicaps? Go ahead and remove your gravity spells."*

There was a collective mental sigh of relief as they dismissed their spells, followed by a shock when they surged faster through the air.

"This is incredible!" Eliza exclaimed, spinning herself in a wild corkscrew. *"I feel as light as the air itself!"*

"You were right, Cole," Valen said. *"Increasing our body weight was a remarkably effective method of accelerating our training. It's only costing me a fraction of my Wisdom to maintain flight, nearly negligible."*

"We will need time on the ground to acquaint ourselves to the change," Lileth said. *"It would be unwise to jump into battle without first testing our new limits."*

"We'll have time," Cole said. *"We're going to skirt around the city for a while. During my mission to Brimhallow I did a week's worth of*

reconnaissance before setting foot in the village. Borla Dign is bigger, but with the five of us I bet we'll be done in a day."

"At least this is not our first Devotion," Valen said. "We already know our targets; the Chosen, the priests, the odium, and the tower itself."

"The odium may not be necessary if they use Hatefire," Lileth said. "An Arch Priest of Sorronis could wield it. Or Sorronis himself, but if he's already there then we'll have bigger concerns than disrupting a Devotion."

"I don't know," Sitra said. "Cole beat the piss out of Sorronis last time they fought, and now Cole's a master of Passion as well as Rage. Not to mention we're all a bit stronger now. I think I like our odds."

"The odds are not as good as you think," Valen said. "You forget how the power of The Three works. They have each crowned their Harbinger, which means The Three are much more powerful than before. When Cole fought Sorronis, Roth had yet to submit to Grotton, and so Sorronis was not at full power. Cole barely survived the encounter. Had Roth given in even a minute sooner, we would likely not be here having this discussion."

"Not to mention I was only facing Sorronis's Hatred for most of the fight," Cole said. "It took only a touch of Despair to cripple me. No, Lileth is right. If even one of The Three shows, then we need to bail as soon as possible, though I wouldn't mind having a few minutes alone with Kreed."

"I still can't believe Roth's gone," Sitra said. "I know he's Harbinger, but are you sure he's not still fighting? The Roth I knew would fight until his dying breath, then keep fighting even after that."

No one had the heart to tell her the truth. After a moment, however, Eliza breached the silence.

"The Roth we know is indeed gone, Sitra." Eliza's tone was gentle, yet firm. "He is Grotton now. Understand this and accept it, for if you ever face him in combat, Grotton will turn your deepest wishes against you and devour everyone you love."

"I know how dangerous Grotton is!" Sitra lashed. "All I'm saying is that Roth would never completely submit to anyone. No matter what. He'd find a way to resist, no matter how small. We shouldn't be *talking about The Three anyway, we should be talking tactics and strategy. How much longer till we get there?"*

After an hour the Unbound had exhausted every possible plan of action. Whenever someone brought up an insurmountable scenario, such as the appearance of an Alpha Colossus, the answer was always the same: Let Cole handle it. Cole didn't like this answer, instead suggesting that they just run away, but the Unbound wouldn't have it. It wasn't that he was afraid of their enemies, rather he didn't want to stay in Borla Dign any longer than they had to. If he was there when The Three showed up, they would likely capture him and use him to unlock the Aethers. Entire worlds were at risk, and he only made it worse by putting himself closer to The Three.

Conversation thinned as the flight wore on. After several hours following the Borla River, the finally saw the lights of the city winking at the edge of the horizon. As they drew near they saw a flock of birds over the island city, a telltale sign of mass death. With dread tickling their hearts, they sharpened their eyes with Wisdom to get a better look. What they thought were birds turned out to be Corpulants of the same flying variety they encountered in Fangshard Valley. An aerial ingress was now out of the question, and so were half their plans. If even one Corpulant caught scent of their Wisdom, it would alert the rest, and the Unbound's window of opportunity would become exponentially smaller.

Once they were a mile outside Borla Dign, the Unbound parted ways to cover more ground, though they kept their Passion network wide open. Valen gave each of them a potion he'd crafted in Cole's lab. The potion would make the drinker invisible for an hour, which would allow them to penetrate the city bounds unseen, and more importantly without alerting the Corpulants to their Wisdom. Cole contacted Wareen and informed the Heart Tree of their arrival.

The Unbound gleaned a great deal from the sky. By augmenting their vision with Wisdom and sharing their observations with Passion, they pieced together the layout of the city and estimated the numbers of their enemies. Borla Dign was cradled by the Borla river, which forked around the city and rejoined on the other side. Empty docks surrounded the island where cargo barges ought to have been moored.

The streets and roofs reflected the stars above as if constructed from mirrors, making Borla Dign look like a patch of the sky itself. The city was arranged in a pattern of ever-larger concentric circles, the buildings evenly spaced, and the streets embellished with odd pale-blue spires that looked like naked trees. While their observations had been helpful, they were still no closer to finding any of their targets. The elusiveness of one target in particular was most troubling.

"*Has anyone seen the tower yet?*" Cole asked the group.

"*No,*" they replied in unison. Then Valen spoke alone. "*We are either very early or very late. Either way, I believe we have seen enough to warrant deeper investigation.*"

"*We better not be late,*" Sitra said. "*I've got a couple of presents to leave under that tower.*"

"*What sort of presents?*" Eliza asked.

"*I don't want to spoil the surprise,*" Sitra said in a playful tone. "*Let's just say they'll be enjoyed by everyone in a one-block radius of the tower.*"

"*Sitra,*" Lileth said, framing her words like a threat. "*We are about to enter a city under the control of the most dangerous force on Aeneria. Now is not the time for surprises or tricks or experiments. The last thing we need is for you to blow up half the city while we're in the middle of fighting for our lives. Please tell me you understand this.*"

Sitra was stubborn in her silence, eventually responding in a subdued voice. "*It wouldn't be half the city.*"

"*Sitra!*" Eliza exclaimed. "*Are you carrying bombs in your bag?*"

"*They're not bombs,*" Sitra scoffed. "*They're fulminating cells with a time-delayed fuze.*"

"*That explains why you have been collecting expired gratia stones,*" Valen sighed. "*Had I known your intended use for them I certainly wouldn't have agreed to help you.*"

"*Stars, Sitra! We flew in tight formation the whole way here,*" Eliza said. "*Overcharged gratia stones are by nature unstable. One bump in the air or one misplaced spell…you could have killed us any minute! Drop them in the river before you vaporize yourself.*"

Guilt and embarrassment twisted out from Sitra's mind. *"They're not unstable and I'm not dropping them, and I would appreciate it if you would all stop talking to me like I'm some idiot child. Wisdom might not be my best subject, but I'm not as stupid as you all think I am. Have any of you even read Chiron's book on fulminators? No, you haven't, but I have. Three times in fact. I know what I'm doing."*

Eliza, Valen, and Lileth bombarded Sitra with their collective rebuttals. Sitra was of course not stupid, but even a clever person would have a difficult time debating three minds at once.

Before their emotions could churn themselves into a storm, Cole interrupted them with a jarring blast of Passion. *"Enough. We're wasting time. Sitra says the stones are stable and that's good enough for me. Let's keep our spacing and touch down on the shores on the far side of the river. Swim across to Borla Dign and wait until you're in eyeshot of the Domina before you take Valen's potion. Keep yourselves centered and report everything you see through the Passion network."*

The Unbound cut a wide path around the Corpulants and touched ground far back from the water, spacing themselves out evenly around the city. Cole's toes sank into cool soil under the shadow of a nearby forest, and Varka's cape rippled into a broad cloak of woven ferns. He dismissed every spell of Wisdom, leaving him feeling nearly blind and deaf as his senses dulled to their normal acuity. It was uncomfortable, but necessary, as Corpulants could detect Wisdom from as far as a few hundred yards. He relied instead on the flow of Passion, using the life candles of the surrounding flora and fauna as reference points. Life was so abundant around him that oddly enough he felt even more sure-footed and oriented than ever before. Ants crawled in jagged highways up and down each tree. Winged serephs and bugle birds slept in the canopy above, their candles blazing brightest of all. Below his feet and under his toes, fungi and their spores permeated every inch of soil as far as his Passion could sense. The forest was alive, and Cole felt the vibrance of his own life candle burn along with it.

Cole passed through undergrowth unseen and unnoticed by any living creature. He reached the edge of the woods and stepped into the wet muck of the Borla shore. After encouraging a few predatory reptiles to wait for prey elsewhere, Cole waded out into the Borla. The water was uncomfortably warm, and carried the sour stink of decomposition into his nostrils. He took a moment and gazed out at Borla Dign. The shore of the island city was about a quarter mile away, a long swim without the aid of Wisdom. Grudgingly, he dove headfirst into the pungent water and started the journey.

The water felt like warm oil over his skin as he cut through the river. It sloshed dully in his ears, and seemed thicker than it ought to be. When the flying Corpulants drew near, Cole tilted and dove to the river bottom, using his Passion to guide him in the motionless murk. When his feet made contact with the opposing shore, Cole wanted nothing more than to cleanse himself with Wisdom, but refrained. He was certainly within range of the Corpulants' senses now. Cole plodded through water weeds and lilies, hiding himself beneath an empty dock as he waited for the others to find the shore. Valen was already in hiding, then came Eliza and Sitra. Lileth took nearly twice as long, but she eventually made it. At Valen's command, they downed the potion, rendering them each invisible without Wisdom.

Cole opened his watertight rucksack and plucked the potion from an inside pouch. He peeled the wax seal, uncorked the vial, then held the potion up to a distant light. The liquid was sky blue and bubbled as if carbonated. Cole downed the vial in two quick gulps. The potion tasted like icy mint, yet it burned his toes as if he'd stepped in a scalding bath. The heat itched its way up his legs and abdomen. Cole rose his arm out of the water and watched as a glittery wave ran over his wrist and hand, leaving open air in its wake. The water rippled around him as he gave the surface an experimental splash, but his body and armor were entirely invisible. Securing his rucksack to a support beam, Cole contacted Wareen one last time before climbing up the stone wall beside the dock.

Hoisting himself up onto a steel-paved walkway, Cole noticed all too late the water dripping profusely from him. Though he was invisible, the water falling from his body gave him the appearance of a dripping ghost. Two figures down the walkway paused, then hastened towards him. Cole darted in between two buildings, his wet feet slapping on the metal street. The figures were close enough now for him to hear their voices.

"Surely those aren't footprints?" said a voice. "I could have sworn we cleared these docks yesterday."

"There's always a few stragglers in a city this size," said a second voice, female. "Come on out, little pretties! Give up easy and I promise we'll have you quick. Run away and you'll burn long and sticky on the tower."

If Cole ran now they would hear his footsteps, but if he stayed put, his footprints would lead them right to him. It was far too early to engage. Varka's cape rustled on Cole's back, and before he new it the spell had already left his hands. The Wisdom came and went in a flash, imbued with a single ironclad rule. Every drop of water in Cole's armor evaporated in a cloud of cold steam. Just as he heard footsteps rounding the corner, Cole leapt into the air and grasped the footing of a third-floor balcony.

"What's all this then?" snarled the male voice. "Smells like that river muck."

"Quiet!" hissed the woman. "Did you feel it, just now? That was Wisdom."

Cole dangled from the balcony as the man walked through the cloud of steam hanging below. The man gave the vapor a curious prod. Cole's fingers began to slip, not because his grip waned, but because his munisica started to sharpen them into blades.

"*I have two priests right below me, though I can't tell which of The Three they serve,*" Cole said to the Unbound. "*Their robes are solid black and they're both bald as river rocks.*"

"*Those are Arch Priests,*" Valen replied. "*The Three place great value on Borla Dign to deploy them here.*"

Lileth's mind chimed in next. "*It is also possible that the Arch Priests are no longer needed on the Light Side, and so their entire force is now available to assault the Dark Side directly. Be careful, Cole. They are The Three's equivalent to us, well-versed in all dark magics. Do not attack unless you can end it quickly and quietly.*"

"*I'm not worried about these two,*" Cole said, glancing up at the sky. "*Can Corpulants smell Rage?*"

Eliza beamed her warning across the network, *"The Corpulants we know cannot, as they are minions of Decreath. But as for this flying variety, let's not chance it yet. Just wait for those priests to pass."*

"Fine," Cole said. His fingers returned to their normal state as he quelled his Rage.

The man below sniffed deeply. "There's something else here. Something sweet."

"Probably one of the Corpulants' leftovers," said the woman. "There were quite a few casualties during the invasion thanks to those bumbling fools in the Divine Guard. That experiment is turning out to be more trouble than it's worth. So far they've proved themselves no more than a bunch of incompetent children. I hope that smell is one of their hides."

The man scanned the alley. "No, it's sweeter than rot. I smell the whisperings of Passion. Fresh Passion. Someone's nearby." He caressed the wall with his thumb, then brought it to his nose. His eyes narrowed as he looked up at Cole's invisible body. "What is that?"

The woman shuffled closer, her hands now churning with a viscous cloud the color of an old bruise. Fear. "What's what? I don't see anything."

"That's because you're looking with your eyes, dolt," said the man. "There's someone up there. Call the Corpulants."

The woman smiled. She dismissed her Fear and brought a hand over her head, sending a bolt of emerald lightning up into the sky. A moment later, a tortured howl ripped through the air, multi-toned and hoarse, like a dozen old men screaming for death. Another howl came, closer than the first. Then another. The Corpulants answered their dinner bell in earnest.

Wind rushed through Cole's hair as he fell. He landed behind the two priests, though their eyes were still scanning the balcony. The man turned, alerted by the clap of bare feet on the metal surface. Hoping Valen's potion was still in effect, Cole kicked off the alley wall opposite, extended his arm and threw his whole body into a punch. His fist collided with the man's chin. There was a crunch of bone, then the man's feet left the ground and his head clopped against the wall, crumpling into a lifeless heap.

Cole clutched his hand, feeling his misplaced knuckles and broken skin. The priestess jumped back in alarm at her partner's unexplained collapse. Her face hardened as she surveyed the scene before her. Her eyes caught the blood dripping from Cole's hand, and she summoned the mottled purple gas back to her hands. Before she could launch the attack, Cole swung his leg around in a powerful kick, breaking her knee inwards. She fell to her good knee, her scream cut short as another invisible kick landed to the side of her neck. The Corpulants' moans neared, closing in from all directions.

There was no time to hide the bodies. Throwing caution to the wind, Cole healed his hand with a quick burst of Passion and he sprinted away from the scene. A cacophony of snapping wings and tortured howls filled the alley. Cole glanced back as he ran. Three Corpulants landed among the priests, shaking themselves like dogs as clumps of flies exploded from the flaps of skin hanging from their chests. They looked like insects wrapped in soggy human skin. Their hides were pale and hairless, their eyes lifeless black glass. They shuffled about on stout legs too short to lift their bellies off the ground, and so their bulging girth slid across the metal walkway, leaving glistening trails of sweat in their wake. One of the priests began to stir.

Cole slowed and stopped. He would have to kill the priests and the Corpulants quickly, and for that he would have to use magic. He turned, ready to unleash just enough Rage for the job, then slowed.

The priest rose to his feet, blood pouring from his nose and broken mouth. He muttered a command at the Corpulants, but his jaw was too mangled to articulate the words. Flies began to accumulate on his face. He swatted them away, now shouting his unintelligible commands. One Corpulant cocked its head, jiggling its curtains of loose neck skin as it took a curious step forward. The priest took a step back, conjuring a handful of blood-red fire.

The Corpulant spread its pale wings, uttering a hoarse wail of defiance. Two of its fellows took a step towards the priest, long spindly fingers twitching in anticipation. They would have their meal.

As if by command, the entire swarm of flies descended upon the priest. He whirled his Hatefire about, searing the cloud of insects before they could touch him. His eyes were ablaze with malice as he shouted insults through his broken jaw. He jabbed a flaming finger at the Corpulants as though aiming a gun.

The lead Corpulant stopped. Its purple lips quivered as though it were about to speak. Its brow knitted together and its lips parted as if to convey its apologies, but then its mouth opened wide like a fish and a shiny appendage launched itself at the priest, punching him in the chest. The Corpulant's tongue withdrew slowly, revealing a six-inch spike, its tip dripping with venom.

The priest looked from the hole in his chest to the monster before him. The Corpulant's shoulders shook as its spired hip bones flexed wider, creating space within its sagging abdomen. Hatefire flashed across the alley, piercing straight through the neck of the lead Corpulant, which fell in a flapping heap of skin and wings. Before the priest finished his attack, the remaining two Corpulants were upon him, lancing him over and over with their venomous tongues. Their howls of victory drew several more from the sky, who joined in on the feast.

Cole did not leave the alley until the Corpulants swallowed both the priests. He reported the event to the Unbound as he continued his search for targets.

"That explains why every Corpulant in the city just took off," Sitra grumbled. *"I Hate those things. You'd better get out of there, Cole."*

"I'm already gone," Cole replied.

"Were you seen?" Valen asked. *"Did the potion hold up?"*

"Your potion worked just fine," Cole reassured them all. *"It was just dumb luck. We should be in the clear now. As far as anyone else can tell, these Corpulants just had a disagreement with a couple priests. They should be done cleaning up the evidence now."*

"It's no coincidence that dumb luck followed you ashore," Eliza said. *"I just overheard a conversation between another pair of Arch Priests. They were expecting trouble from The Sill. Someone tipped them off."*

"Larkin." Cole said the name like a curse. *"I can't believe I trusted him! When we make it to Oberon Temple he and I are going to have a nice long, private talk."*

"*Do not judge him yet,*" Lileth said. "*We don't know if it was him, and if it was, his mind may not have been his own. No one man can resist the combined power of The Three.*"

"*Whatever, it doesn't matter now,*" Cole said. "*Let's hurry up before we end up facing the combined power of The Three.*"

The Unbound delved further into Borla Dign, finding no signs of its citizens. The Divine Guard patrolled the streets in squads, looting and yelling, their forms cast in a ghostly blue glow from the luminous trees spread throughout the city. Unlike the Arch Priests, they seemed immature and impulsive, as if they were far younger than they appeared. While there had been no chatter about the deaths of the two priests in the alley, their enemies now seemed extra vigilant in their patrols, eyes often flicking to the sky.

Just when Cole began to doubt the validity of the Devotion, he stepped in something warm and slick. There was a small puddle of ruddy orange liquid in the middle of Borla Dign's commercial district. Bending low, he dabbed the substance with an invisible finger and brought it to his nostrils. The metallic scent burned his nose and stung his eyes. Odium. A trail of orange droplets led away from the puddle, straight to the massive double doors of a warehouse.

"*Larkin was right about the Devotion,*" Cole said. "*I think I just found the odium.*" He flashed an image of the warehouse across the Passion network. "*I'm going in now.*"

"*Do you need assistance?*" Lileth asked, her voice laden with concern.

"*No, not yet at least,*" Cole replied. "*Keep searching for the Chosen and the tower. If the Devotion hasn't started then the Chosen might be locked up somewhere, and the tower might not be built yet. If nothing else we'll take care of the Corpulants and the Arch Priests before we leave.*"

"*Now you're singing my tune,*" Sitra said, flooding the network with her battle lust.

"*The effect of the potion will expire soon,*" Valen said. "*I suggest we act as though it already has. Stick to the shadows and stay out of the open.*"

Even as Valen said it, Cole felt the return of the cold, tingling sensation. He trotted around the warehouse, sneaking between a loading dock and a small storage shed. His hands and feet were now opaque, the glittery wave traveling back over his limbs and torso as the potion wore off entirely. After scanning the skies and the immediate area, Cole hopped up onto the loading dock and pressed his hand into the liquid stone cargo door. It was unlocked. He pushed himself through as slowly as possible, emerging on the other side with a tiny pop.

There was a single open room stretching from wall to wall. Shelves full of barrels were stacked to the four-story ceiling, where convex glass skylights bent Oberon's rainbow glow throughout the place. The stench of odium was thick enough where Cole didn't have to guess the contents of the barrels. He sneaked further in, crouching through the shadows. An odd feeling told him there was something besides odium hidden within the warehouse walls.

"I found the Chosen!" Eliza said, relaying an image of a tall building with evenly spaced glass windows and neon signs. *"There's a hotel near the center of Borla Dign. The roof is covered in Corpulants and Arch Priests are guarding every entrance, but I can see people through the windows. They don't seem to be in any danger at the moment. Valen's potion wore off so I can't get a closer look, but it seems as if Borla Dign's citizens have yet to be Chosen."*

"How can you tell?" Valen asked.

Eliza contemplated for a moment before responding. *"None of them bear the burn mark of the Chosen, and they seem too composed. Chosen typically give in to gratuitous debauchery, or are otherwise too despondent to move. I cannot risk inspecting them with Passion, but I believe these people are whole."*

"Success at last," Valen said. *"That is enough targets to work with. We know where the priests are, the would-be Chosen, and now the odium. How much is in that warehouse? Cole?"*

Cole had been too busy listening for danger to pay attention to the rest of the Unbound. *"Sorry, yes. The odium is here. All of it."* He inched his way deeper into the columns of shelves. He could have sworn he heard someone whispering his name.

"*Are you feeling well?*" Valen asked. "*You seem unusually preoccupied.*"

"*I'm fine,*" Cole said, injecting authority into his words. Apparently Valen thought it acceptable to question the leader of the Unbound. "*Everyone return to the outskirts of the city. I want you to pick off any priests out on patrol, then work your way to the hotel. Don't get caught. I'll meet you there after I take care of the odium.*"

An awkward silence followed. Sitra was first to speak. "*But we're already by the hotel. There's a nice choke point nearby, right in the city center. I could plant one of my fulminators there and take out every priest in the city when they come running. We only need to lure them there. Eliza's Passion would draw them in like—*"

"*Enough, Sitra!*" Cole ordered. "*Your job is to obey orders, not make up your own when you've got a chance to show off. I don't care how hard you worked on those stupid bombs, you're not blowing anything up until I say so. Now do your job, or do I need to remind you why I'm the one in charge?*"

Sitra's enthusiasm flattened at once. "*Nope. Whatever you say, boss.*"

Without another word, the Unbound departed for the shores of Borla Dign. Cole felt them twisting a separate Passion network, excluding him from their whining and sniping. Who were they to question him? It was he, Cole Carter, leader of the Unbound, Master of Passion and Rage, who had saved all their hides from Sorronis. None of them had ever been on a mission of this scale without help. In Costas there were dozens of other strike teams sharing the burden, but when Cole went to Brimhallow he went alone, without help. They had no idea what it took to survive and succeed. How arrogant could they be to question him in the middle of a mission?

Cole considered breaking into their minds to see exactly what they were saying about him, but something inside the warehouse drew his attention away from his subordinates. A sensation of familiarity blossomed alongside his curiosity, giving him the feeling that he'd been here before. His confidence swelled with every step as he delved deeper into the warehouse. The glass domes in the ceiling slowly dimmed as a cloud passed overhead. The shelves were so full and tall they blocked what little light did make it through. He heard the whisper for sure this time, begging or perhaps promising, or was it just in his head? He knew from his lessons with Chiron that in the absence of sensory input, the mind was liable to create its own auditory and visual hallucinations. But this was too palpable, too enticing to be of his own design.

It was almost too dark to see now. Cole longed to call Wisdom into his eyes and ears, but there were far too many Corpulants skulking about for such foolishness. Instead he used his hands, running them along the shelves, feeling the rough wooden slats and the cool metal bands of the odium kegs. He was certain he'd been here before, just as certain as he knew he was no longer alone. Varka had been here. Borla Dign was his birthplace, his home, where he'd first learned about life and love, about tragedy and beauty, all within this little island city. Cole felt as though Varka now walked right beside him, and he too felt at home.

A light came into Cole's periphery. An open door presented itself to him, luring him out of the darkness and into the warmth of Oberon's grace. Excitement trilled in Cole's heart, in Varka's heart. Their home was just outside, not a few doors down the lane. Varka ran as fast as he could, but like all sweet dreams his limbs moved far too slowly, as though the world itself had been slowed by the weight of the moment. He was going home.

Varka crossed the threshold, emerging into a courtyard lined with pergolas wrapped with black hyacinths and ivory vines. Children too young for school chased glow bugs around the fountain while their parents hollered their half-hearted admonitions. A moonbeam owl soared overhead like a passing comet, silent in its search for its next lofty perch. Varka was so enamored with nostalgia that he nearly forgot what he came here for. How long had it been since he left?

Trotting down the lane, Varka laid eyes upon the house of his parents. Welcome lights beamed through the open windows. His sister's playthings lay strewn about the front yard, as if she'd been called to dinner before she had a chance to put them away. The neatly trimmed hedgerows blossomed fresh hyacinths at his approach, welcoming him back home. As Varka threw open the iron gates, time tripped over itself, doubling, then tripling to catch up as his heart thrummed faster and faster. He was going home.

With a joyful leap Varka cleared the front steps, laughing and crying as he pushed his way through the front door. He popped through the other side, filling his lungs in preparation to announce his return. A horrendous stench filled his mouth, clutching his breath in his throat. It was the smell of blood, of excrement, of Fear.

"Surprise, Human," said a malicious voice.

Cole blinked, unable to draw breath. Habbad stood before him in the atrium of what appeared to be a ransacked mansion. The Underkin was as tall as he was, and holding something to Cole's chest. Befuddled, Cole glanced down and saw a shard of something black and jagged sticking out of his breast.

"You made this way too easy," Habbad said with a dark smile.

CHAPTER 14

PHANTOM PAIN

C ole reached for the blade with a trembling hand. It looked like smoke condensed to solid form. If not for the pain shooting throughout his body, he would have thought it some sort of phantom or perhaps an errant shadow.

"I wouldn't touch that if I were you," Habbad said, withdrawing his own hand and stepping back, admiring Cole with a smug look. "Don't worry, it's not a pithing shard, though I Hunger for the day I can make one for you. It's just one of Decreath's little gifts. How does it feel?"

Cole's tongue tried to wriggle out a word, but the air was trapped in his chest, held in place by what felt like a thousand rusty nails. All too late he recognized the Fear spreading through his veins, its venom ushered along by the wails of his shrieking heart. He couldn't move.

Habbad walked around him in slow circles. "Go ahead then, call for help. Use your Passion."

The mere thought of luring his friends into Habbad's trap sent tickling dread up Cole's back. Sweat accumulated on his exposed skin, flash-freezing to little beads of ice. The fog of his breath puffed up around his nose. An overwhelming anticipation welled up and around him, the promise of nightmares yet to break over him. What had he done?

"No Passion? Then why not use your Rage?" Habbad asked in a tone of mock concern. "Have you forgotten Master Roth's lessons so soon? Go ahead, let the monster loose. Kill me, before I kill you and everyone you love."

Habbad's words shed light through Cole's Fear, revealing his stores of red magic. The Rage struggled against its shackles, longing and blood-blind, demanding its payment in unrestrained violence. Cole buried the power beneath himself, leaving an unsatisfied hollow in its place.

"You've grown," Habbad said. The Hunger in his eyes smoldered with disappointment. "Unfortunately for you, so have I."

With a flash of green Wisdom, Habbad knocked Cole flat on his back. He gripped Cole's ankle and dragged him through the house. Cole watched the ceiling pass by as the Underkin pulled him along like a corpse. He tried calling his own Wisdom to his aid, but every time he reached for it, Habbad's Fear jolted through him, jarring his rationality with maddening terror. He began to imagine his own torture, a symphony of agony conducted by Habbad, his old friend. The once-diminutive Underkin now wielded unknown proficiency with the dark magics, enough to leave Cole crippled and helpless. The only limit to Cole's suffering would be Habbad's imagination.

The unmistakable scent of gore rushed into Cole's nose. He slid to a halt on a wet floor. Something warm soaked into his hair and armor. The smell told Cole it was blood.

"Do you recognize this place?" Habbad asked. "Look around. Take it in."

The Fear relented just enough for Cole to regain control of his head and eyes. At first he thought there was a mirror on the ceiling, reflecting his sprawled body back at him, but as his eyes focused he realized it was something much worse. The skin of some unknown person had been tacked to the ceiling. Its hands and feet dangled like empty gloves. Its torso and limbs were unmarred, other than the bent nails that held the pale canvas in place. The face stared into Cole like a crude mask, distorted and stretched flat with a mat of shiny black hair. Dark blood dripped from the eye holes, smacking Cole in the mouth before he had a chance to close his lips. Habbad allowed him several minutes to appreciate the gruesome sight.

"W-what have you done?" Cole managed.

Habbad stood over him. "I tricked you, trapped you, and paralyzed you. The Corpulant did the decorating for you, or for Varka I should say. This was Varka's home."

Even as Habbad said it, Cole felt memories that were not his own swim to the fore of his thoughts. They were the nightmares of another life, of Varka's youth. His vision began to blend with Varka's recollections. Screams echoed in his ears. People ran for the lives. He had to find his family, needed to make sure they had escaped. Cole jerked, forcing himself back to the present. He lifted his head. Habbad was now across the room, standing beside a robed Corpulant, which was busy feasting on what could only be the insides of the person whose skin dripped from the ceiling.

Fresh Fear tickled Cole's insides. "Is that what you're going to do to me?"

Habbad scooped something off the ground. He walked back to Cole, cradling it carefully between his hands. He loomed over Cole, clutching a portion of broken skull like a bowl of soup. "No, though you deserve far worse after what happened to Lexy. My job is to get Varka ready for The Three when they arrive. This is a Devotion after all, but Borla Dign's citizens are only the appetizer. The Three will have you and Varka, and I will be rewarded at last."

Cole's mind raced, incoherent with terror. He tried with all his might, but his legs and arms remained as immobile as the empty mask staring down at him. Desperate, he resorted to his Rage, but couldn't remember where he'd left it. The sound of his heartbeat sloshing in his eardrums dominated his senses. He couldn't recall what Habbad had just said. The Fear had consumed the words of the Underkin before Cole could consider them. It anchored Cole to the razor's edge of the moment, overwhelmed him with the finality of his doom. But there was something important in Habbad's words, something that gave Cole hope. Cole opened his mouth to speak, to beg, but Habbad's evil smirk stopped him dead.

"Enough talk. Come Varka, embrace your shame." Habbad tipped the skull forward, pouring hot crimson blood onto Cole's face.

Cole lay paralyzed as the blood of the dead filled his mouth with a coppery tang. His throat constricted upon itself, but it was too late. The fluid splashed into his lungs, drowning him from the inside out. He fought for air, but his throat remained clenched, as though determined to prolong his torment. Seconds burned by. Black stars fell like snow before his eyes. Varka's memories battered through his fading vision, drawing him to another life from long ago.

There they were, piled up in the atrium like discarded meat. A mist of blood and agony hung in the air, thick and pungent. Varka could taste them. His sister's tiny dress lay scattered about, torn to pieces by vicious hands. His Father watched their suffering from the ceiling, his skin tacked to the plaster in some perverse tapestry. The bigger pieces could only have belonged to his mother. Every detail took a lifetime to run through Varka's mind, so long that he noticed all too late the other people in the room. They wore cloaks with strange markings and reeked of wrong magic. Each cradled smaller versions of the monsters that tormented the people out in the streets, encouraging the beasts to feed on the bits of flesh chopped about the room.

"NOO!" Cole's scream reverberated through the house. Blood erupted from his mouth like a fountain. He pulled himself from Varka's memories, though the present moment granted him no solace. He screamed again.

"I hope it hurts," Habbad said, hovering a gnarled hand above the black shard in Cole's chest. "I hope you die a thousand times before this is done. A death for every moment of her suffering."

Cole gathered his remaining strength, to say the thing that might save his life, but only managed to utter a single word. "Lexy…"

"You dare!" Habbad twisted his hand. Another smoky blade appeared between his fingers. He gripped it, then thrust it into Cole's chest next to the first. "You dare say her name!" He removed the blade, then drove it back down, again and again, each stab jolting Cole with maddening Fear.

Darkness crept in from the edges of Cole's vision. He couldn't tell if he was fainting or dying, but either way the pain and Fear began to give way to sweet nothingness.

"Oh no you don't," Habbad gasped. His hair was slick with sweat and stuck to his forehead in shiny strands. He removed the ethereal blades from Cole's flesh and threw them against the wall, where they splashed harmlessly in puffs of smoke. "You're going to be lucid for this, Human. I don't give a damn what The Three have planned for Varka, I'm going to take my payment from you, right here and now."

With one hand, Habbad gripped the front of Cole's armor and hoisted him into the air. His other hand stretched and creaked into a fan of ruby-red blades. The munisica of Hatred.

With the phantom daggers gone, Cole regained enough clarity to realize what was about to happen, but the paralyzing effects of the Fear had yet to wear off. His limbs dangled uselessly as Habbad brought the claw to his face. A ruby blade poked through the skin on his cheekbone with a sharp snap. The flesh beneath sizzled and popped, seared by the Hatred. A low moan fluttered from Cole's lips. Then, with indulgent slowness, Habbad dragged the claw down Cole's cheek, splitting the skin like an overcooked sausage. Cole felt his scream escape through the burning gash in the side of his mouth. His training had desensitized him to the pain of far worse wounds; however, the Hatred seemed to amplify the agony one hundred fold, as if augmented by Habbad's own malice.

"Don't scream your throat out yet, we've still got days and days before The Three arrive. Just you and me, friend." Habbad brought his ruby munisica to Cole's other cheek.

With a supreme effort of will, Cole corralled his Fear and looked the Underkin in the eye. "Habbad, listen to me. Lexy is alive. She is no longer Chosen."

The wicked mirth melted from Habbad's face as his brow contorted. The Hatred returned with a twitch as he bared his teeth. "I think I'll cut your tongue out next."

"No, it's true!" Cole gasped. "I'm not lying. Go through my memories, see it for yourself!"

Habbad's eyes narrowed. "Even if I could use your wretched Passion, I already know you are a master of the lover's magic. Do you think me foolish enough to hand myself over so easily?"

"Then use *your* magic," Cole pleaded. "Use Fear, use Hunger, there has to be something. I swear on her life she's whole. Please Habbad, it's not over. There's still hope for all of us."

"Don't! Don't you..." Habbad's words faded as his eyes fell to the ground, searching for an answer. Fury mixed with desperate yearning, painted his face in a twisted grimace. The expression drained as if he'd pulled a plug, then he locked eyes with Cole. "You want me to see your memories? You desire this above all else?"

Cole felt the Hunger snaking about the edges of his mind, and immediately regretted his suggestion. He closed his eyes and whispered, "Yes."

Habbad's voice took on a charming, rich tone unlike anything Cole had ever heard, as if Habbad's tongue had been gilded and polished. "The deepest wish of your heart is a rare treasure, which I shall grant, but only if you pay my price. You must surrender yourself to me in exchange for this, your ultimate desire. Will you submit?"

Doubts mingled with Cole's hope. It was his only chance. "Yes," he breathed.

Ravenous and foreign, Habbad's Hunger tunneled through Cole's mind like a starving mole. To Cole's surprise, Habbad started with the memories of Cole's arrival, when they first met on the woodland trail outside Costas. Habbad paid close attention to the minutia of Lexy's enthusiasm. It was as if every moment not spent humming her song and twirling her dance was a moment wasted in her eyes. Lexy was first to reach him in Kreed's palace, calling him *naked one*. Cole never would have guessed such a relentlessly joyful creature had ever experienced true suffering. Habbad gave a cursory effort with the memories after Lexy became Chosen, but when he reached the Fangshard Valley he panned through every detail with utmost care. He felt Cole's Passion swell as it agonized over Lexy's tortured form, then reveled in Cole's relief as he escaped the Valley with Lexy in hand. Habbad then rushed to Cole's return to The Sill, playing and replaying Cole's memory of freeing Lexy. He scoured Cole's thoughts and intentions, poring over details that Cole didn't even recall, as though determined to catch him in a lie. When he reached Cole's most recent visit with Lexy, Habbad's Hunger seemed to falter, replaced by something too painful to hold.

The world spun to a stop as Cole fell from Habbad's eyes, returning to the room painted with gore. Tears chased each other through the web of wrinkles sprawled about Habbad's face. Cole felt the Underkin's iron grip loosen from the front of his armor. He fell, landing sloppily on his feet. Habbad made no move whatsoever, though the Corpulant behind him nosed its way closer, eager for a fresh meal.

Habbad's face was devoid of all color and expression, as if all purpose in life had just fled from him. He spoke in a voice barely higher than a whisper. "Go. I am done here."

Confused, Cole inspected himself. There was no trace of damage from the smoky daggers, nor did his chest feel wounded. The gash on his face shocked him like lightning, but he was otherwise fine. His Wisdom, Rage, and Passion all came rushing back to him, just as strong and reliable as ever.

Cole hardened the defenses around his mind, then donned every protective spell he could think of, including the shroud of his Master's Rage. He wouldn't be caught off guard again. "She misses you. If we could free her then I know we could free you too. We've learned much since you left. Join us, Habbad. Be Lexy's brother again."

Habbad showed no reaction to Cole's shroud, nor his words. At last he spoke. "The Three have no hold on me. I am in their service by my own choice. Lexy might be whole, but if she saw what I have become, knew what I have done, it would destroy her. No, I cannot return to my past life. I am too far gone."

"You know I can't just let you go," Cole said.

"You can't stop me," Habbad sighed. With a lazy twirl of his hand, the floor around him bubbled, producing a slick puddle of dark liquid. He jumped into the puddle, vanishing to depths unknown. Habbad was gone.

Cole swore. The Corpulant moaned as it shuffled its way across the room, reaching with its pale stick fingers. Flies shook from its robes with every step. They swarmed over Cole, battering fruitlessly against his shroud. Emerald light blazed in Cole's bladed hand as Varka's cape rippled across his back. The Corpulant stumbled and tripped, but instead of falling it floated gently into the air, as if carried by an invisible hook. Its robes stretched tight across its frail arms and fat belly. The monster bellowed in pain, then fell silent as its form crumpled in on itself, condensing to a ball the size of a rucksack. Bones snapped with muffled pops and a sound like stretching rope. With another flick of Wisdom, Cole shot the balled-up Corpulant through the air, smashing it through the liquid stone door. As soon as he stepped through the threshold to the outside, Cole felt the minds of the Unbound pop back into his awareness. Their life candles had somehow been masked while he was inside the house.

Lileth's mind wailed into his own. *"Cole! What happened to you?"*

Cole centered himself and reconnected with their Passion network. *"I fell for a trap. A stupid one too. What's going on?"*

"We circled around the outskirts of the city like you ordered," Valen said. *"We managed to ambush and eliminate a good number before triggering an alarm. These Arch Priests are more capable enemies than we are accustomed to, but fortunately the same is true for us."*

Guilt splashed against Cole's heart. *"Is anyone hurt?"* he asked.

Sitra lashed at him. *"Every damn one of us got hit thanks to your orders, oh wise leader. We're not used to facing this kind of magic. They all use that red shroud Talin had, and it burns right through ours. If not for Eliza's Passion and dumb luck we'd all be dead right now."*

"I'm so sorry," Cole said. *"To all of you. I think Habbad's Hunger was already in my head when I gave that order. I should have recognized it."*

"Wait a moment, Habbad's here?" Valen asked. *"I thought the Underkin died in Fangshard Valley?"*

Cole sent them a sliver of his recent memories. *"He's alive, but he's not here anymore. Where are you all now?"*

Eliza's mind strummed into his own, familiar and warm. *"We are back at the hotel. The Divine Guard retreated, but we believe they're only regrouping. We were waiting for you before we attempted to free Borla Dign's citizens."*

"I'll be right there," Cole said.

Lileth's mind washed over him, breathing her Passion into him as she spoke. *"Hurry."*

Varka's cape snapped to clear crystal as the air exploded around Cole. He tore through the sky as fast as his Wisdom would carry him, shattering the windows below as he flew. The hotel came into view within seconds. Cole slowed, then rendered himself invisible so he wouldn't give away the position of the Unbound. Fortunately there were no Corpulants flying about to sense his blatant use of Wisdom.

"Took you long enough," Sitra grumbled as Cole's invisible munisica clicked on the metal-paved sidewalk. "Did you even kill anything on your way over?"

"I missed you too, Sitra," Cole said. He dismissed his invisibility spell, as well as the shroud. His cheek stung. He clapped a hand to it, fingering the wide-open gash left by Habbad's ruby munisica. "Damn," Cole hissed. "The shroud usually heals stuff like this."

"Not when the wound was caused by Hatred," Eliza said. She rolled her sleeves as she approached Cole with her hands aglow with fuchsia Passion.

"Excuse me." Lileth shouldered her way past Eliza, then placed a rosy palm against Cole's cheek. Eliza faltered and withdrew as the light of her own Passion dimmed. "I've already proven I'm best suited to heal Cole's injuries." Lileth's eyes reddened and her jaw trembled as she worked on the wound. She looked as though she were on the brink of cracking into a sobbing mess.

The pain lifted from Cole's gash as the familiar itch of accelerated healing tingled across his face. The most relieving sensation of all was Lileth's touch. The way she gazed at him made Cole feel as if he were the best version of himself that he could ever find. The world could end right this very moment and he would die content and without regret. All too soon Lileth finished, and her Passion vanished, leaving him with a lingering longing for her.

"Not even Passion can fully heal the wounds of such brutal magic," Lileth said, cupping his cheek. Her fingers ran over something new on Cole's face. "I think it makes you look even more handsome." She then gripped Cole's wrist and brought his hand to the wound.

There was a strip of something dead and hard attached to Cole's face. It was smooth and straight, like a thin, rubbery snake, stretching from his cheekbone to the tip of his chin. Varka's cape nudged his curiosity and he conjured a small mirror into his free hand. Cole peered at his reflection and beheld a white scar, a mark he would carry until the end of his days.

"You're beautiful enough for the both of us anyway," Cole said, pulling Lileth into a snug embrace. "I'm glad you're safe."

"And I'm glad you're still with me," Lileth whispered as she kissed him on the scar.

"Oh don't mind us," Sitra interrupted in a boorish tone. "We're only waiting on you to finish canoodling so we can fight a small army and liberate an entire city. Please, take your time licking each other's faces, we're in no hurry."

The Unbound conjured their emerald wings and took to the sky. As they had in Fangshard Valley, they cloaked themselves in fire to keep the Corpulants' flies from stinging them. The Corpulants, however, seemed to be intentionally keeping their distance, flapping in a wide circle a quarter mile around them, as if waiting for something. Cole and Eliza stretched their awareness out as far as they could, but their Passion revealed no sign of the priests, Divine Guard, nor even the visible Corpulants. The dark magics shielded them from their mind's eye.

"We cannot rescue the citizens until we eliminate the threats," Valen noted. *"Our enemies will certainly use them against us."*

"Whatever we do needs to happen soon," Sitra said. *"Every second we wait brings The Three closer. That's if they're not here already. Let's just go down there and save who we can."*

Sitra had a point, but he also wasn't eager to put innocent lives at risk, not if there was some way to avoid it. *"Sitra's right. If there's a trap we'll just have to trigger it. We can't wait any longer."*

"Wait, that has to be it!" Valen's excitement beamed through the network. *"There is obviously a trap, and they expect us to fall for it, but they do not expect us to expect it."*

"What are you saying?" Cole asked.

"I am saying we walk right up the front steps and trigger the ambush," Valen said, his Rage flaring hotter with every word. *"We know their magic, and how to defend against it. Eliza, can you maintain a Passion shield like Alvani used in Fangshard Valley?"*

"It's called an aura, but yes I can," Eliza replied. *"Cole is capable as well."*

"Perfect," Valen said.

They discussed their plan in flight, landing in the middle of a decadent marble courtyard in front of the hotel's main entrance. Dead fish floated in the ponds on either side. Towering ferns leaned heavily on their sides, their leaves yellowing and reaching for the wilted hedges. Around the courtyard stood several tall commercial buildings, each lined with shadowy tunnels and alleys throughout their footings, too many avenues of approach to count. Soot-stained windows gazed down upon them like the black eyes of a Corpulant.

The Unbound climbed the front steps, deliberate and cautious, each maintaining his or her portion of their protective spells. Cole and Sitra trailed behind the others, just beyond the reach of Eliza's aura, munisica bared and eyes wide. The courtyard was deadly quiet. The only sound to be heard was the steady hum of their spells and the distant bubbling of the water jets in the ponds. Eliza, Sitra, and Valen halted before an array of towering liquid stone doors, each twice as wide as a person and framed with bands of plated steel.

"Should we knock?" Lileth asked.

"Are you a warrior or not?" Sitra hollered over her shoulder. "Kick the damned doors in!"

Lileth sighed, then raised a hand to the middlemost door. There was a flash of emerald light, then all sound in the courtyard seemed to have been sucked into a single point. Barely a second later, a violent explosion rocked the face of the hotel, jarring the heavy metal steps beneath their feet. They flinched, stunned by the blast, then beheld the destruction. All seven doors were gone, as well as their frames and a portion of wall several feet around them. Peering through the dust, they saw large chunks of the missing material scattered throughout swaths of devastation that carried deep into the first floor.

Valen huffed. "That was reckless, Lileth. You could have killed civilians."

"I sensed no life forms in the immediate area," Lileth said in an offhand manner.

"Still, you ought to exercise some restraint. There's no telling—" Valen's words were cut off by Eliza, who gasped as she pointed up at the sky.

"Corpulants!" Eliza shouted.

Hundreds of winged Corpulants cascaded from the roof like a grotesque waterfall of pale flesh and snapping wings. Their tortured howls reverberated throughout the courtyard, deafening and mortifying in such numbers. Shining yellow horns protruded from the gap in their maws, begging to be buried in tender flesh. Valen and Lileth wove their arms in wide arches as they reinforced Eliza's aura with layers of Wisdom, but Sitra and Cole were still at the bottom of the steps, well outside their shield. The Corpulants crashed over the dome of protective magic, bouncing off as if it were made of Morthainian glass. The swarm flowed around them, almost like a liquid, pouring down the steps by the hundreds.

Cole and Sitra were paralyzed in silent terror, their munisica hanging uselessly by their sides. There was a cacophony of scrabbling wings as every Corpulant amassed upon the two warriors, forming a mountain of hobbled flesh two stories high.

"Looks like they took the bait," Cole said to Sitra as they hovered safely a mile above Borla Dign. They watched in disgust as the Corpulants engulfed the phantom Cole and Sitra on the steps below. "Valen's illusions were inaccurate though. The real you is way uglier."

Sitra flashed him a toothy grin and punched Cole in the gut with the back of her munisica. "And the *real you* is way slower. Race you to glory?" She folded her emerald wings and tipped into a dive.

Cole chuckled through a moan as he rubbed his belly. Varka's cape tuned his Wisdom to the perfect pitch as he plummeted after Sitra, catching up to her in a few seconds of howling wind and rippling cloth. As they tore through the sky like two falling stars, Cole zoomed his vision toward the mound of Corpulants, noticing a sudden shift in their churning.

"They're about to disperse!" Cole said into Sitra's mind.

"Our timing's off! I told you we shouldn't have flown so high," Sitra scolded.

Cole ground his teeth in concentration. *"Brace yourself!"*

Sitra's reply gave way to a grunt as Cole's spell hit her, accelerating her faster than the speed of sound. A shockwave of vapor exploded around her and she shrank to a tiny speck in Cole's vision. He surged after her, terrified he'd just plunged her to a violent death, but a second later he saw a pair of emerald wings unfold above the pile of Corpulants, then a brilliant flash of light as her fulminator ignited. A sphere of blinding cobalt energy veined with tongues of orange flame filled the courtyard. The chaos subsided as the fulminator's wrath dissipated. The ponds, hedges, and metal-paved walkways were gone, and in their place was a neat crater. Cole double-checked the life candles of the Unbound, finding them shaken but safe. Not a single Corpulant had survived the blast.

Cole joined Sitra and the others atop the stairs. Flaming bits of fern trees fell gently around them like an amber snow. Eliza and Lileth panted and sagged with exhaustion. Their spells had taken the brunt of the blast. Valen had a line of blood coming from each of his ears. He placed a bead of magenta Passion into each ear, then turned his head side to side as he worked his jaw open and shut.

"I neglected to remove my hearing spells before the blast." Valen said, placing another marble of Passion into each ear. "My eardrums tore themselves to shreds. It appears you got them all, however. Well done, Sitra."

"I told you the fulminators would work," Sitra said with a proud nod.

"That they did," agreed Eliza. "And what's more, the shockwave caused the nearby priests to fumble their spells of concealment. Cole, did you sense them?"

"I counted eleven," Cole said, scanning the buildings across the courtyard. The tinted glass in their windows had been blown out, though the darkness within still hid their enemies.

"As did I," Eliza said. "Sitra, would you be so kind as to invite our friends out to play?"

Sitra gave a dramatic bow, folding her emerald wings around her in a dignified manner. "Why, it would be my pleasure, good lady. She spun on the spot and took flight in a whirlwind of charred fern leaves. She hovered halfway between the hotel and the buildings where the enemy life candles were last detected, then spoke in a magically amplified voice. "We know you're in there. Come out and die in battle, or keep hiding and die like cowards. I've got enough explosives to level half the district and I don't feel like carrying them back, so you'd better make up your minds." Sitra didn't bother waiting for an answer before reaching a hand into her rucksack, pulling out a sizeable crimson fulminator. *"Which building has the most?"* she asked, directing the question to Cole and Eliza.

"The one on your right," Eliza said.

Sitra flapped her emerald wings three times and rose even higher, then shot for a three-tiered office building on the far side of the square. She hurled the fulminator like a bullet, sending it straight through a shattered window in the middle. She cut back up to the sky, then another explosion shook the metal streets. Crimson light poured from the darkened windows as the building leapt a yard into the air. It disintegrated like a sand castle as it settled back to the ground in a heap of wreckage.

As Sitra looped back around, something violet shot out of the broken windows of another building, whistling through the air as it flew for Sitra.

"Sitra!" Valen cried into her mind.

"I see it," Sitra replied in a fierce tone. She twirled in the air, dodging what looked like a dozen violet needles. *"I think our friends are joining us at last."*

"Finally," Eliza said. Sprinting forward, she leapt twenty feet into the air, conjuring her emerald wings as she took flight.

Lileth and Valen shot after her. Cole was about to follow, then paused as he saw a flicker of movement across the square. Seven figures in dark robes emerged from the remaining buildings. Moving fast as shadows on the wind, they drew their ruby munisica and readied other evil magics. All seven pairs of eyes were focused on the Unbound in the air. They would never see an attack coming from the ground. Cole relayed his intentions to the others, then drew his master's shroud and sprinted as fast as he could, his bladed feet gouging the metal pavement as he ran.

Lileth responded with a flashy display of lightning, raining bolts of electricity down upon the metal street. One Arch Priest negated the torrent with a wave of sickly purple Fear. The electricity fizzled and faded before reaching its target, but the job was done.

The Arch Priests were running full tilt, but to Cole they appeared to be standing still. He lunged at one of the cloaked figures. A female voice grunted as their bodies collided, tumbling together in a mess of limbs. Cole held on tightly as they rolled, feeling the muffled cracks of her breaking body as they tumbled. Her weakness fueled his Rage even further. The red magic continued to slow things for him, and when the time was right, he righted himself and kicked off her torso with the force of a cannon blast. He felt her life candle fizzle and vanish as the void consumed her.

While he flipped to his feet, something hot and painful seared across the back of his neck, then a bladed ruby claw whipped across his field of view. Varka's cape seemed to react for him, commandeering his Wisdom and sailing him away from the danger. His back smashed into the side of a building, buckling the metal wall around him. The priestess he tackled lay lifeless in the street while five of her comrades fired magic at the Unbound in the air. There was a thundering of heavy feet as a tall figure charged at him like a rampaging Domina. Cole's Rage purred. Finally, a worthy opponent.

The man trotted to a stop ten paces away, sneering with Hunger in his eyes. Cole knew this was no priest, but a member of the Divine Guard. He was head and shoulders taller than Cole and appeared to be enormously obese, or else harboring several people under his robes. His arms and body were concealed by a vast fur cloak, which Cole only now realized was made from hundreds of Aenerian scalps, some of which still oozed with dark blood. A ruby munisica emerged from the hairy folds. The man gripped the cloak and cast it aside, where it fell to the sidewalk with a wet slap.

Cole nearly dropped hold of his Rage.

The Divine Guardian was no giant. He was encased within a suit of armor comprised of countless Chosen, giving him the appearance of a miniature Colossus. The armor propped him up to nearly twice his height. Wrapped around his arms and legs were the hobbled limbs of his victims, and plated around his body was a cage of charred flesh, black and smoking, ribs still quivering for air. Every piece of the grisly armor of the Chosen had a sheen to it, as if the flesh and bone had been glazed in amber.

One of the man's hands was a munisica twice the size of Cole's. Each bladed finger was the length of his arm and growing longer by the second. He reached behind his back with his other hand and produced a shield nearly as tall as he was. Cole's heart stung as he beheld the naked bodies of seven Aenerian children, each asleep and banded to the shield with spiked wire. Cole's Passion revealed that they had yet to be Chosen; however, their injuries were so gruesome he was sure something else was sustaining them. He also sensed the harsh edges of their dreams, nightmares no child should be capable of having.

"Lay your shield down and I'll give you a quick death," Cole said, his voice a fiery wind. He thought he felt something roll down his shrouded cheek, but dared not check.

The Divine Guardian rolled his tongue along the inside of his lips. "Don't tell me the great leader of the Unbound is afraid of kiddies. They're the softest things, and though their blood be thin it's all the sweeter for it. Fear not the child, human. Fear *for* the child." The man tapped his ruby munisica along the brim of his shield. The spiked wire tightened, digging and tearing its way deeper into the pink flesh. The children woke to the sound of their own screams.

Cole ground his teeth as desperation mingled with his Rage. Action took hold of him at last. He began in a slow circle, his bladed feet clicking over the metal street. The man followed with sharp eyes and a wicked smile, hoisting and slamming his shield to keep it in between him and Cole, eliciting fresh agony from his victims with every thud. The screams of the children tore through Cole as they strained against their bonds. He wanted nothing more than to help them, to free them from the pain, but one wrong move would surely be fatal for both them and himself. He must be smart. Now was not the time for a fragile heart.

Cole continued around, studying the Divine Guardian's every move, watching and waiting for any sign of weakness. There was none to be found. "I just figured out what you are," he said in as carefree a voice as he could muster.

"Oh did you now?" he replied. He took a step closer to Cole, then another. His bladed fingers were each now as long as a spear.

228

Cole moved away to maintain his distance. "You're a coward of course, that's why you use children to protect yourself. But that's no surprise, really. The Three rely upon others for their power, so it's natural for you to do the same. I am a bit surprised at how stupid you are, however. If this is what I can expect from the infamous Divine Guard, then The Three have disappointed me."

"But we haven't even begun our dance," he said. He hoisted his shield once more, slamming it with deliberate force against the metal street to face Cole. "Don't judge me too soon. The kiddies haven't sung my favorite song for you yet."

Cole quickened his pace, feeling his Rage tugging against its restraints. "That's the disappointing part. You think I'm going to hold back for the sake of a few mangled children. This war is much bigger than that—even you, as stupid as you are must know that. Those kids would probably welcome death with open arms."

Fury twitched at the corners of the priest's mouth, twisting it into a snarl. "Come give it to them then!" He lifted the shield to face Cole once more, raising it higher than ever, and Cole saw his opportunity.

Cole broke into a dead sprint. His Rage finally unleashed, time slowed for him, revealing every detail of what needed to be done. He aimed for the gap under the shield, which was now large enough for him to fit under. It seemed to take seconds for him to close the distance to his enemy, though his heart had yet to complete a full beat. The shield had started its descent, but he had plenty of time, plenty of room.

In his eagerness, the Guardian had made the mistake of bringing the shield up in front of his face, temporarily blocking Cole from view. Cole lunged, bringing his legs out in front of him as he slid under the brim of the shield. He aimed his bladed feet for the shining bundle of limbs that was the priest's shins. Cole kicked with all his might, only to come to a dead stop as his munisica collided with the armor of the Chosen.

There was a dark chuckle from above him. Cole threw his bladed hands up, catching the shield before it could strike his neck. Anticipating a counterattack, Cole twisted himself to the side and rolled away from the man. There was a screech of metal. Cole jumped to his feet and saw the Guardian yank his ruby munisica from the street. Cole lunged again, this time aiming for the head, but the man brought the children around just in time. Cole swore. He kicked off the street and leapt over the man in a high arch. The Divine Guardian followed him around, munisica raised, ready to strike.

Cole barely had time to get his hands up. Ruby munisica met black in an explosion of sparks. He deflected several jabs, astonished at the speed and power of the priest's attacks. Hatred bit into his hands and fingers, but it was only pain. His own shroud held fast, fueled by his master's Rage, which burned hotter by the second. The Divine Guardian was impossibly swift and hellishly strong, but his attacks lacked technique and flexibility, simply jabbing over and over at Cole's chest and head. Cole deflected a few more attacks before returning with his own, managing several probing attacks on the armor, which for reasons unknown did little to no damage to the flesh of the Chosen. He needed to land a proper blow, but the priest's shield prevented him from getting close enough. He couldn't bring himself to harm the children, and the Guardian knew it.

Anticipating another stab of the ruby spears, Cole leaned to the side while trapping the ruby arm under his own. With a quick flash of Wisdom, he cast a protective barrier over the children, then clenched his munisica around the arm and dug his feet into the street. He twisted with all his might, launching the man through the air. The man spun like a child's toy before he smashed into the wall on the opposite side of the street, tearing through the metal exterior to the offices inside. Cole knew it wouldn't be enough to kill him, but perhaps it would be enough for him to drop the shield. To his disappointment, the Guardian exhumed himself from the rubble with the shield still in hand. The children were thankfully unharmed. The Guardian's armor of flesh hung loose in places, and he now had a pronounced limp in his left leg. Cole dismissed his protective barrier from around the children and shot a bolt of emerald Wisdom at the shield, intending to break them free, but the Guardian countered the spell with a flick of Fear.

The man limped closer, conjuring up a tiny cloud of orange Hunger between the tips of his munisica. "How noble of you, Human.

You Fear for the children. Tell you what, stand still a moment and keep that Rage burning, and I promise I'll kill them quickly. Won't taint them or nothing. Nice and clean."

Cole knew there was no other way. He might be stronger and faster than the man, but with the children in the way he would never get close enough to do any real damage. He nodded gravely to himself as he accepted what he had to do. Flexing his munisica, he set himself in a low crouch and prepared to charge, but just then Varka's cape fluttered excitedly across his back. It felt as if something bloomed within Cole's Wisdom, and then the answer came to him.

"I accept your offer," Cole said, standing up straight.

Maintaining his shroud, Cole's body pulsed with a gentle jade glow, then his form grew fuzzy, as if he were submerged in water. His outline bent and split as two identical Coles detached themselves from his hazy body, each striding around the man. The copies halted, then all three Coles crouched into a low fighting position, munisica bared.

"Your move," the three Coles said. "I promise I'll stand still."

"Wisdom again? How boring," the man drawled. His ruby munisica receded as the cloud of orange Hunger gave way to a dark purple flame. With a lazy wave of his hand, he sent two flaming daggers of Fear into the copy Coles, who cried out in agony before vanishing in a wisp of emerald vapor. The Guardian sneered as he limped his way over to Cole. He snapped his free hand out and his munisica returned. "You ready to give me that Rage?"

"What about your end of the bargain?" Cole demanded.

"You want my shield? Then take it!" the Divine Guardian roared as he flung the massive shield at Cole like a disc, charging just as fast behind it.

Cole ducked as the children screamed over him. He cast a desperate spell over his shoulder, catching them before they struck another wall. The spell cost him precious time, however, and the Guardian was now upon him.

The man flung a hand out, cackling madly as he bathed Cole in Grotton's Hunger. Cole doused his Rage before the Guardian could steal it, then called Wisdom to his aid, but he wasn't quick enough. The ruby munisica shot forward, and stabbed Cole through the heart.

Cole's face went slack as he brought his trembling hands to the bloody shroud of the priest's wrist. His feet left the ground as the man lifted him into the air, bringing him close to the fetid stench and the yellow teeth.

"Don't go dying on me just yet," the man said in a wet, gravelly voice. "I'm gonna make a full meal out of you, with all the fixings and sweets your little heart can muster."

The color drained from Cole's face. His head fell forward and his body went limp. The Divine Guardian readied a dirty blue spell in his free hand, hoisting his prize up to the stars, then cursed as Cole's body disintegrated in a wisp of emerald smoke.

"What trickery is this?" the Guardian growled as he spun on the spot, munisica and magic at the ready.

A black shadow appeared above the priest's head, and ebony munisica sank into his armored shoulders. Cole roared as he swung a killing blow at the helmet of patchwork skulls encasing the priest's head. His munisica struck true, cracking the helmet down the middle. He had the leverage he needed now. With another savage blow he cleaved half the skulls away, exposing the terrified face within. The man offered a sloppy thrust of his ruby munisica. Cole caught the spears under his arm once more, locked them in place, then brought his ebony hand down like an axe and severed the fingers in a cascade of ruby shards. Grasping the length of one of the ruby swords, Cole spun it about and plunged it through the Divine Guardian's eye.

Whatever bonds held the Chosen to the shield vanished at once. Cole descended several feet, now standing atop a small mound of broken bodies. The length of ruby munisica in his hand melted to a sticky mess. He glanced behind and cast his Passion towards the children, silencing their screams with a heavy, dreamless sleep. They were hurt, but alive. Nothing he and Eliza couldn't mend. The thought of his friends brought his attention to a nearby fountain pool of knee-deep water, where the rest of the Unbound were still locked in battle with the remaining Arch Priests. Lileth, Eliza, and Valen each fought a single priest while Sitra danced with two.

Cole took flight, sensing an unusual weakness in his green magic. Varka's cape was slow to react, almost drunk, tired from the exertions of the illusion spell. Once above the pool, Cole dismissed his Wisdom and landed with a dramatic splash, drawing the attention of each of the priests. Instead of joining the fray, Cole commanded his Passion into the air, galvanizing the rest of the Unbound in an aura of fortifying magic. Cole felt the priests attempt to smother his Passion with Despair, but his Rage kept his aura aloft. The tide of the battle shifted, and the Unbound dispatched the remaining priests with a quick thrust of their munisica, or in Sitra's case by holding her last opponent underwater until he fell still.

With their enemies finally slain, they dismissed their Rage and tended to each other's injuries. Their wounds caused by the priests' ruby claws were slow to mend as the lingering Hatred resisted their Passion. Cole sensed a budding of concern, then saw Lileth rushing to his side, lavender Passion at the ready.

"You are hurt," Lileth said. "Be still, love." She clasped her palms to either side of his face and kissed him.

Cole swayed on the spot as her Passion crashed into him, suffusing his body with blissful warmth while washing his mind of every care. He didn't feel like he was injured…but in that moment he didn't really care. Everything else ceased to exist, and he and Lileth were no longer in Borla Dign, but somewhere inside each other. When she pulled away, Cole felt refreshed and ready to take on the world, as though she had created a new day just for him.

Lileth's brow scrunched together as her gaze drifted over Cole's shoulder. "Are those children still alive?"

"Yes, but barely so," Cole said.

"Stars no," Lileth breathed, then sprinted after the children, Wisdom and Passion at the ready.

Cole wanted to help her, but the looming threat of The Three weighed heavily on him. He looked to the others, finding them already walking back to the hotel, where countless faces peered out from its many windows.

CHAPTER 15

FAREWELL, LOVE

The Unbound returned to the hotel, eyes and ears sharpened for any sign of danger. They vaulted the crater that used to be the front steps and took up defensive positions around the entrance. Cole approached the front doors to find a man in pale blue robes waiting for him. The man's hair was as white as snow, but his face was smooth and young, as though he were no older than Cole himself. The man did not walk, but rather floated, his feet unseen beneath the hem of his robes.

"You are not welcome in Borla Dign," said the man. His face was void of emotion save for a slight smirk.

Cole hardened the defenses around his mind. "I think you mean to say *thanks*."

The man ignored Cole's remark, though his smirk remained. "Forgive me, I should have said Varka is not welcome within Borla Dign. He was exiled long ago, and judging by your prowess in battle it seems the rumors are true, that he lives on within you." The man's smirk broke into a wide smile as he raised his chin and spread his arms. "However, considering you and your Unbound just saved the entire city from becoming offerings in a Devotion, I hereby declare Varka pardoned and welcome you to Borla Dign."

"Thanks?" Cole shrugged, peering around the man to the people gathered behind him. "What's your name, and who's in charge here?"

"My name is Brinleaf, and if you mean to ask who our head of government is, we have none." He cupped his hands together and gave Cole a little bow. "However, if you need to convey a message to the people of Borla Dign, then consider me at your service."

Lileth settled herself at Cole's side. She gave Brinleaf a shrewd look. "He is the Speaker for Borla Dign. Wisdom-predominant cities tend to operate by cognitive consensus, much like the Celestial Council."

Cole nodded and looked at Brinleaf through a new lens. "Well, you haven't put me on trial, so you're doing better than the last Speaker I met. Do you know the status of your people? Is all of Borla Dign in this Hotel?"

Brinleaf's smile faded. "All survivors are within the hotel. We lost twelve percent during the invasion. As your companion stated, we are predominately Wisdom users, and so all of our military fell to the Corpulants within the first few hours. We have made great strides in expanding our consensus to embrace the magics of Rage and Passion, but I am afraid we still have much to learn."

"So you were defenseless to Fear?" Cole asked.

"Quite," Brinleaf said in a dispassionate tone.

Sitra's mind hissed her displeasure to the group. *"Great. Now we have to send untested whelps out here to hold the city. And for nothing in return."*

"Borla Dign has some of the greatest minds outside Oberon City," Valen said. *"Their spellcrafters and scientists could be of great value to the war effort."*

Sitra gave a sardonic chuckle. *"That's if they have the sense to join us. And how the hell are we going to get everyone out of here before The Three roll through??"*

"Some will certainly join, and others will certainly follow," Eliza said. *"This city has a flame in it. We just need to give it a little help."*

Cole blinked, bringing his focus back to the Speaker.

"I see you have a consensus of your own," Brinleaf said with an appraising nod. "A network of Passion, if my own serves me right. Not quite the same as a consensus of Wisdom, but most effective in small numbers such as yours. We have a class in the Passion arts in one of our satellite colleges, though I am afraid our instructors lack your conviction. Should any of you feel in the mood to instruct a class of your own you would be well compensated, I assure you."

Cole was saved from having to ask what the difference was between a Passion network and a Wisdom Consensus by Sitra, who shouldered her way to the fore of the group. She stopped a few inches from Brinleaf and jabbed him in the chest with the flat of one of her bladed fingers.

"We're not here to chat," Sitra growled. "We came here to stop the Devotion, activate your Seer Jar, and recruit some help for the war. Our first task is done, so unless you're going to help us with the second two, I suggest you go back to counting the stars, or whatever the hell it is you Wisdom nerds do."

"My apologies," Brinleaf sighed. "The citizens of Borla Dign are somewhat exhilarated at your presence and their enthusiasm is difficult to corral. Twenty-four percent of us are ready to join The Sill at this very moment, and our Seer Jar is located at the base of the citadel."

"We didn't see any citadels during our reconnaissance," Lileth said.

"That is because our citadel is underground," Brinleaf replied, extending a hand toward the middle of the square. "The entrance is in the pond you were just fighting in. That is where The Three would have held their Devotion had you not arrived."

Valen stiffened. "The Three are still coming. We must evacuate the city immediately. Do you have any boats left?"

"All our watercraft were destroyed in the invasion," Brinleaf replied. "However, we do have quite a—"

"There's no time!" Cole shouted. "We need to get your people out of here now!"

Brinleaf shook his head. "I appreciate your urgency, though you should know—"

"To the skies then," Eliza said. "Borla Dign is a Wisdom city, so most of their citizens should be able to fly, right?"

"That is correct, though it wouldn't be the most—" Brinleaf's mouth hung open as he was interrupted yet again.

"Get your people out here now," Cole demanded. "Two of the Unbound will lead your fliers to The Sill. The rest will stay behind to escort whoever's left. Are there any sun lily trees around here?"

"My *dear* guests," Brinleaf said in complete exasperation. "If you would but listen for one moment you will learn of a much better way. Please, be silent and grant me leave to explain!"

Half the Unbound had summoned their emerald wings, and Sitra had already leapt into the air, only to come crashing back down with obnoxious force. Cole pinched his lips and gave Brinleaf a heavy nod, indicating that the Speaker now had their ears.

Brinleaf adjusted the high collar of his robes. "Thank you. As I said, our Seer Jar is at the base of the citadel, which I will raise from the ground in a moment. Before The Three's minions invaded, we discovered a means to upgrade our Seer Jar to not only transmit light and sound, but matter as well. I believe it was one of the reasons The Three targeted Borla Dign in the first place."

"How did you test this magic?" Lileth asked. "The Sill's intelligence teams found every Seer Jar on the planet deactivated, including yours."

"We have yet to run trials on a living creature; however, we are quite sure it will work," Brinleaf stated. "The spell is sound."

"That's not very reassuring," Cole sighed, glancing at the sky. "But we have to try something quick."

"Of course," Brinleaf said.

Lileth shook her head. "No, that won't work. Unless I'm mistaken, The Sill's jar would need to be upgraded as well. We can't afford to waste time experimenting when The Three could arrive at any moment."

Brinleaf's smile returned. "There is no need to experiment. The spell is sound. Do any of you have contact with someone in close proximity to The Sill's Seer Jar? The person would need to be an expert in either Passion or Wisdom."

"Yes," Cole said. "Eliza or I can contact someone."

"Excellent," Brinleaf said. "Then if one of you would be so kind as to join our consensus, we can duplicate the knowledge in your mind. Whilst connected to us you must then contact your friend at The Sill. The spell is easy enough to learn for an expert of Wisdom, and implementing it should only take but a moment."

Unease stirred about the group. Cole didn't need to sense the Unbound through the Passion network to see how unwilling they were to open their minds to a city full of strangers. Cole glanced at Eliza. She stared at the ground, grimacing lightly and hugging herself, as though she knew a terrible secret. Cole sent a tendril of Passion to her mind, but it was blocked by an iron wall of indifference.

"I'll do it," Cole said, breaking his gaze from Eliza. "I'll join your consensus and contact The Sill. When do we start?"

"Cole you're not serious?" Lileth said, gripping his arm. "We're talking about an untested spell. It's too risky."

"It is, but I agree with Cole," Valen said. His brow hardened as he rubbed his chin. "We can assume the priests have means to communicate with one another, which means our interference here has likely reached The Three already. They will either hasten their arrival or set up ambushes between Borla Dign and The Sill, though we should assume both. This means of teleportation may be our only means to get the entire city out alive."

Lileth shook her head as her eyes fell to the ground. "Fine, but none of us should go first. If anything goes wrong the repercussions could kill the one who goes through. Let's just hope we don't destroy The Sill and Borla Dign in the process."

"Oh come on, Lil," Sitra said as she clapped Lileth on the buttock. "It's good to take a little risk every now and then. When's the last time you risked your life for something?"

Lileth swatted away another smack from Sitra. "About ten minutes ago."

"Oh that was just a scrap," Sitra scoffed and inclined her head toward Brinleaf. "Let's go, Pine-bean, get this party started before The Three come spoil our victory. I can't wait to see the staff's face when we dump a whole city in their chamber. You guys better wipe your feet before you go though."

Brinleaf gave Sitra a queer look. He closed his eyes and clasped his hands behind his back, then floated down the steps. The Unbound followed, eyes scanning every alley and patch of sky along the way. The pool was knee-deep and bordered with a low stone wall encompassing an area as large as the training grounds at The Sill. Brinleaf stopped at the edge of the low wall and extended a hand over the water. A tiny green star sparked to life at the tip of his first finger. With a flick, the bead fell into the water, though instead of splashing, the entire surface of the pool blinked with green light. The stone floor of the pool folded itself downwards in neat triangular segments like slices of a pie, but the clear water remained, held aloft by unseen magic. A gaping chasm beckoned from below the shallows, dark and deep.

Cole leaned forward and peered over the edge. Something was rising. Something massive. A black cylinder ten yards across rose from the center of the hole, then crashed through the surface of the pool. A second cylinder followed at the base of the first, twice as wide and rushing up for the stars. Then another, and another, each wider than the last. When the structure finally ceased its ascent, Cole found himself looking at a smaller version of Oberon Temple.

Water cascaded down the entire structure. It rushed up over the low walls bordering the pool, though instead of spilling out into the streets, the water gathered itself in fist-sized globules and rose back to the peak of the citadel. Tens of thousands of jiggling globes shimmered with moonlight as they rushed back to the top of the citadel, as if eager to keep the water flowing down its black walls.

"You should contact The Sill now," Brinleaf said to Cole in a quiet voice. "Borla Dign's citizens are on their way out."

"Right," Cole replied. Brinleaf gave him a significant look and floated towards the citadel. Cole followed. The Unbound walked close by, keeping their minds close as well, ready to jump to his defense if the consensus should go awry.

Cole sensed life candles stirring behind him by the thousands. They flowed throughout the hotel in a neat and organized manner, not wasting a single step or second on their way out the door. Cole glanced back and saw the first woman step out. She held her chin high and proud, but Cole didn't need Passion to sense the dread radiating from her, chilly and wild like an icy flame. Resisting the urge to soothe her as well as the throngs queing up behind her, Cole focused his Passion instead on the life candles of the staff at The Sill. The sheer distance gave him some trouble, but only for a moment. Cole's presence rang throughout the minds of the staff like a bell, eliciting a flinch of Fear from each of them, then faint voices too soft to understand. After a moment Wareen's mind had calmed enough to make a weak, yet comprehensible connection.

"What is it, Cole?" Wareen asked. *"Are you safe?"*

"We are," Cole replied, assuaging her worry with comfort and confidence. *"The mission was a success. We cleared Borla Dign and stopped the Devotion, but we're pretty sure The Three are going to show up any minute. We need to work a spell on The Sill's Seer Jar. Do you have it handy?"*

It took Wareen several seconds to summon the Passion necessary to respond. *"Yes. I am looking at it now."*

"All right," Cole said. *"Dispel any magic currently active on the jar and stand by. I'm going to transmit a spell for you to cast over the jar."*

Seconds passed. *"I am ready,"* Wareen replied, sure and eager.

Cole sent a burst of gratitude and serenity to her. Though she could barely transmit spoken word to him, Cole's mastery of Passion allowed him to speak to her as easily as if she were standing next to him.

"The Sill is ready," Cole said to Brinleaf, suddenly aware of how far they had walked. They were at the base of the citadel. Behind him, hundreds of Borla Dign's citizens strode in a tight line, each stepping perfectly in sync with the woman in front. They were all tall and thin, and each wore a plain set of high-collared robes of pale blue or grey.

"Then let us hasten our pace," Brinleaf said in a loud, clear voice. "Follow me into the citadel, and be welcomed into Borla Dign's consensus."

"How do I..." Cole fell silent as something enormous made contact with his mind.

The presence dwarfed his own. Even the minds of Chiron and Roth would barely register compared to it. Powerful and deliberate, it pressed eagerly over the entirety of his consciousness. Though it certainly could have overwhelmed him if it wanted to, the presence held itself back in respectful silence, as if it were a polite stranger waiting to be invited into his home. Cole was sorely tempted to withdraw and send them all away, but he steeled himself and opened his mind.

He expected an onslaught of thoughts and emotions. However, what came to be felt more like an absurdly complex puzzle piece fitting itself into his own simple one. The foreign thoughts came, though they felt as much his own as anything else. Emotions rose here and there, but they were gently plucked and cast aside like weeds in a garden made of knowledge and logic. Cole opened his eyes, not realizing he had ever closed them. The world seemed slow and simple to him, almost as if he were fully shrouded with Rage, only now he could see so much more.

Cole followed close behind Brinleaf, and together they led the Unbound and Borla Dign to the citadel entrance. A hole opened in the black stone wall, stretching into a neat door frame. The hole deepened and cut itself into a stairwell wending down to the right, illuminated by a sourceless white glow.

As his connection to Borla Dign strengthened, Cole's awareness broadened and sharpened simultaneously, revealing small errors and flaws around him. It was as if the world had been laid bare before him. Things previously hidden or unnoticed now stuck out to him as if they had been painted neon and bedecked with bells. As the Unbound descended through the stairwell, Cole noticed an inconsistency in the sounds of the footfalls behind him. Sitra had the slightest limp, indicating an injury she was too obstinate to request help in healing. Cole whisked a quiet spell over her knee, disguising it as a normal crack of the joint, and healed her torn ligament. Scanning his own body on a whim, Cole discovered several dozen flaws in his own composition.

Through genetics and the numerous injuries of his youth, Cole's body had grown or healed uneven in places. While their individual effects were mostly negligible, the sum of the flaws amounted to a quantifiable deficit in his body's efficiency, which of course couldn't be ignored. With the consensus guiding his magic, Cole remedied each flaw within a few steps, then proceeded to do the same to each of the Unbound. Within a minute the consensus assessed a cumulative increase of four percent in the Unbound's flexibility and balance.

The winding stairs leveled out and opened to a wide chamber, as Cole knew it would. Towering bookshelves lined the room, each sparkling with thousands of cyphers arrayed in organized grids on their shelves. In the center of the room was a tiered dais with a hollow carved out in its middle. Brinleaf floated up to the top of the dais, and a pedestal containing an olive-green Seer Jar rose up from the hollow to greet him.

Cole waited at the bottom step and motioned for the rest of the Unbound to do the same. While Brinleaf labored over Borla Dign's Seer Jar, Cole drew the consensus into his Passion link to Wareen, where he felt her awaiting his command. Cole broadened his link to her and began the flow of knowledge. The spell was complex, but not so much that Wareen needed help from the rest of the staff. Within a minute she had it memorized, and then within another she had it implemented. Once he was quite sure the spell would hold, Cole withdrew the knowledge from Wareen's mind, just as the consensus would do to him when it was his turn to withdraw.

Brinleaf gave Cole a nod of appraisal, then flicked the teardrop glass of the Seer Jar, producing a shrill chime. The olive-green gas within the jar shifted to seafoam as it shot out of the pointy tip of the container. The vapor thickened and spread itself over the dais, concealing Brinleaf and the Seer Jar from view. Tiny pockets of light flashed from within the seafoam-green cloud, as if a silent lightning storm were taking place. Cole shut his eyes and offered his thanks to Borla Dign before surrendering the spell and withdrawing himself from the consensus. Profound silence fell over Cole's mind.

"Where's Pine-bean?" Sitra asked. "I can't feel him anymore."

"Brinleaf is already waiting for us at The Sill," Cole replied. "Watch out, there's about three thousand people waiting behind you."

Sitra hopped to the side as Borla Dign's citizens flowed into the chamber, now levitating instead of walking, which turned out to be much quicker. There was hardly an inch of space between them, and as each person vanished in the seafoam cloud there was a dull, deep thud that shook the room.

"This is certainly more efficient than flying or walking," Valen remarked, counting the passing citizens with his eyes. "Can you sense anything on the other side?"

Cole squinted in concentration. "Thessi is angry, but Rayn is furious. It's definitely working."

"I had better go through and smooth things over," Valen said as he sized up the cloud on the dais. "Rayn could bring this whole movement to a grinding halt if he wanted to." Valen approached the front of the queue, clearly unsure of how to insert himself into the flow.

All at once, the thousands within the line came to a brief halt, as if they had been expecting Valen all along. Valen blanched and jumped in front, then vanished with a deep thud. A moment later the line began to move even faster. Hundreds passed through every minute.

"It won't be long now," Cole said to the others. A grin tugged at his cheeks as the golden warmth of victory finally erupted within his chest. "I can't believe we did it! We stopped a Devotion! This is a true victory."

Lileth seemed unable to meet his eyes, focusing instead on the children she had levitating in conjured emerald litters. Sitra was quiet as well. It was only then that Cole realized Eliza wasn't in the chamber with them.

"Where is she?" Cole demanded.

"We couldn't stop her," Sitra pleaded. "She used her Passion on us."

"What do you mean?" Cole asked. "Where the hell did she go?"

Lileth put her hand on his arm, offering him a look of deep remorse. "She overwhelmed us, but even if she hadn't I wouldn't have stopped her. It is the only way."

Cole threw Lileth's hand from his arm. "Tell me what happened. Now."

"I'm fine, Cole," Eliza chimed into his mind.

At her presence, Cole pinpointed her location with his Passion, then drew his munisica, not in fury, but in eagerness to reach her. *"Why in the hell are you flying above Borla Dign right now? The citizens will all be through in a couple minutes and we need to be gone right after. Do you plan on fighting The Three all by yourself or something?"*

"Go to your center and clear your mind," Eliza said in a calm tone. *"You know why I must stay behind."*

Cole's Rage burned too hot to center himself, and he knew the reason already. *"A citizen from Borla Dign already volunteered to stay* behind and destroy the Seer Jar. No one is about to follow us through."

"And what of the Chosen scattered about the city?" Eliza asked. "The Divine Guardian you fought wasn't the only one to use the innocent as armor."

"Acceptable losses!" Cole roared. "This is war, we can't save everyone."

"But that doesn't mean we shouldn't try," Eliza replied. "I will use my Passion to release the Chosen, then I will use Sitra's fulminators to destroy both the citadel and the warehouse of odium."

Cole shook with restrained contempt. "Eliza, I'm sorry but this is the worst idea you've ever had. How could you know about the warehouse anyway? I thought I shut you all out of my mind when Habbad poisoned me with Hunger."

A sad chuckle emanated from Eliza's mind. "You did indeed exile my mind from yours, but you can never shut out a person's heart. I've given you a part of myself, Cole, whether you feel it or not. My heart is anchored to your own. I don't know exactly when or how it happened, and I couldn't take it back even if I wanted to."

Cole's vision blurred as hot tears raced down his cheeks. His Rage dissipated, replaced by the familiar emptiness of Despair. "So that means you have to throw your life away? You're so heartbroken that I'm with Lileth that you're going to abandon all your friends and wait for The Three to come kill you?"

"Of course not," Eliza said, soothing him with a wave of Passion. "This war will likely kill us all, but I'd rather my death be at your side than anywhere else. After I complete my task here, I plan to fly back to The Sill and join you once more."

"But that's the flaw in your plan!" Cole exclaimed. "I should be the one who stays behind. With Varka's cape I stand the best chance of making it back alive. No, I'm coming up now and you're going through this portal. I'll force you if I have to."

"No, you won't," Eliza replied. "Not if you value the lives of this world and every other. You are the key, Cole, to all of it. With you The Three will unlock the Aethers once more and wreak unchecked *havoc. You will go and I will stay. I've already seen to the odium and the Chosen anyway. Only one more task left."*

"*Eliza...*" Cole begged, unable to summon a response. He knew she was right.

"*The last citizen just entered the citadel,*" Eliza said with sudden urgency. Something close to Fear began to bleed through her end of the link. "*She'll be down in a moment.*"

Even as she said it, a woman in steel-grey robes hovered past Cole, the last in line. She hesitated, looking to Cole as if she wanted to say something, then seemed to think better and vanished into the seafoam smoke. It was only the three Unbound and the children in the chamber now.

"*At least come down here and say goodbye to us,*" Cole said. "*You know Sitra won't—*"

The walls shuddered as hundreds of cyphers tumbled free from their shelves, smashing to the ground in bright flashes of light and memory. Sitra, Lileth, and Cole all crouched into fighting positions, their munisica coming out of their own accord.

"What is that?" Sitra gasped, her long braid whipping about as her head snapped this way and that. "I've never felt anything like it. It's... powerful."

Cole sensed it too. A presence drew near, so immensely vast that he felt himself dwindling as it approached. They were here. As powerful as he had become, there was no doubt that he wouldn't pose more than a minor inconvenience to The Three, let alone stand any real chance in battle. Even with Varka's cape, he and the rest of the Unbound would only be another meal on their bloody road to domination. A hurricane of Fear, a legion of Hunger, and a boiling ocean of Despair and Hatred united above Borla Dign just for him. They truly were gods.

"The Three are upon us," Lileth said in a grave tone. With a quick jab of Wisdom she gathered up the children, sending them zooming through the air while still fast asleep in their litters. One by one they vanished through the seafoam smoke. "We must leave. Now."

Sitra bared her teeth and flexed her munisica, eyes boring up through the ceiling. "Dammit!" she shouted, then leaped up the dais.

Cole didn't move. Lileth's munisica clamped down on his arm.

"Don't be stupid, Cole!" she commanded. "You don't stand a chance. None of us do. Get in that portal."

Cole looked into the depths of Lileth's eyes, each a burning gem with equal facets of ferocity and intelligence. With a sad smile and a whisper from Varka's cape, Cole cast a silent spell, and sent Lileth flying into the portal.

"Cole don't!" Lileth screamed before vanishing with a dull thud.

Cole readied another spell, one designed to obliterate all things material, and aimed it at the dais. An orb of blue light crackled to life within his munisica. He was about to release it when a presence charged its way into Cole's mind. Consuming and unrelenting, it battered its way through his defenses and commandeered his mind and body. Cole marshalled his defenses in preparation to battle the evil magics, but it was not The Three who had entered his mind. It was Eliza.

Images flashed through Cole's mind like gunshots. Jolting and jarring, they revealed three immense and separate clouds gathering over Borla Dign. Somewhere in each loomed a god, brought to this world by their Harbinger. He felt Eliza tearing through the sky, emerald wings ablaze as she dove for the citadel like a racing falcon. Cole couldn't stop himself. Eliza had him now. The spell in his hand dissipated as his legs carried him to the top of the dais. Static energy caressed his cheeks as the seafoam vapor wrapped itself around him, welcoming yet chilly. With a thud from somewhere deep within his chest, he was gone.

Chapter 16

Rule Breaking

By the time Cole regained control of his body, he could hear the voices of the staff through the seafoam smoke. Tiny sparks of electricity zapped him, annoying and stinging. He spun on the spot and ran back to where he thought he came from, only to emerge from the cloud and into the staff chamber of the Heart Tree. Cole dug his munisica into the polished bark floor, turned around once more, and charged back into the Seer Jar's cloud. The vapor dissipated before he reached it.

"No!" Cole roared. He closed his eyes and clenched his bladed fists as he attempted to connect to Eliza with Passion. Like the Seer Jar's vapor, she too vanished before he could reach her. Cole tried again, but she was gone, as if she never existed in the first place. Cole wheeled about. The Unbound and the Heart Tree's staff were there, as well as Brinleaf and the woman who was supposed to stay behind. The room was quiet. All eyes were on him, each brimming with Fear, save for Brinleaf's and the woman's.

"It was the most logical option," said the woman in the steel-grey robes. "I would have happily laid down my life for the greater good, but your friend's sacrifice was much more productive than my own. You may be upset now, but in time we hope you will see as clearly as we do."

Cole turned his head slowly and locked eyes with the woman, loathing everything about her. He dismissed his munisica and walked with deliberate, heavy steps and stood before her. She opened her mouth to speak again, but Cole struck her in the chest with his naked fist, sending her tumbling over the staff table and crashing into the wall behind.

"Eliza's worth more than your whole damn town!" Cole bellowed. "And now The Three have her!"

The woman shuffled to her feet, rubbing her chest with a web of emerald magic from her palm. Her face paled at the sight of the fresh crimson streaking from her nose.

Cole took a step around the table, but Valen gripped his shoulder, injecting him with soothing Passion.

"I hurt too, Cole," Valen whispered, sending another pulse of magic into Cole.

There was a sound of cracking wood as something streaked across the room. Sitra landed before the woman in a bladed fury, her munisica bared and needle hair gleaming.

"You said she would be fine!" Sitra roared. The woman conjured a crystalline barrier in defense. Blind with Rage, Sitra smashed through the shield with a clawed hand, showering the floor with fading green chips. "You said the risk was negligible!"

The woman conjured another barrier, then another, both of which Sitra smashed just as easily as the first. There was a blinding flash of jade light, then both women were in the air. With a flick of his hand, Valen sent Sitra to the opposite end of the room, where she continued to swipe and reach in an attempt to get to the woman.

"Go," Valen said, lowering the grey-robed woman to the floor. She cupped her nose and bolted for the door.

Sitra closed her eyes and her face went blank. She dropped heavily to the floor, dismissing her munisica. The only sound in the room was the dancing of wind and leaves through the open ceiling.

"Would anyone care to tell us what in Oberon's bloody light just happened?" Rayn said at last. He approached Cole with caution in his eyes and magic ready in his hands.

Cole bit back his sorrow and looked at Rayn through watery eyes. Lileth wrapped her arm around his shoulder, squeezing him tightly. He barely had the strength to speak. "We stopped the Devotion."

"I...surmised as much," Rayn said, a drop of disdain souring his tone. "But that doesn't explain how a few thousand people came to appear in our Council chambers, or what we are supposed to do with them now that they are here. *What happened?*"

Cole blinked out hot tears, but his voice was steady. "I kept Wareen in the loop the whole time. Didn't she relay everything?"

Wareen hugged herself and shook her head. "Your thoughts came through just fine, but it taxed my Passion to its limits to process it all. I am not as proficient with the Passion link as I had hoped to be. The rest of the staff has yet to be informed of the details of your mission." As though she couldn't bear the weight of all the eyes in the room, Wareen took to fidgeting with the hem of her robes, then rushed to replace the Seer Jar from the floor to the center table.

Cole sighed. He slid out from under Lileth's arm and slumped into a chair. He wasn't ready to relive Borla Dign just yet, but circumstances demanded it. A gentle hand grasped his shoulder. He opened his eyes and looked up, expecting to see Lileth, but found Sitra instead, standing tall and proud with her chin held high. Cole massaged his forehead, then drew a long, steadying breath.

Though it was less than a day ago, the flight to Borla Dign felt like a memory from another lifetime. The words came easily enough, however. Cole gave the staff a cursory brief of the mission, sticking to the important facts. The others filled in the gaps in his tale with details of their own. Cole had to stifle another swoop of Rage at the smug look on Rayn's face whenever their story came to a difficult part.

When Cole arrived at his entrapment in the warehouse, he felt a mortified tension wring its way through the Unbound's Passion network. Fear robbed the breath from his throat. Cole took a moment in the stone room of his center to cleanse his shame, then spoke in a dispassionate tone.

"I believe Habbad knew I was coming," Cole said, now more curious than anything. "I don't see how else he would have been at that exact place and time. He worked his Hunger over me from a distance, and I fell right for it like it was my first day on the job. That's when I became a little bad-tempered with you guys."

"You were a complete ass," Sitra snapped.

"I was," Cole said with a nod. "And I blocked you all out when I needed you the most. Habbad used my own Hunger against me. My mind shifted, like I slipped into a dream, and before I realized it I wasn't me anymore. I was Varka. Habbad evoked Varka's memories and lured me into his house. All of a sudden I was myself again, but Habbad's magic was already well underway. I was helpless."

"You were foolish is what you were," Rayn said. "Arrogance of the highest order! I'm surprised any of you survived the mission, if you can even grant this disaster such a title."

Cole felt Sitra back away from him. His Rage flared once more, but he dismissed it. Now wasn't the time. "You're right," Cole sighed. "It was stupid to go off on my own. I made a mistake, one that I don't plan on repeating any time soon."

"How did Habbad survive Fangshard Valley?" Valen asked. "Half a mountain fell on him, and that was after Sorronis struck him with Hatefire."

"More importantly, how did *you* survive?" Sitra said, giving Valen a sharp glare.

Cole delved into his Passion and offered his suspicions to the Unbound, urging them not to talk about their potential traitor in front of the staff. "I don't know how Habbad came to be in Borla Dign, but I'm positive he had help. As for me, I reminded Habbad that there was still some hope left in his world. He let me go."

Lileth let out a quiet sob. Cole looked to her, but she hid her face from view.

"But he had you on a gilded platter," Debjornik said. "Don't get me wrong, I couldn't be more relieved you all made it out unscathed, but what kind of hope would make an agent of our enemies let you go? You're the damned key to the Aethers!"

"Habbad's sister lives here in The Sill," Cole said. "We rescued her from the belly of a Colossus and brought her here to cleanse her of Sorronis's magic and keep her safe."

"Do you mean to tell me you're harboring Chosen within our walls?" Rayn demanded. Cole answered with a steely frown. "This just gets better and better. I suppose you have a herd of Domina tucked away in here as well, or perhaps a few Corpulants. I hear they make wonderful pets."

A sliver of Rage pricked Cole's heart and his voice became a fiery wind. "Lexy is no longer Chosen. Nor is she the topic of this conversation. Now keep your mouth shut or I'll shut it for you.

Permanently." Cole waited until the color fell from Rayn's face before continuing. "I got lucky and I escaped. The rest of the Unbound had already cleared most of the city, so we met up and took care of the Corpulants and a few straggling priests."

"You are too modest, Cole," Brinleaf said. "They were Arch Priests, and a member of the Divine Guard. The Unbound fought a heroic battle, and through sheer power and skill they rid Aeneria of a great evil while denying The Three a tremendously profitable Devotion. We will immortalize our memories of your battle in the halls of our next library, wherever that may be."

Excluding Rayn, the rest of the staff gazed upon the Unbound with newfound admiration bordering reverence. Cole ignored the whispers of their thoughts, instead retreating to his center where he prepared himself for the worst part.

"I take it this is when you had me cast that spell over our Seer Jar?" Wareen asked.

"Yes," Cole replied, twitching as he returned to the present. "After all the civilians went through, Eliza decided to stay behind to take care of a few things. Last of which was destroying Borla Dign's Seer Jar so no one else could follow us through."

Thessi cleared her throat and sat up in her chair. "Not to diminish the nobility of her act, but why wouldn't you keep the portal open? This portal could have saved us a great deal of logistical grinding; what with all the equipment and personnel needed, we could have transformed Borla Dign into a satellite fortress within hours."

Cole's gaze dropped to the table. "Eliza destroyed the Seer Jar for the same reason three thousand civilians are now sheltering outside this building. The Three are in Borla Dign this very second."

The room staff let out a pained sigh. The faces of the entire staff now matched Rayn's pallor. Silence filled the room, heavy with darkening thoughts and dripping with Fear.

It was Debjonik who spoke first. He looked to Cole, not as the leader of The Sill's Intelligence Axis, but as a man hanging upon the final strands of his fraying hope. "Borla Dign... is not far from here. Just a few weeks' travel on foot. I... I don't know what this means. Is this the end of The Sill?"

The congregation deliberated for a while longer, but it soon became clear that no one had the slightest idea for a way forward. However, another more immediate issue soon sparked another debate: What was to be done with the population of Borla Dign? Falinor couldn't wait to get started with recruiting and training, which raised Debjornik's spirits as the Intelligence Axis would benefit the most from the new recruits. Rayn offered a plethora of hurdles and problems brought on by the refugees, though when asked for solutions he retreated into silent brooding. Thessi complained at length about how she was to feed and support such a number. Wareen left for the Communications Web before long, stating that she needed to work with her propaganda team to promulgate the success of the mission.

Brinleaf remained politely silent throughout the discussion. Only when Rayn suggested that Borla Dign set up camp outside The Sill's walls did he chime in.

"We have but two things we would like to say to you all, if we may be so bold as to interrupt your discussion that is," Brinleaf said in a firm, yet calm voice.

"Please, go ahead, Brinleaf," Cole said, silencing Rayn with a glare.

Brinleaf gave a grateful nod. "Firstly, we would like to offer our sincere appreciation for your aid in this, our darkest hour. We would all be burning on the towers right this very moment if not for the actions of the Unbound and the hospitality of The Sill." He then looked directly at Rayn. "Secondly, we would like to assure you all that Borla Dign will be no burden to The Sill whatsoever. Quite the opposite in fact, we intend to integrate into your organization and augment your existing assets with our own. All with your permission and guidance of course."

The skepticism on Thessi's face lifted, revealing a forgotten smile. "Borla Dign operates off a consensus just like the Celestial Council, right?"

"That is correct," Brinleaf said. "And we also frame our government in a similar manner to your own. As the Unbound already know we are not proficient in battle, but it would be no trouble at all to assimilate ourselves into your intelligence, logistics, planning, and communications staff. The Sill will be more capable than ever."

Debjornik stood, surveying Brinleaf with sharp eyes. "We would have to inspect you all for duplicity. Every mind, down to the last child. Do you consent?"

"Of course," Brinleaf said with a slight bow, as though this were the only obvious option.

"Then we vote," Debjornik said with a triumphant grin.

With the exception of Rayn, the entire staff agreed to Brinleaf's offer. Wareen presented the results through a formal Passion link to the entire room. All eyes went to Cole, and it was only then that he remembered the power of his position. The fate of thousands rested on his shoulders.

Cole approached Brinleaf and shook his hand. "Welcome to the team."

With the matter settled, the Unbound departed the Heart Tree, leaving the staff and Brinleaf to their own devices. Though their mission in Borla Dign was by all rights a victory, a muddled layer of defeat had settled throughout the Unbound's Passion network as Eliza's absence grew more apparent by the minute. She had always brought a certain vibrancy to their group, imbuing even the most mundane occasions with the color and warmth of her soul. They had all grown accustomed to the gentle and constant caress of her mind, the way she meandered between their worries and wonders, soothing pains and stoking hopes. With her gone even Oberon's vivid hues seemed grey and dull.

By unspoken consent the Unbound retreated to their barracks, not to sleep as everyone except Lileth had consumed the dreamsource, but to be alone. The stress of politics and battle had taken a toll on all of them.

Though she was in desperate need of sleep, Lileth spirited the sleeping children to Naythan's, where they could begin their journey of healing. Cole watched their interaction with his Passion from afar, observing things through Lileth's eyes. Indignant and impatient as ever, Naythan flat-out refused Lileth's request to care for seven additional children. However, when Lexy laid eyes upon their sleeping faces, her resultant pleading melted all reservation from the old hermit's heart. A knot of worry twisted between Lileth and Cole as

Amorinanis rushed over to the children. She woke them with her mysterious magic, then paralyzed Naythan and Lileth. Berating himself for his lack of forethought, Cole threw on Varka's cape and prepared to fly to Naythan's, only to halt before reaching the door to his apartment. As before, Amori's strange, dark magic had been used for something beautiful. Cole flew to Naythan's so he could see it with his own eyes.

"Took you long enough," Naythan grumbled as Cole landed beside the old hermit. "For a moment there I thought Amori had finally given in to temptation."

"She is alarmingly effective with Fear," Lileth said. She hugged herself and rubbed her arms as though unable to shake a chill. "Are you certain it's safe to keep her in The Sill?"

"She hasn't actually harmed anyone yet," Cole said, surveying all the children with disbelief. Lexy, Amori, and the seven from Borla Dign were busy chasing each other around Naythan's yard. "She's a sponge for dark magic, but every time she expels it she creates something good." He gave Naythan a nudge with his elbow. "Any idea what she did this time?"

Naythan drew his voluminous fur coat tighter around himself. Frowning, he crossed his arms and cradled his chin in his tattooed hand. "Not without months of observations, but if I had to guess, it seems as if she removed every malignant memory from all seven children, a feat you once attempted on her, only she did it right. As for their unusual coloring, it seems she infused their flesh with some sort of crystalline material. Quite impenetrable, even more so than your black shrouds, and the protection extends to their minds as well. Unless I am mistaken, Amori has made it so no one will ever be able to harm these children again."

Cole nodded and watched the kids for a time. The skin and hair of each child was a different color, appearing as statues carved from Oberon itself. Their faces gleamed like polished gemstones and their vibrant hair looked like freshly dipped paint brushes. Cole extended a silent tendril of Wisdom, probing the strange material with a gentle touch. He inspected them with Passion next, but the magic glanced off a slippery and impenetrable barrier that coated their minds.

Cole and Lileth stayed for a while, each enjoying the simple joy of being near such innocent happiness. After getting herself acquainted, Lexy approached Cole and tugged him along by the hand, introducing him to her new friends. Cole couldn't remember all their names, but he would never forget the feel of their little hands in his: warm and malleable, like blown glass that had yet to fully cool and harden. Cole played chase games with the kids for a while, but all too soon his obligations came nagging in the form of several urgent messages from the staff of the Heart Tree. Hugging each child goodbye, Cole and Lileth made to leave, but the sharp thwap of a wooden staff stopped them in their tracks.

"You're out of your skulls if you think I'm taming all nine of these animals for free," Naythan growled. He adopted a dramatic tone as he stared longingly back at his house. "This herd will eat my house after they clean out the pantry. Speaking of, I'll have to expand the living quarters before bedtime. Expensive magic that is."

"I should have known you couldn't go more than a day without payment," Cole said. "You know, you're not very generous for a man of Passion."

"Never said I was," Naythan said with a matter-of-fact nod.

Cole and Lileth departed for the barracks after paying the old man. Exhausted beyond her limits, Lileth begged Cole to lay with her as she slept; however, Cole only had time to stay with her until she nodded off. He longed to stay wrapped up with her, to indulge in the beautiful serenity of her slumber. Her eyes wiggled behind closed lids, with her black petal lashes fluttering like butterfly wings. Her full lips were parted, an inviting doorway to the sweetness of her breath and the soothing song of her voice. He watched the rise and fall of her chest, imagining his heart beating alongside hers, losing itself in the rhythmic dance of her soul. It was with difficulty that he finally slipped away, silent as a shadow.

The next few weeks passed under the pervasive shadow of looming annihilation. Everywhere Cole went he heard chatter of war, of fleeing and hiding, of monsters lurking behind every tree. Paranoia settled in the air like a heavy fog, choking and wringing the trust out of friends and family alike. The Unbound returned to their normal routine;

training students during the day, honing their own skills at night, and searching for a means to build The Sill whenever they could. Cole spent far more time than he liked within the walls of the Heart Tree. The staff seemed unable to make up their minds on large-scale problems. They claimed they needed his authority for big decisions. However, Cole knew it was because none of them wanted to take the blame for the repercussions of these big decisions. That privilege had been reserved for him alone.

After the people of Borla Dign had their minds inspected with Passion, a task which Cole himself took the lion's share of, their integration commenced with seamless ease. Borla Dign's consensus resolved the food shortage within a week by sending a sizeable workforce to assist in the cultivation of the Unbound's blackstout garden. While they lacked the raw power of Passion, the Wisdom users were able to alter the physical structure of every root, leaf, and stem, improving upon the plants with microscopic accuracy. With a little nudging from The Sill's Passion users, the small clutch of blackstout bushes exploded into a sweeping grove of sustenance. The refugees from Borla Dign expanded their influence across all of The Sill, re-opening every shop and laboratory, making improvements everywhere they went. With Thessi's permission they transformed a corner of The Sill into a passable impression of Borla Dign, complete with shining buildings, metal streets, and flowing ponds.

Cole made a point to stop in at Naythan's every few days despite his other obligations. Amorinanis had yet to show any inclination or interest in verbal speech, choosing instead to communicate through actions and gestures, a language which Lexy had become the resident master of. Lexy questioned Cole about Habbad every time he went to visit, as if she knew of Cole's recent encounter with the Underkin, or Underking, as the rumors now called him. Cole refused to lie to her, though nor did he want to tell her the truth, so whenever the subject came up, he distracted her with displays of magic or funny stories.

Naythan had only just finished the addition to his house when he was approached by Lileth, who presented him with one of The Sill's growing problems. There were a great number of orphaned children from the battle at Borla Dign, all of whom needed a home and a proper upbringing. As expected, Naythan vehemently refused, even going so far as to threaten Lileth with magic. Lileth left without a word, returning an hour later with what must have been half the population of Borla Dign. The Wisdom followers filled every gratia stone Naythan had, then foisted additional stones upon him after they overcharged his original stock. Only then did the old hermit concede to their pleas. The refugees volunteered their aid in expanding his house further, but Naythan summoned a swarm of carnivorous fungal spores and sent them sprinting back to their far corner of The Sill.

Lileth continued to drift behind the rest of the Unbound with her training. She never seemed to put forth her best efforts, an observation that Cole had yet to act on despite the disapproving mutterings of Sitra and Valen. They had long given up trying to shed light on the blind eye he had for Lileth's actions. Nor did they bother chastising him for shirking his duties in favor of indulging in so much time with her. Lileth continued her schedule of resting every other night, and Cole was there every time to see her off to sleep as well as tend to the needs of her body and soul. While Lileth's interest in her training diminished with each passing day, in Cole's mind she made up for it with her contributions in meetings within the Heart Tree.

Another odd change was her newfound devotion to the rescued children from Borla Dign. She pestered Naythan every day over things such as the ongoing construction projects, curriculums, and ensuring there were sufficiently stimulating activities for play time. When she wasn't being a thorn in the old hermit's side, she could be found out in the yard playing along with one group or another. Cole never let anyone see it, but he felt a pang of jealousy whenever he went to visit Amori and Lexy and saw Lileth giving the most beautiful parts of herself to others.

Eliza's fate weighed heavily on Cole's thoughts throughout the passing weeks. Not an hour went by without reminders of her absence slipping into his periphery. More than once the other Unbound had to subdue him with magic to stop him from flying off to find her. He made several attempts a day to find her with Passion, but not once did he ever find a hint of her life candle. His hope told him that she was still alive, and merely suppressing her magic in order to remain hidden.

His Wisdom tried to tell him otherwise, that she was far beyond saving, but he chose not to listen to such thoughts.

Aeneria left the house of Cigni and entered the house of Amikar. There had been no sign of activity from The Three, and so the traditional celebrations commenced without interruption. The Arts District put on its usual festival of theatrics, music, and cuisine. The citizens of Borla Dign joined in, marveling at how the artisans blended Passion, Rage, and Wisdom in their various crafts. Though the Unbound had granted all their students leave to attend the celebrations, they themselves had barely noticed the changing of houses. They remained shut away in Chiron's house, which thankfully remained on the other side of The Sill on the quiet canopy of the Necropolis. They pored over Chiron's library in an attempt to discover some spell or trick that might help them in the rising tides of war.

"Chiron and Varka had *cycles* to train before ever facing The Three," Sitra whined, snapping a thin book shut. "The Three could come knock down our walls any minute and there's nothing we could do to stop them. There's no way we're gonna learn enough from these books in time. I can't even remember half of what I already read, let alone find time to practice any of this junk. Look at this one." She whipped the book to Valen, who caught it without looking up from his own heavy volume. "This one's all about bending light, but it's all in Chiron-speech. We already know how to make ourselves invisible. Why even keep something like that in here?"

Valen flicked a web of Wisdom from his hand, enchanting the Volume to levitate among the flock of books currently floating around his head. After another hour of silent reading, every book crashed to the floor. Cole glanced up to find Valen holding Sitra's thin book in his hands.

"Sitra, this is remarkable magic!" Valen said, thumbing through another page. "This could give us the edge we need."

Lileth and Cole set their own books in their laps, eager to hear what Valen had to say. Sitra gave a sigh of annoyance when she saw the book in Valen's hand.

"I told you, that one just tells you how to bend light, Chiron just had an insane way of describing it." She emphasized her point by shooting an emerald spark from one of her fingers like a bullet.

The spark zapped the book in Valen's hands, rendering it invisible. "Not exactly an expert-level spell."

Valen shook his head. "Chiron's vocabulary obviously scared you away from reading past the third page. This book describes far more than bending a single rule. It is about warping reality itself. Unless I am mistaken, this book is Chiron's notes from when he and Varka created the Everglen in Oberon Temple."

"Isn't the Everglen just a bit of forest they planted inside the temple?" Cole asked. "That's not very hard to do. I bet we could figure it out."

"Not even remotely," Valen said, shaking his head. He flipped faster through the book, his eyes darting back and forth in a dizzying blur. "The Everglen is a partition of space and time crafted independently from this world. It has a bit of The Sill in it, yes, but only in concept. Besides the entrance and the back door Sitra found, the vast majority of the place is…" Valen closed the book and donned a faraway gaze.

Sitra's face twisted into a derisive sneer. "So were you going to finish that sentence or…"

"It's another dimension," Valen said in a quiet voice. "Another reality."

"Another reality?" Lileth asked, holding her hand out expectantly. She caught the book and began flipping through it. "A portal to one of the local planets perhaps?"

"No," Valen replied. "This was a pocket dimension, independent of any known reality. Varka and Chiron made it. The spell, or spells I should say, are far beyond my Wisdom to fully comprehend, but the concepts are easy enough to grasp. The pocket dimension is entirely modular."

"I think I would have known if there was any booze in that place," Sitra huffed. "I scoured every inch of that little forest."

Valen pinched the bridge of his nose. "Sitra I swear your ignorance is intentional sometimes. I am not talking about modella wine. I said *modular*, meaning the dimension was pieced together by design. Gravity, magnetism, light, even time. These were all rules crafted by the creator of the pocket dimension."

"They weren't gods," Sitra said. "You can't just make a world from nothing."

"It seems you can," Lileth said. Her eyes scanned the pages with dizzying speed. "I... I don't fully grasp it either, but it's all here. Something about reflective hallucinations and inverse cognitive projections. I... I can't believe what I'm reading. Did they dream the Everglen?"

"That is as much as I could surmise," Valen nodded.

"So what good does that do us?" Sitra asked with a mixture of intrigue and befuddlement.

"It means that we can make our own Everglen," Cole said. The implications struck him one right after another. "We could lure The Three into one of these pocket dimensions and trap them there forever. Or create a safe place for everyone to hide. The possibilities are endless."

"None of it is possible with our current state," Lileth said. "The knowledge it would take, the conviction behind the spells, not to mention the sheer focus required for such Wisdom. This magic is beyond any of us. Even if we could manage it, one mistake could cause unknown havoc among our world. The rules of reality are perilous to meddle with."

"Here we go again," Sitra scoffed.

Lileth raised an eyebrow. "And what Wisdom do you bring to the conversation?"

Sitra rose to her feet. "It's Borla Dign all over again. You hesitated when we first talked about using their Seer Jar as a portal. Not only were you dead wrong, you wasted time. Slowed us down. You broke Roth's rule. Don't ever hesitate."

Lileth shot to her feet. The air between her and Sitra became electrified with mounting fury. "Roth had another rule. Give everything you have, which means giving not only your blood and sweat, but your intellect as well. I refuse to believe he would begrudge me a moment to consider the safety of his students."

A dark grin crept over Sitra's mouth. "Not that moment. That moment could have been spent working out a better escape plan than letting Eliza stay behind to get violated by The Three. Is that what you wanted? To have Roth give her one last lesson before her end? Or did you just want her out of the way so you could have Cole all to yourself?"

There was a loud crack and flash of green light. Cole was first to react. Donning the shroud of his master's Rage, he appeared behind Sitra, wrestling her to the floor in a full-body hug before she could charge. Valen stood in front of Lileth, arms wide and hands shimmering with fuchsia Passion. The cold fury on Lileth's face melted, and the emerald flames snaking from her fingertips dissipated at once. Cole's Passion permeated throughout Chiron's house. Within seconds the tension in the air unraveled, and the four regarded each other as family once more. Cole pulled their minds into the stone room of his center and cleansed them of their Hatred and Despair, reestablishing streams of understanding and empathy to their Passion network until no apology was necessary from any party.

"I think we've gotten everything we need from the library tonight," Cole said. "I'll have a chat with Brinleaf about what we found. If anyone can help us it's the people of Borla Dign. In the meantime, how about we release a little stress down in the training grounds?"

"That is a wonderful idea," Valen said.

The Unbound departed Chiron's house and made for the training grounds. The grass was clipped and clean. The air had a comfortable chill to it, perfect for the heat of an intense sparring session. The towering pines watched them from the borders of the training field, swaying and waving at them as they soared down through the canopy. There was a verdant, earthy scent in the air, another reminder of Eliza, who after seeing the destruction wrought by the new students, had implemented a policy where every lesson ended with healing the wounded flora.

Cole landed ahead of the others and took a moment to enjoy the feeling of the grass between his bare toes. The rare chill brought a sheen of dew upon the entire field. The low-cut grass shimmered like a calm lake and the bordering pines glittered as if they had been frosted with diamonds. Oberon burned the sky with tones of rich azure and keen silvers, haunting the training grounds with a ghostly hue.

Their evening training started with the usual brawl, only now it was not a competition of who was the better fighter, rather it was who could fight with the greatest handicap. The others had expounded upon Cole's theory of increased gravity, adding further hindrances like thin air and limited light. The fetters were not only effective training aids, but necessary, as they had now sparred so extensively with one another that they knew each other's every move.

Cole paired up with Valen for the majority of their session. He chased his friend up the first tree they ever climbed together, determined to kick him from the top in the name of good-natured revenge. Valen anticipated Cole's motives however, and used Wisdom to bend the tree until the tip touched the ground, granting him a safe landing. Cole responded with Wisdom of his own. With the aid of Varka's cape he uprooted the entire tree, roots and all, casting it towards the stars with both of them still on it. By the time Valen summoned his wings, Cole's bladed foot kicked him square in the back, shattering wing and bone as he sent the Aenerian to the ground. Cole knew Valen would survive the fall, but he wasn't sure about a sentinel pine dropped from two hundred feet in the air. Varka's cape whipped flat in response to the danger and helped him guide the wooden behemoth to a safe landing.

The training grounds were unrecognizable after an hour. The crisp lawn had been tossed and shredded, with dark mounds two stories high and small pools where groundwater had been exposed. Nearly every surrounding tree had been knocked over, used either for shield or weapon. To the passerby it looked as if the training grounds had been pummeled by every cannon in Morthain's navy. By the time they concluded their sparring session, Valen, Sitra, and Lileth had each healed themselves of enough injuries to decimate a small army. Cole remained uninjured as his shroud had protected him inside and out. It was tedious work, but they managed to restore the training ground to its pristine condition, though they couldn't remember exactly where each tree should be replanted. The task left their Passion drained, even Cole's. They departed the training grounds buzzing with a fatigue-induced euphoria, completely devoid of the stress they started with.

"We still have another two hours!" Sitra called out. "Don't tell me we're stopping already."

"Sitra, come on, we're exhausted," Cole began. "We've got no Passion and no one has any Rage left besides me. Unless you all want to gang up on me again I don't see a point." Sitra's eyes fell to the side as a shadow of guilt flooded her face. Sighing, he trotted back to her and threw a brotherly arm over her shoulders. "What else do you have in mind?"

"It's stupid," she said. "Just an idea I got from one of Chiron's books."

"Then it can't be stupid," Cole said, giving her a little shake. Lileth and Valen appeared on either side of him. "Chiron's the smartest person I've ever met, and you're far from the dumbest. What do you have in mind?"

Sitra regarded him with a half smile, then extended a hand. Green light crackled in her palm as four stones unearthed themselves from the soil in the treeline. She caught them without looking, then proceeded to preen the dirt off while carving into them with blades of conjured Wisdom. A fine dust collected in her palms as she worked. At last she blew the powder away, then tossed them each an identical sphere of smooth granite.

"Lileth," Sitra said in a tone of command. "I want you to levitate your rock about chest height, then use your Wisdom to place a single rule on it."

"And what rule is that?" Lileth asked, suspicious.

"Do-not-move," Sitra stated.

Lileth appeared confused at first, then held her stone in front of her. A jade sheen flickered over the surface of the stone, then she released it, leaving it floating in midair.

"Good," Sitra said with a curt nod. She screwed up her brow in concentration and rolled her rock between her palms. "Do everything you can to hold that spell."

"What exactly are you going to do?" Lileth asked, taking a small step back.

"I'm going to cast my stone at yours, only mine will have a different rule: Keep-moving." Sitra's face suddenly became as hard as the granite in her hands. "Ready?"

"Of course," Lileth replied.

"You impress me, Sitra," Valen remarked. "I have seen true Wisdom Walkers play this game, though their contests were limited to a debate of theory. I am surprised Lileth agreed, however. This may result in one of those reality-breaking rules she is so fond of protecting."

"Oh yes," Lileth said with a smirk. "The age-old question, what happens when an unstoppable object meets an immovable one. There is only a risk when both forces are equal, though I doubt that will be the case here. Come, Sitra, throw your little rock."

Sitra's lips mashed together as her brow tightened. The granite sphere began to tremble with magic. A cool breeze danced around them, and Sitra's long braid whipped about like an angry snake. She closed her eyes and the muscles in her face relaxed as she adopted a look of profound serenity. Her hand snapped open in a flash of emerald light, and her stone did not race for Lileth's as Cole expected, but crept forward with steady determination.

Cole and Valen watched with mounting anticipation. Lileth waited in a relaxed pose with a hand on her hip, her eyes wandering about the field. After thirty uneventful seconds, the two stones touched, and Lileth's eyes widened with disbelief. She brought one hand up, then the other, each palm ablaze with emerald light. Sitra's expression remained impassive, almost dreamy. A light grinding and popping noise filled the air as fragments flew from between the stones. For a full minute nothing happened, then both stones began to move away from Sitra. Lileth swayed drunkenly and fell to her knees. The unstoppable object had won.

"I don't believe it," Lileth gasped as she pushed herself to her feet. "You're an expert with Wisdom?"

"You would be too if you took the dreamsource cypher," Sitra said. "It's only my conviction that's stronger than yours. I'll never be as quick on my feet or creative with my spellwork as you."

Lileth blinked rapidly as her stoic demeanor returned. "Still, I never thought I'd be so thoroughly overpowered by you. Well done."

Sitra acknowledged with a quick nod, but otherwise didn't gloat as she usually did. She then turned to Cole and Valen. "What are you two waiting for? Get to work."

Impressed by Sitra's command over the lesson, Cole and Valen took to the task with newfound respect for their friend. By unspoken agreement they started with caution, adding only a modicum of conviction to the rules of their spells. After a few rounds of half-hearted attempts they poured greater reserves of focus into into their rules. Cole was forced to use Varka's cape far sooner than he hoped, but it was the only way he could keep up. Valen gave a slight smirk when he saw the cape flickering excitedly, and Cole knew why: Even if Cole were to win, it would be Varka who earned the victory, not him.

After losing two rounds in a row, Valen sat himself cross-legged in the grass and closed his eyes, his breathing so slow that he appeared frozen. Cole knew Valen was currently in his center, bolstering his Wisdom with every reserve of conviction he possessed. It was what Cole would have done anyway. Cole sat himself so close to Valen that their knees touched. Varka's cape drew itself around Cole's shoulders in a blanket of lush grass. Cole took full command of his Wisdom and levitated his stone in the air between him and Valen, imbuing it with an ironclad rule: Do-not-move.

Valen's eyes remained closed. His hand opened with the patience of a blooming flower. The stone rose from his palm. The smooth granite surface flickered jade, then began its journey toward its opponent, deliberate and confident.

Cole sensed a massive spike in Valen's Wisdom, so he bolstered his own spell with every shred of focus he and Varka's cape could manage. The air around him and Valen hummed with magic, and Cole suddenly regretted sitting so close.

The stones touched, but did not grind against each other as they had before. They vibrated with tremendous force, emitting a deafening buzzing sound that shook Cole's ribs and made his hair stand on end. Valen showed no reaction whatsoever. The force applied to the stones ought to have caused a small explosion, or shattered them at the very least, but they droned more loudly with each passing second, vibrating so violently that they appeared as a singular blurry object. The spell drained more and more of Cole's Wisdom, replacing his focus with a drunken sense of detachment. Darkness crept in from his periphery, fuzzy and wonderfully empty. Just before he reached the edge of unconsciousness, he felt something slip in his spell, something that should not be. Fearing the worst, Cole released his spell just as Valen did.

A single stone fell to the gap between their legs, bumping into their shins with an odd heaviness.

"Where'd yours go?" Cole said, hefting the granite orb with a triumphant grin.

"You are holding it," Valen said. "That one is mine."

Cole regarded the stone with a half frown. "I don't think so, bud. The residuals from my spell are still hanging in the granite. Feel for yourself."

As Valen took the rock, his mouth fell open in a look of astonishment. "Incredible."

"What?" Cole asked. Sitra and Lileth had paused in their own match and drew closer.

"This *is* your stone, but it is also mine." Valen gently placed the stone at his side and scooted away, as though it were one of Sitra's fulminators. "Both stones are occupying the same space. Exactly the same space. Every particle is sharing itself with another. I cannot fathom how they continue to remain stable in such a form. This may very well be the most dangerous thing we have ever done. Lileth was right. Some things ought not to be trifled with."

"Seems pretty stable to me," Sitra said, walking over and scooping the double stone up in her hand. "Heavy though. But just to be safe..." She summoned her shroud and searched the stars for something. She let out a triumphant cry, then hurled the stone with a mighty throw. The sphere screamed through the air and vanished over the treetops in a blink.

Lileth shrugged. "What was that all about?"

"Borla Dign's that way," Sitra said, pointing with a bladed finger. "If those rocks turn themselves into fulminators then that's the best place for them. I hope it hits Decreath right in the deka seeds."

Chapter 17

Baby Steps

"I don't need every little detail, just tell me where we stand," Cole snapped. Conversation came to a standstill, all eyes now looking expectantly at him. He attempted to massage the headache from his forehead before it found a place to settle. His morning appointment in the Heart Tree had already gone half an hour past its allotted time, and was now cutting into his lesson for his students. If only he could sleep. "If The Three came knocking right now, with every Colossus and Domina they have, what are our chances? What are our options?"

Rayn's annoyance was apparent, but since the Unbound's return from Borla Dign he seemed to lack the will to argue with Cole directly. "Our chances are poor and our options are limited, but we're not as doomed as we once were. Falinor at least has some good news on the matter."

Falinor showed no reaction. He gazed off beyond the chamber, it seemed to something only he could see. Thessi gave Falinor a swift elbow to the ribs. He jerked upright in his chair, jumping as though waking from a daydream. "Sorry, sorry. A flock of soul flies just landed in the training grounds and put half our students to sleep"

"Do they need help?" Cole asked.

Falinor waved his hand dismissively. "No, not unless help involves something more invigorating than the bolt of lightning administered to the buttocks. Our recruits have taken to knocking themselves out whenever there's a soul fly around. Apparently the fools get a decent high off the ambient dream wave. Don't get me wrong, I enjoy getting a little buzz just as much as the next guy, but the middle of a lesson is hardly—"

Cole cleared his throat. "Your report, Falinor."

"Sorry," Falinor said. "Overall, I'd say the students are making fantastic progress ever since your victory in Borla Dign. Wareen's propaganda team took Brinleaf's memories and crafted training shows down in the Arts District. The students get virtual training by taking turns playing through the entire battle as one of the Unbound. There's currently a weeklong waiting list to play through as you."

Cole sighed. "As long as they're learning something from it. We weren't perfect."

"No real battle is," Falinor said.

"So they're ready then?" Cole asked, though he already knew the answer. "They're ready for the real thing?"

Falinor's eyes fell to the table. "We could train them for a full cycle and they wouldn't be as ready as I would like, but they're not so helpless as when they first started. They've learned enough that they would no longer be a total liability in battle. Their Wisdom is especially robust, what with the Borla Dign folk augmenting my training staff, but they lack Passion and Rage. We need more muscle and heart to win this fight."

Cole's headache took root at last, filling his head with a hurricane of rusty hammers. "Thank you, Falinor. That's... better than I hoped. Thessi, what about you? How are we doing on the logistics front?"

An unabashed grin bloomed on Thessi's face. She spoke with an exuberance Cole never would have thought possible from the previously careworn woman. "Marvelous. I'm not ashamed to admit that the Logistics Arch has gained the most from our friends at Borla Dign. Food is a non-issue. The markets are now fully staffed by competent and motivated teams instead of self-serving individuals, so every apothecary, laboratory, and weaponsmith is producing in excess. We still have some kinks to work out with our local storage and distribution, but our estimates predict The Sill will be entirely self-sustaining within a couple of weeks."

"That is great news," Cole said with as much of a smile as he could manage. "The Logistics Arch is probably the most underappreciated pillar of The Sill's success. Our whole force would have come to a crippling halt weeks ago if not for the efforts of your department. This is huge, Thessi."

"Thank you, Cole," Thessi said with a seated bow.

Debjornik let out a mirthless chuckle from across the table.

"Don't tell me I hurt your feelings, Debjornik," Cole grumbled, then adopted a patronizing tone. "I promise you're just as important as Thessi and everyone else. Why don't you go next?"

A smile broke free from Debjornik's scowl. "It will take more than words to unsettle me, especially from a half-human mutt who can't use Wisdom without Varka's favorite blankie." The table laughed, including Cole. Spirits among the staff had lifted considerably with the successes of the last month. "While the Intelligence Axis hasn't yielded nearly as much fruit as the Logistics Arch, I am pleased to report some good news. The Three have just been spotted in Amoskeag, one of the larger cities on the Light Side, well on the other side of the planet. While I wish no one the misfortune of playing host to those demons, my heart beats a note softer knowing they aren't about to jump over our walls any second."

"That *is* good news," Cole agreed. "We need all the time we can get."

"Of course." Debjornik took a generous gulp from his tankard before continuing. "Moving on... my agents abroad have seen evidence of mass disappearances in the cities on the Dark Side. It was only a few dozen at first, barely a blip on our scans, but after a few weeks that number was well into the thousands. At first we assumed the vanishings were simply victims of Corpulants or Chosen Colossi, but their numbers were far too great, not at all sustainable for our enemies. It wasn't until last week when we saw a surge in people immigrating to The Sill that our hypothesis solidified into theory. We noticed the numbers immigrating were growing proportionately to the numbers vanishing. I questioned the immigrants myself, and they confirmed it at last; we are in for a serious population problem. We expect our numbers to double this month and triple the next. All of Aeneria knows of your victory in Borla Dign. They want to fight."

"Oh let them come," Thessi said, setting her tankard on the table with a thud. "I assure you they'll have warm beds and full bellies in our walls."

"Just make sure no one gets through without an inspection," Cole said. "It would be all too easy to slip a spy or an assassin in among a crowd of refugees. I'll help if you need it."

Debjornik offered a gratified nod. "That won't be necessary, but I'll remember you said that. Now to wrap up my report, I can confirm that our friends in Morthain are not as dead as we all thought. After wading through the rumors and lies, I managed to send a few agents to the White Sands, where they observed several lone ships assaulting every enemy convoy that passes through. The Light Side refers to them as sand pirates, but judging by their patterns and strategies we believe they are the remnants of Morthain's fleet."

"How are you so sure?" Cole asked. Hope swelled in his heart.

"Because my agents cannot lie to me," Debjornik said, settling the matter.

"Good enough for me then," Cole said. His eye twitched as an excited voice jolted through the Unbound's Passion network.

"Looks like we know where our next mission is!" Sitra said with savage glee.

Cole acknowledged Sitra and returned his attention to the staff room. "Thank you, Debjornik. Morthain has some powerful Rage users. They could be the muscle Falinor was talking about." Cole then took a small swig out of his tankard and turned to Wareen. "It seems like everyone's been singing your praises lately. How's the Communications Web doing?"

"As well as we could be," Wareen replied, gesturing to the others. "The rest of the staff has already canvassed our success, though I daresay I can add a few additional nuggets of good news. As Falinor said, we've been helping with the training simulators in the Arts District, but the bulk of our efforts have been focused on our propaganda machine. Your victory in Borla Dign proved The Three can't just go where they please and take what they want. Ours is a story of revolution, and Borla Dign was just the first page. There are plenty of people out there willing to be a part of our story."

"How exactly are you spreading this news?" Cole asked. "Aren't all the Seer Jars down right now?"

"Baileen airdrops," Wareen said. "We link up with them as they pass through our lagoon to cleanse soul flies. Four have consented to bear a few of my staff and a small payload of cyphers. The baileens travel in the upper atmosphere most of the time, so by the time our cyphers land in a city, the baileens are miles and miles away. There is still a risk, of course, but the baileens are willing to do their part. They have suffered losses of their own."

"They certainly have," Cole said, remembering the abomination of the baileen-Domina. "I'm glad they're still on our side. Do you have anything else? Do you need anything?"

Wareen flashed a look of annoyance to the edge of the room where Brinleaf stood alone. "No, nothing new to report. Though I'll have you know our request to Borla Dign's consensus remains unfulfilled."

"And your request will remain unfulfilled until you consent to join our consensus," Brinleaf said as politely as ever. "We guard the knowledge of our magic not out of jealousy, but for the safety of all, including The Sill. Cole can attest to our ethics. You were indirectly connected to our consensus during our escape, were you not?"

"You know I was!" Wareen snapped. "And you had Cole revoke my knowledge of the Seer Jar upgrade, just as you revoked it from him. If you trust us with your people then trust us with your magic!"

Brinleaf gave a small bow. "I am sorry, Passion follower, but it is not within my power. The consensus will not allow it. If you simply join us, the knowledge will be yours."

"And we're back where we started," Wareen sighed. "I'm quite finished. Please Cole, bring this meeting to a close so we can get back to work."

Cole released an aura of soothing Passion throughout the room before he spoke, not enough for anyone to notice, but just enough to unwind the tension in the air. His headache was getting worse.

"Brinleaf, do you have anything?" Cole asked.

"Only for you," Brinleaf said.

Cole gave a quick nod. "Fine. We'll talk after. Rayn? Anything from the Strategy department?"

"Remembered me at last have you?" Rayn said with half-hearted spite.

"I never forgot about you," Cole said. He forced his voice to remain even and respectful. "Strategy and Operations encompasses every other department here. I wanted your report last because it's the most important."

The gloom on Rayn's face lifted somewhat. "Before you stirred things up, the staff used to report to me, then I would give my report to Chiron, Rothael, and Alvani. You've been doing my job for me for quite a while now, and I can no longer ignore the fact that I've become nothing more than a middle man. Operations and Strategy is now obsolete. You are overseeing The Sill's day-to-day operations, and no matter what strategy or plan my team comes up with, you and your Unbound will do what you see fit. With all that said, I wish to formally resign and disband my team. Falinor can see to dispersing us wherever his team sees fit. I have a few young men and women who show great promise for work in the Intelligence Axis."

"You can't abandon your duties," Cole said in a firm, but not unkind voice.

"I am not abandoning anything," Rayn said. "And neither is my team. We have discussed it at length and we are all of the same opinion. We must acknowledge the truth. We must be flexible enough to bend along with the times, lest we resist and shatter into irrelevance. No, my team and I will resign. Unless you would force us to stay?"

"Never," Cole said. "But I will make my case if you'll hear it. Are you Passion-linked to your team right now?"

"Always," Rayn said.

Cole nodded. "I realize the Unbound can be a pain in the ass. I know it more than most actually. They put me in charge even when I flat-out refused, but after a while I came to realize they were right in doing so. And the job wasn't as bad as I expected because I was never alone. They were with me then, are they are with me now, every second of every day. I'm never alone, Rayn, and neither are you. The Unbound needs the Strategy and Operations department, and more importantly so does The Sill. I only see the big pieces, and I have no idea about the thousands of steps it takes to move one of those big pieces. The Unbound can come up with a plan or two, but only you have the resources to find every variable, to see every possible outcome. We need you for that. I can't promise the Unbound won't go against your advice from time to time, but we only do it because we know more than we can tell you."

"You expect us to follow you blindly, though you won't trust us with all the information?" Rayn asked.

"It's not a matter of trust," Cole said. "Aeneria still has a few secrets, and they are just as likely to win this thing for us as they are to cast us into an age of shadow. In the event of our deaths these secrets will find their way to the Heart Tree, then it will be up to you to save us all."

Rayn clenched his jaw and his eyes fell to the table. "Eliza held a special place inside us all. My heart weeps for her." He then brought his teary-eyed gaze to Cole. "That is why we advised you not to go. The Unbound are too important a thing to risk in such perilous missions. You are our only hope."

In that moment Cole saw the staff not as diplomats, but as children, as his family. A triggered memory yanked him from the Heart Tree, to the dank alley where someone he loved needed him more than anyone had ever needed him. Joshy's smile swam to the fore of his thoughts. His ginger hair was a mess, and he still had a bit of food stuck on his cheek, but his eyes, his eyes were on fire. They brimmed with such fathomless love that conveyance was only possible through two words.

I know

Cole sent another pulse of Passion throughout the room, blatantly this time, infusing their life candles with the strength of his compassion. Droplets of lavender light appeared around the staff, teeming and shimmering, and settled about the room like a heavy snow. Profound relief replaced the worry on their faces. Brinleaf began to sway in his corner of the room, as if the Wisdom follower heard music no one else could.

"The Unbound isn't defined by any person or group," Cole said, addressing them all through Passion. *"The Unbound is a path, and as long as there are those still treading it, there will always be hope."*

Cole turned to leave, then stopped at the door. "Please Rayn, just give it another week. If you still feel obsolete then do whatever you feel is right. Brinleaf, if you want to talk to me you'll have to do it on the fly. I'm very late for training."

"Of course," Brinleaf chirped. His robes hissed across the polished bark floor as he hovered after Cole.

Cole and Brinleaf popped out the main door of the Heart Tree. The two guards at the entrance flinched at his sudden appearance, clearly unaccustomed to their new positions. Cole shot them a stern look. They resummoned their munisica and stood a little taller. Cole turned to Brinleaf and asked, "Can you talk in the air?"

"My feet rarely touch the ground, so yes I can," Brinleaf said with a smirk.

Varka's cape snapped to liquid crystal and Cole shot off to where he felt the seven life candles of his students. Brinleaf caught up to him within a few seconds.

"Why didn't you just fly out of the roof?" Brinleaf called over the wind.

With another twist of Wisdom, Cole summoned a shield to block the air around them so he didn't have to shout. "Because it's rude. And I'm trying to play nice. What did you have to report?"

"That your request has been fulfilled," Brinleaf said. "We have created your Everglen."

"But I only gave you Chiron's notes a week ago!" Cole said. "The Unbound haven't even discussed what we needed from it. I hope you didn't do anything that can't be undone. We don't have time to waste."

"We couldn't agree more," Brinleaf said. "We have but laid the groundwork for the pocket dimension. They have made the rules, and are awaiting your approval before they agree upon a reality for the place."

"Who are *they*?" Cole asked, banking left to avoid a broad residential tree. Faces in the widows cried out as they saw him and Brinleaf fly by.

"We think it best if you see for yourself, when you have time that is," Brinleaf said.

Cole wondered where he was going to carve time out of his schedule. "Do you sleep?" Cole asked, hopeful.

"Yes, I do, and so do the people of Borla Dign," Brinleaf said. "And before you ask, no we will not partake in the dreamsource cypher as the staff of the Heart Tree has. The consensus would unravel if we did not take the time to sleep and recover."

"Fine. We'll find the time somewhere," Cole said, knowing full well he would have to miss yet another trip to see the girls at Naythan's.

Brinleaf gave Cole a playful elbow to the arm. "I didn't say I wasn't above sneaking out while the rest of Borla Dign sleeps. Your friend Valen makes a stimulating elixir, does he not?"

"Yeah," Cole replied with a half smile.

"Then I shall take my leave and find Master Valen," Brinleaf said with an awkward mid-air bow. "I will be ready to show you our project at your convenience. Good day, Master Cole."

Cole put on a burst of speed after Brinleaf departed. *Master Cole.* The words didn't sound right to his ears. It didn't even have a ring to it, like Master Valen or Master Sitra. While he loathed the title, he decided to tolerate it because of what it meant to the people of The Sill. A few seconds later Cole landed in the small clearing in the center of the barracks trees.

To his pleasant surprise, Cole found Wilkin's unit well underway with a lesson of their own design, which at the moment appeared to be a half-speed sparring session. Six of the unit were paired up, striking and blocking with deliberate forms straight out of Roth's handbook. Wilkin circled about the unit, observing with a keen eye while offering critique and encouragement in equal measure. Perhaps there was hope for their unit after all.

Wilkin's head perked up once Cole walked within range of his Passion. He cupped his hands over his mouth and called over the din of the mock battle, "That's enough! Line it up!"

The unit froze and, upon seeing Cole, dismissed their munisica and formed themselves into a single line. Sweat glistened on their foreheads and their chests heaved like fireplace bellows.

"Master Cole," Wilkin said with a quick bow.

"Have you meditated yet?" Cole asked.

"We did," Wilkin said eagerly. He then bit his lip as his eyes fell to the side. "We meditated for a whole hour. I know we're supposed to keep going until you show up but you'd never taken so long before so I..." Wilkin shook his head, his eyes now squarely staring at his feet.

"Took initiative," Cole said, finishing Wilkin's sentence for him. "That was the right call. I should have contacted you with Passion to let you know I was going to be late, but I was distracted, and so I failed you."

Wilkin looked up at Cole with a slightly shocked expression. "Master, of course you didn't—"

"Yes, I did," Cole said. "And you all picked up my slack. I would have started you with combat drills anyway. Actually, since you're all warmed up, how about a practical exercise?"

Their eyes lit as excitement trilled across their Passion network. Cole gave no reaction to their mental whispers. They had no idea he could hear every word, and even though he couldn't *not* hear them, he wanted to at least give the illusion of ignorance to preserve their privacy. Cole smiled and reflected for a moment on all the things he and his unit muttered in front of Roth, Chiron, and Alvani, wondering if they'd heard everything as well.

"I'll take that as a yes," Cole said. "Now, one of the most common enemies you'll face is the Dom—"

"Master Cole?" squeaked a tiny voice from the far end of the line. She was the smallest in the group. Narrow-shouldered and with short-cropped hair like Eliza's. She hopped out of line and approached Cole. Her stride bespoke confidence with every step. Her head was barely as high as his elbow, though she looked up at him without a hint of intimidation.

"Yes, Kamilah?" Cole asked.

"You are in hurt, Master Cole," she said. "May I heal you before we begin our lesson?"

Confused, Cole smiled and dropped to a knee so he was looking right at her. "I appreciate your concern, but I think I would know if I was wounded. You might not know it, but I'm pretty good with

Passion." Cole waved his hand and sent a cascade of lavender beads over Kamilah's head.

Kamilah gave an annoyed flinch as one of the lavender motes zapped her on the nose. "No, not a wound. Your head. It is in hurt." She huffed, then a decision clicked in her eyes, and she clapped her hands to Cole's head.

Cole suppressed an instinct to shield his mind. Her magic worked its way through his skull, subtle and light as a feather, leaving him with a minty taste in his mouth. Cole laughed as his morning headache fizzled into nonexistence. Kamilah inspected him for a moment longer, then removed her hands and gave him a satisfied nod.

"Thank you," Cole said. "I never learned that Passion spell. Where did you find it?"

"My mother gave it to me," Kamilah said. "She is dead now. She and father both died in the assault on Costas. You were there."

Cole hid the emotion from his face, forcing it into a warm smile instead. He knew that her parents were likely not dead, but Chosen. Most everyone from The Sill burned on the towers in Costas. Kamilah would learn this soon enough, when life's bitter winds replaced her innocence with cold truth. Cole only hoped her parents were among the scant few he and the others had managed to free from their bodies, granting them a true death through Passion.

"I was," Cole said, giving her a squeeze on the shoulder. "And I have them to thank, for helping me survive so I can teach you today." He sent her back to her place in line with a tilted nod, then stood and addressed the whole unit. "Now that we're *all* ready, I thought I'd show you all what it's like to fight a Domina. Not a real one," he added quickly, seeing the looks of terror on some and bloodlust in others. "You'll be fighting me, and I'll be doing my best to fight like a Domina, which in itself is kind of a strange concept. Can anyone tell me why?"

The unit was quiet for a moment, but then Kolric, a bald boy who rarely ever spoke answered in a shaky voice. "B-because you never know what kind of animal the Domina are made of. One could be covered in fur while another is covered in scales."

"Or wings!" chimed a girl whose name was Serra.

"Exactly right," Cole said. Kolric and Serra glanced at each other, sharing the pride of the moment. A tiny grin cracked in from Cole's hardened-teacher mask. "The animals are called *thralls*. The Domina all start out as regular Aenerians like yourselves, most of which are weak in body and more importantly weak in spirit. Like all scrawny cowards, they yearn for power, which they find in others by stealing it. Using Grotton's magic, Hunger, they trick an animal into swearing itself into service in exchange for a promise, usually food or guaranteed breeding. The number of thralls is very important, because with every additional thrall the Domina becomes more powerful, but it also loses more of its Aenerian mind."

Wilkin stirred. "Master, what's the largest number of thralls you've seen in a single Domina?"

"Three,"Cole replied. "And they were more confused beasts than anything else. I'm sure there are some with even more thralls, but it would take someone with incredibly powerful Hunger to control it."

"Like Grotton?" asked Bennit.

"Let's hope not," Cole said. "If you want to know more, I suggest you spend some time in The Sill's library. While you're there it wouldn't hurt to look into Corpulants and Colossi too. You might even be able to teach me something like Kamilah just did, but that's enough chat for now. It's time to dance."

Cole walked a short ways away from the group and found a small boulder jutting up from the grass. At his command, a satisfying ache stretched his fingers into black blades as the shroud of Rage covered his hand. Cole plunged his munisica into the boulder, then tugged. The boulder heaved grass and earth aside as it revealed a body as thick as Cole's chest, veined with bloody iron ore and spackled with quartz. Cole spun the boulder between his munisica, clearing it of all dirt, then called forth his Wisdom. Ripples shivered up the grass of Varka's cape as the hunk of stone melted and molded itself into a crude, yet enormous mace.

"It's a little small, but you'll get the idea," Cole said as he gave the weapon a few experimental swings, producing a deep *whoosh, whoosh*.

By now Wilkin's unit knew not to wait for a signal. They lunged at Cole head-on, which was exactly what they shouldn't have done

THE UNBOUND

when facing a Domina. With a simple, yet swift overhand swing, Cole flung the mace at the middle of the unit. The group scattered, jumping and rolling in every direction, and all but one dodged the attack. Viness caught the mace solidly to her chest, flew backwards several feet, then landed with a muffled crunch in the grass, motionless. Viness was not only the oldest and wisest of the group, she was the best healer. Her loss would cost Wilkin's unit dearly. Cole charged after the wounded, just as a Domina would to finish its kill. A clawed foot struck him in the side, sharp and tiny, but powerful enough to knock him off course before he reached Viness. It was Grant, the unit's best fighter. Cole hid his proud smile behind a savage grin as he thundered towards the new challenger.

Grant and Kolric both sustained crippling injuries from Cole's munisica before Wilkin corralled his unit into something other than a chaotic melee. Cole kept his attacks simple and his tactics single-minded, providing the unit with patterns they could take advantage of. Cole charged after Wilkin next, who stalled him with perfectly executed evasive maneuvers. It took the remaining three students to lift the mace from Viness, but once they healed her Cole noticed a marked change in the unit's strategy. Disorder gave way to fluid motion and established techniques. Two to distract and evade, two to attack and probe, and two to heal wounds. Wilkin orchestrated from the edges of the battle, giving orders and inserting himself whenever an opportunity appeared.

As the minutes dragged on, Cole sensed a flagging in the unit's strength. They managed to mark him with a collection of injuries, magical burns and countless cuts, though none were serious enough to do any more than enrage a strong Domina. They needed more. They needed motivation. It was then that Cole realized they had been holding back. Master Cole, their teacher and beloved mentor, would never hurt them beyond the aid of a quick spell.

Cole let out a roar so loud the entire unit flinched. His shroud shot over his limbs and raced up his neck as his hair gathered itself into bundles of ebony daggers. With another roar the shroud rushed over his face and torso, covering him inside and out with the master's Rage.

Wilkin barked his orders throughout their Passion network, but Cole was too quick. In the blink of an eye Cole closed on tiny Kamilah. With a mighty upward swing, he caught her between the legs and sent her sailing like a rag doll to the tree tops, then leapt after her, smashing her in mid-air back to the ground. She collided with the ground in a jumbled pile of broken limbs with her head twisted in an odd angle. The unit hesitated.

Rage rising, Cole wasted no time. He charged at Bennit, who stood with his arms at his sides, paralyzed with his own Fear. Cole whipped the mace around and took Bennit's legs out from under him, cleaving them from the knee down. The severed portions flew among the rest of the unit like bloody sticks.

One by one Cole pounced upon the unit, crushing a skull, opening a throat. His Rage would not be denied. The unit was no longer fighting back, but running for their lives, though none could run fast enough to escape the black death that hunted them.

Only Wilkin was left now. Sprinting and panting, the boy cried out into the forest for help, but not a soul came to his rescue. It was his turn to face death now. Wilkin stopped running and turned around.

Cole slowed to a lazy saunter now that his prey had given up. His eyes were black and insensate. A grin stretched across his armored face, wicked and victorious. His clawed feet had elevated him several feet taller than Wilkin, and his bladed hands had grown so large that the tips skimmed the grass. He was Rage incarnate.

"Master..." Wilkin begged. Tears welled in his eyes. "Master... how could you?"

A savage growl grumbled from deep within Cole's chest.

"No..." Wilkin gasped. "Not them. They didn't deserve..." He looked to the stars for answers, but found none.

Cole stalked closer still. The mace ascended for its final blow.

Wilkin's face twisted into a manic grimace. His mouth moved, but no sound came out, for there were no words appropriate for what Cole had done. He closed his eyes and seemed to find an answer within himself. Wilkin released a bellow born in the throes of injustice; the soul's defiance against death itself. His shroud snapped from his palms to his elbows while his munisica tripled in size, forming ebony claws with barbed joints and bladed fins on the backs of his hands.

The mace descended.

Wilkin flattened one hand into a knife and plunged it into the mass of rock and iron. The mace exploded around him in a shower of sparks. Before the first fragment hit the ground, Wilkin leapt into the air, straight through the cloud of smoke and flame. With a mighty roar he brought his bladed foot straight up into Cole's chin.

The force of the kick knocked Cole flat on his back. His shroud receded and his hands turned back to normal. Before Wilkin could land another blow, Cole stopped him with a flash of Wisdom, holding the young Aenerian in midair.

"Now *that* is Rage," Cole said. "Well done, Wilkin."

Wilkin grumbled something incoherent as he thrashed against Cole's spell.

"They're not really dead," Cole said, no longer able to hide his smirk.

Wilkin stopped fighting, though his shroud and munisica held fast. "Prove it," he snapped.

"Only if you stay out of sight and don't interfere," Cole replied. "Climb up a tree or something, and block your mind from their Passion. I'm going to try and get the rest of your unit to dig a little deeper into their Rage as well."

"Fine," Wilkin said, clearly unconvinced.

"Wilkin, your Rage," Cole laughed. "Release it."

Wilkin strained for a moment, then shot Cole a furious glare. "I don't know how."

"We'll have to work on that next," Cole said. He rose to his feet and sent a pulse of lavender light into his student's chest. Wilkin's eyes closed halfway as his shroud and munisica receded. "Now go hide, and watch closely. They're each going to think their entire unit has just been killed, and you need to know how they're going to react."

Wilkin hesitated, but only for a second before trudging off and leaping up a nearby tree. Cole heard the chopping of munisica keeping pace with him from the canopy as he approached Bennit. With a wave of green magic, Cole dissolved the illusion. Bennit's shins and feet popped back into existence, whole and unmarred. Cole then placed a palm on the boy's forehead and implanted a potent false memory with a blend of Wisdom and Passion. As soon as the memory sprouted, Cole jumped back and summoned his shroud and munisica once more. Bennit woke with a start, spinning swiftly to his feet, as if he'd only just fallen to the ground. Cole fueled his munisica until his bladed fingers caressed the ground, then approached Bennit with murderous intent, just as he'd done to Wilkin.

Bennit needed a bit more coaxing than Wilkin had, but he got there in the end, producing respectable munisica and a shroud halfway up his forearms and shins. It wasn't much, but it was certainly more than the tiny cat's claws he had minutes ago. After convincing Bennit that all was well, Cole continued the exercise with the rest of the unit.

One by one the unit fell victim to Cole's trick. They all made marked improvements with their Rage, though as with Wilkin they needed assistance controlling the heat of the red magic. Each student turned on Cole, attacking him with every intent of killing him. They all offered vehement apologies afterwards, but Cole couldn't be more proud, and he let them know it.

Of all their reactions, Kamilah's was the most ferocious and the least expected. The tiny girl with an aptitude for healing had attacked Cole with a torrent of fuchsia stars, screaming her battle cry while momentarily wielding an expert's Passion. Everywhere her magic struck left him numb and tingling, and Cole had to counter with his own Passion to keep from succumbing to full paralysis. Cole subdued her as gently as he could, wrapping her arms and legs around her with a full body hug, but not until she saw the rest of the unit standing before her in perfect health did she finally relent.

Though the whole skirmish had lasted less than twenty minutes, Cole spent the next hour discussing the lesson in detail. Just as Roth had so long ago, Cole investigated every choice the unit made, analyzed every strike, examined every spell. By the end of the hour, the unit had a better understanding of Domina tactics as well as their own Rage. Once they had learned all they could from the encounter, Cole attacked them again, this time as a double-thralled Domina.

After long hours of battle and even longer hours of lecture, it was time for Cole to end the day's lesson. The unit begged Cole to teach them through the night, and he wished he could, but there were other matters demanding his attention. After saying his farewells Cole took to the skies. Almost as soon as he left, his Passion sensed savage laughter, clashing munisica, and crackling spells from the group. He considered turning around and ordering them all to bed, but thought better of it. He wouldn't be the one to spoil their fun, though neither would he go easy on them tomorrow should they stay up all night.

Cole went straight to his apartment rather than stop at Naythan's. The day's training had started and ended late, and Naythan would only just be tucking the girls in for the night. Another day had come to a close and Cole felt only marginally more ready to face The Three or their armies. He wrestled facts against possibilities until his mind knotted itself in a tangle of brooding questions with no answers. The Sill was well on its way to being stronger than ever; however, he couldn't shake what he felt before departing Borla Dign; the unbridled power of Decreath, Grotton, and Sorronis. He had only felt the faintest sliver of their presence before he entered the Seer Jar, and even that had nearly overwhelmed him. The warriors of The Sill continued to sharpen their claws and practice their magic, and for what? To stand tall and brave in the face of gods? If they had a whole cycle to prepare then The Sill's forces could handle any number of lesser minions, but never The Three. If even one of the gods showed himself in the battle, there would be no amount of Rage, Passion, or Wisdom that would save them.

Cole's perseverating carried on through his nightly rituals. He showered, changed and washed his clothes, then ate a few blackstouts. He fell onto his bed and stared at the whorls in the wood grain that decorated his ceiling, losing himself in the patterns. If only he could sleep. Sitra and Valen were probably starting on their nightly training. They had long given up waiting for him to join. What Cole wanted more than anything else in this moment was to be with Lileth, to lust away the night, but tonight was her night to sleep. He would have to wait. But he didn't want to wait. He wanted her now. Springing out of bed, Cole stormed out of his room and pushed his way through the liquid stone door.

The flight to Lileth's apartment was slow and unsteady as he had forgotten Varka's cape in his wardrobe, so he trundled along like an overburdened bumblebee. He landed heavily on the platform just outside Lileth's apartment, hoping she had left the door unlocked. She had.

Cole pushed his way through with a faint pop. There she was, curled up with her back to the door, her bed surrounded by unfinished paintings and crumpled canvas. Her naked shoulder peeked out from the blankets, a beacon in the dim gratia light. Cole brushed his feet off and slid into bed with her. She stirred at his jostling. She turned over, eyes still closed as she reached for him through the sheets. Her hands flowed under his shirt to his back, and she pulled herself close.

"I thought you had forgotten about me," she breathed into his ear.

"Never," Cole said in a low voice. "How was your day?"

Lileth's breathing slowed, light and rhythmic. "I would rather not speak on it. All I want is right here, right now." She wrapped a leg around him and nuzzled closer.

"I'm sorry I've been so busy," Cole said. "This job is pulling me in every direction that's not yours. I feel like my days are not my own."

"You are the key to the Aethers," Lileth whispered. "Aeneria is tearing itself in half to get to you. This world cannot survive another war, and neither can we. I feel it in my heart. When destinies collide you will be there at the fulcrum, holding the key to it all. I don't want to lose you, Cole." She uttered a soft moan as her chest began to shudder with quiet sobs.

"I'm not going anywhere," Cole said with a reassuring hug. "We're going to find a way through this mess. Look how far we've come since Borla Dign. It's only been a few weeks and The Sill is almost as strong as it was when Chiron was in charge. Give it a couple months and we'll be unstoppable. Did you hear about Morthain?"

Lileth was so long to respond that Cole thought she'd fallen back asleep. When she spoke again he could barely hear her words. "I don't have much more fight left in me."

"What are you saying?" Cole demanded.

"I am saying I can't do this anymore," Lileth admitted. "The battles, the stress, the death, there's just no end to it. It is an ugly way to live."

"I know," Cole said. And he truly did. Every week seemed to take more from him, leaving him tired to his bones. "But still, we can't just give up. Aeneria's counting on us. All the local planets too."

Lileth reached farther up Cole's back, raking her fingernails up his neck and into his hair. She dug her nails into his scalp and pulled his lips to hers, then kissed him with wild abandon, as though this might be the last time they held each other. She pulled away and opened her eyes. Tears clung to her black petal lashes.

"Travel for me, Cole," she said. "Right now. Take me with you. I want to see the other worlds. I want to see your world. Take us away from it all."

"I wish I could," Cole said with a pang of guilt. He could never leave Sitra and Valen to The Three, nor Naythan and the girls. The Sill needed him. "There is another way I can take you. And I promise you'll forget about everything outside this room."

"Oh really?" Lileth said.

Cole cupped her face in his hands and kissed her deeply. His lips wandered to her neck as his hands slid down the tight skin of her back. She let out a sharp breath as her flesh burned hot under his touch. With a single fluid motion she was on top of him, her hands ripping the shirt from his chest. The blankets fell from her shoulders. Lithe muscle rolled under her skin, eager and capable, every delicate swell accentuating the curves of her hips and shoulders. Fine droplets of sweat beaded on her breasts as though they had been sprinkled with diamond dust. Her chest heaved as gyrations worked through her stomach and down into her thighs. She gazed upon him with the smoky look of a wild huntress, ravenous with desire. She snatched his hands and slapped them to her chest. Cole's palms glowed lavender as his lust mounted, sending pulse after pulse of seductive energy quivering through her frame. Lileth's eyes rolled as she let out a growling moan. Her hands dove between his legs next, impatient and firm, she un-lashed his belt and explored his aching sex.

Passion flowed between them like two storms colliding at sea. Their minds and bodies joined, melding in the heat of the now, mixing magic and flesh with animalistic fervor. They lost themselves in each other, and for one small moment nothing in this world or the next mattered so long as they burned together.

CHAPTER 18

FIGHT, LITTLE CANDLE

Something pressed against Cole's mind. It felt significant, but surely not as significant as what he and Lileth were engaged in. Probably just the staff of the Heart Tree with yet another bureaucratic issue. The thing pressed again, harder this time. Cole tried to ignore it, but its nagging persisted, haunting and familiar. He realized what the thing was. It was an approaching life candle. Two approaching life candles.

"Eliza!" Cole shouted.

Lileth went rigid under him, then jerked away as though he'd suddenly burned her. "What did you say?"

Cole stood up on his knees. "Eliza! She's alive! She's outside the Lurkwood Gate right now!"

Confusion mingled with the horror on Lileth's face. "I sense nothing."

"She's still suppressing her life force," Cole said as he began looking around the room for his clothes. "I can't believe it!" Lileth wrapped her arms around herself and watched him in stony silence as he dressed. Once clothed, Cole stopped at the door. "Aren't you coming?"

"I'll catch up," Lileth said, though she looked like she wouldn't.

Cole bolted through the door and launched himself into open air, falling three stories to the ground below. His munisica erupted from his hands and feet as he collided with the woven root path. He considered running to get Varka's cape so that he might fly with all haste, but decided his Rage would get him there sooner. His bladed feet tore over grass and rock as he sprinted along.

"Cole, what is the matter?" Valen's mind rang into his. *"Where are you off to in such a hurry?"*

Broadening his Passion to encompass all of the Unbound, Cole responded with bubbling mirth. "Eliza's back! She's approaching the Lurkwood Gate now!"

"*But I don't sense anything,*" Sitra pointed out. "*Why wouldn't she reach out to us?*"

"She's probably suppressing her presence," Cole replied. "*She would have to if she sneaked all the way back from Borla Dign without getting caught. Are you two coming or not?*"

"*We are already in the air,*" Valen said, broadcasting a snapshot of himself and Sitra in flight.

Not wanting to be the last one to arrive, Cole uncorked a larger portion of the red magic, covering his entire body in the master's shroud. His bladed hair whistled around his ears as he leapt over a swath of metal buildings constructed for the citizens of Borla Dign. He tried contacting Eliza as he ran, but her mind was shut to him, probably locked by the power of her own master's Passion.

"Whind! Open the gate!" Cole cried as he skidded to a halt. He took a few steps back and looked up the massive wall of airtight trees in front of him. The trees were thicker than most buildings, and grown so close together that not even air could pass between them. Cole could barely see the tops without drawing Wisdom to his eyes, but he was sure he could clear them in a single bound. He scanned the ground for a good place to launch from. "Whind, open up or I'm jumping over!"

A rustling of leaves heralded the arrival of The Sill's gatekeeper. Whind's figure melted out from the base of the wall, pushed along by thick ropes of crawling vines and tangles of roots.

"This is no cat flap, Wisdom Walker," Whind said in his usual ethereal tone. "These trees are as old as The Sill itself. Grant them a moment and they will open themselves for you."

"It's not for me," Cole said. "There's someone trying to get in."

"I sense nothing and no one approaching," Whind said, but then his head turned slowly to the wall. "Ah, I feel them now. The roots and rocks remember their feet. Your compatriot, Eliza approaches. The Old One is with her."

"The Old One?" Cole asked.

"Indeed." Whind nodded slowly. He extended his hand toward the wall and several bright vines as thin as wire grew from his palm. They shot for the bark and wormed their way through the wall tree.

A second later came a titanic crack. The earth shuddered beneath Cole's feet as two of the enormous trees creaked slowly from the ground, forming a smooth tunnel from which Cole could smell the ocean air. The gratia lights flicked on inside the underpass and Cole ran through without another word to the gatekeeper. He emerged on the other side and summoned a beacon of white light above his head. It wasn't as bright as it should have been, but then he didn't have Varka's cape with him. He ran forward, dismissing his Rage while sending out waves of Passion to sense the life about him. Animals scurried through the underbrush and birds squawked at him over the distant crashing of waves.

"Eliza!" Cole cried out. His breath trailed behind him in wispy vapor as he ran. "Eliza, it's me!"

For a moment the only response was the wild noises of the forest around him. Cole stopped, sure this was the right place. Two silhouettes appeared farther up the trail. One stood tall and proud, while the other wore a thick traveling cloak and leaned heavily on a walking stick. Cole pumped more of his focus into his magical light, revealing a careworn Eliza and an annoyed-looking Ka Reine.

"Eliza!" Cole cried out. His vision blurred as he ran to her. Eliza's face lifted at the sight of him, and she embraced him in one of her warm hugs. Her armored robes were dirty and frayed, and she felt far too bony.

"What in the world are you wearing?" Eliza said with a laugh, pointing at Cole's torn shirt and silken shorts. "You honor my return from enemy lines with shabby night-wear and body odor? I ought to send you away and wait until you are more presentable."

"Wait if you want. I'm starving," Ka Reine grumbled as she ambled past them.

"It's wonderful to see you too, Ka Reine," Cole said with a smile. The old storyteller replied with a dismissive flick of her hand, as though turning around wasn't worth the trouble.

There was a sound of snapping wings, then Sitra and Valen landed beside them.

"I don't believe it!" Sitra shouted. She dismissed her wings and dove at Eliza, tackling her at the waist. "You crazy bitch, I thought you were dead! Why would you scare me like that? And why didn't you contact us sooner?" Sitra's tirade crumbled into incoherent sobs as she hugged Eliza, rocking her side to side on the footpath. Eliza's munisica sprang free and her shroud crawled up her arms, though it was clearly out of self-preservation as Sitra was now squeezing her with enough force to crack a tree.

"Sitra, Eliza just survived an encounter with The Three," Valen croaked. His eyes glistened, though he spoke through a smile. "Let's try not to kill her just yet."

"I *am* gonna kill her though," Sitra sobbed. "You stupid, stupid, girl, I'm gonna..." Her hysteria melted into silent relief as she nuzzled into Eliza.

"I missed you too, Sitra," Eliza said with a meek smile. "And you too." She unraveled herself from Sitra and bounded over to embrace Valen, who patted her awkwardly on the back as if he had never been trained in such open displays of affection.

"What happened to you?" Valen asked once she let him go. "Cole said The Three were on top of Borla Dign as we left. That was you who destroyed the Seer Jar, right?"

"It was," Eliza said. A splash of Fear fell over her face, fleeting yet unmistakable, and for a moment her eyes appeared to see beyond them. "The Three were indeed upon me, and they had fresh armies with them, including several Colossi. As soon as I destroyed the Seer Jar I suppressed my thoughts and magic in hopes that they wouldn't find me, but they did."

"How did you get away?" Sitra asked.

"I ran," Eliza replied in a quiet voice. The Fear came back, indicating she wasn't yet ready to talk about the details. "The power of The Three was beyond my ability to comprehend, and I didn't even sense them directly, only the smallest drop of a shadow as I fled. I felt my mind twisting and unraveling, but I couldn't tell if I was running away from my insanity or towards it." Eliza's hands started shaking as the color drained from her face.

"We're glad to have you back," Cole said, throwing an arm around her shoulder.

Cole nudged the others through the Unbound's Passion network. Valen's and Sitra's minds flowed along with his own, and together they enveloped Eliza's body and soul with the lover's magic. She resisted at first, which confused them, but the reason became apparent as they seeped through her layers of mental armor. Her emotions flooded into them. Potent and raw, they exploded from her in ever-increasing cascades. Fear, Hunger, Hatred and Despair. The sliver of dark magic she felt from The Three had been eating her from the inside out, and she had been suppressing those evils since her escape. The magic bolted from her like it had a mind of its own, eager to infect others and spread the grace of The Three, but the collective power of the Unbound was more than a match for it. Cole felt the arms of Sitra and Valen slide alongside his own, and together they embraced Eliza inside and out. Rage smothered Fear, Passion dissolved hunger, and Wisdom set order to the chaos of Hatred and Despair.

Something poked Cole in the small of the back. He turned to see Ka Reine looking at him, expectant and impatient. She beckoned him away with a flick of her eyes.

"Go," Valen urged. *"We will tend to Eliza. She will be right as moonlight before you know it."*

Cole offered Valen his thanks and unraveled his arms from the group. Ka Reine had already started hobbling way, not towards the Lurkwood Gate, but off the side of the trail. Trees and their underbrush moved aside for her, creating an open path that looked as if it had been there for cycles. She led him to a secluded grove of pale birches. Starlight trickled through the canopy and poured over the blanket of clovers that lined the ground. Apparently satisfied with the spot, she stopped and whirled around to face Cole. Her dull cloak spun with her, though miniscule gems twinkled in the fabric like the night sky. As if the moment brought her back to her youth, her hunched back straightened itself as she rose to her full height and set her fists squarely upon her hips.

"You, young man, have some explaining to do," Ka Reine snapped.

The last time Cole had stood before Ka Reine, she was well over a foot taller than him, and now even though their size difference was quite the opposite, he still felt miniscule before her ancient gaze.

"What have I done now?" Cole asked, not bothering to hide his offense. "I've been pretty good since the last time we met."

Ka Reine stretched up on her tiptoes and rapped Cole on the forehead with a wooden finger. "Not you, *you*," she repeated, jabbing Cole in the chest instead. "Varka! I know you're in there, you arrogant son of a bog angel."

"What did Varka do?" Cole asked, bracing himself for another poke of her stony fingers.

Ka Reine huffed and shrank back to her usual hunched posture. "It's not a matter of what he did, boy, that's long in the past, though we're still dealing with the ramifications of that blunder. I'm referring to what he *should* have done, when he had you in Oberon Temple. Do me a favor and conceal us from sight and sound, and block your mind from your little ensemble. I don't want anyone stitching our words to their tongues."

Cole did as he was told, plying his Wisdom to the air about them, though the magic didn't come so easily without Varka's cape. After letting the Unbound know he would be silent for a time, he looked to Ka Reine and nodded.

"It's done," he said.

"Not so keen on Wisdom without Varka's rag, are you?" Ka Reine said, sneering at the translucent olive-green barrier around them. The magic was sound, but the diameter of the barrier was barely large enough for the two of them to stand in. She gave Cole another sharp prod to the sternum. "What, too busy brooding to show the boy how to cast a few spells?"

Varka was as silent as he had been since the last time he showed himself, a moment so long ago that Cole couldn't even remember.

"How did you and Eliza meet up?" Cole asked in an attempt to bring the conversation back to something he could comprehend.

Ka Reine kept a suspicious eye on Cole's chest as she spoke. "I like to be where things are happening. I sensed a disturbance in Borla

Dign, and so I decided to investigate. In my travels I found the girl hiding up a tree like a frightened cat. She suppressed her vitality to the edge of death's door, but I know one of Chiron's kids when I feel one nearby. I coaxed her down and we've been sneaking our way back here ever since. The Three's minions plagued us every step of the way, too. I don't care for fighting anymore, but I wasn't about to let myself miss a good story because of this Divine Guard, or whatever the hell those fools are calling themselves nowadays."

"Chiron's dead," Cole said. "So are Roth and Alvani."

"I'm afraid you're only one out of three with that statement," Ka Reine said. She brought her attention to the limited space around their feet and shook her head disapprovingly. She rolled her eyes at the magical shield around them, then rapped her knuckles on it, as if asking it to move aside. The shield swelled several times larger as she twirled another finger over the ground. A comfy chair erected itself from the surrounding roots and clovers, and she plopped herself down with a moan of relief. "Alvani is dead thanks to you, which is a far better fate than what that pithing shard had in store for her. Chiron is gone, not dead, though where to I can't begin to fathom. He's probably swimming in the Aethers as we speak. As for Rothael, that's a problem my nightmares will have nightmares about. He was the most ferocious and cunning warrior this world has ever known, and now he is Harbinger to Grotton, a slave to his own power."

"You seem to know an awful lot about what happened in Fangshard Valley," Cole said in a slow, careful cadence. "There were only a few people there, and even fewer when Alvani died. How do you know all this?"

"Suspicious are you?" Ka Reine said with a smirk.

"Sorry," Cole said quickly.

Ka Reine pulled a long pipe from her sleeve and clamped it between her teeth. "Don't be. You know as well as I that there's a traitor in your ranks. Habbad's little trap in Borla Dign was no accident. That's where Varka was raised, did you know that?"

"How do you..." Cole asked, incredulous.

"They don't call me The Old One just because I look like a dried-up frog. I have my means," Ka Reine said as her crooked smile climbed up to her eyes.

There was a flicker of light overhead, and a soul fly dropped from the sky. Sporting a hue of fiery honey, it alighted on Ka Reine's shoulder, then rolled down her arm to where her hand cradled the bowl of her pipe. There was a flash and a sizzling spark from the golden orb. With the pipe lit, Ka Reine shooed the creature away, and it spiraled up the nearest birch to chase its fellows in the canopy.

Cole waited while she indulged in several long pulls. The smell of fruit and spices thickened about him, and he found himself suddenly relaxed and open to the flow of the moment.

"Better?" Ka Reine asked, sending a great cloud of wine-colored smoke to the treetops.

"Much," Cole said.

Ka Reine gave a sharp nod. "Perfect, because what I'm about to tell you is going to cook your brains. Deep in the heart of Oberon Temple lies a series of Vaults, one for each of our magics; they are called—"

"I already know about the Vaults of the Soul," Cole said. "Chiron left me a note."

"He did *what?*" Ka Reine fell into a fit of coughing, which she cleared up by patting herself on the chest with pink magic from her hand. "He left the greatest and most powerful secret this world has ever known *in a note?*"

"I'm pretty sure he enchanted it so no one could read it other than me," Cole assured her. "And the note destroyed itself as soon as I put it down."

"What did it say?" Ka Reine asked.

Cole had read the note over so many times, he recalled it as easily as if it were in his hand at this very moment. "That there's a Vault for each of our magics, but there's one for each of the dark magics as well. The Three went into each of their Vaults and Varka went into the Wisdom one. The Vaults contain the essence of the magic they are named for, and the only way to win this war lies inside one of them. Chiron said Varka and I need to go there and pick one."

"And did he mention that each of these Vaults is a one-way trip?" Ka Reine asked.

"He did," Cole said. "And that's not going to stop me."

She inspected him once more with that same look that made Cole feel like a child. "If the only way to stop The Three lies in a place that is not here, then why are you still here?"

Cole rubbed his forehead as he pondered his answer. He inhaled another deep breath of the pipe smoke, then settled himself onto the plush clover beside Ka Reine's chair, leaning back so he could get a better look at the soul flies bounding about the canopy.

"As it stands right now, taking a step towards Oberon Temple would be taking a step away from victory." He waited a moment for Ka Reine to refute the statement, but she did not. "I'll become the strongest person in The Sill, and The Sill will soon be stronger than it has ever been, but if we move on Oberon City now, we'll only be another meal for The Three. You know how powerful they are now that all their Harbingers have been crowned. I'm pretty sure they're only waiting us out so that we'll be a fatter pig to slaughter when they do finally come."

"So your hesitance is out of cowardice?" Ka Reine asked in a mocking tone. "Rothael would be most disappointed."

"I think Roth would be more disappointed if I charged headfirst into the biggest fight of my life," Cole said. "And I doubt I could sneak my way into Oberon Temple. We're going to have to bring the fight to them, once we're ready for it that is."

"And when do you think that will be?" Ka Reine asked.

Cole sighed and shook his head. "I really don't know. We might not ever be truly ready. Borla Dign was a huge win for us, especially now that Eliza's back safe, but Wisdom can only carry us so far. The entire city was crippled by a few Corpulants. We need more heart and muscle on our side. We need Passion and Rage."

"Rage," Ka Reine said with a hint of disdain. "The least useful of our magics, but quite necessary for this endeavor. I assume The Sill has heard about Morthain?"

Cole let out a chuckle. "You probably already know the answer to that."

"Of course, but omniscience can be misconstrued as rudeness if one is not careful," Ka Reine explained. "The Morthainians will be a tricky lot to find, but you're clever enough to figure it out I'm sure. Just don't wait too long. Grotton will likely be influenced by Rothael's history with the people of The White Sands. He won't wait to collect them."

Cole was silent for a moment as he thought back on his time with Roth. "Were you there when Roth invoked the Trial of Honor upon Morthain?"

Ka Reine shook her head as she exhaled another cloud of smoke. "No. It wasn't the most interesting thing happening at the time, but I was well aware of the happenings as they were happening. I *was there* however when Roth invoked the trial upon the Unbound."

"He *what?*" Cole said, sitting up straight and looking Ka Reine in the eye.

"Oh yes," Ka Reine said with a smug grin. "Rothael stacked quite a high opinion of himself after conquering a whole civilization with only his munisica and that giant rock of a skull of his. He set his sights on the greatest power in the land; the fabled heroes of the local planets who called themselves Unbound."

"What happened?" Cole asked.

"Varka whooped him," Ka Reine said in an offhand manner. "Whooped him like the rambunctious child he was. Until that point Rothael had managed to solve every problem in his life with violence and obstinacy, but Varka was better at both."

"That means Varka won the trial of honor, doesn't it?" Cole asked. "That would make him Roth's king, and the king of all of Morthain!"

Ka Reine let out a wheezing laugh. "I'm not surprised Rothael never told you that little story. Yes, for a moment he did rule over Rothael and Morthain. Rothael begged Varka to kill him as the shame was unbearable, but Varka had a much better idea. He ordered Rothael to repair the damage they'd caused to the town they fought in, then made him join the Unbound for a whole cycle. After Rothael's sentence his honor would be returned, and he would regain authority over himself and Morthain."

"If only I had known," Cole said through a smile. "I would have had Varka command him to cook my breakfast and do my laundry. What made him stay after a cycle?"

"Alvani," Ka Reine stated.

The name hung in Cole's mind, and he was silent for a moment. Sparks raced through Cole's memories, connecting things hidden in plain sight. "When Alvani died, the last word she spoke was *betrayal.* She talked about the pithing shards too. I have a feeling that whoever betrayed us in Borla Dign had something to do with those shards."

"Caught on at last, have you," Ka Reine said. "What do you know about the pithing shards?"

"Not much," Cole admitted. "I can't find anything on them in The Sill's library, nor Chiron's."

"Nor would you," Ka Reine said. "The pithing shards are made from broken pieces of Oberon that fall to Aeneria. They carry a great deal of energy from the soul flies' dust. Normally, the pieces are just a rare treasure found by accident, but in the hands of the Cold Crows they can be crafted into weapons, and with the proper ingredient these weapons can be paired to the soul of their victim."

"Betrayal," Cole said.

"Betrayal most foul," Ka Reine said. "It comes from someone with whom the victim shares a relationship of unreserved love and trust. It can be a son or daughter, a romantic partner, a dear friend. This person injects their love into the shard, pairing it to its victim. Someone very close to your circle bonded those pithing shards to your elders."

Cole's heart went still. His first thought was of the safety of his friends, then The Sill. The traitor could be inside the walls of The Sill this very moment, plotting and scheming, or waiting for the right moment to strike again. Or perhaps he or she was right outside? He turned his head and looked to where he'd left Eliza and the others. No, it couldn't be one of them, his heart wouldn't allow it. He had felt each of their minds through the Passion, which left little room for treachery and lies.

"Before your mind runs away with your worries, I will tell you this," Ka Reine said. "Your friend Habbad was the one who brokered the trade with the Cold Crows. He acquired the shards, but he was not the one who bonded them to your elders. He couldn't have. You know as well as I that he was too damaged to love anyone after his sister burned in Costas."

Despair welled up beside Cole's Fear, dousing what little hope he still nurtured for his friend. By failing in his promise to save Lexy from burning on the towers, Cole had killed what little good was left in Habbad. He had created a monster.

"How am I supposed to find the traitor?" Cole asked in a quiet voice. "The Sill's got to have dozens of people who were close to the elders. Hundreds maybe. I can't go around rummaging through people's minds. Everyone has secrets, and they have every right to keep them to themselves."

Ka Reine stowed her pipe and stood, shrinking her chair back to the ground with a twirl of her crooked finger. "You're a clever kid. You'll figure something out, and if not then the traitor will make himself known before the end, of that I'm certain. But in the meantime, I have a job for you."

Cole was slow to his feet. He had quite enough going already. "What sort of job?"

CHAPTER 19

FROZEN HEARTS

"We have to go. Now," Cole said after popping through the door of Eliza's room. Valen and Sitra had taken her back to her apartment while he spoke with Ka Reine.

"Go where?" Sitra whispered in an angry tone. She was crouched beside Eliza's bed, rubbing warmth back into her friend's hands. Valen was perched likewise on the other side of the bed, massaging Passion into Eliza's temples.

"To Vol Karinn," Cole said. He brushed aside a hanging vine as he stepped deeper into the room. He had never been inside Eliza's apartment before. Like the upper chamber of the Heart Tree, this room was open to the starlit sky, only it seemed as if nature had entered through the roof to reclaim it. Live branches grew from the bedposts and the sides of the armoire, while ferns and flowering weeds sprouted from patches of dark soil around the edges of the floor.

"Never heard of it," Sitra whispered.

Valen stood. "Nor have I. What did Ka Reine tell you?"

Cole's sense of urgency sputtered as he beheld Eliza. The grit had been washed from her face and her short hair was combed smooth to the side. She had changed out of her travel-worn armor and into silken comfort clothes like what Cole had on. Her cheekbones stuck out far too much for Cole's liking.

"How are you feeling?" Cole asked in a delicate tone.

"There's no need to whisper," Eliza said with a smile. "I'm not on my deathbed. I am perfectly fine. Promise."

"No you're not!" Sitra said in a boorish whisper. "That was serious dark magic tearing you up. And you still look like a skeleton. Eat another blackstout." She pulled another of the black fruits from nowhere and thrust it into Eliza's hands.

Eliza humored her with a grateful smile and a small bite of the dark fruit. She looked back to Cole. "I've heard of Vol Karinn, but what's *our* business there? They are not exactly our kind of crowd."

Cole blinked, suddenly remembering they were supposed to be gone by now. "It's a city full of Passion followers. They're well-hidden, so The Three haven't found them yet. We need to get there before they do. Winning them over would be a victory for The Sill."

"That would be a *huge* victory for The Sill," Sitra agreed. "The elite units are doing well enough, but our regular troops are garbage in the healing department. I've seen some of them walking around at the end of the day still carrying wounds that look a week old."

"But how are we to win them over?" Valen asked. "If they have avoided conflict thus far, then why would they agree to join us?"

"We'll have to figure that out on the way," Cole said. "Are you two ready?"

"You mean *you three*," Eliza corrected. She twisted out of Sitra's grip and leapt from the bed, landing on the far side of the room in front of her armoire. The wardrobe burst open, and a satin sheet erected itself between the two doors, shielding her from view. "I just spent nearly a month apart from you all. I am going."

Cole, Valen, and Sitra left Eliza's apartment to change and pack. As Cole checked his armored robes in the mirror, he couldn't help but admire the seamless work of Amorinanis's magic. The material was cool and smooth, like strands of glass made flexible, but so tough he couldn't tear it with his bare hands alone. A swath of Varka's cape billowed from Cole's wardrobe, waving to him through the still air of the room.

"What would you do?" Cole asked the cape.

He waited for Varka to respond, but it merely continued its wave, as though eager to set off on another adventure. Cole sighed, then brought himself to the stone room of his center, washing himself over and over through its cooling waters. Layers of stress which he neglected to notice until now melted from him. When he opened his eyes he felt lighter, but there was a slight weight upon his shoulders that hadn't been there a moment ago. He looked to the mirror and found Varka's cape clasped around his neck, ready to go.

"Where's Lileth?" Eliza asked as Cole joined the Unbound in the center grounds of the barracks. "I thought Valen's potions stalled her sleep for important occasions like this."

As soon as Cole's feet touched the ground he felt Varka's cape tickle his neck as the fabric shifted to spiky grass. "She's not coming. I tried waking her but she wouldn't budge, and we can't afford to wait."

"If that girl spent half as much time training as she does sleeping then she'd be stronger than all of us," Sitra said with a scowl. "Leave her. She's only slowing us down anyway."

No one said a word. Cole wanted to defend her, but there was no arguing that Lileth hadn't been putting in the same effort as she always had. She missed countless training sessions, even with her own elite units, and when she did show up she was aloof and empty. The others were convinced Lileth had caught some sort of virus, but Cole knew the real reason. He'd known it since they escaped Fangshard Valley, and their last conversation in her bed confirmed it.

"Are you sure she cannot be roused?" Valen asked Cole quietly while Sitra waxed on to Eliza. "We may have need of her skill."

"I'm sure," Cole lied. He had tried waking her, but changed his mind before she fully woke. There was a strong part of him that agreed with Sitra. If this mission turned out to be a dangerous one, then he didn't want Lileth there. She wasn't as strong as she used to be. "We need to leave."

Valen clapped him on the shoulder and gave him a brotherly nod. Without another word, Cole brought his Wisdom to action and his feet left the ground. He felt Valen ascending behind him, leaving Sitra and Eliza chatting in the grass behind them, too distracted by their reunion to notice their mission had already started.

Valen opened a link directly to Cole's mind. *"Should we wait? We are quite far."*

"Eliza's Passion is so powerful she could find me even if I hid myself on the back of Oberon," Cole replied. *"And they look like they're enjoying each other for the moment."*

"I see," Valen said. They passed the canopy layer, emerging into the salty air and broad starscape above. Valen tilted his emerald wings and glanced back toward the ground. *"I assume we won't be checking out with Whind before we go?"*

"Nope," Cole said, keeping his eyes straight forward. *"And we won't be telling the staff of the Heart Tree either. Ka Reine agrees there's a traitor among us. By leaving abruptly our absence will go unnoticed for a while, and if there's no traps or ambushes waiting for us, then we can rule out a few suspects. The Heart Tree is going to be furious with me."*

"Not if they have any sense," Valen pointed out. *"At this point it is obvious we have a turncoat in our midst. They would have to be blind beyond reason to ignore the fact that they are the most likely of our suspects. They and Wisdom Walker Larkin. Has there been any word from him since our Victory in Borla Dign?"*

"No," Cole replied. He didn't trust any of the Celestial Council, especially since they were now under direct control of The Three, but for some reason he knew the traitor was closer than that. *"I think it's Rayn."*

"The director of Operations?" Valen asked.

"And Strategy," Cole added. He then sent Valen snapshots of a few of his memories of Rayn, the ones showing how implacable and oppositional he had been. *"And he tried to resign. Recently."*

"Did he really?" Valen said with genuine disbelief. *"I thought he lorded over his position. He always seemed a bit of an asshole to me."*

Cole dropped a few feet, then played it off as if he were merely stretching in midair. Valen never swore. *"Yeah, he did. Every time someone from the other offices reports even the smallest success, he broods and whines like a child who doesn't get enough attention, then he refuses to contribute for the rest of the meeting. It's almost as if he doesn't want us to get better."*

"Perhaps he does not," Valen agreed. *"Do you have any other suspects? Ka Reine perhaps?"*

Cole paused. The thought had crossed his mind. *"The tricky thing about her is, even if she is the traitor, she's so powerful I doubt any of us could stop her anyway. She doesn't like to show it, but she is an absolute master of Passion and Wisdom. I felt it when she and I were talking."*

"I suppose we shall have to wait and see." Valen glanced back to The Sill once more. *"I purchased a rather expensive geography cypher*

from the Cordial Compendium not long ago. I am disappointed this Vol Karinn was not included. Where is it?"

Cole was about to respond, then he realized he forgot to ask Ka Reine where Vol Karinn was. But then he felt a tiny bump in his memory, obvious yet seamless, sitting right where the location of Vol Karinn ought to be as if he learned it from a map. As Cole delved into the bump he was struck by an unbidden and strong scent of spiced fruit and pipe smoke.

"It's on the far side of the Fangshard mountain range," Cole said with certainty. *"The Fangshards angle away from Oberon City, so we shouldn't have to come within a hundred miles of the place."*

Valen went quiet for a moment, his thoughts heavy. *"I do not get feelings of premonitions or intuition very often, but something tells me that when we finally return to Oberon City it will be the end of a great many things. Perhaps the end of all of us. It is a fulcrum of fate."*

Cole didn't respond. He wasn't ready. Only now did he fully appreciate the significance of that final moment, when The Sill made the final push to Oberon Temple; it would indeed be the end of many things. It would be the end of his life at the very least. His friends, his adventures, his time with Lileth. He would either die in the battle against evil, or succeed, and lose himself forever to whatever Vault claimed him. Every step and breath he took brought him closer to death.

Valen took his silence in stride. *"Fate has a cruel sense of irony it seems. During the last war, the Unbound were the ones defending the temple from The Three, and now it is the other way around. Chiron is right. The solution must lie in those Vaults. That is where Varka found his answer, and I know you will find an even better one. It might kill us all to get you there, but I want it known that I intend to see you through to the end. Whatever end."*

Cole didn't respond. He surged faster, letting the wind pull the tears from his eyes so Valen couldn't see. He wanted to turn back. He wanted to gather up everyone he cared about and shut them away until he figured out how to unlock the Aethers, then they could all Travel together, far from the shadow of The Three. Every successful mission was another step towards Oberon Temple, which now more than ever felt like his own personal gallows. Every day on Aeneria had been a struggle, a struggle which he bared his teeth and pushed through, not realizing that every victory had brought him closer to the end of his life.

Something tore through the air directly below them, then two sets of emerald wings appeared. Cole felt a rush of warm compassion as he beheld a smiling Eliza and Sitra. He missed them already.

The Unbound indulged in the intimacy of their Passion network as they flew, exchanging emotions and memories as easily as spoken word. They had a long flight ahead, which would easily be the farthest any of them had traveled by wing, but they had an abundant supply of blackstouts and plenty of funny stories to catch Eliza up on. Cole contacted Wareen at the start of The Sill's work day, informing her that he and the Unbound would be gone, but to where and for how long he couldn't tell her. Wareen grudgingly accepted, leaving him with a standing request for any and all information he could give her.

While no one openly admitted it, Cole knew the others were glad for Lileth's absence. They often remarked on how swift their journey would be without the need for sleep, and complimented each other on their various contributions to the mission. Valen crafted a spell that pulled water from the air, which was meticulous and required constant focus, but he kept them all hydrated throughout the flight. Sitra maintained a barrier that blocked the wind while ensuring the air remained thick enough to breathe. Eliza warmed them all with a nourishing blend of Passion and Wisdom. Cole kept quiet most of the flight. He regretted leaving Lileth behind, but the more he thought about it, the more certain he was that she would have only been a liability. Before he left he placed a letter at Lileth's bedside. The letter was brief and vague, merely explaining that they had to leave on an urgent mission, and asking her to contact him with Passion when she woke. She deserved a proper explanation, but he couldn't leave such information lying around on a piece of paper.

The next day came and went, and he never felt the slightest stroke of her thoughts. He considered reaching out to her instead, but refrained, thinking she was likely too upset to talk. Another day passed without her touch. By the end of the third day Cole had had enough.

He called to her with his Passion, but she was gone, lost to him. Fearing the worst, Cole asked Eliza to contact her, but she was unsuccessful as well. The group concluded that she was merely upset at being left behind, and she was suppressing her Passion as Eliza had done.

By the fourth day Aeneria left house of Amikar and entered the house of Mecelland. The Unbound took a brief respite in the air, but it was only to slow enough to enjoy the view of the changing houses and each other's company. Halfway through the fifth day, their feet touched the ground for the first time since leaving The Sill.

They alighted on an escarpment high in the Fangshards. The mountain range looped back on itself, encircling a frozen lake like a dragon sleeping around a massive blue gem. The lake was solid azure blue, and the surrounding mountains were covered in a spiky coat of green pines, right up to the peaks.

"I don't get it," Cole said, stepping to the edge of the cliff. His bladed toes gripped the rock and root beneath his feet. He sharpened his eyes with Wisdom and searched the land below. There were no signs of civilization. "There should be a city down there. Ka Reine's memory led right to this spot. She didn't show me anything about a lake."

"Perhaps the city is hidden somewhere below? If these people were able to elude The Three then it might not be so easy for us to find them," Valen said. "Though with the Fangshards on all sides it is likely not worth it for anyone to invade here. Corpulants certainly can't fly this high."

"Or this whole thing is a trap," Sitra said as she hurled a boulder off the ledge. "How do we even know Ka Reine's on our side? She could be next in line for Harbinger for all we know."

"Ka Reine had plenty of opportunities to betray me while I traveled with her," Eliza said. "I was crippled from being so close to The Three, but she stayed by my side and escorted me to The Sill on foot. I trust her, and you should too. She fought alongside the Unbound when The Three first laid siege to Oberon Temple."

"True, but so did Kreed," Cole said, still scanning the canyon below. "Kreed used to be one of Chiron's students. He betrayed the

Unbound right in the middle of the siege. Probably switched sides as soon as The Three broke through."

"Was this a tale from one of Chiron's books?" Valen asked.

Cole shook his head. "No. Chiron told me when I first met him. One of the rules Varka placed on Aeneria was that The Three's forces were banished to the light side of the barrier, never to feel the warmth of Oberon again. I met Kreed on the light side before I wrecked the barrier."

"A nuisance since day one," Sitra said with a smirk. "Well then, we better get down there and poke around. It's been a whole week since you've stirred up trouble on our planet. Wouldn't want you getting rusty." Without warning she shoved Cole hard in the chest, sending him sailing out into open air.

The Unbound made several laps around the enclosed valley, scanning with Passion all the while. The air grew warm and humid as they descended, a contrasting comfort in comparison to the flight over. Their Passion revealed a thriving ecosystem of plants and animals, including many species not found anywhere else on the planet, but still there was no sign of Aenerian life. Determined, Cole led them to the very center of the frozen lake, which was the only place they had yet to examine. Their munisica crunched over the ice as they peered into the azure depths below.

"That's strange," Cole said, kicking chunks from the ice. "The entire canyon is as warm as the lagoon outside The Sill, so how can the lake freeze over?" He looked up to Oberon. The moon rested atop the peaks, ablaze with ever-changing hues blooming like flowers. Its warmth kissed his face as fierce and hot as a midday sun back on Earth. "There's certainly plenty of moonlight here."

"The ice is indeed cold. Something must be drawing the heat out of the water," Valen said. He crouched low and placed his naked hand against the mirror-smooth surface. "There is something else very odd about this lake. Life persists everywhere on Aeneria, yet I sense nothing whatsoever below us. Not even the faint glow of fungi or bacteria. What about you, Eliza? Cole?"

Curious, Cole shut his eyes and dismissed his other spells, focusing all his efforts instead on Passion. His awareness stretched to the very limits of the bowl canyon, revealing teeming masses of life candles both large and miniscule, but there was nothing at all below him. Not even at the very bottom. It was as if life had forgotten this lake, leaving it an empty, frozen void. He opened his eyes and glanced at Eliza, who looked just as confused as he felt.

Eliza shook her head. "I sense nothing."

"Me neither," Cole said. "Ka Reine wouldn't have lied. I'm sure the city is here."

"Then perhaps we are not looking properly," Valen said. He conjured his emerald wings and took flight in a gust of wind, leaving a small twister of ice chips in his wake. He then spoke to them all through their Passion network. *"Pay attention as I cast this spell. I only just recently discovered it in Chiron's library."*

"What does it do?" Eliza asked as she craned her neck up at Valen, who was already so high he appeared to be a distant bird.

"It is another way to look at the world," Valen stated. He kept his mind wide open to them as his Wisdom began to bend the rules of reality.

Cole sensed a twisting pressure in Valen's eyes, much like the spell used for night vision, only this spell had vastly different results. Valen sent them all an odd image which no one seemed to understand, then urged them all to duplicate the spell. Amused, Cole took hold of his Wisdom and gave it a try. With a flick of thought, a bead of jade light popped into existence on the tips of each of his index fingers; he then transferred the light into his eyes. Cole blinked as the magic took hold, and for a few seconds everything went black, leaving him utterly blind. Then there was light, only it was unlike anything he had ever seen. It bloomed about him, revealing Sitra and Eliza. Their skin and eyes were almost blinding, while their armored robes and hair were so dim he could barely see them. The light had no color, and could only be described as...

"Heat!" Sitra gasped. She extended an arm and admired her hand, twisting it about. It was as bright and detailed as a metal sculpture pulled straight from a furnace. "This is heat-vision! Winged serephs use this to hunt."

"And so will we," Eliza said. She conjured her wings and took flight.

Sitra didn't need telling twice, not when there was a competition at stake. She shot into the air as if fired from a Morthainian cannon, her munisica leaving deep gouges in the ice.

Cole took to the air without the aid of wings. He felt the ice crack from Varka's cape as it shifted to liquid crystal. The spell over his vision left him disoriented, and the drain on his focus was much more taxing than he expected. The night sky looked like an empty void, like a black ocean looming above. The oddest thing of all was Oberon, however. Cole had become so accustomed to its fickle hues, always mixing and shifting its way through the rainbow, but now the moon stared down at him with a single, flat tone painted across its face. He angled back towards the ground, and after being momentarily blinded by the vibrant heat of the surrounding valley, began his search for inconsistencies in the ice.

The lake was barely bright enough for him to see, but after a few seconds his eyes adjusted and revealed details below the solid ice. There were veins beneath the surface, flowing and churning with what had to be liquid water. Here and there, bright objects darted about like fireflies with patterns similar to fish chasing prey. There was life beneath the surface.

"Found it!" Sitra said. Her pride rang through their minds like the obnoxious peal of a bell. *"There's a warm spot near the shore with a trail hidden in the woods. Hurry, or I'll start the fun without you."*

Cole banked towards Sitra's life candle and put on a burst of speed, anxious that she might do something rash without them. She came into view soon enough, and so did the others, each appearing like a statue made of white-hot metal. Below them was a triangular patch of ice ten paces across. It was warmer than any portion of the lake he'd seen so far.

Sitra greeted them with a deep bow when they all landed beside her on the pebbly shore. "Thank you, thank you, it was no trouble at all. Now, if you'll follow me sirs and miss, we have a city to liberate." She spun around on the spot and strutted into the woods towards a paved road, which was heavily overgrown and looked as if it hadn't been used in cycles.

Eliza cupped her hands around her mouth and called out, "Sitra dear, I think you're going the wrong way. Actually no, I *know* you're going the wrong way. Vol Karinn is under the lake."

Without missing a step Sitra spun on the spot, still maintaining a smug grin and cocky strut. "I knew that. Just getting a running start." She took two quick steps and launched herself with a powerful kick off the pavement, sailing high over them, stretching herself into a spear as she summoned her munisica. She smashed through the center of the triangle as easily as if it had been made of thin glass.

"Sitra!" Cole shouted as he sprinted after her. Valen and Eliza joined him around the jagged hole in the ice. Sitra's life candle was gone. Cole dismissed the spell in his eyes and the world resumed its normal hues. He held his hand flat above the crevice. "Stand back."

Valen and Eliza obeyed, and Cole called his Wisdom to action. Varka's cape creaked as it froze, and emerald light exploded from Cole's palm like a firehose. The ice hissed violently as the frozen water shifted straight to vapor, skipping its liquid form. The three of them instinctively hovered themselves in the air as the ice beneath their feet vanished. After half a minute there was a gap in the ice large enough for a baileen to land in. Cole sent the vapor to the sky, where it condensed into a cloud that billowed over half the valley.

"*Stop stop stop!*" Sitra's voice clamored through their minds. "*I can't breathe!*"

Cole ceased the flow of magic and descended through the mist. With the ice gone, Sitra's life candle became immediately apparent. Emerald light shone from Cole's hand and the air cleared, revealing Sitra sitting at the bottom of the lake, covered in mud and clumps of algae. Eliza and Valen floated down beside him as they approached Sitra.

"What in the bloody Aethers was that about?" Sitra said as she rose to her feet, dripping from head to toe in lake muck. "I was perfectly fine. Landed on a nice ice path, safe and sound, then you come barreling through like a vapor dragon. Is this one of your pranks or something?"

Cole was about to land next to Sitra and help clean her off, but thought better of it. "Your life force vanished as soon as you fell through the ice. I didn't know what else to do."

"Sure sure," Sitra scowled at him as she began cleaning herself with Wisdom. Clumps of detritus leaped from her skin and robes as if zapped by an electric shock. She levitated beside Cole and took care to ensure a few pieces splattered on him. She pointed at the cloud of vapor still hanging beneath a shelf of ice. "There's a tunnel over there, or I should say there *was* a tunnel. Who knows what's left of it now."

Valen waved his hand and the cloud vanished, revealing a large triangular cutout in the ice, easily wide enough for all four of them to walk through. He beckoned to the rest of the group with a sideways nod. "Shall we go introduce ourselves?"

Once everyone was clean and dry, the Unbound entered the icy tunnel, which angled downward at a gentle, yet slippery slope. They all summoned their munisica to keep from sliding, gripping the ice with clawed toes as they walked. The temperature dropped with every step, chilling their lungs as their breath hung in the air like floating bundles of cotton. Oberon's glow bled through the ice above them, casting iridescent shafts of light that refracted all about them in prismatic displays.

"Is that running water?" Sitra asked, pointing to a shimmering portion of the wall with a clawed finger. Gurgling noises rumbled from the other side.

"And fish too," Eliza said as a fleeting shadow darted across the wall. "It's strange. My Passion couldn't detect them from above the surface. There is something very odd about this ice. It should not be here, not in such a temperate part of the Fangshards."

"I expect we shall find our answers at the bottom," Valen said with a tone of mistrust. "We should keep a few spells at the ready for underwater breathing. One misplaced strike or spell could have us submerged in no time at all, though it might be a good way to drown any enemies we encounter."

"Always the tactician," Sitra said. "Hey Liza, didn't you say you knew a thing or two about Vol Karinn? Anything we ought to know?"

"I suppose it's time for me to come clean," Eliza said with a sigh. "*A thing or two* might be stretching the truth a bit. I was born in Vol Karinn. It is sometimes known as the dessert bowl, so called because it's contained by the surrounding mountains and because many treasures lie within. Vol Karinn is indeed a city of Passion followers, but they are not the craftsmen and songwriters of the Arts District in The Sill. The people here focus their efforts on a very narrow facet of Passion, one that travelers and warriors pay the highest price for."

"What facet is that, healing?" Cole asked.

"Sex," Eliza stated. She raised her chin as her face flattened to an emotionless mask.

Sitra looked as if she wanted to make a joke, then seemed to realize the implications Cole and Valen had already caught on to. Vol Karinn sounded like a city of prostitutes. A brittle silence filled the air around them as discomfort began to bleed from Eliza's portion of the Passion network. Eliza cast sideways glances at them, daring them to make the usual joke or stupid comment.

"The lake wasn't frozen the last time you were here, was it?" Cole asked in an attempt to change the subject. "You didn't know where the entrance was."

"No," she replied. "It has been a cycle and a half since I last stepped foot in Vol Karinn. It seems that much has changed."

The awkward silence resumed once more, this time broken by Valen. "There is no use delaying what promises to be an uncomfortable reunion. Shall we speed things up?" Valen plopped himself down on the icy slope and slid past them all. His hair rippled as he accelerated.

"He's been acting weird lately," Cole noted.

"I like it," Sitra said. She took a running start and dove headfirst, sliding on her belly. Her voice echoed back, shaking with laughter. "See you at the bottom!"

Cole put an arm around Eliza and squeezed gently. Her lip gave a single twitch, but otherwise her face betrayed no emotion. He searched within himself for the special place where their old fraternal bond used to be. It felt dim and hollow, but he could still hear the echoes of laughter and comfort. Cole sent a soothing beam of Passion through, conveying everything he wanted to say since they last touched minds.

When he finished, he waited for her heart to reciprocate its Passion for him, but there was only quiet. Disappointment fell over Cole. He looked to her, though her watery eyes remained straight ahead, as if determined to drill holes through the ice in front of her. Cole took his arm from her shoulders and called his Wisdom. His bladed feet lifted from the frozen path as the green magic whisked him down the tunnel, leaving Eliza alone in the ghostly light.

CHAPTER 20

TEMPTATIONS

The ice darkened as the tunnel dove beyond Oberon's reach, eventually giving way to tones of gentle rose and amber that grew brighter as the slope relaxed to a flat path. As Cole caught up to Sitra and Valen, he noticed signs of artifice inlaid on the tunnel walls. Someone had carved images into the ice. Cole slowed for a better look, discovering images flowing seamlessly from one to another. The scenes varied from epic battles to depictions of Aenerians arriving on exotic local planets, falling from the skies amid rivers of soul flies. Cole could have spent hours perusing the artwork, but Sitra beckoned to him from farther ahead.

"It's just like Morthain!" Sitra rang back. "They put a whole damned thing under the lake!"

Sitra and Valen were silhouetted against a bright backdrop that could only be the tunnel's end. Cole shot down the tunnel with a quick blast of Wisdom, landing beside Valen as he beheld Vol Karinn.

Hundreds of feet above was a frozen expanse of solid ice stained with broad colorful strokes of Oberon's whim. It stretched across the entire bowl-shaped valley, forming the ceiling of a crater with steep walls of rough stone. Frozen waterfalls lined the crater walls like pillars of pale sapphire, each carved into a titanic figure of what appeared to be Aenerian deities cast in heroic poses. The frozen gods stood sentinel around a city even larger than Borla Dign. Nearly every structure was carved from the same pale blue ice. There were countless towers, each finished with a pointed tip and reaching for the sky, as if hoping to someday poke through the frozen ceiling. Shining cathedrals sat comfortably atop hills scattered throughout the valley floor, four in all, and each was surrounded by a brood of smaller ice houses.

In the very center of the valley crater was a proper lake, only it wasn't frozen and pale, but shimmering with dark blue water and bordered by a lush shoreline. An island jutted out of the middle of the lake, covered in trees and fresh growth, and home to the largest building of all; a hall with walls of dark wood and a roof of black slate. At each corner of the hall was a towering lighthouse with golden bonfires blazing at their heads. A gentle snow fell over the entire valley crater, its fat flakes riding currents through the enclosed sky in sweeping white ribbons.

Cole stood in awe for a moment as he took in every detail. Vol Karinn reminded him very much of a snow globe. He leaned out from the edge of the tunnel and discovered they were standing atop one of the titanic waterfall statues of the valley wall.

"Does any of this look familiar to you?" Sitra asked Eliza as she landed beside them with a gentle flap of her wings.

Eliza gazed upon Vol Karinn for a full minute before responding. "Only the Summit," she said, indicating the warm hall in the center of the island. "The ice is new."

"And very peculiar," Valen noted. He placed his palm flat against the frozen mouth of the tunnel. "There is some spell in it, but I cannot tell which, or even what school of magic it comes from. It is the reason we could not detect the city from the surface."

Cole projected the awareness of his Passion as far as it would go. Pin pricks of life shone to him from the bottom of the statue they stood on. He enhanced his vision with Wisdom. What looked like ants crawling about the statue's feet sharpened into fat people in furry brown coats. They worked nets with long poles at the edge of a river set against the valley wall.

"There's people down there," he announced. "Let's go introduce ourselves."

He leapt out of the tunnel, controlling his descent with Wisdom. With a flash of emerald wings the others joined, cutting wide circles around him as he fell. Cole turned in midair to get a closer look at the statue whose head they had just jumped off of. It was a man with fine knives for hair and jagged munisica for hands and feet, with clothing of the same make as the armored robes of The Sill. The sculptures managed to capture the primal ferocity of a master's Rage in the eyes of the man, though the rest of the face was set in the calm repose of Wisdom.

The people below cried out in alarm as the Unbound landed among them. They dropped their poles and nets and fled in an awkward shuffle hindered by snow shoes.

Cole's feet sank into white powder. The ground was blanketed by knee-deep snow with tufts of straw grass sticking out. He uncorked just enough of his Rage to protect his feet and shins from the bite of the snow, then set off after the fleeing people, bounding like a deer through the powder. He called out to them, but upon glancing back they ran faster, their Fear renewed. One man tripped in a splash of white.

Cole grabbed hold of his fluffy coat and hoisted the man to his feet. "Easy there, we're not here to hurt you." The man took one look at Cole's munisica and promptly fainted. He fell backwards in another muffled puff of powder. "You've got to be kidding me," Cole muttered.

His eyes followed a trail of freshly churned snow to where the rest of the people had made it to a clear stone path and struggled out of their snowshoes. Cole swore and leapt from the snow, extending his jump with Wisdom and landing on the path between the fleeing people and the city. Eliza and Valen landed behind him, and Sitra at his side carrying the man who had fainted.

"We're not here to hurt you," Cole said as he twisted his palms to face the crowd in a gesture of peace. "We're here to help."

The crowd looked ready to bolt, but Eliza strode forward, munisica aglow with fuchsia Passion. She extended a clawed hand and cast a wave of pacifying magic at the crowd, who threw their arms up in an attempt to shield themselves, only to lower them a second later. The worry on their faces melted, giving way to serene acceptance and smiles.

"Fear not, my brothers and sisters," Eliza said with a tone of command. "We come with peace in our hearts and an offer of aid in these dark times."

A woman stepped forward and took Eliza's munisica into her hands, regarding her with warm familiarity. Her face was gaunt and sallow, as if she had been sick for some time, but she emanated a surprisingly potent aura of soothing Passion.

"Greetings stranger, I am Arinell," she said, placing a palm to her fur-padded chest. Like the crowd behind her, her face looked disproportionately tiny amid her voluminous coat. "Vol Karinn hasn't played host to outsiders for quite some time. You must be freezing. Please, take my coat." She then removed her jacket with fervor, as though it were a matter of life or death. Three of her companions removed theirs as well, and approached the others with looks of utmost concern. As their sunken faces had suggested, their bodies were skeletally thin.

"No, thank you," Cole said to a man incessantly offering a coat. His arms looked too skinny to even hold the garment. Cole looked to Arinell. "Please, we don't need your coats. We use Wisdom and Rage to keep us warm. What we really need is to speak to whoever is in charge of Vol Karinn. Your city is in danger."

Arinell's brow scrunched with worry, but her tone was gentle. "You speak of war and danger, yet you brandish magics used for exactly those things. I mean no offense, but I would know more about you before we take this encounter any further. Please, strangers, tell us who you are and where you hail from."

Cole stood a little taller. "We're from The Sill. We're the Unbound."

Silence fell over the path as the people of Vol Karinn adopted expressions of disbelief, which quickly lit to wild delight. Before Cole knew what was happening, the crowd converged on the Unbound, cheering with cries of elation and raucous applause.

"Eliza, what's this all about?" Cole asked, projecting his voice across their Passion network. *"Are we celebrities or something?"*

"No, they think we're gods," Eliza said with a tone of annoyance. *"The majority of Vol Karinn are religious to the extreme, and all are superstitious. They recognize The Three as gods of Aeneria's Light Side, though they do not worship them. They see the Unbound as Harbingers for Wisdom, Rage, and most importantly, Passion. The statues around the crater are carvings of our predecessors."*

316

"This should be easy then," Cole replied. *"If they worship us then we should have everyone out of here by the end of the day."*

"But we are not gods," Eliza said in a warning tone. *"We should not abuse their trust, not when their hope and lives are at stake."*

Every hand in the crowd found Cole's bare skin, each offering a generous measure of Passion. Cole accepted the offerings grudgingly, offering a reluctant thanks and in many cases transferring a portion of his own Passion back, unnoticed by the giver. Judging by their look of general malnourishment, the people needed the magic far more than he did. After greetings and names were exchanged, they plied Cole with questions about his life and showered him with compliments. They admired his munisica, taking the razor-sharp claws into their hands with curiosity and open awe. They grasped his magically warmed skin and armor and begged for more displays of Wisdom. It was as if they knew nothing whatsoever of the outside world. Cole looked to the other Unbound and saw they were likewise engaged. He shouldered his way to Arinell, intent on putting a stop to the mounting hype. He had to use his Passion to find her life candle among the forest of furry coats. When he found her his words went unheard, as the crowd had broken into song and dance, drawing others out of the snow with their jubilation. With the din rising louder by the minute, Cole grasped Arinell's shoulder and prepared to project his words directly into her mind, but paused as three deep explosions shook the air.

The crowd fell silent at once. Three more explosions thudded into Cole's chest. He and the Unbound reacted out of instinct, drawing munisica and taking to the air, scanning for the source of the danger. Farther up the path, a woman stood with a hand raised. Jade magic crackled between her clawed fingers. She wore elegant crimson dress robes, and was trailed by two men dressed in robes of plain brown wool. Chiron's lessons on Aenerian politics told him this woman was a Cardinal, an enforcer of religious edict. Cardinals were not inherently malicious, but any transgression against the gods they served were typically met with swift action.

With a calculating glare, the Cardinal surveyed the crowd in the path, then the four Unbound hovering in the air. Without a word, she brought her hand down and pointed it at the crowd. The magic in her palm shifted from crackling jade sparks to a pulsing orb of lavender Passion as she sent waves of pacifying magic over the entire area.

Cole and the others recognized the spell at once. They hardened their minds with ironclad Wisdom, nullifying the Passion before it could paralyze their bodies. At his urging, the Unbound dismissed their munisica and joined him on the path in front of the Cardinal and her Ulrichs.

Cole approached the woman, dismissing his shroud and showing her his empty hands. "Our apologies, Cardinal, but we had no way of alerting you to our arrival. The Three are—"

The Cardinal's face twisted with concentration as she loosed another wave of Passion far more potent than her first barrage. Cole's hair stood on end as the magic passed through the Unbound, again with no effect, but he heard dozens of soft thumps behind him. He glanced back. The entire crowd had fallen to the stone path, unconscious. Disbelief lifted the Cardinal's eyebrows as she fumbled to find her words.

Though Cole could sense the Fear leaking from her, her voice was steady and clear. "In the name of the Cascada, you are hereby detained for inciting disorder and using unauthorized magics. Dismiss whatever spells you have active and submit to the grace of the Goddess or you shall suffer my retribution." Her jaw clenched as her fingers darkened into black claws. Cole felt the heat of the woman's Rage extinguish her Fear; however, her shroud barely covered her hands.

"That's gonna be a no," Sitra said with a sneer. "But by all means, bring those kitten's claws over here if you're feeling frisky." To emphasize her point, Sitra beckoned to the Cardinal with a single finger, which lengthened to an ebony blade the size of a small sword.

"That's enough, Sitra," Cole said. He looked to the Cardinal, adopting a gentle yet firm tone. "Cardinal, listen to me. Vol Karinn is in danger. The Three are spreading across Aeneria like a plague. Sooner or later they will come here, and when they do it will be too late for anyone to help you. Please, take us to your governors so we can discuss Vol Karinn's future."

The Cardinal dismissed her munisica with a sigh of defeat, though she kept her chin up high. Her Ulrichs appeared relieved at her decision. "Who are you, and where do you hail from?"

"We are the Unbound, and we are from The Sill," Cole repeated, wondering how many more times he would have to introduce himself. "Please, take us to whoever is in charge of Vol Karinn."

The Cardinal shook her head. "Impossible. The Unbound were decimated thirty cycles ago, and the four of you look as if you've barely seen the end of your third. And even if you were the Unbound I couldn't fulfill your request because Vol Karinn has no central government."

"Who's your boss then, scarlet?" Sitra demaded. "Who are you so afraid of disappointing?"

The Cardinal let out an annoyed huff, then spoke with what sounded like a line memorized from text. "Every citizen of Vol Karinn serves Cascada, the Goddess of Passion. They need no hand to guide them, for they all walk the path of Passion. Let no evil taint—"

"He means the Conclave," Eliza interrupted, then spoke to the Cardinal. "I was born in Vol Karinn. Take us there, or I'll take us there." She held the Cardinal's gaze as jade wings unfurled from her shoulders.

"Put those away!" the Cardinal hissed. Her head spun from side to side as she scanned for passersby. "Fine, I'll take you, but for Cascada's sake keep your magic hidden. The last thing we need is a city-wide riot on your account."

"Then you might want to call off the other Cardinals you just called over. We don't want another misunderstanding." Cole projected his words so all could hear, speaking in a tone of polite indifference. For a moment he enveloped her mind with his own, though he made no move to penetrate it. He merely showed her a glimpse of his Passion, which far exceeded the defenses of Rage and Wisdom. He strode forward and brushed past the Cardinal without waiting for her response, then stopped. "Please, Cardinal lead the way. We don't have much time."

The Cardinal rushed ahead and led them down the path to Vol Karinn. She had ordered one of her Ulrichs to stay behind and erase

319

the recent memories of the unconscious fishers. Cole felt an urge to stop her, but he was in a foreign city and had no right, no matter what his morals told him. The other Ulrich trailed close behind their procession, casting disapproving glares at the Unbound's attire. Cole and the others were barefoot as usual, which along with the cut of their robes set them in scandalous contrast to the heavily clothed people of Vol Karinn. The air around them rippled gently on account of the spells they used for warmth, though Sitra went so far as to keep a rolling ball of orange flames in her hands, tossing it brazenly back and forth as if daring the Ulrich to object. He did not.

Impatience tingled over Cole's skin as they slogged along, igniting within him an urge to summon the biggest wings he could and slice the skies in half. The walk was so painfully slow that Cole was forced to retreat to the serenity of his center. It had been too long since he'd properly meditated anyway. He cleansed his mind of clutter, surprised at the sheer mass of stress that had accumulated in his psyche, the vast majority of which was centered not around the war, but Lileth. Every moment since he'd left her was a moment half lived, dulling the charm Aeneria once captivated him with. He wished now more than ever that he'd Traveled with her, to live out the end of their days in some quiet oasis far away from here, like two shadows in the Aethers. He closed his eyes and searched the quiet of his mind for her special place and called to her with all his heart, but once again there was nothing.

Swallowing his disappointment, Cole returned his focus to the present. They were now strolling through what appeared to be a market district, with men and women alike hauling baskets of moss and fish eggs into wagons, which sat on blades instead of wheels. Children on ice skates chased each other through the legs of their parents, carving and crunching tight circles over the frozen streets. Starved faces peered out from billowing fur cloaks and hats, but so did warm smiles and eyes glinting with compassion. Cole had no doubt that any one of these people old or young would welcome a stranger to their table with open arms and their last bite of food. He didn't need his Passion to tell him these people were worth fighting for.

Cole quietly offered magical nourishment to each person they passed, but found each of them already brimming with Passion, which made him wonder at the reason for their frail and infirm appearances. Cole shelved his concern, for now at least, instead casting his eyes through the snowfall to the distant ice statues that lined the valley crater.

A familiar face measured him, hard with controlled fury, with thin knives for hair and fire in his eyes that could only come from one who has dominated his own Fear. A young Roth watched over the people of Vol Karinn, poised and ready for whatever enemies may come. The statue was an accurate depiction of the Roth Cole remembered, with the only exception being the spark of mischief tugging his cheek into a wolfish grin. Cole heard a sniff behind him. He found Sitra gazing unblinkingly at Roth's statue, her lips pressed hard together and her forehead a tangle of muscled knots. Tears clung to the ends of her lashes.

Cole looked around the valley walls to the other statues, eager to see another familiar face. He found Chiron, who even in youth emanated a sense of infinite patience and compassion. He held his arms loosely behind his back, and his face was lit with the beginning of a smile, as though he had just locked eyes with an old friend. His neck showed no sign of the scar, however. Cole recalled seeing the scar during his first and only sparring lesson with the elder. White and glowing, it wandered from under Chiron's chin to a jagged path over his torso, ending in a neat spiral around his navel. It was a scar caused by the loss of someone he'd loved, someone his soul had been bonded to with Passion. Cole's fingertips went unbidden to his own scar. The deformity was just as thick and rubbery as the day he received it, an incurable mark of Hatred for all the world to see. Cole wondered what the elder would say to him now, if he would approve of the choices Cole had made, or the inexorable journey Cole had set The Sill upon.

Several other statues lined the valley canyon. Cole expected to see Alvani among them, but remembered she had been too young to serve with the Unbound. There were a few other women, however, each more beautiful and imposing than the last, with one flourishing munisica even larger than Roth's. Cole took a minute to appreciate each of them, then stopped in his tracks when he beheld the statue they had just come from. It was Varka. The sculptors had managed to polish the ice to display the master's shroud of Rage, which covered every inch of exposed skin and sharpened every hair into a fine needle. A cape was draped over his shoulders, the same cape that was now a sheet of soft snow over Cole's back. Varka's face betrayed nothing of the overwhelming pressures that no doubt besieged him, rather he looked confident and shrewd, as though he had just worked out an answer to a riddle. Though it was merely a depiction of the man, seeing Varka's likeness in such a tangible form made him much more real to Cole, instead of some obscure manifestation of his imagination.

"What are those people doing at the feet of the statues?" Cole asked, pointing to a cluster of dots perched about Roth's bladed feet.

"Offering Cascada's gifts to our gods," stated the Cardinal.

The Cardinal led them through the city, keeping the curious citizens at bay with her stern glare. All about him Cole sensed a flutter of talk spoken through Passion. He tried not to listen, but it was like trying to ignore people yelling to each other from across the street, so he settled for feigning ignorance as he did with his students.

They came to the lake set into the heart of Vol Karinn, stopping before a line of docks laden with transport shuttles bobbing in the blue water. Steam rose from the lake in winding ribbons, and as soon as they stepped into their boat, they passed through an invisible barrier, entering a climate as balmy as The Sill's.

"I thought you said Wisdom and Rage weren't authorized here," Sitra said, slapping the side of the boat as they glided along. "What moves this thing then, hopes and dreams?"

The Cardinal stood at the front of the vessel. One of her hands rested upon a gratia stone set into the base of the bowsprit. She kept her eyes on the center island as she spoke. "*Unauthorized magic* is unauthorized. The citizens of Vol Karinn may apply for temporary licenses to use Rage and Wisdom, though they seldom do. Passion keeps the peace within our walls and evil from our hearts. Occasionally we require spells outside of Passion to aid us in our service to the gods."

"Like moving this boat through the water when you're too lazy to paddle yourself," Sitra offered in a would-be tone of innocence. "It's funny, I don't remember seeing you apply for a license before you attacked us back there. I think I have a piece of yarn in my pocket if you ever want to sharpen those claws of yours."

"That's enough, Sitra," Cole said aloud before addressing her mind directly. *"Let's wait until after we've talked to their leaders before we really piss them off. I want to at least give them a chance to play nice before we get nasty."*

"Oh you're no fun," Sitra said with a chuckle. *"But you are the boss."*

"Glad to see your memory's not as dull as the rest of your brains," Cole said, flashing her a smile, which she returned. Her eyes were still a little wet, but he was glad her playfulness had returned.

The boat came to a smooth halt on the docks of the center isle. The Ulrich hopped up onto the gangway, offering a hand to help them off, though no one took it as they followed the Cardinal up a set of zigzagging stone steps. The masonry showed obvious signs of Wisdom manipulation. There were elegant patterns woven throughout its grain, thin, looping bannisters that grew along the steeper portions, and the entire staircase was made from one continuous piece of rock. Cardinals and other important-looking people walked the footpaths carved throughout the island, popping in and out of buildings made of dark wood and bedecked with flowering vines.

The steps ended in a stone archway that framed the big hall atop the hill. It was both the highest and largest structure in Vol Karinn, and unlike the surrounding districts of ice houses, this building exuded warmth and comfort. Soft turquoise light pulsed from stained glass windows running up all four stories. Fruit-laden trees lined the grounds outside, their branches sagging to the ground with the weight of their bounty. At the entrance to the hall, two golden statues stood on either side of the oak double doors, one depicting a gorgeous woman with voluptuous curves set in an inviting pose, the other a shirtless man with lithe features and a look that promised to please.

The Cardinal spun to a halt before the double doors. "You are about to enter the Summit, outsiders. Mind your mouths and keep your magic to yourselves, for behind these doors reside our most devout. Cascada will not tolerate threats of violence. Touch no one unless they touch you first. You have been warned." The Cardinal gave a nod to her Ulrich, who approached the doors and slammed his fist on the heavy oak.

"What are we about to walk into?" Cole asked Eliza.

"*I can only guess,*" she replied with a trickle of apprehension. "*I have never been inside the Summit.*"

The doors glided open on oiled hinges, uncorking a symphony of scents and sounds that came rushing out like the waters of a broken dam.

The Ulrich gave a small wink, then his mind rang into Cole's like a deep gong. "*Welcome to paradise.*"

The Cardinal stormed forward as if she were late for a business meeting. Cole followed with the Unbound in tow. Unlike the exterior of the hall, the interior looked as if it were carved out of the inside of a jungle cave. Luminescent turquoise mushrooms lined the stone walls in between clusters of vines with shiny leaves, bathing the whole chamber in a dim, sultry glow. A brook of mint-green water weaved throughout the cave, and on its surface were water lilies carrying plates of fruit or drink with pot torches in their centers. Half-naked, or in some cases fully naked, people lay strewn about the grotto, either floating and laughing merrily in the brook or half-hidden behind within a copse of ferns.

With every breath the balmy air smelled of a different perfume, each more tantalizing than the last, instilling in Cole a desire to find the source. Music pulsated throughout the chamber, pounding against his heart with deep drums and tickling his ears with lusting strings. The hairs on Cole's arms stood on end, electrified by the energy in the air. His eyes couldn't seem to open wide enough to take in all the sights.

"*Wisdom,*" Eliza said, jolting his mind like a splash of ice water. "*Go to your centers and clear your minds before the Passion takes you.*"

Cole did as he was told, and while the alluring sensations didn't entirely subside, they no longer overwhelmed his reason. Beside him Sitra panted slightly, flexing her naked fingers in the air like a predator ready to pounce. She blew a sharp breath out through pursed lips and shook herself.

"*What sort of Passion is this?*" Sitra asked.

"*The basest kind,*" Eliza replied in a dry tone. "*Keep up.*"

Cole held firm to his Wisdom as he trotted after Eliza and Valen. He accidentally bumped into a woman as he rounded a corner. The softness of her bare breasts pressed into him as her fingers twirled their way under the folds of his armored robes. She looked up at him with a wild, inviting smile, but Cole pushed his way along before his Passion caught fire again. The Cardinal led them deeper into a network of tunnels and grottos so expansive that Cole wondered if the Summit was another pocket reality like the Everglen. He glanced through a fissure in the ceiling and saw a starry sky beyond.

"The Conclave awaits you," the Cardinal whispered into Cole's ear. She nodded to a curtain of hanging flowers. Torchlight flickered through the gaps in the petals. "I am not welcome here, so I will take my leave and give you one last piece of advice. Do not lie to the Conclave. They know your truths even before you do." And without waiting for a response, the Cardinal threw her shoulders back and strode off down the tunnel with her Ulrichs close behind.

Cole looked to the others, who each gave him a solid nod. He took a steadying breath and swallowed a fluttering in his chest, then pushed his way through the flowery curtain.

Torches danced with amber tongues along the walls. The ceiling was open to the stars, displaying constellations Cole had never seen before. Lounging in their own separate pools were men and women wearing tunics made of sheer fabric, and circlets upon their brows. There were other people in the pools with them, but whether they were men or women or even Aenerian, Cole couldn't tell, for they seemed to be made of translucent azure crystal. They fawned over the Aenerians, massaging every inch of their bodies with hands of sapphire. Instead of hair, they had luminous ghostly tendrils that passed through skin and flesh like a phantom's kiss, caressing the Aenerians from the inside while their hands worked outside. Everyone seemed too preoccupied with giving or receiving their pleasures to notice the Unbound walking through the moss-covered walkway that split the room in half.

Cole was about to ask one of the dignitaries for assistance, but then he heard a soft chuckle and saw a glint of a smile through a fern tree. He pushed the leaves aside and found a woman in a hidden alcove sitting comfortably upon a luxurious throne of suede pillows. Torchlight tickled over a sheer black dress that left nothing beneath to the imagination. Under each of her arms, one of the crystalline beings nuzzled itself, each being working its hands over her thighs as its phantom tendrils probed everywhere else. Unlike everyone else in the grotto, this woman's eyes were sharp and alert, and aimed directly into Cole's. There was no doubt this was the person he was supposed to find.

Cole's foot had barely entered the alcove when the woman rose from her plush throne. She dismissed the crystal people with a graceful wave of her hand, then stepped down a carpeted dais towards Cole, her eyes unblinking all the while.

"The Summit welcomes you, warriors of The Sill. My name is Visellis. I speak for all of Vol Karinn with the voice of Cascada, the goddess of Passion." She spoke in a tone of rich honey, sultry and alluring. Her words rolled easily into Cole's ears like hearing his favorite song. Ribbons of fair blond hair flowed down her shoulders, her hair doing a better job of concealing her breasts than the insubstantial material of her gown did. "It has been far too long since we've had any visitors. You must be exhausted, coming all the way from The Sill. What is your name, warrior?"

"I am Cole, and our journey was fine," Cole said, choking as she embraced him with an intimate hug, squeezing the muscles of his shoulders and pressing herself into him. She gave him a warm kiss on the side of his lips before pulling away. "We managed to avoid The Three's minions at least." Cole watched as she gave each of the Unbound the same familiar greeting. Valen went rigid as a frozen pine when she embraced him. Eliza had backed away with a little bow, which Visellis deemed appropriate to ignore. When her eyes wandered back to his own, Cole asked, "Visellis, are you aware of what's going on outside your borders?"

"Please, call me Vi," she said, squeezing Cole's arm.

"Okay, Vi," Cole replied, as a pleasant shiver ran from her touch over his skin. He wrestled his Wisdom back to the moment, clearing his mind. "Do you know what's happening on Aeneria right now?"

"What happens outside our world is of little concern to us," Vi said with a girlish giggle. "We offer ourselves to Cascada, who in turn provides us with her grace and shields us from harm. Whatever quarrels stir above shall eventually pass, and when they do Cascada will open our world to Aeneria once more."

"Quarrels...," Cole said, not bothering to hide his disbelief. "Aeneria is at war. The Three have each crowned a Harbinger, and they control almost the entire planet, even Oberon Temple. The fact that Vol Karrin hasn't been razed yet is only because The Three are busy with easier meals. We found you without a problem, and so can they. Do you have any idea what a single priest of Sorronis could do to a city full of Passion followers?"

Sadness fell over Vi's face as tears began to well in her eyes. Cole felt a sudden urge to comfort her. "I know what you think of us. Vol Karinn used to be open to all of Aeneria. Drifters and pilgrims wandered freely into our valley crater, stealing our hearts after enjoying our bodies, only to move on and regale the world with tales of the Lost City of Whores. We cannot resist Cascada's calling. The pleasures of soul and flesh are the greatest of life's gifts, and to offer that gift to another is the grandest treasure of all. Cascada has blessed us with her Passion, and it is our duty to see that Passion shared."

She was avoiding the question. Cole's eyes wandered over her body, his gaze swimming through the gossamer lace to the supple charms of her breasts and hips. The rolling torchlight revealed odd shadows covering every inch of her skin, neat little lines scattered without rhyme or reason. Cole blinked and saw they were scars. He resisted the urge to offer to heal them, but Vi must have seen the desire through his gaze.

"Some scars cannot be healed, even by Cascada's grace," Visellis cooed, tracing a finger along the scar on Cole's cheek. "A lesson it seems you learned the hard way."

Cole splashed his mind with icy Wisdom several times more, though it seemed to have a diminishing effect. "Vi, I don't really care about Vol Karinn's rumors or whatever duties you are bound to. You deserve the right to live however you please, which is exactly what The Sill is fighting for. It's only a matter of time before The Three's minions find you, and when they do they'll take everything you love and twist it against you in violation of your souls. Honestly, there's so much Passion throbbing in the Summit, it might even bring Sorronis himself. My point is, Vol Karinn isn't prepared for even the smallest invasion. I saw your people out there. This is a city of lovers, not fighters. Sick lovers by the looks of it. The Sill can help."

Pity scrunched in Visellis's brow. "Dear warrior, you cannot understand the depths of Cascada's grace until you have felt it yourself. Our lady Passion will provide as she always has. As for Vol Karinn's citizens, I assure you they are quite healthy, despite the meagerness of their appearance. It is by the strength of their Passion that Cascada's ice came to be. They offer themselves at the statues of the Unbound, providing the strength needed for the enchantment that hides us from the outside world. Those who prove themselves earn time at the Summit, where they are rewarded with Cascada's higher gifts. Some even go so far as to join bodies with the crystal nymphs, that they might better serve the goddess through pleasing others." With a graceful gesture of her hand, she pointed to the crystalline people. They wore looks of pain mingled with restraint, as if standing idle had caused them an itching agony that could only be assuaged by pleasing another.

Cole shook his head. "I already told you, we found your city easily, even with your enchanted ice. When The Three find you, they'll make your every moment a living nightmare. You'll wish you were dead, but they'll take even that from you. We aren't asking you to give up your lives, what we're asking is that you live them at The Sill, just for a while until we win this war. You can worship and love and lust however you like. The Sill is plenty big enough for all of that. We can have you all out of here within a day, and you can return as soon as it's safe."

Visellis slinked around Cole, pausing in front of him as though allowing him a good look at her, then stood behind him and slid her hands over his shoulders. Passion tingled through her touch, trickling and soothing its way down his spine.

"It is always thus with the warriors," she said. Cole could feel the hot sweetness of her breath against his ear. "Your lives are fraught with dangers that would break lesser men, yet you harden your hearts and trudge on, fighting a war within yourselves long after the battles are over. Life doesn't have to be so. This is a holy place, a safe place. We can show you the richness of a life you have never known, a life where simple pleasure is the currency." She then dropped her husky whisper so that only Cole could hear. She dragged a nail down the side of his neck, pulling his ear closer to her mouth. "Tell me, warrior, have you ever felt a whole-bodied orgasm? From your head to your toes, every fiber, every bone, writhing and squirming and pulsing with unbridled euphoria. It is… transcendent."

Visellis drew away, and at her gentle command the two crystal nymphs converged on Cole. Their every movement bespoke lust as their eyes begged for his body. The torchlight danced inside their glassy bodies, refracting and reflecting. The ghostly tendrils that were their hair reached for him.

"Stop," Eliza said in a steely voice. A bubble of jade Wisdom crackled to life around Cole, preventing the advance of the crystal nymphs. Denied, the nymphs recoiled and wept at the sight of the barrier. "We are here to save your city, not indulge in its wanton lust. You heard Cole's reasons for our visit. Give us your response."

"It has been over a cycle since that voice last kissed my ears," Visellis said as she returned to her cushy throne. The nymphs rushed back to her side and resumed their task, plunging their ethereal tendrils deep into Visellis's body. Her eyes rolled as the pleasure bloomed, then she set her gaze upon Eliza. "You have been on pilgrimage for a long time, Eliza Thornheart. So long that I thought you had abandoned Cascada forever, but now I see your time was well spent. Two seed-bearers and a flower is quite the harvest."

"What is she talking about, Eliza? What pilgrimage?" Valen asked in an undertone. Cole sensed Wisdom and Rage boiling up inside him, which at first seemed to be directed at Eliza, but then Cole realized it was *from* Eliza. She had injected the counter magics into their mental network to stay the effects of Visellis's Passion. "Never mind. You can tell me after our business here is concluded."

"A pilgrimage," Visellis started, dropping her seductive tone and adopting a much more business-like one, "is a journey taken by our adolescent. We send them out into the world, blessed with Cascada's gifts and with a single task: to bring back suitable mates. Each completed pilgrimage makes Vol Karinn stronger. When we sensed Aeneria's barrier had fallen, we recalled all our pilgrims to shield them from the coming plagues, and they all returned in haste, some even with mates. Eliza, however, ignored our summons. We were then forced to construct the Frozen Sky and shut her out of Vol Karinn." Visellis gazed upon Eliza with compassion bordering on indulgence, as a perversely obsessive mother would look upon her child. "It warms my heart to see her returned to us now, safe, whole, and her pilgrimage complete. You have done well, Eliza Thornheart."

Sitra looked at Eliza with a mixture of shock and hilarity, as if she were seeing her for the first time. She gave Eliza a couple prodding jabs with her elbow. "Eliza you little scoundrel you. So where should I plant my seed? No, wait! I'm the flower, aren't I?"

Eliza ignored her and took a step towards Visellis. "My pilgrimage ended the moment I left Vol Karinn. I am a citizen of The Sill now, as well as a member of the Unbound."

Visellis stroked her fingers over her chin, then shook her head, tousling her ribbons of blond hair with a giggle. "Tripe. The Unbound are the demigods of a dead age. I find it hard to believe that the likes of Chiron and Rothael would count mere children as their equals, but that does raise a question. If The Sill is attempting to uproot Vol Karinn, why wouldn't one of the surviving Unbound come themselves? Too busy wringing out the final dregs of their youth no doubt. Oh what I wouldn't give for five minutes alone with the Bonebreaker."

"Roth and Chiron are dead," Sitra snapped, jolting Visellis from her reverie. "We're the Unbound now, so you might want to show a little respect seeing as we're your only chance to avoid burning on a Devotion tower."

"Those are some lofty claims," Visellis said, amused. "But you'll forgive me if I'm not so gullible as the fishing folk you beguiled with your grand entrance. You are no Unbound."

Sitra's munisica flared as a menacing growl rumbled in her chest. "You ignorant old bitch! You really have no idea what's going on out there."

"She's not ignorant," Valen corrected in a polite tone as he gripped Sitra's shoulder. "Ignorance by choice is stupidity. She is stupid. Perhaps we should enlighten her with a few of our memories. Fangshard Valley ought to do the trick."

"No," Cole said in a stern voice. They could of course overpower Visellis and force any number of memories into her mind, but something about her told him that wouldn't work. If it came down to it, he would commandeer her mind and have her set certain things in motion so they could evacuate the city, though Cole would rather not recruit followers through force, at least not as their first option. "If she wants to shut herself away from the world and ignore the truth then so be it. It's not our job to tell people how to think."

"This one continues to impress me," Visellis said to Eliza. Her eyebrow went up as she surveyed Cole. "Where did you find such a fine specimen of a seed?"

"From Terra," Eliza said with a proud smile. "In the final hour of the last age, Varka cast his soul into the Aethers and brought Cole to us. You could say *that* act was the most successful pilgrimage in all of history, wouldn't you agree?"

The color fell from Visellis's face as it hardened with disdain. But then a thought lit in her eyes and she snapped her gaze back to Cole, looking at him through a lens of awe. "I disagree, but agreement on all matters is no requirement for friendship. Why don't you and your friends stay a while. You have traveled far, and Vol Karinn is bound to have something that tickles your fancies. Indulge in us for a day or two. Perhaps in that time one of us will have a change of heart."

Eliza and Visellis then quipped back and forth like an overly polite chess match of words, never breaching etiquette, though it was clear each held a deep contempt for the other. Cole searched for answers while they went at it, but none were forthcoming. He conferred privately with the others through their Passion link, though they were just as stumped as he was. Their options were sinking beyond reach with each passing moment, bringing them closer to what promised to be a contentious ultimatum. One thing was certain, however: They were wasting time.

"I think," Cole said, interrupting the two women as tactfully as he could, "that we have gone as far as we can here. Visellis isn't about to change her mind, and neither are we. Back on Terra we call this *spinning our wheels.* This should have been a friendly reunion of The Sill and Vol Karinn, but instead we've greeted each other with debate and contention. Vi, on behalf of The Sill I would like to apologize for our embarrassing behavior."

Eliza went stone still and Sitra looked as if she were about to hit him. Valen seemed to have caught on, however.

Visellis folded her hands over her lap and sat up on her soft throne, smiling broadly. "No apology necessary, my dear Cole. Debate is natural for those who allow Wisdom and Rage into their hearts. There was little you could do, but *you* at least saw the light in the end. I am more disappointed by Lady Thornheart as she was taught better, but all can be forgiven. Her time among brutes and bureaucrats has obviously meddled with the purity of her heart."

"Don't say a word," Cole commanded the Unbound. He continued to beam pleasantly at Visellis. "I would be disappointed if we parted ways now without gaining anything from each other. Our journey has not been easy and we could use a break. With your permission, I would have us remain in Vol Karinn for a few days. We may not agree with each other, but I'm sure we could find some common ground and appreciation during our visit."

"We are of the same mind," Vi said, resuming her seductive tone. "Vol Karinn has many pleasures to offer such bright and young minds as yourselves. As you and I are leaders of our separate parties, it would be appropriate for me to show you a few of these pleasures myself, though you'll have to come to me after-hours. As gratifying as it is to serve Cascada, there are a few ministrations that require my full attention during the day."

"That sounds lovely," Cole replied with a bow of his head. "We won't take up any more of your time then. I do have one request, however. May we use our Rage and Wisdom during our stay? Within reason of course. We are accustomed to certain comforts, just a few simple spells that your people won't even notice."

Visellis cast a wary eye over the rest of the Unbound, then returned her lustful gaze to Cole. "Normally it is forbidden, but so long as you supervise your party then I see no harm. All I ask is that you try to keep the mayhem to a minimum." She flashed Cole a smirk, then spoke directly into his mind so that the others couldn't hear. *"And don't forget my offer. I want to be alone with you."*

Cole kept the pleasantness on his face. "Of course. Take care, Vi." He gave her another small bow and led the Unbound out of her chamber. The crystal nymphs reached out to him with looks of unrequited lust as he left.

He could feel the heat of Sitra's and Eliza's eyes raking over his back as they navigated the mushroom-lit passageways out of the Summit. As soon as the heavy oak doors closed behind them, Sitra punched Cole hard in the kidney, halting the group as she rounded on him.

"You're away from Lileth for a few days and you get the hots for the first slut that flashes her tits and Passion at you?" Sitra's shouting carried down the hill, drawing horrified looks from the people bustling along the walkways below. "Do you know what you catch when you dip your dick in a swamp? You catch things no Passion in the world can clear up. Stars, the entire city's probably been through her legs."

"I'm sure Cole has a very good reason for being so friendly with that snake," Eliza said in an icy tone. "And I didn't hear much from you, Valen. Perhaps you were hoping she would include you in her offer?"

"Your mind is clouded," Valen said with his usual neutrality. "Had you been watching for it, you would have seen the room Cole gave us to maneuver while exchanging pleasantries."

Eliza turned to Cole. "Room for what exactly?"

"To pull Vol Karinn out from under her feet," Cole replied to everyone with hushed Passion. He turned and continued down the stairs. *"Keep up. We've got work to do."*

CHAPTER 21

AGAINST THE CURRENT

The Unbound departed the Summit, restricting themselves to less-obvious magic. They took one of the small boats back to the main city and followed their noses in search of a place to eat. They still had a few blackstouts left, but they were just as bland and boring as ever, and as queer as Vol Karinn was, they were all eager to try the local cuisine, and planning was best done with a properly full stomach.

The first place they popped into was a coffee and tea shop which was made entirely of ice and just happened to double as a brothel. The counters, stools, booths, flooring, all looked like ornate crystal. The other patrons, with their voluminous fur coats and gloves, were well-insulated, and had no issues sitting for hours in a frozen booth while sipping from steaming granite mugs. The Unbound, however, ruined the booth they sat in. Their spells for warmth seeped into the furniture, turning their bench and stool into a half-melted mess. Oddly enough, the proprietor couldn't have been happier with the ruined furniture, exclaiming that it gave him a legitimate excuse to employ Wisdom to fix it. He removed a white rod from a pedestal below the shop's gratia stone, then, wielding it like a wand, funneled all the water back to its proper place and froze it with a pulse of emerald light. Giggling like a child with a toy, the proprietor thanked them with offers of free drinks and an hour each with his crystal nymph, who seemed to appear from nowhere at the mention of its name. They gave their polite refusals and finished their drinks, standing this time.

They came upon a bakery a short while afterwards. The bakery had some stone worked into its construction and also happened to serve as a brothel. Sitra urged them along, insisting that they find something with meat, though Eliza pointed out that meat would be hard to come by in a city of Passion followers.

Following a savory aroma around a towering spire, the Unbound came upon a restaurant with a carving of a fish set above its door. The restaurant had a warm, rustic tone. Wood planks were set into the floors and countertops and sleek fur lined the chairs and booths. Heavy iron brackets along the walls held clutches of spiked mushrooms, which glowed like cherry embers when flicked. They settled into a corner booth behind a spiral staircase climbed by the occasional patron with a concubine in tow.

"Are you sure I can't tempt you with one of our lovecrafters?" the waiter asked for a third time after taking their orders. "Nothing stirs up an appetite quite like the hands of our nymphs."

"We're hungry enough as it is," Eliza replied. "I am curious about your menu though. When did Vol Karinn start serving the flesh of animals? I thought Cascada forbade the killing of the innocent."

The waiter flinched at the word 'killing', as if Eliza had just uttered an abhorrent swear word. "Stars no, nothing has to suffer to fill our kitchens, I assure you. The fish come to Vol Karinn to spawn, and right after nature takes its final breath from their gills we harvest them, along with any unfertilized eggs. The Summit has blessed the harvesting with Cascada's approval."

"A convenient interpretation of edict, but understandable," Eliza said. "Edible plants must be hard to come by with all this ice. The citizens would starve without another food source."

"We do not partake in the fish," the waiter replied as he cast a covetous look at another server carrying a tray laden with steaming meats. "The duties of the Conclave are taxing to the extreme, and so only they are allowed the exception as their bodies and brains require the extra nourishment. The rest of Vol Karinn finds sustenance in the fungi and moss farms at the base of the valley walls."

"Convenient indeed," Eliza replied in a sour tone. The waiter took this as a compliment and departed with a deep bow.

"So what's your plan, boss?" Sitra asked once the waiter was out of earshot. "Should we tackle evacuation first or animal rights?"

Cole set his elbows on the table and massaged an ache from his temples. "I told you to stop calling me *boss*, remember?"

"Sounds familiar," Sitra replied, distracted. She cast a furtive glance over her shoulder at the nearest table, then gave a covert flick of her wrist. Her palm flashed with jade Wisdom. A steaming morsel shot from one of the plates onto their own table, unnoticed by anyone but the Unbound. Sitra leaned her head back and opened her jaw as the hunk of fish slapped into her mouth. "Ow, ow, ow, tha's hah."

"As uncouth as ever," Valen sighed. His hand glowed emerald as he waved it over the table, but instead of stealing food, a bubble of green light shimmered and faded around them. "Our words are now guarded. Go ahead, Cole."

"Thanks, Valen," Cole replied, then addressed the table. "Do we all agree that we're not going to get anywhere with Visellis?"

They all nodded, and Eliza elbowed a giggling Sitra, silencing her before she could start on whatever joke she was about to say.

"Aside from pleasures of the flesh," Cole said, rolling his eyes. "Visellis isn't going to cooperate, or even compromise by the looks of things. That leaves us with a couple options. We can take her mind by force and order her to evacuate Vol Karinn, or we can turn around and chalk this up as a failure. We all know what The Three will do to this place."

The table fell silent for a moment. Cole saw the memories of Costas and Borla Dign flashing behind their eyes. After a quiet moment, Valen was first to speak.

"This issue is one of ethics and morals," Valen said in a slow, careful manner. "Your first option would be quickest and it would save a great many souls, but beginning a relationship with deceit and force would only sow distrust further down the path. In this case coercion and possibly violence would be the ethical choices, though we would be compromising our morals."

"But nor can we leave Vol Karinn to its own devices," Eliza interjected. "It is too easy a target for a Devotion. The valley canyon protects them from most intruders, but it also serves as a cage, especially with the frozen sky in place. There would be no escape."

Cole sighed as another poor idea came to him. "If we stayed here we could wait for The Three's minions to arrive first and ambush them."

"No," Valen replied. "Aeneria needs us to be productive. We cannot do that here. And if The Three decide to make a personal appearance, then this valley canyon will be our cage as well. Sitra, what on Oberon's backside could you be laughing about at a time like this?"

"And they think I'm the stupid one." Sitra chuckled. "Look around you. They love us. Listen, they're talking about us right now, even after that scarlet witch wiped the minds of those fisherfolk."

Cole turned his head in a would-be casual manner. Every eye was upon them, every mouth grinning wildly or whispering behind a cupped hand. Some stood at their tables with determination etched on their faces, as if gathering the courage to come speak to them. "How did they find out?"

"It doesn't matter," Sitra said as she displayed one of her hands before them in a slow flourish. Rage answered her summons as the hand became black as the void, stretching and sharpening into a bladed weapon. The shroud continued up her wrist and slid under her armored robes. She bared her teeth in a half smile and spoke with a voice of honed steel. "We're the Unbound. Let's play the part."

"Sitra, put those away!" Eliza reached across the table in an attempt to force Sitra's hand down, but the munisica might as well have been made of Morthainian glass. Eliza then called upon her own Rage, but Sitra's shroud had already spread throughout her long braid and eyebrows. The table creaked in protest.

"We don't hide who we truly are," Sitra said. Her voice surprisingly calm and measured given the current depth of her Rage. "And we don't ask permission. If those Summit sluts have an issue with it, they can come climb down from their satin thrones and deal with us themselves." Still resisting Eliza's munisica, she gave Cole a look of controlled fury that reminded him very much of Roth. "You know it's the right move."

Noticing her own shroud had crept up her arms, Eliza yielded and sat back down, flustered and glowing. The damage was done, however.

Half the restaurant was out of their seats and some were already walking over.

Cole cracked a smirk as he failed in his attempt to give Sitra a chastising glare. "We're going to be respectful."

"Of course," Sitra declared, clearly pleased with her victory.

"And we're *not* going to use violence or coercion," Cole said.

"That's my concerns dealt with," Valen said with a thoughtful nod. "Count me in."

Cole put a hand on Eliza's shoulder. Her muscles were clenched and hard, trembling under his touch. He waited for her to look at him. "No one is going to get hurt on our account. We're simply going to introduce ourselves and make our case, then whoever wants to escape can take the Seer Jar back with us."

Eliza closed her eyes and took a steadying breath. Then another. She stopped shaking as calm washed over her, though she managed to keep her munisica. She opened her eyes and looked to Cole, offering him all the trust and hope she possessed in a single gaze.

Their meals came just ahead of the tide of curious onlookers. Valen dismissed his muffling spell and the Unbound welcomed all who approached their table, urging more tables and chairs from the icy floor with their Wisdom. The staff seemed worried at first, but their concerns gave way to their own budding intrigue, and they too joined the growing table. The Unbound spent the next hour answering questions about Rage and Wisdom, even the dark magics, all while displaying their emerald wings and munisica. The crowd swelled as more people flooded in from the streets. Valen cast a spell to warm the air within the restaurant while Cole cast another to raise the freezing temperature of the ice, allowing everyone to abandon their puffy coats so more people could cram in. After regaling the crowd with tales of their training under Roth and Chiron, Cole asked for quiet and explained the perils of The Three as well as the current state of the Dark Side. In the grim silence that followed, Cole presented his offer for escape and the Unbound departed, leaving them to ponder their future.

"I told you this was going to be easy," Sitra muttered into their Passion network as they neared the exit. *"If a single one from that*

crowd doesn't show up tonight then I'll strip naked and go join the Conclave."

"They certainly were captivated," Eliza remarked. She stopped by the entrance and placed her hand on the Passion stone embedded at the checkout counter. A keen ringing filled the air as the stone shone bright as a Light Side sun. *"I worry that a single day won't be enough to convince them all, however."*

"It is all the time we can afford," Valen said as he filled a second Passion stone. *"Our students need guidance and the Heart Tree will undoubtedly have a list of tasks ready for our attentions. I shudder to think what would happen if The Sill were to be attacked and we weren't there to help defend it."*

Valen's words put haste in their step. They popped through the liquid stone door, eager to get to work. As Cole emerged to the chilly streets of Vol Karinn, he beheld the statue of Varka looming between two spires of ice. A small weight tugged at his heart, dragging it an inch towards a place of hopelessness. The Unbound of old had been powerful beyond their comprehension, and they had Traveled to every local planet, honing their skills while learning the secrets of the Aethers. Cole and his friends seemed like mere hatchlings taking their first flight in comparison to the ancient warriors. If Varka, Chiron, and Roth couldn't stop The Three, then what hope did they have?

"Stop!" cried a stern voice from behind.

Cole turned to see the same Cardinal who escorted them to the Summit. Her face was flush, her hair slightly disheveled, and she appeared to be struggling between running as fast as she could and maintaining the dignified image of her position.

The Cardinal stopped before them, finally posting her hands on her knees as she heaved for air. One of her Ulrichs placed a hand aglow with pink Passion on her back and her breathing slowed. She straightened up and fixed the front of her robes, speaking in a steady cadence. "The Conclave has decreed that I shall escort your party during your visit. This is not to be seen as a punishment, rather I will be at hand to assist with your navigation of our nuanced customs." She cast a sideways glance at a group of boisterous people exiting the fish restaurant. Arm in arm, they clamored in excited voices as they skipped down the street, shouting and singing about the Unbound and the wonders of The Sill. The Cardinal brought her harpy's eye back to Cole. "You are clearly wanting for assistance in this matter."

Cole placed a hand saturated with calming Passion on Sitra's shoulder, quelling what would undoubtedly be an inflammatory verbal assault. He maintained a polite smile for the Cardinal, however. "We would be delighted to have you and your Ulrichs along for the tour. It's good there's three of you because our group can't seem to agree on which areas to visit first. We'll be splitting up into two groups I think. I hope that doesn't cause you any trouble. We could wait for another Cardinal to help?"

"We're splitting up?" Eliza asked in a worried tone.

"Just go with it," Cole hissed.

The Cardinal's eyes darted to each of the Unbound several times, as though she kept losing count of how many were in their party. She blinked rapidly and shook her head. "No no no, I have been assigned to your party so my Ulrichs and I will assist you."

"Great," Cole said. Without another word, he and Sitra turned on the spot and continued down the street while Eliza and Valen walked past the Cardinal.

"What is your name, Cardinal?" Cole asked when her labored breathing came within earshot. His Passion revealed the life candles of her Ulrichs trailing close behind Eliza and Valen.

"Cardinals and Ulrichs forfeit their names when they take their oaths of service," she replied.

Cole's Passion revealed a trace of bitterness emanating from her, as well as a subsequent effort to cram the resentment back to where it slipped out from. Cole usually did his best to ignore the hidden emotions of others in order to preserve their privacy, but as there was a whole city at stake he chose to relax this rule. Ethics and morals, as Valen said.

"What was your name before you took the oath?" Cole said in a gentle tone. "I promise I won't turn you in."

A sadness flashed across her face, quickly replaced by a stony mask. Once again Cole detected a flicker of emotions before she crammed them in the same place in which she kept her resentment.

She loathed the position of Cardinal, though her sense of honor denied her the ability to feel such things. It had been a very long time since she felt genuine love and kindness from another, the very gifts she was sworn to preserve.

She checked behind and beside her, then replied with a private mental touch, *"My name is Olavia."*

"It is a pleasure to meet you, Olavia," Cole replied, offering her a measure of his compassion. Her mind soaked it in like a starved desert plant tasting true water for the first time. Pity welled up within Cole, though he concealed it from her awareness.

Olavia was much more relaxed from there on. She offered suggestions as to where they should visit first: museums, monuments, and towers with scenic views. However, Cole was only curious about places with thick crowds and heavy foot traffic.

She led him to a market square bordered by stalls and carts stocked with various wares. One cart sold a thing called a shaper stick, which was nothing more than a focusing shard embedded in a piece of wood, allowing the user easy use of Wisdom spells. Next to it was a Cardinal issuing licenses to use the shaper sticks. Other stalls displayed collections of frozen fish, eggs, moss, and ice-carving tools. Another vendor guarded a paddock of squat, hooved creatures with sleek voluminous fur. As each customer paid the gratia stone, a woman hopped over into the paddock and used a broad set of mechanical clippers to shear a swath of fur. After the transaction she patted a fuchsia hand between the creature's horns, and the fur grew back within seconds, just as shiny and full as it was before.

Cole and Sitra hopped up onto a tall plinth at the base of an ice statue depicting a baileen, a much better position to view the hustle and bustle of the market. Olavia looked only slightly discomforted by this. A chill crept into their hands and feet, and so they called forth their munisica and ebony shrouds. Sitra's long braid became a sweeping rope of woven needles, matching her spiked eyebrows. Her bladed feet gripped the ledge of the plinth while her clawed hands rested on her hips, setting her in a proud, heroic pose. Galvanized by her display, Cole brought forth the entirety of his master's shroud, covering himself inside and out with the midnight armor of Rage.

"Don't you think that's overdoing it a bit?" Olavia called up from beneath the statue. "You two are making quite a scene."

"C'mon, red," Sitra scoffed, crossing her arms. "We're freezing our asses off, and can't keep ourselves warm with Wisdom forever."

"I'll get you some coats then," Olavia replied. She darted off to a nearby vendor.

That was all they needed. Within seconds a family of four took notice of Cole and Sitra. The children hopped up and down like baby birds as they cried out in delight, their cheery faces barely visible from the depths of their puffy jackets and hats. At first the questions came at a steady trickle, then they surged into a relentless deluge as more people took notice, gathering in throngs beneath the baileen statue. Just as they had done in the fish restaurant, Cole and Sitra recounted their more romantic adventures and exploits, which eventually brought them to the subject at hand. Cole felt another granule of his hope break off into the wind, where it joined the fat snowflakes swirling about the market. He felt the eyes of the other Cardinals burning into him, searing him with their disapproval, but he also felt a sense of wonder hiding behind their solemn masks. The fact that they made no move to stop him told Cole that he was safe to go on, though he was quite sure they would wipe the minds of everyone in the crowd as soon as he left.

As Cole explained the coming dangers and breeding nightmares, he couldn't help but brace himself for an imminent sting of dejection. He didn't need Passion to sense the excitement churning about the gathering crowds. They hung on his every word, right up until he suggested they uproot their entire lives, leave everything they know, and start life from scratch among strange people in a strange land. The joy fell from their faces, replaced by a disturbed brooding and raw silence. With no idea what else to say, Cole nodded to Sitra. Magnificent emerald wings erupted from their backs like fans of knives. The snowy air whipped up about them as they took flight.

"We definitely get entertainment points," Sitra sighed as they landed a block away from the market. "I ran out of good stories but they didn't seem to mind. They would have listened to the *legend of how I put on my pants this morning* or the *epic of what Cole had for dinner last night.* They're naive. And blind. I thought this was gonna be easy, but now I don't think there's a fire big enough to burn their asses into leaving."

"I know what you mean," Cole said as he dialed back his Rage and dismissed his wings. Varka's cape became weightless on his back as it transformed into a blanket of soft snow. "We're asking thousands of people to leave everything they know and love because there are monsters coming. Monsters they've never seen and have no reason to believe exist. We might as well try to convince them the stars are falling. I know I wouldn't budge if I were in their shoes. You haven't broken the Seer Jar yet, right?"

Sitra patted the space between her breasts. "Couldn't be in a safer place."

"You keep it in there?" Cole asked, astonished.

"Have a better idea, genius?" she snapped, defensive as usual when her intelligence or competence came into question. She ground her teeth and averted her eyes from him. Cole tore his eyes away before she accused him of gawking at her chest.

The people of Borla Dign had worked with The Sill's Communications Web to craft a much smaller version of the Seer Jar, which they could keep in a pocket and take with them on missions. It was only good for one use, after which it would self-destruct and close the portal behind them. The Seer Jar still required the knowledge of Borla Dign's consensus to operate, so the Wisdom followers created a cypher that granted a temporary understanding of the magic. Of everyone in the Unbound, only Valen was trusted with their spell. Cole preferred this option over entering Borla Dign's consensus again, which had left him feeling numb and emotionally empty for hours afterward.

"No, you're fine," Cole replied, then made a stab at another subject. "Should we even bother wrangling up another crowd, or should we just go home?"

"I don't know. You're in charge," she said, still not looking at him. "I'm just the village idiot."

"Sitra, please. You know I didn't mean anything by it. I was just surprised, that's all," Cole pleaded, but she shrugged him off and stormed away from him. "You know what, you're not stupid, you're just getting soft. I wonder what Roth would say if his favorite student allowed herself to be hurt by mere words."

Sitra whipped around so fast that her bladed hair struck the side of a lamp post, producing an explosion of ice chips that nearly cleaved the post in two. Her munisica closed into fists. "Since when did you start caring about what Roth would think?"

Cole gaped at her. "What the hell are you talking about?"

"Well that makes perfect sense," Sitra said, rolling her eyes. "Of course you wouldn't remember a conversation that didn't revolve around you like everything else has since you barged into our lives."

"Enough," Cole said, voice rising. "Either tell me what this is about or go find yourself a comfy place to hide while we save this city."

"That's just it!" Sitra barked. "You're busy saving cities full of lovers and scholars when you should be out recruiting warriors."

"Are you talking about Morthain?" Cole asked.

Sitra gripped the air in front of her, as if wishing her claws were around Cole's thoat. "Of course I'm talking about Morthain! Roth charged me with invoking the Trial of Honor upon them should he die in this war. Since we all agree that he's as good as dead, that means I, not *you*, have a job to do. Instead you've got us on the other side of the planet begging help from whores. But then again, it's *my* Trial of Honor. There's no glory in it for you, so I see why this one slipped through the cracks."

Cole was speechless. Her tirade had come on so abruptly, so unexpectedly, that he couldn't find the words to make it better. He had fully intended to search The White Sands for what was left of Morthain, and there were plenty of good reasons he had yet to do so, but at the moment he could not recall any of them. He felt like a child again, inadequate and lost, grasping at things far beyond his realm of comprehension. He felt his hope bleed from him like sand through a broken hourglass. Most painful of all was the new sorrow welling up in him, chilly and withering. He loved Sitra like a sister since the day they met, but apparently she held only contempt for him. He wondered if the others felt this way as well.

"There you are!" cried an exasperated voice.

Cole turned to see Olavia bustling up the street. He sighed, shaking his head at the ground. Now he would have to suffer her displeasure for his use of 'unauthorized magic'.

"I hope you didn't wipe their memories," Cole said to Olavia as she trotted up beside him. "They have a right to know what's going on in the world."

"The crowd dispersed soon after you left," Olavia said with an an air of would-be indifference. "There were too many for the other Cardinals and me to corral, so no, we did not modify anyone's memories. The other Cardinals will likely report you for your use of Wisdom and Rage, however."

"And what about you?" Cole asked, watching Sitra disappear around a corner. He thought he saw tears in her eyes.

Olavia was silent. Cole looked back to her, finding tender curiosity budding in her eyes. Her mind nudged his. *"Were all those stories true?"*

Cole broadened the connection between them, shedding a fleeting light over every facet of his mind so she could feel the truth for herself. She quailed as a few of his memories rushed into her. *"Every word."*

Olavia's mouth fell open. Her eyes drifted into a faraway gaze, her breath quickening as implications fell into place. After a moment she gave Cole a stern look and whispered, "We have to leave Vol Karinn."

Cole reconciled with Sitra after finding her in a bar. She hadn't been gone long, but she was already on her third glass of something called starfire brandy. She had been crying. He downed the rest of the liquor for her, regretting it at once as it seared him from his tongue to his toes. He wrestled her into a hug, which she resisted, then broke down in earnest. Once calm returned to her, she left the bar with her chin up high. As Cole paid the bartender he noticed a word carved into the frozen counter where Sitra had been seated.

Bonebreaker.

With Olavia now firmly on their side, they found a few choice places to give their speeches. The Cardinal's support extended to her Ulrichs, hastening Eliza's and Valen's progress as well. Cole had difficulty conjuring the motivation he had when he first arrived. Cries of awe rose and fell in tumultuous waves as they told a story or showcased a flashy display of Wisdom, but when it came time for the ultimatum the crowds always fell silent. It wasn't enough. They needed something more, but shy of bringing a Colossus through their frozen sky, Cole couldn't think of a good-enough spark to light this fire.

The day was half over by the time Cole and Sitra left their third crowd in brooding quiet. Olavia did her best to mitigate reprisal from the other Cardinals, but they were already patrolling the streets in teams, wiping minds as they went. Accepting failure at last, Cole reached out to Eliza and informed her of their lack of progress.

"I'm afraid Valen and I fared even worse than you and Sitra," Eliza said, her words heavy with loss. *"We ought to have known the Cardinals would intervene. Vol Karinn will fall to The Three."*

"This has been an enormous waste of time," Valen added. *"We should not have come. A single envoy could have told us what the four of us just spent a precious week learning. Aeneria will suffer for our lapse in judgment."*

"Let's get out of here then," Sitra said. *"We can't win every fight."*

The Unbound met at the base of Chiron's ice statue. A horseshoe pond half-glazed with ice was wrapped around his feet, steaming and simmering from the hot springs beneath. A herd of the sleek-furred animals chomped away at the golden tufts of grass sprouting from a nearby field of white powder. The snow fell heavily around them, thickening the air with a muffled quiet.

Valen cleared a patch of ground and conjured a fire for them. Sitra dug through her bag and tossed each of them half a blackstout, the last of their stores. Eliza siphoned water from the pond, collecting it into an orb beside the fire where she began purifying it with Wisdom.

"What are you doing?" Olavia asked Cole as he warmed his hands by the fire. Her Ulrichs closed in behind her.

"Setting up camp," Cole replied as he warmed his hands. "This is where we told everyone to meet us by the end of the day. This is where we'll activate a portal to bring them all to The Sill."

Olavia took a step closer. "But the day is only half over and you haven't spoken to everyone yet. There's still the Lowfields, Harper's Corner, Deerun Bridge, why have you given up already?"

"Because, Cardinal, Vol Karinn doesn't want to be saved," Eliza replied. "To join us means to take a stand in a war they don't want to believe in. This is a place of lovers, not fighters. Had I not been sent to The Sill and enlightened to the dangers of our world, I would be right alongside them. No glitzy magic or tale of heroism would have made me leave my life behind."

"I'm sorry, Olavia," Cole said. The others perked up at hearing the Cardinal's name for the first time. "We've done everything we can. The other Cardinals are erasing our words faster than we can utter them and we have no right to interfere with Vol Karinn's law, even if thousands will burn for it. We will wait here in case anyone does come. You are of course welcome to join us."

Olavia tensed, her hands balling into bladed fists. "But you're the Unbound! It *is* your right, no, your obligation to save Aeneria. Use your powers to force the minds of the Conclave. Stars, I'll help you put the rest of the Cardinals in a coma if that's what it takes."

Cole gave her an empty smile. "We could do that, but answer a question for me first. As benign as we think we are, if we force an entire civilization to bend to our will, then how does that make us any different from The Three? They use dark magic, but Passion, Rage, and Wisdom can get the job done just as well. We've been fighting for a long time, Olavia. I'm sorry to say we don't have enough fight left in us to save Vol Karinn."

One of the Ulrichs tapped Olavia on the shoulder. She looked to him, annoyed at first, but then he offered her a series of intricate hand gestures. Her face lifted with each passing second.

"What's he doing?" Sitra asked through a mouthful of blackstout.

Cole watched for a moment, but couldn't glean a word from the Ulrich's silent language. "The Ulrichs have their tongues removed when they take their oaths of service. They communicate with their hands instead of their voices."

"Well whatever he's saying it seems like good news for us," Sitra said.

The Ulrich finished, offering Olavia an optimistic shrug. The Cardinal nodded, then approached Cole and grasped each of his shoulders. "Bannerdean Hall," she said through a smile.

JOSEPH PARADIS

"What's that?" Cole asked.

Olavia squeezed him, unable to contain her excitement. "It's a place where you can show Vol Karrin the truth, just as you showed me. It is also one of the few places where Wisdom is not only allowed, but celebrated. Bannerdean Hall is named after the city where Walker Chiron was born, who embraced both Wisdom and Passion. Within Bannerdean Hall we emulate his union of the two magics, blending them together in such a way that memories can be brought to life before a stage for all to see. The magic allows the audience to mingle their sub-selves with yours, and experience your memories as their own. Bannerdean Hall is typically used for entertainment, but it is also used by the Conclave to disseminate edict. Deceit and embellishments are impossible, which makes the display that much more potent. This is how you will give them the truth. Show them what you know."

"We're familiar with this magic," Cole said, eyeing the blooming hope on the faces of the Unbound. "I'm just worried if we'll have enough time. How many people can we fit into Bannerdean Hall?"

"Everyone!" Eliza gasped, clapping her hands together and shaking them. "Bannerdean Hall was built to host the entire city for the end-of-cycle festivals, but there's also an alarm in case the Conclave needs to draw everyone in for an urgent message. Why didn't I think of this before?"

Another idea came to Cole. He gazed openly at Sitra's chest, eliciting befuddled looks from the group. "We can set up the portal right on the stage as soon as we're done. How soon can you get everyone in there?"

"Within an hour once the calling horns are blown," she replied. Her Ulrich tapped her on the shoulder again, then his hands became a blur of symbols and forms. "Right. We'll head out now and start plying our way through the staff at Bannerdean Hall. When you hear the horns, come straight over. The ceiling is open so you can fly right in. The Conclave will take longer than the rest of Vol Karinn to show up, but that will only give us another fifteen minutes or so. Whatever memory you choose, be sure to make it as concise and compelling as you possibly can."

Calling their Rage into action, Olavia and her Ulrichs sprinted for the city, their clawed feet crunching over the ice and snow as they sprinted along.

"How about Borla Dign?" Valen suggested. "It is freshest in our minds, and it certainly showcases a few of the horrors plaguing our world. It is also a prime example of our success as the new Unbound."

"Success would work against us in this case," Eliza said in a steely tone. "Remember, this is a city of Passion followers. It may be indelicate, but we need to play on their sympathies. The battle in Fangshard Valley would be a better choice. Oberon City lost an entire battalion to Sorronis's Hatefire while we nearly succumbed to his rain of Despair, not to mention we lost two of their fabled Unbound. Fangshard Valley will also validate Cole as Varka's heir and us as the new Unbound."

"Our powers do that for us already," Sitra said in a would-be casual tone. Her wolfish grin didn't quite meet her eyes; she clearly wasn't ready to relive Roth's ascension to Grotton's Harbinger. "And anyone who's seen Cole in his master's shroud and felt his Passion will know he's the real deal. Not to mention he's wearing the same damned cape as Varka's statue over there. I think Costas would be the best memory for these people. It shows them what they're in for. We all smelled those towers and saw what those Underkin became. And... and that's where we lost Storn." Her voice broke as her jaw trembled in a struggle to find the words. "If that doesn't convince people to escape, then nothing will."

Sitra, Valen, and Eliza waxed on about their chosen memories while Cole stared into the depths of the fire. He played through each scenario in his mind. Each was powerful and pivotal to their journey, but none affected him as much as his mission in Brimhallow Village, nor were they as applicable. Brimhallow was a society of Passion followers after all, which meant The Three would dismantle Vol Karinn with similar, gruesome efficiency. In Brimhallow, every citizen had been captured and consumed, their bodies Chosen and dismantled for evil rituals within their own temple. He recalled the eerie quiet of the streets, the atrocity of a thousand skins tacked to the temple walls, and the nightmarish red glow of the temple interior. He didn't need to delve further into the memory to know that this was the one. Brimhallow's demise would be used to save Vol Karinn.

The calling horns echoed throughout the valley crater, so loudly that several small landslides cascaded along the valley walls. After some difficulty grasping their magic, the Unbound conjured their emerald wings and took to the skies. Their Wisdom didn't seem to want to flow as it usually did, and even their Rage took some prodding to grant them munisica, as though something in the air suppressed their magic. They discussed their symptoms in flight, but even their Passion had been affected, making their words dim and hard to hear. They were all the more eager to get back to The Sill and take a well-earned break.

Eliza led them to Bannerdean Hall, but the snow was now falling so thickly that they made two loops around the entire city before she found it. Cole glimpsed it through a river of fat white flakes; a stadium of dark stone, cut deep into the ground with rows upon rows of seats encircling the stage like tree rings. As they neared, he saw droves of fluffy brown coats marching through the streets and filing into the stadium. Smaller ice sculptures of the old Unbound stood guard at each entranceway, set in heroic poses or casting powerful spells. He heard Eliza utter something through their Passion network, then saw her cut into a steep dive toward Bannerdean Hall. Cole and the others followed.

The Unbound landed roughly upon the stage, gouging the stone with their munisica. The seats were already half full, and judging by the vacant looks coming from the brown coats, none of them remembered the Unbound's campaigning in the streets. The Cardinals had been efficient in their cleansing.

"There you are," Olavia cried as she and her Ulrichs came trotting onto the stage. "No sign of the Conclave yet. The other Cardinals are asking odd questions, but once the show starts they'll see the truth as plainly as I did. The whole stadium is enchanted so anyone within its confines will live your memory. You do have a good memory for them don't you?"

"Yes," Cole replied, hoping she didn't notice the shaking in his voice. He never liked being in front of crowds. "It's one of my own.

I've given the memory to the other Unbound, so they'll be able to help flesh out details and strengthen the magic."

"We'll need you to hold on to this for us," Valen said, giving her the cypher. "Projecting the memory will put too much Passion and Wisdom into the air, and will likely corrupt the knowledge in that cypher. Do be careful with it. It is our key to get home."

"Indeed I will," Olavia said. She took the cypher with gentle fingers as one of her Ulrichs handed her a strip of cloth. She wrapped the orb and tucked it safely into the folds of her crimson robes. "The stage is charged and the spells are ready. Once you delve into the memory, the Passion and Wisdom will trigger themselves and Vol Karinn will join you. I will be up there, which is where the Conclave will sit once they show up." She pointed up to a marble balcony partitioned from the rest of the rows. "You'd better get started soon actually, they're filing in faster than I anticipated."

Cole looked up and around. In the brief moment they'd spoken, nearly every seat had been filled. A wall of brown fur and expectant faces surrounded him on all sides. He took a sharp breath, wondering how long he'd forgotten to breathe, then worried how many people noticed him standing there, panting like a fool. A drop of sweat rolled down his back, and his heart felt like it was trying to bash its way through his ribcage. He looked to Olavia to tell her he was ready, but could only manage a nod. She understood and took off at once.

"You gonna make it there, noodle legs?" Sitra asked as she clapped him on the shoulder, nearly knocking him over. She lowered her voice and gripped his shoulders, steadying him. "Are you afraid to go back into that cellar? We can take the memory from there if you want."

"No," Cole croaked. "I'm... just nervous in front of crowds."

"You're shitting me," Sitra said with a disgusted sigh. "The great and powerful Cole, heir to Varka's might, leader of the Unbound and The Sill, the man who fell a Colossus by himself and—"

Cole shoved her away. "I get it, I know I'm being stupid!"

Sitra continued on as though she hadn't heard him. "...and nearly killed Sorronis singlehandedly, the only one on Aeneria who's mastered Rage and then had the balls to master Passion, and who just happens to be the most dangerous person I know... You're telling me this man is scared of speaking in front of a few Passion lovers."

"Glory to Varka's heir! The Unbound have returned!" cried a jubilant voice from a few rows up. A dozen people throughout Bannerdean Hall echoed the words.

"It appears the Cardinals missed a few minds," Valen said with a rare smile.

"And it looks like Cole's legs have stopped shaking," Sitra chuckled. "Thought I was going to have to set your pants on fire to get you out of your own head. Works like a charm, right Val?"

Valen replied with a contemptuous grunt.

A hand slipped into Cole's and held it tightly. Eliza beamed at him as he felt her Passion massage its way up his arm, warm and soothing. Her voice fell gently over his mind, instilling him with a sense of calm and safety. *"We are with you."*

And before Cole knew it, a gold and pink haze had surrounded him and the stage gave way to tall ferns and creeping vines. He was just outside Brimhallow Village, learning what he could from the safety of the shadows. His reconnaissance was near an end, however, and it was time to enter the village. There were signs of violence and struggle: broken furniture, claw marks in the door frames, blood spattered on carpets, but there was no sign of life. Cole pushed on. Fear welled up inside him as he neared some unknown source of evil, so he called upon his Rage, burning the crippling magic faster than it could blossom. Then he saw it. The temple covered in skins. It was at this point that Cole felt the presence of the citizens of Vol Karinn, watching through his eyes, listening through his ears. Horror, revulsion, and even Rage emanated from the Passion followers as they beheld the demons' nest.

With a captivated audience in tow, Cole spared no detail as he delved further into the memory. He felt his friends with him as well. Drop by drop, they maintained the ocean of particulars that ran the background of the memory, such as the sweet tang of rot or the phantom whispers that lured him deeper. Cole brought them to the basement, through the wall of arms with its hundreds of scrabbling hands and thousands of jagged fingernails. He dispatched the Domina on the other side, then went even deeper beneath the temple. The collective Fear of Vol Karinn began to plague his mind on the stage, infecting his heart and chilling his spine, but Cole couldn't call his Rage to quell the tide, not without tainting the memory.

He had always recalled his torture with a sense of pragmatism because he had made it out just fine; however, this time his Fear and Despair were nearly as potent as they were during the event. The other Unbound made attempts to help him, only to recoil and retreat, stung by the dark magics. Cole wanted to stop the memory, to simply explain the rest to Vol Karinn through spoken word, but he couldn't. He was stuck. Cole plodded through the rest of the memory, inflicting one agonizing detail at a time upon himself and everyone else, as though he were dragging them all through a swamp filled with barbed wire. But pass through he did. Before the magic faded, Cole brought forth another memory, one just as painful. He brought Vol Karinn to the ledge in Fangshard Valley and showed them the last moments of Roth, Chiron, and Alvani. Too weak to go on, Cole withdrew at last.

The stage swam before his eyes, then solidified in full. It was done. They now knew their fate should they stay, the dangers that waited beyond their frozen sky. He felt sick. His legs wobbled and his stomach churned. The other Unbound seemed just as beleaguered by the memory. Snow fell in thickening clumps. A few inches had accumulated while the memory played, changing the sea of brown coats around him into a wall of white.

"Valen, can you do anything about this snow?" Cole asked as he put a hand over his eyes and peered around. "I can't see Olavia."

Valen rubbed his hands together, inspecting them with a troubled expression. "At the moment, no. I think the vestiges of that memory have weakened my Wisdom. I... I need to recover."

They had precious little time. They had to act or else all would be for nothing. Commanding his own Wisdom, Cole brought the green magic to his throat with the intent to raise his voice loud enough for all in the stadium to hear. The magic was slippery, however, and it took him several tries before he could grasp it. Varka's cape hung over his back as useless as a dish rag. Grunting with the effort, Cole managed the spell at last.

"People of Vol Karinn," Cole started, his voice booming like thunder. "You saw it through my eyes. The Three have slain the Unbound of old. We were students of Roth and Chiron, and upon their demise they transferred their responsibilities to us, the new Unbound. Our enemies have already taken most of Aeneria, but their Hunger is insatiable. They will come for Vol Karinn, and your great city will suffer the same fate as Brimhallow Village." Cries of terror and outrage erupted around him. Cole looked to Sitra and nodded. She took the Seer Jar from its hiding place and held it up for all to see, though the thick snow occluded it from the eyes of many. Cole waited for a lull in the clamor, then continued, "We offer you an escape from The Three. We will open up a portal on the stage, which will take you to The Sill, our home. There you will be surrounded by able warriors who can protect you, and should you choose to, you can join us in the fight. The portal will only be open for a short while, so you must come with us now, or stay and brave the storm alone."

The din of the crowd rose once more, only this time it was with an air of action and intent, leaving Cole with no doubts that he had the vast majority on his side. Hope took root in him at last.

"Valen, the cypher," Eliza said in a hushed tone. "Now is the time."

Valen reached for his pocket, but dropped his hand halfway. "The Cardinal still has it. Where did she go?"

Cole peered through the heavy snow. The white flakes were so thick that even the middle rows had been blocked from view. But then he saw it at last, a flash of scarlet robes. He spoke with his mind and showed the Unbound where to look. *"Up there! See the red?"*

"I see it," Valen replied . With his palms glowing jade, he twisted his hands before him and the snow cleared between the stage and balcony.

Garbed in tight leathers the color of old blood, was Visellis. Her blond hair had been yanked back into a formal braid, but her posture was relaxed and perfectly at ease. She regarded Cole with a dark smile, and he knew they had made a terrible mistake.

CHAPTER 22

EVIL UNMASKED

"It seems we have a different understanding of the word mayhem,*"* Visellis said. Her mind felt like chilled oil creeping through his thoughts.

Cole stood tall and defiant. *"At least your people were open to the truth. We simply went a little further and showed it to them."* He dropped his veneer of courtesy and broadened their conversation so the other Unbound could hear, and bathed every word in threatening intent before it left his mind. *"If you try to wipe their minds again, or prevent anyone from leaving, you will be stopped. This isn't the way to learn how we earned the title of Unbound."*

Instead of recoiling from the minds of the Unbound, Visellis wove her own throughout theirs, embracing them. *"Leaving? But we haven't had our time alone together. And how will you leave without this?"*

Visellis raised her hand in front of her. Even from a distance Cole could make out the glittering shine of the cypher. She brought it to her lips and kissed the glassy orb as though it were the most seductive thing in the world, then crushed it between her fingers in a puff of viscous light.

"No!" Eliza shouted. Her fingers stretched and darkened, but the shroud barely covered her hands.

Her dark smile returning, Visellis extended an arm and Olavia appeared on the balcony, her Ulrichs trailing right behind her. Infinite sadness filled their eyes, painting their faces with the emptiness of those who had lost all hope. They turned to the stage, but their hollow gazes stared beyond it. Visellis caressed the air before her with a tender stroke. Tendrils of magic the color of blued bruises snaked from her fingers, extending across the balcony and licking Olavia and her

Ulrichs on their cheeks. With one unified motion, the Cardinal and her men raised their bladed hands, and before Cole could utter a word they plunged the black claws into their own throats, and tore them out.

Cole watched in horrified disbelief as their life's blood erupted from their wounds. Their empty expressions showed no signs of pain, not even when death laid them upon the balcony floor. It was in that moment Cole felt it pool up inside him. It was the same magic carried by the snow and woven into the frozen sky, only apparent now that he'd seen it out in the open. Despair.

"Can we kill her now?" Sitra demanded. Her eyes burned with Rage, but she didn't seem to notice the heavy snow had changed to a light rain. A black, oily rain.

Cole looked at his hands and watched as flecks of tar spattered across his palms. He then gazed out to the sea of people around him. They sat motionless and expressionless, their oil-covered faces showing no reaction to what had just happened on the balcony. Rather, they looked as if they didn't care about anything in that moment. Neither did Cole.

Eliza was first to act. Her tears mixed with the tar on her cheeks as she charged across the stage. She leapt into the air, falling far short of what Cole knew she was capable of, and landed among the crowd. She leapt from seat to seat on her way to Visellis, who stood on the balcony with her arms open wide in welcome.

"No, Eliza," Cole mumbled. He had almost summoned the Rage to join her, but then a dozen figures in blood-red leathers climbed up on the stage wielding ethereal daggers of mottled purple; Fear willed into solid form. Sitra and Valen noticed them too, but the black rain of Despair had already soaked through their armor. They wiped their faces and eyes, though it only served to spread the sticky tar. They would die, just as Olavia died, just as Cole would die.

The concept of death was all the spark Cole's Rage needed to ignite. The familiar ache creaked through his fingers and toes as they became black knives, but the shroud was slow to spread. His mind clearing, he immersed himself in the minds of the Unbound, bolstering them in the furnace of his Rage. Sitra and Valen shook their heads, baring their teeth, then strained as they attempted to summon their own munisica.

"Liza!" Sitra roared. Eliza was almost to the balcony. Sitra crouched into a sprint, but the figures in leather were upon her. She rolled away from the slash of a dagger, only to put herself in the path of two more glinting blades.

Something whistled near Cole's ear. He ducked instinctively as a dagger hissed through the air where his neck had been. Two women stalked toward him while two men flanked him from either side. Their ghostly daggers stretched into swords. Cole flexed his hands, urging his munisica to grow larger, but the Despair slowed the red magic.

The two women charged, swinging their blades in wild arches over their heads. The attack was as crude as it was deadly, but it told Cole they had no real training, that they had never faced a real enemy who fought back. He caught a blade in each hand, stopping them in midair, but a stab of paralyzing terror caught him on either side of his chest. He saw the men in his periphery, each drawing back for another thrust. Using the swords for leverage, he yanked himself forward and leaped between the women, landing on the far side of the stage. He felt his ribs. They were tender and felt broken, but whatever magic Amorinanis had woven into the threads had stopped the blades from penetrating. The wounds hurt, but his Rage burned all the hotter for it. His shroud crawled steadily up to his elbows and knees.

The two men charged this time. Cole deflected each blow with his shrouded wrists, kicking straight through the shin of one man in a burst of flesh and leather before rolling toward the women, who had just begun circling around to flank him. They were faster than the men. Their attacks came like a hail of angry snakes, then doubled as they summoned a second sword apiece. Cole reveled in the challenge. Time slowed for him as he felt his shroud slide up to his shoulders and thighs, revealing opportunities at last. Flattening his hand into a blade, Cole waited for a brief pause between their ungainly attacks, then Cole stabbed one of the women through her neck. The second woman never saw him coming. The blood and victory fueled his Rage further still, and by the time he returned to the men his master's shroud had come at last, sharpening his mind and body.

"M-monster, monster you are," babbled one of the men, who had just had his leg healed by the other. Cole indulged in the man's weakness. He sensed Fear bleeding from him like a child's piss.

Cole's lip curled in disgust. There was no challenge here. He raised his arm and aimed his palm at the men, who balked and fled as though he'd aimed a cannon. Two orbs of fuchsia light pulsed from his hand, each striking a man in the back before they made it off the stage. They fell to the ground in a tangled, twitching heap. The spell wouldn't kill them, but the seizures would last for hours and leave them conscious to the agony of their flesh. Plenty of time to measure themselves against the might of the Unbound.

Cole snapped his attention to Sitra, who still had two enemies, then Valen, who still had three. He raised his palm again, then stopped. There was no real danger. The scales of battle had tipped in their favor seconds ago, an eternity in combat.

"Cole! Help Eliza!" Sitra boomed after winning herself one of the conjured swords and burying it in its owner's mouth.

A ripple snapped violently down Varka's cape, shedding the oil and revealing the flowing-glass cloth beneath. The stage cracked beneath Cole's munisica as he leaped into the air, fueled in equal parts of Rage and Wisdom. The balcony was less than a hundred feet away, but time moved so slowly for him that it seemed to take half a lifetime to get there. Eliza stood before Visellis, covered in tar from head to toe, but as Cole landed beside her he noticed parts of her that were several shades darker than the black rain. Her munisica were larger than he'd ever seen them, and her short hair was a rose of bladed obsidian.

"How long?" Eliza growled. The rain continued to fall. "How long have you been quartering Vol Karinn's Passion to The Three?"

Visellis looked perfectly at ease, a lazy smile upon her face, her arms open and inviting. "My arrangement with The Three is far better protection than the so-called 'might of the Unbound'. When the barrier came down it was I alone who saw the opportunity for safety, and I alone who had the foresight to act. Better to live in ignorant servitude than die as heroes."

"You've been paying tribute to The Three?" Cole demanded. "How?"

Visellis flashed Cole a seductive look and spoke in a sultry tone. "Join me, warrior. Taste the secrets for yourself. There are powers I can teach you, pleasures I can gift you. I promise you, ten minutes alone with me and your mind will truly be *Unbound*."

"The Three promise only pain and death," Eliza said through bared teeth. She crouched into a low fighting position. "You are alone with me now, and I promise you both."

"That's what I was going to say," Cole said to Eliza.

"No, she's mine," Eliza said, her mind a hurricane of seething Rage. Cole nodded and took a step back.

"Then I await your justice," Visellis cooed.

Time slowed once more. Eliza lunged, her arm extended like a spear aimed directly at her enemy's chest. It was then that Cole saw it, the Hunger waiting in Visellis's eyes, the Hunger that was the counter to Eliza's newfound Rage. It was too late. His friend was already beyond his reach. Tendrils of orange Hunger exploded from Visellis's palms and mouth, wriggling and dripping as they enveloped Eliza. Eliza's eyes popped wide, then her shroud vanished like a shadow before a flame, replaced by an emerald-green film. She stopped in mid flight as the tendrils slapped over her, unable to find entry through her barrier. Landing back on the balcony, she shot a pulse of green light at the floor beneath Visellis's feet, then jabbed her glowing fist toward the sky.

A cluster of stone needles shot up from the balcony between Visellis's feet. They passed through her body as if she weren't even there, continuing up several feet above her head. The tendrils of Hunger fell from her hands and mouth, where they melded in foaming puddles on the marble floor. Cole felt her life candle flutter, then fade into the void.

Eliza jumped to her feet, stoic in her triumph. She approached Cole and placed a palm on his chest. Passion jolted throughout his shrouded body, caressing and invigorating parts of him that he didn't realize were tired. Her eyes flicked to Olavia and her Ulrichs, but she knew as well as Cole did that there was no saving them now. The rain continued to fall.

"I thought she had you," Cole said.

Eliza clenched her jaw and her munisica reappeared, as did her shrouded hair. Her emerald barrier stayed the rain. "It was she who fell for my trap. Our Rage was too tempting an offer."

Cole nodded.

Below them, the stage was a mess of inky puddles, shreds of red leather, and gore. Valen hovered in the air, painting a protective umbrella of Wisdom over the stage while Sitra healed a wound on her chest with a palm aglow with soft pink. The remains of the Conclave lay strewn about the path around the stage. Cole and Eliza flew down to join Valen and Sitra, dismissing their shrouds after passing through the umbrella of Wisdom. They all took turns cleaning the tar from each other with jets of steaming hot air from their palms.

"What do we do now?" Sitra asked as they cleaned her off. "Bannerdean Hall is about to become Bannerdean Pond if we don't stop this rain. That's the same stuff Sorronis used on us in Fangshard Valley, right?"

"It is not as potent, but it is indeed a rain of Despair," Valen said. He glanced up at Vol Karinn's frozen ceiling. The tar ran down his conjured dome in viscous ribbons. "The Despair is woven into the ice. It is subtle magic, diluted just enough that no one would notice, but in such a large mass the magic is substantial. It is the reason our Passion couldn't sense the people below."

"Despair was snowing down upon the entire city," Eliza agreed. "Undetectable, but steady enough to accumulate and poison every soul in Vol Karinn given enough time. They have been under its influence for months, possibly an entire cycle. Valen, could you extend your barrier to cover the entire stadium?"

"It would be all I could do," Valen replied as he looked around. The people of Vol Karinn were still in their catatonic state. Every person sat motionless, half awake and black from head to hands. "It will take days to cleanse them all. There must be close to three thousand. We could try to melt a hole above the stadium."

"That'll take even longer!" Sitra said. "Remember how long it took us to walk through it?"

"Then Cole may have to fly back by himself," Valen offered. "He could beg another cypher or bring one of the Borla Dign people. Alone he is much faster than we are in a group."

"So have you gone entirely insane or are you just plain stupid?" Sitra said in a scathing tone. "Sorry Cole, but we're not letting our *Key to the Aethers* out of sight. If you get yourself killed on another solo mission then there'll be zero brains left in our group. I can't be the smartest one wherever we go, that's way too much pressure."

Sitra and Valen began bickering, dismissing each other's ideas for either taking too long to execute or being downright impossible. The biggest issue with their proposals was the fact that they no longer had the cypher, which meant their portable Seer Jar was useless. Without the portal, the people of Vol Karinn would have to walk, which would take months, and that was if they were strong enough to make it out of the valley canyon. There was only one option left.

"Are you praying?" Eliza asked Cole. Sitra and Valen circled around each other as their debate continued to gain in momentum.

"In a way," Cole replied. He kneeled and pressed his forehead to the stage. He shuffled around, searching for the right spot, then swore. "This won't work."

He hopped off the stage to the walkway surrounding it, summoned his munisica, then sank his claws into the dark stone beneath his feet. With a grunt, the stone cracked and he pried free a chunk the size of a table, tossing it aside before sinking his claws in for another. Eliza watched him with mounting curiosity. After a minute he'd cleared a hole deep enough to stand in, exposing the soil and rock beneath. Cole knelt in the earth and pressed his head to cool dirt. This spot would do.

"What's he doing?" Cole heard Sitra say to Eliza after a few minutes had passed.

"Praying, in a way," she replied coolly.

"To whom?" Valen asked.

"Hopefully you'll all find out soon," Cole shouted into the dirt. "Now leave me alone for a minute. I need quiet."

"Valen, I take back what I said," Sitra said in an exasperated tone. "Cole's insane, not you."

"Quiet, Sitra," Valen hissed.

Half an hour passed. Then an hour. Then two hours. Sitra and Valen continued their debate, though they eventually gave up after circling back and repeating options which had long been disregarded. Eliza watched Cole the entire time, who hadn't moved since settling in. His stomach groaned in ravenous protest, his back and hips ached to the bone, and a sharp rock had been poking his knee the whole time, but still he persisted. Finally, after two and a half hours, Cole sprang up on his knees and punched the dirt, then loosed his cry of victory.

"Yes!" Cole shouted, triumphant.

Sitra and Valen came rushing over.

"This better be good," Sitra demanded. "We could have walked there and back by now."

Valen hopped down into the hole with Cole. He inspected the dirt and rock. "What did you do?"

Cole grinned ear to ear. "Something big."

Eliza looked up, her brow furrowing with worry. Her eyes narrowed, then snapped wide. She let out an involuntary squeak of terror as a massive shadow passed over the frozen sky.

An explosion echoed throughout the entire canyon as five dark spikes penetrated the frozen sky, each larger than the largest building in Vol Karinn. There was another explosion, this time followed by a million cracks as a swath of the icy ceiling came loose and rose to the heavens. A chunk broke free and fell right above them, larger than Bannerdean Hall itself. A titanic stone hand shot through the first hole and caught the hunk of ice, cradling it with almost tender care as it withdrew into the starry sky above. A shadow moved over the hole in the ceiling, then two gargantuan ruby eyes blazed down upon the city with the ancient fury of the Fangshard Mountains.

"OOOOOOOO-CHAAAAAA"

Goran's thunderous greeting filled the valley crater. The ground beneath their feet shook as several landslides rolled down the crater walls. He returned his attention to the frozen sky and resumed his excavation, snapping and plucking the ice away with surprising delicacy. Within minutes there was nothing left of the frozen sky other than a single crusty ring around the valley wall. The black rain was gone at last.

Goran stepped down from the mountains and set his paws safely in a straw field at Vol Karinn's edge. There was no sound and the ground didn't so much as tremble in his wake. Goran moved with such beguiling grace that had they not watched him climb in, they would never known he was there.

Tears ran freely down Cole's eyes as he gazed up at his old friend. Goran's legs and arms looked to be made entirely of living stone, as if the bones of the Fangshards had become his own munisica. The brindle over his chest looked like rippling autumn forest blazing its pattern over his flanks and back. The tuft of snow on his head was nearly as high as the peaks surrounding the city. The mirak leaned in and brought the tip of one of his claws to the stage, setting it right in the middle.

Valen and Sitra moved aside so as not to be squished, while Cole and Eliza leaped up to join them. The claw was nearly as wide as the stage itself.

"I remember you," Cole said as he placed a palm on the column of living rock. The others followed suit, hands glowing with pink and fuchsia Passion. Goran rumbled his pleasure.

Sitra gave Goran's claw a playful punch. "He's bigger. Must be the steady diet of Domina and small mountains. Remind me why we don't just ride him to Oberon Temple and let him squash our enemies for us?"

"Because his influence only stretches as far as the Fangshards," Eliza said. "Isn't that right, Cole?"

Cole pressed his forehead to the stone. It was warm. "Yeah, that's right. I had to convince him that the ice here would eventually infect the entire mountain range. He can't stay long. It costs the Fangshards quite a bit to put all of Goran in one place like this."

"It's a shame we couldn't get him to carry us back to The Sill," Valen remarked. "The entire city could sit comfortably on his shoulders."

Goran withdrew his claw and brought it to his nose for a sniff. His ruby eyes shone brighter at the scent. He gave a satisfied grunt and sauntered around the city to the nearest monument of one of the old Unbound. The statue was as tall and thick as Goran's fore leg, but toppled as easily as a card castle when the mirak gave it a nudge with his paw. A waterfall sprouted from where the statue's head rested against the valley wall. Cole thought the destruction an accident at first, but then Goran tossed the pieces out of the valley and worked his way over to the next monument, repeating the process.

"Well that takes care of the Despair," Eliza said as she watched Goran work. "The citizens will rouse from their stupor soon. Should we fly back to The Sill and procure another cypher for the Seer Jar?"

"That's our only option at this point," Cole sighed. "Vol Karinn will be vulnerable though, so two of us will have to stay behind to protect them. If The Three were receiving tribute from the Conclave then they'll likely come investigate soon. I worry we may have doomed everyone instead of saving them."

"We did the right thing," Eliza said. "Had the people known the truth they would have gladly sacrificed themselves rather than continue supporting The Three. I don't—"

"*OOOOOOOO-CHAAAAAA.*"

Goran's thunder shook the air. He called out once more, a hint of urgency apparent this time. The Unbound conjured their wings and took to the sky without another word, finding Goran where Varka's monument had been moments ago. Once he deemed them close enough, he nudged his snout to a low spot on the valley wall, sniffed, then plunged a claw into the rock. When he removed his claw, the hole he created rippled and shifted, stretching wider and deeper as a neat tunnel revealed itself to them. Cole felt a concept sink into his mind from Goran's.

"*Thank you,*" Cole said as he hovered in the air. He wasn't sure how a tunnel would help them traverse half the planet, but he trusted Goran implicitly. "*I miss you.*"

Goran brought a fiery ruby eye to Cole and gave him a single, slow blink. With a farewell snort, the mirak turned and walked straight into the valley wall. An earthquake's roar filled the canyon as the mountain face churned and rolled, swallowing Goran whole before shifting back to plain rock.

"I have an odd feeling that tunnel doesn't simply lead to the other side of the mountains," Valen said. He swooped over and landed before the opening. The dark hole was twice as tall as he was and four times as wide. "There is magic here," he called back to them. "Goran meddled with the space. It has been bent, or perhaps stretched."

As Eliza had predicted, the people of Vol Karinn began to stir shortly after Goran left. They were confused and disoriented, but once the Unbound came back to the stage, all eagerness to leave returned to them, especially after seeing the slain members of the Conclave strewn about. The air grew substantially warmer without the frozen sky, and soon the ground became littered in oil-soaked coats, revealing thin, skeletal bodies and pale faces. Augmenting his voice with Wisdom, Cole explained the duplicity of the Conclave and how Goran had removed their frozen sky and monuments of the old Unbound, but they only seemed to half-listen. The people of Vol Karinn had eyes only for the moon and stars above. It was as if they had forgotten what the natural sky looked like and were only now gazing upon the wonders with virgin eyes. Upon mention of the new tunnel, however, excited murmurs and terrified whispers broke across the crowd. Cole didn't get a chance to tell them of the uncertainty of its destination before the first rose from their seats and made for the exits. Fortunately there was a small contingent of Cardinals left to maintain a semblance of order, who after experiencing Cole's memories for themselves, were just as insistent to be off.

"*You dropped the snowflake that started the avalanche,*" Valen said, speaking through their Passion network. "*There is no stopping them now. Two of us should go in ahead of the throng.*"

"*You're right,*" Cole admitted. "*I just hope Goran knew what he was doing. There's no way the four of us can guard a few thousand Passion users out in the open, and we all know how ineffective their Cardinals are in battle. Speaking of, we should take Olavia and her Ulrichs with us. We'll give them a proper service as soon as we can.*"

The crowd filed out of Bannerdean Hall and flooded the streets within minutes. The remaining Cardinals had already summoned litters for Olavia and her Ulrichs and covered them in death veils. As the masses poured through Vol Karinn, the streets and buildings began to melt in earnest. The frozen streets and walkways became slick and wet, eliciting countless falls and spills from the citizens as they stopped by flooded shops along the way, filling their pockets with food and supplies. Cole worried they would take too long and lose their resolve, especially after seeing folks grab non-essentials such as toys and cases of liquor, but before long he sensed life candles nearing the mouth of Goran's tunnel. After helping the Cardinals refreeze and resurface the streets leading out of Vol Karinn, Cole took to the sky and followed the river of people below him, who cried out in delight as they saw him flying overhead.

"Sitra's up front," Valen shouted from the entrance of Goran's passage. He and Eliza stood with their sleeves rolled, drying people off with blasts of Wisdom as they passed through. The citizens had each taken a dunk in a gathering pond at the base of the nearby waterfall, cleansing themselves of any vestiges of the black rain.

"Head on in. We'll see the rest get through," Eliza said to him, then turned to a pair of Cardinals beside her. "Tell the other Cardinals to check the city for stragglers on their way out. In this chaos it would be all too easy to forget about an infirm in bed or a child hiding in a closet. The melting ice will swallow the city within an hour."

"But what of the Summit?" asked one of the Cardinals. "There's likely a few Conclave members still in there, and crystal nymphs would never leave without permission."

"I will clear the Summit," Eliza said. The Cardinal began to protest but Eliza silenced her with a glare. "Go now. There is too little time and too much to do."

The Cardinal nodded and summoned respectable munisica, then shot down the path to the city like a streaking red comet. Cole landed beside Eliza and put a hand on her shoulder. *"Promise me you'll be careful."*

"I'll make that promise when you do. Go on now, Leader of the Unbound. Aeneria needs you." Smiling, Eliza turned away from him and put another hand into her drying spell.

Cole entered the tunnel and weaved his way through the crowd, keeping his feet on the ground so as to not disrupt the flow of traffic with a display of Wisdom. Their progress was slow enough as it was.

The passageway was lit with shining beacons of light stuck to the ceiling by someone farther up. Peeking over heads and shoulders as he ran, Cole saw Sitra trotting along with an arm in the air, shooting balls of white light up every ten paces or so. The crowd thinned as he neared her, and soon it was just the two of them jogging into the empty black.

"Kind of freaky, huh?" Sitra laughed as she hurled another fistful of light ahead of them. "Can you sense anything ahead?"

Cole cast his Passion out as far as it would go, but there was nothing for miles, other than the crowd behind them and Goran's dim presence permeating the rock. "Nothing at all. It's strange, I can't even sense Valen or Eliza anymore. We can't have gone that far." He glanced back and saw Sitra's string of lights, but there was no sign of the entranceway.

Sitra's chuckling echoed into the void ahead. "Where the hell is that furball taking us?"

After what felt like an hour, a faint blue speck appeared ahead of them, just a pinprick of light. Sitra raced ahead, leaping off the walls and punching the ceiling with light as she went. Cole kept his excitement in check and continued scanning with Passion and Wisdom. Now was not the time to stumble into trouble. The blue light grew steadily larger as a tranquil breeze carried the familiar scent of the sea. A broad smile tugged at his cheeks as he watched Sitra's silhouette dance and twirl ahead of him.

Cole's toes sank into the moon-baked sand as he joined Sitra on a beach. Oberon beamed overhead, welcoming them with triumphant ambers and blossoms of azure. Gentle waves lapped at the shore, eager to greet them. A few miles over the water, Cole beheld the dim glow of the Arts District and felt the teeming sea of life candles bustling about The Sill.

"I don't believe it," Sitra gasped. Slick with sweat, her long braid swished across her lower back as she sauntered up to the water's edge. She crouched and allowed a wave to crash over her hands. "I don't believe it."

Cole turned and looked back to the low foothills behind him. "The Fangshards must have roots that end here. I guess Goran gets to make his own rules when it comes to these mountains."

The citizens of Vol Karinn emerged onto the beach carrying bundles of supplies and sleeping children in their arms. The sight of the ocean left them speechless. They approached the rolling water with curiosity and wonder mingled on their faces, like animals seeing fire for the first time.

"Keep it moving!" Sitra shouted across the beach. "Stop clogging the tunnel, there's three thousand people right behind you!"

As they helped usher people down the beach, Cole kept close watch over the treeline. They weren't far from the place where they had their first encounter with Domina. After a few minutes he felt Valen's and Eliza's life candles appear from deep within the passageway.

"Cole, Sitra, is that you?" Valen asked in an urgent tone. *"We've been calling out to you for half an hour. I was worried something happened. Are you on the other side yet?"*

"We certainly are," Cole sighed. *"You're gonna love it here."*

Eliza pressed her curiosity into them. *"Where did you come out?"*

"We'll let you see for yourselves," Sitra said. *"Wouldn't want to spoil Goran's surprise for you."*

After flying a loop over the surrounding forest to check for danger, Cole and Sitra found a quiet spot farther down the beach to sit and relax while they waited for the others. Soon they would be tangled in the webs of bureaucracy and politics, but for now they were content to dip their feet in the water and enjoy a well-deserved break. They were home.

CHAPTER 23

THE TRIALS OF THE DEAD

Eliza and Valen were last to emerge from Goran's passage. As soon as they passed through, a grating sound filled the air while the sand rumbled beneath their feet. The tunnel collapsed upon itself and sank into the beach, leaving no trace that it ever existed. The incredulity was slow to fade from their faces, but after regaining their bearings they joined Cole and Sitra at the water's edge and enjoyed the moment of peace. Children played in the water, taking turns jumping over the waves or riding them in while their parents watched from the shore. The Cardinals patrolled up and down the beach distributing food and offering words of prayer while their Ulrichs kept watch. Cole hopped up and showed them a spell to desalinate the water from the ocean. Shoals of clean water bubbles soon bobbed among the crowd, soothing parched throats and cleansing sweaty brows.

Cole wished the moment could have lasted forever, but his Wisdom urged him on before long. Aeneria was still at war. They needed the safety of The Sill. Reaching out with his Passion, Cole found Rayn busy in his office at the Strategy and Operations center. The staff member was so busy poring over reports from the other departments, he didn't notice Cole watching from the edge of his thoughts.

Cole gave Rayn's mind a gentle nudge so as not to startle him, but Rayn jumped with a violent start, sending a stack of loose paper sprawling across his office floor.

"Starfire! Cole is that you?" Rayn demanded.

"Yes," Cole replied, reassuring Rayn with a wave of soothing Passion. *"We just returned from a mission. Everyone is perfectly safe. I'm sorry we left without telling you, but our secrecy paid off in the end."*

"We can discuss your reasons later, just get back here!" Rayn said. *"The Three have not been idle during your absence."*

"Actually, we need your help getting back," Cole explained. *"Do you know of a city called Vol Karinn?"*

"Vol Karinn?" Rayn asked, his confusion sprouting from him like a leaky bucket. *"Yes, it's a sizeable city somewhere on the other side of the planet. A whore's exile if I remember correctly. What of it?"*

"We have them with us," Cole said, showing Rayn an image of the crowded beach.

"How in the..." Rayn's thoughts trailed off as the concept struck him numb.

"Send one of Falinor's companies out to secure the beach," Cole said, speaking now as the leader of The Sill. *"We'll need Thessi's transport ships, and housing prepped once they all arrive. Get Debjornik's team ready at the Lurkwood Gate. We'll need to inspect everyone's minds upon entering."*

Ideas slowly began to spin in Rayn's mind, accelerating to the whirring pace of a well-trained Wisdom user. He then spoke with confident alacrity. *"It shall be done, Wisdom Walker. How many immigrants should we expect?"*

"Roughly three thousand citizens, including about a hundred Cardinals and Ulrichs, and twenty crystal nymphs," Cole stated.

Cole could tell Rayn hadn't the slightest idea what a crystal nymph was, but it mattered not for his calculations. Numbers and figures whirled through Rayn's mind as he disengaged from Cole to contact the rest of the staff.

"Are they on their way?" Valen asked as Cole's thoughts returned to the beach.

"Yes," Cole replied. He leaned back and stretched out on the sand. Varka's cape massaged his back with gentle ripples of crushed shells and granules of coral. "It's going to take them a while to get The Sill up and moving. We should do another loop over the coast to make sure no Domina come creeping through the trees."

"Sounds like a perfect job for our elite units," Sitra said as she dug a hole in the wet sand with her toes. A wave rolled gently up the shore and swirled up into the hole, then receded, leaving a hissing puddle of foam between her feet. "What do you think? Time for their first real mission?"

The Unbound contacted the leaders of each of their units. Within minutes they saw flocks of emerald wings and sun lily leaves rising up from the Lurkwood Gate. By unspoken consent the others had nominated Cole to contact Lileth. Cole didn't know what he Feared more, Lileth's reprisal or her continued silence. Swallowing his doubts, he reached for her with his Passion, only to realize he couldn't find her. She wasn't at The Sill at all. Dread tickled his heart. Hopefully she hadn't gone out looking for them. Relief washed over him as he contacted the leader of one of Lileth's units, who explained that their master had taken ill and was currently asleep in her apartment.

Wilkin pressed his location directly and privately into Cole's mind. The unit arrived dressed in fresh cloth armor and ready for orders. They stood tall and proud, flexing their munisica and budding emerald wings. These were not the same softlings grasping at magic and wishing for glory whom Cole had first met. Discipline and duty hardened their features as they surveyed the scene before them with keen eyes, scanning for weakness and vulnerability as their lessons had taught them.

"I apologize for leaving without an explanation," Cole said, addressing the whole unit. "Our mission required complete secrecy. Not even the staff of the Heart Tree knew about it. We were successful, as you can see."

"No need to apologize, Master Cole," Wilkin said. "It is not up to us to question the Unbound. It is our job to keep training and make sure we're ready for your return."

"And you did your job well, judging by the number of wings I saw on your flight over," Cole said as he walked among them. "Only Kolric was able to summon wings during our last lesson. Maybe I should disappear more often." He gave Kolric a pat on the shoulder and saw the boy's bald head flush with pink.

"Then maybe Bennit won't have to ride on a leaf like a child," Viness snickered.

Bennit wagged a bladed finger in warning. "Careful Viness, or I'll just clip yours and slap them on my back."

There was a smattering of chatter through the unit's Passion network. Cole pretended not to notice.

"That's enough! We're on mission!" Wilkin barked, silencing them. "Master Cole, what are your orders?"

"Thank you, Wilkin," Cole said. "The people on the beach are now citizens of The Sill. Your task is to protect them. You will work with the other elite units to patrol the ocean, skies, and surrounding forest for threats. If a threat should arise, kill it. If you can't, call for me and I'll do it for you. Begin now."

They stared unblinkingly at him, eyes wide and mouths slightly parted, then Wilkin roused them with a mental shout and they took off running. As Cole watched them go, he almost wished a pack of Domina would attack, just to see how they would fare against a real enemy.

A half hour later, a fleet of battleships arrived carrying Falinor and one of his assault companies, then Thessi and a few cargo vessels. They were sloppier and slower than Cole would have liked, but within another half an hour they had the beach secured and all the immigrants aboard.

Eliza had been working with the Cardinals while they were waiting, and after some deliberation she'd accepted their nomination of ambassador for the people of Vol Karinn. Once docked at The Sill, she went ahead with a few Cardinals to make preparations for everyone to check in through Debjornik's teams. Sitra's unit had spotted movement back on the beach, and so she worked with Falinor to lead a patrol deeper into the mainland woods. Wilkin's unit unanimously pleaded to go on the patrol as well, which Cole allowed, but only after reminding them that they still had training with him in the morning. Valen decided to go have a word with Brinleaf about sharing the knowledge of the Seer Jars, leaving Cole by himself at the Lurkwood Gate.

"You have been busy as a river in a storm, Wisdom Walker," Whind said in his airy voice as Cole emerged on the inside of the gate. The Gatekeeper was dressed in his usual living garments of bark and woven leaves, and he stared through Cole instead of at him.

Cole suppressed his initial flinch at Whind's sudden appearance from a nearby tree, then sighed and composed himself. "How are you, Whind?"

Whind aimed his faraway gaze up at Oberon. "The shadows darken, but The Sill burns all the brighter for it. The trees stand strong, Wisdom Walker."

"Right," Cole said with a respectful, albeit confused nod. "It's good to see you, Whind."

"And you as well," Whind said, bowing low. A patch of clovers at his feet wiggled in undulating waves as they crawled up his legs and covered his whole body. Whind stood upright, every inch of him clad in tiny green leaves, then walked straight into The Sill's outer wall, vanishing in a fluttering shower of clovers.

Cole shook his head and continued on. Varka's cape trailed lazily behind him, hardening into stiff, wooden knots as the enchanted cloth emulated the root path beneath his feet. Cole was in no rush to get to the Heart Tree, so he plodded on foot, taking in the sights and sounds of his home. Faces peered out from the lit windows of nearby trees while onlookers leaned over the network of canopy walkways above, all yearning for a look at the newcomers. Cole ducked behind a row of hedges to avoid a boisterous crowd from the Arts District, who judging by their carts full of food and clothes, were on their way to greet the refugees. He didn't have the energy to entertain a crowd of enthusiastic artists at the moment, not when there was so much work to be done. They passed him by, singing an emotive melody that hung in his thoughts long after the music faded from his ears. He trotted on, but instead of following his duties to the Heart Tree, he followed his heart to the barracks, where the other half of his soul lay waiting for him.

As Cole climbed the ramp to Lileth's apartment, the tickling dread resumed its tattoo over his heart. He thought about how she must have felt to wake up abandoned by the few people whom she loved. She probably thought them all dead. The thought of hurting her sent a knot of guilt twisting through his gut and left a sour taste in his mouth. Heart hammering on, he held his breath as he pushed his way through her door.

He found her sprawled gracefully on her bed, her chest slowly rising and falling under a thin silk shirt. Dim gratia light showed her fast asleep. Her eyes rolled gently behind closed lids, making her black petal lashes flutter like flowers in a breeze. Her face was set in such profound tranquility that Cole wished he could join whatever dream she was having, even considering casting a spell to do just that. He sat at the desk beside her instead, content for now to just be near her.

The room was an absolute mess. As his eyes adjusted to the low light, he saw clothes and crumpled bits of paper strewn about the floor among precarious towers of books. Cole recognized many of the volumes from The Sill's library. They were tales of old Wisdom Walkers and their adventures on the local planets. He smiled and took a moment to indulge in fantasies of getting lost with Lileth on faraway worlds, living out a life where war and suffering were merely long-forgotten memories. He looked back at her. The faintest smile curled a corner of her plump lips, as though she knew exactly what he'd been thinking.

Something sharp snagged Cole's wrist. He turned and inspected her desk. It was covered in thousands of tiny, broken bits of colored glass. Standing in the middle of the table were figurines made from the fragments, children set in playful poses, each a different color. After a moment Cole recognized them. They were the children they'd saved from Borla Dign, the ones Amorinanis had charmed into living gems with her odd magic. He looked closer, marveling at the meticulous detail taken in portraying the mirth in their smiles and the wonder in their eyes. As he looked the figures over, Cole realized the colorful fragments weren't bits of glass at all, but shattered fragments of gratia stones. There were flecks of blood dried up on the table as well.

He returned his gaze to Lileth and felt a mournful longing akin to homesickness rush up inside him. He missed her, even now with her so close. Wherever she was, that's where he belonged, and he'd do everything he could to never leave her side again. She turned over and faced him, still asleep. Her hand draped over the edge of the bed, revealing a collection of thin, raw slices on her fingertips. As silent as a shadow, Cole touched each of her fingertips with a drop of lavender Passion, healing them as she had healed him during their first training session so long ago.

"I thought I felt someone," Lileth said, waking at last. Her lips smiled for him, but as her eyes bloomed, they revealed the depth of her sadness. "Come to me."

Cole rose obediently from the chair, then stopped. "I haven't showered in a week."

"And I don't care," she replied, tugging at his hand.

Cole unclasped Varka's cape and draped it over the back of her chair, where it hung as grey and lifeless as a dusty curtain. He tore his armor off next, refusing to soil her bed with the gore of dead enemies. She pulled him into the bed and nuzzled close, unaffected by the smell of him. Now he was home.

"I knew you'd come back to me," Lileth said in a choked whisper. "I'm sorry I didn't come."

"No," Cole said, Hating himself. "I'm the one who should be sorry. We could have easily taken the five minutes and woken you, or I could have left a message with the Heart Tree. My note certainly didn't explain much. I just left you alone in the dark." Cole bit back his guilt and prepared his tongue for the truth. "I left you because I Fear."

Lileth sat up a little. "What hope does Fear have to affect a master of Rage?"

"It's not Fear for me, but for you," Cole muttered. "Lileth, I love you more than anything in this world or any other, but the thought of you going into battle ignites a Fear that no amount of Rage can manage. Ever since the elders died, you haven't been the same. You've… diminished. You are no longer fit for battle."

Lileth was quiet for a time. Eventually, she rose from her bed and walked over to her wardrobe, where she pulled out her cloth battle armor. She flicked a gratia stone embedded in the wall, bringing the lights up a bit, then inspected the garments.

"I have known those words to be true for longer than my pride will admit, but the time has come for me to accept them in full." She ran a jade finger along the length of the armor, which then rolled itself into a large ball in her outstretched hand. With another touch of Wisdom the ball shrank until it was smaller than her fist. She tossed it aside, where it knocked hard against the wall then cracked to brittle pieces over the floor. She looked up to Cole with watery eyes. "Thank you for helping me see the truth."

Cole sprang up from the bed and wrapped her tightly between his arms. Her tears flowed down his chest, warm and heavy with guilt. He felt as if he'd just killed part of her. He cupped her cheek in his hand and brought her chin up to his, then kissed every inch of her face until her tears stopped.

Lileth blocked his next kiss with one of her own, then gave him a serious look. "Have you checked in with the Heart Tree yet or did you come straight to me like a moonstruck fool?"

Cole shrugged. "I gave them enough to chew on after the mission, though Rayn's been attempting to contact me ever since I crossed though Lurkwood Gate. It's probably some risky decision he doesn't have the guts to stake his reputation on. He knows I'm no better at guessing my way through The Sill's problems than he is."

Her eyes fell to the side. "I ought to chastise you for neglecting your duties, but I'm not one to judge. I have been lying to my elite units and telling them I've fallen ill, when the truth is they surpassed me in all magics nearly a month ago. I can no longer keep pace with them."

"And you don't have to," Cole said, squeezing her. "Valen and the others can take them on, or I can. I'm the lazy one who's only got one unit."

"That is only because you are burdened with leading The Sill out of this nightmare," Lileth said. "Remember how often Chiron missed lessons? Not even he had time to manage a unit to himself, yet yours is perhaps the most capable of them all."

Her praise filled him with pride. "He was gone an awful lot, even when it was just me and him. It seemed like he spent half his time out on his own missions."

Lileth's eyebrows met. "Speaking of, how fared you on this last mission? Where did you go?"

Cole told her of Ka Reine's return, of the intel she provided and her suspicions of betrayal inside The Sill, and explained their need for secrecy. While summarizing the mission, he felt Lileth tense in his arms whenever he mentioned Eliza, so he attempted to steer his narration away from her whenever possible. The account almost took as much out of him as the actual mission, leaving him drained and wishing now more than ever that he could just curl up with Lileth and sleep. When he finished, she met him with a gaze that washed all his burdens away.

"You are an amazing man, Cole," she said, beaming at him. "Not even Varka's legends can compare with what you have done."

"I wouldn't go that far," Cole said. "He was more powerful than Chiron and Roth, both of whom made a joke out of me in our last sparring matches. Chiron didn't even use magic against me."

"I am not talking about strength or skill," she said, shaking her head. "I'm talking about what you have done. No one in recorded history has united so many people in so short a time. The Unbound of old meant for The Sill to be a home for people of all our magics, yet none of them, not even Varka or Chiron recruited whole cities. I may no longer be much use in battle, but I have seen with my own eyes what real progress is. The Sill is stronger today than yesterday, and it will be stronger tomorrow, and every day after. It is all because of you, my love."

"Thank you," Cole managed before his throat suddenly became too tight to speak. He felt himself unraveling as the stress of recent events twisted up inside him. She pulled him close and kissed his tears away, just as he had done for her. "What will you do then, if you really are done with the whole warrior thing that is?"

"I will spend my time gleaning fulfilment where I can, and offering it to others when I can." Her eyes went to the crafted figures on her desk. Their colors popped brilliantly among the browns of the table and wall. "The Arts District always has much to offer, and the orphans at Naythan's house are in need of love and guidance. That is where I have been spending most of my time while pretending to be ill. Lexy is quite the little charmer. The girl you rescued from Brimhallow refuses to talk to me, however."

"Amori is a bit of an oddball," Cole said. "She doesn't talk to anyone, though I suspect she and Lexy have some secret language only they understand. I wish I had more time to play with them." Cole's mind drifted for a moment as he thought about the two girls. Lileth's stiff silence drew him from his reverie. "What's wrong?"

"Another truth I have been choosing to ignore," Lileth said, her tone grave and quiet. "The success of your last mission confirms it.

We indeed have a traitor in The Sill. From what you described Vol Karinn sounds like the perfect place for an ambush, yet there was none. Everyone in The Sill is suspect, including me."

"If you're the traitor then why don't you ambush me now?" Cole said with a smirk. "You've got me with my pants down and everything."

"I am serious," Lileth said. "You must inspect the minds of everyone in The Sill, including the Heart Tree and the Unbound."

"But we've been scanning everyone as they come in," Cole explained. "Every Borla Dign immigrant has been cleared and Vol Karinn is being checked as we speak. But that does leave all the natives of The Sill..." Cole's brow furrowed as the seeds of future headaches scattered about his head. If the traitor, or traitors had been within their walls the whole time, then The Sill was never a sterile place, and they had only been adding clean minds to a pool tainted with treachery. Their recent population growth would make the task of re-scanning all the more arduous, and unpopular.

"Begin with me, right now," Lileth said, backing away from him and closing her eyes.

"Lileth I'm not—" Cole flinched as she shot him an icy glare.

"The lives of thousands depend upon you having the conviction to make difficult choices," she said. "And this will hardly be the most difficult decision you ever make. Now, set your emotions aside and scan my mind. I will not let you leave until you do so."

"And what if I don't want to leave?" Cole slid his hands over her shoulders and attempted to pull her close again, but she remained rigid and implacable. He let out an exasperated sigh. "Fine."

Blending Wisdom and Passion, Cole ran through the halls of Lileth's mind, scanning room after room in a half-hearted attempt. She hid nothing from him. In places where he only gave a cursory glance, she forced him to stay and peruse further.

"Satisfied?" Cole demanded, removing himself several minutes later.

She raised a sharp eyebrow. "That depends, are you?"

"Not even close," Cole said. He flashed her a smirk and leapt across the room, landing atop the bed. "Come lay with me."

"No," she said, crossing her arms. "Go inspect the Heart Tree and the other Unbound. Time is wasting."

After several failed attempts to persuade her, Cole gathered his things in a single lump in his arms and stormed out of her apartment wearing only his silken undershorts. He had just spent a week on mission, which by all accounts was a massive success, and now he had to go straight back to work. All he wanted was a couple hours, even a couple minutes to relax with someone who demanded nothing from him other than his love and affection. Fuming, he retreated to his apartment to shower and change. If he wasn't allowed a break, then he would at least be clean and comfortable. He left his battle armor in a stinking pile and donned a pair of well-worn trousers and a shirt meant for the most casual of occasions, an outfit not at all befitting the leader of The Sill.

On his flight to the Heart Tree, he summoned the staff and the rest of the Unbound to the meeting chamber, though he didn't explain why. Within minutes everyone other than Sitra had arrived. She was embroiled in a battle with an enemy scouting party, and assured Cole that under no circumstance would she deny her students a chance to fight real enemies for the sake of a meeting. She then sent him snapshots of memories from the battle, showing him how well the units were doing, and that they were perfectly safe under her watch.

The staff of the Heart Tree scoffed at his plan to inspect everyone's minds. The only one who didn't outright refuse him was Debjornik, who claimed to have been clamoring for a proper inspection from the start. Valen and Eliza hesitantly agreed to his plan, but he could tell they were only acting out of loyalty. A debate ensued. Falinor and Wareen seemed to have prepared for the topic beforehand. They bombarded him with a litany of reasons for which an inspection would undermine the morals of what they fought for, to which Valen replied with an explanation of the difference between morals and ethics. Thessi didn't care either way so long as she could get back to work as soon as possible. Rayn said nothing the whole time. Silent as a waiting viper, his look of disgust said everything for him. The contention settled into bitter acceptance after Cole declared he would replace anyone who didn't abide the inspection. In an attempt at appeasement, Cole volunteered to go first. He opened his mind, laying his every thought and memory before the entire staff, no matter how private or intimate. Eliza and Valen went next, then each staff member. None of them was the betrayer.

Upon finishing, Cole tasked Debjornik with coming up with a plan to scan the rest of The Sill by the end of the day, including Sitra. To Cole's pleasant surprise, the Intelligence Axis had a plan laid out for just an occasion, which Debjornik had already begun to orchestrate through telepathic Passion.

Though morning was still hours away, the group rolled right into their usual start-of-day meeting. Valen and Eliza left to join their units fighting alongside Sitra, though they remained actively connected with Passion as they always did.

"Now that I've got you all good and angry, I'd like to get right to our reports," Cole said, bracing himself for the likely backlash.

True to his character, Rayn answered with a derisive chuckle. "What's the point of verbal accounting when we just scoured every inch of each other's minds? Or are we just pretending as though we didn't just violate the privacy of everyone in this room?"

Debjornik slammed his fist on the table. "Always the victim! If you would deflate your ego for just one minute you would see the truth plain as starlight. We need to discuss what we know in order to decide what's best for The Sill. Sharing our memories is a small price to pay for the survival of Aeneria's last free souls."

"Don't fret, Rayn," Thessi said in a bored drawl. "Our discussions likely won't involve the memory of a scared little boy wetting himself on stage before the dancer's guilds."

Rayn went a deep shade of red as the air around him hummed with energy. Cole stood from his chair and sent a wave of nullifying Passion throughout the room, replacing the colliding storms of emotions with quiet tranquility.

"I think I'll start then," Cole said, taking his seat. The staff looked at him with expressions of solemn curiosity. "You now know where I went and why I left in secret. The mission was an obvious success, but how does that affect us now? Falinor, let's start with you."

Falinor gave a pleased shrug. "The Sill was already well off before you left. I don't want to get anyone's hopes up, but if even a fraction of these Passion folk join our ranks as healers, then I doubt there's a force alive that could contend with us. Unless The Three pay us a visit themselves that is, but that's what you Unbound are for."

"And we'll be even stronger after we find the Morthainians," Sitra chimed in, speaking only to the Unbound.

"That's better than I hoped for," Cole said. "Debjornik?"

Debjornik straightened in his chair. "As you all saw in my memories, there has been a significant dip in Domina forces across all of the Dark Side, starting just after the Unbound returned from Borla Dign. Since there are no bodies, we can assume they went back to the Light Side, but for what gain we can only guess, seeing as The Three have had outright command over the Light Side for cycles. I suspect the Domina are being relocated to make way for another more powerful threat."

"What threat is that?" Rayn asked. "Your memories showed nothing of the sort."

"My memories show whispered rumors collected from all over Aeneria," Debjornik explained. "It's largely a jumbled mess, but when added together we can glean certain things from the muck. We have confirmed Council Member Larkin's reports of the indoctrination of Aeneria's children. After conquering a city, The Three's Divine Guard kill anyone older than a toddler and destroy all recordings of their history with the intent of creating a fresh, malleable generation of loyal followers. This we knew for some time, but something odd has been happening over the last couple of months. Adults are appearing in the conquered cities, and there are more children than ever. Overall populations are greater than they ever were, but we are confident there have been no major migrations other than Borla Dign and Vol Karinn."

"How is such a thing possible?" Thessi asked. "Are you sure they aren't trickling over from the Light Side?"

Debjornik shook his head. "There are far too many. We believe The Three have accelerated the growth of the indoctrinated children, much like the girl Cole rescued from Brimhallow did to herself, but on a much larger and faster scale. The children reach physical adulthood within a month, then join the Divine Guard, who are proficient in all of The Three's dark magics."

"They're copying us," Falinor said. "They've seen how effective the Unbound have been against single-magic enemies like Domina and Corpulants so they're making Unbound of their own."

"The similarities don't end there," Debjornik said. "The Divine Guard has somehow mimicked the effects of our dreamsource cypher, so their most dangerous fighting force now works against us around the clock. And, there's this." Debjornik removed a dark lump from his robes and threw it in the center of the table. The object landed with a heavy thud.

"A blackstout?" Rayn asked. "Why should a disgusting fruit concern us?"

"Because that blackstout came from Oberon City," Debjornik explained. "This variety of blackstout is of course native to The Sill. Our traitor has been busy."

The room fell silent as the gravity of Debjornik's words rattled implications through their minds. Cole silently berated himself for not acting on his suspicions sooner. Only time would tell the extent of the damage his neglect would cause.

"Is there anything else, Debjornik?" Cole asked.

Debjornik nodded. "Only a request that you personally see to the inspection of your child from Brimhallow, and the Old One, Ka Reine. The Old One will likely refuse our inspection and I'd rather not risk the sanity of my teams. She is too dangerous. The child even more so."

"I'll take care of it," Cole said. "Thessi?"

Thessi stared far past the table, still digesting Debjornik's report. After a moment she sighed and shook herself back to the present. "The Sill will be far beyond our capacity for food and housing once Vol Karinn finishes in-processing. Fortunately for us they are Passion users. So long as they are willing to pitch in and learn a few spells, they should be able to help cultivate more blackstouts in the hanging gardens and expand the living quarters of our residential trees. From a logistical standpoint we won't have a problem supporting the new immigrants. Equilibrium should occur within a week, but as I said we will need their help."

Eliza's voice rang into Cole's mind like a clear bell. *I will ensure my people earn their refuge. Tell Thessi she will have all the help she needs.*

Cole relayed Eliza's words, which seemed to put Thessi at ease. He then turned to Wareen.

"What does the Communications Web think of all this?" Cole asked.

Wareen pulled a miniature Seer Jar from her robes and twirled it between her fingers. "Vol Karinn's additions will likely resolve our personnel issue, so after this meeting I plan on shutting down propaganda operations and focusing on our other efforts. If the Unbound are willing, I'd like a copy of the memories of your mission in Vol Karinn. There was a bit of fighting in there, but that Despair in the rain is something they need more exposure to. Your previous memories have been a boon for teaching Falinor's students how to fight without putting them in real danger."

"Too right you are!" Falinor exclaimed. "They're applying their education on the mainland now with those scouting parties. It's a shame there's only enough action for one assault company."

"We'll be sure to stop by as soon as we can," Cole assured Wareen. "Is there anything else."

She tossed him the Seer Jar. "I'd consider it a personal favor if you convinced Brinleaf to share the knowledge of upgrading our Seer Jars, as well as anything else that might help us. Had Goran not been there, then your return would have been delayed another week, and saving Vol Karinn would have taken far longer and been far less fruitful. Appeal to his logic. Our forces would benefit immensely."

"I'll see to it personally," Cole said, giving Valen a mental nudge.

Valen's reply came at once. *I made our plea to Brinleaf. He is consulting the consensus as we speak, but wishes to speak to you personally. I believe he is waiting outside the Heart Tree for you now.*

Cole's Passion revealed Brinleaf's life candle burning neatly right where Valen suggested. Rippling and complex, teeming echoes of thought exuded from Brinleaf's mind, indecipherable to anyone listening. The consensus must have still been in deliberation.

Cole returned his thoughts to the round table. "Rayn, do you have anything to add before we wrap this up? Your memories showed some promising ideas. Were those outposts?"

"You've already seen them," Rayn said in a dismissive tone. "Nothing but plans and contingency plans. There's no need to discuss them further."

"We saw them but we need your opinions," Cole said, his tone optimistic and encouraging. He felt as if he were trying to cheer up a recently reprimanded child. "Where do you think The Sill should go from here?"

Rayn frowned, then let out an annoyed sigh and tapped the table with a jade finger. The wood grains undulated for a second, then settled into a topographical map complete with tiny trees and real water. Cole watched in awe as The Sill and the surrounding lands materialized in front of him. Rayn then stood and tapped dozens of tiny cities in quick succession, his fingers a blur of fluent motion.

Laying his hands flat on the edge of the table, Rayn leaned in and looked Cole square in the eye. "We are ready to take the fight outside our walls. We have been for some weeks now, but with Vol Karinn's healers augmenting our forces I see no reason for further delay. Unless The Three show themselves, we will have no problem taking back some of the closer cities. The Three's minions have grown accustomed to easy victories won from people who only practice a single school of magic. Debjornik's reports show increasing complacency in their tactics. They don't prepare to defend against counterattacks, ambushes, or flanking maneuvers of any sort. If Brinleaf is amenable to sharing the knowledge of the Seer Jars, then it would be all too easy to set up outposts throughout the Dark Side. Personnel and equipment can be transported instantly and efficiently. If an outpost were to be overwhelmed it would be all too easy to move our assets to a neighboring outpost, or back to The Sill itself."

"Rayn this is huge," Cole said, genuinely astonished. "How soon can we make our first move?"

"Right now," Rayn said. "Falinor has two capable assault companies on standby. Send one out now. Keep the second just outside The Sill to secure the nearby ocean and the mainland, and the third can remain inside our walls to train and rest. Once an outpost is secured, rotate the companies so that fresh warriors assault the next outpost while the tired return to The Sill to recover and train."

Cole stood, unable to contain his excitement. He felt the other Unbound listening closely through his ears. "Rayn, you're a genius! Are you sure we're ready? It seems like only yesterday our warriors had trouble climbing trees and lighting campfires."

Rayn waved his hand over the table and the map flattened itself back to plain wood. "It's my team's job to assess and plan. You have our assessment and we've offered our best plan. Do with them what you will."

Cole left the meeting in high spirits. As he walked down the spiral steps leading to the exit, he tuned his Passion to watch the events on the mainland through the eyes of the other Unbound. Sitra, Eliza, and Valen mingled throughout the elite units, observing and coaching as they routed the remaining enemies through the forest. Their enemies were mostly Aenerians, low-level scouts adept in deception and swift travel, though there were a few Corpulants and single-thralled Domina skulking about as well. The elite units were remarkably effective, using their magic in equal measures while countering the magic of their enemies, just as they had been taught.

Cole beamed with pride as he watched Wilkin's unit through Sitra's eyes. Their chase inadvertently brought them within range of a newborn Colossus. At three stories tall, the Colossus was far from harmless, but nor was it beyond their abilities. They dismantled the titan with careful attacks, though Viness and Grant sustained crippling injuries that Sitra had to heal. After Kolric and Serra broke open the bone nest and exposed the priestess within, Wilkin paralyzed the woman with Passion and scoured her mind for information.

"Master Cole!" Wilkin said, his words fuzzy as he was at the extreme range of his Passion.

Cole responded with a hint of impatience, as though he had been busy with something important. *"Yes, Wilkin, how goes your first mission?"*

Wilkin spoke in a hurried voice. *"We just captured a priestess inside a Colossus. I know you don't want us breaking into people's minds yet, but I had a feeling she might know something useful. She just killed herself with Fear, tried to take me with her too but I pulled out."*

"One of the many risks of delving into an evil mind," Cole said. *"I wouldn't make a habit of it until I've trained you properly in the art, but I'm glad you weren't an example for the rest of your unit. What did she tell you?"*

"That there's a camp not far from here," Wilkin said. *"There's more Colossi and Corpulants and about one hundred priests. I don't think we can take them all ourselves, even with the other elite units."*

Cole was quiet for a moment, incredulous that this was the same arrogant boy who not a few months prior was too cool for Passion. *"Wilkin, why didn't you tell Master Sitra this information? Isn't she close by?"*

It was Wilkin's turn to be silent. Cole sensed hope flutter from the boy, fragile yet yearning. *"This is important, and so are you. I wanted you to be the first to know, Master."*

Cole allowed a sliver of his emotions to shine through their link. *"I am very proud of you, Wilkin."*

Wilkin's mind beamed with golden warmth, but he stifled it at once, shelving it for later use when his unit was celebrating safely back at The Sill. When he spoke it was with calm repose. *"Thank you, Master."*

Cole severed the connection and relayed Wilkin's information to the rest of the Unbound, as well as Rayn and the other staff members. He popped out of the Heart Tree at last. Oberon's light splashed its warmth over his face and arms. Brinleaf stood at the base of the stairs, arms crossed behind his back.

"Greetings, Wisdom Walker," Brinleaf said. He wore his usual high-collared formal robes, though Cole recognized a white spiral pattern painted over one of his eyes.

"That's a new look for you," Cole said, pointing to Brinleaf's eye. "Been enjoying the Arts District?"

"I find the festivities an enchanting way to expand my perspective of the world," Brinleaf replied with a small smile. His eyes flickered over Cole's plain t-shirt and faded trousers. "I see I am not the only one who enjoys a change of outfit."

"I find wearing battle armor all the time *limits* my perspective of the world," Cole said.

"Indeed," Brinleaf agreed. "Would you care to join me on a walk?"

"I've got a couple hours to burn," Cole said. "Lead the way."

Brinleaf was quiet for a while. He hovered inches over grass lawns and woven root paths as he led Cole in a straight line across The Sill. Cole's curiosity was overshadowed by wondering how he was going to debate Borla Dign's consensus over the knowledge of the Seer Jars. Even with the other Unbound helping him, they would only be a few beggars against a cohesive machine made of thousands of minds.

"I don't need Passion to see the question burning a hole through your ears," Brinleaf said. "Our answer is yes."

"You'll share your knowledge of the Seer Jars?" Cole asked, incredulous.

"Chief among our reservations was our suspicion of betrayal among your ranks," Brinleaf said. "We hid this from you because we predicted it would sow mistrust if suspicions originated from the people of Borla Dign. Valen told me of your inspection process on his way to join the fighting on the mainland. The Consensus was wrong. You are more logical than we gave you credit for."

Cole let out an irritated sigh. "In the future just tell me in private if you have any more of these *reservations*. I give you my word I'll handle it as diplomatically as possible. I'm the last one who wants to deal with the staff and their whining, so that makes me the last one who wants to sow mistrust."

"Noted," Brinleaf said, gliding a little faster now.

Cole commanded his Wisdom to carry him in the air so he wouldn't have to trot to keep up. "Where are we going?"

"To your Everglen," Brinleaf stated. "They have been waiting for you. They require your confirmation before setting the rules for the reality within the pocket dimension."

"Ah, I finally get to see who *they* are," Cole said, suddenly nervous. Lileth's warnings about manipulating the laws of nature popped to the fore of his mind. "Where is this place, behind the Hanging Gardens?"

"No. It is within your Necropolis," Brinleaf replied.

After a short and quiet flight, they had arrived. Cole dipped his feet in the shallow pond, which shimmered with gentle cerulean light. The cool water felt good on his feet. Lavender flower petals rushed across the surface to greet him, flapping excitedly like tiny water beetles. The surrounding trees watched over him like wizened old men with their gnarled branches and beards of glowing moss. The lavender petals rushed up Cole's back and covered Varka's cape, just as they had done for Chiron so long ago. Cole took a moment to reflect on their fallen before following Brinleaf farther in. He paid quiet tribute to each gratia stone embedded in the trunks of the old trees as he passed them. Birds keened their mourning songs overhead while tree frogs whooped along.

Brinleaf led him to a place in the Necropolis he had never seen before. Cole stepped up onto a patch of soft roots that rose above the water, forming a small island void of trees or flowers. In the center stood an archway made from the same roots, with tiny gratia stones woven throughout, held in place by golden wires bent in the shape of flowers. Cole peered through the archway. He saw the Necropolis on the other side, but it seemed different somehow, ethereal in a way, as though it were merely a dream of the place around him.

Brinleaf stood next to the archway, his expression grave. "Approach, but do not enter."

Cole obeyed. He felt apprehension flow into him from the other Unbound as they watched through his eyes.

"Wait, and one of them will approach you," Brinleaf said.

Cole was just about to ask what Brinleaf meant, but then he saw it. Movement beyond the distant trees. There were people, hundreds of them, all walking in the dark just beyond his vision like shadows cast by ghosts. Cole leaned to the right and looked around the archway, but there was nothing. When he returned to the center there was a figure striding towards him, confident and graceful. The figure stepped up onto the root cluster island. It was Deekus.

"It's been quite some time, hasn't it?" Deekus said. He stood tall and proud, wearing the same cloth armor Cole saw him in half a lifetime ago. There was no trace of the trauma from his death on the ocean floor. He beamed at Cole with an infectious smile. It was Deekus as Cole remembered him. "You've come a long way from the boy who didn't believe he could do magic."

"Deekus," Cole breathed. "Are you alive?"

Deekus laughed. "Not even close, my friend. What's left of my body lies in the veins of the tree you planted over it, and in the insects and animals that consume its fruits. No, I am dead."

"Then how is this possible?" Cole asked. He felt the other Unbound pressing firmly against his mind, though Eliza's presence was so insistent that his heart began to ache with her loss.

Deekus's gaze searched the Necropolis in open wonder, as though the lavender petals falling about him were the most interesting thing he'd ever seen. "The world remembers. The air and the trees, the rocks and the soil, they all hold an imprint of every moment, no matter how insignificant." The faraway stare vanished from him as he gave Cole a wry grin. "That's what the others say at least. Truthfully, I think the contributions you all made to my gratia stone carried memories of me, and after a time I just sort of came to be, in this place. Then this doorway appeared, and your friend Brinleaf asked us to help him with a spell. We've been waiting for you ever since."

The questions flooded from Cole before he could stop them. "Are you a ghost then? Is Storn in there with you, or Chiron?"

"I'm afraid not," he said with a sad smile. "Only those whose bodies were laid to rest in the Necropolis walk this place. And no, we are not ghosts. If I had to limit us to a single label, I would say that we are more akin to condensed love."

Cole's heart was pounding so hard he could feel it in his ears. He took a steadying breath. "Brinleaf said you were waiting for me, waiting to confirm the rules of some sort of pocket dimension. I'm not sure what that means."

"What you see through the archway is the reality in which The Sill's fallen exist," Deekus explained, donning a more serious tone. "What we and Brinleaf have created for you is another reality in which you and the others may enter, after you accept our conditions that is. We call it, The Havenflow."

"What are your conditions?" Cole asked, though he dreaded the answer.

"The Havenflow can accept two souls at a time," Deekus said. "Once inside, the gateway will close for a day, and you will be at the mercy of the dead. Some were warriors, who seek to test and temper your mettle in the fires of combat. Others were the fabled Wisdom Walkers of their day, who wish to show you secrets garnered from the local planets, should you earn them that is. Many wish to expose you, to lay bare every facet of your soul and judge them before impartial eyes. The ordeals of the Havenflow are perilous to those feeble of soul. Those who enter will emerge with profound gifts of prowess and self-understanding, or their minds will collapse within their own cascading layers of insanity."

"Won't you be there with us?" Cole asked. "Can't you keep us safe?"

"I am but one of many," Deekus said. "I will do what I can, but once you agree to our terms I will cease to exist as I do now. I will join the consciousness of the Havenflow and become part of the trials within."

"You don't have to do that," Cole said. "There has to be another way. You've already given up your life, you shouldn't have to give up what's left of you now."

"We lived in service to all that is good in this world and every other," Deekus said. "Such a contract doesn't end for something so trivial as death."

Uncertainty welled up inside Cole like water in a leaky boat. He felt just as much unease from the other Unbound. Even Sitra was at a loss for words. To enter the Havenflow would be gambling not only with their lives, but with the fate of Aeneria and every local to boot. But then again, it might be just the thing they'd need to match the might of The Three.

"There is one more thing you should know," Deekus said. "The dead have agreed upon one necessity for the Havenflow's reality. The sheer volume of our knowledge is far too great for a single day's worth of trails, and so we have agreed to distort the stream of time within the Havenflow. From The Sill, the gateway will appear to close and reopen in a day; however, once inside, a cycle will pass before you can leave."

An entire cycle. Cole hadn't even been on Aeneria that long. He resisted the urge to take a step back from the archway. "You've given us a lot to consider. We will need some time to think this over. Is there anything else you can tell us about the Havenflow? What exactly will we find inside?"

"Yourselves," Deekus said. He gave Cole a sad smile, then turned away and strode back to where he came from, vanishing among the shadows of The Sill's dead.

CHAPTER 24

THE SHADOW TIDE RISES

Two months flew by with such speed that Cole wondered if Deekus had accidentally meddled with The Sill's time instead of the Havenflow's. The house of Mecelland gave way to Elliyan, which then passed over to Oruun. As Rayn's assessments had predicted, The Sill outmatched The Three's minions at every turn, yielding two or three new outposts every week. They even reclaimed Borla Dign, though its citizens chose to remain dispersed throughout The Sill's forces until the war was decided. True to his word, Brinleaf shared the knowledge of Borla Dign's Seer Jars, though only to the elite units. Still, the portals provided dramatic improvements to The Sill's mobility as they pushed the battle lines back towards Oberon City. Debjornik's hunt for The Sill's traitor took far longer than the day Cole originally assigned his team. After a week of systematic quarantines, they'd managed to scan every mind, producing no results whatsoever other than an air of mistrust amongst once-friendly neighbors. Unwilling to accept defeat, Debjornik attempted to initiate another investigation, but Cole put his foot down, diplomatically of course.

The elite units had proven themselves proficient enough to strike out on their own. They provided recon and fighting support for Falinor's assault companies, and in some cases dominated entire outposts on their own, a task they had become most adept at. When The Sill's forces came within reach of the White sands, the flying ships of Morthain remained ever elusive, merely ghosts in the wind. Falinor assured the Unbound his assault battalion was fine without additional Rage users, as they had recently grown from three companies to five, but Sitra was still determined to find the Morthainians.

With Wilkin's unit spending a larger portion of their time outside The Sill, Cole was free to make regular visits to Naythan's, often with Lileth at his side. Amorinanis became even more taciturn than usual, and would often withdraw into her room with Lexy when Cole and Lileth came around. Naythan surmised her change in behavior was due to her continued growth, which had slowed down quite a bit, but by the time they entered the house of Oruun she appeared to be of middle adolescence. Most disappointing of all was the change in Lexy's demeanor. She had grown as well. No longer was she the sweet little girl who thought every moment not spent singing and dancing was a moment wasted. Her tongue had become as sharp as her wit, both of which stung with the sardonic impatience of a moody teenager. She reminded Cole of Habbad. He found himself nursing a deep regret for the days spent working and training instead of taking time to enjoy the fleeting wonder of her youth.

Lileth had separated herself from the Unbound entirely. The others asked for her whenever Cole showed up alone for training, but his reply never changed. After a month of Sitra's pestering, Cole managed to draw Lileth out of the safety of her routines to confront the others. With a heavy heart she explained the toll her duties had taken on her, as well as the risk she posed by going out on missions in such a state. Cole knew the others weren't convinced, that they were more of the mind that she simply wasn't trying anymore, but they all loved her enough to respect her wishes. At their insistence, however, Lileth did agree to stay connected to their Passion network so that she might continue to help out in lessons and meetings, if only from an advisory position.

As the days wore on, Cole felt a looming sense of doom drawing near. Even though The Sill was gaining ground nearly every day, he still felt something terrible was coming for him. The Sill had come into an age of peace and prosperity it had never before seen, with trade routes reopening and its military swelling larger by the week. Wareen's Communications Web had 'accidentally' leaked a theory that The Three's powers relied upon the negative emotions within the hearts across Aeneria, and the Arts District had not been the same ever since. Daily festivals spilled across The Sill, filling the markets and barracks with mirth in the forms of song, food, and masterful craftsmanship. The Unbound knew the celebrations didn't directly help their cause, but Cole couldn't help but wonder why The Three continued to allow them to gain ground, and didn't fly out to annihilate them at their leisure. Perhaps they were not so omnipotent as they seemed.

One day after Wilkin's unit set a new record by claiming two outposts in an afternoon, an ominous reminder dragged Cole's hopes back to the ground. Every victory, no matter how small or large was another step, or in some cases a leap, towards the end. His end. He alone would eventually find himself within the Vaults of the Soul, never to return. This ominous feeling became the foundation of a generalized anxiety that stalked his every step throughout the day, like a demon hiding within his own shadow. Cole had no desire to infect the rest of the Unbound with his worries, and so he limited his catharsis to his private moments with Lileth. She had a way of soothing him with a single touch or word, as though she knew him better than he knew himself. Whenever his schedule permitted even the slightest opportunity, he would race back to her apartment and lie in bed with her, shutting out the rest of the world. He spent hours with her every day, making love, indulging in fantasies of their quiet escape to a local planet, or venting his concerns from a previous meeting with the Heart Tree. She was there for him every time, listening and loving him no matter what.

One day while his unit was out and the rest of the Unbound were busy with their personal endeavors, Cole made his way down to Naythan's to see the girls and check on the orphans. On his way he popped into the markets and bought a pair of stuffed miraks for Lexy and Amori, a toy crafted after stirring legends of 'The Man of the Mountains' reached The Sill. The toys bore a passable resemblance to Goran when he was the size of a house cat. The brindle fur was sleek and the white mohawks had been made from tufts of down feathers. For eyes the toys had little marbles of ruby gratia stones which fueled a spell to keep bad dreams away.

Cole strode up the front walkway, eager to see Lexy's and Amori's smiles. Naythan's house was unrecognizable from when Cole had first come asking for help months before. Countless additions had been added to make room for Aeneria's orphans, who now came through the Seer Jars in droves whenever a new outpost was claimed. The trees lining Naythan's yard had been pushed back and hollowed out for classrooms, their windows spiraling up to the very top branches. Cole popped through the front door of Naythan's vine-covered house, emerging not into the cramped and stifling quarters of a hermit, but a great hall lined with tables and open windows stretching up to the ceiling. A breeze of something sweet wafted from the kitchens as a stout woman from Vol Karinn chased a flock of giggling children around the fireplace mounted in the center of the room. Cole's Passion revealed a tiny ocean of life candles brimming about the grounds.

Keeping his Passion flowing, Cole followed the magic up a set of stairs to an office, where Amori, Lexy, and someone very old were currently mingling with Naythan, pestering him no doubt. Cole was about to knock on the door frame when a voice inside the office shouted, "Come in, come in. I sensed you coming a mile away."

Cole smiled and pushed himself through the liquid stone door. The office had no windows and looked to be one of the smallest rooms in the house. Lexy sat on Naythan's desk while Amori stood beside it, resting her elbows on a stack of papers with her chin nestled in her hands.

"You can spend your time doing other things too, you know," Lexy declared in her squeaky voice. She wore white Underkin's wrappings under a pale blue dress, and her curly hair had been tamed to curtains of silk trailing over her narrow shoulders. She stared at Naythan with hard eyes that didn't notice who just entered the room. "You used to spend all day with us, but now all you want to do is look at charts and talk about boring stuff with the other teachers. We were supposed to go to the markets today, remember?"

Naythan sighed and leaned forward in his chair. His fluffy fur jacket hung on a rack in the corner of the room next to his staff. Covering him now was an ornate set of emerald and auburn robes. The formal raiment suited him far better now that he was headmaster of The Sill's first academy for children. "Sweet ones, there was once a time when this old man had only two children to care for, and he was the happiest man on this world or the next, but war has taken that from us. Our little flock has grown, and continues to grow every day. There are many children who lost everyone they love and they need someone to guide them, to nurture them, and show them that they are not alone in this godless world. You wouldn't take that away from them, would you?"

Lexy huffed, unconvinced. "You're the boss. Make someone else in charge for a while. A promise is a promise."

"The sprout has a point, Naythan," croaked a voice from the corner of the room. Ka Reine sat in a high-backed chair, motionless and calculating, like an ancient bird of prey watching over her land.

Naythan rubbed his fingers into his forehead. Bangles of shells and painted pebbles slid down his wrists, crafts made with the care and whim of tiny fingers. "I promised nothing! I merely told the girls that I may have some time this afternoon to take them out for a treat. How was I supposed to know Falinor's barbarians would take two outposts in one night? I haven't even finished tallying up bedspace for the incoming orphans."

Ka Reine surveyed Lexy and Amori, measuring them as if they were up for auction. "I'm not talking about promises you may or may not have made, though dangling such a treat in front of two precocious girls is dancing with disaster if you can't guarantee a follow-through."

"Don't I know it." Naythan cursed at the papers in front of him. His eyes snapped up. "Are you suggesting I entrust my duties to someone else? I won't have one of those idiots from Vol Karinn tainting my operation with swooning and fawning. They care more for giving the children what they want instead of what they need."

The girls deflated as they watched their chances dashed by the grumblings of grownups. Cole would have taken them himself, but his other obligations wouldn't sit idle for that long. He noticed a few trinkets on the girls which suggested they hadn't missed too many trips to the markets. On each of their right hands was a black glove with hard resin claws; a toy munisica. They wore necklaces and bracelets as well, and there was something inscribed on them. Cole sharpened his eyes with Wisdom and recognized some of the names of the members of the elite units. Apparently Lexy was a fan of Wilkin.

Ka Reine turned her gaze to Naythan. "You're counting linens and putting butts in classrooms, don't make it sound like you're unraveling the mysteries of the Aethers. Hand the tasks off to someone else. You should be training your senior instructors to replace you anyway. If old age takes you tomorrow, who would be able to fill the prestigious and demanding role of seed counter? My stars, who would be willing?"

"Old age huh?" Naythan grumbled, cracking a smile at last. "You're so ancient you could be my grandmother's grandmother."

"And I'll outlive your grandchildren's grandchildren, because I know how to live," Ka Reine replied, raising her chin with a proud nod. "I'll see to your charts and numbers. Go play with the girls. They'll be adults in ten minutes and you'll be left fumbling through your ledgers, wondering where the time went."

Naythan flashed her a halfhearted sneer, then looked to the girls, who bounced so quickly on their toes they appeared to be hovering. "Go take those rags off and put something nice on. I won't have my personal guard looking like a pair of trolls while I peruse the markets."

Lexy squealed with delight while Amori let out a sharp breath through her smile. They sprinted from Naythan's desk and bumped straight into Cole.

"Naked one!" Lexy cried, calling Cole by the first name she ever knew him by. She threw her arms up for him while Amori looked up with a mulish grin.

"Noticed me at last have you?" Cole reached down and scooped both girls up in a single arm. Lexy hadn't grown an inch, but Amori was now taller than his waist.

"Are you coming with us?" Lexy asked. "Please say yes, I want to hear about the adventures of the elites. They're supposed to be as powerful as gods, and beautiful too." Lexy giggled as Amori twisted and gave her a playful shove. Cole noticed a fake scar drawn on Amori's cheek, identical to his own.

"I'm afraid I'll be busy this afternoon," Cole said. "But tonight I promise I'll come back with Lileth and we'll put a memory up on Naythan's stage for you. It's from a mission I went on with my elites last week. And, I've got these for you." Cole then uncurled his arm from behind his back, producing the two stuffed Gorans.

Disappointment bloomed in the girls' faces. Lexy gave Cole a patronizing look. "We don't play with toys anymore, Cole. We're not kids."

"Then what are those for?" Cole demanded, indicating their munisica gloves.

"These are not for playing," Lexy said as she twisted her claws with a flourish. "These are for looking pretty."

Now more than ever Cole regretted not spending more time with the girls. Stung, he set them back on the floor. "All right then, I'll just have to find someone who still likes toys."

"And come back with some good memories!" Lexy cried, hugging his leg before darting out of the room. "Come, Amori, we need to get ready for the markets!"

Amori stood rooted on the spot, her lips pouted in uncertainty. Lexy called out again from the hallway, and Amori snatched one of the stuffed Gorans from Cole's hand and sprinted through the door. He sensed their life candles twist up the stairs and up to their room, wondering what would really happen if he simply stayed with the girls and abandoned the day's meetings and training sessions.

"You look like you could do with some delegation yourself," Naythan grumbled from behind his desk.

"I just might," Cole sighed. "I could put Rayn in charge one day a week. Maybe then he'll stop calling for a dozen meetings a day just to whine about the rest of the staff."

"Spread yourself too thin too early and you'll wind up just like Rayn, irascible and grating," Ka Reine said as she snatched her pipe from her robes and lit it with a spark of Wisdom. She took a deep pull and expelled a great cloud of green-purple smoke that smelled of spiced fruit. "I remember Rayn when he was a child. Precocious, but attention-starved. Never could stomach the taste of failure, especially not in front of his friends. Every step and breath he took was measured for safety and surety before he committed to it. A useful trait, especially for his current position, but he hasn't grown much over his life. You're a good kid, Cole. Don't let a job ruin that."

"Hear hear," Naythan agreed. He fanned his hand in front of his face and coughed as the aromatic smoke wafted over his desk. Annoyed, he jabbed a jade finger towards the wall, where two small holes appeared. Air rushed in one hole while only the smoke raced out of the other.

"I think that's a lesson I'm going to have to learn the hard way," Cole said, plopping himself in a cushy armchair beside Naythan's desk. "With certain things at least. There's some jobs I can't trust to other people, no matter how ornery the job makes me."

Naythan removed his glasses and cleaned them with the sleeve of his robes. "Nonsense. All jobs can be delegated. Chiron did it all the time. Seems every cycle he tried to put me in the Heart Tree as head of the Training Center. Poor Falinor took the job instead, damned fool." Naythan paused in his polishing and gave Cole a sharp look. "I should have known. You're here on task, aren't you? Well spit it out then. The quicker you say what it is you need, the quicker I can ignore it and get back to my own obligations."

"I'm not here to beg anything of you, Naythan," Cole said in a calm voice.

"He's here for me," Ka Reine said with a smug look.

Naythan whipped his glasses back on and looked back and forth between them, eyes narrowing. "Is this true?"

"I'm afraid it is," Cole said, keeping his eyes on the Old One. "I put it off as long as I could, but you know how annoying the staff can be. They're starting to accuse me of hypocrisy."

"That *can* be annoying," Ka Reine said, her lined face blank except for a single eyebrow raised high. She bit at the end of her pipe absentmindedly, though her eyes were locked into Cole's.

"What on Oberon's backside are you two yapping about?" Naythan demanded.

"The boy wants to have a peek into my mind to make sure I'm not the traitor," she said in a casual tone. "He thinks I'm the one harvesting The Sill's secrets and selling them to The Three."

Naythan turned his gaze to Cole, a question frozen upon his lips.

"You have me wrong," Cole said. "I want to prove you're *not* a traitor, but that's kind of hard when everyone in The Sill has submitted to an inspection except for you. Our forces run into ambushes that our enemies could have no way of preparing without help. Enemy outposts are empty or under evacuation by the time we reach them. People are dying. This inspection is our first line of defense against treason."

A smug grin returned to Ka Reine's face as she took another long pull from her pipe. "Tell me, oh sagacious Wisdom Walker, did your suspicions begin with my return to The Sill, or before?"

"Good point," Cole agreed. "Betrayal was obvious long before your return, one of the many reasons I don't believe you to be a traitor. However, you know as well as I do that your mastery of Passion and Wisdom allows you to pass undetected over Whind's walls, and once inside it would be all too easy for you to swindle lesser minds into revealing their secrets. We can't let subjective truths get in the way of ensuring the safety of thousands, no matter how compelling the evidence might be. I don't like it, but at the moment an inspection is our only means of proving innocence."

"You sound like Chiron," Ka Reine said with a hollow laugh. "But unlike Chiron, you have no idea of the folly of what you suggest. My mind is not that of some simpleton staff member who hasn't seen her third cycle. I was ancient before the previous Unbound took their first steps, and I was old before the construction of Oberon Temple. I've spent more time on each local planet than any of you have spent on Aeneria. We will enter the next age before you get through half of what I am. To enter my mind is to surrender yourself to the fathomless history of all our worlds. The attempt would drive you mad."

Cole sighed. "Madness is a small price to pay for the future of every world Aeneria touches. But if it's the safety of others that's your only reservation, then I believe we can mitigate that risk. The people of Borla Dign have agreed to conduct your inspection through their consensus. Their minds act as one, and so they can process things magnitudes faster than an ordinary—."

"I don't need you to explain the conventions of a consensus," Ka Reine snapped. "I know more than you can imagine. There's nothing you could say that would be news to me, boy, and there's no way you could convince me to allow those lack-hearts into my mind."

Cole's eyes fell to the floor between his feet. "I take it that means you won't consent to the inspection. Not even as a personal favor?"

"Not for all the stars in all the skies," Ka Reine said, taking another drag from her pipe. "So, shall we lock our thoughts and battle this out like warriors? I think you'll find my mind isn't so easy to conquer as an enemy outpost."

Cole moved his gaze from his feet to hers. "No. Though the Heart Tree demands it, I try not to make a habit of forcing myself into other people's minds, not that I imagine myself strong enough to compete against yours. Suspicion doesn't prove you our enemy, but unfortunately your concealment doesn't prove you our ally. So long as you refuse the inspection I can't allow you to remain among us. Please, leave now in peace."

Tension grew so thick in the air, Cole could feel it pressing against his skin. No one spoke, but the room seemed louder than ever. A timepiece whirred and ticked the passing seconds on a shelf behind him. Naythan's breath fluttered between lips still frozen with incredulity. The distant laughter of children snaked through the two holes in the wall. Cole looked up and braved the eyes that had been boring into him, daring him.

"Let's say I do leave," Ka Reine said, not bothering to hide her derision. "What's to stop me from sneaking back in? You said it yourself, I could fly right over the walls and swindle my way through The Sill as I please."

"We have ways of keeping you out," Cole said plainly.

Ka Reine grinned, as if excited by the challenge. "And let's say I won't leave? Aeneria is a dangerous place now. What if I say I'm safer in The Sill, where I can provide my advice and powers to those who would fight The Three?"

Cole kept his eyes firmly in hers. "I sincerely hope you don't."

Silence reigned over the little office once more. Naythan had scooted his chair into the far corner next to his coat rack, as though wishing for safety within the confines of his old fur. Cole felt as if his own heart was the loudest thing in the room now.

"I'm no fool, especially when dealing with one," Ka Reine said. She twisted her pipe between crooked knuckles, upending it and tapping the bowl against the arm of her chair. The ashes fell to the floor. "I have a few trappings squirreled away that I must collect, but I will leave. Give me the rest of the day to see to my affairs and I'll give you my back."

Cole uncorked a drop of his Rage, burning his rising anxiety to cinders. The hour was too late for half-measures. "You will leave now. Tell me what you need done or collected and I will see to it personally."

"I see," Ka Reine said with a slow nod. "What I wouldn't give for another peek inside *your* mind. You are not the same scared little human I met during the last passing of Allias. You have grown. I just hope it will be enough to weather the coming of the Shadow Tide." She sighed, then stood, straight-backed and with her chin held high. "I take it you'll be escorting me to the gate?"

"That's the plan," Cole said, rising and offering her his arm.

She ignored him and strode past with no trace of her hunched back or hobbling gait. If the effort pained her, she didn't show it. Ka Reine reached the door, then turned back and looked to Naythan, her eyes glistening with a shadow of sadness. She took a slow breath and opened her mouth to say her farewell.

"Now!" Cole shouted into the minds of the Unbound.

Ka Reine's brow hardened to a bundle of knots. Her head snapped from side to side, eyes scanning for danger.

An explosion tore through the room.

Donning his master's shroud, Cole leapt across the room in a blink and stood over a cowering Naythan. A net of green Wisdom appeared above them and yanked the ceiling straight off the walls. Valen hovered in the open sky, emerald wings spread wide, the lines of the net connected to his outstretched hand.

Fury seared the shock from Ka Reine's face as she wheeled around. Green light flickered inside her fists. Another explosion shook the room as Eliza erupted from the wall beside Ka Reine, sending debris tearing through the air. She brought her munisica together and a thick beam of fuchsia Passion shot from her palms, vibrating the air and rattling the entire house. The beam struck Ka Reine full in the chest.

Ka Reine stumbled as the magic poured into her. Before she could collect herself, the floor behind her erupted in a geyser of wood and metal fragments as Sitra emerged from below. In a flash of black shroud and munisica, Sitra reached around Ka Reine, grabbed each of her wrists and crossed her arms, locking them in a hug around the Old One's body.

Tossing the roof aside, Valen descended into the room and landed beside Eliza. He brought his palms together and shot a broad emerald ray at Ka Reine. The magic joined with Eliza's and the two streams formed a potent river of Passion and Wisdom.

Arms locked at her sides, Ka Reine's face relaxed to an expressionless mask. A translucent white film covered her skin and clothes, a barrier, but of what kind Cole couldn't tell. With a flash of Wisdom, Cole blasted another hole in the wall behind the desk, then levitated Naythan through it and lowered him safely to the yard.

"It's not working!" Valen shouted over the roar of the magic. "Help us!"

Valen and Eliza shook with the effort of their spells. Ka Reine's eyes had gone all white and something began flickering overhead, drawing Cole's eyes up. A glassy orb solidified high above them. Smooth and shiny, the orb showed Oberon's image like a warped reflection. A strand of gleaming rainbow light unraveled itself from the orb and whipped across the room. Cole's Rage slowed things for him. He jumped aside as the strand sizzled past him, cleaving the floor, desk, and wall in a neat smoking line. The strand curled back for another attack, splitting itself into several whips that would no doubt slice the entire room and everything in it to ribbons. With Varka's cape aiding his Wisdom, Cole took a wild guess and bent the world to his will. Emerald light roiled like fire between his munisica as a swath of air above the room hardened into a mirror. The rainbow whips lashed at the barrier, halted by their own reflected energy. Cole twisted the spell, bending and broadening the mirror until it encapsulated the orb. There was a hollow thud, and his and Ka Reine's spells shattered each other into nonexistence.

The light faded from Ka Reine's eyes and she went slack in Sitra's shrouded arms. Cole felt the air stir once more, the split second of warning that preceded a magical attack. Without hesitation he dismissed his shroud and thrust his palms towards Ka Reine, hitting her with a beam of emerald from one hand and lavender from the other. His heart ached with Passion while Varka's cape rippled across his back, tuning his Wisdom to the proper frequencies.

Pain twisted Ka Reine's features as her shields vanished and the four beams of magic contacted her body at last. Sitra yelped and leapt back. A translucent sphere of seafoam green materialized around Ka Reine, frictionless and impenetrable. Her feet slipped and she fell, sliding about the bottom of the sphere like wine inside a crystal glass.

"I have it," Valen said, panting as he took control of their barrier. The beam of Wisdom faded from his hands. Cole and Eliza ceased their attacks as well.

"All right, let's get her out of here," Cole said as he levitated himself out of the open ceiling. The others followed in a gust of wind and a flash of emerald wings. Valen trailed close behind, carrying the seafoam-green prison with a leash of Wisdom.

They landed on the far side of Naythan's property, away from the Arts District towards a secluded portion of The Sill, where Falinor stood ready with one of his assault companies. The warriors formed a circle around the yard, munisica and magic at the ready. Half the warriors stood guard on the forest floor while the rest were perched in trees or hovering on sun lily leaves. While Cole could see them plain as day, they had suppressed their life candles to such a degree that it rendered them invisible to his Passion. Cole saw the relief on their faces, but he also saw tempered discipline. These men and women had been ready to fight to the death if Ka Reine had overpowered the Unbound.

"Is the area clear?" Cole called out to the tree line. A quick scan with Passion revealed nothing, as it should have if Naythan's staff had correctly masked the children's life candles before evacuating. This was not a thing for young eyes to see.

"Lileth rounded up the last two shortly after you entered the house," Falinor said as he emerged from behind a clutch of ferns. He was in full battle dress, shining olive and brown robes with alloys woven throughout the fabric and thick metal plates over his chest and shoulders. "You sure that barrier will hold?"

"So long as the spell is fueled properly, nothing magical or material shall pass through," Valen said. With a gentle wave of his hand he rolled the orb over the grass to Falinor. Ka Reine hovered within the seafoam prison, arms and legs crossed and face inscrutable. "The draw is quite severe, however."

"I've got twelve experts in Wisdom ready to work around the clock to maintain the spell," Falinor said. "And another twenty set up for guard rotations. Never thought I'd see the day... the Old One too. Our first prisoner in The Sill's first prison." He leaned close and wrapped his shrouded knuckles on the surface of the barrier. Ka Reine stared through him as though he weren't there.

"I don't want her treated poorly," Cole said. "She's only our captive until she allows us to inspect her mind. Bring her whatever she wants and make sure she's comfortable. There's no proof she's done anything wrong."

"Debjornik will find out soon enough," Falinor sighed. "If our enemies stop predicting our moves before we make them, then that's all the proof we need. Rayn just reworked our plans for new outposts. We should know within the hour if Ka Reine is our traitor."

Eliza approached the sphere and pressed her palm to it, her face heavy with guilt. "I'm not sure we're doing the right thing. Part of me can't accept that Ka Reine is our traitor. She's been a stalwart ally of The Sill since its inception, and to the Unbound before that. It feels wrong."

"Well why don't you climb in there with her and have a little chat?" Sitra said with a scowl. "I don't care what we can prove, no innocent person would have attacked us with magic like that, not when we only hit her with pacifying spells. She would have cut us all in half if Cole had taken another second to find a counter to whatever the hell those whips were. If she tries anything like that again, I won't hesitate to relieve her of her head."

• • •

The Unbound spent the rest of the day in the Heart Tree monitoring The Sill's forces through Rayn's map table and Wareen's Seer Jars. Falinor's support company repaired the damage to Naythan's house within an hour, improving it with rare materials and artwork imported from the far reaches of Aeneria's Dark Side. Naythan had been utterly incensed by the brawl in his office, not for the damage to his home, but because he wasn't informed beforehand. He also flat-out refused to believe Ka Reine had betrayed The Sill. Naythan pummeled Cole with a tirade for the better part of the day, stating how he had known her longer than anyone else alive, and regaling him with countless tales of her heroism among the Unbound. He even threatened to leave The Sill and strike out on his own, but Cole knew the threat to be empty. As offended as the old hermit was, he would never trust The Sill's orphans to another. Especially not Cole.

By the end of the day Naythan ate his words as Cole knew he would. The Sill's forces encountered six fully-manned enemy outposts, all of which showed no indication of evacuation or knowledge of Rayn's plans. The Unbound set out with their elite units and reclaimed every single one, their efforts taking them well into the following morning. The battles were longer and bloodier than the easy victories of evacuated outposts, but enemy casualties far exceeded their own.

Thunder clapped against Cole's chest as he returned to The Sill through the murky cloud of a Seer Jar. The outpost they'd just liberated had been heavily defended by the Divine Guard, who had proven too dangerous for the assault companies, and so it took the combined forces of the Unbound and every elite unit to earn a victory.

Cole heard the urgent voice of Kamila from just beyond the Seer Jar's smoke. "Don't try to heal it, just stop the bleeding until Master Cole comes through. Stars, there's so much blood."

Emerging from the cloud and into the training field, Cole found his unit crowded around Wilkin, who was lying in the nearby grass. Great puddles of shining crimson led from the Seer Jar to his students, covering the hands and armor of everyone in the unit as well. Cole wished he had listened to Eliza before the last raid and only taken the Unbound. It would have taken far longer with only the four of them, but the chances of anyone getting hurt would have been nearly zero.

"I've got one critically injured, but I'll have him patched up in a minute," Cole said. *"Anyone else hurt?"*

"Three in each of my first and second units," Valen replied quickly.

"Checking now," Sitra said.

Eliza had been too busy healing her units to respond. Cole hurried over to Wilkin and shouldered his way through Grant and Viness. "Move," he ordered.

The unit snapped at his command, each leaping back several paces and giving him plenty of room to work. Wilkin was on his back, eyes half-open and head bobbing to the side. Red froth gurgled between his lips with each shallow breath. The right side of his chest worked frantically while the left side was sunken and still. His battle robes were so dark with blood, they almost appeared black. His left arm was badly broken, bent in a way that made it look like he had another elbow above the first. His hand twitched as munisica extended and retracted across crooked fingers, Rage battling against the siren call of the void.

Kneeling over his student, Cole whipped an emerald hand over Wilkin, and the bloody robes tore themselves from his broken body, landing in a wet heap several yards away. "Release your spells," Cole demanded.

The unit did as they were told. The open chasm in Wilkin's chest came loose, releasing a tide of dark blood and spilling glistening organs out into the dirt. Wilkin's working lung went still and his fingers ceased their twitching. Cole ignored the anguished cries of the others as he drew upon his vast reserves of Passion. Closing his eyes, Cole withdrew to his center and conducted himself from the quiet of his stone room. He reached for Wilkin's mind, cradling it gently away from the edge of the void, then took the boy's pain into himself. The agony was pure, captivating all five of Cole's senses. He siphoned it all as swiftly as he could. Placing his hands over Wilkin's broken form, the Passion flowed from him at last, radiating from his palms in a brilliant downpour of lavender. The air hummed with magic and the faint trill of wind chimes. Blood retreated back to where it came from and flesh wove itself anew. Varka's cape vibrated over his back as Cole trickled Wisdom into the spell, placing things where they belonged, and removing things that didn't. A minute passed and Cole ceased the flow of the magic. Wilkin's skin was whole and smooth, save for a bulbous scar that stretched from his armpit to his hip, a vestige of inflicted Hatred that he would carry for the rest of his days.

Wilkin's eyes cracked open, then he gasped and tried to rise. Cole set a palm on his chest, pinning him to the ground, but Wilkin lashed at him with black claws.

"The battle is over," Cole said in a soft voice as he filled the air with pacifying magic. He observed Wilkin's expression as it softened, then gave way to confusion. "You're back at The Sill. You're safe."

Wilkin looked down at himself. "I'm naked."

"That you are," Cole said with a grin. "Now if you'd be so kind as to remove your munisica from my arm, I can go help the other units."

Wilkin grimaced as he pulled his claws from Cole's arm. He stammered an apology and tried to heal the wounds, but Cole was already sprinting towards Valen's unit on the other side of the training field, healing himself and mending his armor as he ran.

Most of the wounded were in as critical a state as Wilkin had been, though some were far worse. One girl had lost a foot and Sitra had to go back through the Seer Jar to retrieve it. Another boy had his spine so badly twisted that it took Eliza and Cole the better part of an hour to fix all his damaged nerves. No one had died though, and for that they were grateful.

Tired and shaken, Cole and Eliza dismissed the units and met Valen and Sitra in the middle of the training grounds. The field had been altered to accommodate the increased traffic through the Seer Jar network. Around its border were dozens of stations, each designated by a small pavilion grown from the ground, with supports and walls crafted from stiff vines and roofs made from woven ferns. In the center of each station was a stout brass pedestal with a Seer Jar perched on top. At the far end of the field loomed the same three sentinel pines where Cole had his first lesson with his unit.

"What a disaster," Eliza sighed as she took a seat next to Sitra and Valen in the soft grass. Cole fell in next to her. "I knew bringing the students was a bad idea."

"What are you talking about?" Sitra asked with a look of disgust. "That was the best outcome we could have hoped for. Real battle with real consequences. Do you think they're just going to skip off to their rooms for a snack and a nap? No, they're gonna go discuss tactics and iron out their mistakes so they don't get chopped up so badly next time. Look, there they go now."

The Unbound turned their heads and sharpened their eyes with Wisdom. Every single unit had gathered under the sentinel pines in tight circles around the trunks. Cole didn't need to sharpen his ears to know what they were talking about. One unit watched a pair locked in a slow, demonstrative sparring session, pausing now and then while someone corrected their form. Another unit was busy taking turns wrapping themselves in shadows as they practiced a basic concealment spell.

"I suppose you're right," Eliza admitted. "But I'd rather not have so many close calls in the next battle. I didn't even engage the enemy. There were too many wounded to heal."

"Nor I," Valen added. "I spent half my time countering spells and casting shields over our units. I worry we may cripple their survival skills if we continue to pull them out of the fire before they get burned. They still have much to learn."

Sitra huffed. "Next time I'll ask Debjornik to find us a more suitable enemy. Not too soft, not too hard. Something just right for our little band of sapling warriors. What we really need is... hey is that Lileth?"

There was movement beyond the sentinel pines. A tall figure strode down the path that led to the dancing gardens, surrounded by a cluster of much smaller figures. Cole's Passion had revealed Lileth's presence long before his eyes did, though he refrained from saying anything because she held a deep guilt for her resignation from the Unbound, and usually avoided their group whenever possible.

"What is she up to these days?" Eliza asked.

"She tends to the children at Naythan's academy," Cole replied as he watched Lileth and her class handing out food and drinks among the units. "When she's not doing that she's working on her sculptures and paintings. It's really good stuff, better than most things in the Arts District, but she always destroys her work before finishing it."

"The muse is ever an ephemeral thing, or so I have been told,"
Valen said. "Did she ever find out what her ailment is? Why she sleeps
so much?"

"No," Cole said, bitterness slipping into his words. More often
than not, whenever he went to visit, she would fall asleep in front of
him, or already be asleep by the time he arrived, unresponsive to his
love. "I've looked her over more times than I care to count. Naythan
gave it a shot too. As far as we can tell there's nothing wrong with her."

"I could take a look at her," Eliza offered with a gentle smile. "I
have some skill with healing, as you might know. It's possible I could
find something you and Naythan missed."

Cole shrugged. "I'll ask her, but I don't think she'll consent. She
doesn't like other people poking around inside her. She snapped at
Naythan the other day, and she refused to go anywhere near Ka Reine
because of her ability to see into the souls of others."

"Or maybe because Lileth knew Ka Reine was a filthy traitor,"
Sitra scoffed. "She come clean yet?"

"I don't know, I've been busy with our raids," Cole replied. "And
we still don't know if she's done anything to hurt us. I should go check
on her and make sure she's all right. If she wasn't our enemy before,
she certainly will be after our scuffle." Cole rose to leave, but a familiar
mind caressed his own.

"Wait a moment. The children want to come say hello." Lileth
locked eyes with him from across the field. Even from so far away her
gaze still managed to steal his breath away.

Cole stood rooted to the spot, a smile slowly spreading across his
face as she strolled across the field with her little army. He noticed a
couple of the gemstone children from Borla Dign among their
number; a girl with deep sapphire skin and a boy of fiery garnet.

Lileth halted several paces from them and the children bunched
up behind her, hissing with furtive whispers. Lileth seemed to have
expected this, however.

Lileth spoke to the children with a matronly voice that drew a
raised eyebrow from Sitra. "You are now in the company of my dearest
friends, also known as the Unbound. They are not so fun as Naythan,
but that is only because they are too shy. Go on, say hello." The children

gave their greeting in an unsynchronized yet enthusiastic chorus, after which a few of the braver souls leaned around their classmates for a better look. Lileth urged them with a gentle pulse of rosy Passion from her palms. "Give them your gifts then. They need them the most, for they are the most boring and shy people in the world."

A stampede of giggles and leaping legs rushed at them. Valen, Sitra, and Eliza rose to their feet, hastily scouring the blood from themselves with a blast of steam from their palms. Cole scrubbed himself as well, and not a moment too soon. The children cheered as they collided with their legs. A dozen or so clambered up Sitra's armor, bringing her laughing back to the ground like a fallen tree. Tiny hands foisted gifts of stone carvings, wooden charm bracelets, and cakes made from sweetened blackstouts, each given along with a demand for more magic or a story of their journeys.

"You were quite right, Lileth. We needed this very much," Eliza said into their Passion network while managing several children in a game of tag. *"Thank you, for showing us something other than fighting and suffering. We have seen too much of both lately."*

"I only wish I could join you," Lileth replied. A stinging guilt emanated from her. The Unbound smothered her pain with their Passion without hesitation.

"Ah, don't worry about it," Sitra said. *"At least Valen looks like a master of Wisdom without you around. And whatever you're doing with Cole in the bedroom's been paying off big time in the Passion front. I swear he could raise the dead after a night with you."*

"Thanks, Sitra," Cole said aloud, shooting her a warning glare.

"I would wager you are of best use to The Sill right where you are," Valen added. *"Tending to the next generation within The Sill is no less important than what we do outside The Sill. Your advice is very helpful by the way. I never would have thought to—."*

A pulse rang through their minds, keening and urgent. Wareen's voice came next.

"You must come to the Heart Tree now," Wareen said with trembling thoughts. *"Larkin has appeared in our Seer Jar. He is acting odd. Come quick."*

"We're on our way," Cole replied. He then directed his thoughts to the Unbound and Lileth. *"Get in the air."*

Varka's cape snapped to a pane of clear crystal as Cole shot up into the sky. Using only the power of their legs, Valen, Eliza, and Sitra leaped two stories into the air before conjuring their emerald wings and joining him. Though he wished she hadn't, Lileth remained on the ground with her class. The children cried out in awed cheers as the Unbound vanished from sight.

"Do not worry, I am still with you," Lileth said directly into his mind. Her words loosened an anxious knot in his gut that he wasn't aware of until now.

Forgoing the courtesy of the front door, the Unbound descended through the open ceiling of the staff chamber, passing through a tingling invisible barrier meant to keep the forest out. The staff was already seated, each staring so intently at the Seer Jar mounted in the center of their table that they seemed not to notice the Unbound's arrival. Debjornik's assistant was seated at the table as well, encapsulated in a sensory barrier that covered her and the Seer Jar. Cole took his seat between Rayn and the girl while Valen, Sitra, and Eliza stood behind him.

"What have we missed?" Cole asked, peering into the teardrop crystal nestled within its ornate brass stand. The darkness within the Seer Jar looked like a pocket of night sky.

Rayn spoke without looking at him. "Nothing yet. We hear Larkin's voice from time to time, but most of it is garbled muttering. The only thing we can understand is when he says your name."

"All right then, let's see if I can't draw him out." Cole stood to enter the sensory barrier, then paused. "This Seer Jar has been downgraded, right?"

"Of course it has," Rayn said dismissively. "The last thing we need is a physical gateway between The Three's hive and the Heart Tree."

Wareen chimed in with a reassuring tone. "The risk was negligible, but we had Brinleaf downgrade this Seer Jar on the off chance the knowledge reached an unsecure node in our network. Nothing will come through this jar other than light and sound."

"Good to know," Cole said as a wave of gratitude washed over him. He reached through the sensory barrier and tapped Debjornik's assistant on the shoulder. She jumped at his touch, then nodded and scooted out of the chair. Cole sat in the chair and the staff chambers vanished. Thick silence filled his ears. A dim ambient light illuminated him and the portion of the table which the Seer Jar sat upon, but outside that was a black void as far as he could see. Leaning in, Cole grasped the brass wire handle and pulled the Seer Jar closer to himself, then spoke in a low whisper. "Larkin, it's Cole."

The murk within the Seer Jar gave no response.

"Larkin," Cole repeated, louder this time.

Shadows stirred within the crystal. There was a sigh of pain, then a grunt as something large and grey moved within. Cole recognized a swath of Larkin's robes, stained with unknown filth from his months of imprisonment. Larkin's face came into view, his eyes sunken and uncaring, his face slack and pale. He looked like he'd been dead for days, yet somehow his peeling lips moved as words hissed between them.

"The key to the Aethers," Larkin whispered.

"Yes," Cole replied. "It's me, Cole."

"Terra," Larkin said, voice cracking. The corner of his mouth twitched as though it wanted to smile but lacked the strength. His faraway gaze looked beyond his prison, to somewhere happy and warm. "I remember Terra. Earth. Couldn't stop the Hunger. Greedy empires, raping and gorging. But there was beauty in the eddies. Passion helped. Philosophy. Understanding. Art. I failed them all, just as I fail Aeneria now."

"But you haven't failed," Cole said. "You're still alive. You're still fighting, and because of you we're winning! Just hold on a little longer, I swear we'll get you out of there."

"It is too late for me," Larkin said with a leaky chuckle. "They have me now. I am theirs. They knew all along, saw me sneaking, but they allowed it. Encouraged it. Didn't even bother to find out what I was saying. What I learned." His eyes closed as he labored to find his breath.

"Don't you dare give up!" Cole commanded, grasping the brass mount with both hands. "You have to keep fighting! We're going to save you!"

Larkin's eyes opened halfway and found Cole's. His words came strong and clear. "The Shadow Tide is nigh. The Three come for you now."

An icy snake of Fear tickled Cole's insides. "How do you know this?"

A familiar voice that did not belong to Larkin came next. Thunderous and dripping with malice, it rumbled with such force that it shook the table and cracked the Seer Jar.

"WE COME."

The scene within the jar widened to reveal the rest of Larkin's body. His waist and legs were gone. Holding him upright like a grotesque puppet was a massive ebony hand, its bladed fingers buried deep up into his torso. The view within the jar followed the munisica as it carried Larkin up the length of an enormous belly and chest, naked and covered in the shroud of Rage.

Roth's face appeared, fully shrouded and impossibly large. He opened his mouth as if to speak, lips pulling back to reveal the gates of some forgotten circle of hell; black teeth large as shovel heads and sharp as chipped obsidian, with clumps of hairy grey flesh and severed fingers wedged between. A putrid smell filled Cole's nostrils as an otherworldly howl rose from nowhere. Cole tried to get up, to look away before it happened, but something held him fast to the chair. The teeth parted and Larkin's head vanished into the black maw, his face set in a perverse grin, his eyes locked in Cole's. There was a wet snip as the jaws closed, then a hollow pop as rusty blood gushed out from between the black teeth. The body rolled out of frame as hot stench poured down the back of Cole's throat. Grotton's song rose to an unbearable howl, shaking Cole to the bone and threatening to shatter him from the inside out, then the crystal filled with dirty red. The Seer Jar melted in a puddle of dark blood, hissing and boiling as it poured across the table.

CHAPTER 25

BORROWED TIME

Strong hands gripped Cole's arms and yanked him backwards before the blood could spill onto his lap. Darkness enveloped him, then light. His eyes told him he was in the staff chambers, but the putrid stench clinging to his throat and Grotton's howl ringing in his head told him he was somewhere else.

"Cole!" cried a voice. "What's wrong with him?"

"Let me at him," said another.

Clean Passion surged through Cole and he felt as if someone had rung an enormous bell inside his head. He jerked free of the arms and rolled to his hands and knees, then vomited on the chamber floor.

"I'm fine," Cole gasped, shrugging off whoever was rubbing his back. Trembling, he rose to his feet.

Eliza stood before him, with Sitra and Valen right behind her, their faces awash with horror. The staff stood against the chamber walls as if they had been glued there.

"What in the high hells just happened?" Rayn said in a queasy voice.

"Grotton spoke to us," Cole said. He took a few steadying breaths, then kicked a fallen chair up with his foot and sat himself in it. "Did you all see what I saw?"

"Yes," Sitra replied. "We felt it too. Roth… he's…"

"That was not Roth," Cole said in a stern tone. "That was Grotton."

"How can we hope to fight something like that?" Falinor asked. "You four are the strongest among us, and you can't even bear the utterings of even one of the black gods."

Cole had nothing to say. The others looked just as dumbfounded and frightened as he felt. There was no magic, no weapon at all that

JOSEPH PARADIS

could contend with something so overwhelmingly vile. The last few months of training and preparing seemed like nothing more than childish dreaming.

"What happened to The Seer jar?" Debjornik asked, eyeing the melted mess that was currently hissing and boiling its way across the table and floor. "I thought only sight and sound could be transmitted. How is this possible?"

"I… I don't know," Wareen stammered. "That's a new Seer Jar too. It's never been touched with Borla Dign's upgrade."

Valen shuddered, then resumed his usual mask of stoicism. "I think we should turn our focus to our next actions. Grotton has given us his message. Now we must decide what to do with it."

Calm returned to Cole at last. He thanked Valen with a nod, then turned to the staff. "The Three are coming. Debjornik, you're The Sill's eyes and ears. Do you still have agents in Oberon City?"

"Yes," Debjornik replied. Cole sensed whisperings of thought flit between Debjornik and the life candles a few floors below. "But nothing strange has been reported yet."

"What about our outposts?" Cole asked, directing the question to Wareen.

Wareen gave him an uncertain look. "Nothing yet, but why would they? I thought The Three were inside Oberon Temple."

Cole pointed to the puddle of smoking blood on the table. "We obviously have no idea what The Three are capable of. They could pop up anywhere, even inside The Sill for all we know. Falinor, put our forces on high alert and make sure they're ready to bounce to other outposts if there's any sign of The Three. They might be able to handle low-tier enemies but there's no point handing lives over to something stronger."

Falinor gave a quick nod. "It will be as you say."
"Colossus!" Debjornik shouted. "Rising from the waters around Oberon Temple. Alpha or larger, it's too big to tell."

"Show us," Cole said. He extended a tendril of thought to Debjornik, a temporary invitation to the Unbound's Passion network. Debjornik's face twisted with concentration as he struggled to show them images which had been relayed through two minds before his own.

416

Cole shut his eyes and Oberon City appeared before him like a hazy daydream. The image sharpened, revealing metal streets and buildings, their sharp angles rising high. The sky was dark, an inky canvas of roiling clouds so thick that even Oberon's glow was nothing more than a feeble grey smear. Debjornik's agent gazed out from the roof he stood upon, beyond the orderly skyline of port warehouses and piers, to the looming monolith that was Oberon Temple. Stacked up to the stars, the temple's charcoal black tiers formed concentric cylinders, each a mile high with the smallest resting at the very top. Something lumbered about in the water, kicking widowmaker waves with each step. It was not one Colossus, but three Alpha-class Colossi. They stalked their way to the shore, with the smallest one still taller than the first tier of the temple. One titan for each of The Three.

Cole withdrew from Debjornik's mind, and so did the other Unbound. Judging by the hopeless looks of the other staff members, they too had seen the coming nightmare. A light rain began to patter against the barrier above the chamber.

"We can't fight that," Sitra stated. The staff wilted on the spot, their eyes falling to the floor. These were clearly not the words they had hoped to hear. Sitra, however, didn't look hopeless; rather she looked curious, as if the vision had raised a question that needed answering.

"We cannot defend against them," Valen said. "Not even one such titan, not when they can simply step right over The Sill's walls. Our options are running thin."

Debjornik's mind pressed against the Unbound's Passion network once more. An image appeared to Cole. The Colossi had laid themselves prone in the water, setting their heads on the shore with their mouths stretched wide. A great horde flooded the streets below; legions of the Divine Guard marching in orderly columns, swarms of Corpulants both winged and legged, and smaller Colossi striding shoulder to shoulder passed Oberon City's buildings. The streets were churning rivers of the damned, flowing and funneling into the mouths of the three Alpha Colossi on the beach.

Eliza's hand found Cole's. She squeezed hard. Her eyes implored him for deliverance from the coming nightmare. She spoke directly into his mind, revealing the true weight of her Despair. *"Sitra and Valen are right. The Three are beyond us. We cannot hope to stand against such evil."*

"Not as we are," Cole replied, bolstering her with an invigorating blend of Passion and Rage. "We will have to grow beyond ourselves."

"You're not suggesting..." Eliza's voice trailed off as realization struck her. It was the only option.

Cole gave her hand a squeeze before releasing it. He turned to the staff. "I'm sorry to cut this short, but the Unbound have business elsewhere. Valen, Sitra." Cole's feet left the polished wood floor as Varka's cape fluttered behind his back. The rest of the Unbound summoned their emerald wings and leapt out of the chamber.

"Where in the world do you think you're going?" Rayn spat. He charged across the room and reached out as if to snatch Cole's ankle and stop him from floating away, but then he seemed to think better of it and withdrew his hand. "Your business is right here! Fate has brought the hour of our annihilation to our doorstep and you think you can just run off without an explanation? Thousands of souls are at stake! I swear if you leave now, I will ensure The Unbound are stripped of all authority and lead The Sill myself."

Cole paused in midair and sent a pulse of soothing Passion throughout the chamber, blending it with Rage as he did for Eliza. "Relax, Rayn. There might be a time when The Sill calls you to lead it, but that time isn't now. We're only going to the Necropolis."

The fury on Rayn's face softened to a mild frown. "And what do you think to find among the dead?"

"Answers," Cole said with a reassuring smile. Rayn's hand went to his forehead, as if the weight of the moment were too much to keep his head upright. Falinor, Debjornik, Thessi, and Wareen each gave him a nod of grim acceptance.

Brinleaf and a small team from Borla Dign were already waiting for them beside the archway of the Havenflow. The Unbound touched down with gentle splashes in the shallow water, its surface a rippling expanse of glowing turquoise under the rain. The lavender petals that usually swam up to greet them had sought shelter beneath the bearded trees, huddling up around their trunks in blankets of fluttering petals.

"You haven't been waiting here the whole time, have you?" Cole asked as he stepped up onto the island of roots.

Brinleaf replied with a look of polite calm. "The Havenflow is ready. Are you prepared for what lies within?"

"We are," Cole said in a serious tone. "The Three are coming, and when they get here they'll have every demon in this world at their side. We can't put this off any longer."

"Can't we?" Sitra asked, casting a suspicious glare at the archway. "This whole thing could be a waste of time. You never did tell us what we'd be facing in there. What if this place kills us, or what if we survive and it still isn't enough?"

"Then The Three will kill us when they get here," Valen said with a resigned sigh. "Either way we are quite doomed, so we may as well take our chances in the Havenflow. It is time to fight or flee."

A low growl rumbled in Sitra's chest. "Don't be stupid. I never said anything about running away, I just find it hard to trust the fate of The Sill to a bunch of Wisdom users and dead people who were too weak to survive whatever killed them in the first place. I'll go in this thing. Hell, I'll even go first, just don't ask me to be happy about it. At least we'll really only be gone for a day."

"And Deekus will be there, watching over us," Eliza said. She walked up the dais and placed her hand on the archway, giving it a look of longing. "If the Havenflow is made from the memories of the dead, then he must be a part of it as well. I trust this place."

Cole shifted to the side and peered through the archway, expecting to see Deekus striding up to greet them from the ethereal world beyond. He hadn't told Eliza about his recent encounter with Deekus, and he wasn't sure exactly why.

"The Havenflow can accept two souls at once," Brinleaf said. "Once you enter, the gateway will close behind you and you will be trapped inside with the trials of the dead. The gateway will open after you endure one cycle inside the Havenflow, though only one day will have passed in our world. These are the terms. Who will be the first to accept them?"

"I already said I'm going first," Sitra grunted as she pushed her way to the front of their group. She shot Brinleaf a hard look.

"Pinebean, If this thing doesn't open in a day I'm going to rip your heart out through your ass."

"Naturally," Brinleaf said with a polite nod. "Who will be the second?"

A twinge of anxiety quickened Cole's heart and brought sweat to his palms. He knew the Fear was childish, just his sub-self's reaction to facing the unknown, but it gave him pause nevertheless.

"I will go," Valen said in a flat tone of unconcern. He looked at Cole. "I figure you and Sitra are the best fighters, so we may as well split the two of you up. And since you and Eliza have traveled furthest down the path of Passion, the two of you can heal whatever damage The Three manage to cause in the next day. Does this make sense?"

Relief soothed the icy Fear in Cole's limbs. "It makes perfect sense."

"Do be careful," Eliza said. She gave Valen and Sitra each a long hug, imparting upon them her farewell gift of Passion. "We will be right here when you get out."

"I hope not," Sitra said, pushing Eliza off with a playful shove. "Our enemies are marching on The Sill, so that means you two are going to be a pair of rocks in their boots every step of the way." She punched Cole squarely in the chest and flashed him a mischievous grin. "That's an order, boss."

Cole rubbed his chest. He managed half a smile and muttered, "Understood." He wasn't sure what scared him more, the evil bearing down upon The Sill or the unknown dangers his two friends were about to face. He wanted to hug them both, to tell them what they meant to him, to give them words of advice and fill them with nourishing Passion as Eliza had, but their feet were already moving.

Before Cole could find the words, Valen and Sitra were through the archway, their outlines dulling and rippling like the dead air around them. Cole leaned to the side and peered around the arch, expecting to see them, but there was nothing. They were gone. When he looked back through the portal, a violent storm had kicked up around Valen and Sitra, ravaging the phantom Necropolis with back-breaking winds and flashes of lightning. They huddled at the edge of the dais, shielding themselves with Wisdom as the shallow water twisted up in towering cyclones and bearded trees bent sideways, tearing free from their roots. Lightning flashed through the archway as the air within became so thick with mud and debris that Valen and Sitra were no longer visible. Panicking, Cole readied a spell to yank them back, but the gateway crumbled before his eyes as the storm ravaged the woven roots and vines. The archway collapsed upon itself as its tiny gratia stones clinked loose over the island at Cole's feet. The gems dimmed as light faded entirely from their cores.

Cole fell to his knees and attempted to scoop the broken roots and loose gratia stones back into a pile. "Help me!" he shouted to Brinleaf. "Fix this thing, we need to pull them back!" Eliza appeared at his side, plucking and weaving the pieces of the gateway back together with strands of emerald Wisdom.

"It is impossible," Brinleaf said. The lack of emotion in his voice sent a hot flame of Rage roaring through Cole. "The dead have them now. They will either survive the challenges within, or join the dead and become part of the Havenflow. Those are the terms. The gateway will reform itself in one day, and only then will we know their fate."

Cole's munisica came forth on their own as the black shroud wrapped up his arms and legs. He glared at the useless pile of sticks and spoke in a tone of deathly quiet. "What are we supposed to do then?"

"Get up," Eliza said, her voice fierce and confident. Cole looked up at her, surprised to see her munisica drawn and ready as well. "They've been in there for days already. Either they are already dead, or they are doing everything they can to make themselves harder to kill. No matter their fate, they are not wasting their time, and neither should we waste ours. Get up." She extended an ebony clawed hand.

Cole grasped her munisica and hoisted himself to his feet. She was right. There was nothing they could do.

"Thank you," Cole groaned. He cleansed himself in the stone room of his center before speaking again. "Let's go back to the Heart Tree. Valen would be disappointed if we weren't productive."

She grinned at him. "And Sitra would have our heads if she knew we hadn't killed something yet."

Cole turned to Brinleaf, who hovered at the edge of the dais, arms crossed and just as motionless as before their arrival. "Let me know if anything changes."

Brinleaf gave a solemn nod. "Of course, Wisdom Walker."

Back in the Heart Tree, Cole found each staff member laboring within their separate offices. Falinor was issuing evacuation orders to certain outposts. Debjornik was gathering intel on the Colossi, which had already departed Oberon City, their bellies full of The Three's minions. Thessi worked on consolidating resources from various outposts while Wareen's team monitored their Seer Jar networks. Cole and Eliza joined Rayn in the Strategy and Operations room, a clean chamber lit with harsh white gratia lights. Surrounding the chamber were partitioned offices where the people within digested information gathered from the other departments. Rayn was in the center of the chamber, leaning over a map table with his eyes closed. The air about him was a flurry of telepathic activity.

"You're back sooner than I expected," Rayn said after Cole and Eliza had stood in silence for a full minute. "Don't tell me you've lost your taste for adventure already. Or perhaps you finally realized there is plenty of glory to be had from the comfort of your home?"

"Straighten your tongue, Rayn, before I take it from you," Eliza snapped. The sneer melted from Rayn's face as he eyed her munisica. "Just because you aren't privy to our every sacrifice doesn't mean they aren't being made. Two of the Unbound are risking their lives as we speak so we might weather the coming storm."

Rayn stammered as he struggled to find words. "I... I had no... you never informed me of what Brinleaf concocted."

"Nor will we," Cole said as he approached the map table. "Where do we stand? I got the general picture on the way in, but I want your take on it."

Rayn swallowed back a retort and waved a glowing hand over the table. The Sill and surrounding landscape vanished and the stone surface rippled like water, then a model of Aeneria rose from the table, two yards in diameter with carvings for every city, highway, and body of water. Cole traced his eyes over the Fangshards, a toothy scar that wrapped around half the planet.

"The Colossi have begun to split up, but there is no doubt they are headed for The Sill," Rayn said, pointing to each of three black dots near Oberon City. "We've surmised something else as well. Debjornik's agents have reported musterings in all enemy outposts between here and the Capital. We believe the Colossi will be stopping briefly along the way to pick up additional forces. They've already ignored a few of our outposts, and one has already stopped at one of their own. And they must have heard about your friend in the Fangshards because they're skirting the entire mountain range. Not that it matters—their speed is incredible."

"How long until they get here?" Cole asked, watching a black dot as it vanished from one city and reappeared miles away in the middle of a grassy expanse.

Rayn looked at Cole, Fear plain in his eyes. "Two or three days, depending on how many stops they make."

Cole shook his head. "How is that possible? They're big, but they still have to walk to get here."

"We don't know," Rayn admitted.

Silence fell between them. Cole noticed Rayn's staff had been quiet as well, each turning an ear in hopes of hearing something that contradicted the doom written in their reports. Rayn shot them a look of reproach and they resumed their work, though they lacked the fervor they had just a few minutes prior. Rayn then painted the air around the table with a quick muffling spell, shielding their words from eavesdroppers.

"Have you considered surrender?" Rayn asked, his tone fragile and cautious. "We can likely hold off the Three's minions indefinitely, perhaps even win with enough time, but one fact still remains as true as the day this war started: If The Three enter the battle themselves, we will all die. Seeing as they're crossing half the planet to come to us, I think we can count on their direct involvement. That leaves evacuation. The Sill can spread out among our outposts, but then we'll have to leave someone behind to destroy our Seer Jars, and we'll be defending multiple fronts with far softer defenses. Eventually we'll run out of places to hide and, well, that will be that."

"Let me ask you something," Cole said with a tone as hard as Morthainian glass. "Have you ever been inside a Corpulant?"

Rayn blinked several times before responding. "What?"

"A Corpulant," Cole repeated. "Have you ever been inside one?"

"Of course not," Rayn replied. "I wouldn't be here if I had."

"Well I have, and so has Lexy," Cole said. "Not a very fun place to be, especially when you're paralyzed. Their stomachs stretch to almost any size, so when they swallow you there's a good chance you won't even be the first thing in there. The acid works very slowly, but when the burning starts it certainly doesn't feel that way. You'll try to kick and scream and cough, but you can't move an inch, not even when you're choking on bits of other people. Even if you could move, the first thing you'd do is tear your own flesh off, just to stop the burning. Then you realize your only escape is to drown in your own soup of melted skin and piss, and so you take that first breath, hoping it brings the end. If you're lucky you'll get that end, unless you were Chosen like Lexy was when the Corpulant took her. She lived in a perpetual state of dying until Kreed took her out of that thing and stuck her on a tower, where she was first to burn in her town's Devotion. That will be the terms of our surrender. Every man, woman, and child, innocent or otherwise will suffer like Lexy."

Rayn had grown pale as a corpse. He gripped the edge of the table as if it were the only thing keeping him from flying away. "How did you escape?" he asked in a quivering whisper.

Cole commanded his master's Rage, and in a blink covered himself fully in the ebony shroud. "I fought."

After a brief yet constructive discussion, Cole, Eliza and Rayn came to a compromise. They would recall the majority of their forces back into The Sill, where they would prepare for siege operations while a few sentinels would keep their outpost Seer Jars ready for evacuation. If they were to stand and fight, The Sill was certainly the best place to do it. Rayn prepped the orders for the rest of the Heart Tree departments while Eliza and Cole made for the barracks, where they would rally the elite units for another task.

"There is another option," Eliza said in a private stream of thought as she flew beside him.

"I'm not leaving The Sill to fend for itself," Cole stated, cutting sharp turns between the trees of the markets. *"Not while every enemy in the world is bearing down on us."*

"Keep that in mind should this siege turn against us," Eliza said. *"You may never get such an opportune moment to enter the Vaults of the Soul while The Three are occupied elsewhere. If all seems lost, you must harden your heart and make for Oberon Temple with all haste."*

Cole didn't respond, though he knew she was right. He surged faster through the air, wishing he had spent more time with Lexy and Amori, and most of all Lileth. He reached out to her but found her mind embroiled in a storm of emotions brought on by what she had just heard through his ears. He wanted nothing more than to go to her now, but he had responsibilities to The Sill, and she to her children, whom she was still in the middle of a lesson with.

"Don't worry, I'll come to you before we head out," Cole assured her, caressing her mind with affection. He poured more of himself into her, wrapping her in a warm mental hug, then withdrew at once. Despair welled up from within her so quickly that she had to excuse herself from her class, leaving the children alone in the Arts District as she ran for her apartment.

Cole swallowed back a mouthful of guilt as he realized what had upset her so. He would be entering the Havenflow with Eliza, the two of them alone for an entire cycle to face the challenges within. He had grown so accustomed to the long days and months that a cycle didn't seem so daunting to him until this moment. The equivalent of seven Earth-years would pass while he and Eliza toiled in the Havenflow. He wanted to believe that he would stay true to Lileth, that he would never forget how he felt about her, not even in the weakest moment, but seven years was no small span. He had grown so much in his handful of months on Aeneria that there was little chance of him emerging from the Havenflow as the same person. He tore faster through the air, shaking the thoughts from his head and forcing his mind to the task at hand.

"Congratulations," Cole shouted. He kept himself fully shrouded as he paced in a slow circle about center field of the barracks. Swaying from exhaustion, the units gazed at him with glassy-eyed stares. Many had just been pulled out of bed. "Thanks to our overabundant success on the battlefield, The Sill has earned itself the direct attentions of The Three. They are on their way here now, and will arrive in as little as two days."

The haggard expressions around him vanished, giving way to looks of shock and panic.

Cole continued, urging Rage into his voice in hopes of galvanizing the units. "This is it. This is the moment we've been working towards. This is why you joined The Sill's most elite fighting force instead of taking up jobs as basket weavers and bakers. We have never been more ready or more deserving of a chance to strike back at the hearts of our enemies." Cole paused. Even through the shroud of his Rage he could feel the Fear stirring about him, carried by telepathic whispers of uncertainty. They weren't stupid. They knew what it meant to stand before a god.

"Still your Fear and draw your munisica," Eliza commanded in a tone of fiery wrath, her own munisica gleaming in the moonlight. "The Three feed on every drop of your Fear, Hunger, Despair and Hatred, whether you feel it or not. Deny them these gifts, for you are warriors of The Sill and they have not earned them from you."

Cole waited as they took command of their Rage. The Fear in the air evaporated like fog before a rising sun. Smiling, he took a second to look each of them in the eye as he spoke. "When The Three get here they'll have every minion and monster you haven't killed yet, saving you the trouble of hunting them down yourselves. While you're cleaning up the easy targets, the senior Unbound and I will play host to Decreath, Grotton, and Sorronis. I'm sorry if this comes at a disappointment to any of you, but as the ranking warriors it's only fair we get first choice of enemies."

A smattering of laughter echoed among the units. A tall girl whose shroud had just begun to sharpen her hair stepped forth. Cole recognized her as the leader of one of Valen's units.

"Master Cole," she said in a serious tone. "Where are Masters Valen and Sitra? The other unit leaders and I can no longer sense them with our Passion."

Cole chose his words carefully. He didn't want the existence of the Havenflow to be common knowledge until he knew just how dangerous it was. "Masters Valen and Sitra are currently on a mission, the success of which could have a tremendous impact on the fate of The Sill."

"When will they return?" demanded a stout boy with thick munisica, one of Sitra's unit leaders. "If things are heating up here we can hardly afford their absence. We need Master Sitra's Rage."

Wilken shouldered his way to the front of his unit. "Open your eyes, Brunthorn, Master Cole's Rage is without equal. You should wait until your claws grow a bit longer before you speak on things you don't understand."

Brunthorn's hands balled into bladed fists as he took a step towards Wilkin, but members of his own unit held him back.

"It's a valid question," Cole said in a loud, clear voice, putting an end to a scuffle before it began. "Brunthorn, your Rage burns hot enough to melt the wings off a Corpulant, but don't forget your other magics." He then addressed the entire group. "Masters Sitra and Valen have a job to do, and they will return when it's finished. We will do our best to defend The Sill in the meantime. Unit leaders, get your warriors a decent meal and restock on supplies. I need you ready and patrolling The Sill's borders as soon as possible. Keep Falinor informed of anything unusual. You aren't a part of his assault companies, but you may need them if The Three surprise us earlier than expected. Go now." The units dispersed without hesitation. Cole caught Wilkin's eye and beckoned him over before he got too far. "Wilkin, prepare your unit and gather them in the training fields in half an hour. You'll be coming with Eliza and me."

"Yes, Master Cole," Wilkin replied with a quick nod, then turned on his heel and ran after his unit.

"And what will you and I be doing while they prepare?" Eliza asked once the last warrior was out of earshot.

"We're going to load up Sitra's fulminators into that cart over there, then grab whatever stimulants Valen has left in his store." Reaching his hand out, Cole extended his Wisdom to a heavy cargo wagon at the other side of the clearing. The wagon shuddered, then floated through the air where it alighted at the base of Sitra's apartment.

"She might not be here to enjoy our trick, but she's certainly going to be a part of it."

"We'll have to ensure we get a good view of the explosions," Eliza said, flashing him a mischievous smirk. "Sitra will be most disappointed if we don't at least give her a memory of her hard work."

As gently as they could, they levitated the bombs out of Sitra's apartment and into the wagon, filling it within a few minutes. They loaded two more wagons, strapping the fulminators down with vine clippings grown into broad webs with Passion. Cole secured a vat of stimulating potions to one of the carts, as well as a rattling case of empty vials.

"I'll take these," Eliza said in a quiet voice. "You probably want to go say goodbye to Lileth. You shouldn't leave her while she's so upset."

Guilt twisted in Cole's chest. "There isn't time. She'll understand, and we'll be back soon enough."

Eliza frowned at him. "There is plenty of time. Go." She turned to leave, tugging the wagons with green strands of Wisdom as she went.

Cole watched her go, his guilt boiling up into frustration as he gazed over at Lileth's apartment. What was he supposed to say? He had no choice but to enter the Havenflow with Eliza. He could ask Brinleaf to go with him instead, or perhaps go alone, but then he'd be compromising the fate of The Sill for the sake of assuaging Lileth's jealousy. Not to mention he wasn't sure his sanity would survive an entire cycle with Brinleaf, or by himself. He was fuming by the time he reached Lileth's door. He would simply tell her what had to be done, and she would have to find the strength to deal with it for one measly day. If it bothered her that much then she never should have left the Unbound, for then it would have been her and Cole alone for a whole cycle, just like they had fantasized about during so many nights together.

Cole pushed himself through the door, his arguments in hand. Her room was quiet and so dark he couldn't see his own nose. Running his hand along the wall, Cole found a gratia stone and charged it, flooding the room with soft white light. Lileth was on the floor, her back to the bed and her head hanging limply to one side. Blood trickled from both her eyes.

"Lileth!" Cole shouted. He bounded to her side, crouching and calling her name as he shook her. She wouldn't rouse. He tried to connect with her mind and force her awake, but her thoughts were such a roiling storm that he couldn't find her center. Placing a palm on her chest, he sent a pulse of Passion into her. Her body jolted at the magic, but otherwise didn't respond. He closed his eyes and dove his mind into hers, pouring all his Passion into the storm while calling out to her, but it was like trying to fill a bucket with no bottom. His cries went unanswered, his Passion unrequited. Cole felt something dark creeping up around him, something alluring and dangerous, whispering to him from the shadows of Lileth's mind.

Scooping Lileth up in his arms, Cole carried her out the door and leaped off the ramp. Varka's cape snapped from cloth to crystal as the air exploded around him.

"Naythan!" Cole shouted with all his mind.

Naythan's alarm echoed back. *"Falling stars, boy! You scared the tattoos off me. What is it?"*

"Lileth's hurt," Cole said, his tone pleading. *"I think someone attacked her."*

"Bring her in then," Naythan replied.

With Naythan's thoughts guiding him, Cole flew through an open window in an uninhabited wing of the academy. The room had a warm glow, with lavish furniture and enchanted wallpaper that mimicked a sky set in eternal sunset. Cole set Lileth down on a squishy suede couch.

"Tell me what you know," Naythan said as he rolled the sleeves of his headmaster's robes.

"I- I don't know," Cole stammered. "I found her like this. I tried Passion on her body and her mind, but..." Cole's voice trailed off as a fresh crimson tear fell from her cheek and soaked into the couch cushion.

Naythan moved Cole aside with a firm hand. He adjusted his glasses, flicking the frames several times with a tattooed finger. The lenses flashed through different colors with each click of his nail, finally settling on an opaque amber. He looked her body over, scanning her while holding two fingers above her forehead. He gave his glasses a final flick and they returned to clear.

He spoke without taking his eyes off her. "Body's perfect, so's the brain. But the mind... There's something brewing in there. Feels like dark magic, but for the life of me I can't put a finer point to it. Any idea who might have attacked her?"

"You think she's been attacked?" Cole asked.

"That's what you said, wasn't it?" Naythan replied with a raised eyebrow. "Dark magic is the only thing I've ever seen put a mind in a state like this. Lileth's as private a person as I've ever seen, so you'd be better than me at guessing who might have done it. Does she have any enemies out there? Anyone she might have spurned?"

Cole's panicked thoughts immediately went to Eliza, then he berated himself for even considering her. Then there was Ka Reine. It was no secret in The Sill that Cole and Lileth had a relationship far beyond acquaintances. Ka Reine could have hurt Lileth to get back at him, or perhaps lure him into a trap. He extended his Passion to the guards outside Ka Reine's prison, forcing his way into their thoughts without bothering to conceal himself. Locked away in The Sill's only metallic prison, a single-story box with thick walls and no windows, was the Old One. Using one guard's eye he peered through a pocket-sized Seer Jar. The room had been lavished with darkwood furniture, plush carpets, cold chests stocked with The Sill's finest cuisine, and shelves overflowing with books and cyphers, but Ka Reine ignored it all. She hovered in midair, frowning, her eyes shut, arms and legs crossed. Cole withdrew from the guard's mind, leaving him confused and rubbing his head.

"Ah, so you *do* have someone in mind," Naythan said in a casual tone as he beheld Cole's pensive expression. "If you wouldn't mind destroying someone else's house this time, I'd appreciate it."

Cole ignored him. He inspected Lileth, whose eyes were still crying blood. He placed his palm on her forehead and used his thumb to gently tug her eyelid open. The eye was whole and unmarred, though it darted back and forth as if she were locked in a nightmare.

"Can you stop the bleeding?" Cole asked.

"It's not her blood," Naythan replied. "We could plug up her tear ducts, but then whoever's blood that is will have nowhere to go."

"If it's not her blood then-" Cole paused as Eliza pressed against his thoughts.

"*Cole, where are you? Everyone is ready.*" Her focus had been elsewhere, but now nearly all of it was on the link between the two of them. "*Stars, what happened to Lileth?*"

Cole suddenly remembered what he was supposed to be doing, and a wild anxiety stole half a breath from his chest. The Three were well on their way and precious minutes were rushing from him like birds in the wind. He pushed his recent memories into Eliza's mind and turned to Naythan. "I have to go. Can you watch her?"

"That much was obvious," Naythan said. "I'll have to move her from here, however. I don't want Amorinanis picking up any of... whatever this is."

Cole offered his thanks and dove out the window and flew towards the training grounds, wishing he could split himself in two.

He found his unit assembled around the wagons in the middle of the training field. Eliza strode among them, handing out Valen's potions and words of encouragement. She hugged Grant and the two of them shared a laugh, then turned to Cole as he landed among them.

"We are ready," she said.

Cole nodded. He hopped up onto one of the wagons, careful not to kick any of the fulminators, then addressed the units. "As some of you probably noticed, these wagons are not full of normal gratia stones. They are a specialty of Master Sitra's, which she calls fulminators."

"They're bombs," Viness said in a bored voice. Excited murmurs broke out among the rest of the unit. Serra and Kolric backed away, eyeing the wagons nervously.

"That they are," Cole replied. "There are three Alpha Colossi headed toward The Sill, and we're going to be dropping these bombs on their heads with the intent of slowing them down enough to allow Masters Sitra and Valen to complete their task. We suspect that one of The Three lies within each Alpha Colossus, so we can't get too close. Master Eliza and I will each carry one wagon. The rest of you will carry the third."

Wilkin leaned in and spoke in a low voice, though every ear in his unit was clearly listening intently. "Master, I don't mean to question your judgment, but are you sure we are the best for this job? I ask not out of cowardice, but in regard for the importance of this mission. The fate of The Sill depends upon us, and we were only students not long ago."

Cole placed a hand on Wilkin's shoulder, but his words were for the whole unit. "Wilkin is right, this is a job for the senior Unbound, but seeing as we're a little short I chose the next best thing. You have distinguished yourselves as the most effective of the elite units, and believe it or not, combined you are nearly as powerful as I am." Cole paused as the unit let out a collective, empty laugh. He continued through a rueful smile, "I said *nearly*. Truly though, together you are more powerful than I ever was when I trained under my old masters, and I was the strongest in my unit. You're learning and progressing faster than my unit ever did. I'm proud of each of you, and I wouldn't trust this mission to anyone else."

The unit replied with solemn silence this time.

"I agree with almost everything Master Cole just said," Eliza added, hopping up onto her own wagon. "Even the Heart Tree has remarked upon your progress. And while I won't speak ill of my units or any other, I will admit there may have been a few requests from the other groups to train alongside you. But as for Master Cole being the strongest in his unit, I'd say that depends on how you define strength. Is a mastery of Rage an asset when a mere expert in Wisdom can hold you aloft like a child's kite?" With a snap of her fingers she uprooted a nearby boulder the size of a dresser and levitated it above the unit, sprinkling them with dirt. This unit laughed as they shielded their eyes.

"*Why wasn't I told about the requests?*" Cole asked with his mind. "*I would have loved to join our units for a few sessions.*"

Eliza raised an eyebrow. "You were... occupied at the time. The requests have been filed in your office at the Heart Tree."

"Right..." Cole said, turning himself from her amused gaze. He knew of course what he had been occupied with.

Careful not to jostle the fulminators, they spent a few minutes trimming the wheels and axles off the wagons, lessening the load they would have to carry with Wisdom. Cole contacted Rayn while they worked. Even in the brief time since he'd last seen their positions, the Colossi had covered an astonishing distance. Debjornik's original estimation of two or three days now seemed desperately optimistic. Though Rayn was loath to lose both Cole and Eliza for any period of time, he carried out his job to the letter and provided three targets for their bombing mission; a trio of coastal towns within relatively close proximity to one another. Cole gave his thanks and said his farewell to each member of the Heart Tree, then activated the Seer Jar that would take them closest to their enemies.

Eliza went through first, sitting atop her now-wheelless wagon as it floated into the mist. She vanished with a snap of hollow thunder. Wilkin's unit went through next, all perched atop their payload of vine-wrapped fulminators like a family of birds. With Varka's cape guiding his Wisdom, Cole hefted the last cluster of bombs, wondering if Wilkin's unit would be able to hold their load while maintaining other spells. Even without what they trimmed off, each wagon weighed as much as several large Domina.

The concussion shook through his chest as he emerged from the mist alongside the others. The outpost captain greeted Cole with a small team of warriors, offering refreshments and supplies, but there was no time for such things, and no need. However, Cole did take a few miniature Seer Jars, handing one each to Wilkin and Eliza. Should either team become overwhelmed, they would have a way to get back to The Sill.

They took to the skies, and soon the forest village of Simulhost was nothing more than a clutch of brick huts and winking torchlight. Cole had no trouble maintaining contact with Eliza, and he designated Kamilah as Wilkin's conduit of communication, as she was the most Passion-gifted in her unit. The inexperience of Wilkin's unit came to light sooner than Cole expected when he felt the effects of Kamilah's chills and shortness of breath creep in between her thoughts. The unit was so distracted with carrying their load that they had forgotten the basics of high-elevation life-support, such as pressurizing the air they breathed and keeping their bodies warm. After a not-so-gentle reminder from Cole, Wilkin's unit slowed commensurately with the added strain of their enchantments. As the minutes dragged on, the unit showed no sign of stopping their steady plod towards the closest target, which was the harbor town of Belfas.

Once assured Wilkin's unit wasn't going to fall out of the sky, Cole checked the vines securing his wagon, then flew underneath it and put on a surge of speed. He sensed Eliza do the same as she sped off towards her target. A nervous worm wriggled in his gut as both wagons vanished beyond the range of his magically enhanced vision.

The air billowed around Cole's barrier, fluttering and gentle, as though he were in a canoe gliding over smooth waters. He pushed himself higher, until the crisp features of the landscape were no more than vague smudges passing so slowly, he wondered if he was moving at all. A rare quiet permeated the air around him, and while he still kept a firm hold on Eliza's and Kamilah's minds, he couldn't help but appreciate the serene solitude of the moment. He flew out from under the bed of the wagon and did a few slow, graceful loops, flipping until his front faced the sky. An ocean of stars and distant galactic bodies flickered for him in a dazzling show of pale beauty.

His mind wandered unbidden to Earth's starscape as he tried to find familiar constellations, a habit he had fallen into more and more lately. Earth seemed like another lifetime ago, as if his past had been experienced by another person. Giddy wonder swelled in him as a thought struck him for the first time. Should he somehow survive until Aeneria returned to Terra's house, he could venture out with astronomy equipment and observe Earth, perhaps find his hometown if the telescopes were strong enough. He could even join minds with Earth's soul flies and glean some information from their dreams. He realized then that he'd never made a conscious attempt at Traveling, and promised himself to learn the magic from The Sill's libraries as soon as events permitted.

As the minutes turned into hours, Cole retreated to the stone room in the center of his mind, where he reflected on matters closer to his current home. Lileth's fate was his foremost concern, followed by Sitra and Valen, then Eliza and Wilkin's unit. He worried for Amori and Lexy too, not that they were in any immediate danger, but for what kind of women they would grow up to be. Naythan was a busy man, too busy to watch and guide them every minute of the day, and

Cole had never taken the time to really get to know his staff at the academy. The girls deserved mentorship and structure, but most of all they deserved love. They deserved a parent. Cole's thoughts wandered throughout the rest of The Sill, to friends and acquaintances, and to all the people he had yet to meet. The last report from Thessi revealed that with the missions at Borla Dign and Vol Karinn, along with the constant trickling of immigrants, The Sill's population had just reached over ten thousand, a number twice the highest count in history. The achievement was regarded as a testament to their success, but right now it seemed only a reminder of how many relied upon him.

Cole's target came into view at last. Kilkerran lay crowded about the mouth of a river, its hardwood huts and walls darker than the surrounding landscape. Normally he could have crossed the distance within minutes, but with the bulk of the wagon slowing him it was another hour before he arrived, hovering two miles directly above the delta town. Eliza arrived at her target soon afterwards, but Wilkin's unit took another hour still.

"We're still going strong, Master Cole," Kamilah assured him. Cole sensed a drunken haze in her mind, the sort that accompanied an over-exertion of Wisdom. Upon further inspection, Cole discovered she alone was maintaining the spells necessary for her entire unit to see in the dark. Her memories showed the rest of her unit had been similarly affected. *"We can see Belfas."*

"You need to go higher," Cole warned. He projected his thoughts to the entire unit, who were beyond the limits of their Passion and could only listen to his words. *"That Colossus is about a mile tall, and I don't want you within two miles of its head. If you encounter any trouble, any issues at all, drop the bombs and use that Seer Jar. Keep in mind that your exertions will affect your judgment and reaction time."*

There was a brief pause before Kamilah responded with slow, thin words. *"Of course, Master Cole."*

Eliza's worry bled into Cole. *"Are you close enough to take direct control of their minds?"*

"Maybe one or two of them, but not the whole unit," Cole replied. *"Kamilah has the Seer Jar. I'll have her activate it if there's any trouble."*

Cole circled above Kilkerran as he waited for Wilkin's unit to reach their target. He scanned the waters beyond the shoreline, but there was no sign of his Colossus, just distant storm clouds and the dark mounds of an archipelago. He reached back with his mind and contacted the leader of outpost Simulhost, who then relayed his words back to The Sill.

The outpost commander's response came within a few minutes. The mental transmission was weak, but coherent. *"Debjornik says the Colossi should be arriving any minute, and Master Eliza should be there already."*

Cole relayed the words to Eliza. Her shock came at once.

"Stars!" she swore. Cole sensed a sudden dip in her Wisdom as Fear flooded through her. *"Cole, I'm so sorry, it's been here the whole time. I thought it was a part of the landscape. Oh no, I don't think I'm high enough."*

Cole was about to soothe her, but then a sudden motion caught his eye from below. One of the islands was moving.

A figure waded through the ocean. A cloud followed just above it, wispy and streaked with orange stains; Grotton. The surface of the ocean churned from the Colossus as it charged, propagating into towering waves large enough to swallow entire fleets.

Grim determination took hold of Cole as he rose higher to assess his target. *"Eliza, get to height and wait there. Wilkin's unit isn't ready yet, but my Colossus will arrive in a couple of minutes. We need to attack at the same time if we can."* He then turned his Passion to Wilkin's unit. *"Kamilah, how long until you reach Belfas?"*

Kamilah was once again slow to respond. Her words were sluggish and weak, as if her mind had been filled with molasses. *"We are... far. We are... too late? The Colossus is going. Going somewhere else."*

Cole swore. He watched as Grotton's Colossus laid itself down before Kilkerran. Orange clouds gathered in thickening sheets over its bulk. Its head alone filled the entire mouth of the river as swarms of black dots flooded from the streets and into its gaping maw.

"Eliza, can you still hit your Colossus?" Cole asked.

She took a moment to judge her target. *"Yes, but it looks like it's getting ready to leave."*

"*Get ready to drop it,*" Cole replied, then broadened his thoughts to include all of Wilkin's unit. "*Drop your wagons on my command. Set them on the right path with Wisdom, then activate your Seer Jars and get back to The Sill. Kamilah, your unit will have to drop as close as you can. Is everyone ready?*"

"*Ready,*" Eliza responded.

Kamilah's mind swam with confusion. "*But... but... we're not at Belfas yet.*"

"*I know,*" Cole said, funneling as much of his own Wisdom as he could into her mind, but she was too far away to make sense of it. "*Just drop the wagon when I say. Promise me.*"

"*Yes,*" Kamilah said.

Eliza's urgency spilled into Cole's mind as her window of opportunity began to close. Cole floated atop his wagon and took aim at the gargantuan figure below him. "*Release at my command. Three... two... one... RELEASE!*"

The wagon rushed away from him, leaving behind a hollow whistle and a trail of dancing leaves. A measure of Cole's Wisdom returned, bringing everything into sharp clarity. He took hold of his Rage, which further slowed things for him and allowed him time to think. He guided his wagon with gentle nudges of Wisdom, steadying it as the payload tumbled lazily towards the center of the Colossus's back.

Once certain his aim was true, Cole dug through his robes and took out his Seer Jar, then checked on the others. Eliza showed him her wagon, which was seconds away from a direct hit with the head of her Colossus. Kamilah's eyes showed their wagon dropping a mile away from Belfas, but it was somehow moving laterally towards the retreating Colossus. Kamilah's hands fumbled with her Seer Jar as a horrifying revelation rang through her mind.

"*Wilkin!*" she cried, and through her eyes Cole saw a tiny speck racing alongside their wagon. Wilkin flew like a spear, arms outstretched in a green glow as he pushed the wagon towards the Colossus with every ounce of Wisdom he had.

"*Kamilah, stop him!*" Cole shouted into her mind, but her Fear echoed back in waves of crippling dread.

A blinding light flared from below. Cole squinted and threw a hand out to shield his eyes. A few seconds later a shockwave struck him with the force of an avalanche, ripping his eardrums and stunning him so that he dropped his spell for flight. Varka's cape flapped uselessly behind his shoulders as he fell headfirst towards Kilkerran.

CHAPTER 26

TRUTH AND TREACHERY

The roar of wind felt like daggers twisting in his ears. Cole's eyes stung and watered, blinded as by a thousand midday suns. Heat seared his face. Confusion mingled with worry, replacing coherent thought. Was he falling?

The light before him dimmed, revealing a boiling sphere of coalescing colors a mile below him. Eddies of green bloomed among erupting reds and dancing lavenders. The ball faded and realization yanked Cole back to reality as he beheld the Alpha Colossus. In the middle of its back was gaping hole a quarter of a mile wide, through which was nothing but scarred earth streaked with char.

Cole brought Wisdom to the moment and stopped himself in midair, then healed his ears with quick bursts of Passion from his fingertips. He reached for Eliza with his mind, but she was gone, hopefully back at The Sill. He searched for Kamilah and found her frozen with a Fear not of her own. The Colossus began to stir below him. Its wound churned as bodies of the Chosen poured forth to replace the ones the fulminators had vaporized. A sharp wave snapped through Varka's cape and Cole shot back to the sky.

"Kamilah, can you hear me?" Cole asked, though he had a feeling she couldn't. His words echoed back, dripping with Fear.

Suffusing himself in the mastery of his Rage and Passion, Cole rushed his mind through the link to Kamilah. He emerged in her thoughts like a torch, shielding her from the darkness within her mind, which he recognized at once as Decreath's presence. Cole found Kamilah huddled in her center, a bubbling pool set at the base of a small waterfall. He enveloped her with his Passion and took command of her body and mind.

Cole opened Kamilah's eyes. She was falling. Bloated clouds of purple passed her on all sides. Using her Passion, Cole located everyone in her unit, even Wilkin, who was now well over a mile away. Too far for what he must do. The rest of her unit was nearby, but they were saturated with Decreath's presence, each walking the razor's edge between life and death. There was no time. Without further hesitation, Cole took command of Kamilah's Wisdom and yanked them close, then with her hands he activated the Seer Jar.

Kamilah's mind vanished as Cole's focus returned to his own body. The Colossus was back on its feet, staring directly up at Cole, a grin of Hunger twisting its misshapen head. Clouds thick as vomit rose up in columns of billowing orange smoke as guttural laughter began to fill Cole from the inside out.

Defiant and heartbroken, Cole hung in the air and withstood the maddening presence for as long as he could.

"I see you, Grotton," Cole said, projecting his thoughts for the dark god to hear.

The laughter grew louder as seductive forces began to worm their way through Cole's mental armor.

Cole shut his eyes as tears rolled down his cheeks. He hugged his Seer Jar tight against his chest. "I'm so sorry, Wilkin."

Hollow thunder rattled him, then Cole's feet struck solid ground. A flowery breeze carried the Seer Jar's mist away from him. He was back in The Sill, standing in one of the pergolas surrounding the training field. He felt Eliza before he saw her. She was ministering to the unit, who stood huddled together in front of the pergola next to Cole's, their faces perplexed and eyes searching. Cole stepped off the platform and onto the cool grass.

Eliza looked at him, eyes wide. *"What happened?"*

"I couldn't save them all," Cole said, his words heavy with Despair. Rather than explain, he showed her the brief moment in which he commanded Kamilah's body and mind. Eliza winced as his shame and heartache stung her.

The unit stirred as talk broke out among them. Judging by their questions, they had no idea what had just occurred, why they were at

The Sill. Kamilah was the only silent one. She stood quiet and still as she stared beyond the field to her memories.

Grant approached Kamilah and gave her a pat on the shoulder. "Good call activating that Seer Jar. I owe you one. We all do."

"That was the worst thing I've ever felt," Kolric said, hugging himself. "Was that Decreath?"

"Had to have been," Bennit replied. "That Fear was far too powerful to be anyone else. I blacked out right after that cloud came up. I wanted to see that explosion too. Wilkin, how close did you get with that bomb anyway?"

The unit shuffled around as they scanned for their leader. When they couldn't find him they looked farther out, as though expecting to find him hiding behind a distant tree. Cole sensed their Passion cast out for his life candle, then saw the horror bloom on their faces.

Viness shook her head slowly, then looked to the small figure who had yet to blink. "Kamilah," she pleaded through a sob. Grim silence fell over the unit.

Serra stormed across the grass. There was a flash of black and suddenly Kamilah was in the air, held aloft by Serra's munisica. The bladed fingers were wrapped snugly around Kamilah's neck as her feet kicked out for support.

"You left him behind!" Serra screamed in wild Rage. "You left Wilkin to die!"

"Release her, Serra," Cole said. He would have used Passion on her, but at the moment the magic was beyond him. "Kamilah had no part in it. I was the one who chose to leave Wilkin behind." He heard Eliza let out a quiet gasp beside him.

Serra lowered Kamilah to the ground, though she still kept a firm grip on her neck. Disgust soured through the fury on her face. "You... ordered her to do it?"

"I made her do it," Cole said with a grave nod. He then turned to his left. "Eliza, please."

Blinking herself back to the present, Eliza noticed Serra and Kamilah at last. Her face softened as the air stirred. She exuded Passion, soothing and comforting them all as it spread throughout the area in waves. Relief washed over the faces of the unit. Serra's munisica retreated as her shoulders and head drooped with guilt, then Kamilah pulled her into a tight embrace. The two girls held each other, each shaking with sobs as grief took them.

"Please, Master Cole," Grant began with disbelief in his eyes. "Explain what you mean by that. You were miles away, weren't you?"

"I was," Cole said, struggling to keep the sorrow from his voice. "But not far enough where I couldn't take control of Kamilah's mind and body. I made her activate the Seer Jar, then used her Wisdom to pull you into its mist. Wilkin was too far away, and I…" A gasping breath escaped his throat before it snapped itself shut. His vision blurred as the tears came at last. He wasn't supposed to show weakness in front of them, a lesson he once taught Wilkin.

Cole didn't quite recall what happened next. Apologies were exchanged through touch or choked voices, then Eliza sent the unit back to the barracks, leaving her and Cole alone. She put an arm around him and guided him behind the sentinel trees, away from the view of the open field, then held him. Cole's legs crumpled beneath him as he fell to his knees, hugging her legs. He cried for a long while, so long that he knew he was wasting what little time they had left. Eliza kept a steady stream of Passion flowing into him, easing his Despair the best she could, but it was as effective as turning a desert into an ocean one bucket at a time. Cole grieved not only for whatever undying torture Wilkin would endure; he grieved for the fate of everyone he loved, for the end times had come at last.

When it became apparent his anguish was inconsolable, Eliza extended the familiar music of their old Passion link, the private one they first created on their mission in Costas. Cole knew he shouldn't, but her soul felt like a ray of warm sunshine piercing through his Despair. He grasped it, attuned his song to hers, then their old link reignited in a blaze of friendship and something deeper. He tried to hold his Despair back so as not to overwhelm her, but she took it all, sharing in every thorn of grief and guilt and dread that racked him. The storm lifted at last, leaving nothing but pure golden light.

Cole rose to his feet and gave her a rueful smile, then withdrew from the link. "Thank you."

Eliza appraised him for a moment. Cole thought he saw a shadow of regret pass over her face, but it was gone before he could be sure. She gave him a curt nod. "Roth told you this would happen, at Deekus's funeral. He was right; it never does get easier."

"He also said to stop making friends," Cole said. "But I don't think he was right about that. Thank you, Eliza, really."

"Of course," Eliza said with another sharp nod. "Shall we go debrief with the Heart Tree? I'm curious to see what sort of affect we had. If your fulminators were anywhere near as potent as mine, then The Three will think twice about walking over our walls."

Back in the Heart Tree, Eliza and Cole each projected their memories on a portable stage set in the corner of the room, rather than explain the details of their mission. Thessi's initial outrage at the loss of so many gratia stones was quickly stifled when she saw the damage done to the Alpha Colossi. By the time they finished their accounts, Debjornik had already begun to receive encouraging reports. Of the two Colossi they hit, there was a marked decrease in their speed, and Rayn's team assessed their overall mass to have diminished by twenty percent. However, the Colossus they missed was moving faster than ever, and had ceased making stops to pick up reinforcements. While discussing what to do next, Falinor stood up suddenly and informed them that his naval scouts reported sightings of enemy ships heading towards The Sill. Cole rose to his feet and readied his Wisdom for flight, but Falinor stopped him.

"Whoa whoa whoa," Falinor shouted, waving his hands in the air. "Unless you two plan on fighting every rotten monster on this planet, I suggest you have yourselves a seat. Have a meal and a nap while you're at it."

"What are you talking about?" Cole demanded.

"You're bushed," Thessi said in a matter-of-fact tone as she stood and walked over to a tall cabinet. She threw open the doors and withdrew a couple of potions, then tossed a blackstout to each of them. "We may not be as keen on our magic as you are, but even we can see when you need a break. Especially you, Cole. I doubt you have the Passion to heal a bruise right now."

Confused, Cole and Eliza caught the blackstouts and looked to the other members of the staff.

"It's not sustainable," Debjornik said, shaking his head.

"Not at all," Wareen agreed, scanning Cole and Eliza with piercing eyes.

"We'll replenish on the flight out," Cole protested. "There isn't time to sit here and wait.

Rayn cleared his throat and folded his hands in front of him, then spoke in a tone that suggested he was explaining something to a child. "We are in siege. That means our tactics must change from taking ground to holding it. Resources must be managed differently. Time, food, energy, even you are a resource that we must use efficiently so that we might exhaust our enemies through attrition. The Sill's walls will hold back all but The Three themselves, and our warriors can manage whatever foes attack from the sky. Our strategies show that The Unbound would best serve The Sill as a final line of defense. That way if The Three or one of their more powerful minions assaults us from an unexpected front, you will already be within The Sill, where you will be in the best position to react."

"At the very least don't go squandering yourselves on the front lines," Falinor said. "We've got grunts for that."

Frustration tightened the muscles in Cole's neck and balled his hands into fists. He knew they were right, but he also knew that he and Eliza could sink a fleet of ships without a single casualty. Each of their warriors had cherished loved ones, colorful histories, and plans for the future. He might be nothing more than a resource, but so were the lives of their people. He couldn't allow another Wilkin.

Eliza's words strummed into his thoughts. *"If you want to go then I will of course be right behind you, but keep in mind Sitra and Valen will emerge from The Havenflow in a few hours. They may need our help, or perhaps they'll be so powerful that they'll eliminate The Three's forces with ease. Either way we need to enter as soon as possible, especially with Decreath's Colossus approaching so swiftly."*

Grudgingly, Cole set aside his emotions and agreed to stay behind. Eliza left to tend to her duties for the people of Vol Karinn, leaving Cole to monitor things with the staff of the Heart Tree, who had dispersed back to their separate offices in the floors below. To his annoyance, his Passion was so depleted that he couldn't join the mental network with the staff, and so he wandered from floor to floor observing the operations of each department in person. Each office was a swarm of activity, the chaos of which overwhelmed Cole at first, but after watching for a moment, a flow of productivity revealed itself to him, putting some of his worry to rest.

He stayed in the Training Center the longest. Magic had been mingled with the natural construction of the room. Gratia stones embedded in the walls powered various devices. Holographic displays contained charts and graphs used for tracking locations and statuses of the assault companies. A collection of Seer Jars sat in cubbies cut into the walls, one for each outpost, though most were empty and dark now that siege operations had begun. A map table dominated the center of the chamber. Cole watched it for a while. Blinking dots showed the progress of their fleets patrolling in defensive formations around The Sill. One of Falinor's assistants informed him that it would be at least an hour before the enemy ships would arrive. Feeling helpless yet hopeful, Cole left the Heart Tree and set out for Naythan's.

The Sill was oddly dull without his Passion. Cole was blind to the gardens of the life candles, and deaf to their symphony of emotions. The routine spells that heightened his senses left him far from insensate, but his lack of Passion unnerved him, especially when Naythan's academy came into view and he was unable to discern the activities within. He knew something was wrong before he entered through the window he departed from. An ominous shadow seemed to reach out from the depths of the room, empty and dark, like a ghost from some forgotten crypt. Something had happened.

Cole landed beside the empty couch. There was no one in the room. "Lileth!" he shouted. "Naythan!"

No one answered. He suddenly remembered Naythan saying he would have to move her. He pushed through the liquid stone door and delved further into the house. Following the muffled sounds of activities around him, Cole wandered through halls and popped into a classroom, startling the students within. To his great relief, Naythan stood at the front of the room, a look of mild shock upon his face.

"Where's Lileth?" Cole demanded.

Naythan stared up through the ceiling and spoke in an airy tone: "Lileth? Why I left her sound asleep up in my…" his voice trailed off as he began scanning the walls and floor. "Well that can't be right. I can't sense Professor Lileth anywhere. She's not in the building, or anywhere on the academy grounds, but where else could she have gone?" He then looked to Cole, shaking his head with a little smirk as if Cole was overreacting. "I wouldn't worry yourself overmuch. I'd wager she merely wandered off to the Arts District for some crafting supplies. You should see her work, there's quite a bit of it displayed on the grounds. She made this one tree out of brass wire, marvelous thing, thousands of strands all twisting out from the trunk like real wood."

Something wasn't right. Cole stared at Naythan. It was most unusual for the hermit to teach classes himself, and Cole was positive that his Passion was more than capable of scanning the whole of The Sill's island. The most worrying thing of all was Naythan's cavalier attitude towards Lileth, whom they had just seen crying blood a few hours ago.

"Thank you, Naythan, I'll go have a look in the Arts District now," Cole said, bowing out of the room. Naythan jabbered on as if there had been no interruption at all, seamlessly directing his rant back towards the class, who sat eagerly on the edge of their seats.

In the hallway, Cole shut his eyes and searched within himself for his Passion. A small pool had replenished itself, just enough to work the most basic of magic. He extended his mind out as far as it would go, his head throbbing with the effort, but his Passion only revealed the life candles within ten paces. Cole scanned through every room as he tore through the halls of the academy on the off chance Lileth was merely concealing her life candle. Munisica sprouted from his feet as his Rage hastened his stride. His search brought him up to Naythan's office on the top floor, which gave him an idea. He knew the room was empty before he entered, but there was something else in there he needed.

Cole yanked open the drawers in Naythan's desk, riffling through papers and crafts from the girls, casting them aside. He yanked on the doors to a tall cabinet in the corner of the room, but they wouldn't budge. A quick scan revealed the cabinet had been both reinforced and locked with Wisdom. Cole couldn't guess how to counter the spells, but with the help of Varka's cape he was able to circumvent them. Hidden latches snapped within as the cabinet door sprang open. Lying upon the shelves were hundreds of cyphers, their brass labels describing various memories or parts of convoluted spells, but they weren't what he was looking for either. Cole was about to abandon his search when his Wisdom sharpened, and his ears picked up a faint hum he could feel vibrating his toes.

Wrapping his Wisdom around the heavy cabinet, Cole slid it across the floor, revealing a hidden door. He tugged on the iron-ring handle and the door creaked open, exposing a fat omnistone brimming with energy. Cole slapped his palm to its glassy surface and drew Passion into himself, Passion he recognized as his own, payment for Naythan's services. Cole thought it curious that the old hermit had yet to use the vast majority of the magic within the stone. With half his Passion replenished, Cole ceased the flow of energy and shut his eyes, expanding the touch of his mind throughout The Sill to the ocean beyond. A teeming hive of lights popped into existence as life candles of The Sill's citizens revealed themselves before his mind's eye. Thousands swirled about him in a galaxy of activity, but not one carried Lileth's song. He was about to ask Eliza for help when he felt an odd gap in the world, a fragile void out by the docks. He couldn't be sure it was her, but someone was indeed hiding himself or herself from magical detection.

After replacing the cabinet to the corner of the room, Cole created a window in the wall and sailed through, Varka's cape fluttering gently across his back as he shot up towards the stars. The outline of Cole's body shimmered and vanished as he cast a spell to make himself invisible, then suppressed his own life force so whoever was hiding at the docks wouldn't sense him coming. He passed through layers of chilled cloud vapor as he neared the towering canopy of The Sill's walls. The world was quiet at such a height, as birds rarely expended the energy to fly so high. Cole stretched out an invisible hand to stroke the needle tips of the pines, then recoiled as a face smiled up at him.

"Off again I see," Whind said. He stood perched in a thin upper branch while holding onto another with a single hand. A thick coat of pine needles replaced his usual attire of woven leaves and soft bark. His body swayed in the breeze as if he were just another limb in the tree. "It is not wise to circumvent my gates, even for a Wisdom Walker such as you. Had I not recognized you before you hid yourself from view, I might have thought you hostile and attacked."

"I'm sorry, Whind," Cole said. "I'm just hopping out for a minute and didn't want to be seen. I'll come back in through a gate, I promise."

"Of course," Whind said with a polite nod at the bodiless voice above him.

Cole took Whind's silence as permission to pass, and so he continued over the canopy, still invisible, but paused as a question came to him. "Have you noticed anything odd lately?"

Whind's eyes remained on the horizon as he spoke. "The Sill is an odd place, even for Aeneria. I have observed many queer things within its walls, especially in recent months."

"I mean have you seen anything odd *today*," Cole said with a prickle of Rage. "Did anyone sneak out recently?"

"I would not know if they did, now would I?" Whind said. By the tone of his voice, Cole could tell he wasn't being difficult on purpose. Whind was a strange fellow as long as Cole had known him.

"Please let me know if you do," Cole asked.

Whind gave a slow nod. "Of course, Wisdom Walker."

Without waiting for a further reply, Cole plunged over the canopy of the wall trees like a spear, aiming for the docks where he felt the void. Part of him wanted to warn Eliza in case he ran into trouble, but if the void was Lileth then he'd rather not trouble her. Their most recent connection with Passion revealed that her feelings towards him hadn't faded in the slightest.

Cole hovered over the docks, invisible and silent. He followed his Passion to where he felt the void, a tired old canoe which floated a little lower than its fellows. Alighting on the edge of the dock, Cole found a shivering lump of rough canvas nestled in the craft's hull. His eyes followed the mooring rope, where it hung loosely halfway up a deck post, as if someone had started freeing the vessel but suddenly lost the strength to do so. With a flick of his hand he tossed the canvas to the other side of the boat. Lileth was curled up under the seat, fast asleep and trembling all over. Cole shed his spells and scooped her up into his arms. Her skin felt like stone pulled from a frozen river.

"Where am I?" Lileth moaned.

"You are with me," Cole said in a soft voice. At his command, Wisdom brought warmth into his arms, and within seconds the chill fled from Lileth's body as if she'd been basking by a roaring fire. Cole poured his Passion forth next, easing the shakes of starvation from her body.

Coherence returned to her as the magic did its job. Lileth blinked in her surroundings, then flexed herself out of Cole's arms and stood tall and dignified, but when she spoke it was with a voice of one in deep hurt.

"Ka… Ka Reine," Lileth stated, voice cracking. She winced with some unseen agony, then steadied herself with a sharp exhale. "It's been her all along, tormenting me in my dreams. Fear, Hunger, Hatred and Despair, she's been using them all against me while I sleep. Stars, I've been so foolish. She must have been worming her way in for months. I can still feel her." Tears welled in her eyes and she let out a sob. She blinked, and a single drop of blood ran down her cheek.

Cole pulled her into a tight hug. "It's okay now, you're safe. I've got you."

"*What's going on?*" Eliza's voice beamed into Cole's mind, tight and alert. "*What are you doing outside the walls, and who is that with you?*"

"*I found Lileth,*" Cole said.

Confusion fluttered throughout Eliza's thoughts. "*I didn't know she was missing. Wasn't she at Naythan's?*"

"*She was,*" Cole replied. "*Meet me at my apartment and bring one of your units. I'll explain on the way.*" Cole began streaming memories to her as he returned the majority of his mind to Lileth.

"Am I going mad?" Lileth asked into Cole's chest.

"Of course you're not," Cole said, rubbing her back. "Let's get you somewhere safe. Can you walk?"

Lileth shook her head. "I don't think I can trust my legs. I can't trust anything."

Cole swept his arm under her as his feet left the ground, his Wisdom lifting them both into a gentle flight just a few feet above the ground. He used the Lurkwood Gate, where Whind was already waiting with the tunnel raised. The gatekeeper betrayed no look of surprise, rather he simply inclined his head in acknowledgment as they passed.

Eliza stood at the base of Cole's apartment tree accompanied by one of her units, who under Cole's relayed orders, took up defensive positions around the trunk. Cole landed on the ramp and urged Eliza to follow as he passed through the liquid stone door. He set Lileth on his bed, then he and Eliza wove spells throughout the tree, encapsulating the room with barriers against mental and magical penetrations. They tied the magic to an omnistone embedded in the wall, which brimmed with energy Cole had squirreled away since his arrival.

"Here, take these," Cole said, offering Lileth a blackstout and one of Valen's stimulating potions. "She can't get to you if you're awake."

Lileth downed the elixir in a long, graceful swallow, then began peeling the blackstout absentmindedly. "I'm not sure I am. None of us are while Ka Reine still draws breath. Has anyone checked on the children?"

"All is well inside our walls," Cole said. He had already used his Passion to check directly with the Heart Tree, as well as Naythan and Ka Reine's guards. "The children have no idea what happened, and additional guards have been summoned to Ka Reine's cell. They tell me she hasn't moved or made any apparent attempts at hostility since we put her in there." Cole knelt down beside the bed and put a hand on Lileth's knee. "Are you sure it was Ka Reine and not some other demon bred by The Three?"

Lileth slouched and hugged herself as if a chill had just crept into the room. "When it first started happening, I hadn't the slightest inkling that I wasn't alone in my mind. The dreams came and went like some foul wind, but they began to linger into the waking hours, weighing me down with the most horrible sensations. It happened so gradually that I didn't notice. All I wanted to do was sleep, even though I knew it was making me worse. During my last dream state she made her presence quite clear." Lileth's hands balled into fists, then hardened into knots of black knives as her munisica sprang forth. "She must have known the rest of the Unbound were gone and decided that was her chance to take me."

"Ka Reine has one of the most powerful minds on Aeneria," Eliza said. "The fact that you resisted for so long is incredible. I do wonder though, how in the world did you end up outside The Sill? Whind would have noticed if you wandered out. Even if you flew."

Lileth's eyes darted about, reconstructing what looked like broken memories. "I remember crawling. Dirt, blood, and darkness. I had terrible urges not of my own, urges to hurt myself and others. I held on to what little of myself she couldn't take, the part of me made from Cole and you and the others, and I used that to push my body as far away as possible."

"How did no one notice you?" Eliza demanded, fury hammering in her words. "The Sill is overpopulated, why didn't anyone see you and help?"

The answer came to Cole in a flash of revelation. "I found her, but it was more of a lucky guess. I couldn't sense her with my Passion, but I could sense a void in the world. Her life force had been stifled to the edge of death, just like what happened to you when you escaped Borla Dign. The Three do that to you. I felt it happening to me on our last mission when I got too close to Grotton. It seems now that they all have their Harbingers, the mere presence of one is enough to kill a person. Ka Reine has become a hand of The Three."

"What I'm most concerned about is how she was able to affect me while she's in prison," Lileth said. "Brinleaf's spellcasters assured us that nothing magical or material would be able to pass through the walls of her cell."

"Dreams are a thing beyond the magic and material," Eliza said in a quiet voice. "Soul flies and Wisdom Walkers use dreams to pass between the limits of realities. It would be no great feat for a potent mind such as Ka Reine's to dream her way through a prison wall, no matter what spells or material is used." Eliza shut her eyes for a moment as her tone shifted to one of defeat. "How in Oberon's grace are we supposed to fight something like that?"

Cole knew it wasn't really a question, rather a statement of the daunting challenges bearing down on all of them. He had endured

Grotton's presence, and could have for some time longer, but that would be all he could do. To fight or work magic while battling an essence of evil was still beyond him.

Lileth reached over and took Eliza's hand in hers, their intertwined fingers glowing with pink light. "We fight by standing together. I have been idle for too long. I will rejoin the Unbound, if you will have me that is."

Eliza hesitated for a moment, as if she might say no, but then shook her head with a soft chuckle. "Of course we'll have you. You never left us, not really."

"Are you sure you're ready for this?" Cole asked in a gentle tone. He winced as he thought about what to say next as it wouldn't be easy for her to hear, but now wasn't the time to soften his words, not when lives would depend on her. "The Unbound have grown while you've been teaching at Naythan's. We've taken our training far beyond where it was when you resigned, and it's not like we'll be training anymore. We'll be faster and stronger, and some of our techniques will be new to you. Lileth, I love you and I want nothing more than to have you at my side, but we have to be certain you can operate at an effective level. There can be no doubt here."

Lileth's eyes bowed a little lower with each word, but her back remained straight and proud. "Ka Reine's shadow still lingers in me, but now that I know it was her all along and not my own mind unraveling on itself, I can take steps to cleanse and heal. She made a mistake in assuming I was weak enough to succumb to a direct attack. She's not as powerful as we thought she was." She then brought her eyes to Cole's, her gaze steadfast and burning with desire. "I am ready to fight alongside the Unbound."

Cole nodded. Part of him was relieved to have her back, though another part of him dreaded what he must do next. "This means we have to kill Ka Reine. Now, before she can infect anyone else."

"Agreed," Lileth said.

"Well I *don't* agree," Eliza said.

"Why not?" Cole demanded. "I loathe killing as much as you do, but she's a danger to everyone we're fighting for, and a drain on our resources with the number of guards we have to keep at her cell.

We have all the proof we need." Cole then spoke directly and privately into her mind. *"Do you not trust Lileth? Is this a jealousy thing?"*

Eliza's cheeks flushed as her eyes went wide. "Because we don't have the proof we need. Ka Reine is one of The Sill's oldest and most trusted allies. I'm not saying she's beyond suspicion, especially since she won't submit to a mental inspection, but we have no proof that she is acting of her own free will. You said it yourself, only The Three have displayed the power to poison someone's life force to the brink of death. For all we know she has been enchanted by some powerful priest, or even one of The Three."

"I am ashamed," Lileth said, her brow tightening, "that I was so quick to prescribe execution before considering all the possibilities. Perhaps I am not ready to rejoin the Unbound if my desire for revenge outweighs my sense of logic. Thank you, Eliza, for correcting me. What do you suggest?"

"At the very least we ought to break her mind and pry the answers from her," Eliza said. "But we should wait until we have Sitra and Valen with us. In the meantime you have to stop sleeping."

"That... seems fair," Lileth said. Cole thought he saw a shadow of regret pass through her eyes. "I'm not sure I can afford the dream-source cypher in my current state."

Without a word, Eliza plunged a hand into a pocket in her robes, then tossed an object the size of a bird's egg to Lileth. Eliza surveyed Lileth with a look of challenge.

"How long have you been carrying this?" Lileth asked as she held a dreamsource cypher up to the light. The inside of the orb bloomed with viscous greens and hazels.

"Not long," Eliza said. "Cole told me what happened right after he found you at the docks. I knew there was a good chance we'd have to stop you from sleeping, so I flew up to the Cordial Compendium before meeting you here. If you really want to rejoin the Unbound, then commit, right here and now."

Cole took his hand from Lileth's knee and rose to his feet. "That's not necessary. She just downed a whole bottle of Valen's potion. Give her a day to recover at least. She won't be able to sleep tonight anyway."

"There is no time," Lileth said as she rolled the orb in her fingers. "The Three will be here by then. I must do this."

The cypher dissolved in her hand, spilling like a liquid through her fingers, only to reform into tendrils of gaseous light that twirled back up into her eyes. Lileth was quiet for a moment. Her eyes snapped shut, though they darted about under her lids as the knowledge settled in her mind. When she opened them, it was with a sad smile.

"How do you fe—" Cole gasped as Lileth fell forward of the bed, collapsing in his arms. "Lileth!" He shook her and shouted her name again and again, but she hung there, limp and lifeless.

Eliza swooped low and cradled Lileth's head in her hands. A few seconds later she turned her gaze to Cole, alarmed and incredulous. "This is impossible."

"What is it?" Cole pleaded.

"She's asleep," Eliza said.

Cole extended his mind towards Lileth's, intent on wrenching her back to the waking world, but something lashed back at him. He dove back in, and the thing struck once more, painful and powerful. Cole tried to focus his efforts in order to overpower the foreign presence; however, it had no focal point. It permeated her entire mind and flitted between evil magics too quickly for him to react to it. Despair-Rage-Hunger-Passion-Despair-Fear-Hate. There was no way to counter it. The thing entwined itself about her mind like a snake protecting its eggs, ready to strike at anyone who got too close.

"What is that?" Eliza said, horrorstuck.

Cole didn't answer. He scanned Lileth's body to ensure nothing else was awry, then lifted her and set her on his bed. Cole made for the door. Rage the likes of which he had never felt seared through his limbs, scalding him from the inside out.

"Wait, where are you going?" Eliza asked, rising to her feet and following him to the door.

The shroud of Rage bloomed over Cole's skin like a wave of black death. He thrust his bladed fist and hit the liquid stone door faster than it could react. The door exploded outwards in a hail of heavy rock and dust. Varka's cape snapped to flat, clear crystal, and Cole shot out into the sky.

He could hear Eliza's voice fade behind him, feel her mind press against his own, but this moment was not for her. This was a moment for action. His Passion yielded to him like a loyal hunting dog, showing him exactly where to go. The air exploded around him as he commanded his Wisdom into speed, causing the titanic pines around him to shudder and rain swarms of needles. Rage slowed things for him, and after several slow seconds, he arrived at The Sill's first and only prison.

The prison was set in a far corner of The Sill, hidden in a bare glade devoid of vegetation, a stain on the land made by an errant spell cast long ago. It was a single dome-shaped building made from metal harvested from deep within Aeneria's crust, large enough for several people to live comfortably inside, though only one person lay within. Rage stones were embedded along its sides, fueling spells that laced the metal walls with its black shroud. Twenty-one guards were lined up around the prison wall, warriors plucked from Falinor's elite. At Cole's approach, the guards flinched and readied offensive spells and munisica.

Cole's bladed feet plowed through the earth as he collided with the ground like a falling star. Seamlessly, he continued on in a steady stride as the debris fell around him, revealing his identity to the guards, who dropped their spells at once.

The leader of the watch came trotting up to greet him, a tall, capable-looking woman garbed in armored robes plated with Morthainian glass. They had never met, but Cole knew of her feats on the training field.

"Master Cole!" she cried out in relief. "What brings you all the way out here?"

"I'm going in," Cole said. The shroud in his throat cast his voice in sharp menace.

The guard winced, then trotted alongside Cole to keep up. "But... your orders. It was your decree that the prison was to remain locked until the Heart Tree voted otherwise, that not even you—"

"I know what my orders were," Cole snapped. "Unlock it or I'll break it."

The woman stopped, and Cole detected the strumming of Passion through the air. He kept walking. He was only a few paces from the prison wall and had no intention of waiting for her. He flexed his munisica. His whole body ached with the challenge of tearing into something worthy of his destruction.

"Unlock the cell!" the woman cried from behind him.

Two guards rushed forth, halting in between Cole and the metal wall. They faced each other and wove their hands in intricate patterns, producing geometric patterns of green light between them. One guard fumbled with the cooperative spell, obviously nervous at the sight of Cole's shrouded state. After another attempt they had the spell properly formed, and they levitated the web of complicated patterns into the wall, where it slid perfectly into a series of thin cutouts. There was a sound like a bell, then a portion of the wall beside them rippled in the shape of a doorframe. He felt protests of mental chatter against his mental armor, like insects battering a screened window for entrance. Cole ignored them and pushed his way in through the door.

The life candles of The Sill winked out of his awareness as a single pyre erupted in the prison before him. The door popped behind him as Cole stepped into the cell. As he had ordered, the room was designed to be as comfortable as possible so Ka Reine wouldn't want for anything. Artifice had been blended masterfully with nature, giving the room the appearance of a cozy, secluded corner of The Sill. The floor was carpeted with plush moss and woven-root walkways laced over runnels of fresh water. The ceiling and walls had been enchanted so the room was much larger inside, and seemed to continue on forever with open skies and views of glens farther in. Here and there furniture had been plied from living trees and giant mushrooms, including a hammock of vines, a chair and desk made from a cluster of braided saplings, a hulking tree stump with a glass door displaying various dishes, and several full bookshelves which looked untouched. Behind a tree, sitting on the ground, Cole saw two buckled boots sticking lazily out away from him, one tapping rhythmically against the other. The rest of the Old One's body was hidden behind the trunk of the tree.

"Brave of you to come here," Ka Reine said, her voice fuzzy and full of pipe smoke. A plume of violet billowed from behind the tree. "Stupid to come alone. What if I decide to take my revenge out of your mind?"

Cole stopped several paces behind the tree. "You and I are not as equal as you think. Last time we did our best to keep you alive, a much harder task than simply killing you. I'm not feeling so generous today."

Ka Reine let out a soft, scratchy laugh. "Found your traitor at last, have you? Got all the proof you need?"

Cole slashed his hand through the air. A whip of emerald light tore through the tree, severing it cleanly in half just above where he guessed Ka Reine's head to be. The top portion of the tree slid and collided to the moss floor, then tipped and crashed through a bookshelf and the hammock. Another plume of smoke rose from behind the trunk.

"Submit to an inspection now, or the next one's going across your neck," Cole said. Magic crackled between his claws.

"You've got a long way to go before you've earned the right to my thoughts, or the ability to behold them," Ka Reine sighed. "I'll strike a bargain with you: If you somehow manage to quell the Shadow Tide and win this war, then I'll let you have a go. Be warned, however, my mind is not some novel you can skim through on a cozy rainy day. I have watched eons pass through the local planets before humans learned to walk upright. I'm guessing you don't have that kind of time, seeing that The Three will be here in less than a day."

Curiosity blossomed before Cole's Rage. How could she know about The Three? The walls of her prison should have blocked any and all communications inside and out. The only explanation was that she had gleaned information through meddling with the dreams of everyone at The Sill. He knew he ought to kill her now and rid The Sill of one of its greatest threats, but there was a chance that he would need Ka Reine to undo whatever spells she was currently tormenting Lileth with.

"What have you done to Lileth?" Cole demanded, walking around the severed stump. He wanted her to see him, to see death standing before her, to know her life depended on her answer.

Ka Reine regarded him with a fleeting, expressionless glance, then took a moment to pull off her pipe again. "I didn't do anything to the girl that she didn't deserve. I'd kill her now for pity's sake, but she's too far gone. By the looks of it she's already taken you with her. Should have killed her proper the first time I found the two of you traipsing about Aeneria stealing everything you could get your hands on."

"Untie your tongue and give me the truth," Cole barked, taking a step closer. His munisica stretched even longer, itching with gratifying pain.

Ka Reine scoffed and waved her hand dismissively. "Truth! If you can't see the truth even when it's spreading its legs before you every night, then this age is already beyond saving. Why don't you ask Varka about the truth. He's in there listening to every word we say, but he's too cowardly to come out and show you. He still pines for her."

Cole paused. Deep within himself he felt a longing agony that was not his own. Ghosts of memories flitted about the periphery of his mind; of days spent on the open ocean, of ceaseless wonder and adventure, of a profound love as wild as it was thrilling. An odd, flowery scent filled his nose. He recognized the fragrance as a black velvet hyacinth, a plant he had only smelled once during a private lesson with Chiron far away, but now the scent felt like the comfort of home. He opened his eyes, not realizing he had ever closed them, and looked to Ka Reine. "What... what are you talking about?"

Ka Reine's wrinkles deepened as she grinned, clearly amused by his confusion. She spoke in a slow, clear voice. "Binary souls."

"What is that?" Cole asked, now struggling to maintain the hold on his Rage as something else more dangerous began to spread like brush fire.

"This life is not the first time you and Lileth have met," Ka Reine explained. "The last time I saw the two of you was in your prior lives, and you went by the names Varka and Vex. Varka was as precocious as he was lonely, but he was a good boy all the same. Vex on the other hand had a shadow of evil in her that could only be sated in the lust of sex, thievery, and search for power. Rotten slattern she was. Hunger ruled her heart, just as it rules Lileth's now. I should have recognized

Vex's melody in Lileth's soul long before you threw me in this prison, but it seems I've grown complacent. Lileth is not who she seems to be. I doubt she even fully understands who she is. If you have any desire to save this world, end her life before her betrayal bears any more fruit. Kill me too if it pleases you. I'd wager a death by your hands would be preferable to whatever The Three have planned for me."

"Liar," Cole snarled. The thing that kindled inside him was now a roaring inferno. It wasn't true, couldn't be true. He loved Lileth, and even now felt her love thriving within him. It was a love born in battle and sacrifice and saving each other's lives. Ka Reine was merely trying to stall him to give The Three more time, and Lileth's torment continued every second. No, he wouldn't hear another word. Not one more lie. The fire inside him spread across his shroud, searing him into a maddening fury that could only be doused with the suffering of the one to blame.

Cole raised a munisica, savoring the moment before he struck. Ka Reine sat there, smoking her pipe and tapping her feet together in some stupid melody, mocking him. Just before he indulged, someone else entered the room.

"Cole!" Eliza's voice rang out.

Cole ground his armored teeth, incensed. How dare she interrupt, now in the heat of his moment.

Eliza ran to him, then stopped and recoiled. Horror splashed across her face as her eyes flitted over his munisica and face. "Your shroud... What have you done?"

Cole lowered his hand and looked at his claws. Glowing crimson veined his shroud like jagged lightning bolts. The veins cracked and spread, pulsing in synch with his desire for Ka Reine's suffering. Sickening shame pooled up in his belly as he realized what it was.

"Hatred?" Cole asked, looking to Eliza for confirmation.

Eliza took a step away from him, closer to the door.

"It seems Lileth isn't the only one you don't know so well," Ka Reine said with a derisive chuckle.

Cole looked to his hands again. The shroud receded and his body shrank back to normal. His Hatred and Rage smoldered in a wasted pile, smothered by shame. "Eliza," he said, pleading to her. "I... I'm sorry."

If Eliza was disgusted or disappointed, her face didn't show it. She took a steadying breath and gathered herself before speaking privately into Cole's mind. *"Brinleaf contacted me directly. The door to the Havenflow is reforming. Sitra and Valen should be coming out any moment, if they survived that is."*

Cole nodded and urged Eliza towards the door, following her. He glanced back at Ka Reine, who sat peacefully among the rubble of her room, still smoking and tapping her feet.

"My offer still stands," Ka Reine said as Cole reached the door. "Quell the Shadow Tide and my mind is yours."

Cole ignored her and pushed his face into the cool stone.

CHAPTER 27

THE STRENGTH OF GODS

T he flight to the Necropolis was as short as it was silent. Cole sensed Eliza flying right behind him, but her mind felt distant and wary of him, as if he were a rabid animal in her midst. He felt dirty. Hatred was something they were supposed to be fighting, not wielding. How could something so foul just sneak up on him? He tried to find an excuse, anything at all to relieve him of his shame, but one fact remained as looming and immovable as a mountain: The Hatred came from him, and was his alone.

As the Necropolis came into view, Cole broke the silence. *"How was Lileth when you left her?"*

"The dark magic relented as soon as I sensed you arrive at the prison," Eliza replied in a guarded tone. *"She's still asleep somehow. I had my unit return her to Naythan's so he could look after her. I thought Naythan was supposed to be watching her in the first place. Wasn't she critical when you left her with him?"*

"Naythan was acting very strangely after I discovered Lileth was missing," Cole said. *"I have a bad feeling. Really bad. There's something wrong here. Something among Naythan, Lileth, and Ka Reine. I don't know who to trust anymore, and after the stunt I just pulled I can't even trust myself. I just wish we had more time."*

After a moment of silent pondering, Eliza extended strands of warm golden friendship through their link, easing the tension between them. *"You're a good person, Cole. One act of Hatred doesn't define you, not when you've brought so much good into this world. Think of where The Sill would be if you'd never washed up on our shores. Thousands of people owe their lives to the goodness of your soul, and countless more depend upon it still. Never forget that."*

Her words assuaged his shame, sending it back to the pit it had crawled out from. He couldn't find words adequate to convey his appreciation for her, and so he flipped and slowed himself mid-flight, joining her in the air. He wrapped his arms around her and hugged her tightly. They embraced for a moment, then she withdrew, smiling through her sorrow.

A flock of amber soul flies scattered as Eliza and Cole descended through the canopy of the Necropolis. Brinleaf hovered on the little island of roots in the exact same spot where they'd seen him last. At first glance the archway appeared fully formed, but as Cole landed beside it he saw the slightest gap between the sprigs at the very top. The egg-sized gratia stones had been replaced among the woven vines, glowing and pulsing.

"Are they okay?" Cole asked Brinleaf.

"We shall find out in a moment," Brinleaf replied, hovering closer to the archway. "I have been listening and I have been watching, but the Havenflow remained beyond this world and my faculties."

Cole and Eliza watched in brittle silence as the wire-thin vines at the top of the archway wove through patterns and loops. Cole resisted the urge to speed the process up with Passion. Finally, after a minute dragged by, the vines touched and their wriggling ceased. But nothing happened.

"Did it work?" Eliza asked, peering through one side of the archway. Cole stepped around and looked through the other side.

"I am afraid I am just as ignorant as you are," Brinleaf replied. "This is the first time I have witnessed this step of the process."

"I don't sense anything, it's just a bundle of vines and gratia stones," Cole said as he reached for the archway.

"Stop!" Brinleaf said, his eyes wide. "The archway may collapse and there is no telling when it will open again."

Cole withdrew his hand. "But nothing's happening."

"Yes, something is happening," Eliza said, squinting through the gate. "Reach deeper with your Passion, not farther. Someone approaches."

As Cole attempted to untangle the meaning of her words, two figures appeared in the archway, distant and vague. Cole looked around the vines to the actual Necropolis and saw no one.

The outlines of the two figures sharpened as they strode confidently towards the gate. Cole recognized Valen at once, who looked unchanged except that his body had a faint emerald glimmer to it. Sitra on the other hand looked so different, Cole had to enhance his vision with magic just to be sure it was her. She was at least a foot taller, her munisica far larger with each claw the size of a sword. She was shrouded head to toe with a master's Rage.

Valen stepped through the archway first. He regarded Cole and Eliza with a curious grin, as though he had almost forgotten who they were. Sitra came through next, head high and proud, and as Cole only now realized, completely naked. Her shroud was thicker over her breasts and hips, masking the details of her anatomy.

"Right where we left you," Sitra said. The ebony needles of her hair clinked as she looked from Cole to Eliza. "You didn't kill The Three without us, did you?"

"No," Valen replied for them, casting his gaze somewhere under Oberon. "They come. Decreath will arrive first. What happened to Grotton and Sorronis?"

"Oh never mind that now, you fools," Eliza said through a laughing sob. She leaped across the little island and embraced them both in turn, crying tears of happiness. "You had me so worried. I thought you died as soon as the archway vanished."

"Why, what happened?" Sitra asked. As she spoke, Cole watched her, awed at her new appearance. He himself had donned the master's shroud more times than he could remember; however, seeing it exemplified in her was astonishing. Her teeth were like obsidian gems, and her eyes were solid black as well, making it difficult to tell exactly where she was looking.

"A violent storm kicked up around the two of you. Was it too long ago for you to remember?" Cole asked.

"It's not just that," Sitra said, frowning with a pensive expression. "They altered our minds so most things wouldn't stick. Dammit, I can't even remember what we were doing ten minutes ago. It's leaking out like a dream after waking up."

"Wait, so you don't remember what you learned in there?" Cole demanded.

"Not entirely," Valen said in a calm tone. "The Havenflow allowed us to retain what we gained from the dead; self awareness, understanding of our new powers, and whatever spells we learned. However, the actual memories of our training no longer belong to us. It must have been a precautionary measure to protect the secrets of the Havenflow. The last thing I recall was entering the archway."

"What sort of powers and spells are we talking about here?" Cole asked, casting an envious gaze at Sitra's form. "I see Sitra's obviously made some progress."

Sitra and Valen shared a private glance, and Cole could have sworn he felt something akin to telepathic Passion, but he couldn't quite make it out, nor could he sense their life candles at all for that matter. Something was very different between the two of them.

Valen returned his gaze to Cole. "That is a difficult question to answer, for we do not recall how and when we attained a spell or skill, so our gifts will not be apparent until the moment calls for them. But to paint it with a broad stroke, we are far greater than we were."

"What he means to say," Sitra said, butting in, "is that I mastered my Rage and he mastered his Wisdom, and at some point we both mastered Passion." She flashed Valen a mischievous grin, and Cole could have sworn he saw Valen's cheeks flush pink. "It's so strange. It's as if all I did was walk through a doorway, but I now I feel like I could crush ten of the old Sitras without breaking a sweat. Hell, give me an Alpha Colossus and I'll have that thing dismantled before Cole gets his wings out."

"This is wonderful!" Eliza gushed, hugging them both once more. Cole had a feeling she wasn't simply congratulating them on their new powers.

Cole leaned close to Valen while Sitra and Eliza drifted away and exchanged excited whispers. "Do you think you're strong enough to make a difference? Chiron, Roth, and Alvani had countless cycles of training and their combined strength wasn't enough."

Valen nodded. "True, but they did not have the Havenflow. Trust me, we are far beyond any evil we have yet to face, save for The Three themselves, and I am confident Sitra and I can hold them off at the very least. And when you and Eliza emerge we shall give all of Aeneria reason to hope once more."

Cole smiled, relieved. "Why does she still have the shroud on?" he asked as he watched Sitra chatting animatedly with Eliza. "I'd like to think she just lost her clothes in there, but knowing Sitra she's probably just showing off. And what's with the barrier you've got on?" Cole asked, indicating the emerald sheen over Valen's skin and robes. "Is that part of mastering Wisdom?"

"I know not, other than Sitra and I are both more than what we once were," Valen said, looking over himself as though he too had only just noticed the glimmer. "It seems that at a certain level of proficiency our magics manifest uniquely for each individual. I do know that mastery is relative, as there is always more to learn about oneself. For as long as I live I will continue my journey down the paths of Wisdom, Passion, and Rage."

Cole sighed, feeling as though a horrible weight had been lifted from his shoulders. No longer was he solely responsible for Aeneria's fate. He had never been alone of course, but no one else had possessed the strength of magic to stand against the toughest of their enemies until now. While he couldn't grasp the enormity of their new abilities, they each gave off an aura that left no doubt that they were the two most powerful beings on Aeneria, perhaps even more so than The Three. On the outside, however, Sitra and Valen exuded profound calm and confidence, as though winning this war would be no greater trouble than weeding a garden.

"I suppose we shouldn't put this off any longer," Cole said to the group. "I'm ashamed to admit it, but I was too scared to go in first. Even after seeing the two of you come out stronger than ever, I'm still not sure I can do it. Can you remember anything that happened in there? Anything at all?"

Valen looked to Sitra, and his expression grew soft and tender, as though the ghosts of the most wonderful dream had graced him at her sight. "I remember nothing, but I am quite sure it was not all trials and turmoil. I imagine the dead have no desire to see this world fall into darkness, not when there is such beauty and warmth left in it." He turned to Cole, placing a hand on his shoulder. Cole's entire body shivered with energy at the contact. "You must go now. Aeneria will need all of its Unbound before long."

"I should fill you in before I go," Cole said. "You've only been gone for a day but a lot has happened. Strange things. Unlock your mind so I can transfer the knowledge with Passion." Cole probed his thoughts towards where Valen's life candle should be, but there was still nothing there.

"There is no need," Valen said. "I have already gleaned the events from the last day from the eddies of your thoughts, and I will not unmask my vital essence just yet. To do so would reveal the extent of my new powers to anyone with the ability to sense it. I would rather The Three not know what they are walking into."

"But how?" Cole asked, incredulous. "To sneak something out of my mind... your Passion would have to be—"

"You will understand once you travel the Havenflow," Valen said with a nod. "Please, Cole, go now. We will tend to Lileth and Ka Reine and whatever demons have the temerity to dance with us."

There was no way he could put it off any longer. Eliza was already waiting for him at the archway. The look on her face told him she was just as nervous as he was.

"Ready?" she asked.

"Almost," Cole replied. He reached around his neck and unclasped Varka's cape, which shifted from a tangle of roots to plain fabric in his hands. He rolled the cape and tossed it to Sitra. "Make sure Lileth gets that."

"You got it, boss," Sitra said with a warm smile. "Now get your asses in there and do us proud. In the end it'll feel like no time at all. Promise."

Cole nodded and stepped toward the archway. Eliza's hand found his, and he grasped it as if it were the only thing keeping his heart from fleeing out of his chest.

"Breathe with me," Eliza's voice rang through his mind, slow and steady.

Cole took one last look at Valen, Sitra, and Brinleaf, then held his breath as Eliza pulled him gently through the archway.

CHAPTER 28

DIVINE LANDING

Sitra watched her friends pass through the archway, feeling as though part of herself had left as well. Even without her Passion she could tell there was something special between Eliza and Cole, something similar to what she and Valen now had.

As if he knew she was thinking about him, his mind chimed into hers, bright and clear. *"You didn't forget absolutely everything from the Havenflow, did you?"* His shoulder bumped softly against hers as he joined her at the edge of the archway. Cole and Eliza had walked off the island on the other side. They didn't notice it yet, but the turquoise water had begun to rise above their ankles.

"Don't be stupid," Sitra replied. She gave Valen a playful shove with the flat of her munisica, then yanked him back into a tight, one-armed hug. She rested her head against his as they both gazed into the Havenflow, which for some reason felt more like home than The Sill did. *"My memories have been washed away, but the feelings are still there. Yours better be too."*

"That they are," Valen said as he coiled an arm around her. *"I think I just realized why I had this barrier up. Your hair could skewer Morthainian glass."* Waves of mirth and contentment passed between them as they embraced mind and soul. *"We are bonded, are we not?"*

"To the bones," Sitra replied.

With their minds entwined, a sense of danger reverberated between them as the water around Cole and Eliza surged in earnest, rising above their heads in a twisting column twenty paces wide. They could see two figures spinning within, floating in the violent whirlpool amid pieces of shattered branches and mud.

"I do not envy them," Valen said.

"It's only a bit of water," Sitra scoffed. *"And rock. And trees. And fire somehow? Huh, they'll be fine."* The tower of swirling water had both frozen solid and lit itself aflame like a massive torch, trapping Cole and Eliza within like a snapshot of two dancers. She could see spells crackling in their hands, but another cyclone had already begun to rush about their frozen prison. The churning forces tore a tree from its roots, which smashed the trunk into the archway, shattering it across the island of roots. The gateway was gone. *"They'll be fine,"* Sitra repeated in a tone of forced confidence.

"Valen, Sitra, a word if you please," Brinleaf said, hovering over the root island to greet them. He kept his eyes on them, but he worked Wisdom with his hands, conjuring up an emerald basket and plucking the loose gratia stones with delicate flicks of his fingers, as though playing an invisible piano.

"Why does Pinebean float around like that all the time?" Sitra asked Valen. *"It's like his feet are too noble to touch our ground. Can I dunk him real quick?"*

"Be nice, Sitra," Valen said, giving her shoulders a squeeze before detaching from her and facing Brinleaf. He raised his chin and spoke in a voice of utmost respect, though Sitra could feel he was just as annoyed as she was. "Of course, Brinleaf, what can we do for you?"

Valen already knew what Brinleaf wanted, just as Sitra did. Their mastery of Passion left little to secret from an unguarded mind, though Valen was always better with the diplomatic things.

"The people of Borla Dign would like to invite you into our consensus," Brinleaf said. "The consensus is in no small part responsible for the creation of the Havenflow, and so we beg a moment of your time to glean what we can from your minds. We ask not for some presumption of debt owed, but for our custodial duties to the Havenflow. The Sill's dead deserve every comfort and ounce of optimization we can provide, and the safety of those who enter is paramount. Any information you could share would be invaluable to the war effort."

"And?" Valen said, his tone hardening.

"And nothing," Brinleaf said in a flat tone. "We have made our case as plainly as we could."

"Your words are as plain as they are true, but they are not the whole truth," Valen said.

"You can't hide your intentions from us, Pinebean," Sitra said in a mocking tone. "Just come out and say it so it at least seems like you're being honest."

Brinleaf's eyes narrowed, then he resumed his expressionless visage. "On behalf of the consensus, I offer our sincere apologies. In our eagerness for self-preservation, we will at times overlook things such as trust and manners. The consensus is very much interested in any spells you learned while inside the Havenflow, particularly from the school of Wisdom. Knowledge is a power we have grown fond of."

"That wasn't so difficult, was it?" Sitra said, crossing her arms.

"Not literally," Brinleaf said. "So what is your response? Will you share your knowledge with us?"

"No," Valen said. "At least not until you pass through the Haven-flow yourself. I deny you not out of spite, but out of honor for the dead. It would be an insult to their memory to pass their knowledge to the uninitiated."

Brinleaf nodded, as if Valen had responded precisely the way he expected. "We disagree with your reasoning, but we understand it. Perhaps in time we will send a pair through, though I am afraid that will not be for a while. I am not sure any of us will survive the Havenflow with our current ineptitude at Passion and Rage. Many of us still adhere to the path of Wisdom."

"Then get angry for once!" Sitra said.

Without further warning, Sitra conjured a ball of fuchsia Passion between her bladed fingers and sent it flying at Brinleaf faster than he could react. The magic collided with Brinleaf's chest as though it were made of liquid, but instead of splashing about, it soaked into him, sending him careening backwards into the water as he dropped his hold on Wisdom. Sitra watched with mounting gratification as Brinleaf sat up in the water, several emotions blooming on his face like the colors on Oberon; alarm, confusion, anger, then finally, glee. Soaking wet and laughing to his belly, Brinleaf hoisted himself to his feet.

"I forgot how marvelously quiet the world could be!" Brinleaf said, glancing about the Necropolis as though seeing it for the first time. "I cannot remember the last time I disconnected from the consensus." He then looked at Sitra and his eyes went wide. "Mistress of Rage and Passion, the enigma of the night, she who is as terrifying as she is beautiful. See how the moonlight sparkles in her hair!"

"Why thank you, Pinebean," Sitra said with a little curtsy.

"You may have broken him," Valen said with a sliver of caution. "This better not be a permanent affliction. He still has a job to do."

"He'll be dull as a river rock in no time," Sitra scoffed. She withdrew Varka's cape from under her arm and clasped it around her shoulders. The fabric creaked as it shifted to a blanket of curly roots. She felt the enchantment at once, tuning and tinkering with her Wisdom in an attempt to elevate it. "Well that's disappointing."

"Not quite the god-tier power you imagined," Valen asked as he helped Brinleaf pick up the gratia stones he dropped.

"It's working, but I'm not getting much out of it. It's Varka's cape, so maybe it only works for Cole." Sitra waved her hand before her and conjured a flock of doves made of jade flames. The birds swirled high above their heads, drawing the attention of nearby soul fies, then dove to the water, where they vanished in little puffs of steam. *"Oh well."*

"You feel as though you are beyond expert with Wisdom as it is," Valen said. "Perhaps there is a limit to what the cape's enchantment can do." He conjured his own basket from Wisdom and deposited the gratia stones into it, then handed it to Brinleaf. "Shall we tend to our jobs now? I assume you would rather pass on consulting with the Heart Tree?"

"I'd rather sleep inside a Corpulant for a night than chum it up with those bureaucrats," Sitra said. "I'll see to Lileth and Ka Reine."

"Please call upon me if you need help," Valen said.

"Only if you promise *not* to call on me if you need help," Sitra replied. Then with the speed of her Rage and a twist of her Passion, she sprinted across the island and kissed Valen on the cheek, penetrating the barrier over his face as she ran by him.

Her foot found a solid rock beneath the water. She leapt into the air and took flight, not with the aid of her Wisdom, but with the sheer force of her Rage. The jump carried her out of the Necropolis, up through The Sill's canopy layers, where she swore she saw Whind watching her from the top of a tree. Sitra guided her descent with her munisica, using them like rudders in the air. She landed in the far edge of the training fields, sprinting off again before the dirt from her impact had even begun to rise. For the fun of it, she avoided the ground for the rest of the trip, simply leaping from trunk to trunk as she went.

Sitra landed atop Ka Reine's prison, jarring the metal dome with the sound of a deep gong. The guards circling the prison leapt back in alarm, spells and munisica at the ready. Sitra disarmed them with a broad pulse of Passion, then broadcast her identity to each of their minds, allaying their Fear entirely. She found the leader of the watch and reviewed the spells woven throughout the prison walls, and as she suspected there was little room for improvement. The enchantments had been laid out in complex arrays of Rage, Wisdom, and Passion, which would react dynamically to counter any source of magical interference, friendly or malicious. Nor had there been any sign of tampering or stress of any kind. As far as Sitra could tell, nothing had occurred within this prison that shouldn't have. However, following Cole's and Eliza's theory on dreams, Sitra embedded another spell into the prison, one that would make it impossible for anyone to sleep within; that way Ka Reine would have no way to contact anyone through her dreams. After charging every gratia stone in the prison walls, Sitra took flight, with Wisdom this time, and sailed gently towards Naythan's.

Following Lileth's life candle, Sitra popped through the front door of Naythan's house. She felt Lileth upstairs surrounded by people Sitra recognized as one of Eliza's units, but for some reason Naythan was down in the basement. Alone. Even from a distance she could sense Lileth's body was in perfect health, though her mind was besieged by a maelstrom of dark magic and horrible dreams. Curious, Sitra made her way down to the basement first, concealing herself with an invisibility spell so as not to alarm the students as she passed them through halls.

Judging by the hum of telepathy in the air, the academy had finally received word of the coming of The Three, and were now ushering the children to safe houses under the roots of The Sill's oldest trees.

Sitra stalked her way down a winding set of stone steps leading to the basement. The sound of clinking bottles and frustrated grumblings met her before she reached the bottom landing. She sent an obvious pulse of Passion through the basement. Naythan's life candle resonated with the contact, flaring bright for a heartbeat, but otherwise the old hermit showed no reaction to her presence.

"What the hell are you doing down here, old man?" Sitra demanded, shedding her invisibility spell, though she kept her mind concealed. Naythan had an armful of vials full of what looked like alchemy ingredients.

"Be careful, Sitra, something is wrong with him," Valen chimed into her thoughts. She didn't need him to tell her that.

Naythan acknowledged her with the slightest nod. "Oh you know, just the usual mid-cycle cleaning. Gutting out the old to make room for the new. Would you believe some idiot arranged all our stock in the Terbelkin method? What am I supposed to do, reference the charts every time I need a snip of fireweed? It's utter calamity I tell you." He waxed on about the state of the shelves around him, talking more to himself than anyone else.

"You know The Three are coming, right?" Sitra asked. "As in we have less than a day before all of Aeneria's nightmares break upon our walls? Don't you think you should do this another time?" Naythan gave no response. What bothered Sitra wasn't his rudeness, but rather the fact that he showed no reaction to someone fully shrouded appearing next to him out of thin air. Curious, Sitra nudged one of the shelves with a bladed toe, tilting it over. The shelf clacked to the stone floor, its contents shattering and filling the room with pungent aromas. Naythan didn't even flinch.

"Now I know you've gone crazy," Sitra said. She then cast her mind out towards Naythan's, cradling it as gently as she could so as not to startle him. She scanned his body first, finding it whole, then delved into his mind. His thoughts were utterly consumed by the task in front of him, as though nothing else in the world existed. They felt fanciful, dreamlike, but there were hints of something more sinister guiding them from afar. Sitra attempted to isolate the suspicious thoughts, to trap and identify them, but they vanished like vapor in her claws. Growling mad, Sitra retreated from Naythan's mind and pointed her claw at his backside, striking him in the flank with a bolt of white lightning.

Naythan jolted upright, dropping his armful of vials. He blinked rapidly as he surveyed his surroundings, then uttered a high squeal at the sight of Sitra. "Help! Demons take us!"

"It's me, Naythan," Sitra said, emitting another pulse of Passion so he could properly identify her. "You were sleepwalking."

"Sleep... what... how in the world did I get down here?" Naythan smoothed out the front of his headmaster's robes, absentmindedly cleaning off the powders and broken glass with jets of steam from his hands. "Wait, Lileth! Where is she?"

Sitra scanned Naythan's mind once more to be sure he was awake. There was no trace of dream or the dark presence. "Upstairs where you left her, though she hasn't been there the whole time."

Naythan's brow knitted with confusion. "The last thing I remember is trying to enter the girl's dreams. Whatever madness she's embroiled in must have leaked into me. Strange, it doesn't seem like she's sleeping now." He let out a sharp hiss and winced. "Heavens! Her mind is boiling hot. Sickly, sickly thing."

"Well then get your ass back up there and help me fix her!" Sitra barked.

"Oh all right then," Naythan huffed. "Where's my staff?"

Annoyed, Sitra grasped Naythan with Wisdom and levitated him through the basement and up the stairs. He thrashed his arms in unbalanced protest while jabbing at her mind with his, then eventually gave up and resigned himself to floating cross-armed and frowning all the way up to Lileth. Sitra forced the liquid door into its frame and entered the room, setting Naythan down within.

Eliza's unit stood around Lileth. She lay sweating and trembling in the bed, apparently asleep. Various tints of pink and lavender emanated from their hands as they bathed Lileth with Passion.

"Begone, all of you," Naythan snapped. He found his staff leaning up against the couch and had begun jabbing it into the ribs of anyone close enough.

The leader of the unit looked to Sitra, clearly awed by her fully-shrouded state. She gave him a nod, which he returned, then one by one his unit flew out the open window.

Naythan plopped himself on the side of the couch and grasped Lileth's head with his tattoo-laden hand.

"Wait for me," Sitra said, crouching at his side. She extended her mind alongside Naythan's, bringing him into her and Valen's link.

Naythan paused and regarded the two of them with a mixture of admiration mingled with apprehension. *"My my my, you two have been busy. Mastering magics like the latest fashions. And I see you've gone and bonded to each other in Passion. Risky, but there's no sweeter thing from what I hear. I'm curious though, where did you find the time to learn all this? Such growth would take cycles."*

"In a place not of this world," Valen replied for both of them. *"We have not the time nor the liberty to explain, but know that we are more than we once were. Please, Naythan, be quick. The Heart Tree has need of Sitra and me."*

Valen's voice rang in Sitra's mind, filling her with several sensations at once; the thrill of victory in battle, her favorite song from the Arts District, the smell of a beachside fire, the safety of her friends. She knew they had somehow fallen in love in the Havenflow, but this was something more than a swooning of the heart. She felt his energy inside her, just as hers lived inside him, one ocean of magic and thoughts surging between them in a shared tide.

Embracing their bond, Sitra and Valen delved into Lileth's mind with Naythan as their guide. Though together they were far more powerful than Naythan in every regard, the old hermit's memories contained vast libraries of knowledge in healing maladies of the mind and of the flesh.

"Ah, this is where she got me last time," Naythan said, halting their progress before something that felt like a heavily protected safehouse. Even as he said it, an image of a hallway appeared in Sitra's and Valen's minds, finished with a heavy wooden door at one end.

"You can sense where my footprints end, just before the door, then something clearly happened, there. Interesting. This entire portion of her mind is vast beyond comprehension, but it only exists while she sleeps. She may not even be aware of its presence. What chills my marrow the most, however, is that this door and whatever lies beyond were made by someone other than Lileth."

"How can you tell?" Sitra asked, taking a step towards the door.

"Not so close, Sitra," Valen said, pulling her back. *"Look at the design used to manifest this place. It doesn't match the rest of her mind, and as far as I know Lileth has never spent time aboard a luxury ship."*

"Precisely," Naythan agreed.

As Sitra surveyed the hall around her, more details came into focus. Long planks of polished dark wood lined the walls and ceiling while a sleek red carpet covered the floor. The finish and trim work had been filigreed with elegant patterns of Morthainian glass and precious metals. The door at the end of the hall was shut, though flickering lights could be seen inside its keyhole and along the edges of the frame, as though someone were moving just on the other side. There was a hint of salt water in the air, and lively party music thumped from somewhere above them. Sitra could feel the floor swaying gradually beneath her feet. She twisted and looked down the hall opposite the door, expecting to see more of the ship, but the walls and ceiling gave way to a moonlit grove with soul flies chasing each other along a chuckling brook.

A painting materialized on the wall beside Sitra. It was of a marvelous ship, as beautiful as it looked capable, with pale blue sails and a hull of rich dark wood. Etched in a brass label along its frame was a single word.

"Ecstasy?" Sitra asked, running her fingers over the name.

"The name of the ship perhaps?" Naythan said. *"You're both quite sure Lileth has never been in such a place?"*

"Lileth grew up in a town of strict Wisdom users," Valen explained. *"They would have no use for a comfort ship such as this one. She came straight to The Sill from there. Our unit spent some time on a Morthainian ship, but it was nothing like this."*

"Hmm." Naythan approached the door, stopping where he had pointed before. *"Then there are only a few explanations left to us. I am going to attempt to open this door again, which will likely trigger the same magic as before. I have no idea how to counter the trap , but the two of you ought to be able to figure something out. Hopefully glean something useful from my blundering. Guard yourselves now."*

Valen and Sitra hardened their minds. As Naythan's consciousness neared the door, his body materialized out of thin air, wrapped in his fur coat and staff in hand. Naythan pushed his glasses up and peered so close to the door that his nose almost touched the handle.

"Well bless my stars, I'm a genius," Naythan said with a wheezy laugh. *"I can't believe I fell for something so crude. My sisters would be ashamed."*

Naythan hooked a tattooed finger through the air in front of the door, snagging a shiny gossamer thread which led to a broad web covering the whole frame. The web detached and attempted to envelop Naythan, but with a lazy flick of his hand, the web vanished in a puff of emerald smoke.

Naythan looked back and gave them a wink, then grabbed the glass door handle. His body went rigid, then a purple flame erupted from the floor around him, swallowing him whole.

"Fear!" Sitra bellowed. Her body materialized in the hall. Shrouded with her master's Rage, she charged at Naythan.

Naythan fell to his knees and screamed like a child. The flames tore at him like they had a mind of their own, only instead of burning him, they tore pieces from his clothes and flesh, scooping them away in clean handfuls to be consumed in the growing fire. Before Sitra could reach him, Naythan fell to the floor and the rabid fire consumed him entirely, leaving nothing behind.

Sitra roared. She prepared to charge through the door, then Valen's presence blossomed inside her, sweet and pure.

"We must go, my love," Valen said. *"We cannot save him from in here. Come with me."*

His words settled her Rage back to a manageable temperature, and together they left the ship and returned to their bodies. Sitra blinked, and she was back in Naythan's room. Lileth was on the couch, sweating and shivering with lines of blood running from her closed eyes. Naythan was on the floor beside the bed. Dead.

"He's gone," Sitra said to Valen. *"He's dead."*

She scanned Naythan with both Passion and Wisdom, showing Valen the world through her senses. There was nothing but a rotten void where Naythan's life candle ought to have been. His body was cold and hard as stone, as though he'd been dead for hours.

"I'm going to kill Ka Reine," Sitra said. Though she still wore her master's shroud, her tone was calm and even. *"First Lileth and now Naythan. She's gone too far. I don't care what she's done for The Sill in the past. There's no coming back from this."*

"Agreed," Valen said. *"There are no other viable options for us at this point. I shall be right there."*

Sitra bent low and kissed Lileth on the brow. "I'm so sorry, Lil. This will all be over soon." She transferred Varka's cape from her own shoulders to Lileth's, hoping its enchantment would help in some way.

A minute passed and Valen still hadn't arrived. From his mind she felt a flurry of activity about him; panic, disappointment, contention. Something was happening in the Heart Tree.

"Change of plans," Valen said.

"Obviously," Sitra snapped, glad she wasn't the one dealing with the bureaucrats. *"Did I hear something about our navy not pulling its weight?"*

"Something of the sort," Valen replied. She sensed he was storming mad, but he somehow kept an even demeanor to the outside world. Sitra liked his angry side. *"Our naval forces just engaged The Three's, and we are losing at every turn. It seems Ka Reine's treachery runs deeper than we knew. The enemy ships know exactly how to counter our tactics on open water, and so they are currently making a mockery of Falinor's fleets. A great many lives have been lost already. They need us."*

"And what about Lil? And Naythan?" Sitra demanded. *"She's infected and he's a corpse. We can't just leave them here. Dammit, there's still so many children in the building."*

There was a pause in which Valen exchanged words with someone, then he returned his attention to Sitra. *"The Logistics Arch is already crafting another facility similar to Ka Reine's prison, for Lileth. Two of my elite units are on the way to pick her up. As for Naythan…"*

"I'll have one of my units bring him to the Necropolis," Sitra said. "It's a shame. I really liked him. I think I'll feed Ka Reine to a Corpulant after I take what she owes Naythan out of her soul."

Sitra waited in grim silence for Valen's units to show up. They were young, as all the units were, but the smattering of battle they had already seen had stripped them of their innocence and naivete. Careful not to touch her, they conjured webs of Passion and Wisdom around Lileth and carried her gently through the open window. Sitra's unit came shortly afterwards. Normally they would have praised Sitra for her newfound Rage and begged her to fight them, but their current task left them with no such luxury.

Sitra felt a sudden and unexpected pang of loss. Not so much for herself, but for The Sill. Naythan had done his best to cultivate the title of 'Hermit', but nearly everyone in The Sill had encountered the old man at one point or another. Whether it was healing some incurable illness, or sneaking sweets to children in the markets after their parents had denied them, he was always there to lend a hand to those in need, though he would certainly grumble about it the whole time. He alone was responsible for The Sill's first and only academy, a haven for Aeneria's orphans of war. Countless children who had lost everything and everyone now had a proper home where they could learn and grow into good people. Sitra took heart knowing his legacy would live on so long as the academy survived.

Two of the unit lifted Naythan's stiff figure from the floor and levitated him outside, where the others had cut a slab of granite from a boulder in Naythan's yard. They laid him on the slab, straightening his headmaster's robes and setting him in dignified repose with his staff nestled in between his tattooed fingers. Without the aid of Wisdom or Rage they hoisted the slab onto their shoulders and carried Naythan in a slow procession towards the Necropolis. They held their heads high and proud, unashamed of their tears as they flowed freely from red eyes. Sitra had never felt so connected to the Old Hermit as she did now that he was beyond this world.

Only after she was sure the academy's children were well on their way to The Sill's bunker did Sitra take flight. She followed her heart to the shore outside The Sill, positive this time that she saw Whind gazing at her from the canopy as she flew over The Sill's outer walls. She found Valen standing alone on the rocky shore nearest Oberon, staring up at the moon as if Aeneria's oldest sentinel held the very answer to this war. She came to a rough landing on the jagged rocks beside him. His eyes had plenty to say, but Sitra wasn't in the mood to hear anything at the moment. She wrapped him up in a bone-crushing hug, placing one clawed hand behind his head as she pulled his lips into hers. Her shroud receded, leaving her fully naked and allowing her to touch him properly. His skin was firm yet smooth, and his embrace made her forget every woe and whim she'd ever had. There was only now.

"Thank you," he said after some time.

"Shut up," Sitra said as she buried her head into his chest. She didn't like how short she was without her munisica, but the way she fit into him felt right. If only this moment could last forever, just the two of them and Oberon. "Do we have to leave now?"

"No actually," Valen said, squeezing her. "I advised Falinor to pull his navy to deep waters and let the enemy ships through. It took some convincing, but assured the Heart Tree that you and I could handle the enemy ships ourselves. I was rude to them. You would have been quite proud of me I think."

"Rude huh?" Sitra growled. "Do you think there's enough time to show me just how rude you were?"

Valen raised an eyebrow. "There is time enough. Though I wager you could handle a bit more than the thrashing I gave those bureaucrats."

Sitra purred in his arms.

"Draw your shroud, Mistress of Rage and Passion," Valen whispered in her ear.

Sitra felt the blades of his munisica scratch across the muscles of her naked back. She indulged in the sweetness of the pain for a few seconds before her shroud crawled over her limbs and hair, halting it at her torso. Valen's shroud matched hers, sharpening his eyebrows into little serrated knives of midnight black.

The tips of the first sails poked up from the horizon an hour later. After donning his armored robes, Valen took Sitra's face in both hands and kissed her deeply, then took flight, soaring high above the oncoming ships. Sitra donned her shroud once more and waited in plain view on the shore. She felt Rayn's mind reaching out for her, somehow managing a nagging tone through his panic.

"Will you wipe his ass for him before I fly back and flay him?" Sitra asked Valen.

"Stay your forces, Rayn," Valen said after removing his mind from concealment. *"Sitra and I will handle this alone."*

"Finally!" Rayn snapped. *"If you insist on fighting an entire fleet by yourselves, then you need to keep your minds open to me. How are we to know if you get yourselves killed or overrun? Shall we wait until our enemies knock on the front door?"*

Sitra felt Rage flare through Valen, as well as an urge to commandeer Rayn's mind just to shut him up. Sitra tried to stoke this urge into action, but Valen's will was indomitable. *"We will not be overrun and you will keep The Sill's forces behind its walls. Use whatever means you want to observe the skirmish from within, but Sitra and I must conceal our minds in order to ensure a swift victory."*

Contempt thickened in Rayn's thoughts. *"You have yet to explain how you suddenly have the means to defeat a legion of the Divine Guard, especially when they gave you so much trouble in Borla Dign. Not even Cole could defeat them outright. Speaking of, where did he and Eliza wander off to?"*

"As I told you before, we are more than we were," Valen said. *"And so too will Cole and Eliza be when they return, which will be less than a day."*

Valen severed the connection with Rayn, then concealed his mind. Sitra did the same, though their Passion bond ran deeper than telepathic communications. She could still feel him within her heart.

Sitra watched the ships grow larger as they neared, counting one hundred and fourteen in all. The waves hissed over the rocks before her while birds bickered from the treeline behind her. Battle lust tingled in her bones and simmered in her blood. Once the ships were within a mile, she felt a foul presence wander over the beach; the collective minds of the Divine Guard probing for fresh victims. Hundreds of mental tendrils wormed about like leeches in search of warm flesh. Sitra called her Wisdom to the air, illuminating her shrouded form. The mental probes lashed over her, foul and full of perverse intentions, but they found nothing, as none but the most powerful minds could touch hers or Valen's while they were so concealed. Sitra watched in savage delight as several of the ships angled directly for her. The rest followed right behind.

The nearest ships anchored themselves a hundred yards off the shore as countless barges detached from the vessels, each laden with enemy warriors. The barges wasted no time. They formed up into a row a half mile wide and charged at the beach. Just a few minutes later, wood scraped over rock as The Three's forces stepped foot on The Sill's island.

Every member of the Divine Guard was garbed in the armor of the Chosen—undead limbs and torsos forged in Hatefire and reinforced with dark magic. The shortest among them were still chest and shoulders taller than Sitra, giving them the appearance of miniature Colossi. True to their name, Sitra detected all four evil magics festering in equal measure among them. Hundreds of them ambled onto the shore, and hundreds more followed behind as the rest of the ships and barges moved in.

Sitra stood motionless as they circled around her, apparently unsure if she was a black statue or a promising victim. Those nearest her stopped, though one strode forward, confident and grotesque, halting right in front of her. The figure reached up and peeled the lid back of a helmet made from molded skulls, revealing the face of a pale woman with no eyebrows or hair.

"Don't tell me you're the only one out here to greet us," said the woman. Her voice was scratchy and wheezy, as though her throat were made from wind-beaten cloth. Her breath reeked of rot as she leaned close. "Well sweetness, what are you waiting for?"

"Just you," Sitra said. She raised a bladed hand and extended a single claw, the tip of which gleamed with emerald light.

"Oh you're gonna be delicious," she rasped, then conjured up a barrier of purple Fear in counter to Sitra's Wisdom.

A heavy boulder detached itself from the ground behind the woman and collided with her back, causing her to lurch forward. The woman gave an ungainly wobble and her head slipped right into Sitra's waiting claw, piercing herself through the eye before falling in a lifeless heap of her own disintegrating Chosen. Incensed at last, the rest of the Divine Guard converged on Sitra, brandishing weapons of molded bone, conjured blades, and the ruby munisica of Hatred.

Sitra closed her eyes and emitted a pulse of Passion, which spread from her in a blinding wave of fuchsia. The Divine Guard weren't ready for it, as they were prepared to exploit her Passion, not defend against it. Thirty of them fell to the ground, stunned. Sitra moved among them like a speeding falcon, slipping through the plates in their armor and giving them each a quick, mortal wound to the head or neck. They were dead before their comrades even knew what happened. Sitra tore down the beach issuing a swift death to those too slow to react. Her Rage demanded that she smash through their armor with thunderous blows, but her Wisdom and Passion tempered the red magic, and she opted for clean, lethal jabs to vulnerable spots. Even through the haze of battle she could feel Valen's approval at her efficiency, which she found immensely gratifying.

The few who had the potency of Hatred to see her coming met her with ruby munisica and thick clouds of Hunger, both of which ought to have been a proper counter to her Rage, but they could only exchange a few blows before her claws found their flesh. She was simply too quick, too powerful. After a minute she was already running down stragglers from the first wave. She wondered if these were the weaker of their forces, merely meant to test and probe, but her sense told her otherwise. These warriors of the Divine Guard were just as strong as those they faced in Borla Dign, some even stronger. The only difference here was her newfound powers.

The second wave of barges slid up onto the rocky shore, with the third close behind. Sitra swept through their numbers even more quickly than the first wave. The Three may have endowed their Divine Guard with unnatural levels of dark magic and forced them to adulthood; however, these were still children, some of whom her Passion revealed to be less than a few months old. Nothing in their short lives could have prepared them for the wrath of black claws before them. Sitra hardened her heart as she lost count of how many she killed.

By unspoken command, the Divine Guard began their retreat, as Sitra and Valen knew they would. They fled for the barges, leaving even before their fellows could clamber on. Sitra tended to the stragglers, who had broken ranks and lost all composure; she killed them with simple bolts of condensed fire. The rocky beach was a mess of bodies, both dead and undead. The waves continued hissing up onto the rocks as if a massacre had never occured, only now the water was solid red. Sitra used the lull in the battle to free the Chosen, whose limbs still writhed on the rocks, thrashing their Hatred at the world. Levitating herself, Sitra made a pass over the half-mile stretch of bodies, bathing the beach in a curtain of fuchsia magic and granting true death to those who had earned it long ago.

As the retreating barges mingled among the rising anchors of the navy, a figure descended from the sky, sparkling with a sheen of pale emerald. Explosions rang over the beach as deck guns shot javelins of solid metal, each missile as long and broad as a man. The rounds exploded into harmless dust long before reaching Valen, neutralized by an invisible barrier surrounding him by thirty yards on all sides. The Divine Guard hurled spells from the upper decks, though they proved just as ineffective as the javelins. Even the screaming bolts of condensed Fear weren't potent enough. The jagged purple magic passed through his Wisdom barrier and struck him true, but the magic splashed harmlessly over him like buckets of spoiled milk.

Sitra watched as Valen inventoried the scene before him. Her sharpened vision showed his face as an expressionless mask, though his eyes held a shadow of regret. Sitra knew he would take no pleasure in what he was about to do.

Hovering just a hundred feet over the water, Valen brought his hands up from his sides as though praising Oberon. The moon loomed over the horizon, its surface a riot of amber and cobalt. The bloody waves along the beach ceased their hissing as the water receded, and for a moment all was quiet.

Two enormous serpents of white water erupted from among the ships like inverted waterfalls. Swelling as broad as the thickest trees in The Sill, the snakes reared hundreds of feet into the air, then struck, mouths agape. Two ships exploded as the titanic snakes crashed through their frames, shattering them as though they were made of dried leaves. The snakes struck again and again, each blow annihilating another ship as though struck by the fist of a god. A cluster of ships which had yet to set anchor wheeled about on the spot and shot farther down shore, beyond the reach of the leviathans, but Valen raised his hands yet again and two more snakes reared up a mile away to greet them. In an act of desperation, or perhaps by accident, one of the ships released a swarm of flying Corpulants into the chaos, though instead of attacking Valen, the beasts fled for the open ocean. Valen aimed his palm toward the swarm. Blinding white light dominated the entire battlefield as a bolt of crooked lightning leapt from his palm and branched among the flock of Corpulants. Smoking bodies and crisped wings dropped from the sky as the entire flock splashed into the water, dead.

With nowhere else to go, the fleet returned to The Sill's shores, their retreat folding back down the path of their initial assault, straight into Sitra's waiting claws. The remnants of the fleet seemed unable to choose between the crushing death of the giant serpents, or Sitra's bloody whirlwind on the shore. In the end it mattered not. Within half an hour every ship was floating in a thousand pieces, or sinking to the shallows. When the last serpent returned to the water, Sitra levitated herself up to Valen, approaching him with caution in case he had lost himself to his battle lust, as she had so nearly done. Never had she seen destruction on such a scale. To her relief she found him calm and coherent, a sad smile tugging at his cheeks. With their enemies now dead or dying, she dropped her mental defenses and nudged her mind into his. Solace eased the sadness from his features as their minds entwined, their two souls dancing as one.

Sitra didn't bother slowing down. She crashed herself into Valen and knocked the breath out of him. He laughed and embraced her, spinning them both in the air. After a moment she pulled away and they gazed upon the aftermath of the battle.

"Snakes huh?" Sitra asked.

"They were effective," Valen remarked.

"That they were," Sitra said. "That was the most impressive bit of Wisdom I've ever seen. I doubt even Chiron could have managed something that big. How do you feel?"

"Terrible," Valen admitted. "Did you feel their minds? They were just children. Stupid, powerful children."

Sitra thought for a moment before responding. "Not really. These children were grown like plants in a garden, only instead of water and moonlight they were fed dark magic and innocent victims. They shouldn't even exist. Killing them was the right thing."

Sitra and Valen swept over the flotsam, freeing Chosen and dispatching any survivors. It was grim work. Sitra found one woman clinging to a piece of wreckage as she fought for the final moments of her life. She had lost both her legs and all of her armor. With the desperate look of a child who had swum out too far, the woman reached for Sitra, begging for help. Sitra flooded the woman's mind with Passion, easing her Fear and pain before killing her with a quiet spell. Guilt curdled in Sitra's gut as the hours dragged on.

Valen notified the Heart Tree of their success, providing a full report through snapshots of his memories to Rayn. Awed by the Unbound's newfound powers, the staff of the Heart Tree was much more cooperative thereafter. Sitra listened from the outskirts of Valen's mind as he ordered Thessi to send a team out to recover any useful supplies while Debjornik's agents scoured the debris for intel. Rayn informed them that Grotton's and Sorronis's Colossi were last seen heading out into open waters with all haste, fully recovered from Cole's ambush. Decreath's Colossus would be arriving any moment.

"Have you recovered from your exertions yet?" Valen asked Sitra after they landed on the rocky beach.

Sitra's shrouded braid whipped back and forth as she shook her head. "I wouldn't call that little dance an exertion. My Rage is fine, but my Passion is a bit drained, and I hardly have any Wisdom left. I'm more worried about you to be honest."

Valen took a deep breath. "I could use another hour or so to recover my Wisdom, but other than that I am fine."

Sitra inspected Valen's mind and body to make sure he wasn't just saying things to please her. "Should have been more efficient like me."

"I suppose I should have," Valen said with a soft chuckle. He gazed out at the horizon. "Should we tell them now?"

"No, they'll only get in our way," Sitra replied as she followed his eyes. "What do you think it's waiting for?"

Decreath's Collosus had been standing in the waters some twenty miles off shore. It was so large the deep waters only came up to its waist, and it seemed as if it could reach up and touch Oberon if it wanted to.

"At first I thought it was waiting for Grotton and Sorronis to show up, but now I think not." Valen glanced back towards The Sill. "I think Decreath is waiting for Cole to come out of the Havenflow. That is the sole reason for their journey. They need the key to the Aethers. They need Varka."

"How in the hell could The Three know that?" Sitra hissed, but in her heart she knew he was right. "We should run back inside and kill Ka Reine before she can steal any more of our secrets."

"It matters not," Valen sighed. "The damage has been done. Our only hope now is to hold Decreath off until Cole and Eliza return."

Sitra huffed. "Hold him off? Did you see what we just did to their navy? I bet Decreath's just waiting for Grotton and Sorronis to show up because he knows he can't take us both on."

"I hope you are right," Valen said, then his brow knitted with worry. "Shall we fly out to meet him then? Cole and Eliza will be out soon, but we may never get another chance to fight just one of The Three."

"I thought you'd never ask." Sitra gave Valen a swift kiss on the lips, then scooped him up in her bladed arms and took flight.

"Sitra!" Valen gasped through the wind. "What do you think you are doing?"

"Oh shut up and let me carry you," Sitra snapped. "You just sit tight and relax. Recover some of that Wisdom you wasted on your snake show. Think of this as your punishment."

The wind tore Valen's laughter from his mouth as Sitra put on a burst of speed. His words bloomed into her mind like fireworks. *"Had I known this would be my punishment, I would have started squandering my Wisdom ages ago."*

Sitra hugged him tightly. Even through her shroud she could feel her heart pounding away at her chest. This was it. All their training and sacrifice and preparation had led up to this moment. Though her battle lust roared and her Rage purred at the challenge before her, Sitra knew that this very well may be their last fight, their final act of defiance against Aeneria's evil. Still, she wished they had just a little more time. Cole and Eliza would have at least doubled their chances. She took heart knowing that if this were to be her end, at least she would meet it with Valen in her heart.

Halfway to the Alpha Colossus, Sitra slowed. The titan stirred. Its arms swung back and forth as it gained momentum. Its head dipped through hanging purple clouds. It waded through the water, slowly at first, then charged through the ocean as easily as if it were sprinting over flat ground.

Sitra slowed and released Valen, who conjured emerald wings and levitated by her side.

"It would be easier to pick up a mountain than stop that thing," Sitra said, keeping her eyes on the titan. "Any ideas?"

Valen shook his head. "Even at my full strength I could only slow it, and that's without Decreath's Fear countering my Wisdom. I do have one idea, but I'll need your help."

"Hurry up then!" Sitra snapped. The Colossus had halved its distance to them since they stopped.

Valen twisted his hand before him as though tying a knot, then a strand of silvery light sprouted between his fingers. He held the strand with the faintest touch of Wisdom.

"Take one end, but do not let it touch your skin," Valen said. "You will have to hold the other end of the spell too."

Sitra took hold of her portion of the spell, and as she did, Valen's plan became plain to her. It was a simple rule; a strand of magic just a hair thick meant to cut through anything solid. The only problem was that cutting through an Alpha Colossus made of armored Chosen would require an astronomical level of focus. It would have been easier to make another attempt with the giant water serpents.

"If we hide our minds and bring the spell underwater, Decreath might not notice us," Valen said. "We will have to dive deep. Will you have enough Wisdom to breathe?"

"No, but I can just hold my breath," Sitra replied, casting a wary glance at the Colossus. She could sense Valen's unease. "We're out of time. Get in."

Sitra took a deep breath and dropped into the water, then shot away from Valen. The strand of magic trailed close behind her. The demand on her focus increased commensurately with the increasing length of the spell, filling her head with a fuzzy, drunken, fog. She stopped about a quarter mile away from where she started, lowering herself deeper into the safety of the dark below. Ghostly shafts of moonlight waved to her as she descended. She waited.

A dim roar came from nowhere, punctuated by thunderous explosions above. Sitra's throat clenched as she beheld a shadow charging through the space between her and Valen. She urged what little Wisdom she had left to flatten her eyes and broaden her pupils, sharpening her vision for the haze of the dark water. She could only make out the first few feet of the gossamer spell, but the drain on her focus told her it was still active, and the Colossus was nearly on top of it. As soon as one of the shins passed between her and Valen, a crushing weight enveloped her mind, smothering her with emptiness. Her vision went black as all thought began to vanish. She was only dimly aware of the thread of magic snapping from her grasp, but when it did the crushing weight lifted at once.

The spell had dissipated entirely, but it had passed through three quarters of one of the Colossus's shins before it did. The leg crumpled and snapped around the wound, and the rest of the Colossus came down on top of it. For a moment Sitra was tossed about like a piece of seaweed as the titan displaced the water around her. She collected herself and made her way to the surface, swimming with only her Rage and what little air was left in her lungs.

She broke the surface, gulping great lungfuls of air as hundred-foot swells threw her this way and that. Seemingly unconcerned, the

Colossus rose from the water and resumed its march, only now it was hampered with a severe limp. Once a sliver of her Wisdom had returned to her, she levitated herself out of the water, relieved when she saw Valen rising as well.

They met in the air, their minds still concealed.

"We'll have to take the other one off the old-fashioned way," Sitra said, flexing her munisica. "The stupid leg's thicker than a city block. I'm not sure if my Rage is strong enough to cut through it in time."

"Your Rage could be ten times as strong and you would still be limited by the size of your tools," Valen said. "And Decreath is sure to notice us if we try something so obvious."

"Better us than The Sill," Sitra snarled.

"Very true," Valen said through a scowl. He drew his own munisica, and his robes rippled as his shroud snapped up his arms and thighs. His hair and eyebrows glistened like black razors. "We shall give Decreath a taste of his own Fear."

Sitra growled in approval. They flew after the hobbled titan, catching up to it within a minute. The Colossus stopped. Sitra felt a wave of Fear pass over her so potent it nearly peeled the shroud from her skin. Valen shuddered as his shroud receded, then he bared his teeth and the black armor returned.

The Colossus twisted on the spot. Hundreds of feet above them, a gargantuan face made from tens of thousands of severed heads turned to greet them. It peered at them through glistening mounts crafted from teeming multitudes of Chosen eyeballs. Sitra couldn't begin to guess how many there were, but there was no doubt they were all looking directly at her. There was a squelching sound of something being pulled out of mud, then the mouth of the Colossus peeled open in a grotesque smile, revealing a forest of broken bones for teeth.

Fear gripped Sitra's heart as she felt her own shroud begin to recede. Then Valen's minds rang through hers, galvanizing her resolve.

"No point hiding our minds now," he said into her.

"Hold on to me," Sitra said.

Valen's Rage burned with hers, and together they formed a torch that no shadow of Fear could penetrate.

"Until the end," Valen said.

Sitra felt her old battle lust rise up from deep within, greeting her like a friend in her final hour. She released a savage cry so loud that several corpses shook loose from the outer shell of the Colossus, falling and splashing to the waters below. The titan's smile vanished. Sitra and Valen charged, shooting at the monster's head like twin spears.

The Colossus made no move to stop them, but rather it swung one of its massive arms backwards, bending slightly at its knees. With a dull whoosh it brought its arm forward and hurled something at The Sill. The object was bright and looked to be the size of a loaded wagon. Sitra watched it as it spun out of sight; she noticed dozens of egg-shaped orbs, each one shining red or green or lavender.

Sitra changed course, shooting around the torso of the Colossus. She tore after the flying object as fast as she could, but her Wisdom had yet to recover. She wasn't going to make it.

"Sitra!" Valen called into her. *"What was that?"*

Sitra slowed, giving up at last, then replied in a tone heavy with defeat, *"My fulminators."*

Chapter 29

Betrayal

"It is time," Eliza said, taking a step onto the mound of roots. The gateway had reformed at last. The final vines had joined in an intricate knot at the crest of the arch while others carried tiny gratia stones into place. The air between the arch seemed to thicken. Eliza turned to Cole, her smile bright and vibrant. "We can go home at last."

Cole stepped out of the turquoise water and joined her, glancing around at the moss-covered trees and soul flies of the Necropolis. The tiny lilac flowers blanketing the surface of the water drifted away, their petals flapping softly and sadly, as though they grieved their departure. Cole squinted and inspected the archway, as well as the surrounding waters. This wasn't the first time the archway had reformed. The Havenflow had tricked them countless times before, each ploy resulting in a trap which they had barely survived. One of the Havenflow's favorite tricks was to allow them to pass through the archway and beguile them with convincing illusions. On one such occasion he and Eliza returned to The Sill and defeated The Three with Sitra and Valen, then lived on for several months before The Three found new Harbingers and killed them all. Cole and Eliza woke back in the Havenflow, and time had henceforth lost all relatable meaning to them.

"You know this might be another trick," Cole said as he bounced lightly on the roots, testing them. He considered obliterating the entire necropolis with a spell. He often found it was better to catch the Havenflow off-guard than walk into one of its traps. "We might have only been in here ten minutes."

"I think this time it's for real," Eliza said as she approached the archway. Her short hair was a bundle of ebony knives, a clear sign of one who had nearly mastered Rage, though her hands and feet were bare. Better to feel the world with, as she would say. She caressed one of the egg-sized gratia stones on the arch and gazed back to Cole. "I know it's real because my heart aches for it. Things will not be the same after we pass through. You and I... our life we have together. It will all be gone. The Havenflow will take it from us, just as it did to Valen and Sitra."

Cole stepped to her side and put an arm around her, his truest friend. Her hair jabbed into his naked cheek as she rested her head on him, but he didn't care. He embraced her within the confines of their Passion link, the same link they'd created on their first mission to Costas. *I don't know what we'll find on the other side of this gate, but one thing I do know is that what you and I share runs deeper than magic or memories. No matter what happens we will have this for as long as we live.* To emphasize his point he released a beam of Passion across their link, lacing it with trust, hope, and love. She reciprocated the Passion, adding her own facets to their link. He took her hand into his and spoke aloud. "Let's go save Aeneria."

They squeezed each other's hand and anchored themselves into their link. They pooled their memories together and wrapped them in every protective measure they could think of, forming an impenetrable fortress of mental armor. Nothing the Havenflow had presented them with so far would have even the slightest chance of stealing their memories. Holding their breath, they stepped through the archway.

Nothing happened. Cole released Eliza's hand and found Brinleaf floating next to them, expectant.

"Welcome back," Brinleaf said.

Cole laughed and hugged Eliza, picking her up off her feet and spinning around. "See, I told you!"

Eliza laughed with him. When he put her down, she gazed up at him with curious glee. "Told me what?"

"What do you mean?" Cole asked. He felt the smile fade from his face. His eyes whipped to the Havenflow's archway. "I just... we just..."

"What's wrong?" Eliza asked in a soft voice.

"I... I don't know," Cole admitted. "I forgot what I was about to say. That's so strange. It feels like we just went in. Do you remember anything?"

Eliza's smile melted, replaced by a mild interest at his question. Her eyes lit with recognition, then faded into a frown. "No, nothing at all. It feels as though I'm waking from a dream. The memories are dissipating before I can begin to reach them."

Brinleaf stroked the side of the gateway with a hand aglow with jade Wisdom. The vines unraveled themselves as the arches crawled back into the roots of the small island. He collected the gratia stones with a flick of his finger, placing them into a conjured basket.

"Your memories of the Havenflow exist within the Havenflow," Brinleaf said at last. "They do not belong to this world, though as with Valen and Sitra your new powers and magic are your own, which is most fortunate because Aeneria needs them now more than ever. There was an explosion on the other side of the markets not two minutes ago."

Cole's shroud snapped over his skin before Brinleaf finished. He sent out a scanning wave of Passion. He recoiled as he felt something enormous just outside The Sill's walls, a mountain of agony with a heart of Fear so pure and potent that he barely noticed two life candles blazing beside it.

"Decreath is here," Cole said, locking eyes with Eliza.

Eliza nodded, grim yet confident. "Sitra and Valen are with him."

They took flight, leaving Brinleaf alone on the island of roots. Cole reached out to Sitra and Valen, but their minds were too encumbered by their battle for them to notice his touch, and he didn't want to distract them by forcing his way in. The fact that they were fighting at all and not simply dead was heartening. He contacted the Heart Tree next, bringing each staff member into a single telepathic network with himself and Eliza.

"Where in the black stars have you been?" Rayn shouted across their minds. *"Decreath is here! The Sill is under attack! We—"*

"Try to relax," Cole ordered. *"We don't have time to talk. I'm going to pull all of your recent memories."* As gently and quickly as he could, Cole sifted through their memories of the previous day,

circumventing their mental defenses with ease. Naythan, dead. Lileth, imprisoned, her mind hidden behind metal and magical barriers. Decreath, arrived. A breach in the wall. Grotton and Sorronis, arrival imminent. Cole changed course in midair. Eliza followed. *"Falinor, disperse our assault companies evenly inside our walls. We need to be ready for another breach. Thessi, gather supplies and meet Wareen at the training fields. If we lose The Sill then we'll need to use the Seer Jars to jump to other outposts. Debjonik, put eyes in every tree, including the outer walls. I don't want anyone sneaking in or out."*

"Already done," Debjornik replied.

Cole sensed Thessi and Wareen carrying out his orders.

"And what of me?" Rayn demanded, his tone ringing with urgency.

"Fill in where you can and make adjustments where you see fit," Cole said. *"I'm going to be too busy fighting to keep track of all the chaos and I'll need you to act in my stead as things develop. I don't want anyone outside our walls besides me and the Unbound. All our elite units are yours to command."* Cole then sent the imprints of every unit leader's life candle to Rayn so he could find them with Passion. *"The Sill is in your hands, Rayn."*

Rayn was speechless for a moment as he tried to bottle up his awe and maintain his composure. *"As you command, Wisdom Walker."*

Cole dissolved the Passion network as they executed his orders, leaving a thin yet clear strand between himself and Rayn.

"Where we going?" Eliza asked. *"Shouldn't we go help Sitra and Valen?"*

"They are diminished, Valen more so," Cole replied. *"Go to the markets and grab a few gratia stones for them. The Cordial Compendium should have a full Wisdom stone after everyone purchased all those dreamsource cyphers."*

"And what will you be doing?" Eliza asked, but Cole's guilt answered for her. *"Be quick about it then. The fate of Aeneria is more important than any one person, even one of the Unbound."*

The air exploded around Eliza as she shot towards the markets. Cole sensed traces of disappointment and jealousy through their link, but ignored them. He had to know if Lileth was safe. According to

Debjornik's most recent memories, the explosion and breach in the wall happened right next to Lileth's prison. Weaving around trees, he scanned the area ahead of him with a more focused cone of Passion, and to his horror he found Ka Reine's life candle burning right where the hole in the wall ought to be. His unit was there with her, as well as one of Eliza's and one of Sitra's.

Rage, Passion, and Wisdom flared in unison as Cole put on a burst of speed, smashing through trees instead of dodging them. The gap in the outer wall came into view within a few heartbeats. Four of the hulking trees were gone, broken and scattered over a swath of charred destruction. A heartbeat later he beheld a metallic dome structure, cracked roughly in half, its fragments strewn over the surrounding wreckage. There was no sign of Lileth's life candle.

The earth erupted around Cole as he landed, fully shrouded and ready to end Ka Reine's life once and for all. Green sparks crackled from him as he strode towards her. The Old One stood in the middle of the gap in the outer wall, leaning on her cane and regarding him with a haughty expression. He felt the Hatred from their last encounter boil up, but he suppressed it before it could manifest into tangible magic. His unit and two others stood around Ka Reine in defensive positions, munisica and magic at the ready.

With snap of his Wisdom, Cole yanked all three units off their feet and sent them flying away from Ka Reine, dropping them a hundred yards away and holding them in place. Ka Reine opened her mouth to speak, but as she did all the jagged fragments of Lileth's prison came flying at her. Metal plates three feet thick clanged together with ear-stabbing reports, forming a tight shell around her, then the edges of the fragments shone white hot as they melted together, sealing her in.

Cole heard Rayn in the back of his mind, his voice quiet before the significance of the moment. *"Debjornik's team spotted a great host moving up the shore to the break in our wall. They have Colossi, smaller ones, and an army of Divine Guard. Are you listening? They are almost inside!"*

"I'm here now, Rayn," Cole replied in a voice of molten fury.

Cole drained the heat from the metal before it could cook Ka Reine alive. He heard shrill voices calling from the elite units, but they could wait just another minute. He needed to know. With a single bound he landed beside what was left of Lileth's prison. The air was rank with burning and death. The inside of the metal dome looked even worse than the outside.

He cast his Passion over the area, revealing faint echoes of fourteen life candles from two of Valen's elite units. They had died a quick and violent death. His heart sank for them, then sank even lower when he couldn't find the slightest trace of Lileth's life candle. He looked around. The destruction was concentrated around the prison, as if whatever had blasted through the walls had been aimed directly at it. Something crunched under his bladed feet. With a spark of Wisdom he levitated several pieces of what looked like broken egg shells before his eyes. Sitra's fulminators.

"Master Cole!" cried a shrill voice Cole recognized as Kamilah's. Cole released the magic holding the elite units in place. "Master Cole they're here!"

There was movement on the far side of the gap in the trees. A sixty-foot-tall Colossus lumbered in. It was surrounded by twenty or so members of the Divine Guard, each adorned with his or her own grotesque armor made from charred bodies of Chosen. Armed with the magic of The Sill, Kamilah and the others ran straight for their enemies, defiant in the face of death.

Faster than thought, Cole shot through the air like a javelin thrown by a god. He smashed through the heart of the Colossus, killing the priest within. The rest of the Divine Guard had barely registered his appearance when he swept his munisica among them, cleaving through armor and necks as though they weren't there at all. They were all dead before the first Colossus hit the ground.

Shadows moved beyond the gap. Ambling up from the shore were hundreds more Colossi of various sizes, some of them so tall their heads would have scraped The Sill's canopy. Winged Corpulants flapped about their shoulders like flies around a tower of excrement. At their fore was a line of Divine Guard forty wide. Upon seeing Cole they peeled spears of bones from their backs, charged them with purple and blue flames, then hurled them through the gap in the wall.

There was no time to counter the missiles directly with magic, not while they were dripping with unknown Despair and Fear, nor could he catch them all with his munisica. Calling his Wisdom once again, Cole summoned a net of magic over the heavy rocks on the beach, lifting them up as a physical shield. Most of the spears shattered harmlessly among the rocks, though several made it through. Cole flitted through the air, slashing and kicking them to pieces, but there was one he knew he'd missed.

Spinning and upside down, Cole glimpsed the spear heading straight for Kamilah. Cole aimed a spell to push her out of the way, but missed, striking an unsuspecting Grant instead. The spear was ten feet in front of Kamilah before she even saw it coming.

"No!" Cole roared as he landed in a sprawl, then bolted towards his unit. He was too late.

A cloud of silvery glitter appeared before Kamilah. The spear halted a few inches from her chest, then the blue-purple flames sputtered and died as the length of bone fell at her feet. Cole watched with disbelief as Ka Reine floated out from the metal orb in which he'd encased her. Her body was insubstantial and hazy, as though she were made of thick fog, then condensed back to solid form. Quick as lightning, she threw a gnarled hand out at Cole, a ball of silver fire flaring between her fingers.

Cole raised a barrier between himself and Ka Reine, then felt something clack to the rocks behind him. He leapt back and found another bone spear lying right where he had been standing. Silvery glitter hung in the air above it.

Stymied, Cole lashed out at her with his mind and magic, lifting her off her feet as he overpowered her mental barriers with a pulse of hardened Passion. She was his.

"Master Cole don't hurt her!" Kamilah screamed. "She saved us from the explosion! She tried to save Master Valen's units but something inside the prison stopped her. I think it was Lileth."

"Who are you?" Cole demanded, ignoring Kamilah's protests.

"*I… am not the one… to whom you need to pose that question,*" Ka Reine replied in a choked tone. Cole loosened his hold on her mind so she could speak clearly.

"*Explain,*" he said.

"*There is no point,*" Ka Reine answered. With her eyes alone she pointed towards the gap in the wall. "*She is already gone. Walked off. Belongs to The Three now.*"

"*Who?*" Cole said, shaking her.

"*Your Vex,*" Ka Reine spat.

Hidden in the layers of his sub-self, Cole felt a pang of longing not of his own. Varka's grief flooded him, and he felt tears race down his shrouded cheeks.

"I don't believe you!" Cole roared. Heaving her through the air, he brought her close until her eye was level with his, then formed his thoughts into single point and stabbed through her mind, intent on tearing the woman's memories from her no matter the cost. However, unlike the minds of everyone else he had encountered, Ka Reine's mind was a profoundly tangled quagmire of memories both ancient and alien. He would need a week in the Havenflow just to begin to make sense of it.

"*Kill me then,*" Ka Reine whispered with the speed of thought. "*Or let me go so I can defend the children. Choose quickly. Those pitiful wretches just threw another volley, and we all saw how great of a job you did stopping the last one.*"

Cole gnashed his teeth as indecision itched in his marrow. Precious seconds ticked by. He swore, then spun Ka Reine through the air, placing her in front of the next volley of spears. Cole raised her arm and commandeered her magic, forcing her to repeat her spell, this time augmenting it with his own unruly Rage.

A great gout of silver fire erupted from her hand as a glittery cascade blazed across the entire gap in the wall. Forty spears halted in midair, then their flames changed from blue and purple to a seething crimson. Ka Reine let out a savage cry, then there was a barrage of thunderous reports as the spears shot back at their owners, exploding like fulminators and killing dozens with each impact. The advancing line faltered, panicked and confused, unaware of the Colossi trampling everyone who had stopped in their paths.

"Cole, what's going on over there, and why have you been blocking my thoughts?" Eliza popped the questions into his mind, simultaneously prying her answers directly from his memory. *"Oh my stars, is that Ka Reine? Hold her right there, I'm coming."*

Cole set Ka Reine down, then bent low and picked up her staff, handing it to her. "I'll be keeping an eye on you."

"Just be sure to keep the other one on Vex," Ka Reine said, her tone indignant. She flattened the front of her robes with a wrinkled hand as she waited for Cole to respond.

Cole was ready to believe Ka Reine wasn't the traitor, but he wasn't ready to believe that Lileth was. She may have been poisoned by evil magic, and the tale about this Vex woman might have had some truth to it, but none of that mattered at the moment. He would stop The Three, then he and the others would use their newfound powers to find and cleanse Lileth.

"Are you sure you can hold the line here?" Cole asked.

Ka Reine set her shoulders back and stood as tall as her rounded back would allow. "By myself no, but with the children helping I believe so. I can cast a few auras that will heighten their abilities far beyond their normal levels. We will hold the line."

Cole nodded, then took flight before his regrets could sprout. He transferred his memories to Eliza and met her in the air. They flew side by side through the gap, towards the towering nightmare that was Decreath's Colossus. Cole contacted Rayn along the way, informing him of recent events in rapid bursts. Cole sensed Rayn withhold judgment and incredulity, focusing his thoughts on more pressing concerns.

"The battle goes well for Sitra and Valen," Rayn said, transmitting an image of the Colossus lying prone in the shallows, so vast it appeared as its own island. Divine Guard, flying Corpulants, and smaller Colossi burst out holes in its back by the thousands. The Corpulants took to the skies, but every other enemy was slowed by the water. *"They felled the Alpha Colossus and nearly have it open. Whind is on his way to repair the hole in the outer wall. He says he could have it mended in an hour, but that was before those Corpulants began flying in from the skies. It's taking nearly all his efforts to stop them."*

"The elite units can handle a few Corpulants," Cole said. *"Send them up there, then have Whind work on that hole, but tell him to leave a gap one tree wide. It's better to funnel the ground forces through a small hole than have them pop up somewhere unexpected."*

"Blast it, I should have thought of that," Rayn said. *"Never mind, I'm working it now."*

Cole and Eliza flew through the gap, then over the crowded coastline, relaying images of enemies back to Rayn so he could keep track. Once they reached the cool air above the beach, Cole's jaw dropped. An ocean of enemies churned the surface of the water, a sickly boiling mass of evil, all sloshing steadily towards the gap in the wall. The air was black with Corpulants, and there were too many Colossi to count, each laden with dozens or hundreds of Divine Guard clinging on to the smaller titans.

Halfway to the horizon Cole beheld the fallen Alpha Colossus lying prone in the water, a black island of squirming undead. He enhanced his vision and saw two pairs of emerald wings slicing through the air above the dark mass. Cole and Eliza surged onward as fast as their Wisdom would carry them. Sitra's and Valen's minds were still beyond their reach.

"Please, please, just a little longer," Eliza pleaded. *"We're coming."*

"They made it this far," Cole said with budding hope.

"Yes but this is just one of The Three, and by the looks of it Decreath has yet to truly show himself," Eliza said. Shock rebounded between them as they saw Grotton's and Sorronis's Colossi appear on the horizon. The titans loomed impossibly taller by the second, monoliths of the undead. Bleeding dread flooded from Eliza, not for what they were about to face, but for an idea that suddenly came to her. *"Cole, I think you should flee."*

"Not a chance," Cole stated plainly. He knew her reason, but it wasn't nearly good enough for him to abandon everyone he knew and loved. Eliza shot in front of him, forcing him to a stop. Cole tried to fly around her, but she drew her munisica and punched him in the chest, hard. Cole tried again, and was met this time with a kick to the head. "What the hell do you think you're doing? They need us! Now!"

"Cole, think about it!" Eliza screamed. Tears welled in her eyes and her voice shook with fury. "This is what they want. You are the key to the Aethers. The Unbound might be a little stronger than we were yesterday, but there is still every chance we're marching to our deaths. This world and every other will suffer if you hand yourself over now, including Terra. Then there'll be no point in us saving Lileth, and the two of you won't be able to live out your lives together, happy, and in love... and..." her voice broke as sobs stole her breath away.

"Eliza," Cole muttered as her sorrow bled into him. Their Passion link left no doubt that she believed every word of what she said. Even in the war-torn chaos of this world she placed his happiness before her own. He wished he could give her another answer, wished he could give her the world, but he couldn't. He wouldn't. "Eliza, even if I fly straight to Oberon Temple and find a way to win this, the victory will mean nothing if everyone I love is dead. I'll have nothing left to live for."

"That's the most selfish thing I've ever heard you say," Eliza said in an icy tone. "You'd put your own happiness before the fate of billions because you're too scared of living the rest of your days without your friends. Shame on you, Cole Carter. Shame on you for your cowardice." She waited for him to respond. When it became apparent that he wouldn't, she seemed to deflate and resumed in a tone of defeat. "If that doesn't convince you, then hear this; you will never get an opportunity like this again. All of The Three are here, far away from Oberon Temple. With your powers you could be there in less than a day and search for an answer without anyone to stop you."

She was right. And Cole knew it this time. But there was one more piece to the puzzle which he had yet to tell anyone. It was the hidden reason for his reluctance, though the results were the same. He wasn't ready to say goodbye. He wasn't ready to meet his end. She was right, that if he left now there would be no one who could stop him. The Three would be right here, killing his friends. He would without a doubt never see any of them again, but if he stayed and fought, then perhaps they would win, and by the time the next Harbingers were crowned, the Unbound would be even more powerful. The chance was too tempting to pass up, however slight it was.

He looked into her eyes, Hating himself for the pain he was about to give her. "The Vaults of the Soul is a one-way trip, Eliza. Anyone who goes in never comes out. Ever. Chiron told me. Ka Reine confirmed it too. That is why I'm afraid to go. I'm not ready to say goodbye to everyone yet."

Eliza frowned as she tried to form words, but they wouldn't come. Cole felt the arguments well up inside her, seething and explosive, only to be stifled by her love for him. She wasn't ready to say goodbye to him either.

"Tell you what," Cole continued. "You and I will go over there and give it our best shot. If the battle turns against us at any point then I'll flee for Oberon Temple, no matter the cost."

"I'll go with you into the Vaults," she whispered. "I'll go with you into the end. Please…"

A desire to deny her rose up instinctively, but Cole disguised it, twisted it into a desire to have her at his side until the end of time. A beautiful lie that Cole knew he would regret until his final hour. The lie wasn't far from the truth, as he knew there was a caged part of him that wanted to love her freely as she loved him, but there was no way he would let her go with him. Not to the end.

"What a beautiful end it will be then," Cole lied. "Come on, our friends need us."

Cole watched relief wash over Eliza's face as they flew off again, and it took every ounce of focus he could spare to hide his disgust at himself. Even in the face of death he was too cowardly to tell her the truth, just so she would go willingly with his plan. What would Lileth say if she could share his mind now? Would she approve of his manipulation, or would she Hate him for his budding feelings for Eliza? He berated himself for not searching for her before leaving The Sill. She was delirious, poisoned with unidentified evil magic, and if the explosion hadn't killed her then the Divine Guard certainly had. The finality of the concept hit him true in the quiet of flight, twisting his heart with Despair. Lileth was—.

"No, don't believe it. Not yet." Eliza's words crashed into him like cold water. *"The last time she wandered off, her mind was a void,*

which you could feel by its absence. I scanned the forest on our way out, and my Passion is greater than yours. She was not there."

"It feels like a lifetime since I felt her soul," Cole said. "I miss her."

"Me too," Eliza said.

Cole knew she meant it.

Cole flew closer to Eliza and grasped her hand. Her touch anchored him to the moment, preventing his thoughts from slipping back to Despair.

When they came upon the fallen Colossus at last, they found Sitra and Valen making diving loops over the island that was its exposed back, alternating between carving a hunk of armor away with their claws and wings, and killing any Divine Guard foolish enough to crawl up to greet them.

"Damn freaks just keep coming!" Sitra bellowed. "How the hell are we supposed to draw Decreath out of this mountain of shit when they keep popping out!" She dove again, kicking the head and shoulder off a man as he clambered up over a fallen comrade. "That's it, I'm going in."

"Sitra!" Valen cried, diving after her.

Now that Cole could see they were in no immediate danger, he struck Sitra and Valen with an affectionate, yet jarring burst of Passion. Sitra angled her wings and looped up once more, cleaving the head off yet another victim before riding up to meet them.

"I'm gonna kill you two!" Sitra hollered as she locked eyes with them. She crashed into them and wrapped them in a single shrouded hug. She laughed as tears streaked down her blackened cheeks. "I thought the Havenflow killed you both."

"I think it might have at some point," Eliza said, unable to hold her laughter in despite her own tears.

Valen flew up beside them. Like Sitra's, his emerald wings had been elongated and sharpened, with extra blades jutting out from every feather. And like Eliza, his shroud seemed to cover every portion of his body except parts of his face and neck.

Valen smiled from ear to ear, but his voice was as calm and monotonous as ever. "Warm greetings, Cole and Eliza. You are—"

"More than we once were?" Cole chuckled, flying over and giving his friend a hug.

The four friends joined minds at last. Warmth and compassion rang between them like notes to an old song. Their collective mastery of Passion bolstered their fraternal links like never before, hastening thoughts and shielding their minds with thick mental armor. Within a few heartbeats they exchanged a full account of recent memories as well as an estimation of their new powers.

"So if Eliza mastered Wisdom, that means Cole is the only one who didn't master anything inside the Havenflow," Sitra stated. One of her black eyebrows went up as she looked Cole up and down. "We expected you to walk out a master of all magic. Looks like you're even with me now. If we make it out of this alive, you and I need to square up and find out who the better fighter is."

"I have to admit," Cole started, knowing he would be blushing if he weren't fully shrouded, "I may have been using Varka's cape a bit too much. It was a crutch, and my magic suffered for it. The Havenflow just gave me a chance to catch my Wisdom up to where it should be, maybe a little further even. My Passion and Rage are stronger than ever though, so you really wouldn't stand a chance against me. I was already miles ahead of you before I went into the Havenflow."

"Really?" Eliza snapped, incredulous. "You're about to face the fight of your life and all you two can think about is the next one?"

"Well, that and where our next meal is coming from," Sitra said, patting her armored belly with a clink. "Don't suppose Thessi could run some food out to us? Hell I'd even go for a blackstout right now."

"Children," Eliza huffed.

While their life candles burned all the brighter at their reunion, Cole's flame didn't quite match the rest of theirs. It was like his happiness was a bird trying to fly with only half its feathers. He missed Lileth.

"There has been no sign of her," Valen said, breaking the silence. "Which means she is not dead for certain. When we finish here, we will find her. With four masters of Passion searching we will find and cleanse whatever poison ails her soul. You have my word."

Cole's heart swelled with gratitude and hope, humble gifts he offered to the others through their fraternal link. He turned his attention to the horizon. The two Alpha Colossi lumbered ever closer. *"Sorronis and Grotton will be here soon. We need to get to work. Decreath lives in Kreed's body, which can be broken just like anything else, so let's break him."*

"I'm afraid you and Eliza will have to do most of the work," Valen admitted. *"Sitra and I used up a good portion of our Wisdom just to drop Decreath's Colossus. I still don't know how to—"*

"Here, I brought this for the two of you." Eliza reached into her robes and pulled out a small bundle wrapped in silken cloth. She tossed it to Valen. *"It may be small but trust me it's very full. I transferred power from every gratia stone in the markets into it. It should convert into fuel for whatever magic you're lacking in."*

Valen unwrapped the stone and they all shielded their eyes. It looked like he held a brilliant white star in his clawed hand.

Valen dismissed his munisica and placed his palm flat to the stone. It shone bright green for a moment as the magic flowed into him. He repeated the process and replenished his Passion and Rage, then tossed the stone to Sitra. *"Does Rayn know you took that from the Operations center? It is very valuable."*

"If we live long enough for him to find out, I will gladly accept his retribution," Eliza stated.

After Sitra took her fill, Cole and Eliza topped themselves off for good measure. The Omnistone was still too bright to look at, as though they had barely drained it at all.

"What a waste," Sitra said as she squinted at the stone. *"It would have made a fine fulminator. Imagine the look on Rayn's face."*

Eliza tossed the omnistone back to Sitra. *"That's exactly what I was thinking."*

Sitra flashed them a mischievous smile, then wove her claws over the stone, covering it with webs of emerald and crimson. A ringing filled the air as cracks splintered across the surface of the omnistone. Cole floated back several feet, not entirely confident his shroud would protect him from so much unstable energy. When Sitra finished a moment later, she cocked her arm back, taking aim for one of the massive fissures in the Colossus's back.

"Ready?" Sitra asked aloud, grinning wide.

"Thow it," Cole commanded.

Sitra whipped her arm down, hurling the fulminator with a blast of Wisdom and raw strength. The bomb ripped through the air as it went. Below them, the Divine Guard shielded their eyes and summoned barriers and ruby shrouds as they dove aside in a panic. The fulminator missed them all, vanishing through the crevice, then they rose to their feet spitting insults and spells back at the Unbound.

Faster than Cole thought possible, a four-acre swath of the titan's back suddenly rose into the air, then a concussion struck him like a punch from the Colossus itself. Brilliant white light shone from the fragmented carapace as a wave of heat seared across his robes and face. Pieces of Chosen, Corpulants, and Divine Guard swirled up around the Unbound as if they were suddenly transported to the inside of a gruesome snowglobe. As the light faded and debris fell away, Cole beheld what looked like an entire city inside the now exposed portion of the Colossus's back. Structures of bone and steel were laid about in an organized grid, complete with furniture and carved statues. The damage was immense, even for an Alpha Colossus.

Something stirred within the settling mess. Waves of crippling Fear radiated from a single point of churning bodies and debris, then a broad structure began to rise. A spire of charred flesh and dirty steel emerged, and at its tip was an altar surrounded by several thick columns, capped with a pointed slate roof. A pale figure floated above the altar.

Before Decreath had a chance to strike the first blow, the Unbound gripped their Rage and dove in a tight formation. At Cole's urging, the others pulled back just behind him, granting him the room he needed to collide with the pale figure with all the Rage he could muster. The tower rushed up even faster, as if eager to greet them, then the pale figure turned to face him.

"*Stop!*" Cole shouted, halting himself in the air twenty feet above the altar. He felt the others stop just behind him.

Wilkin spun slowly atop the altar, naked, suspended by invisible hooks of Fear. His eyes were stuck wide open and his breath came rapidly and shallowly. He appeared unable to move his body, but his eyes darted about incessantly, searching for a way out. When he found the Unbound, Cole saw the Fear of Decreath burning behind his gaze.

"Master, I'm sorry, I'm sorry, I'm sorry..." Wilkin breathed in a voice barely loud enough to hear. As he spun around, Cole beheld a neat laceration running from the back of his head to the bottom of his back. A faint blue wire was braided along the wound like stitches.

"No," Cole gasped. He glanced around, searching for a source of the danger. He sensed potent Fear mingled with other magics, but it was too convoluted to understand.

The tower shuddered to a stop. The Unbound circled around, searching for a way to free Wilkin, but no one could make sense of the magic. A door opened nearby. Cole whipped around to see who it was, but he could only catch a glimpse of white vanishing behind another column. Cole heard the footsteps of dress shoes clack over the metal surface, as well as the shuffling of something wet with four legs.

"Enough," Cole said to the others. "If there's a trap then let's trigger it before Grotton and Sorronis get here."

Following his lead, the Unbound spread themselves around the tower, then with a collective jolt of Wisdom, they tore the slate roof and every column off the top of the tower. Kreed stood next to the altar in his snow-white suit, twirling the blue wire from Wilkin's back around his index finger. At his side was a horrible winged creature made from a collection of bones forced onto four legs and a tail. Strands of flesh and flaps of skin clung to the creature's frame, torn and ragged, as though something had nibbled its body away.

"How long has it been?" Kreed gushed. He gaped at Cole with indecent interest, twirling the slack out of the thin blue wire. "It feels like an age, doesn't it? We've both grown and done so much, oh and the tales I've heard!" Overcome with a fit of glee, Kreed rapidly clapped his fingertips together, twitching the wire even tighter. "Tell me, is it true you have a child? Amorinanis I believe? Immensely powerful with limitless potential. Well, I wouldn't expect any less given who her father is. I can't wait to meet her and see those gifts firsthand."

"Don't indulge him, Cole," Valen said to the group. *"Grotton and Sorronis will be here in but a few minutes. He is only stalling us."*

"I know that," Cole replied. *"I'm just trying to figure out how to help Wilkin."*

"Wilkin isn't going to come out of this alive, Cole," Eliza said as gently as she could. *"You must harden your heart. We haven't much time."*

As if he could hear their conversation, a shivering whisper slipped out of Wilkin's lips as he spun around. His frantic eyes found Cole's.

"I'm sorry, Master Cole. I messed up. I'm sorry. I'm sorry. I'm sorry…" Wilkin continued muttering to himself as his face spun out of Cole's sight once more.

Sickening grief struck Cole's heart. It was his fault. By assigning Wilkin to that pointless mission he had caused untold suffering to a boy whose only desire was to make his master proud.

"Oh hush now, you've done a fantastic job for your masters," Kreed chuckled as he followed Wilkin around. He bounded over to Wilkin and wrapped him in a tight hug, nuzzling their cheeks together. "We would have been here a couple hours sooner if I wasn't having so much fun with you. Very brave student you have here, Master Cole. And what a performer! You should be proud." Kreed gripped Wilkin's head and kissed him on the brow, and as he did the thin blue wire began to tumble loose from the skin behind Wilkin's head. Dark blood oozed in earnest. Kreed detached himself from the boy and tripped over a piece of broken column, then stumbled upright, causing another inch of the stitches to dance free.

"Dammit Cole, if you don't do something I will!" Sitra shouted, her Rage flaring across their minds.

Sheets of blood ran down Wilkin's back, covering his feet before racing to the altar in a solid line. The bone-creature sniffed the air, then clicked its jaw excitedly as it ambled up the altar to nip at Wilkin's toes.

"Down, Baedine!" Kreed snapped, aiming a kick at the creature. "I said down! That's not yours!"

A ball of fire streaked from the sky to the altar. It splashed harmlessly across a gleaming blue barrier around the bone creature, which twitched and leaped back in shock. Kreed looked up with a surprised smile. Sitra loomed above, flames licking between the long blades of her munisica.

"Really now? Wisdom?" Kreed said with a disappointed sneer. "Didn't your masters teach you anything? Do you even know whose Harbinger I am? It would take a far more powerful—" Kreed threw an arm over his eyes and leapt back as a solid beam of fire ten feet wide roared from Valen's outstretched claw. There was only the faintest yelp before it struck the bone creature, obliterating it and the section of the tower it stood on. Kreed lowered his arm slowly and spoke with a voice of oiled malice. "If you were bored of the pleasantries then you should have just said so."

"Now!" Cole shouted.

Gathering their minds into a cohesive thought, the Unbound enveloped Wilkin's mind with Passion, shielding him from the Fear while drawing all his pain into themselves. With Wilkin's mind safely in their embrace, they charged at last.

As if he had been finally granted his deepest desire, Kreed's eyes rolled and his lips pulled back in an indulgent smirk, then he yanked the blue wire. Cole, Sitra, and Valen screamed as Wilkin's agony reverberated across their minds. The wound opened like a book as his skull slipped through, glistening and red, followed by his entire spine. Eliza maintained stoic composure as she dove into Wilkin's mind, saturating him with his own pleasant memories as she carried him to the void.

Wilkin's body fell to the altar while his skull and spine flew into Kreed's waiting hand, splattering his white suit with red. Tendrils of bruised purple snaked from Kreed's fingertips and sank into the bones like starving roots. The spine stretched several times its length as the vertebrae broadened and sharpened into jagged blades. Kreed's head fell back. Mottled smoke billowed from his mouth and eyes, then he emitted a noise that had no business in the world of the living. It was the drenched nightmares of the damned.

The Unbound took solace in the safety of their joined thoughts. They shared in each other's Rage, the only thing hot enough to stay the chilling dread and keep their minds from twisting themselves into insanity. The voice of Decreath rose in intensity, then leveled out to a nearly tolerable wail, unable to pierce their hearts with deadly terror.

"That's the worst thing I've ever heard," Sitra said in a warbled tone. *"At least we can listen to it without dying."*

Cole blinked and steadied himself. Sorronis's and Grotton's Colossi were each within a mile. He wasn't sure the Unbound could stand the presence of all of The Three at the same time.

"Kill him now, before the other two get here!" Cole shouted as he dove for Decreath.

Wielding the spine like a whip, Decreath lashed out with unnerving speed. Cole ducked under the attack and landed on the tower, then kicked off to the side and dodged another blow. Purple Fear glinted between the blades of the whip. The others surrounded Decreath from the sides and the rear. Sitra landed directly behind him, but Decreath spun around and spewed a cascade of liquid smoke over her, and she leaped back, blind and scratching at her eyes. The whip tore around in great circles, keeping Valen and Eliza at bay as they flew just out of reach. They shot beams of fire and lightning that fizzled before reaching their target. Cole waited for an opening, then charged as fast as his Rage could carry him.

As fast as Cole was, Decreath was somehow faster, and quickening with every beat of the battle. With absurd ease, the god of Fear brought his whip around and struck Cole full in the chest, stopping him on the spot. Cole winced and glimpsed at the damage. His reinforced armored robes had been torn completely off, and his shroud had two deep furrows dripping with violet liquid. The wound stung as if he'd been laid open by a frozen sword.

"How is he so fast!" Sitra said as she too failed to dodge a blow from the whip. Another lash came down on her before she hit the ground. She recovered, seething as her Rage repaired the gashes in her shroud. *"Fear isn't supposed to make a person faster."*

Cole watched as Eliza danced gracefully over the tower, using bursts of Wisdom and Rage in equal measure as she dodged the whip with an incredible display of acrobatics. She twirled to a low, crouched position beyond the inner limits of the whip, which at the moment was chasing Valen through the air. Just a few feet away from Decreatch, she flattened her munisica into a single blade and stabbed it outward, but once again Decreath displayed speed beyond their understanding. With a lazy wave of his free hand, ghostly purple tendrils erupted from the floor beneath Eliza's feet, halting her mid-strike and constricting around her whole body. Eliza's scream snapped short as one of the tendrils buried itself in her open mouth.

Without conscious thought, Cole charged once more at Decreath, who seemed to expect the attack and brought the whip cracking down once more. Cole feigned left, then rolled to the right, earning a few inches and a miss from the whip. Valen and Sitra came in at the same time, each taking a splash of the smoking vomit full to the face, which took them out of the fight but allowed Cole to reach Eliza before the whip came around again. Cole snipped the tendrils from Eliza with his munisica, then threw her out of the way with a burst of Wisdom. He noted an odd slowness to her as she flew from him, as if she were moving through water instead of air. As Cole spun to face Decreath, he noticed the strange torpor in his own limbs as well. Rage fueled his every motion, but it felt as if he were moving about unaided by magic of any sort.

The answer came to him a fraction of a second too late. The bone whip coiled around his arms and legs, pinning him strait as a rod. His feet left the ground as Decreath dragged him close. The mouth was open and gurgling, ready to shower him with the debilitating vomit, the same smoke that permeated the air with numbing Fear.

"*Valen, burn him with fire!*" Cole shouted into their minds. Even his thoughts were sluggish.

"*But I can't see a thing,*" Valen gasped as he tried to remove the viscous Fear from his face. The magic racked him with crippling spikes of pure terror. "*The Fear, it's too great. I can't use my Wisdom.*"

"*You can! Light the whole tower on fire, just do it now!*" Cole said. Bruised violet smoke bubbled from Decreath's mouth, which was only inches away now. Cole shut his eyes and shifted his mind to Valen's, pouring a measure of Rage into his friend.

Trembling and blind, but stable, Valen rose to his feet and ignited the spell. Cole imbued the fire with the Rage from his own soul, urging Eliza and Sitra to do the same. The entire top of the tower burst into rich crimson flames, searing away the haze of Fear. The fire carried no heat, but rather a concentrated essence of Rage, the soul's denial of death and Fear. Decreath's scream shifted from creeping torment to shrill pain as alacrity returned to Cole's limbs. Seizing his Rage properly, Cole's limbs exploded through the bone around him, and he stabbed his munisica three times into Decreath's chest. Decreath wailed and withdrew, holding his hands over the wounds in his breast, each oozing with dark violet liquid.

Valen's fire burned the taint from his and Sitra's skin and brought Eliza back to her feet. Rage blazed in their eyes. Decreath stumbled back from Cole, spells failing in his hands as the fire consumed the Fear. The liquid gushing out of his wounds sizzled and evaporated before hitting the ground. Now Decreath was the one too slow to react. Sitra's munisica slashed across his back, slicing ribbons from his white suit as her blow sent him flying into Eliza, who met him with a bladed foot to the face. Decreath landed sprawled on the tower floor, screaming at Valen's feet.

"End it, Val," Sitra growled.

Crimson flames rolled within Valen's claw as he raised it high. Decreath tried to crawl away but Sitra, Eliza, and Cole stepped on his hands and feet, pinning him to the tower.

There was a great gust of wind as the flames covering the tower suddenly rushed upward in a swirling vortex. Cole looked up and saw two figures floating in the sky above. One was small in comparison to the other, with ruby shroud and munisica, and a bundle of cloth cradled in one arm. The other was fully shrouded in black and the size of a small Colossus.

Menacing laughter thundered through the air as Valen's fire coalesced into a ball between Roth's munisica. The magic solidified and shifted to a rusty orange before he cast it back at them.

"Move!" Cole shouted as he took flight.

Raw and ravenous, the ball of Hunger roared through the air, rattling Cole's armored teeth as it neared. Their feet had barely left the ground when the spell collided with the tower. As Cole ascended for the stars something struck him in the back, and he was no longer flying away from the tower, but towards it, almost too quickly for his Rage-sharpened senses. The pressure on his back increased, and in a blink he collided with the tower, smashing through the explosion of Hunger to the bone and dirty steel beneath. Flashes of stairs and bloody light flicked across his vision in between periods of deafening black. After a few seconds of thunderous carnage he felt himself come to a halt somewhere near the bottom of the tower, which judging by the din above was currently collapsing on top of him. In the chaos he realized the pressure pinning him in place was the weight of a massive bladed foot.

With Rage flooding him in searing waves, Cole thrust his arms down with the intent of overpowering whoever was standing on him, but the pressure increased a hundredfold and he only succeeded in digging himself deeper. Cole shut his eyes and delved into his Passion. He was still connected to the rest of the Unbound, but barely. Their minds were too preoccupied with battle for him to ask for help.

At last the foot released him and the immense weight lifted from his back as a fading clamor told him that whoever had been standing on him was plowing their way out of the rubble. Cole righted himself in the dark mess and found a solid piece of frame with his bladed feet, then jumped as hard as he could, aiming himself towards the life candles of the Unbound.

Cole emerged from the rubble, whole but shaken to his core. Black swords pierced his peripheral vision as a bladed hand the size of a small tree enclosed around his head, lifting him off the ground. Cole pried at two of the claws, each as long as his leg, but they didn't so much as tremble at his power. Up he went, twice his height, then three times until he was level with Roth's shrouded face. Hunger surged through the claws, washing over Cole in a river of will-bending power. Cole felt his Rage leaking from him, weakening him. He wanted to give up.

"Don't tell me you've forgotten my rules, Human." Roth's voice rumbled into Cole's chest like thunder. He spoke through a mouth easily large enough to swallow Cole's head and shoulders in a single bite. "I want everything you got. Every drop of blood and sweat you own belongs to me."

"You're not Roth!" Cole growled as he kicked out at open air.

Roth let out a chuckle like a rolling avalanche. "You're right. I am much more than he. He tempered his Rage with Passion instead of feeding it what it needs. Hunger knows what Rage wants. Hunger knows what everyone wants. Right now you want to give up, but your heart tells you to hold on for your friends."

Cole's eyes flicked up. Above Roth's head he saw Valen and Sitra fighting Talin, Harbinger of Sorronis. Talin was shrouded head to heel in the bloody armor of Hatred. Slicing through the air on emerald wings, Sitra and Valen dodged beams of Hatefire, clashing black munisica against red. Eliza was nowhere to be seen, which meant she was fighting Decreath alone.

"Let's say they all die, right now," Roth rumbled, pulling his lips back into a demonic grin. Clumps of pink and white flesh hung between his obsidian teeth. "What would you want then? What would be your heart's desire?"

"To kill you!" Cole shouted.

Roth's black eyes shut halfway as his mouth opened in laughter, an open window. Cole's Wisdom came at the speed of thought. A crackling ball of destructive green energy appeared in his hands, so powerful that he could feel the shroud in his palm begin to splinter. He shoved the spell into Roth's open mouth, then kicked upwards as hard as he could, smashing Roth in the jaw. The claws on his head slackened as the force from his kick shot him towards the ground in the blink of an eye. Cole landed and leapt back at once, detonating the spell.

The Colossus's back shuddered as a brilliant white explosion erupted from Roth's face. Roth stumbled back and cradled his face in his hands, then an otherworldly sound filled the air as Cole heard the alluring power of Grotton's song.

Cole shot up into the air and found Eliza a hundred yards away battling Decreath, who had somehow fully recovered from his wounds. She was on foot and surrounded by a dozen members of the Divine Guard as well as a forty-foot Colossus, but something was odd about their behavior. Lavender light shone from their eyes and they weren't attacking Eliza at all. They were attacking Decreath. Several more warriors emerged from a crevice in the ground, all hell-bent on rushing Eliza, but she dove from between the legs of the small Colossus and sent a blast of Passion into each of their faces. The enemies doubled over in agony, only to rise a moment later with Passion shining in their eyes as they aimed their weapons at the god of Fear.

"I don't need help!" Eliza shouted to the Unbound, but her words were for Cole. *"Decreath is mine."*

Valen's voice came in a calm, measured tone. *"Nor do we. Sorronis is slowing already."*

"Focus on Grotton!" Sitra urged. *"He's used Roth's body long enough."*

Cole brought his attention back to the shrouded giant beneath him. The enormous munisica lowered, and Grotton gazed out at Cole through Roth's eyes, which now glowed a dull, rusty orange. Half his jaw was missing, blood dripping from the shattered remnants of shroud. Though the wound began to repair itself, Cole took heart knowing that he could at least damage the god.

While Grotton took a moment to heal himself, Cole withdrew to the stone room of his center. With each inhale he filled the room with cool, peaceful air, and with each exhale he let the water flow down over his Fear, Hunger, Hatred and Despair. He repeated the process until all that was left was a perfect balance of Rage, Wisdom, and Passion.

Cole opened his eyes. A lazy smile stretched over Grotton's armored face, then he threw his shoulders back and drew breath. Air and debris rushed into his mouth in vast quantities as his portly belly swelled until it was larger than the whole of his body. A gout of what appeared to be orange insects erupted from his mouth, billowing up forty feet into the air, thick and turgid. As the magic neared Cole, he saw that it was not a swarm of insects, but rather a cloud of miniscule faces each ruddy orange with a mouth full of razor-sharp teeth, gnashing and biting everything in their path to include each other. The rising ocean of Hunger billowed and gathered around Cole from all sides, occluding the stars and Oberon's light. He could hear their tiny laughing snarls as they buzzed closer.

Cole shut his eyes again and hovered in the air. Rage was not the answer, not in the face of Hunger. Cole summoned his Wisdom to the moment, fueling it with a trickle of Rage. There was a deafening snap as a violent cyclone appeared around him. Lured by the taste of Rage in the air, the entire swarm flew eagerly up into the twisting sphere of magic. Cole pushed the spell away from himself and the swarm followed, then he twisted the magic into an impenetrable barrier of pure Wisdom, trapping the Hunger within. Cole held his hand up and began to close his fingers, compressing the emerald barrier until it was no taller than he was. He then placed a single munisica against the sphere and filled it with a potent surge of Passion, erasing the Hunger within. He dismissed his spells and the barrier dissipated in a thin fog of sparkling lavender.

He looked down at Grotton, expecting fury, but the god's smile was even broader, as if he were pleased by Cole's performance. Cole smiled back, hoping to incite Grotton into another obvious attack that he could counter with Passion. The lover's magic was the perfect antidote to Hunger, but he couldn't think of a way to attack Grotton with it. There was no way Passion could pierce a Rage master's shroud, and even Cole's most powerful blast of Wisdom only broke the armor for a few seconds before Grotton healed himself. He needed more time to think. Letting go of his Wisdom, Cole landed several yards in front of Grotton, well within reach of those giant munisica.

As Cole looked up at Roth's stolen body, he couldn't help but think of his first encounter with the Bonebreaker many months ago. During that occasion he was shorter than Roth's waist. Now though, he was barely taller than Roth's knee.

Towering above him, Grotton raised his fist to the stars. A fire ignited between Grotton's bladed fingers, which roared and hardened into a flaming sword the size of a small bus. Cole felt the heat of the magic through his shroud. Then, faster than he thought possible, the arm descended and the sword was inches from his eyes. Rage blended with instinct and he dove to the side, rolling straight into a kick from Grotton's massive foot. Head ringing, Cole stopped himself in midair and fell back to the ground. Grotton bellowed and the sword came down again, only this time Cole was ready for it. He flipped out of the way as the sword smashed through the ground, producing a geyser of white-hot lava from the hide of the Alpha Colossus. As Cole sprinted around Grotton's backside, he summoned a barrier over his shroud, covering himself with a sheen of jade ice, linking the spell to a steel support beam he sensed buried in the rubble and corpses beneath him.

Feigning fatigue, Cole allowed the sword to hit him with glancing blows as Grotton drove him to the edge of the Colossus's back. With each strike the sword dimmed as its heat was transferred to the steel beam, only to surge back brighter and hotter than before. Before long genuine fatigue dragged at Cole's mind, making his thoughts and reactions sluggish, and Grotton's slashes were no longer glancing, but direct. It soon became a battle of Wisdom, Grotton's sword against Cole's barrier, and Cole knew he couldn't keep it up much longer.

Cole raised his munisica and caught the sword between his claws. His barrier vanished as the sword sputtered and melted harmlessly between them. The hiss of crashing waves behind him told Cole he was near the edge. From between Grotton's legs he saw a column of smoke rising from the back of the Alpha Colossus a hundred feet away. Cole hoped he had enough Wisdom left for what needed to be done.

The sword lifted as a bladed foot came flying at him. Cole shut his eyes and threw a hand up, conjuring a blinding beam of light directly into Grotton's face. The kick missed and Cole rolled to the side, then heaving up the final dregs of his Wisdom, he grasped the steel beam with his thoughts and cast it as hard as he could at Grotton.

Corpses and metal framework exploded from the back of the Colossus as a thirty-foot beam of glowing steel screamed through the air. Grotton stumbled around, blindly rubbing his eyes with one hand while holding the other out to shield himself. Cole's aim was true, but just before his attack landed, a barrier of pale blue and bright emerald magic appeared before Grotton. The spell turned the beam to chilled powder that scattered like snow over the armored chest. His Wisdom depleted, Cole cursed Decreath and charged at Grotton. There was only one way now.

Cole let his Hatred flow through him. Seething and potent, the evil magic granted him speed and strength beyond the limits of Rage, imbuing him with the power and desire to inflict relentless suffering on

JOSEPH PARADIS

the ones who wronged him. Cole struggled to contain the magic as he ran, but he had suppressed it for so long, it caught like fire in a drought. His right hand burned as its munisica bloomed a beautiful ruby red. The shroud of Hatred traveled up his arm, and it was all he could do to halt it at the shoulder. Searing agony rang from his bones, promising release through the exchange of pain. Cole's feet covered the distance in two bounds, then he jumped.

Grotton blinked as he regained the use of his eyes, but it was too late. Cole's ruby munisica slashed across his chest, rending the ebony armor as easily as dried leather. Shards of black and red shroud exploded in a shower of sparks, snapping the bones in Cole's hand and exposing Roth's bare chest, as well as the stump of the pithing shard buried in his heart. Time slowed as Cole wrestled with the magic storming within him. Rage and Hatred tore at each other, fighting for dominance of his soul. He couldn't control it. He couldn't stop it. He had missed his chance.

Cole felt something stir within a forgotten corner of his mind. A boy with Velcro shoes and a crooked hat looked up at him with adoration gleaming in his eyes, but there was something else behind his gaze, an answer.

I know.

Passion surged through Cole like a tidal wave, soothing the unruly duo of Rage and Hatred bickering like children. In their place blossomed a love so pure and deep that for a sliver of a heartbeat Cole felt an intimate connection to everyone around him, alive, undead, and even whatever The Three had become. The connection expanded beyond the battlefield, beyond The Sill and surrounding lands. It continued past the farthest reaches of Aeneria until Cole felt himself falling into the limitless wonder of the Aethers. He touched every mind on the journey out of himself, losing his sanity in a wonderful symphony of chaotic bliss, until there was nothing left but a singular, yet nebulous concept that connected them all: Love.

When Cole returned to his body he was wrapped in one of Grotton's munisica. Both his black and red shroud were gone, leaving him defenseless, but an ingot of what he had just experienced remained in the form of Passion. Just as Grotton's claws began to slice their way into his flesh, Cole placed his hand against Roth's bare chest and transferred Joshy's gift.

There was a brief flash of lavender, then a concussion with no sound. Grotton's munisica relaxed and Cole fell to the ground, shaking and weak. His Wisdom and Passion were gone, and without them he was afraid to summon his Rage, which was still too closely entwined with his newfound Hatred.

Grotton crashed to his hands and knees. The ruddy orange glow vanished from his eyes and his black shroud faded and bloomed in waves as he struggled to maintain hold of his Rage. He looked up, and Cole saw tears pooling in his eyes.

When he spoke it was in a voice very much like Roth's. "How... how can you bear it?"

"I couldn't," Cole gasped. "Not alone."

"No," Roth growled through bared teeth. He winced as the shroud receded from his face in tiny twitches. "No, no, NO!"

The orange light blazed back into Roth's eyes and Cole knew he had no choice. He had to end it now, no matter the consequences. Sighing with regret, he delved within himself and approached the cages to his Rage and Hatred. Hopefully one of the others would be able to stop what he was about to become.

A flicker of movement caught Cole's eye. A pale, thin hand gripped a piece of bone jutting out from the very edge of the Alpha Colossus. Drenched and trembling from head to heel, Lileth hoisted herself up onto the battlefield. Equal parts of Fear and intent lined her face as she gazed at him. Clumps of seaweed hung over her nightgown, and she had a small leather satchel draped over one shoulder. Her skin was pruned and raw, with fresh crimson scrapes over her hands and knees. Varka's cape hung slack over her back, plain and grey. Her whole body shook with chilled exhaustion, though her eyes were clear and lucid.

"No!" Cole shouted, and he bolted around Roth's hulking form, anxious to put himself between her and danger. Not far away he saw the others still locked in battle with Decreath and Sorronis, but he couldn't tell how they were faring. He took Lileth's hand in his. She felt as cold as a corpse. "Lileth you can't be here now. It's too dangerous."

"I came to help," Lileth said in an empty tone.

Roth stirred and Cole swore. He had to end this now before Grotton recovered. He threw open the cages and let the magics loose, but to his surprise the Rage charged ahead of the Hatred, fueled by his desire to save Lileth. The black shroud snapped over him in an instant, granting him his tools of destruction. The patches of Roth's unarmored flesh called out to him. As Cole took the first step, something slapped into his back.

He uttered a soft moan and fell to his knees. His munisica shrank and his shroud vanished. Rage drained from him, stolen by some strange presence. He reached around to his back, but found he no longer had the energy to lift his arms, and his hands swung uselessly by his side as he slumped to his knees. Lileth came into his view, and it took all his strength just to turn his eyes to look at her. He tried to tell her to run, but another moan came out instead.

As she walked past him, Cole saw that the satchel was open, and she had a stout piece of wood in her hand. She dropped the object as she continued her stride, which grew more lithe by the step. The object clattered to the ground. The wooden cylinder cracked neatly in half, revealing a jagged hollow along its length, and suddenly a great many things made sense to Cole. The piece of wood was taken from a tree next to Alvani's grave site, the hollow inside from Alvani's pithing shard, which was now buried in his back.

"Why," Cole breathed.

Lileth paused. She turned her head and looked back, confused and concerned, as though she had merely heard a whisper on the wind. Her brow hardened and she walked on.

Tears flooded Cole's vision faster than his sluggish eyes could blink them away. There was a flapping of wings and a gust of wind, then Cole heard voices around him.

"His life candle is fading!" Eliza shouted. "Lileth, what are you doing here, get away from Grotton!"

"Something is very wrong here," Valen said in a grim tone.

"Well get him back on his feet at least," Sitra growled. "Decreath and Sorronis won't stay down for long, and it looks like Grotton's about to be sick. Lileth, get your ass over here and help!"

Cole felt hands on his back as the others transferred their magic into him. He didn't have the strength to tell them to stop. Crushing agony radiated from his back as the pithing shard ripped the magic from his flesh and soul. Cole screamed.

"Why isn't it working?" Eliza wept as her hand fumbled over his back. "Stars above…"

"A pithing shard!" Valen shouted. "But how!"

"Never mind, just get him out of here!" Sitra snapped. "Lileth what the hell are you doing?"

It was now or never. Cole dug through his memories and uncovered one of the spells from Chiron's book of warning. It was risky in the extreme, as failure could result in unimaginable destruction and permanent damage to this reality, but he saw no other choice. Grasping the failing wisps of Wisdom that the others had gifted him, he brought the spell into the world. One by one he aimed a hand at each of his friends, and they vanished in a cloud of emerald smoke.

CHAPTER 30

A STORY OF PAIN

C ole made an attempt to cast the spell on himself, but his Wisdom had run dry. The fact that he was still in agony gave him some comfort, for it meant his spell hadn't obliterated the world in a black hole. Sitra, Eliza, and Valen were safely back at The Sill. It was him The Three wanted.

Rough hands dragged him by the collar of his armor. How far or where he went he couldn't tell. He was dimly aware of a presence hanging over him, dark and cold like a heavy shadow. The pithing shard drained his life candle all the while, stealing the strength from his limbs, the breath from his chest, and magic from his soul. All that was left was pain. Ubiquitous and overwhelming, its crushing emptiness filled his mind past endurance, erasing all thought and splintering his skull from the inside. Something twisted his guts, churning up vomit he lacked the energy to heave. Stabbing pain radiated in slow waves from his back to the rest of his body, as though several ragged blades were wandering freely from nerve to flesh to marrow. Nothing in training or battle had ever prepared him for this. How he managed to keep existing he couldn't guess. There was a clang, then his face struck something that tasted like metal, or perhaps that was just the blood in his mouth. He was alone. Alone with the pithing shard.

His ears told him someone was nearby. The stench of odium and charred flesh told his nose that he was very near an Alpha Colossus, or more likely, inside of one. Slow, shuffling footsteps echoed all around him. A fleeting urge to see who it was leapt up within Cole like a minnow jumping out of water, but then it was gone with a cold splash. Moving his head was agony beyond endurance, the mere thought of it sending a twisting, jerking blade through to his neck and shoulders.

Opening his eyes was an effort beyond his strength. Hands as hard as bone lifted him into the air, then down again.

"Almost ready," said a female voice. Her tone was sultry and wet, though there was something perverse about it, as though her mouth and throat had been coated with bloody perfume.

Something tapped the pithing shard three times. Each touch was a sledgehammer driving the wedge of lightning through Cole's body. If only he could move. He felt as if he were paralyzed in a bath of open flames.

"Yes, yes, yes, we're nearly there," said the voice.

The bony hands gripped Cole by the hair and yanked his head back. His hope begged for a knife, a claw, something to open his throat and deliver him from the pain. Foul liquid sloshed about his mouth and stung his nostrils, his own vomit or hopefully a poison. Cole let the liquid trickle freely down his throat, where it could choke him to an unfeeling death.

Death did not come for him, however. Instead, a burning sense of panic-driven vigilance blossomed in his heart, the same sensation he had felt so many times in battle when his life danced upon the wire of mortal danger. Cole's eyes snapped open. He was first aware of the potion coursing through his body, fueling it with trembling Fear. He was inside a small, dimly lit room. A sheen of rusty blood covered the walls and ceiling, a dark metallic material with a molded bone framework laced within like tree roots. He rolled his head to the side and saw a plain, empty chair, and carved in the wall behind was a series of drawers and shelves covered in old brown stains. One of the drawers was too full to close. A thin chain dangled out, and on its end was a barbed punch knife with clumps of meat still clinging to it.

Cole heard the footsteps scuffling behind him as someone rummaged through more drawers. He attempted to roll and rise to his feet, but only his arm heeded his will. It flopped to his side, where it dangled off the edge of the table he was lying on.

"Ah there it is," said the oily voice. "The will to live that resists the call of the void. Fight it, human. Fight it like your life depends upon it."

Cole's breath couldn't come fast enough, or deep enough, as if he were drowning in empty air. The Fear gifted him another measure of wobbly strength and he rolled his head to the side, but the stranger was still beyond his periphery. A moan escaped his lips as fresh agony twisted from his neck to the bottom of his spine. The stranger shuffled past his vision, the outline hazy and dark, as though made from liquid shadow.

The stranger paused as his moan lingered in the air, and when it spoke it sounded as though it was through a smile. "Do not deny your pain, human. It's a beautiful paradox, a gift from the gods bestowed only upon the worthy, and no one is more worthy than you. Embrace it, for even as the void tempts you, the pain will anchor you to this world. You have unfinished business here."

Cole heard the footsteps shuffle around the table, then the creak of the chair, followed by the squeaking of wheels as the chair rolled closer. Fear drove him through the barriers of pain, and he turned his head once more to behold the stranger through watery eyes.

Spider-leg fingers peeled back a grey hood, revealing a gaunt, hairless face as pale as a drained corpse. Her body was hidden within odd, ink-black robes thinner than cloth, but thicker than shadow, with little dark tongues licking at the air like flames. Shining orbs glinted from behind a thin strip of cloth set over her eyes. She was bald as a skull, and her ears, nose, and lips looked as if they had been chewed off by a tiny nightmare. The lipless mouth stretched into a demonic smile that revealed a bundle of long, filthy teeth that looked like thin fingers.

"What are you?" Cole managed.

The grin stretched wider as she inched closer. The sour-sweetness of putrid flesh crashed into Cole's nostrils as she spoke. "I am many things to many people. To The Three I am but a tool, a servant born in the grace of the Shadow Tide. To the innocent I am judge, for I unravel the weave of lies which cradles their shame. To the loyal I am the temptress who understands. To the lost I am salvation. I am many things, but to you my sweet, I am a guide. I am a Cold Crow."

Another measure of energy licked through Cole's limbs, fragile and nauseating. He lifted his head off the table and gripped the edges. He almost had the strength to roll himself to the floor, but he didn't want her to know that. The pain from the pithing shard ebbed away as clarity slowly returned to him. "Where am I?"

The Crow's mouth clicked rapidly as she let out a wet hiss aimed at something to her side, then she slowly returned her veiled gaze to Cole, showing every one of her dirty teeth. "The pithing shard in your back is destined for the Vaults of the Soul within Oberon Temple. You on the other hand, you belong to the Cold Crows. My sisters and I are most eager to discover why Varka chose a simple human to carry a sliver of his soul."

Cole's breathing slowed, though his heart still raced out of control. He blinked hot tears away and scanned the situation with a pragmatic eye. A modicum of strength had returned to him, perhaps enough to physically overpower the creature before him, though his magic remained empty and forgotten, as though it had never existed in the first place. He pretended not to notice the long pliers that hung loosely in the Crow's spindly fingers. "You won't win. The Unbound are now stronger than The Three, and The Sill has been taking ground every day. We were winning. We proved Three Three weren't gods, that they could bleed and hurt the same as the most lowly beggar. If Lileth hadn't been charmed against me, I would be doing something far more productive than staring at your ugly face."

The Crow let out a sharp cough that may have been a laugh. She held the pliers to his face and rested the tip just below his eye. "Words. Empty. Ignorant. The Harbingers are merely vehicles for The Three to indulge in the physical realm. Your strength is an illusion cast by our hand. We have nudged you along paths of our choosing so that you would be ready for what is to come. We have all we need now. The Sill will play its true role in due time."

The Crow retched her oily laughter once more, and Cole saw his opportunity. His arm whipped through the air and he ripped the pliers from the Crow's hand, rolling sideways off the table before the pain in his back could cripple him. He fell to the floor and rose unsteadily to his feet, wobbling and crashing into the drawers behind him. Hot lightning sliced through his back and stole his breath as darkness flooded his vision. Gasping, he reached behind his back and secured the tip of the pliers around the pithing shard.

"Don't move or I'll smash it!" he said in between breaths. The pain was almost gone now. "I'll die and you'll never get to use my pithing shard. Now stand up and walk to the back of the room." The Cold Crow didn't move. She stood there staring through the strip of cloth, her lipless smile twitching wider still. Cole knew he didn't have the magic to kill her, but the strength in his limbs would certainly suffice, though he wasn't entirely confident that the shard wouldn't kill him as soon as he withdrew it. It was a gamble he had no choice but to take. "If you think I'm bluffing then keep smiling."

"That pithing shard is not yours," the Crow said in a brittle tone of mock-pity. "It is Varka's."

The room began to spin. Varka's shard? But how? Cole grasped at the concept, but it eluded his touch like a fish in muddy waters. His heart sank as he felt what little strength he had leak out of him. His legs began to shudder. He had to make a choice.

The Crow rose to her feet and took a step around the table, towards him.

"Not… don't…I'll rip…" Labored panting stole his breath away as he struggled to remain upright. He tightened his grip on the pliers and forced his eyes to stay open.

The Crow took another step.

Memories swam to the front of Cole's mind. He saw his leg stuck in a stone door and Goran perched above him, wild and quizzical. He saw Sitra and Storn running up and down the sentinel pines by the training field, laughing and slashing at each other with their new munisica. He saw Valen on the eve of their first mission, swallowing his pride and accepting Cole as an ally and more importantly, a friend. He saw Deekus sitting with him in the sand, a fire blazing beside them as they inspected a tiny rock in Cole's Palm. He saw Lileth's eyes swimming in shadow, burning with equal parts ferocity and intelligence. The memories flooded through him in a never-ending cascade, but it had to end. Now.

"I love you all," Cole whispered with empty Passion.

Cole yanked. He felt the pithing shard slip free, dripping in blood and evil. Before his flagging strength could desert him entirely, Cole heaved, casting the shard down on the metal floor. The pliers shattered in a clang of sparks, but the pithing shard remained inches above the floor, hovering and bobbing. Cole lunged for it. There was a dry cackle and the shard went sailing beyond his reach, right into the Cold Crow's bony hand.

"No," Cole gasped.

"You are truly alone now, human," cooed the Crow. "And now I possess the key to the Aethers. All of Varka's tricks shall be toys for The Three's indulgence. The Shadow Tide is nigh."

The Cold Crow snapped her teeth together, and something hard struck Cole behind the shins, sweeping his legs out from under him. Invisible hooks sank into his skin and hoisted him back up onto the table. He tried to tear them out, but there was nothing to grab, just his own flesh pierced with icy magic. A purple cage materialized around him, trapping him in. He kicked at the cage and a potent spike of Fear shot up his leg and straight into his heart. The room faded as he struggled to remain conscious.

"Tell me a story, human," the Cold Crow said as she shuffled over to the chair and slumped herself in. "I hear the Warriors of The Sill endure pain beyond measure in their training. Gruesome wounds. Destructive magic. Fatigue beyond endurance. I've seen firsthand what pain your warriors can handle in torture, but I wonder, as the strongest warrior the Dark Side has seen in an age, what do you know of pain? Tell me a story."

Cole remained silent.

The Crow chuckled. She removed a crescent-shaped blade from a nearby drawer, inspected it, then exchanged it for a serrated one. "Silence? No matter. They always go silent before we start. But take heart human, for I am here for you. We'll make a new story right here, you and I together. A journey through your pain. First, I'll bend something. Something that's not supposed to bend. Then I'll cut things. Snip them right off, a quick one first, then one so slow it will define who you are. Don't worry about losing the pieces, I'll show them to you as we stroll along. Eventually we'll get to the real art of it, when I take your insides and see how they look on your outsides. Pain can teach you, shape you, change you. We'll travel the story of your pain so you remember who you are, then we'll go to places far beyond, where you will become something more. Something divine." The Cold Crow tugged on a lever on the wall, and a broad sheet of metal slid loose in the ceiling above him, revealing a pristine mirror.

Fear looped in knots around Cole's heart. He scanned his reflection through the purple cage. His armored robes were oddly loose. He gazed down at his hands and feet, but they had vanished inside his sleeves. The room suddenly felt much larger than it had a moment ago.

"I thought that might happen," said the Crow as she peered through the cage, wagging the pithing shard for him to see. "Varka has indeed left you."

Cole couldn't believe what he was seeing. He was shrinking. After only a handful of seconds he was sitting entirely inside the upper portion of his robes, which now felt like a great, filthy coffin. It couldn't be. He was the same size as his first day on Aeneria. He was human in full.

The Cold Crow indulged in his confusion for a moment longer, then hummed a mournful lullaby as she turned her back to him and filled a cart full of tools and bowls.

Cole suddenly couldn't get enough air. Gasping, he pushed the sweat- and blood-soaked armor away from his body. He felt something hard in an inside pocket. He plunged his hand into the pocket and pulled out a tiny vial of jade-green liquid. It was one of Valen's Wisdom-boosting potions. It had been in there since before he entered the Havenflow, well over a cycle, so small he'd never noticed it. Surely it had expired by now, but there was no other option. Cole threw the robes off himself and bit the cork off the bottle, draining it in three quick gulps.

It was as if a light had suddenly been switched on. Bright and clear, energy welled up inside him right where his Wisdom should be, just a thimbleful. It wasn't much, not nearly enough to overcome the Fear of the cage, let alone The Cold Crow, nor was it enough for him to teleport himself to The Sill like he had to the others. There was only one option left; a far less-taxing spell from Chiron's forbidden book, though it was all the more dangerous for it. He would bring an object to absolute stillness. It would cease to move on any plane, ignoring the speed which Aeneria orbited alongside the local planet, as well as the exponentially greater speed of the local solar system hurtling through its star cluster, and the astronomical speed of the entire galaxy itself sailing through the Aethers. The result would be utter annihilation on a scale which he couldn't begin to grasp. He would once again be gambling with not only his own life, but with reality itself. With a flutter of Wisdom, Cole levitated the cork to the far side of the cage. There was no telling where it might go, and he didn't much care, he only hoped it had enough mass to do the job because he lacked the Wisdom to place the spell on anything larger. Clinging to the cork with magic, he crept back into his armored robes and closed his eyes and blocked his ears, then unleashed the spell.

The world unmade itself around him. Heat, light, and sound erupted all around him, occluding all other sensations in a single moment of chaos so powerful that Cole felt as though he had been placed inside a dying star. A full minute passed before the din began to fade, and only when Cole felt something burning against his skin did he begin to believe that he might have survived. He'd never been more grateful to feel pain. His vision steadied as he popped his head out of the neck hole of his armor, revealing debris and fire all around him. The cage of Fear was gone, and the table was nothing more than fine dust. Liquid metal dripped from the ceiling in molten ribbons.

There was an odd quiet in the air. A potent stench of sour char stabbed his nostrils as though he had snorted up a lungful of ash. Cole ran his fingers over his body, finding it whole and unharmed. There was no time to wonder why he hadn't been obliterated like everything else around him. He had to move. The Cold Crow was nowhere to be found.

He rose to his feet and cast off the armored robes, burning his hands on the material as he did. He stood there, naked and trembling as he gazed upon the full scope of the spell's destruction. Everything within ten yards of himself was an unrecognizable cavern, with fine powder raining steadily among the dripping swaths of superheated metal. The cavern extended and tripled in size, forming a tunnel that sloped downwards for what looked like half a mile. There at the end of the tunnel, was the unmistakable prismatic glow of Oberon's light. He ran.

Clouds of fine powder puffed up around Cole's feet with each tiny stride. He felt so small and vulnerable, just a plain magic-less human, and he couldn't hear anything other than a dull tone. Something stirred in the powder beside him as he darted out of the room. He chanced a glimpse over his shoulder as he sprinted.

A hand rose from the dust, then an arm and shoulder, followed by a blackened face. The Cold Crow wiggled upright. The lower three quarters of her body was gone, and so was a large portion of her head, leaving behind wounds that looked like polished obsidian. A tortured grimace twisted what was left of her mouth as she raised a hand and pointed the pithing shard at Cole. A tiny star of mottled copper appeared at its tip, and Cole sensed Varka's magic blending with something foul.

Cole snapped his head towards Oberon's light and redoubled his speed, attempting in vain to urge Rage into his limbs as he dodged puddles of liquid metal and leapt over the crosscut rooms and hallways of the Alpha Colossus. But he was so small, and the tunnel so long. His feet finally found a level surface to run on. He kept his gaze on the rainbow light ahead of him as he ran for his life, but it wasn't there. Rusty copper light saturated the tunnel as the sound of a thousand screams rushed up from behind him. Something struck Cole in the back, entering him. He kept running, though he felt something was running inside him now. He came upon a crevice and prepared to leap, but his legs were no longer his. They weren't even there. He was falling, quickly now, down into the darkness. Down far beneath the world. Beneath himself.

Chapter 31

The Origin of Hatred

Far beneath the world, beneath himself. He was no longer falling, but moving. Cole's body ceased to be, so instead of being, he simply glowed. He pulsed with faint reds and greens and lavenders, along with thin diodes of things more sinister. He was alone now, alone in a river flowing upwards and onwards. Fear had no place in his heart, though he didn't quite feel safe either. He existed in a place between emotions, in between realities. Awareness bloomed within him, and he knew he was not just floating in the river. He was the river, yet somehow he was still apart from it. Alone.

Time meant nothing to the river. The future did not exist, nor did the past. The river flowed deeper within itself, winding endlessly into the fathoms of a single moment. Cole passed through memories; victories, failures, mundane reminiscence, and the silliest little things. Each memory was nothing but a moment, definite yet intangible as a dream, a part of the greater whole. He passed through them all, then again and again until he grasped himself as he never had before. Cole was nothing more than a collection of moments, but what would his next moment be? The curiosity had only just begun to sprout when he felt a shift in the river. He felt himself moving, then rushing, then racing towards a place familiar yet terrifying. There was no telling where it was, but he knew that was where his next moment would be.

A chill ached in Cole's bones. Sour tang coated his mouth. He opened his eyes and coughed. He was lying in shallow, dirty water, and there was brick around him and blue skies above him. There was a dumpster nearby with big lettering that Cole couldn't understand, its contents vomiting up out of its plastic door and into the cobblestone alley around it. At one end Cole saw a street with a broken sidewalk and cars humming by. At the other end was a parking lot, empty save for a single trash tornado chasing seagulls along the pavement. Shivering and naked, Cole rose to his feet. He looked down, expecting to find a red jacket and Velcro shoes, but there was no trace of Joshy. It was as if that moment never existed.

A dizzying sense of deja vu racked him as he scanned the cobble-stone alley again and again. Here? Of all places? His memories of Aeneria were still with him, just as palpable as the scar on his face from where Habbad marked him with Hatred. His whole body was raw and bruised enough that he didn't need to pinch himself to know he wasn't imagining things, but he did it anyway. The pinch barely registered next to the pain from the wound in his back. He felt hot blood turn cool as it oozed from the hole.

He had to move. Rummaging through the dumpster, he tore open plastic bags in search of something to cover himself with. Most of it was rotten remnants of what looked like restaurant food, but eventually he found a strip of cardboard long enough to wrap around his waist. His house wasn't far, just a mile or two, but what would be left of it? Over four years had passed on Earth while he'd been gone. Would his mother even live there anymore? Would she even recognize him? In the end it didn't matter, as he couldn't think of anywhere else to go.

Cole trotted down the cobblestone alley to the busy street. People, real humans gaped open-mouthed at him from behind windows of new cars. Some laughed, though most just gawked. Cole kept his head down and jogged along. He passed a woman on a walk with two children. Her eyes went wide upon seeing Cole, and she swept the children to the far side of the sidewalk, shielding their faces.

"Sorry," Cole said, wincing as he neared them.

The woman scolded him, though Cole couldn't understand any of it. Her words sounded familiar, but he couldn't place the dialect, as though she spoke in a foreign language. He glanced back as he passed. Her eyes were locked on him, and she jabbered briskly into a small phone, ushering the children away all the while. Behind her Cole saw what he knew to be a stop sign, but the letters made no sense at all.

"Damned cypher!" Cole hissed to himself. The Aenerian language cypher must have still been in effect.

He passed several other people before cutting across to a side street. They all took their phones out upon seeing him, either to point the devices at him or make a call. He zig-zagged through the grid of the tree streets in an effort to throw them off his trail, which seemed to work for a time, until he turned a corner and found himself face to face with a police cruiser. The lights came on and the officer came out. He was a large man with a bit of a gut and broad shoulders, and the look of exasperation he gave Cole made it seem as if he'd just trudged through a double shift chasing naked crazy people.

"I'm sorry," Cole said as slowly and clearly as he could. "I'm just trying to get home. It's not far."

The officer acted as if he hadn't heard a word. He began his steady approach, one hand pointed at the ground with the other on his belt, all the while barking commands Cole couldn't understand.

Cole sighed and shook his head, then resigned himself to kneeling on the sidewalk. Another cruiser pulled up behind the first, followed by two more. The officer strode around to Cole's back side and shouted some more. He still couldn't understand a word, but he'd seen enough people getting arrested in his youth to know what came next. He removed his hands from the cardboard and let it fall to the ground, then laid himself on top of it, spreading his arms out wide. The pavement was unforgiving, rough and raw as a knee planting itself in the small of his back. The legs of four other officers appeared around him. Gloved hands guided his arms behind his back as the cuffs snapped over his wrists. They bombarded Cole with what sounded like questions, which became more heated as Cole failed to answer them. Fingers tapped gently around the wound in his back and the numerous scrapes on his body, and one of them checked the pulse in his neck. After a moment of deliberation one officer gave a curt order, and Cole was back on his feet. Two of them helped him into the back of a cruiser, which took off at a brisk pace almost as soon as his bare skin touched the plastic seat.

Tears rolled down Cole's cheeks as the car rumbled over potholes and sewer grates. He had never felt so lost, so helpless. His mind went to The Sill, wondering how long his friends could hold out without him. Their armies could likely hold back swarms of ground and air forces, even the lesser Colossi, but if The Three had regrouped and continued the assault, there would be no chance. Sitra, Valen, Eliza, Amori, Lexy, all could be dead or dying by now, and there was nothing he could do. And Lileth. He refused to believe her betrayal was of her own choice. Grotton must have worked his way into her mind and charmed her against her will. He himself had fallen prey to Hunger, so it was easily possible that Lileth had been tricked as well.

Cole stilled his tears for a moment and retreated to the stone room in the center of his mind. He cleansed himself of all emotion, then reached deep within himself where he knew his Passion to be, where the links to the Unbound should be. There was nothing. He reached for his Rage and then his Wisdom, finding nothing but empty, mundane pieces of himself. He was just a plain human.

The cruiser did not take him to the station as he expected, but to the city hospital. Cole didn't quite understand why, his wounds were nothing he hadn't shrugged off before, though that was with the aid of magic. Magic which he no longer possessed. They stopped outside the emergency room entrance and waited while one of the officers riding up front went inside and emerged a moment later with a hospital gown. They uncuffed him, dressed him, then re-cuffed him to the bars on one of the heavy hospital beds. The officers remained in the room as the emergency room staff ministered to his injuries, took vitals, and drew blood. Cole grew listless as the wasted minutes rolled on. He still couldn't understand a word anyone said, and so he ignored all questions and retreated within himself, making fruitless attempts at his magic all the while. After what felt like no time at all, his back had been sewn up and his various scrapes and cuts had been bandaged. Back to the cruiser he went.

Now garbed in a hospital gown and a wool blanket one of the officers had procured for him, Cole arrived at the Nashua police station. The two officers transferred him to the station staff, who after giving him a brief search, ushered him down a hall to an office buzzing with blue uniforms, clacking keyboards, and a handful of Nashua natives who had run afoul of the law. The sour odor of the unshowered and unkempt permeated the air, the choice scent of those who lived in the squalor of the tree street fringes. Cole had forgotten how much he loathed people of certain parts of town. Though he had just come from a battle atop an island of undead Chosen, he was certain he didn't smell as bad as the stick-skinny man in front of him, with his stained sweatpants and filth-encrusted fingernails.

The staff cuffed him to a long bench behind the smelly man and a few others. Their cuffs ran under a long bar set just under their knees so that they could shuffle down the bench as those in front passed through a processing desk. Cole shut his eyes and returned to the stone room within himself. Minutes dragged on, or perhaps it was hours. Aenerian days *were* far longer than Terra days. The sky through the windows was darker than when he first arrived. He searched the walls for a clock or a calendar, anything to give him some sense of orientation, but gave up after a while, focusing instead on attempting to cast a laser-shower over the man ahead of him.

It was finally his turn to see the desk officer. He sidled up and looked at her, tilting his head back to meet her eye because she was so tall. She looked oddly familiar to Cole, though he couldn't think of whom she reminded him of. She was very tall, with a sturdy frame and strong hands that looked just as capable of working a keyboard as managing a fist fight. Her voice matched her handsome face, matronly and strict, but it was plain that this was a good woman. Still, he couldn't understand a word she said.

"My name is Cole Jonathan Carter," Cole said as slowly and clearly as he could.

The officer shook her head, then hailed one of her coworkers, a muscly Latino man who looked like he hadn't slept in days. The desk officer gestured to Cole, indicating he should try again.

"My name is Cole Jonathan Carter," Cole repeated.

Both officers shook their heads this time. The woman handed Cole a pen and a pad of lined paper. Cole wrote his name and social security number, clear and bold, then handed it back to her. The woman took one look at his scrawl and sighed, then pulled out a small jar of Carmex and applied the balm to her lips with the relief of one taking a drag from a cigarette.

Something warm and calm clicked into a forgotten place within the halls of Cole's mind, but just as he began to grasp it, another officer un-cuffed him and pulled him away.

The desk officer clicked away at her keyboard, muttering to herself. "… second John Doe today."

Cole stopped. The officer at his side squeezed his arm and pulled, but Cole didn't budge. He turned around to face the woman.

"What did you just say?" he asked.

The room went quiet as another officer came running over to secure his other arm. They each threw a leg behind his knees and yanked him back with a barked command. Cole remained rigid and upright, intent on the woman at the desk.

"I'm afraid I still can't understand a word, sir," said the desk officer. "Please move along. You're holding up the line."

Cole stared at her for a few seconds, confused yet thrilled. The muscular officer set himself between Cole and the desk, pointing what looked like a yellow toy gun at Cole's chest. Cole relaxed as a set of long chain cuffs clicked around his ankles, then he submitted to the firm hands guiding him out of the room.

The iron bars clanged shut. Cole took a glance around the cell and counted five others in there with him. Three men slept on the steel benches along the wall, another stood in a corner talking to himself, and one paced circles around the center of the cell, eyeing Cole's blanket with a look of longing. There was a single toilet set behind a concrete half-wall, accompanied by a stainless steel sink that looked far from stainless. Cole shuffled over to an empty spot on the bench at the feet of a sleeping man and sat down. The pacing man stopped pacing. He took to standing cross-armed, alternating between staring at Cole and casting furtive glances to the officer sitting at the desk just outside the cell.

With the only light coming from the buzzing fluorescent bulbs above, Cole once again lost sense of time. After what felt like an hour, the man in the corner curled up under a bench and slept. A mousy teenage boy came in soon afterwards. He stayed at the door, clinging to the bars as he became the new target for the man with the staring problem. Eventually both found separate spots on the floor, each sitting against the bars and nodding off with their chins on their chests. Sleep never came for Cole, as he knew it couldn't.

A meal came on paper plates in the form of powdered eggs, two plain pancakes, and a bottle of water apiece. Cole wasn't hungry, but he downed the water. Throughout the next day his fellow detainees were swapped out for other Nashua natives, each somehow more disheveled and smelly than the last. Meals came and went, which served as a way for Cole to mark the time. Eventually a man in a suit came and spoke to Cole through the bars, but his words were just as jumbled as everyone else's besides that woman at the processing desk.

At the end of the second day, Cole heard a male voice approaching from down the hall. The words of the man sounded clearer than those around him, and if Cole focused he could almost make them out. The man walked past the cell with a small contingent of men and women dressed in a mixture of business attire and police uniforms. An unbidden sense of familiarity tickled Cole's memories as he beheld the man, and so he rose from his bench and approached the bars for a better look. He was an officer, but the decorations on his white collared shirt identified him as someone of rank. The black had all but faded from his salt and pepper hair, save for a sable tuft just above each ear. He carried himself as a man whose youthful arrogance had been tempered to the patient confidence of old age and experience.

The group ignored the people in the cells as they strode by, though they all seemed to know the officer at the desk. Cole caught the man's eye just as he was on his way through a door to another room. The man paused as confusion knotted his brow.

"What's with the kid in the blanket?" the man said to the desk officer, clear as daylight.

The desk officer shrugged his shoulders as he gave his explanation.

The man in the white shirt nodded and sighed. "Just make sure you wait till whatever he's doped up on burns off before his hearing. Rodriguez bit my ear off after we brought that last John-Doe-crackhead to court. Damned judges love bureaucracy almost as much as a defense attorney on the ropes."

The desk officer gave a half-hearted laugh and polite nod as he muttered his response.

The man in the white shirt gave a disapproving grunt. "I've known you fourteen years, Jeff. Stop calling me *Chief*. Daniels will do just fine if you need to be all formal. Christ, before the uniforms you and I used to terrorize this place worse than half the scumbags on the bad end of Palm Street." The desk officer laughed for real this time. Satisfied, Daniels turned to leave.

"I know you," Cole said in a loud voice. He knew at once that Daniels had understood him.

Daniels stopped once more and locked eyes with Cole for a few seconds, then addressed the desk officer. "Thought you said he couldn't speak english?" The desk officer shook his head and gave his reply.

"What's your name then?"

"Coleton Jonathan Carter," Cole said. "I used to live at eighty-five Blossom."

The desk officer's eyebrows went up as his fingers danced across his keyboard. The color drained from the face of Chief Daniels as his friend at the desk uttered something Cole couldn't understand.

"Sense of humor huh?" Daniels said in a derisive tone. "I worked the Carter case twenty-some years ago. That's a dead kid's name. Be sure to give it to Judge Rodriguez tomorrow. Hearing him whine brightens my day better than coffee and flowers." The door slammed as Chief Daniels departed at last.

The rest of the day dragged on without event. People came and went from the cell, as did plate after plate of bland food. His belly finally urged him to eat, so he helped himself to dinner long after it had gone cold and everyone else had gone to sleep, including the desk officer. As he ate, a sickening thought wormed its way into the stone center of his mind. What if none of it was real? What if Aeneria and Oberon and all his friends were just a delusion brought on by trauma? Perhaps he went insane after Joshy died, and his mother had no choice but to put him in an asylum where he descended into the madness of his own fantasy world. The thought gnawed at him all night, until eventually he ceased his attempts at magic and devoted himself to counting the minutes until his next meal. He was getting very hungry.

The next day he was given a plain grey shirt and pants with matching slippers, then two officers brought him outside and helped him up into the rear of a police van. The back of the van had no windows, but Cole knew the area well enough to judge the turns and figure out where they were.

The courthouse was a building Cole never thought he'd be inside, especially while wearing cuffs on his wrists and ankles. His escorts brought him through security, then down a dark wood hall to a small courtroom in the far corner of the building. The room was already full of people, some with their own police escort. Cole waited in silence for his turn with the Judge. He couldn't understand a word anyone said, and he was confident he wouldn't be able to communicate when his time came. One of his officers prodded him in the shoulder, then gestured toward a short podium set before the Judge.

His hearing went about as well as he expected. The Judge tolerated a few of his attempts to name himself before his face turned cherry red and he began shouting at Cole's escorts. During the ride back to the station, thoughts of his insanity swam to the fore of his mind. He sobbed alone in the back of the van, holding himself tight to keep from unraveling.

The cell was empty when he returned, and so was the desk in front of it. He was alone. Cole paced around, running his mind through memories of Aeneria over and over again in an attempt to convince himself that they were real, but each time, the memories felt thinner, as though they were dreams fading to the morning light. Frustrated, he curled himself up under a steel bench and gave in to the crushing hopelessness of his situation. His misery deepened as he realized he didn't even have the ability to cry himself to sleep. He really was insane.

Screams echoed from down the hall. A man, fighting and roaring with everything he had, his voice as hoarse as dirty sandpaper. Cole sat up, alarmed. It wasn't the oncoming violence that disturbed him, but the man's words. He could understand them. A door outside the cell banged open. Two officers held a small man between their arms. The man was deathly thin, his skin pocked and scarred, his limbs frail and knotted like old ropes. Cole could smell the man and his blackened, tattered clothes before he even entered the room.

"Let the fuck go a me, let go, let go!" the man wheezed. One of the officers did indeed let go, but it was to open the door to the cell adjacent to Cole's. "I'll fuck your daughters and kill your pig wives. Eat my shit you fuckin' crooks."

The officer who still had a hand on the man half-carried him into the cell without apparent effort, then the other officer shut the door. Cole couldn't make out their words, but they seemed to be chatting lightheartedly and joking, as if they were doing nothing more than putting groceries away or taking out the trash. They continued their conversation as they left from the door they'd come in from, their deep voices echoing alongside their fading footsteps.

Though both cells were lit by the harsh white of the fluorescent lights, the man took no notice of Cole, nor did he stop talking. He directed his tirade at a spot on the back wall next to his toilet. Cole understood every word the man babbled, though after twenty minutes he wished he couldn't. His nonsense shifted from pigs to money to drugs then back to pigs again in an incessant cycle.

Cole ignored the man and mulled over a curiosity that had taken root some hours ago, blooming fully upon this man's arrival. This man, Chief Daniels, and the large woman at the check-in desk were the only people Cole could understand. Why? What did they have in common? Perhaps they all knew each other? Or maybe Cole had met their soul flies on Aeneria? If Aeneria was real that is. No, that couldn't be it. Aeneria left Terra's house shortly after his arrival, and he and Goran didn't meet any soul flies during their early adventures.

The night wore on and the prattling man fell asleep right in the middle of the floor. Cole brooded over dozens of theories to answer his question, but the most likely conclusion he'd managed was that he was truly insane. Standing for the first time in hours, Cole stretched the aching numbness from his legs and back and paced around his cell. He found himself staring at the door Chief Daniels had left through. Cole had met the man long ago, though Cole remembered him as Mr. Daniels, one of the officers who'd frequented his house during his first bout of disappearances. He was only three at the time, but he recalled a few flashes, such as sitting on Daniels's lap in his cruiser, and Daniels playing with Joshy on the kitchen floor. The fact that Chief Daniels admitted to working the 'Carter case' confirmed that this was in fact the same man. Cole had met him before.

But what about the woman at the desk? Cole was certain he had never met her, but as he recalled her large frame and handsome features, a warm light flicked on in his heart. She reminded him of Nana Beth. Her curly dark hair, strong jaw, and capable hands made her look as Cole imagined Nana Beth had in her youth. Cole thought back to his many conversations with Nana Beth over dinner. Didn't she have a granddaughter? She would be about the same age as the woman at the desk, and Cole found it hard to imagine any descendant of Nana Beth taking the safe job of a librarian or a realtor. That could have been it. The two women may have been related.

Cole returned his gaze to the man sprawled out on the floor. Why was he significant? What was so special about him that some part of Cole's insanity recognized him? Had they met before? The man choked himself half awake with a hacking cough, then rolled over, muttering about money as he melted back to sleep. A fresh wave of the man's odor struck Cole like a punch to the nose. Cole had endured old wounds, burning corpses, and the stench of Domina up close, yet this man's stench was worse than all of them combined. It was the chemical smell that blended with sour musk that made it so special, but it was the sneaking familiarity that made it worse. Cole had smelled this stench before. He watched as a puddle of drool formed from the man's quivering lip, and something horrible slid into place in Cole's mind. He recognized his face, his hands, the burnt-out rasp of his voice. He had met this man before.

This man was Joshy's murderer.

Like a spark in a midsummer's drought, Rage pulsed through Cole's chest, hot and wild. His heart seemed to slow with the mounting gravity of the moment as raw power swelled in his limbs. Hatred followed soon afterwards, adding to the coming storm. Energy prickled down his neck in a cascade of searing needles, painful yet gratifying. His fingers jerked of their own accord, and he could almost feel the tips hardening, sharpening into black dragon's claws.

Blind with deadly intent, Cole approached the bars separating him from the source of his Hatred. He wrapped his fingers around the cold iron and pulled. The metal squealed in protest as it yielded beneath his grip, bending wider and wider until the gap was large enough. Silent as death, Cole slipped through the bars and entered the cell. Hatred and Rage lapped at his heart like rabid dogs. For far too long he'd indulged in fantasies about this moment, but never in his darkest dreams had he thought it would happen, that he would be alone in a locked room with the scum of his life.

Cole gathered a handful of the man's shirt and lifted him into the air. The piles of wrinkled skin that were the man's eyes cracked open, revealing penny-brown irises flecked with bits of grey. His mouth popped open and Cole saw Fear blossom in his heart. Cole tightened his grip on the man's shirt.

"Scream," Cole demanded.

The man worked his mouth, his dry tongue quivering behind the chips of rock that were his teeth. His wooden hands scrambled over Cole's wrist while his feet kicked about Cole's shins like a drowning child's.

"You killed my brother," Cole growled. "You killed an innocent little boy, and now I'm going to kill you."

Fear became the man. It dripped from the man's pants, spackling the floor in an acrid mess. It echoed from his throat, tight and shrill as a dying mouse. Ravenous, it stole the remaining warmth from his limbs and the blood from his face.

The man whispered in between wild gasps. "I don't... never... not me..."

"DON'T LIE!" Cole roared, slamming the man to the bars.

The man's wet hair snapped back as his head clopped against the iron. He began wailing, and Cole slammed him again, imagining his skull breaking apart just like Joshy's. The man then went quiet and still, eyes wide for Fear, open for death. Cole brought a hand to the man's throat, intent coursing through his fingers. The confusion and defeat in the man's face brought a fresh wave of Rage crashing against Cole's mind. He had no idea *why* he was about to die. Cole needed him to know.

With an effort of will, Cole suppressed his Hatred and Rage and searched the halls of his heart for Passion. He found it, weak and

THE UNBOUND

wounded, then forced it to the moment. He felt eddies of Wisdom watching from the far corners of his mind, and snatched the green magic, bending it into action.

With his hand brimming with green flames and lavender sparks, Cole took it from the man's throat and slapped it to his forehead. A squeak slipped from between cracked lips. Cole locked his gaze into the man's eyes.

"See me now," Cole hissed through bared teeth.

Cole brought them both back to the place of his nightmares. The cobblestone alley materialized below them, along with two boys and a man. The man was beating the wall with a length of pipe, rambling and cursing. The boys tried to rush by, but the man stopped them. Ricky was his name. He threw one boy to the ground, then turned his weapon on the other, and in an act of brutal finality ended a life so relentlessly pure and profoundly innocent that the world would never shine as brightly again, for its child of love had died. Gone forever.

Ricky's mind thrashed and wept against the unyielding grip of Cole's magic. He compelled Ricky through the memory again, then again, beating the truth into his mind until he had no choice but to accept what he had done. Ricky didn't offer excuses or reasons. Instead he folded in upon himself, burying himself in layer upon layer of guilt and Hatred, shame for what he had become.

A perverse yet overwhelming sense of curiosity seized Cole, and he followed Ricky through the jagged paths of his mind, just out of sight. He saw a boy surrounded by strangers day and night, surrounded but alone. He was always alone. There were no other children, no toys, just him in his closet with no door. His mother would let him sleep in the bed with her sometimes when she was alone too, and sometimes he would sneak under the warmth of her blankets after the strangers left. There were always so many strangers; men who shouted mean and broke things, ladies who scratched and slapped and stung, and people whom he'd never seen before and never saw again. One night the music was so loud it hurt his ears, and so he went into his closet. He had no door and so it wasn't much quieter, but his ears hurt so badly. When he woke up the music was gone, and so was his mother. Gone forever.

Ricky learned that the strangers could help him, but they seemed to slap and sting him just as much. There was always some food in the smelly piles in the sink, and sometimes on the floor after the strangers played music really loudly. They left clothes and toys from their pockets sometimes too. Not real toys but he could pretend. Ricky had never had toys before. He brought them to his closet and kept them in a secret hole in the wall. He kept the money he found too, and the cigarettes. His mother would need them when she came back, and she would be so happy that she'd let him sleep in the bed with her again.

The days stacked up to months and years, and Ricky never saw his mother again, only strangers. He grew smart and hard and learned how to get what he needed. Cops came eventually and took him out of his closet. He went to school and saw more strangers, boys and girls with mean eyes and stupid mouths. It was even easier to get what he needed from them. People in fancy clothes put him into a home with more strangers. They didn't like him much, but he liked it that way. They didn't care when he left to get what he needed, and they probably laughed when he left for good.

He was on his own, and that was the way he liked it. He was the only person smart enough and strong enough to rely on anyway. His teenage years showed him there were others like him. They weren't family, he didn't want a family, but they were good to him so he called them friends. His friends brought other friends and showed him things he'd never known he needed. He always knew what sex was because he'd seen all kinds from his closet, but it wasn't until he got it for himself that he understood why people liked it so much. He felt love for the first time, not with the people he fucked, but for the sex.

School was boring, and so he and his friends stopped going. Instead they went to each other's houses while their parents were gone, and they had parties and played music. Here Ricky felt love for the second time. He felt the heat of it in bottles swiped from liquor cabinets. He felt the rush of it in the pills stolen from nightstands. He felt the bliss of it every time he smoked the brains from his head.

Ricky was eighteen when he felt love for the third time. One of the girls he was fucking woke him up one afternoon and told him she'd missed her period, and she had three sticks to prove him the father. He felt no love for the girl other than the love between her legs.

She wasn't smart or funny or even that pretty. She was just there. But something changed within Ricky as he watched her stomach swell and bulge over the months. There was a child in there. His child.

Though he didn't mean to, Ricky stopped the drinking and the partying. He stopped doing drugs too. None of it seemed important now that he had a kid on the way. He used the bus to get work, then used his car when had enough money to buy one. He got his own apartment in a nice part of the Tree Streets, filled it with clean furniture, clean food, and real toys. He made her move in with him, not because he loved her, but because the child needed a mother. Months flew by, and his love grew stronger as her belly grew bigger. He talked to his baby every night, promised it warmth and peace and adventure.

Ricky became a new person. He had to. It was time to be a man and a father, and while he didn't love his girl he thought he might one day, when she became a mother and a woman. Unfortunately she was still sixteen, and even after all the things Ricky gave her, she didn't change in the least. He could stop her from the drinking and the drugs and the partying, but only when he was home. The doctors' appointments stacked up faster than his insurance could handle, and so he had to take a second job, then a third. He would come home to find her wasted, the house a smelly mess, and with people he had never met dancing to music so loud it made his ears hurt. Strangers in his home. He kicked them out and out they went, but not always. Sometimes he had to fight them when they were too blasted to reason with.

He felt sick at work one day, so he left, but on his drive home he knew the sickness was far worse than something he'd eaten. There was a car in the driveway. It belonged to a guy who came around way too often to just be a friend, and always when he wasn't home. He knew they were fucking, but he'd never caught them before. His heart hammered like a gun as he stepped up to his front door. He knew what he was about to walk in on, that he wanted to kill the guy with the bat next to his coat rack on the other side of the door, but he couldn't. His unborn son needed him.

The house was quiet. There was no music, no annoying laughter or loud strangers, no sound at all. The bat by the door tempted him, but he ignored it and went upstairs. He found them in bed. They weren't fucking or even cuddling. They were fully clothed and lying perfectly still as if asleep. A silence screamed from them. Ricky's heart fell into his stomach when he saw the needle hanging from a bloody scab in the crook of her arm. He picked her up and tried to shake her awake. Her body was light and stiff. Dead. Gone forever, and she had taken his son with her. Ricky was alone. The love drained from him, every last drop, until the golden sun in the windows faded to the orange glow of the street lights. There was nothing left for him. He put her cold body down with the last of his hope, then his fingers found the needle that killed her, and Ricky descended back into the bliss of his second love.

Cole withdrew from Ricky's mind. He didn't need to see the rest of his life to know how he'd become the tortured creature he was today. He removed his hand from Ricky's head and lowered him until his feet were back on the ground. The broken man crumpled at Cole's feet, sobbing and defeated.

"No more, no more," Ricky wailed. "I want it to stop. I don't want to do it anymore. Kill me. Kill it dead."

A storm of magic and emotion roiled inside Cole. It was but a drop before an ocean compared to the full measure of his power, but it was certainly enough for this.

"Get up," Cole commanded.

Sniveling and moaning, Ricky slowly rose to his feet, though his eyes remained glued to the floor. "I can't do it. I don't want to live anymore. Please... kill me dead."

"I promised myself that if I ever met you I would end your life, and that's exactly what I'm going to do." Cole raised his fist and extended his first two fingers. A ball of emerald and lavender crackled to life an inch beyond his fingertips, casting a harsh glow into the Fear that had just returned to Ricky's eyes. "I am going to kill who you are, then it will be up to you to become something else. You remade yourself once before. You can do it again."

A hoarse scream rose up from Ricky's throat, then sputtered into a dry gasp as Cole jabbed his fingers to the man's forehead. Ricky's eyes rolled and his body went limp, but the magic held him upright as it coursed through him, shimmering over his skin with the colors of Wisdom and Passion. Cole shut his eyes and crafted a spell which he had both been warned against using and forbidden his students from ever performing. He altered the core facets of Ricky's mind and soul, mending fractures, purifying taint, closing certain paths while forging others. He wove compulsions that Ricky would have no choice but to obey until his dying day. Never again would Ricky partake in a vice; not one pill, not one sip of the weakest cocktail, nor one moment of sexual desire. He would spend his every waking moment seeking the pain in others, and he wouldn't rest until he had eased that pain. The final compulsion was hardest for Cole to weave, for Ricky's impulse to end his own life consumed him as nothing else had: Ricky would love and care for himself as much as he loved his unborn son.

When Cole finished his alterations, he put Ricky into a dreamless sleep, then cleansed the toxins from his flesh and healed the decades of abuse from his organs, finally ending the connection with a measure of nourishing Passion. He placed Ricky on a steel bench and poured the lavender magic directly into his chest. He was so consumed by the task, he failed to hear the footsteps coming from down the hall.

"Get away from him right now!" bellowed a voice as a door slammed open. "Back away, Cole!"

Cole ceased the flow of magic and turned. Chief Daniels stood on the other side of the bars, face flushed and breathing heavily. He was in plain jeans and a black sweater, and the pistol in his hands was pointed at Cole's chest.

"So *now* you know who I am," Cole said, wondering if his magic would be faster than a bullet.

"Step away from him right now and show me your hands!" Daniels stammered as he eyed the magic still smoldering in Cole's palm.

"He's fine," Cole stated. Slowly, he stepped away from Ricky and slipped through the gap in the bars, back into his cell. Chief Daniels's gun remained locked on him as he bent the bars back together and retreated to the other side of the cell. "Better now?"

"What, what the hell are you?" Daniels asked, lowering his gun to Cole's feet.

Cole considered the man for a second. He might have been able to disable him and be on his way, but the exertions from his work on Ricky had left him too diminished to be certain, and there was no telling if his magic would replenish itself afterwards.

"What do you remember of me?" Cole asked.

Daniels blinked rapidly as memories flashed in his eyes. "You were the kid that kept running away. We all thought it was the girl's fault, your mother's, but there wasn't enough evidence to do anything about it. There were rumors it happened again when you were a bit older, but the truancy officers never caught you at it. Then there was the murder—your brother. You ran away for good after that."

"Is that why you came here in the middle of the night?" Cole asked. "To arrest me for Joshy's murder?"

"Christ... that poor boy." Daniels shook his head and winced, his watery gaze traveling somewhere beyond the room. He sniffed, then turned a sharp eye to Cole. "I came here because I couldn't sleep. To tell you the truth I haven't slept right since you last ran away. Questions keep popping up instead of dreams, questions that won't quit until new questions take their place. Kid, no one is leaving this room until I get some answers. Start talking."

Cole let out a hollow laugh. "What, no lawyer? This all seems a little out of order for the Chief of the NPD."

Daniels holstered his gun and snagged the chair from behind the desk, rolling it to the door of Cole's cell. He plopped himself down and crossed his arms with an obstinate grunt.

"Fine, but you're not going to believe most of it," Cole said. He took a deep breath, then explained everything about his vanishing from his childhood, which wasn't much other than Joshy claiming he saw a bunch of strange lights in the room. Daniels sat up straighter when Cole recounted the mysterious details of his high school vanishings, and by the time Cole got to his final disappearance in the hospital, he was nearly out of his seat. Cole paused then. He wasn't sure if Daniels believed him or not, but he was sure his magic was returning. He would be out of the cell soon either way.

"So what was this place?" Daniels asked, captivated. "Where have you been this whole time?"

Cole sighed, then cast aside his reservations. "It's called Aeneria. There are people there, good and bad, and magic on both sides. There's a war going on, and right now the bad side is winning. If I don't get back there soon, that war is going to spill over to this world and twenty others. Earth and everyone on it will fall prey to an evil you can't begin to imagine. This evil comes in the form of monsters and magic and real nightmares, but the worst evil will come from what they bring out of the hearts of everyone you love."

Daniels fell back into his chair and stared at the ceiling for a moment, then shook his head and ran both hands through his silvery hair. "That's what all this has been? Magic? That's crazy talk, kid, out-of-your-gourd loony babble. The stuff isn't real. Is it?" He begged the question more than asked it.

Cole nudged his head towards Ricky. "You saw me using it when you walked in."

"I don't know what I saw," Daniels scoffed, shaking himself back to reality. "I shouldn't have come here. You're clearly on the crazy train, and I'm not letting myself get dragged along any further than I already have. I can't believe I lied to my wife just to come here and listen to this garbage. Have fun in Corrections, kid. I'm done." And with a final nod to himself, Chief Daniels jumped up from the chair, brushed off, and stormed off towards the door he'd entered from. When he reached for the handle the door gave a quick, splintery screech and his knuckles thudded against bare wood. "What in the world?"

The handle had jumped to the center of the door. Flustered, Chief Daniels snatched at the handle once more, but there was another sharp creak and the handle jumped to the top of the door. Swallowing hard, he took a few steps back and lowered his shoulder, then cried out in dismay as the door shrank to the size of a notebook. He wheeled around to the other door to find Cole leaning against it.

"How did you..." Daniels's voice trailed off as his head snapped back and forth from the locked cell to Cole.

"Magic," Cole stated.

"No no no! Get your ass back in there!" Daniels barked as his eyes flashed over the phone at the desk. "You'll get me fired. I never should've come here."

"Enough," Cole said. He flicked his wrist and the door creaked back to normal size. "If I don't get back to Aeneria soon, then getting fired will be the last thing on your mind. Are you going to help me or not?"

"Help you? How?" Daniels asked.

"I need to find my mother," Cole explained, though in truth it was only a hunch. "Take me to Blossom Street. I can get there myself, but it will be quicker if you drive."

Chief Daniels cut his hand through the air. "Absolutely not. Even if I were beginning to believe you, and I'm not saying I am, there's cameras and staff all over the station, and day shift starts in a few hours. If I don't get you back by then—"

"Then you and everyone you know will suffer a fate worse than Joshy's," Cole finished for him. "I'll take care of the cameras, and the staff. Just get me across town as quickly as you can or leave now and pretend you never saw me."

With worry twisting his brow into knots, Daniels put a hand on the handle of his gun, but didn't draw it. His eyes searched the room for answers, then landed upon the man fast asleep in his cell. "How do I know you didn't kill that guy in there?"

"I did," Cole said in a somber tone. "That man was Joshy's true murderer, but I changed him into someone else. When he wakes up he'll be a new person. A good person hopefully. I worked pretty hard on him, so I'd appreciate if you kept this a secret between us and not go digging back through Joshy's case. See what kind of man he becomes first."

Cole watched the Chief's mouth fall open yet again as he gaped at Ricky's snoring figure. He had had enough. It was time to move. Cole opened the door behind him and left Daniels to his confusion.

"Wait a damned second then, I'm coming!" Daniels shouted from the other side of the door.

Chief Daniels guided him through the dark halls and empty offices, taking him on an annoyingly circuitous route to avoid being seen. Cole only had to use Passion twice to urge people away from their path, but he didn't tell the Chief that. Cole detected the spark of electricity from cameras as he approached the door to the parking lot, so he moved the devices to a safe angle with a quiet nudge of Wisdom. Daniels wasn't convinced, however, and wouldn't let them out the door until Cole made a show of waving his hands in the air and shot a few emerald stars at the wall.

"Don't see why you need me for any of this," Daniels huffed as he slumped into the driver's seat of his unmarked cruiser. He seemed to grow more ornery the further along they went with Cole's plan. "Could have lent you a broomstick or a magic carpet. Surprised that Arnaria place didn't teach you how to fly."

"They did," Cole said as he buckled himself into the passenger seat and shut the door. The engine rumbled to life. "Do you remember how to get there?"

Daniels gave him the stern look of an owl whose feathers had just been ruffled by an errant breeze. "I'm Chief of Police. I know every driveway, walkway, and freeway in this city, though I don't know why I'm still going along with this. I'll be fired before first shift. Wife's gonna flay me alive."

The ride was painfully slow. Cole watched the street signs and buildings as they trundled by. He was certain he could have run faster, even at his current stature and state. Daniels brought them out onto the highway and finally picked up a decent pace. Cole glimpsed the speedometer. The numbers were still beyond his comprehension, but had a feeling the red needle hovered directly over the speed limit the whole time, and not one notch over. They pulled off the highway at the next exit and rolled into the grid of one-ways that comprised Nashua's Tree Streets.

"Of course," Daniels said as they slowed to a halt before a sea of red taillights, slapping the shifter into park. "Gridlocked at four thirty in the morning. I forgot DPW was working nights down here this week. Sorry kid. Blossom's just another block up too. We can walk if you want, but you're not going out of my sight."

"Move up," Cole said.

"Beg your pardon?" Daniels huffed.

"Drive," Cole said.

Daniels closed his eyes and for a moment looked as if he were about to change his mind about the whole ordeal, but when he spoke it was in a calm, measured tone. "Unlike you, I don't have any special powers here. I couldn't budge this traffic even if I had a whole platoon behind me. Unless these folks start hopping up on the damned..." His voice hardened to stony silence as the car in front of them slid sideways up onto the sidewalk, then the next car did the same, and the next, until they had a perfectly clear path to Blossom Street.

"Move up," Cole repeated.

Daniels shook his head and put the car back in drive.

As the car turned onto Blossom, Cole felt an ominous sinking in his chest, as though his heart had turned into frozen lead. All the streetlights had been smashed out and every house was dark and uninviting, as though the entire street had been condemned for a decade. Yet his house was somehow the darkest. They stopped in front of it, and a queasy sense of impending danger snuck up the skin on Cole's neck.

"You don't have to come in with me," Cole said, gripping the handle of the car door so hard he felt the plastic bend. "This might be a one-way trip."

Daniels was silent for a moment. Then he flicked a switch on his side of the dash and the floodlight on the roof of the car blazed to life. He reached up and angled the blinding light at the front door. Every window in his mother's apartment was covered in plastic or cardboard, while every window in Nana Beth's was nothing more than shattered remains of jagged glass and memories. Cole had a horrible feeling that his last nightmare of this place was no mere dream.

"I'm not letting you out of my sight," Daniels grumbled. His granite tone shifted from that of a tired old Chief to something warmer, almost fatherly. "I've been in worse houses in worse parts of these streets. Let's get you up there and see what there is to see."

Cole set his foot on the first of the front steps. Not a single fleck of paint remained on the rotten wooden porch. The screen door was nowhere to be found, and the front door hung ajar just so, revealing a sliver of the black nightmare that lay within.

"I'll go first I think," Daniels said, cool as could be.

Cole couldn't tell if Daniels was just pretending to be brave, but at the moment he didn't care. He was too scared to go first anyway.

THE UNBOUND

Chief Daniels knocked on the door three times, each rap pushing it just a little wider. He shouted into the door with booming authority. "Tara this is the Nashua Police. I've got someone out here you need to see."

There was no answer. Cole silenced his Fear and released a probing wave of Passion through the house.

"There are people in there," Cole said. "Four I think, and I'm pretty sure one is my mom. You should go. You've already done too much for me. Go home and apologize to your wife."

Daniels reached into his pocket and pulled out what Cole first thought was a radio, but turned out to be a flashlight. He clicked it on, and Cole saw he had his gun drawn in his other hand. "After me then."

Chief Daniels pushed the door open and entered. Cole followed, his heart rattling against his ribs as if it were trying to break free. Daniels ran his hand over the wall and flicked the switches up and down, but no light came on. Cole's shoes crunched and snapped over whatever sticky mess coated the floor, and a stench that reminded him of Ricky's childhood memories kicked him in the nose. Daniels waved his flashlight around in a scanning pattern, revealing a cavern of garbage and filth that didn't resemble Cole's home in the slightest. The sheetrock had so many holes, it looked as if the place had been some sort of cage for a rabid animal. Half the kitchen cabinets were ripped out, and there wasn't so much as a leg remaining of the table. Whatever was piled up on the sink may have at one point been dishes, but now looked like something sliced out of a Corpulant. Every appliance was gone, and all that was left of the living room carpet was patches of brown grease. The couch where Nana Beth used to tell him stories had been flattened to the floor, its remaining cushions saturated with the same muck that covered the carpet. This was worse than his nightmares.

Chief Daniels filled his lungs to announce himself once more, but Cole put a firm hand on his arm. His Passion detected a violent and volatile presence charging from just around the corner.

"Put your light out, now!" Cole hissed. "Someone's coming."

Daniels didn't reply. Instead he pointed both his gun and flash-light at the rising footfalls stomping from the first floor bedroom. Cole didn't have time to think. Rage pumped into his limbs, crushing his Fear and bringing clarity to the chaos. Fast as a whip, he snatched both the flashlight and the gun from Daniels and charged at the attacker. He heard a faint whisper of something sharp cutting through the air and dodged to the right, crashing through what was left of the railing on the stairs. He felt the gun slip out of his hands and saw the flashlight spin down the hall. A male voice grunted as a heavy body tripped over him onto the kitchen floor, shaking trash and rotten food from the counters. Guided by the shafts of light pouring through the windows, Cole saw an opportunity and leapt from the stairs. He willed Passion into his fist and punched the man square on the nose. Lavender light beamed from his eyes and the man fell back, asleep. Something metallic clinked away from his hand as he began snoring in earnest.

Cole heard Daniels kicking trash aside on his way to retrieve his flashlight. A few seconds later he saw him standing with his gun out again.

"You trying to get us killed!" Daniels snapped as he kicked a knife away from the man lying in the kitchen. "How many more are there?"

"Three, but they're not going to wake up. Drugs," Cole gasped.

Daniels threw him an arm and helped him to his feet.

"My mom's upstairs."

Daniels took a long look at the man on the floor. The face pulsed with lavender light as the broken nose repaired itself, sucking fingers of blood back up into its nostrils. Daniels nodded to himself, as though what he saw made perfect sense, then turned to Cole. "After me then."

Cole followed once more. Daniels flipped every switch he could find, but no light came to their aid. Cole kept his head and eyes down as they went up the stairs and turned the corner to his mom's room. He had no desire to see further violation of his home. He waited at the doorless frame, staring at the ruddy stains on the floor as Chief Daniels made his sweep of her room.

"Go on, kid," Daniels said, offering his flashlight.

Cole declined the flashlight and entered alone. He waved his hand through the air and filled the room with a dim, sourceless light. She was there, sprawled out among the heaps of clothes and trash covering her bed, wearing nothing but a pair of ripped boxer shorts. Cole bent low and covered her nakedness with the cleanest bit of blanket he could find, then looked over the woman who once was his mother. There wasn't one inch of her he recognized. Her skin was sallow, pocked with countless scabs and bruises. Bed bugs skittered and jumped throughout the wiry nest of her once-blond hair. Her whole body seemed deflated, thin flesh hanging loosely over protruding bone. The face that used to measure him with stern love now looked like an insensate mask of death and lumpy scars, incapable of emotion or expression.

Hesitantly, he placed his palm on her forehead and extended a tendril of Passion towards her mind. A world of Despair revealed itself, an endless storm of loss and hopelessness churning and consuming everything in its path. There was nothing left of her, no redeeming quality or faintest candle of who she used to be. Years of suffering had taken everything from her, leaving her with nothing to fill the void except what poisoned fruits she could harvest from the tree streets. This woman was not his mother.

The decay of her mind was so absolute that he wasn't sure if he could do anything for her. Even Ricky, the scum of his life, hadn't seemed such a hopeless endeavor. Still, he had to try.

As Cole settled himself into the magic, he felt a hand on his shoulder. It squeezed, and he heard a sniffle behind him. Cole started the flow, and as he did he felt an immense ocean of Passion surge from Chief Daniels. Daniels didn't seem to know that part of his soul was spilling forth, so instead of stopping it, Cole acted as a conduit, and directed the Passion into Tara. Minutes passed, and the further Cole toiled, the deeper her wounds seemed to run. Though her body was less than a day from death, he had it cleansed and nourished within ten minutes. The damage to her soul, however, was far beyond mending. Even if all the Unbound worked on her, there would be no bringing her back from the dank hell she had burrowed herself into. There was only one thing left for her. With a heavy heart, Cole removed the vast majority of her memories of Joshy, Nana Beth, and himself. She would have just enough recollection to know that these people were real, and they had once been a part of her life, but when she woke she would attribute the memory loss to drug abuse. It was cruel, but necessary for her rebirth, as these memories were the pillars on which all her suffering stood.

Cole finished. He tried to stand, but the room spun so fast that he lost his balance and fell. Daniels caught him.

"This city could use a thousand of you," Chief Daniels said as he helped prop Cole back on his feet. "Is she going to be all right?"

"I don't know. I've never felt such a broken soul before. I—" Cole grasped Daniels's shoulder as the room lurched once more. He felt a sensation of falling, though his feet were firmly planted. "There's not much time. I'm... I'm about to Travel. I can feel it coming on."

"Say what now?" Daniels protested. "Kid we have to get you back, now while I can still protect you. I'll delay your transfer and make sure you get a decent defendant. Once you identify yourself you'll be back with Tara in a few days. Your mother needs you."

"I'm sorry," Cole said. He held his hand out before him. A wave of tiny emerald beads began to spread from his palm, leaving open air in its wake as it flowed over his body. The river was calling. He returned his gaze to Daniels. "On our way out, I modified the memory of the man in the cell. He will explain that he saw me pick the locks and escape. No one will know you saw me tonight."

"Don't do it, Cole," Daniels pleaded, reaching for him.

"Take care of her," Cole said, then shut his eyes and let the river take him at last.

CHAPTER 32

NECESSARY EVIL

When Cole opened his eyes, he had to blink several times to ensure he'd made it out of the river. Everything was black. He smelled earth and wet leaves, and heard the faint sounds of insects chirping and distant birds whooping. The ground was soft and moist. Focusing his Wisdom into his eyes, Cole gave himself night vision, but there simply wasn't enough ambient light to work with. He could, however, make out a dim glow in the sky and the outlines of treetops. He rubbed the magic out of his eyes and conjured a hovering white star instead, hoping the magic wouldn't draw unwanted attention.

He was in a forest for sure, but other than that he couldn't tell where he was. His Passion detected nothing larger than a rat for one hundred paces around, though the sheer darkness of the beyond and the emptiness of the sky still unnerved him. He rose to his feet, still wearing his plain clothes from his court date, then began walking downhill in search of water. Just as he wondered if he was going in the right direction, his foot sank into something mushy. He pulled it out with a vacuous, squelching noise, losing his shoe. He looked down to see a boulder with a pink hole in its side, hissing angrily as it shuffled away from him. A curious smile spread across his cheeks. He removed his other shoe and took off at a run, uphill this time.

The ground leveled out and a stone cabin appeared to him. A family of chestnut brown miraks peeped out over the roof, then vanished in a flurry of barking protest. Cole approached the font door. It was smooth as newborn ice. He dismissed his werelight and pushed himself through, then waved his hand blindly over the walls. Turquoise light flooded the cabin from each rubbery bell mushroom he rapped his fingers on. He flicked a few more lights on and knew at once this was indeed the same cabin he had lived in with Goran so long ago. The table and chair were missing a leg apiece, and the bowl Goran usually kept full of deka seeds was gone. The sleeping mat was littered with holes and tiny chew marks. The shelves were vacant, their books torn to pieces and scattered about the floor. Cole picked one up, delighted to understand the words scrawled on the pages. It was a journal, a detailed account of someone's adventures in a faraway land. A piece of cloth binding clung to its spine. Cole turned the flap over and found something odd pressed in with bold blue ink.

Terra Chronicles, Volume Five: A Journey of Varka and the Unbound.

Excitement welled within Cole as he skimmed through the frail pages. He recognized an elegant, flowing script in an entry signed by a much younger Chiron. Then there were a few lines written in a bold, heavy script which looked as though the person had carved the words with a knife dipped in ink. Rothael Bonebreaker had signed each of those. There were others whose names he didn't recognize. The majority of the entries had been Varka's. Reading them felt like looking into a mirror, despite having Varka's essense stolen from him by the pithing shard. He had shared his soul with the first of the Unbound for so long, but the two had been woven together so intrinsically that he never noticed. Only now in the quiet of the cabin did Cole feel the emptiness. The loneliness.

He thought of his own Unbound, and Lileth too, and his heart sank even deeper. He missed them, longed for the old days when they adventured together under the capable eyes of their teachers. He missed Lileth most of all, the way she fought with such grace that she could have been dancing, how her eyes seemed to lift him out of his weakest moments, and her touch. Both of body and soul, her touch had wrapped him in a sense of safety he had never known. At times he felt as if he were no longer one person, but two fires burning as one, and all the brighter for it. In her absence he realized just how much she had sustained him throughout their time together.

Cole set the book down on a shelf and resisted the urge to pick up another, vowing to the torn pages and tattered bindings that he would return one day and set the place back in order. He was still alive, and he was back on Aeneria, therefore there was still hope. He was still human-sized, childlike in Aenerian eyes, and he had only a fraction of his powers, but it was something. Hope alone wouldn't be enough, however. He needed food, supplies, a means to get back to The Sill. From there they could devise a plan to get him into the Vaults of Soul within Oberon Temple.

He tried his Passion first, reaching out as far beyond his mind as he could, then deep within himself, where his links to the Unbound had been. Both attempts got him nothing more than a headache. His Passion simply didn't have the potency to connect with their minds at such a distance. He could run and live off the land, but that would take months in his current state. There was only one thing left to do. He would have to go to Costas and steal a transport from one of the high districts.

Guided by his hovering light, Cole left the stone cabin and set off at a steady jog through his and Goran's old hunting grounds. He scaled a few trees along the way and knocked clusters of deka seeds to the ground. The seeds took the shakes out of his legs, but his stomach still grumbled its demands for proper food. It was slow going through the dense underbrush and game trails, especially without any stars to guide him. He glanced up now and then through the canopy, searching for any celestial body that might help orient him, but the sky was as dark and empty as a puddle of oil.

After an hour of plowing through thickets, he emerged onto the trail on which he first met Habbad and Lexy, clothes torn and smudged with dirt and plant matter. He broke into a run, willing fickle Rage into his limbs, and to his surprise he felt a gratifying ache in his hands and feet as his munisica sprouted. He only managed to cover his wrists and ankles in the black shroud, but the strength and speed were substantial. The Rage kicked his hopes up into a wild gallop as he charged down the trail.

In no time at all the forest around the path thinned and gave way to sprawling fields of tall grass. He had hoped the openness of the fields would reveal at least a few stars, perhaps one of the more empty-skied local planets, but there was still nothing. Not one speck of light. There was a glow in the sky over where he knew Costas to be, and so

Cole dismissed his werelight, using his spell for night vision instead. A breeze poured across the empty sky, hissing through the grass in a steady whisper.

Cole bathed himself in shadow as he entered the Underkin's district. He lacked the Wisdom to render himself entirely invisible, but so long as he stayed out of the torchlight and didn't make any noise, his presence would only be detected by a Corpulant, which could sense his use of Wisdom. The district didn't seem to have any Corpulants, however. In fact, if not for the groups of Underkin bustling about, Cole would have sworn he was in another part of Costas. There was no stink in the air or trash in the streets. Every window had shiny glass, every doorway a proper door. Gratia stones shone from the fronts of magic-powered wagons parked in front of houses, each full of supplies, empty crates awaiting supplies, or tiny seats. The biggest difference of all was the Underkin. There was no twinge of Fear in their eyes, no shadow of Despair over their wrinkled faces. Cole even heard bubbly laughter from the children.

As he rounded a corner, Cole's Passion detected a massive trio of life candles headed his way. They were twisted and feral, containing mismatched layers of animal and Aenerian souls. Domina.

Cole ducked under a staircase, nestling himself between a stack of baskets and the wall as he peered out from in between the steps. He had fought enough Domina to be certain he could defeat these three even in his current state, but there was a very good chance they would call for help before he could finish them off. He held his breath and pulled the shadows closer.

Three hulking figures lumbered into view, so close he could smell the tang of their musk. Judging by their fur and misshapen snouts, they had taken thralls from the bear-like creatures that stalked the woods around Costas. They wore Underkin wrappings from the waist down, and two wielded heavy sledges while the other tugged a hovering wagon along with a rope.

The Domina stopped. The biggest and ugliest of the group sniffed the air in Cole's direction. Cole hastily summoned a barrier over his skin to prevent his scent from escaping, but it was too late. One of the Domina grabbed a torch off the wall in front of the stairs and began sniffing his way to Cole, using his sledge as a poker to move baskets aside. With a flash of Wisdom, Cole shattered the casing on the torch, covering the beast's hand and arm in oil, then thick orange flames. The Domina let out a piteous wail as his fellows ran over to beat the fire from him. Cole slipped out from under the stairs and bolted, unseen.

He ran until he couldn't hear the Domina's cries, finally slowing in a market alley. The signs above the doors glowed with dull jade, and through the windows he could see gratia stones embedded in cashiers' pedestals. There were shops for medicine, tools, food, books, even a beauty parlor. While Cole had only ever been to the Underkin District once, he was certain that luxuries such as toy shops were reserved for the Aenerians, not their slaves. The Sill's Intelligence Axis certainly hadn't picked up on the change, though Debjornik had been quite busy elsewhere.

After checking the area with Passion, Cole unlocked the front door of the clothing shop and slipped inside. He passed over the shelves and racks meant for children and formal wear and found a large roll of industrial wrappings, which advertised flame-, shock-, and cut-resistant qualities. He stuffed his prison clothes in the bottom of a trash can and began the tedious process of donning Underkin wrappings. The material was a dark silver with black metal threads woven through. It adhered to itself and snugged comfortably to his skin as his body heat soaked into it. He added extra layers around his vital areas, padding himself in armor up to his ears. He went to pay the gratia stone sunken into the merchant's counter, then thought better of it. He didn't want to leave traces of his magic for the wrong person to find.

Now bearing a passable impression of a very tall Underkin, he walked openly through the streets without the guise of magic. The other Underkin took no notice of him as he strode by, and neither did an Aenerian woman, though Cole cut a wide path around her anyway. As with the Domina she was well over twice his height, and there was no telling what magic she was capable of. As he probed deeper into Costas he noticed more Aenerians and Domina, though oddly enough there were still plenty of Underkin. From what he recalled of his anthropology lessons with Chiron, Underkin in Costas weren't allowed in the Aenerian districts without escorts or a master's token, but that no longer seemed the case.

There were no signs of proper vehicles other than the hovering wagons and the occasional trolley, nothing that would get him across the planet. He needed a flying car or a seaworthy ship at the very least. Cole passed through an unguarded district gate, a set of golden statues of regal Aenerians with their hands clasped in an arch. The street and sidewalks shifted from rough cement to grooved marble, and the buildings were far taller, each clad in shiny golden trim. The Underkin he saw had no escort or tokens around their necks, though their wrappings bore elegant patterns.

After reading a sign post which had an engraved map, Cole doubled back a bit and made course for the port in hopes of finding a ship. He heard shouting up ahead, and saw three Domina storming up the street. One clutched an arm covered in angry cherry blisters while the other two sniffed the air. Concealing himself behind a group of Aenerians, Cole cut into the next open door that presented itself to him.

He was met with rich aromas of wood and savory spices. He stepped into a room furnished with tables and chairs crafted from rough-cut mahogany with dark ebony embellishments. There was a U-shaped counter in the center of the room, and in the center of that was a tower of shelves containing bottles of every color. Vines meandered across the ceiling and down the support beams. The pub was empty save for a lone man behind the bar, who was too busy stocking the shelves to notice him enter.

Cole took a tentative step forward, unsure if Underkin were allowed in such an establishment, but then he saw diminutive ladders built into the sides of the bar stools and a few small tables set off to the side. He strode casually around to the back of the bar and climbed up onto a stool that gave him a view of the door.

"Hungry or thirsty?" asked the bartender without looking up from his crate. Cole thought the man sounded drunk. There was an open bottle of amber liquid on the counter beside him.

"Both," Cole said, glancing up at the door.

The bartender tapped each cork in the crate with an emerald finger, then the bottles rose into the air and found empty spaces on the shelves. He kicked the crate aside and opened another. "Are you paying with coin or magic?"

Cole stretched himself taller and stared at the man's back for a moment. His suit was of the finest cut and his shoes looked like the most expensive thing in the pub. Cole leaned over to try and read the Aenerian's face, but the man turned away.

"Magic," Cole said, trying his best to make it sound like a statement and not a guess. It was not common for Underkin to use magic.

"What about those wrappings?" the man said in a hard voice. "Did you pay for those? Or did you just steal them?"

"I... I didn't steal anything," Cole stuttered. He tightened the headscarf around his face. "I paid for them with magic. Rage actually, not that it's any of your business."

"An Underkin that can use magic. That is a rare thing. One in a thousand at the very least," said the man. He stood to his full height and faced Cole at last. Cole averted his eyes and looked away. "Even more rare for a human from Terra."

Cole leaped up so fast he sent the barstool cartwheeling behind him. He was on the counter in a flash, crouched like a wild animal, munisica bared, magic crackling between his claws. The man showed no reaction whatsoever. He leaned his elbows on the counter and watched Cole with a look of mild interest. His face was handsome yet heavily lined, as though he'd spent his entire life scowling at one thing or another.

"Habbad?" Cole breathed.

Reaching under the bar, Habbad produced a bottle of water and a package wrapped in wax paper and twine. He slid the items over to Cole's feet. "What are you doing here, Cole?"

Cole jumped a step back on the countertop, his munisica and magic still ready. His eyes flicked over a path to the door. "What are *you* doing here?" he snapped.

Habbad sighed and pinched the bridge of his nose, as though the question wasn't worth his time. "I do many things in Costas. Right now I'm filling in for a bartender."

The words almost made Cole lose his grip on his magic. "What are you talking about? You work for The Three. I doubt they ran out of people for you to torture and kill. Unless that's what you're here for, to finish off Costas once and for all."

Habbad gave Cole a patronizing look. "I worked for The Three, but no longer. I defected after our paths crossed in Borla Dign. Over the months I found my way back to Costas. I have been laboring to rebuild the city, not finish it off."

"But that's insane," Cole said. "It can't be true."

"This world is insane," Habbad grumbled. "Now if you don't mind, you're scraping the finish off the counter."

Cole's eyes flicked down to the deep white gouges left by his claws. For a few heavy seconds he didn't move, sure Habbad was about to trick him or attack him. He cast a few barriers over himself, including an explosive trap that would destroy the whole room should his barriers fail, then dismissed his munisica and hopped back onto his chair.

"Feel better?" Habbad asked in a derisive tone that suggested Cole's quiet spells had not been that quiet. He waved a jade hand over the counter and returned the laquer to a mirror-smooth polish. "I don't need poison to kill you. Eat the food, so long as you can pay for it that is."

"What happened to you?" Cole asked.

"You first," Habbad demanded, crossing his arms. "I can answer your question better if I hear your side of things. Besides, you're the guest here. Indulge me."

Cole uncorked the bottle and snipped the twine from the wax paper with a single bladed finger. He took his time unwrapping the food, deciding what he should and should not tell the giant Underkin. The scar on his face began to feel hot and prickly. He took a bite of the food, a hearty loaf of ground meat, rice, beans, and mushrooms. He suppressed a moan as flavor and spices flooded his mouth. He took a few more bites and gulped some water down then looked up at Habbad.

"The Three came for us at The Sill," Cole started. "They each had their own Alpha Colossus. The Unbound met them in battle over the ocean while The Sill defended against their ground and air forces. We were winning, and would have won had I not been hit with a pithing shard."

"You mean Varka's pithing shard," Habbad corrected.

Cole raised an eyebrow. "I thought you said you didn't work for The Three anymore."

A shadow of regret fell over Habbad's wrinkled face. "I know all about that pithing shard, and the person who betrayed you to make it. Lileth provided the betrayal and I brokered the trade with the Cold Crows."

"Lileth wasn't acting on her own," Cole said. "Someone put her under a spell that made her sick, dark magic. It messed with her head and her heart. We noticed the change in her a few months ago."

"Convenient, but not entirely true," Habbad said. "The magic that ailed her was of her own design, symptoms brought on by betraying one she loved. To convert the pithing shard from Alvani's to Varka's she had to channel the soul imprinted on her own. Yes, just as you had a bit of Varka's soul in you, she had a bit of another soul in her. The imprint belongs to a woman named Vex, who from my understanding was Varka's lover many cycles ago. The two used to be thieves of some sort, pirates. Records show them popping up all over Aeneria aboard a ship called the Ecstasy, stealing and swindling the world's secrets with near impunity. Some echo of Vex betrayed Varka to make the pithing shard, just as Lileth betrayed you."

"No, that doesn't mean anything. In fact, this proves Lileth wasn't acting on her own," Cole said, hope fluttering up in his chest. "It was this Vex woman. She made her do it."

Habbad shook his head. "No, it wasn't. And it wasn't the first time Lileth betrayed you. On your first visit to Oberon Temple, you were attacked in your sleep the night before your trial. I sent the Corpulant and Lileth let it in. We meant to capture you and bring you to the Vaults of the Soul that very night."

Cole bored his eyes into Habbad's, searching for an edge of a lie, but found none. His fluttering hope smoldered and sank back through the layers of grief in his chest. "Why though? She loved me. I know she did. Passion doesn't lie."

"It was her love that gave her the power to do it," Habbad said. "Vex's love for Varka allowed her to reconstitute Alvani's shard for use on the part of Varka's soul that rested in you, just as Lileth's love for your elders fueled their shards. Yes, it was her who killed Alvani, Roth, and Chiron. And I helped."

A heavy blanket of Despair fell over Cole's heart. He searched himself for a way out, an explanation to prove Habbad a liar, but it made too much sense. Tears stung his eyes and he spoke in a defeated quaver. "How. How could she do it? How could anyone...." He looked up to Habbad, hoping to find an answer in his stony glare, but to his surprise there were tears in his eyes as well.

"I don't truly know," Habbad admitted. "When I first arrived at The Sill my mind found hers in dream. I don't think she was aware of it at first, but the dreams became too specific, too potent for us to ignore, so we learned to do it intentionally and regularly. We both wanted more from the world. She had her past and I had mine, and in sharing them we discovered unrequited desires within ourselves. Desire to right old wrongs, for balance in the world, for the thrill of adventure, but most of all we desired power. We Hungered for it. From then on we worked our plans to earn Grotton's favor through secret dreams. Months passed, and even after we became separated by fate and thousands of miles, we came together every night in dream. I didn't know what love was at the time, and still don't, but I think I came close to it with her. And I was certain she felt the same way about me." Habbad's jaw clenched as tears broke free from his distant, watery gaze. His sorrow doused some of the jealous Rage that had been twisting tighter in Cole's muscles. There was real pain in Habbad's eyes. True loss that Cole was all too familiar with.

"It was her, wasn't it?" Cole asked. "She was the one who convinced Grotton to take Roth for Harbinger."

"It was supposed to be me," Habbad said. "I earned it. I, a mere Underkin had delved further into Hunger than any Aenerian in history. I planted Grotton's seeds all over the planet, brought his grace to the hearts of countless and so made it possible for him to manifest once more, but it was all for nothing in the end. Yes, she was the one who swayed the god to take the Bonebreaker instead. I should have known it all along. While I was more accomplished than anyone alive in Grotton's arts, I felt glimmers of Hunger though our dreams that hinted she held something more potent still."

Cole couldn't help but feel sorry for Habbad, but there was a limit to his sympathy. There was no ignoring that Habbad had brought every ounce of his regrets upon himself through his own, horrible choices. "Then why do you still use Hunger? I don't need to see how tall you are to know you still have Domina inside you. Dozens at least, by the feel of it. You know better than anyone else the risks of using evil magics."

Habbad's sorrow shifted to a disdainful sneer. "You call yourself Unbound, but your understandings of magic and evil are quite the opposite of your namesake. Evil lies within the intent, not the act. To torture a man would be evil in your eyes, but if the intent was to wring information out of him that could be used to save thousands, then the torture is not evil. The same goes for Fear, Hunger, Hatred and Despair. After the battle in Fangshard Valley, I sought out The Three in the depths of Oberon Temple to demand recompense. Grotton mocked my plea and stripped me of every Domina I had, then compelled me into his service. For months I was his, utterly and perfectly. However, after I captured you in Borla Dign something changed in me. In learning of Lexy's fate I felt the blossom of Passion for the first time in my life, and I was able to break free from him soon afterwards. Yes, I have taken Domina since then, but only the willing. Men, women, and beasts, all broken with nothing left to live for. Many would have killed themselves, but I offered them a release through a new life within me. Evil lies within the intent, not the act."

While Cole wasn't entirely convinced, he was forced to reconsider his stance on morals and dark magics, but now wasn't the time. He still had a job to do.

"Join me," Cole demanded. "Come with me to The Sill and help us set things right. We can still stop The Three."

"There's no point. You no longer have Varka's soul within you," Habbad said. "The Shadow Tide is upon us. Aeneria lies in between worlds, that's why the skies are empty. Soon The Three will unravel Varka's final rule and the Aethers will be wholly open to them. There is no way to stop it, and neither I nor my people will be the ones to die trying. Costas is of relatively negligible influence to this new world. The Three will overlook us and we will thrive in quiet peace."

"You rule Costas?" Cole asked, incredulous.

"I am the Guardian of Costas," Habbad said. "What Kreed should have been."

Cole slammed his hand on the bar. "Give me a ship then. Get me to The Sill and we'll risk our lives for you. I know if I can just get inside Oberon Temple, I can figure something out. I may not have Varka's soul anymore but there's still a chance I've got something inside me that will work. I can still use magic, and I just Traveled to Terra and back."

"You Traveled?" Habbad said, frowning.

"Take my memories if you need proof," Cole said. "Just give me something to get me to The Sill as fast as possible. If not for your people then do it for Lexy."

Habbad's face hardened as his knuckles turned white on the edge of the counter, and for a second he looked as if he were about to attack. He relaxed, and Cole detected the subtle variations of telepathic Passion strumming in the air. Cole tried to keep the impatience off his face as he waited for Habbad to speak. After a minute he returned his distant gaze to Cole and spoke not as Habbad, but as Guardian of Costas. "I'm not giving you a ship because there are none you can man yourself, and I can't give you a flying car because Kreed took them all. Even if I did I wouldn't send you to The Sill."

"Why won't you help me?" Cole demanded, slamming his fist again. "Dammit Habbad, you know what they'll—"

"I'm not finished," Habbad interrupted, rising to his full height. "And I never said I wouldn't help you. My intelligence teams report that The Sill has somehow been sealed off. At the moment there are dozens of lesser Colossi and half an army trying to get in, but something is stopping them. As for your Unbound, they have already marshalled your forces inside Oberon City. That is where you should be."

The need to act jolted through Cole like lightning. He stood in his chair, ready to bolt and run the whole way to Oberon. He looked to Habbad one last time. "Habbad, please. Give me a ship. Have them bring me part way then turn around if they need to."

"You won't get a ship," Habbad said. He planted a hand flat on the counter then leapt over it, landing beside Cole's chair. "I can do better than a ship, if you're willing to bend some of your rules that is."

"What do you mean?" Cole asked, suddenly wary.

Habbad extended a hand and rolled the tips of his fingers together, as though spreading salt over a meal. Thick, shimmering liquid fell from his fingertips in a steady stream the color of dark wine. The magic spattered over the wooden floor. Each dropped snapped wide and formed a patch of smooth crystal, joining with others in painting a broad, circular mirror. Cole's lip curled in disgust as he sensed all four evil magics blending before him, but he also detected traces of Wisdom in the spell's framework. With a final flick, Habbad finished and looked to Cole.

"Jump in head first," he said with no hint of deception.

Cole leaned over the chair and peered down. The spell looked like a pane of dirty glass. He could see the floor through it. "What the hell is it?"

"It's a portal," Habbad explained. "The other end is anchored just outside Oberon City."

"And by what means is it anchored?" Cole asked.

"By an act that fits your limited definition of evil. Do you really want to know?" Habbad asked with a sneer.

Cole shook his head.

Habbad made a satisfied grunt, then reached a hand towards Cole. as though offering to help him down. Cole was about to explain that despite his size he was perfectly capable of getting off the chair, but the words stuck in his throat as his water bottle zoomed into Habbad's outstretched hand. Habbad dipped his finger into the bottle, and as it touched the liquid it turned a bruised shade of blue. He dunked it three more times and the water shifted to ruby red, then flaming orange, then electric purple. He corked the bottle with his thumb and shook it. When he offered it to Cole, the liquid was solid black.

"Drink that," Habbad said.

"Nope," Cole said, clamping his mouth shut.

Habbad sighed, then spoke in a soft tone Cole hadn't heard since Habbad was smaller than him. "It's my way of thanking you for saving Lexy, for taking care of her when I couldn't."

"You still can," Cole offered.

Habbad's eyes fell to the ground, then he turned and walked away, towards the exit. He stopped just before the door and looked over his shoulder. "Head first," he reminded, then left, sealing the door behind him.

Cole set the bottle down on the counter and turned his back to it. He dismissed the barriers he placed over his body as well as the trap. Holding his breath, he bent his legs to leap off the chair, swore loudly, then snatched the bottle off the bar and downed it in several gulps. Before the taste or the effects of the potion could hit him, he closed his eyes and dove for the portal, head first.

CHAPTER 33

ONE-WAY TRIP

As soon as he thought his head would hit the floor, Cole felt an ungainly flip of gravity. He was falling head first, but then he wasn't anymore. He was falling feet first. When he dared to open his eyes he found he was no longer in the bar, but several feet in the air, dropping to a rippled tan something he could barely see. He landed bodily, but the surface was soft. He hawked salty sand from his mouth as he flipped himself over, then let out a howl of agony.

It felt as though an animal was burrowing through his back, slashing and snapping every nerve and bone on its way to his heart. Cole's teeth snipped through the side of his tongue as the pain locked his jaw shut and racked his limbs with violent tremors. Fear stole the breath from his mouth and his lungs seemed to be filling themselves with broken glass. The pain waxed on, twisting and tearing its way through his senses until he felt himself slip to the brink of non-existence. He would have ended his life right there if he had the power. Habbad's drink was no potion. It was poison.

The tumult ebbed with glacial sluggishness, relinquishing his senses back to him one at a time, finally fading to its point of origin; the wound from the pithing shard. There wasn't enough light to make out much of his surroundings, but the briny scent in the air and rhythmic whisper of waves told him he was on a beach. When he could move again he sat upright in the sand and took inventory of his faculties, finding himself whole of body and mind, though his clothes felt painfully tight. With a flick of Wisdom, he urged more light into his eyes and saw gaps of swollen skin choked between the layers of his wrappings. He felt himself rising gradually into the air, and his limbs were stretching longer by the second. He urged Wisdom into the armored fabric and expanded the wrappings as his body continued to grow. After several confusing minutes the growth finally ceased. He was back to his normal Aenerian size. He felt something rise up inside him, terrible yet marvelous, so powerful that he Feared Habbad had betrayed him and taken him for Domina. He retreated to the stone room in the center of his mind, but the strange energy was there already, as it had been all along.

It was as if a crippling pall had been removed from his soul, and with his absence he could finally grasp the full measure of his magic. Rage roared in his heart. Wisdom rushed into his thoughts. Passion sang in his soul. His magic was back more powerful than ever, and it was his alone, not Varka's. He felt other magics stirring beneath as well, untrained and untapped, evil magics he strived to avoid at all costs. He saw them now through a lens of pragmatism, and while he certainly wasn't ready to start experimenting with atrocities, he began to wonder what good they might be capable of with the right intent.

Cole looked up at the sky, where the ghostly pallor that hung over the beach was strongest. Oberon hung almost directly above, large as a dinner plate and surrounded by utter darkness. Its glow was weak and grey, a pale phantom of its former brilliant glory. Cole's heart sank. The Shadow Tide had come.

There were distant voices between the rushing of the waves. Cole snapped his gaze to the water and beheld a fleet of warships racing up the coast, the nearest of which was so close he could count the crew and guns on the top deck. His Wisdom was there in a blink, rendering him invisible and shooting him high above the beach. There were just over a hundred ships, each loaded with warriors in full battle dress, the vessels equipped with massive guns built into their bows. Cole shielded his mind and zoomed his vision, pondering the quickest way to annihilate them all, but then he noticed some of the ships were floating higher than others. Much higher. Some as much as twenty feet above the surface. He saw the familiar glow of gratia lights and reflections from black glass tinted with streaks of reddish brown. Giddy curiosity blossomed in Cole. He cut through the air and positioned himself in front of the lead ship, then swapped his invisibility spell with a beacon of ambient white light.

The bow of the lead ship dipped into the water as it came to an abrupt halt. The rest of the fleet rose out of the water and flowed around it, surrounding Cole with an array of guns of such a large caliber that a grown Aenerian could have stood comfortably inside the barrels.

"Name yourself or die," boomed a female voice from the nearest ship. Cole had heard the voice once before, but he couldn't remember where.

Cole augmented his reply with the strength of his Rage, and watched with satisfaction as warriors all around flinched as his words struck them. "I am Cole, leader of the Unbound. I hereby invoke the Trial of Honor upon the leader of this fleet."

There was silence as some ships moved closer and others backed away. He scanned the nearest ship, looking for the woman who had threatened him. He found her in the crow's nest, leaning halfway out and arguing with the crew below. It was Milette, the woman whose hands he clipped off with his munisica before taking her prisoner and pressing her into service with the Morthainian military. Someone had either given her new hands or her munisica had grown from the stumps he left her with.

At last Milette finished arguing and returned her scowl to Cole. He could tell she recognized him. "Board our vessel. You can take your challenge up with the King of Morthain."

Cole maintained the illuminating spell until he landed on the main deck. There were far fewer Morthainian glass weapons and far less armor than he expected. Instead he saw emerald magic crackling between fingers, jade barriers glowing over lithe bodies, and impressive shrouds paired with sweeping munisica. He kept all emotion from his face and shielded his mind from dozens of probing mental attacks, offering them no crack or fault to slip into. They were surprisingly proficient with Passion. Relief and pride danced in the halls of his heart. He was thrilled so many of Morthain's forces had survived, but even more so that they had begun to use other magics. King Auger must have knocked some sense into his people before he breathed his last. Whoever replaced him must have been a rare warrior indeed.

The doors to the lower deck crashed open, and out strode War Captain Seive, the woman who had given Roth so much trouble during their visit to Morthain. Her silver hair was entirely black, a thin rope of woven blades that clinked down her back as she walked. The fires of a thousand battles blazed in her eyes, casting her aged face in a hardened mask of experience and valor. Her munisica were far larger than the last time Cole had seen them, only instead of thin swords one hand was an ebony hammer while the other was a barbed glove. Judging by the embellishments and cleanliness of her armor, War Captain Seive was now King Seive, or was it Queen?

Seive brought her hammer to her chest in a salute. "Greetings, Unbound One. It has been some time since you last thorned yourself in our hide."

"Hello to you too, Seive," Cole said with a wolfish grin. "Are you sure you want to do this here? I'd rather not destroy a perfectly good war ship. I need every single one to retake Oberon City."

"Funny," Seive huffed. "That's precisely where we're headed after the King coats our deck with your blood."

"You're not the Queen, I mean King of Morthain?" Cole asked.

Seive raised her chin and drew her shoulders back. She cracked a haughty grin. "I was until a few days ago. Someone else beat you to the glass throne, and I'm certain she's not about to lose it, even to the leader of the Unbound."

"Who is it?" Cole asked, looking to the other ships.

The doors banged open again, and a tall, menacing figure clad in nothing but the master's shroud of Rage stormed across the deck, black eyes locked on Cole's.

"Where in the bloody fuck have you been?" Sitra shouted. Before Cole could close his gaping mouth she scooped him into a backbreaking embrace, kissing him squarely on the lips with all the tenderness of a brick thrown from afar. "You stupid, stupid, boy! We thought you were dead! Worse than dead! We searched half the planet looking for you! What happened after you sent us back to The Sill? And where did you get the balls to use one of Chiron's forbidden spells? Answer me!"

"Sitra," Cole wheezed, but she couldn't hear him due to flock of questions and threats flying from her mouth. In the end Cole had to don his own master's shroud just so he could get enough air to talk. His bladed feet tore through the wrappings and stretched to the deck, though he still couldn't break her grip. "Sitra! Where are the others?"

"On the other side of the Fangshards," she said, pointing with her eyes towards Oberon. "They're fighting The Three's forces in the city as we speak. Almost everyone from The Sill is with them."

"Do you have Passion links to them?" Cole asked.

She gave a firm nod. "Of course."

"Bring me in, then," Cole demanded. "There's too much to say with words."

Sitra released him at last from her iron grip, then closed her eyes and unleashed her Passion into him. It was like the first day of summer after a lifetime of bleak winters. The savage beauty of her soul's music thrummed within him, and suddenly he wasn't alone. He felt Valen and Eliza too, and joined in the collective revelry as all four of their life candles burned as one unified flame.

"Thank the Aethers," Valen said.

Relief wept from Eliza in shuddering waves, and she could only manage a single word. *"Cole."*

"If we didn't need him for another round with The Three I'd break his legs to keep him from walking off again," Sitra quipped. *"I think I'll keep my munisica locked around his neck for the time being."*

"We felt your life candle vanish from this reality. What became of you?" Valen asked Cole.

Within the span of ten wild heartbeats, Cole replayed his memories from the moment he teleported them to The Sill to now. His imprisonment with the Cold Crow sent shivers through their minds, and their love poured through him as he recalled his time spent on Earth. He felt their disbelief curdle into disgust as Lileth's betrayal settled into layers of acceptance. His own ambivalence for Habbad reverberated through them, and like him they were just as likely to Hate him as thank him. Habbad had played no small part in the coming of the Shadow Tide, but without him there would be no hope of setting things right.

"That's it, now fill me in," Cole urged.

"It would be my pleasure, Wisdom Walker," Valen replied, offering the appellation with newfound reverence.

Flashes of sensations rushed into Cole at a dizzying rate. Valen, Sitra, and Eliza materialized in the center of the training fields, battle weary and horribly disoriented from Cole's spell. Their Wisdom was too slippery for flight, so they ran for the break in the wall to get back to Cole, but their armies had been outmatched and it was all they could do to help hold the line. Ka Reine fought alongside them, her body phasing in and out of the material world, scooping enemy hearts right out of their chests as she danced through their ranks. The Old One nearly met her end when nine elite members of the Divine Guard bound themselves in suicide to a potent spell, which consumed them along with Ka Reine in a cloud of screaming black fire. For all the knowledge and power the Havenflow had granted the Unbound, none of them could fathom how the Old One had survived such potent evil magic.

Eventually the Unbound reached the limits of their powers, and when all seemed lost, Whind was there to mend the break in the wall, only he wasn't alone. Amorinanis appeared by his side. As Whind regrew the border trees, Amori managed to absorb every ounce of evil magic from the battlefield, killing scores upon scores as her strange gift manifested in a violent gale of death. The evil flowed into her body, and for a moment the Unbound thought her a nightmare worse even than The Three, but then she released it, and the world changed around her. The ground quaked as the walls of The Sill grew rapidly up into the sky, their canopies bending inwards and joining in an impregnable tangle of nature's fury. With the people inside sealed from harm, the battle ceased and The Sill tended to their dead. Amori had been in a coma ever since.

The Unbound recovered quickly enough and left through the Seer Jars to find Cole. When it became apparent he was no longer on Aeneria, they set out for Oberon Temple in a final attempt to stop the coming of the Shadow Tide. Eliza and Valen led The Sill's forces to Oberon City while Sitra ventured to the White Sands in order to execute the last order Roth had given her. When Valen and Eliza arrived at the capital city, The Three had already stolen into the temple, and by the time the two armies met, the skies had vanished as the Shadow Tide moored Aeneria to a place between realities.

The Sill's forces retook most of Oberon City; however, the Unbound couldn't get within a mile of Oberon Temple as the same barrier that Varka had once cast between Aeneria's Light and Dark Sides now hung over the ancient monolith.

"If they're using Varka's magic against us," Cole began, his hope rallying up alongside his daring, *"then maybe I can counter it. I just Traveled completely out of turn, and I unraveled the old barrier by mistake before I knew anything about magic. I bet I can do something with this one."*

"Our thoughts exactly," Sitra agreed. *"But there's a tiny problem in our way. A few tiny problems actually. The three Alpha Colossi are standing guard outside the barrier, and their guts are still full of legions of enemies. Eliza and Valen can't get near without pissing one off."*

"We have tried every spell and underhanded trick we know," Eliza said. *"We can't even enter from above the temple without them shooting us with bones laced with Hatred and Fear. They cut through our shrouds and barriers like a needle through cloth. The Colossi are faster than they have right to be."*

"Then we need to lure one away," Cole said. *"Preferably all three. I bet Morthain's guns would do the trick."*

The idea echoed poorly off Sitra's doubts. *"They could probably blow a hole right through Oberon Temple, but getting there's nearly impossible. The ships can fly up to a mile or so high, but the Fangshards are way taller than that, and thanks to our giant furry friend the valley's still closed."*

Cole's tenacity bent, but it did not break. *"You let me handle Goran. Just get your fleet to the valley entrance."* He gave Sitra a broad smile and punched her in the shoulder, then spoke aloud, *"That's an order, Queen Sitra."*

"That's King *to you, boss,"* Sitra said, punching him back even harder. *"King has a better ring to it."*

The air broke around Cole as he took flight, indulging in the full measure of his Wisdom. The Fangshards loomed along the coastline, menacing and jagged, like the jaw of some great predator. The peaks came to fine points, and each was bleached white with snow that never melted. He had difficulty retracing his course from his last visit as the coast had no distinguishing features, but after a minute he found a rough break in the mountain ridge that could only be the remnants of Fangshard Valley. Cole slowed himself and landed. The broken bones of the mountains towered over him, immovable by means mundane or magical. Some of the fragments were large enough that they could be planted elsewhere and still hold the title of mountain.

Cole dismissed both his Rage and his Wisdom, instead delving into the unique bond of Passion that he and Goran had forged long ago. He spent ten minutes arranging his arguments and galvanizing his appeals. This war affected the entire planet, including Goran and every living thing within his realm. Now wasn't the time to worry about species conservation or soil fertility. When he was ready, Cole laid himself flat on the feet of the Fangshards and prepared himself for the arduous process of seizing Goran's widespread attention. His Passion had barely begun to trickle when a deep rumbling shook the ground.

Cole's eyes snapped wide as Goran's mind gripped his own in feral embrace. Cole's lips pulled themselves into a toothy snarl and every hair on his body stood on end. He felt charged, electrified with ferocity. A thunderous presence roared within Cole's mind.

"OOOOOOOO CHAAAAAA."

Cole laughed aloud, then replied with savage glee. *"It's good to see you too, bud."*

Unlike the last time he'd communicated with the mirak, Goran's consciousness didn't feel vague or distracted by the teeming multitudes of life within the mountains. It felt sharp and purposeful, like a predator the moment before it pounces. Cole could barely grasp the power at Goran's disposal, and it terrified him to think what would happen should it be unleashed. The entire Fangshard mountain range was ready to bring its might against The Three, and Goran would be its teeth and claws, its final storm in the face of death.

Cole was about to make his request to open the valley when a stupendous tremor kicked him up off the ground. Cole threw his limbs under himself and landed on all fours. A grating thunder shook the air with no signs of stopping, growing to such an unbearable tumult that

Cole had to block his ears with magic. He levitated himself off the bucking ground and looked up to see a gap near the top of the rubble miles away. Snow and glacier and boulders of all sizes buckled under some unseen force as a gap appeared and widened. Cole waited, awestruck by the sheer power working before him, and a quarter of an hour later, Fangshard Valley was open.

"You knew all along, didn't you?" Cole asked.

"OOOOOOOO CHAAAAAA."

Goran withdrew from Cole's mind, but his presence remained poised and close. Cole had an ominous feeling that Goran was about to do something even more momentous, and though he loved and trusted his friend, he didn't want to be around when it happened.

It wasn't long before Morthain's ships soared up behind him. He leapt up onto the lead ship and joined Sitra at the prow. She made no remark on the newly formed valley, nor did she care that its walls were near vertical and looked as if they could collapse any minute. Her black shrouded eyes were locked on the other end of the valley, focused on the battle ahead. The fleet was far quicker out of the water than in. Cole worried the flight enchantments would drain the ship's energy reserves before they reached the city, but he sensed the minds of competent spellcasters below deck flooding gratia stones with steady streams of power. These were not the same people Cole had once known.

Cole sensed Eliza and Valen waiting for them in the sky on the city side of the Valley. By unspoken agreement, he and Sitra took flight to greet them. Eliza couldn't wait for them, however, and Cole felt her shoot towards them. Valen trailed close behind her. Cole and Sitra slowed, but Eliza put on a fresh burst of speed, and just a minute later she collided with them, embracing them both with her arms and her mind. The three of them spun through the air in a dizzying hug, then Sitra snagged Valen by the armor and brought him in too. For a moment no one spoke. They held each other tightly as they reveled in the solace of each other's companionship. After a time Sitra and Valen broke away for what Cole assumed would be a private conversation between lovers. They didn't say a word, however. They just embraced each other, eyes closed and foreheads resting together. Eliza held him tighter still.

Cole felt the familiar warmth from a cherished place within his heart. Her mind nudged his, then she spoke privately to him through their old Passion link. *"I thought you were dead."*

"So did I," Cole replied.

There was restraint in her pause, but then she cast her inhibitions aside and flooded his mind with her soothing caress. *"I may never get the chance to say this again, so I'll say it now. I love you, Cole. I've tried my best not to, both for your sake and Lileth's, but my heart sings all the more for it. I know it's too late now, and you don't have to love me back, I just needed you to know before you can't anymore."*

"Eliza…" Cole began, but then didn't quite know how to finish. He knew the Havenflow had changed things between them, something special, but the memories of whatever happened would always be beyond their reach.

The jarring percussion of Morthain's artillery shook him from his thoughts.

"It has begun," Valen said.

Morthain's fleet wasted no time. Charging from the foothills, they sailed over the treetops and split their forces around the city, shooting their cannons all the while. Cole sharpened his eyes with Wisdom as he and the Unbound followed close behind the fleet. The city was ablaze. Columns of turgid black smoke rose up like bloated snakes. Proud towers lay broken and crumbled among the chaos and fire in the streets. There were flocks of Corpulants swarming freely about, but there were emerald wings among them, their owners hacking and slashing the winged nightmares like diving hawks.

"Are we sure they don't need our help?" Cole asked the group.

"Of course they need our help," Sitra said. *"That's why Morthain's flanking the city from either side. Their warriors are going to enter on foot while the fleets pummel the Colossi. Let them handle the city. We have blood to spill elsewhere."*

Following Sitra, they put on a burst of speed and flew several miles above the city, far beyond the reach of the flying Corpulants. As they passed through a cloud of acrid smoke, Cole saw the temple at last. It loomed in the ocean beyond the city, so large and so dark that it would have blended in with the starless sky if not for the faint silvery sheen rippling over it. Its tiers were stacked up in ten concentric cylinders, each a mile high and smaller than the one below. Oberon hung empty and grey directly above.

As they flew, Cole noticed a broad swath of brownish grey running a third of the length up the temple walls. The Alpha Colossus showed no blemish from the battle at The Sill, nor did the second one, which stood guard a third of the way around the temple. Then Cole saw a series of red and white explosions near the city's shoreline. The third Colossus was stumbling through the shallows towards the city, struggling to remain upright as Morthain's artillery battered across its chest like tiny exploding stars.

"Your trick is working," Cole said, pointing to the shore. A sizeable chunk fell from the titan's body, joining a steady rain of corpses and debris. *"Morthain's already baited one out. We should have a big-enough gap to reach the barrier now."*

"It's still not safe," Eliza warned. As she spoke, the Colossus near the shoreline threw an arm up to shield itself from the barrage, then charged forward, leaping the remaining half mile to the coast in a single bound. *"They are much faster than they ought to be. We should wait until they lure out another."*

"Why do they seem even bigger?" Sitra asked. No one had an answer. *"Dammit. Morthain's ships can't move that fast. King for less than a day and I'm about to get them all killed in their first battle."*

"The fleet's damage output is substantial," Valen remarked. The Colossus had broken into a dead sprint, but fell flat on its belly as the fleet shifted fire to its legs. *"So long as they face only one Colossus at a time, I estimate their casualties will be minimal."*

But even as Valen said it, a wall of white erupted from the base of the temple as the other two Colossi charged for the city, thundering through the water with alarming speed. The Unbound watched in grim silence and cut a wide path around the city and the approaching Colossi, knowing full well they were leaving thousands to die.

"I can't find Falinor," Cole said after a minute of searching with Passion. *"If any of you can reach him, tell him to get everyone in the*

air or prepare to breathe underwater. Those waves look like they're going to reach the Fangshards."

Cole sensed Valen's telepathy through the fringes of his mind, then shock, followed by a drop of grief.

"Falinor went dark," Valen said. *"So did the rest of the Heart Tree staff. The Divine Guard razed their headquarters in the foothills not long ago. I hailed an officer in an assault company and she shall spread your warning as far as she can, but the battle goes ill for us. Our forces are starting their retreat. To make matters worse, a legion of Domina and armed Underkin have just been sighted pouring out from the Fangshard Valley."*

"Stars no," Eliza said.

"What the hell are Underkin doing here?" Sitra demanded. *"They're not fighters."*

"Habbad!" Cole said. *"He came!"*

"Should we turn back and help?" Eliza asked. *"Victory in the temple will have little meaning if everyone we're fighting for is gone."*

"No," Cole replied. *"Send an envoy out to greet them. They're here to help."*

"Seems risky," Sitra growled. *"I like Eliza's idea better. It would be nice to tear a few Domina necks before our final battle."*

"No, Cole is right," Valen said. *"About not going back at least. We may not get another opportunity to penetrate the barrier. We must try while the Colossi are occupied."*

Eliza and Sitra gave their grudging acceptance and the group flew on. They skirted the Colossi by several miles, crossing over the city shoreline shortly after the two charging titans emerged from the water. Sitra's Rage flared across their minds as the first Colossus dashed several of Morthain's fleet with absurd ease. Some of them hadn't even offloaded their warriors into the city yet.

The barrier seemed to glow brighter as they neared. It shimmered and waved like a sheet made from woven strands of diamonds. Gentle and calm, its appearance offered no hint of what danger lay hidden within its fabric. They halted one hundred feet from the ghostly veil. The air was heavy with magic.

"Everyone keep a hand on me," Cole commanded. "I'm going to pass through first."

"Wait, that's your plan?" Sitra asked, dumbstruck. "The last great barrier killed anyone and anything that passed through it, and you expect us to just hold your hand and skip on over? Dammit Cole, I thought you knew a spell or something."

"It does seem a tad foolhardy," Valen agreed.

Eliza hovered close and placed a hand on Cole's shoulder. "I'm with you."

Cole locked eyes with her for a moment, wishing they had more time to talk privately, then turned his gaze to Sitra and Valen. "It's how I got through last time. Come on. If it starts hurting me then you all can pull me back." He floated towards the barrier before they could argue any further. Eliza kept her hand on his back the whole time, and after a moment he felt two more press firmly to his shoulders.

He was only a few feet away now. Magic vibrated the air so forcefully that he couldn't hear his own panting breath. A giddy sense of terror flipped about in his stomach, coiling and constricting around his guts. Before the Fear could manifest into hesitation, Cole plunged his hand into the barrier. The ghostly sheet did not break, however. Like last time, it yielded to his touch like taut fabric, tingling and stinging his flesh all the while. He pushed harder until his whole arm went numb with the sensation of being stabbed by millions of electrified needles. He threw another hand into the effort. His ears throbbed, his teeth felt like they were about to rattle out of his skull, and his vision blurred as though the ocean had risen to the stars. He felt a vague shift in pressure on his back as one of the three hands adjusted from supporting him to pulling him away.

"Push...me," Cole struggled, hoping his words could still make it into their minds.

The pressure on his back increased tenfold, then suddenly it was gone. There was a flash of white light and a great rushing noise, then there was nothing. Even the tingling had subsided. He was on the other side. Smiling, he whipped around to share his relief, but found himself staring directly at the ghostly veil. His friends were on the other side.

"No!" Cole roared as he shot for the barrier like a spear. As soon as his hands touched, a jolt of energy tore through him, and he nearly fell from the sky. Head spinning, he hollered for them, but his voice couldn't make it through the hum of the barrier. He tried his Passion instead, first with Valen, then Sitra, but nothing seemed to work. He was alone.

On the other side, Sitra tapped one of her bladed fingers on the veil, producing a flash of white light that made her wince and pull away. A quarter of the black claw had vanished. Enraged, she conjured a ball of liquid fire as large as a baileen. She launched it at the barrier with a powerful kick, but the magic splashed harmlessly across the ghostly veil without leaving so much as a scorch mark. Valen waved his hands slowly about himself as though painting a mural, then hundreds of emerald spears materialized around him, each ten feet long and crackling with energy. With a twist of his hand the spears joined together and shot for the barrier faster than Cole could see. For a quarter of a minute the missiles exploded against the veil in a shower of emerald sparks, though in the end they were as ineffective as Sitra's fire had been. Eliza remained still and quiet the whole time, her eyes pinched shut in concentration.

Her mind brushed against his, soft as a whisper, and he felt her through their link. *"Cole."*

"Eliza," he replied. Their link felt distant and thin. *"Tell them to stop. They're wasting their magic."*

"You can't go alone," Eliza pleaded. *"You can't leave us. Not before the end."*

Cole flew as near as he could to her without touching the barrier. She met him as close as she dared, eyes red and tearful.

"I'm not alone," he said. *"I still have you."*

He held her gaze for a moment as she cried, wishing he could touch her and hold her one more time, but there was no time. Heart heavy, he spun in the spot and soared for the black monolith of Oberon Temple.

CHAPTER 34

FATE OF WORLDS

The ocean air shattered at the touch of his Wisdom, but no matter how fast he flew, the wind couldn't seem to carry his tears away quickly enough. He maintained his weakening connection to Eliza, hoping he could continue to do so once inside the enchanted walls of the temple. Thinking of the temple brought to light another problem. He had no idea where the Vaults of the Soul were held. Oberon Temple was ten miles high, and the bottom tier of its structure was at least that wide. It might take him months or cycles just to navigate a portion of the labyrinthian tunnels and chambers within. Still, he had to try. There was no turning back now. But where should he enter from? Surely The Three would have every entrance well-defended, and while he Feared no lesser enemy, there was every chance his presence would trigger an alarm.

An unbidden and annoying memory of Habbad came to mind, with it a fresh pang of loss, and suddenly Cole knew where he should start looking. He flew to one of the middle tiers and began scanning its surface, glancing back now and then at the city skyline for reference. His urgency hardened into frustration as he couldn't find so much as a blemish on the temple's outer walls.

"It's up one more level," Eliza offered, streaming a trickle of her recollection into him.

Joining his memories with hers, Cole halted before the spot where he was confident it should be, but found nothing other than a seamless expanse of smooth obsidian. Curious, he floated towards the wall and ran his hand over it. The dark stone was cold and rough, but then he felt a patch far warmer, which gave slightly under his touch. Urging Wisdom into his fingertips, he cast the spell for unlocking liquid-stone doors, and a small hole appeared just under his hand. The hole broadened in earnest, and within seconds Cole found himself staring at an open window. Inside, rainbow moonlight poured through lush vegetation and he saw woven tree root paths beyond.

Cole slid into the Everglen, locking the window behind him. The earthy aromas and steady din of the forest life made him feel right at home.

"Can you still feel me?" Cole asked Eliza. Their link felt wire-thin now.

"Barely," she replied, then before he had to ask, she transferred her sight of the battle to him.

The Three's Colossi had eliminated all but a few of Morthain's fleet, but now their attentions were on something on the other side of the city, near the Fangshards. Cole's heart sank as Eliza showed him Goran standing erect on his hind legs at the edge of the foothills, chest out and teeth bared. He was bigger than ever. Only a few strips of his brindle fur remained along his flanks. His granite claws were as large as city squares, the living stone stretching all the way up his limbs like a shroud of Rage. A small forest of mossy growth covered his chest and belly in a verdant green banner. Glaciers ran along the landscape of his craggy shoulders, leading up to the snowy peaks that tufted the top of his head. His eyes were smoldering gems of ruby starlight, locked with deadly intent on the three Colossi now lumbering their way towards him. As vast and imposing as he was, Cole could tell he was only half the height of the undead titans.

Cole withdrew from Eliza's stream of thought. *"I don't want to watch. Just... let me know if he..."*

"I will," she whispered. Her voice was so faint he could barely understand her.

Delving into his Rage, Cole summoned his master's shroud and kicked off with bladed feet. He followed a woven root path and within a few minutes found the small cluster of apartment trees they had stayed in last time he was there. Butterflies floated around the apartments, their wings flickering with rich colors like flakes of stained glass. Nearby was a large boulder jutting up out of a clover patch, a set of double doors crafted seamlessly into its face. Cole knew the doors led to an elevator which would bring him anywhere he wanted, but still hadn't the foggiest idea where he should go.

Cole paced from tree to tree, racking his brain for a spell or scrap of Aenerian history that might help him. The butterflies weren't helping matters. He shooed them away so he could think without distraction, but they kept landing on him, and more seemed to show up every minute. Eventually he cast a barrier around himself, though that only seemed to excite them further. They were stunningly beautiful, he thought. Their wings were painted in striking tones, each pair a different color, as though they had flown in the iridescent clouds of dust cast by the soul flies on their way to and from their local planets.

Cole's meandering and pondering yielded nothing other than the fact he was wasting time, and so he started for the elevator, determined to figure things out as he went. As he neared the lift, a blaze of color caught his eye from a nearby tree. From its roots to the tips of its leaves, every inch of the apartment tree was covered in the rainbow butterflies. It was Chiron's tree.

Curious, he approached the liquid stone door and pressed himself through it. Chiron's room was just as he remembered it, spartan in design with a plain bed, desk, and a wardrobe, just like the barracks rooms at The Sill. Cole scanned the room with his eyes and with his magic, hoping to find some sort of clue left by the elder. His search produced nothing, however, and after ten minutes he chastised himself for wasting even more time. People were dying by the second. He had to keep going.

He halted before the door. A butterfly, smaller yet more beautiful than all the others, was perched just above the door frame. Its wings bloomed whimsically through every color like the surface of Oberon, and it produced a little cloud of viscous light with every flap.

"What are you doing in here?" Cole asked.

As if in answer, the butterfly took to the air. Its wings seemed to beat far too slowly to sustain flight, only one stroke every few seconds, leaving behind a tiny, glittering shower of whatever color it happened to be at the time. Cole dismissed his shroud and held out his hand. The butterfly landed in his palm, but as it did its form began to shift and sway, until it melted into his skin in a puff of rainbow light. Horrorstruck, Cole whipped his hand back and forth in an attempt to shake the creature from him. He examined his hand and found a patch of the same rainbow light painted on his palm, blooming through colors as though he'd been kissed by Oberon. Cole tried wiping his hands and cleansing them with magic, but the smudge of pigments remained, glowing and tingling with unknown purpose.

When Cole left the apartment the butterflies were gone. With nowhere else to go, he decided to try his luck with the elevator. The double doors slid shut behind him as he stepped inside. The last time he had used the lift, he had been in such a Rage that now, he didn't recall how to use it. It had brought him to the Council chambers, seemingly of its own accord, but he was certain he didn't want to go there. He scanned the walls, floor and ceiling, finding no button or lever of any sort.

"The Vaults of the Soul," Cole said aloud, wondering if it was voice-operated.

Nothing happened. He tried a few other places he remembered from old conversations, including the embassies, forums, and libraries, but nothing worked. Frustrated, he readied his Wisdom to move the lift manually, but then his palm started itching. He twisted his hand and saw the smear of rainbow light pulsing excitedly, then the little butterfly emerged from it as if his palm were an open window. The butterfly flapped slowly up to a tiny six-pointed star etched on the ceiling. The carving lit up as the shimmering insect alighted on it. Job done, the butterfly gave a single sharp flap, then made the slow glide back to Cole's hand, melting into his palm once more. The elevator lurched, not up or down, but sideways. After a moment the lift dropped into a sudden freefall, and Cole had to stick a hand up to the ceiling to keep himself from hitting it. It yawed sideways once more, then twisted and rose with such force, Cole's legs buckled and his knees hit the floor. After too many twists and dips to count, he had lost all sense of direction, as well as his hope that he'd make it back out the way he came.

Since there was no point in trying to keep himself oriented, he turned to his link with Eliza, hoping to find some good news outside the temple. A drop of Fear crashed over his heart. He couldn't find her. Determined, he sat himself cross-legged on the floor and withdrew deeper into himself. Like dimming lights, his senses faded one by one until he existed solely within his own mind. He found her at last. Her link was thin as spider silk, but it was there.

"There you are," Cole said, offering her what little compassion he could through their frail link.

Her response was instantaneous. *"Cole! Stars above, I Feared the worst! Are you safe? What's happening in the temple?"*

"I entered through the Everglen and took the lift, but it's taking me somewhere all on its own." He flashed her the memories of the butterflies. *"How goes the battle? Are we winning?"*

"The battle is over, for us at least," she said. *"Both sides are in full retreat. Goran and the Alpha Colossi flattened the city and they're still at it. Right now we're rallying our forces and routing our enemies before they flee into the surrounding lands. Habbad is with us. He is different."*

"Be careful," Cole warned. *"I wouldn't be surprised if he tried something before the end."*

"He won't be a problem," Eliza said. *"As soon as his forces arrived, he allowed us into his mind, or minds I should say. We found no duplicities in our inspection, though that didn't stop Sitra from lacing his internal Domina with Passion traps. If he turns on us he will lose his thralls, but I don't think that will happen. He is with us."*

"Good, good," Cole said, convincing himself that everything would be fine. The lift gave a violent shudder as it dropped once more. *"How is Goran holding up?"* She didn't respond, though he could still feel her. *"Eliza?"*

"Let me show you."

The music of Eliza's mind seeped into him, and he saw the world through her eyes. She was in the sky, miles above the ground. Sitra and Valen were with her, scanning the scene below with fire in their eyes. Sitra's bladed hair chimed in the wind, her shroud covered with angry red furrows still smoldering from dark magic. Blood dripped from her claws. Valen hovered next to her, his armored robes torn and damaged in places, exposing patches of unmarred skin beneath. Floating beside them on wings made from raven-black smoke was Habbad. He had forgone the suit, instead wearing thick ivory wrappings adorned with

Morthainian glass plates on the shoulders, thighs, and chest. His smoky wings rippled, and his hands and feet were massive munisica of crimson Hatred. His eyes surveyed the scene below, calculating yet awestruck. Eliza's gaze drifted downwards, bringing Cole's along with hers.

Had he not seen Oberon Temple looming in the background, he would have thought they were on another planet. Where Oberon City had once stood, four mighty figures were locked in a titanic melee over fields of rubble and flames. The foothills of the Fangshards were now as tall as the rest of the snowy peaks, and expanding outwards as if the Fangshards were reaching out to embrace the devastated city. Cole watched as gentle hills exploded skywards, sharpening to jagged spikes as if hammered by the gods below. Aeneria's breath surged in gouts of fiery ash as each new mountain birthed itself, issuing concussive waves that could be seen radiating for miles around. As the battle of the titans stormed on, the jagged peaks continued to encircle them, until the final mountain grated into place and locked them all in a cage of rock and fire.

Goran was only half the height of the Alpha Colossi, but what he lacked in stature, he more than made up for with ferocity. His granite claws rent acres of corpses from the Colossi with every blow. His enormous jaws and diving canines hacked through limbs as though they were made of rotten wood.

However as prodigious as the damage was, Goran couldn't seem to keep up with the rate at which the Colossi reassembled themselves. The flesh of the titans was made primarily of the mutilated bodies of Chosen, which required a mastery of Passion to release into true death. As soon as Goran cleaved a swath of flesh, the charred mass would gather itself up into a writhing ball, only to be picked up and consumed by another Colossus a moment later. Landslides rolled in from the new mountains to bury the Chosen, but the Colossi exhumed the flesh with a lazy kick and integrated the mass into themselves with routine ease.

As the battle wore on, great fissures cracked open in the ground around them. A molten orange glow pulsed from the depths before Aeneria's blood came rushing out in geysers of angry magma. Though Goran's strength never wavered, it didn't take long for the Colossi to capitalize on their advantage in numbers. While the mirak was busy savaging one, the second repaired itself and the third attacked with a hail of bone spears cast from its palm. The poisoned missiles sank into Goran's hide by the thousands, each producing a river of crimson as they pierced flesh and stone alike. Goran's roar shook the newborn mountains in a tumultuous bellow, pained and furious. His eyes blazed with primal Rage as he charged at his attacker, but the second Colossus was already waiting, and it stabbed him in the flank with a length of metal frame from its severed arm. In response, a shaft of rock half a mile wide erupted from the mountain beside Goran and smashed into the Colossus, knocking it off its feet and sending it careening into a lake of liquid fire. The Colossus attempted to scramble out of the lava, but the solid ground broke apart at its touch and it sank even lower, until it finally vanished in a belch of magma. Goran trembled up onto all fours, took a step forward, then shuddered and collapsed to his belly. The two remaining Colossi lumbered over to him, palms aimed at his brindle back.

Heaving, Goran turned a ruby eye to Eliza. Though he was miles and miles away, Cole knew his first friend was staring at him through her.

Cole felt a voice rumble through Eliza's mind. It was the voice of soil and roots, of snow-capped peaks and verdant valleys, of winds and rain and trickling rivers. It was the voice of the mountains.

"OOOOOOOO CHAAAAAA."

With a bellow of defiance, Goran launched himself up onto his hind legs and raised his claws to the starless sky. Each Colossi unleashed a volley of spears into his mossy belly, piercing him with swarms of tainted bone that passed through his bulk and erupted from his back in a burst of flesh and blood. They were too late, however. Goran's granite claws were already on their way down, aglow with veins of emerald green and fiery crimson. As he struck the ground a shockwave exploded from him, knocking the Colossi flat on their backs a mile away. The earth buckled and broke across the battleground, yielding in massive chunks as Aeneria's blood came flooding up to consume them all in molten wrath.

Eliza tried to turn away, but Cole urged her to keep looking, and so she did, though her view became clouded with tears. The lava rose halfway up the circle valley, filling it like a bowl of soup. It devoured everything in its path, leaving nothing for the Colossi to reassemble themselves with. Where Goran had been, there was nothing more than a fading tower of steam.

Unable to bear it any longer, Cole withdrew from the sight. Eliza wrapped him with tender compassion, sharing what grief she could through their feeble link.

"He was incredible," she whispered. Despair hung thick in her mind, but it was nothing compared to the Passion she felt for Cole and the others still alive.

Cole tried to utter something, but a deluge of grief crashed over him like a rain of lead, burying him beyond reach of his hope. He had no urge or desire to speak of. Back in his body he was dimly aware that the elevator had stopped moving, but it didn't seem to matter. Nothing seemed to matter. He had lost too much. Joshy, Deekus, Storn, Roth and Alvani and Chiron, then Naythan and Wilkin. Each soul was a candle of life that had lit up his sky, but now his sky was as empty as the black void now lurking around Oberon, And now Goran. Goran was his first friend, not only on Aeneria, but in his entire life. It seemed like only days ago Goran had saved him from the cabin door, and then Cole had returned the favor by saving Goran from the giant grubs, sealing their bond in ancient Passion. Goran had nothing to gain, but remained resolutely by his side through the best and worst of times, even when the call of the mountains took him away. Goran's death left a gap in his soul, an empty hollow no one else could ever fill.

Cole knew Eliza felt the Despair gathering inside him, and he tried to pull away to save her, but she didn't shrink from it. She held him fast and poured her love into him. After a moment he felt a change in the pitch of her mind, then another. Sitra joined the connection, followed by Valen and a callus mind that could only have been Habbad. Their minds mingled together as they embraced him through his and Eliza's private bond.

"You'd better not be hesitating in there," Sitra said with mock reprisal. There was restrained sorrow in her voice, and Cole knew she was doing her best to be strong for him. *"Get your ass in there, do*

your job, and get your ass out. No mucking about." Cole uttered a hollow chuckle in reply, but felt his Despair lift considerably as Sitra's Rage seared into him. She bumped her consciousness against his, rough yet loving, then pulled away.

Valen's words rang through next, clear and brilliant. *"I believe in you, Brother. As Eliza once said, your bond with Goran was reciprocal. If his development from tiny mirak to god of the Fangshards is any indication of the evolution of your powers, then The Three are in for the reckoning of their lives. The fate of the Aethers couldn't be in better hands. I believe in you, Brother."* Valen transferred a measure of his Wisdom before withdrawing, bolstering Cole's mind with the green magic.

Habbad's mind approached next, but he didn't say anything. Cole could tell he had much to say, but now wasn't the time. There were too many wrongs between them to right with a few parting words. The Underkin began to withdraw, then paused and broke his brooding silence at last. *"I have shielded my words from the minds of the others, for my words are for you alone. From what I understand this is a one-way trip for you, not that you would be likely to survive anyhow. So with your permission I would like to take custody of both Lexy and Amorinanis. I... I have much to explain to Lexy, and after I'm done she may Hate me anyway. She has right enough to. As for Amorinanis, I believe I can help her. I can teach her how to control her powers, and offer my expertise in using evil magics with good intent. At least that's what some of my Domina are telling me. So long as the girls will have me, I will care for them as though they were both my sisters, and if they refuse me, then I have resources enough to indirectly provide for and protect them for the rest of their lives. What say you?"*

"I say you're a fool if you think Lexy could ever Hate you," Cole replied. *"She's stronger than both of us. If you have the strength to come back to us from The Three's inner circles, then I know she'll have the strength to love you again. As for Amori, be careful. Very careful. She's only a few months old, but I think she might be the most powerful person on the planet. The others will explain what we know so far, and Lexy knows her better than anyone else does. Take both girls and my blessing. You probably need them more than they need you, to be honest, but that's something you'll figure out as you go."* He felt Habbad pull away, but he held him tightly for a moment longer. *"I'm glad I met you, Habbad. You will always be a brother to me."*

Habbad remained silent until Cole released him at last, then Cole withdrew, leaving himself alone with Eliza.

"Are you afraid?" she asked.

"Right now, not at all," Cole replied. *"I'm with you."*

"You know what I mean," she chided.

"I've never been more terrified in my life," Cole said. *"I feel like a kid again, like I'm about to jump off a cliff without knowing what's at the bottom."*

"You are far more than a child," she said. *"I'm sorry for foisting my emotions on you in such a late hour. My heartaches are the last thing you need on your mind when you're trying to save the world. I've been a fool."*

It was Cole's turn to admonish her. *"Never apologize for telling someone how you feel. When you do you're apologizing for the truth. It's what you do with those feelings that matters in the end."*

She beamed. *"How very wise of you."*

"I didn't come up with it," Cole laughed. *"I think Alvani said it at some point, but it resonates with me now more than ever."* He embraced her then, entwining his mind and soul with hers the best he could through the feeble link. *"I don't remember what happened between us in the Havenflow, but my heart tells me it was something important. Too important to ignore. I promise you, no matter what kind of trouble I run into within the Vaults of the Soul, I'll find a way back to you."*

"I'll hold you to it," she said.

A comfortable silence came between them. Cole wished he could hold her and feel her heartbeat against his own, if only for a moment before the end. He considered casting Chiron's teleportation spell to do just that, but then the fate of the Aethers began to weigh heavily on him.

"I have to go," Cole said. *"If I don't do it now, I'll never get the courage again."*

"Just a little longer," she pleaded. Her soul sang into his, tight and warm and right.

Cole suppressed a sob, then hardened his heart. *"I'll find a way back to you."*

Before she could say the words that would surely stop him, he severed the connection and returned to his body in full. When he opened his eyes, the only thing he could see was the faint patch of rainbow still burning in his palm. He rose to his feet and fingered around for the seam in the doors, then pushed them open.

Warm, salty air rushed in as he beheld the interior of a small, single-room hut with wooden walls and a ceiling made of layered ferns. There was a cot pushed against the back wall, and a table holding a few weapons, including a dagger that looked oddly familiar. But Cole didn't care much about the dagger at the moment, nor anything else for that matter. Sitting in a chair next to the bed, was Chiron.

"Master!" Cole exclaimed as he leapt into the room. Trepidation licked up his spine a second too late. Fearing a trap, he closed off his mind and hastily covered himself in his usual protective spells, finishing with his master's shroud of Rage. He crouched into a low fighting stance, and brought his midnight gaze to the man before him.

"*Tremendous*," Chiron said, beaming at him.

"Who are you?" Cole demanded. Magic crackled between his claws. He felt flames of Hatred join the fray, and instead of stifling the magic, he allowed it some room to work. If this was a trap then it was just one thing standing in the way of saving everyone he loved, and *that* he could Hate. Lines of ruby scorched over his shroud in crooked veins, increasing his physical strength by magnitudes.

Chiron's wholesome smile faltered as a mixture of pride and sorrow bloomed over his face. He sighed, then blinked a tear out. It rolled from the corner of his eye, down the sharp angles of his face to the tip of the opalescent scar at his throat. "I am no threat to you, of that I am certain. Please, take one of the weapons on the table if you'd like, though I daresay your munisica are far superior to such crude instruments." Seeing that his words did nothing to assuage Cole's apprehension, Chiron opened his arms and continued on as politely as ever. "You are quite right to withhold your trust, but I assure you there is nothing within this pocket dimension more dangerous than you at this very moment."

At the mention of a pocket dimension, Cole sent out a pulse of Wisdom blended with Passion. The magic returned to him almost instantaneously, revealing nothing and no one beyond the walls of the hut. He was indeed in a pocket dimension, and the man before him felt like Chiron, though he seemed to take no notice of Cole's magical probing. "You're not Chiron."

"You are mostly correct," Chiron said with a nod. "I am merely an imprint of myself, which I left here the moment before my pithing shard killed me. I exist only in this place, and only for one purpose."

"And that is?" Cole asked.

Chiron's expression changed from polite interest to grave urgency. "To ensure you make it into the Vaults of the Soul."

Cole was quiet for a moment, unsure if he should believe a word of it. Just then his palm tickled with an itch, and out of his periphery he saw the rainbow butterfly flutter from his hand, slow and graceful. It landed on Chiron's head, where it flapped excitedly and set to preening itself.

"I see you worked out my clue," Chiron said. "I was worried I may have been a tad overzealous with the spell. There were dozens of the tiny critters before I left my imprint. How many were there when you arrived?"

"Your tree was covered in them," Cole replied.

Chiron's eyebrows went up. "Really? Well, you found your way here so I suppose they did their job well enough."

"What is this place?" Cole asked, adopting a relaxed position as he looked around, though he kept his shroud and protective spells up. "It looks familiar."

"I should hope so," Chiron said. He inspected the interior of the hut as though seeing it for the first time. "I believe this is the hut where we first met. I instructed the pocket dimension to take the form of a moment that you and I would both remember, but told no one else of. That way you would know my imprint to be authentic."

"But I didn't feel anything when I stepped—" Cole started, then stopped and watched the butterfly flapping happily on Chiron's head. "Of course."

Chiron smiled up at the butterfly. "Just a trick of Passion and Wisdom, though a devilishly clever one I admit."

Cole was silent for a moment as events from the long Aenerian months ran through his mind. His consternation must have shown through his shroud, as Chiron raised his hand to stop the flood of information before it could start.

"There is no need to fill me in on what has happened since I imprinted myself here," Chiron said. "I think it is safe to assume you did a great many things and met a great many people, and that someone or everyone you know is already dead, including me. Let us not waste what precious time we have left by regaling me with tales that will fade from my mind as soon as I fulfill my purpose. The only thing that matters now is getting you into the Vaults."

"You know where they are then?" Cole asked. "Can you take me there?"

Chiron raised a winged eyebrow. "I cannot, but you hardly need me. You already know where they are. I can see in your eyes that you have been there countless times already."

"I don't understand," Cole said, quite sure he'd never been anywhere near the Vaults before.

"They lie within you, in the very core of your mind," Chiron said. "I cannot tell you what the place is or what it looks like, but I suspect it is a place of tranquility and reflection. You may house certain memories there, or perhaps all of them."

Cole knew the place. It was the stone room in the center of his mind. But that couldn't be right. There was nothing beyond its confines, and he would know because he was the one who built it. He suppressed an urge to withdraw into himself just to check.

"I have a place like that," Cole said. "But I don't think it's connected to the Vaults of the Soul. It's not connected to anything actually."

"I would take a closer look if I were you," Chiron said with a knowing grin. "You are in the deepest reaches of Oberon Temple. The magic embedded within its walls will allow you to access the Vaults through this special place of yours."

Cole didn't bother hiding the skepticism from his face. "If that's all it took, then why didn't you have me do this sooner? I had already created the center of my mind by the time we got to the Temple for my hearing with the Council."

"You were a bit... unfinished," Chiron said. "The Vaults of the Soul encompass the very foundations of our magic, their source if you will. Visiting them is perilous under the best of circumstances, and it was my estimation that even in our final moments together, you did not know yourself well enough to test them. You were not ready."

"But I'm ready now?" Cole asked, confused.

Chiron nodded. "As ready as you will ever be."

"Why didn't you enter yourself?" Cole demanded, anger flaring in his words "You would have stood a better chance than me any day. People died. A lot of people died. You and Alvani, Naythan, the entire Celestial Council, and thousands of others. Then there's the millions of Chosen that The Three took for their Alpha Colossi. Oh and let's not forget about Roth, but Grotton only took him for Harbinger." As he spoke he saw a shadow of remorse fall over Chiron's face, but that only served to enrage Cole even further. "What was it then, too cowardly to take the plunge yourself? Was that one-way trip a bit too much for The Sill's greatest Wisdom Walker?"

"Yes," Chiron whispered as his face twisted in anguish. The butterfly darted away and hid behind the bed. Above the collar of his robes Cole saw the tip of the opalescent scar throbbing at his throat. He spoke in a choked voice. "Ka Reine and I knew of the Vaults for some time. We tried entering on several occasions, but something stopped us, a lock which we had no key to open. I should have put more of myself into the effort. Stars know I *could* have. I always knew if had devoted just a few cycles to the endeavor, I would eventually find success, but I was too scared to truly make an attempt. Too scared that I would be tempted by the dark magics and plague this world with the Despair that has been rotting in my heart ever since I lost my Saphyra. She would have been ashamed of my cowardice, that I let her death poison my heart until my dying day."

"I'm sorry," Cole muttered, disarmed.

"Do not feel sorry for me," Chiron said, drying his tears with the sleeve of his robes. In that moment he appeared to Cole not as Chiron the Wisdom Walker, nor Chiron of the first Unbound, but Chiron the man, fallible and imperfect. "Feel sorry for those who've suffered because of my cowardice."

"You are not a coward," Cole said. "You knew yourself well enough not to put the world in danger. Had you entered you might have replaced Sorronis, or joined him, and this world and every other would be worse off for it. If there was some sort of debt owed, then you've more than paid for it in my eyes. You brought me here."

"That was quite touching. Thank you, Cole," Chiron said with a small smile. Tears gleamed in his eyes once more, but did not fall. He took a steadying breath and continued. "So, are you ready to face eternity?"

"No, but I don't think I'll ever be," Cole replied. He felt as though his guts had been replaced by a writhing bundle of icy snakes. "I just go to my center?"

"And take a closer look," Chiron said with a wink.

Cole watched as the color in Chiron's skin and robes dulled to grey, then faded to transparency until there was nothing but an empty chair. Chiron's imprint had fulfilled its purpose. Cole was alone.

Steeling himself, Cole sat on the floor of the hut and withdrew to the center of his mind. He dismissed his active magic and began his steady, meditative breathing. At first there was nothing but empty whiteness, as though the stone room was reluctant to show itself. He realized then that it was his own Fear preventing the room from manifesting. He burned the Fear away with a flick of Rage, then recreated the stone room block by block, which for some reason was even more difficult than the first time. When he had a passable impression of his center, he left his body entirely and willed himself into the room, polishing off the finishing touches by hand. After placing the final crystalline bead of memory on the rock cone protruding from the ceiling, Cole brushed his hands together and took a deep breath. Upon his exhaling, water flowed down over the cone and its million marbles, falling in an unbroken line from the tip to the stone pedestal beneath. Cole cupped his hands under the water and splashed it over his face. It was cool and soothing.

Cole paced around the room, inspecting every block and blemish in the walls as he went. Nothing seemed out of place. He checked the crystalline memories, snapping several off and shaking them before a light he had conjured, but there was nothing but the thoughts within, playing over and over in an endless loop. Frustration boiled up inside him and steam began to simmer from the flowing water. Why couldn't Chiron give him a better hint? *Take a closer look?* That could mean anything. Would it have been so difficult for Chiron to give him a simple answer just this once? It was probably some profoundly obscure nuance of Wisdom that required copious amounts of focus and a herculean effort of will. If only there had been a door, or a window, or a set of stairs, something he could make sense of.

There was the gravelly sound of stone rubbing on stone. Cole wheeled around, alarmed. Positive he had not consciously made the noise. He found himself facing a dark hallway made of the same stone as his center. Just as he began to wonder what lay beyond, orange torches flared to life along the walls, revealing a passageway that looked as if it had no end. Cole took off at a sprint, then willed his magic into flight and tore down the hallway as fast as Wisdom could carry him. Miles of stone blurred past him in seconds, and soon a light appeared at the end of the hallway, growing larger and larger until Cole found himself at the entrance of something that was no longer of his mind.

He slowed, landing seamlessly into a jogging stride as he emerged onto a stone walkway suspended by nothing. When his eyes adjusted, he discovered this foreign room was no room at all. The walkway shot out into limitless space that expanded in all directions. An ocean of stars twinkled at him from all sides, so dense with light that there was barely any black to behold, as though all the stars in all the skies had been collected and brought to this strange place. Movement ahead caught Cole's eye. His jaw swung open.

Resting in the crowded starscape was a distant planet as large as his outstretched hand. There were others on either side of it, and more on the other side of those. Cole recognized Wulfmont, Rhunham, Dunhaven, Allias, and Pastori and several others, including Terra. All twenty-one were circled up around him, level with the walkway and spinning gently. As he twisted around to count them he discovered the walkway had vanished behind him, and so had the hall that led to his center. There was only one way to go now.

Cole ran on, wondering if it was air he was breathing or if he was only imagining it. The sound and feel of his bare feet slapping across stone felt real enough, and so did the weight of his wrappings and the sweat on his brow. He wondered what would happen if he dove off the side into the abyss, or where he would appear should he attempt to return to his body. At the thought of using magic, he realized with mounting horror that he had none. He slowed to a halt and attempted to summon his munisica, but his hands remained hands and his feet remained feet. He tried conjuring a flame in his palm, just the smallest candle between his fingertips, but the Wisdom didn't come. Panting, he reached for his Passion and withdrew inwards towards his center, then outwards when that failed. Finally, he tried his link to Eliza, but her special place within him was barren and mundane, as if the link had never existed in the first place. Panting and panicking, he turned to run back. Cole's arms spun in a wild windmill as he teetered over the edge out into limitless open space.

Something grabbed him by the back of his wrappings and pulled him back in a deft motion. Heart hammering against his ribs, Cole spun around and found himself face to face with a man he had never seen before, but there was no doubt in his mind who he was. It was *He. Him*. Varka.

"Took you long enough," He said. "We've been waiting for you." He turned on the spot and walked away before Cole's shock had even begun to settle. He halted after ten paces and spoke over his shoulder. "Are you coming?"

Cole didn't know what to say, so he didn't say anything. He shook himself and trotted after the man, inspecting him with unabashed awe. He stood within an inch of Cole's height, and it was hard to tell from a sideways angle, but Cole imagined they looked somewhat similar too. He wore armored cloth robes of the same design used by the warriors of The Sill, earth-toned with thick padding on the chest, arms, and thighs. A half cape was draped gracefully over one of his shoulders. His hands and feet were naked, free to explode into ebony munisica in an instant.

"I know you," Cole said at last.

"And I know you, Coleton Jonathan Carter of House Terra," he replied, eyes locked straight ahead. "You've made quite a mess of things."

"I had help," Cole offered. "You should know, seeing as you were there for most of it."

"I have been here, as I have been for countless cycles," the man said. "The presence you are alluding to is but a fraction of my soul, one of many which I planted across the Aethers." He waved an arm, indicating the local planets.

"Are you not Varka?" Cole asked, confused.

"Varka is but one of my children," the man said with a sharp edge in his tone. "I am Davos."

"Are you saying there's more out there?" Cole's question was answered by a bored nod. "More people like me?" Another nod. "How many?"

Davos shrugged. "Hundreds. Thousands perhaps. I was very young and very desperate when I cast myself out into the local planets." Davos stopped suddenly and motioned to something in front of him.

Cole was so occupied with the spectacle of the local planets, he hadn't noticed how far they had gone. They stood before a floating platform thirty yards across, with six sets of stairs spaced evenly around it, each leading up to a dais where a large formation of crystal hung motionless in the air. There was a fiery red, a forest green, and a gentle lavender, then there was a mottled purple, a toxic orange, and a sad blue with a bloody crimson heart. One for each school of magic. There were people frozen within the crystals for the evil magics, each stuck in a tranquil pose with shafts of starlight shimmering around them.

Davos's eyes narrowed at the wonder on Cole's face. "The ones you call The Three were the first of my children to return to me. Their Harbingers are currently unraveling the vestiges of the mess created by my last child to enter the Vaults." He nodded up towards the green crystal, and Cole noticed another man frozen within.

"That's Varka!" Cole gasped, sure this time. "He looks just like you. And me." He took a step towards the green crystal. There was a woman in the Vault as well, lying lifeless at Varka's feet. She looked very much like Lileth.

"Careful now," Davos said. An unseen force dragged Cole back several paces from the steps. "Not until I explain things. The man in the Vault of Wisdom bears my appearance for the same reason the others in the Vaults of Fear, Hunger, Hatred and Despair do. It is the same reason you and I look something alike."

"Because we are your children?" Cole guessed. This meant he had not been carrying a bit of Varka's soul, but Davos's.

"Yes," Davos replied. "A fragment of my soul lives in each of them, a key passed from me to their greatest grandfathers, transferred through the seed of life until the fragment found a suitable host. Though you no longer carry it, the fragment that attached itself to you had been there long enough to attune your soul to the right frequencies, and allowed you to return to me. The Vaults are locked to anyone who does not bear my soul."

Cole gazed up at the crystals, or Vaults as Davos had called them. The people trapped inside did indeed look like him, as though they were all close relatives separated by time and worlds.

"What's the point of all this?" Cole asked. "Why split your soul and draw everyone in here?"

"Is it not obvious?" Davos said, and his eyes lit with ravenous wonder. "Can you not feel it? The Vaults are the source of their namesakes. Fear, Passion, Hunger, all of them exist out there, in the local planets. The one who enters a Vault gains dominance over the very source of the magic. In other words, they become a god. Long ago when I walked this world and my soul was whole, I was part of the team who made Oberon temple, including the Vaults of the Soul. Oh, how our genius shined. One of my colleagues had the clever elegance to combine Hatred and Despair into a single Vault, a twist of reasoning I never fully understood until Sorronis arrived. In the end we all agreed that no one person should hold dominion over all six Vaults, but I sensed the webs of deception in the hearts of my partners. In my investigations, I discovered each had planned to kill the others and take the Vaults for themselves. We battled here on this very floor." Grief welled up in Davos's eyes as his memories haunted him.

"How did you survive?" Cole asked.

"I was the better liar," Davos said, shaking his head in disgust. "Yes, I emerged the victor, but I was also trapped. In all our meddlings and double-crossings, one of us had locked the Vaults so that none may enter or leave, not physically anyhow. I was never able to unlock the Vaults, but I did find a way to circumvent their rules. With endless solitude before me, I held out for as long as I could, but eventually I gave in to the same temptation that drove my friends to murder. I fractured my soul and cast the pieces among the local planets so that one day I could return and enter all six Vaults. I would become a god of gods, and use my power to set balance to the Aethers, for I had already seen what evil men were truly capable of. My Aenerian children were first to return, Sorronis, Grotton, and Decreath, marvelously talented and just as ambitious as I. They each took one of the Vaults of evil magic, a noble yet necessary sacrifice, for without them there would be no dark to balance the light. Varka followed them not long after that. He was most disappointing." Davos scowled up at the man frozen in the green crystal.

"How so?" Cole asked. "Our history says he came in here to stop The Three, but I suppose he failed in the end."

Davos sighed. "Varka was perhaps the most precocious of all my children, but limited of ambition. He's been there, swimming in the essence of Wisdom for thirty cycles and has yet to crown a Harbinger like the others. That's why Aeneria is in the Shadow Tide; there's not enough light to balance the dark. The fool even bonded himself with another child of mine, Vex I believe, and so he brought her along with him. She had the ambition I longed for in my children, but unfortunately it was Varka who won dominion over the Vault of Wisdom after he followed her in. They were mad with love, and I suspect that same love is what caused the mess at the end of Aeneria's last war. Instead of embracing the essence of Wisdom, Varka warped it and broke the rules of this reality, one of which prevented anyone from Traveling the Aethers. He thought he'd put a stop to my plan, to use my own Vault against me, but in the end he failed. He couldn't stop you from returning to me."

The Vaults seemed to spin around Cole. His head felt faint and dizzy. Davos grasped his shoulders and held him upright, then pulled him into a fatherly hug. Cole was crying before he knew it. His entire life had belonged to someone else. Every memory was not his own, merely a step towards this, his final moment. Eventually his sobbing ebbed. He pulled away and looked to Davos.

"There's no way back, is there?" Cole asked.

Sorrow deepened in Davos's frown. "I'm afraid not. This is your destiny. A cruel destiny, and for that I am sorry, but soon it will all make sense, and your pain will become understanding."

"I... I don't know what Vault to choose," Cole muttered.

"No one does at first," Davos said in a gentle tone. "The choice is as permanent as it is profound, and no one but you has the right to make it. Take as long as you need, for time does not exist here."

"What will happen to the others?" Cole asked. "My friends. My mother..."

"The Harbingers will find them eventually, and they will all die," Davos said. "That is why you must take your place in one of the Vaults, take command of the essence of one of our magics and bring us one step closer to balancing the Aethers. Through the Vault you will live on in the hearts and minds of every sentient creature in all the local planets. You will become a god. And when the time is right, you can crown your own Harbinger and walk the world again as you see fit. You may choose a Vault that has yet to be chosen, or you may enter one that is already occupied if you feel you could do a better job, but be warned, you will have to pit your soul against the one inside to gain dominance over the magic."

Defeat washed over Cole, burying him with his own wilting hope. Sorronis's Vault seemed to call to him. "There has to be another way. It feels wrong. I have no right to anyone's Rage or Passion or Fear. No one person should have all that power."

"Wrong. You earned the right by making it here," Davos said. "The trials you faced, the suffering you endured, the accomplishments you achieved. I have seen it all, and I deem you worthy, Coleton Jonathan Carter. More worthy than any before you, including The Three."

"The Three are evil," Cole said in a serious tone. "Plain evil. If I take a Vault for myself then I'll only be following in their footsteps."

Davos's brow knitted. "The evil of The Three will remain unchecked as long as there is no light to balance the dark. If you abhor their Vaults then forge a new path in the essence of Passion or Rage, or de-thrown that fool in the Vault of Wisdom. Take as long as you need, but know that while time does not flow in this place, outside events will continue apace. Every moment you spend dithering will only further tilt the balance of the Aethers. Even now, The Three toil to unravel Varka's magic over Traveling, and when they do they shall devour everyone you know and countless more, and the power to stop it will have been right in your hands all the while." Davos's expression softened as he nodded to himself. "Your hesitation is well warranted, and I do not blame you for it, only I wish I could give you the strength to do what must be done. I know I cannot, but there may be someone who can."

"Who?" Cole asked, though he didn't really want to know. A drop of Fear crashed over his racing heart.

Davos's eyes pointed over Cole's shoulder. Cole spun around. Lileth stood before him, whole and healthy and beautiful as the day he met her.

"Hello Cole," she said. Her raven hair fell like dark waterfalls over her shoulders, and she wore a dress embellished with lavender petals like the floating flowers in the necropolis. She strode towards him with a shameless grace, her gaze unblinking and disarming.

His heart slowed at the sight of her. "Lileth," he breathed.

Tears filled her eyes as she embraced him, wrapping her arms perfectly over him as though they had been made for his body alone. She whispered into his ear with a voice of sweet nectar. "I'm so sorry. For everything."

Before Cole knew it he was hugging her too, and all his worries melted from him like dirty ice before a flame. The war, the pithing shards, the deaths, his responsibilities, nothing mattered outside her arms. He was no longer alone. He had her at last.

"Lileth," he whispered.

She pulled back and beheld him with an alluring gaze, equal in intelligence and ferocity. "I need you to know that everything I did was for a greater good. The Aethers need balance. Vex showed me things, things that Davos has confirmed. The ways of this world cannot continue, lest evil run unchecked through the Aethers. You must join us, my love."

Cole's vision blurred as he began to sob with relief. "Will we still be together?"

"Of course we will," Lileth said in a soft tone, wiping his tears away with her thumbs. "There are still two empty Vaults. Choose one, and I'll choose the other, then Davos will exist in all six Vaults and we can help create the world anew with our Harbingers. We will be the light to balance the dark, gods of the Aethers. This is our escape, Cole. It will be just as we fantasized about. Run away with me."

Cole glanced up at the empty Vaults. Rage and Passion were both open to him. He couldn't recall how many times he had used each to defeat and defend against evil.

He tore his eyes from Lileth and looked to Davos. "Are you sure this will work? I don't have the piece of your soul anymore."

Davos looked to Lileth. "If you are certain he is with us, then return to him what you stole."

From the depths of her dress, Lileth removed a jagged length of blackened metal. It was part of the pithing shard, the same one that had been buried in his back. The thing reeked of evil, but Cole could sense something else in there, a sliver of soul.

"Will you come with me, my love? Will you burn with me and stay the darkness?" Lileth asked, holding out her hand.

Cole took the broken shard without hesitation. "I'll follow you anywhere."

Davos approached them and put a hand on each of their shoulders. "You have both made me proud beyond words, but you, Cole, you have gone far beyond what anyone had right to expect of you, and for that you may choose first. Which Vault will you take?"

Cole knew the answer long before he ever stepped foot in Oberon Temple.

"Passion," he stated.

Davos reached for Cole's hand and tapped the piece of the pithing shard. A wave of opalescent light passed over it.

"So be it," Varka said. "Before you enter the Vault, you must first pierce your skin with the shard. Just a prick will do, and my soul will then return to you. And let me remove this." Varka stroked his hand through Cole's hair, and Cole felt a great tension release itself from his mind, as though a rope of braided iron had come unraveled. "There, now you have full use of your magic. I apologize for the deception, but it was a necessary precaution. Now go, my children. Go with my blessing and let us sail these seas of destiny."

Cole pulled Lileth in close and kissed her, deep and long, wrapping her in his arms and his Passion. A moan vibrated from her lips into his. If he could, he would have stayed locked in timeless embrace for all eternity, but destiny was calling. After a final kiss to her forehead he withdrew.

"See you on the other side," he said.

She blinked a tear from each eye and flashed him a wolfish grin. "I hope so."

They parted ways. She went up the stairs to the red crystal while Cole took the stairs to the lavender. Cole's magic pulsed inside him like never before, as though each facet of his soul was trying to dance its way to its respective source. All six Vaults called to him, each alluring in its own way, but with every step he climbed his Passion throbbed ever stronger.

He stopped just before the lavender crystal and glanced over at the red. Lileth was already inside, frozen in silent beauty. If only he could have looked into her eyes just one more time.

Cole held the sliver of the pithing shard up to the stars, watching how the light played off its razor-sharp edges. Just a pin prick. He turned back towards the center of the platform. Davos gave him a solemn nod, urging him on. Giddy with excitement, Cole brought the pithing shard to the tip of his finger. Just then he saw a flicker of movement from a nearby dais, and Cole glanced over at the Vault of Wisdom. Varka stood at the very edge of the massive crystal, his eyes boring straight into Cole's with a look of utmost urgency. There was a woman at his feet. Even in the stillness of the Vault Cole could tell Vex was dead. It looked as if Varka wanted to say something. Curiosity bloomed in Cole's mind. Why had Varka used the essence of Wisdom to stop The Three instead of crowning his own Harbinger? If he'd made it into the Vaults, he was obviously told of the plan in place, knew of his responsibility to balance the Aethers. Why then would he kill his lover and squander his godly powers on things such as the barrier and halting Travel? He must have known something.

"It is time, Cole," Davos called up to him. "Do what needs to be done."

Cole pressed the shard to his fingertip. His flesh was warm and taut, eager to yield to the blade. Curiosity struck him once more, ominous this time, and he stopped. He needed to know. With the speed of thought, he cast his Passion towards the man trapped in the green crystal. He met resistance, a creeping madness he had felt all too often; Fear. Why would there be Fear in the Vault of Wisdom? Cole burned a hole through the Fear with a blast of Rage and plunged his consciousness towards Varka's.

"Stop that at once!" Davos hollered. "That man is a threat to everything we strive to protect!" Emerald wings erupted from Davos's back as a blended shroud of red and black snapped over his skin. His munisica filled with screaming purple flames dripping with blue light. He aimed an unknown spell at Cole, then a cluster of thick jade chains erupted from the platform around him, coiling over his body like dozens of angry snakes.

Cole ignored Davos and delved further into Varka's mind.

A presence rushed up to meet his own, ancient and powerful. *"Listen well, Coleton Carter, for I cannot hold Davos for long. He is mad, tainted by the power that lies just beyond his reach. I saw this madness in his heart long ago, but I was not strong enough to stop him, and so he locked me into the Vault of Wisdom and sealed it with Fear. Before he could complete my imprisonment I managed a few spells using the power of the Vault. You know of the spells I speak of, but the most important one of all was finding you. The piece of Aenerian soul that you were born with was not Davos's, but mine. I sent a portion of my soul to Terra with instructions to find the one who could save the Aethers from this calamity. My soul wove its way through your bloodline until it found one of pure heart. The soul in the shard you hold belongs to him. He put it there just before you arrived."*

"Why should I believe you?" Cole demanded. "Why should I believe a word from either of you? If what you say is true then my entire life has been a lie, one that you wove to bring me here against my will. I could have lived out the rest of my days in blissful ignorance of all this. Why couldn't you choose someone else?"

Sorrow bled from him. *"You are right to Hate me. I burdened you with the fate of worlds before you were even born. If I could take your suffering into myself I gladly would, but I cannot. I made the best choice with what little time I had, but I know in my heart The Three and Davos would have eventually found a way to circumvent my spells and plagued the Aethers until the end of days. I am sorry too, for your Lileth. Vex was the greatest of my failures, one which will haunt both of us until we take our last."*

"It's true then?" Cole asked, gazing at the body at Varka's feet. "You killed her. Your Vex."

"And it killed me to do so," Varka replied with a shudder of genuine Despair. *"I always knew she had an evil in her, but I was so love-blind I didn't see the danger until we met Davos. What I mistook for her wild desires was a Hunger more potent than even Grotton's, only she had the cleverness to bring that Hunger into the Vault of Wisdom. I followed her with the intent to temper her darker tendencies and shoulder the burdens of the Vault, but such power is not so easily shared for those who walk the path of Hunger. The love of my life turned on me, and I had no choice but to kill her, lest The Three become The Four. With her dying breath she used the Vault to cast a fragment of her soul out into Aeneria, where it eventually found your Lileth. I could have stopped her, however I hoped she would return a better person. I have never been so wrong, and both my heart and yours have paid the price."*

Fresh Despair washed over Cole's hope. He felt as though he was losing Lileth all over again. However, he noticed a part of himself that the Despair couldn't touch, a brilliant seedling of Passion rooted somewhere among the garden of mind, right where his memories of the Havenflow should have been. The sliver of pithing shard felt painfully sharp in his hand now.

"What should I do then?" Cole pleaded. *"Should I fight him?"*

"You are one of the most powerful beings that has ever walked this planet," Varka said. *"But you alone are not enough to defeat him, especially not here. He will dominate you, then force you into the Vault of Passion."*

Dreadful finality fell over Cole as he considered another option. He thought of his friends, his mother, everyone he had lost, and grim acceptance clicked in place. *"I'll kill myself. I have to. While there's still time."*

Agreement rang from Varka. *"It pains me to ask it of you, especially after everything you have already sacrificed. Suicide is a choice only you can make, and it will only delay Davos from achieving his goal. Eventually another of his children will find their way to the Vaults."*

"I guess it's better than nothing..." Cole fell silent as he resigned himself to the permanence of the choice, the sinking horror of the act.

"There is light to this darkness," Varka added. *"It is a spell which I have spent the last thirty cycles crafting and polishing. I give it to you now, a final gift and small recompense for the suffering I brought upon you."*

"What does it do?" Cole asked, terrified of the answer.

Varka spoke in a tone of warm moonlight. *"It will kill you. Your body and soul will be shattered, but it will keep the pieces alive for a fraction of a second, allowing you to project them into each of the Vaults. What happens from there I can only guess, but I think it is safe to assume you will have a chance, however slight, to win dominance over each of the six Vaults. Should you succeed you will attain an omnipotence unimaginable and unprecedented. Should you fail, then at least you will have delayed our end a little longer."*

"But that's exactly what he wanted to do!" Cole protested. *"No one person should have all that power. I would be no better than Davos."*

"But you are not him," Varka said. *"You came here seeking to save the Aethers, not to dominate them. Listen not to him, nor to me, but to your own soul, which at this very moment is entirely your own.*

Search it, for it has all the answers you need." There was a sudden and drastic decrease in Varka's presence, as though his mind were a fire that had just been splashed with water. Cole glanced back at Davos and saw the jade chains snapping, their links disintegrating with puffs of smoke. *"Accept the spell. Quickly now."*

Cole opened his mind and felt the knowledge flow into him. He couldn't grasp the intricacies of the spell, but the general concepts were sound enough for him to work with.

"What will happen to you?" Cole asked once the transfer was complete.

"I will be here, waiting to help in whatever way I can." Varka's mind dimmed until his voice was barely audible. *"You cast many shadows, Coleton Carter, for in your heart and in your mind you are many."*

Cole severed the connection and returned to his body. In one hand he held the sliver of the pithing shard. In the other an orb of Varka's opalescent magic hummed between his fingers, resting just above the patch of rainbow light left from Chiron's butterfly. On the platform below, the final jade chain snapped free and Davos took flight with murder in his eyes.

Clenching both hands tightly, Cole shut his eyes and held his breath. He knew what he had to do.

CHAPTER 35

DAWN

"There you go, Val, give it hell!" Sitra shouted.

Eliza took a spot next to Habbad on the prow of one of the few surviving Morthainian ships. They were floating in the waters outside Oberon Temple, as close to the ghostly barrier as they dared. Sitra was in the air, encouraging Valen with her magic and voice as he tried every spell they could think of to breach the barrier. Cole had been inside for half a day, and beyond reach of Eliza's Passion for most of that time. She wasn't worried, however. Though they weren't entirely bonded with the lover's magic, they were both masters of it, and she was confident that should the worst come to pass, her heart would tell her somehow. Besides, he had promised to find a way back to her.

"That's obviously not going to work," Habbad said in a drawling tone. Valen had conjured a spinning emerald saw blade broader than the ship they floated on. Sitra augmented the spell with her Rage, and the whirring edge of the blade ignited with bold red flames. "They already attempted a blend of Rage and Wisdom. I'm telling you, this barrier is going to take more than two or three schools of magic to unravel."

"You are probably right," Eliza sighed. "But I don't think we're ready to indulge your magics just yet, not when we just lost so many to the evil arts. Can you blame us?"

"Yes," Habbad said without looking at her. "Your emotions ought to fall second to the fate of twenty-two worlds."

She gave Habbad a sideways glance and a sour taste seemed to fill her mouth. It was not his appearance that revolted her, for he was actually rather handsome when he wasn't scowling. It was his presence.

She could sense multitudes of thralls within him, each tortured soul more desperate than the last. The prolific Hunger required to enthrall such a number ought to have made Habbad irredeemably evil, but she had scanned his mind and every Domina within, and found no evil intention behind the magic. Every Domina had agreed to join him with full knowledge of the contract and without the lust for power. Many of them would have died had they not been enthralled, either by some grievous wound, suicide, or illness. It was an odd way to save a life, and the act forced Eliza to reconsider her definition of evil.

"This barrier is beyond us," Valen said to the whole group, which now included Habbad. *"The fabric of the magic is unlike anything I have ever encountered. It requires something we lack. Something Cole had."* Accepting defeat at last, he tilted from the sky and returned to the ship with Sitra at his side.

"Should we try another volley with the main guns?" Sitra asked. "If we pound the same spot over and over, then maybe it'll soften the barrier enough for our magic to rip through."

"Don't waste your munitions," Habbad said. "The barrier didn't even flinch the last time you fired at it, and that was with half your fleet. I doubt a few ships would fare any better."

"Oh that's right," Sitra said with a mirthless laugh. "I forgot you were an expert on naval artillery. I hope you thanked the sailor before you ripped the ass off his soul and slapped it onto yours." She walked across the deck and stood before Habbad, regarding him with black fury. "Let me guess, you want us to try a few of your little tricks? I bet there's still a few children back at The Sill, maybe we could bring them here and use their blood and screams to pierce the barrier. Think that'll work?"

"Sitra, please," Eliza implored. The last thing they needed was another fight. "We still have another way in, one that doesn't involve dark magic."

Habbad's lack of response only seemed to further infuriate her, but Sitra turned on her heel and stormed off before her munisica could grow any larger.

"The risk is too great," Valen said. "And I don't know the spell. The first ten pages of Chiron's warnings were enough that I closed his book and never opened it again, lest someone steal the knowledge from me and put the whole world in danger. Cole should never have used the teleportation spell, even to save us. Even if I had the knowledge I wouldn't dare."

"I'm not talking about you," Eliza said. "I gleaned the spell from Cole while we were in the Havenflow together."

"Eliza," Valen said in a tone of exasperation. "The warnings were there for good reason. And the Wisdom required would—"

"Would be no greater than what Cole had when he used it on us," Eliza interrupted. "You forget that I too have earned the title of Master in the green magic, which Cole proved isn't a requirement for this spell. More than that, I too have read the warnings, both on the pages and through Cole's mind. I can do it."

Valen tensed, and for a moment Eliza thought he was going to attack her. The risks of using the teleportation spell were certainly great enough for him to try and stop her by any means. However, Valen was tired and she was not. Though it would destroy her forever, she would kill him without hesitation if it was the only way to save Cole. To her relief, however, he deflated with a great sigh, and looked at her with acceptance in his eyes.

"Can you take all of us?" he asked.

"Of course," Eliza replied.

They spent the next quarter of an hour reviewing the spell in detail. Sitra was of course all for it, but Habbad seemed to inch himself away from the group as he learned more about what they were about to do.

"You might as well come too," Sitra said to Habbad with savage pleasure. "If it goes wrong you'll be dead anyway, even if you ran all the way back to your cushy palace in Costas."

In the end Habbad agreed to join them, though grudgingly so. When Eliza was ready, all four of them clasped hands on the prow of the ship, then she drew upon her Wisdom. Just when she was about to direct her magic into action, something bright ignited in the sky directly above them. Eliza ceased the flow and looked up.

A swirling white light glowed steadily brighter over the surface of Oberon. Its radiance surged until it was so brilliant, Eliza had to squint at her feet, though after a few seconds that became too bright to behold. She cast a spell over her eyes to shade them from the stinging glare, then gazed back up at Oberon, which now looked like a ball of alabaster flames.

"Move the ship," Eliza began with a whisper, then Fear brought her voice to a shout. "Move the ship now, Sitra! Get us out of here!"

Blind to the world, Sitra gave the telepathic command to the crew below, but it was too late. A beam of white fire descended from Oberon, tearing its way to the temple in a column of energy so immense that it would surely destroy the planet. With the speed of thought, Eliza sent a bolt of Passion into each of their minds, commandeering their magic before they knew she was there. She crafted a shield with every facet of magic they had among them, even Habbad's, branding the spell with a simple rule; save us.

The light grew so intense that even with her Wisdom shading her eyes, Eliza couldn't see a thing. A roar filled her ears, consuming every sound in a maddening cacophony as an electrified taste coated her tongue. The wood beneath her feet shook so violently she was sure it would shatter. She sensed a sudden and extreme dip in their collective magic as something touched their shield, bringing them all to the edge of unconsciousness. In the deepest reaches of her mind she felt Cole's touch, sad yet serene, then realized with a start that the overwhelming force had somehow come from him. But then he was gone just as swiftly as he came.

The light was slow to fade, as was the din battering her ears. When her senses returned, she heard the dull rush of fast-moving water. She wrenched herself from the flow of magic and their pearlescent shield covering the ship vanished in a blink, revealing a gap in the world.

The barrier was gone, and so was the Temple. Eliza looked up to where the upper tiers had just been a moment ago, and found an empty void where Oberon should have been. In place of the Temple, a ten-mile crater gaped from Aeneria's crust, with water pouring in from all sides. A foreign starscape glittered innocently across the inky canvas above, stretching from horizon to horizon, it bathed the world in a gentle glow. Eliza worried what else might have vanished. She found the shoreline where it should have been at the water's edge, as well as the Fangshards off in the distance, but there was something else she couldn't find. Her heart tightened in her chest as she suddenly realized what it was. She looked to Sitra and Valen, and the sorrow on their faces confirmed it.

"He's gone," she breathed.

• • •

Eliza's heart continued to beat, and her breath continued to flow, but she didn't feel as though she had survived. Events took place around her, many of which she took an active part in; however, none of it held the same meaning. There was a dullness in the air, as though music which had played throughout her entire life had been ripped from her soul, leaving the world lusterless and grey.

The Unbound and Habbad gathered their remaining forces and made for their nearest outpost, where a Seer Jar would take them back to The Sill. Habbad brought most of his Aenerians and Underkin who had joined the battle. However, his Domina joined the crews of Morthain's surviving ships and departed through Fangshard Valley to the White Sands and Costas beyond.

The Unbound were the last to take the Seer Jar, which had been hastily set up on the roof of an old library. Something warm touched the backs of their necks just before they entered the nebulous cloud of the jar's magic. They turned around to see a local star rising from the horizon. It did not vanish as it should have with the change of house, but rather it continued its steady ascent, painting Aeneria's Dark Side in warm golden light for the first time in all recorded history. Blending her mastery of Wisdom with Valen's, the two of them scanned the far reaches of the skies and what lay beyond. What they discovered was as shocking as it was unnerving. They were in no recognizable house. There was no local planet nearby and the starscape was of another place entirely. Aeneria was in its own reality. Furthermore, there was no trace of The Three. The evil magics still existed, but only in the hearts of individuals rather than the ubiquitous shadow cast from the black gods. The world had balance.

The sunrise was waiting for them at The Sill. Whind had convinced the outer walls to recede, allowing the newborn daylight to trickle in over the canopy. Valen and Sitra set to work immediately, though none of their concerns interested Eliza. Habbad labored to ensure his people were fed and housed to his satisfaction, then he set off for Naythan's Academy without another word. Eliza had her responsibilities as well. There were her elite units to look after, and she was still ambassador for the refugees of Vol Karinn; however, at the moment she didn't have the heart to give herself to them. She wanted Cole.

She wandered The Sill for hours, closing her mind and weaving her way around anyone she saw. Her meandering brought her to the Necropolis, and a strong desire to create a grave tree for Cole stole through her, but there was nothing of him to bury beneath the roots. She went to Deekus's tree and paid what little she had into the gratia stone of her first love. She had given her heart to two men in her life, two of the greatest minds she had ever touched, and fate had taken them both from her. Eliza departed the Necropolis, bonding herself to a solemn vow to never love again.

With no urge or desire to speak of, Eliza trudged on, aimless and hopeless. Hours passed and the sunlight overhead waxed, then waned to starlit shadow. No one came looking for her. Eventually she happened upon something that gave her pause, and her Despair lifted, revealing Cole's apartment tree before her. A need for action flared up inside her, and Eliza sprinted up the ramp to his door. She knew there was nothing inside but painful relics of his life, but part of her wanted to feel that pain. She wanted to feel him again. Passion welled in her, and as she pressed her face into the door she felt a presence within. The melody of the soul was similar to Cole's, but not quite the same. Heart hammering, she pushed her way through the liquid stone door.

There was a small human woman sleeping in Cole's bed. Eliza would have thought her an Underkin had she not known Cole when he was smaller. She was garbed in the finest silk robes with precious metals woven throughout in delicate filigree. Her blond hair fell gracefully over her shoulders like warm honey. She had the sunken look of someone who had recently been deathly ill, but rich, healthy color glowed in her hollow cheeks. She looked like Cole.

Eliza sat herself on the bed. She caressed the woman's forehead with a stroke of Passion.

"Wake," Eliza whispered.

The woman stirred, then her eyes opened like blooming lilies.

"Where am I?" the woman asked.

"In a safe place," Eliza replied, filling the air with pacifying magic so as not to frighten the small woman. "My name is Eliza. You must be Tara."

Tara nodded, then her eyes searched around the room. "I... I lost someone. Someone important. I swear I felt him. Just a second ago. His name was... oh god I can't remember."

"I know him," Eliza said, choking back tears. She dried her eyes and placed a hand on Tara's arm. "Let me tell you a story about the bravest man I ever knew."

END OF BOOK 3

If you enjoyed your journey to Aeneria and want to help make it a real place, please take a moment and give this book an honest review.

For all Hate mail and love letters:

www.AeneriaIsComing.com/contact/

From the World of Aeneria

Website
AeneriaIsComing.com

FROM THE AUTHOR

Greetings Traveler!

I've been writing sporadically for most of my life. However, it wasn't until January 2016 that I began to take it seriously thanks to one of my closest friends. While I'd like to be writing full-time, I (like most independent authors) have a day job, which is a logistician position in the National Guard. I joined in 2005, deployed twice, and have been active duty since 2012. The military lifestyle has had a tremendous impact on my life, filling it with more ups and downs than I can keep track of, as well as some lifelong friends.

My days are spent at a desk or bumbling around in a humongous truck. After work I get myself to a gym and do battle with my inner fat kid for a couple of hours, then rush home and hopefully start writing before 8 pm. I nurture a love for performance arts, especially plays and local stand-up. During summers I don't ride my motorcycle nearly enough, and the same goes for my snowboard during the winters. At least once a year I'll go abroad, usually your typical over-indulgent Caribbean cruise, though recently I spent a week in France, where I had the privilege of officiating at a wedding for two dear friends.

The stories I enjoy the most usually leave me shaken for a few days, not because I'm a glutton for masochism, but because they resonate with the wounded parts of me that I wouldn't ordinarily take notice of. With a somewhat busy lifestyle where stoicism has become my go-to survival tool, I need those stories that derail me from my daily grind, that kick me in the gut and make me feel something.

As of writing this I'm 31 years old and live in Manchester, New Hampshire.